THE MONTAGUE TWINS

THE WITCH'S HAND

NATHAN PAGE AND DREW SHANNON

ALFRED A. KNOPF

NEW YORK

THIS IS A BORZOI BOOK PUBLISHED BY ALFRED A. KNOPF

Visit us on the Web! GetUnderlined.com

Educators and librarians, for a variety of teaching tools, visit us at RHTeachersLibrarians.com

Library of Congress Cataloging-in-Publication Data
Names: Page, Nathan, author. | Shannon, Drew, illustrator.
Title: The witch's hand / Nathan Page and Drew Shannon.
Description: First edition. | New York : Alfred A. Knopf, 2020. | Series: The Montague Twins ; volume #1 | Summary: Orphaned teens Pete and Al Montague and their adopted sister, Charlie, already known for solving mysteries in their small New England town, begin studying magic as they investigate a disappearance connected to a seventeenth-century witch.
Identifiers: LCCN 2018048652| ISBN 978-0-525-64676-1 (hardcover) | ISBN 978-0-525-64677-8 (pbk.) | ISBN 978-0-525-64679-2 (ebook)
Subjects: LCSH: Graphic novels. | CYAC: Graphic novels. | Brothers and sisters—Fiction. | Twins—Fiction. | Supernatural—Fiction. | Magic—Fiction. | Mystery and detective stories.
Classification: LCC PZ7.1.P33 Cur 2020 | DDC [Fic]—dc23

The artwork for *The Montague Twins* was created with traditional and digital drawing techniques.

MANUFACTURED IN CHINA
July 2020
10 9 8 7 6 5 4 3 2 1

First Edition

We would like to dedicate this book to our families.

—NATHAN AND DREW

CHAPTER 1

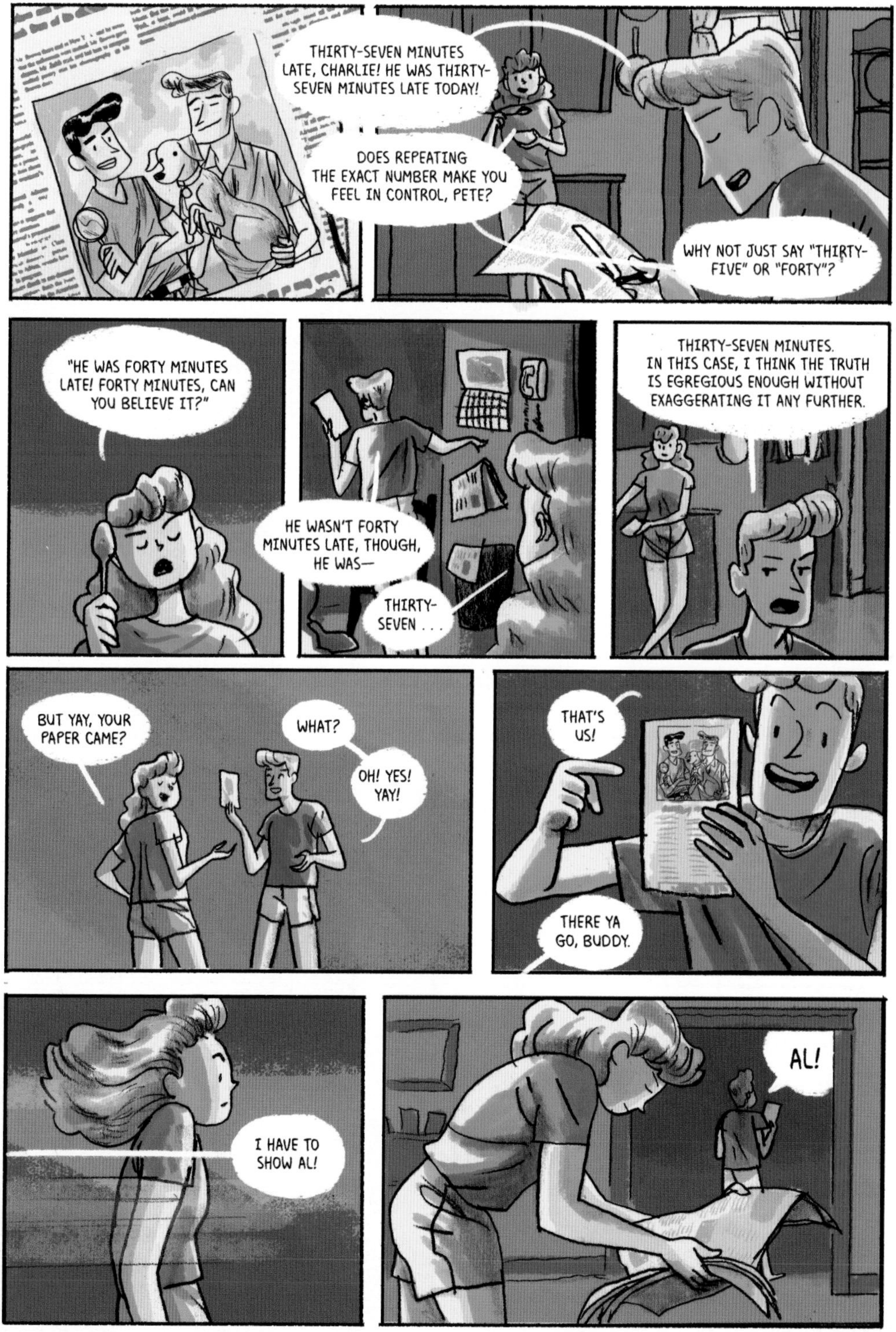
THIRTY-SEVEN MINUTES LATE, CHARLIE! HE WAS THIRTY-SEVEN MINUTES LATE TODAY!
DOES REPEATING THE EXACT NUMBER MAKE YOU FEEL IN CONTROL, PETE?
WHY NOT JUST SAY "THIRTY-FIVE" OR "FORTY"?
"HE WAS FORTY MINUTES LATE! FORTY MINUTES, CAN YOU BELIEVE IT?"
HE WASN'T FORTY MINUTES LATE, THOUGH, HE WAS—
THIRTY-SEVEN . . .
THIRTY-SEVEN MINUTES. IN THIS CASE, I THINK THE TRUTH IS EGREGIOUS ENOUGH WITHOUT EXAGGERATING IT ANY FURTHER.
BUT YAY, YOUR PAPER CAME?
WHAT?
OH! YES! YAY!
THAT'S US!
THERE YA GO, BUDDY.
I HAVE TO SHOW AL!
AL!

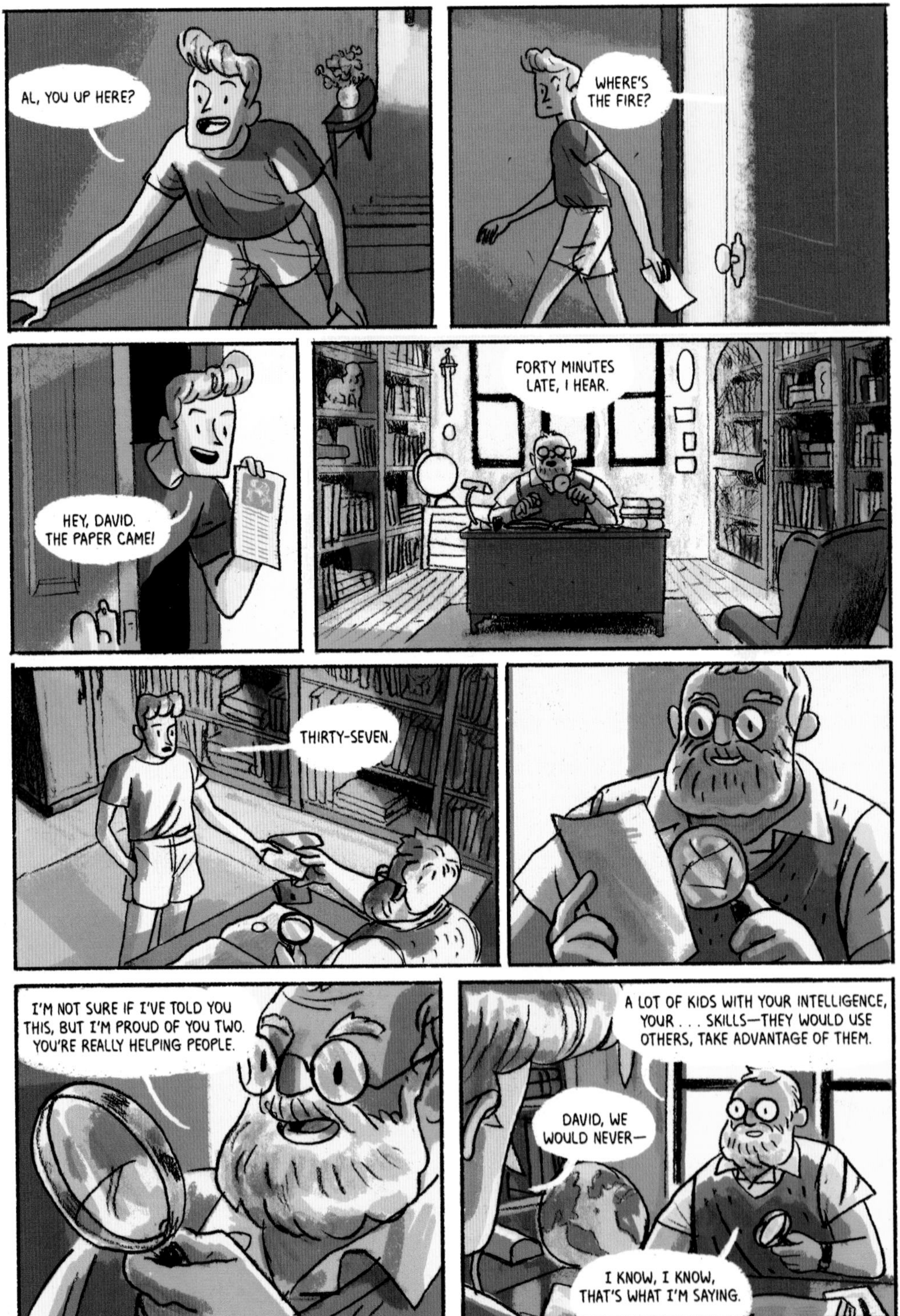
AL, YOU UP HERE?
WHERE'S THE FIRE?
HEY, DAVID. THE PAPER CAME!
FORTY MINUTES LATE, I HEAR.
THIRTY-SEVEN.
I'M NOT SURE IF I'VE TOLD YOU THIS, BUT I'M PROUD OF YOU TWO. YOU'RE REALLY HELPING PEOPLE.
A LOT OF KIDS WITH YOUR INTELLIGENCE, YOUR . . . SKILLS—THEY WOULD USE OTHERS, TAKE ADVANTAGE OF THEM.
DAVID, WE WOULD NEVER—
I KNOW, I KNOW, THAT'S WHAT I'M SAYING.

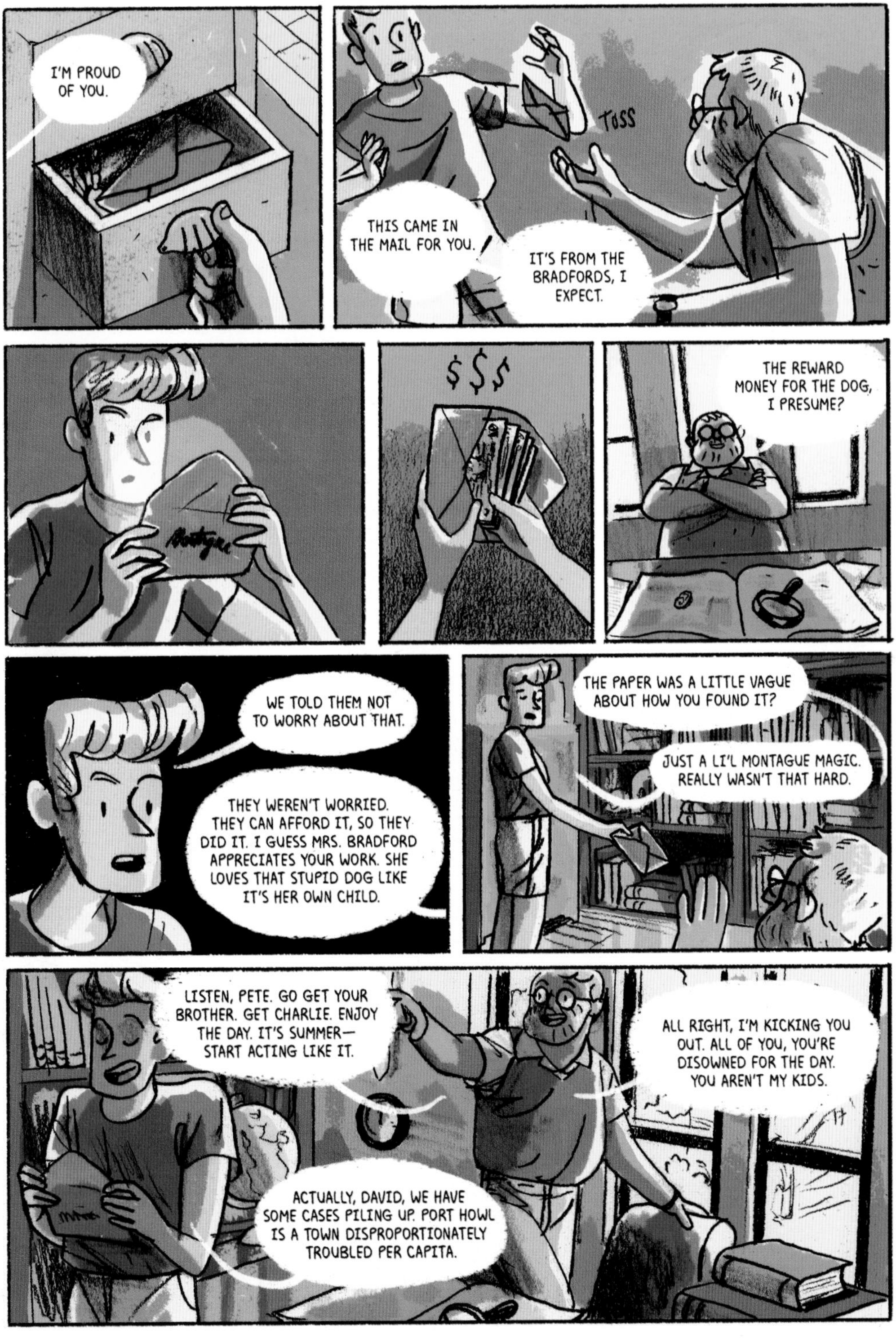
I'M PROUD OF YOU.
THIS CAME IN THE MAIL FOR YOU.
TOSS
IT'S FROM THE BRADFORDS, I EXPECT.
$ $ $
THE REWARD MONEY FOR THE DOG, I PRESUME?
WE TOLD THEM NOT TO WORRY ABOUT THAT.
THEY WEREN'T WORRIED. THEY CAN AFFORD IT, SO THEY DID IT. I GUESS MRS. BRADFORD APPRECIATES YOUR WORK. SHE LOVES THAT STUPID DOG LIKE IT'S HER OWN CHILD.
THE PAPER WAS A LITTLE VAGUE ABOUT HOW YOU FOUND IT?
JUST A LI'L MONTAGUE MAGIC. REALLY WASN'T THAT HARD.
LISTEN, PETE. GO GET YOUR BROTHER. GET CHARLIE. ENJOY THE DAY. IT'S SUMMER— START ACTING LIKE IT.
ALL RIGHT, I'M KICKING YOU OUT. ALL OF YOU, YOU'RE DISOWNED FOR THE DAY. YOU AREN'T MY KIDS.
ACTUALLY, DAVID, WE HAVE SOME CASES PILING UP. PORT HOWL IS A TOWN DISPROPORTIONATELY TROUBLED PER CAPITA.

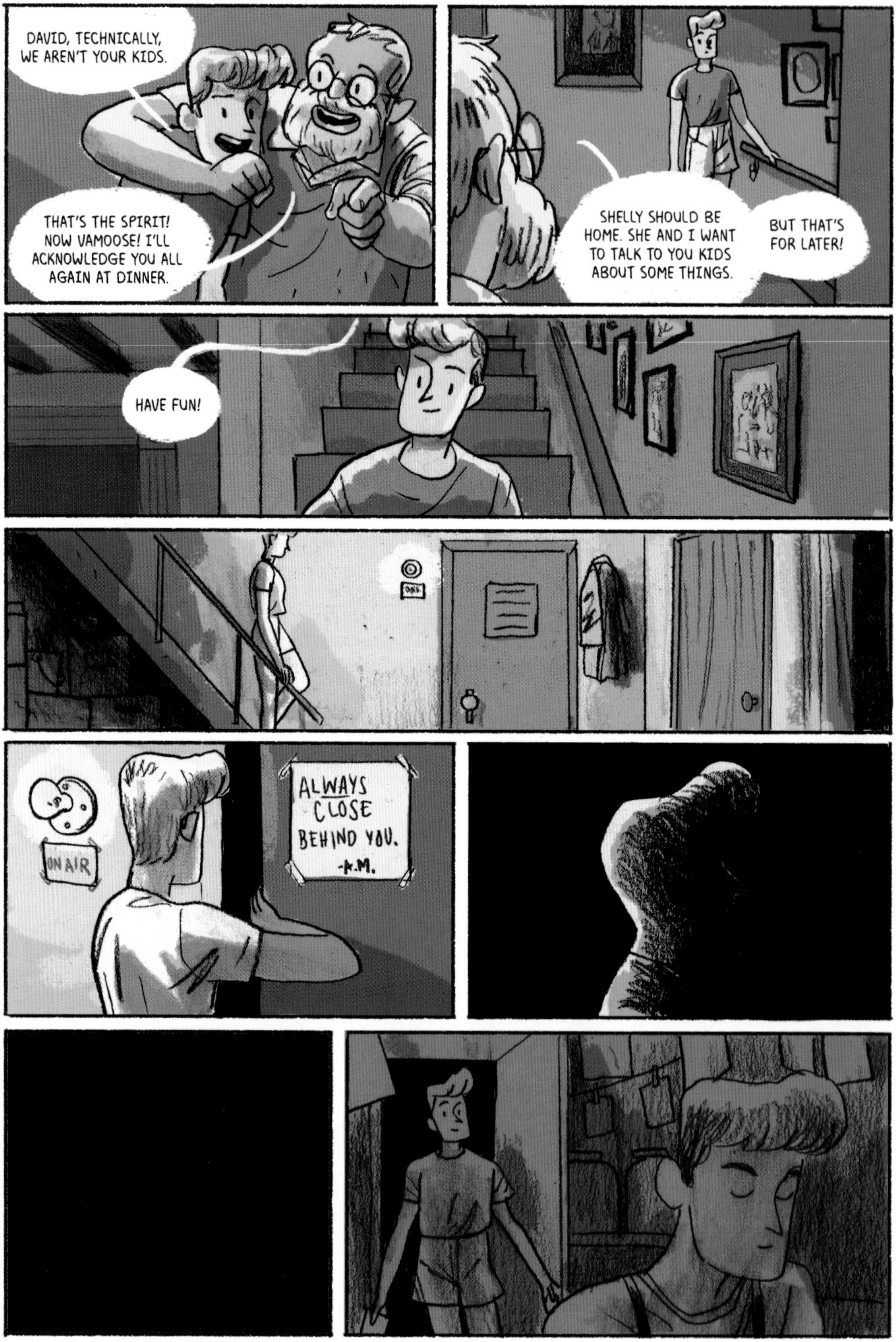

DAVID, TECHNICALLY, WE AREN'T YOUR KIDS.
THAT'S THE SPIRIT! NOW VAMOOSE! I'LL ACKNOWLEDGE YOU ALL AGAIN AT DINNER.
SHELLY SHOULD BE HOME. SHE AND I WANT TO TALK TO YOU KIDS ABOUT SOME THINGS.
BUT THAT'S FOR LATER!
HAVE FUN!
ON AIR
ALWAYS CLOSE BEHIND YOU. -A.M.

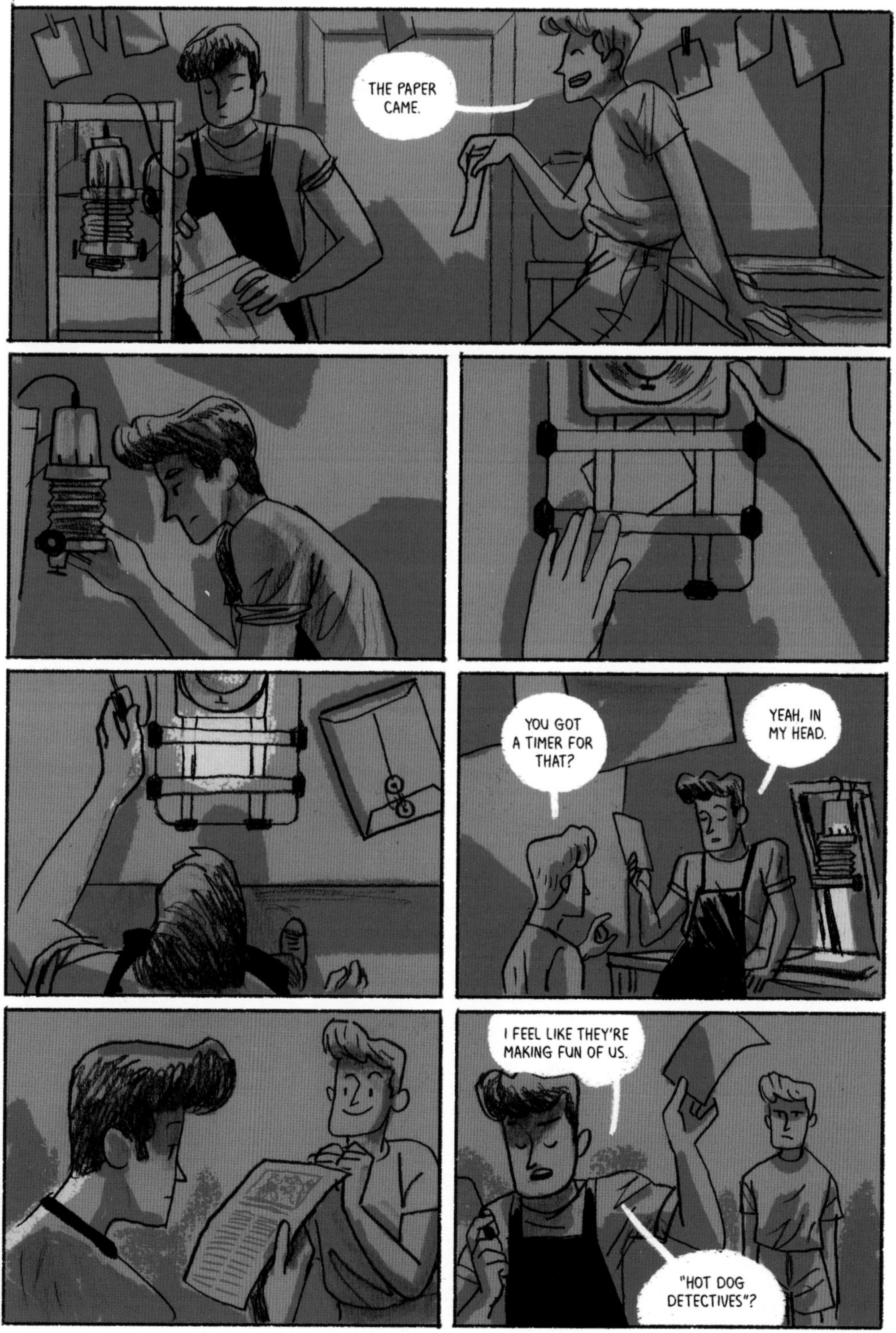
THE PAPER CAME.
YOU GOT A TIMER FOR THAT?
YEAH, IN MY HEAD.
I FEEL LIKE THEY'RE MAKING FUN OF US.
"HOT DOG DETECTIVES"?

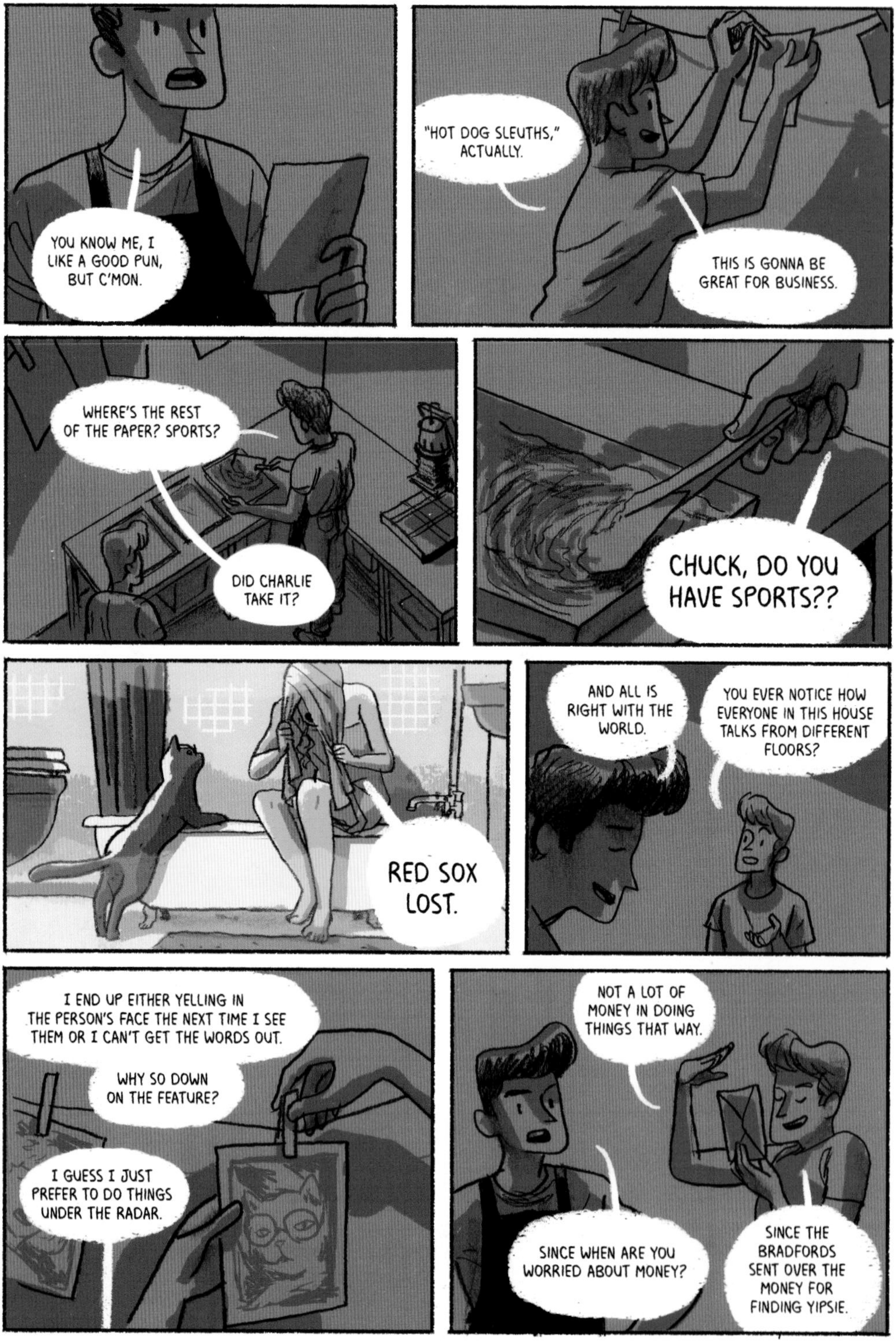
YOU KNOW ME, I LIKE A GOOD PUN, BUT C'MON.
"HOT DOG SLEUTHS," ACTUALLY.
THIS IS GONNA BE GREAT FOR BUSINESS.
WHERE'S THE REST OF THE PAPER? SPORTS?
DID CHARLIE TAKE IT?
CHUCK, DO YOU HAVE SPORTS??
RED SOX LOST.
AND ALL IS RIGHT WITH THE WORLD.
YOU EVER NOTICE HOW EVERYONE IN THIS HOUSE TALKS FROM DIFFERENT FLOORS?
I END UP EITHER YELLING IN THE PERSON'S FACE THE NEXT TIME I SEE THEM OR I CAN'T GET THE WORDS OUT.
WHY SO DOWN ON THE FEATURE?
I GUESS I JUST PREFER TO DO THINGS UNDER THE RADAR.
NOT A LOT OF MONEY IN DOING THINGS THAT WAY.
SINCE WHEN ARE YOU WORRIED ABOUT MONEY?
SINCE THE BRADFORDS SENT OVER THE MONEY FOR FINDING YIPSIE.

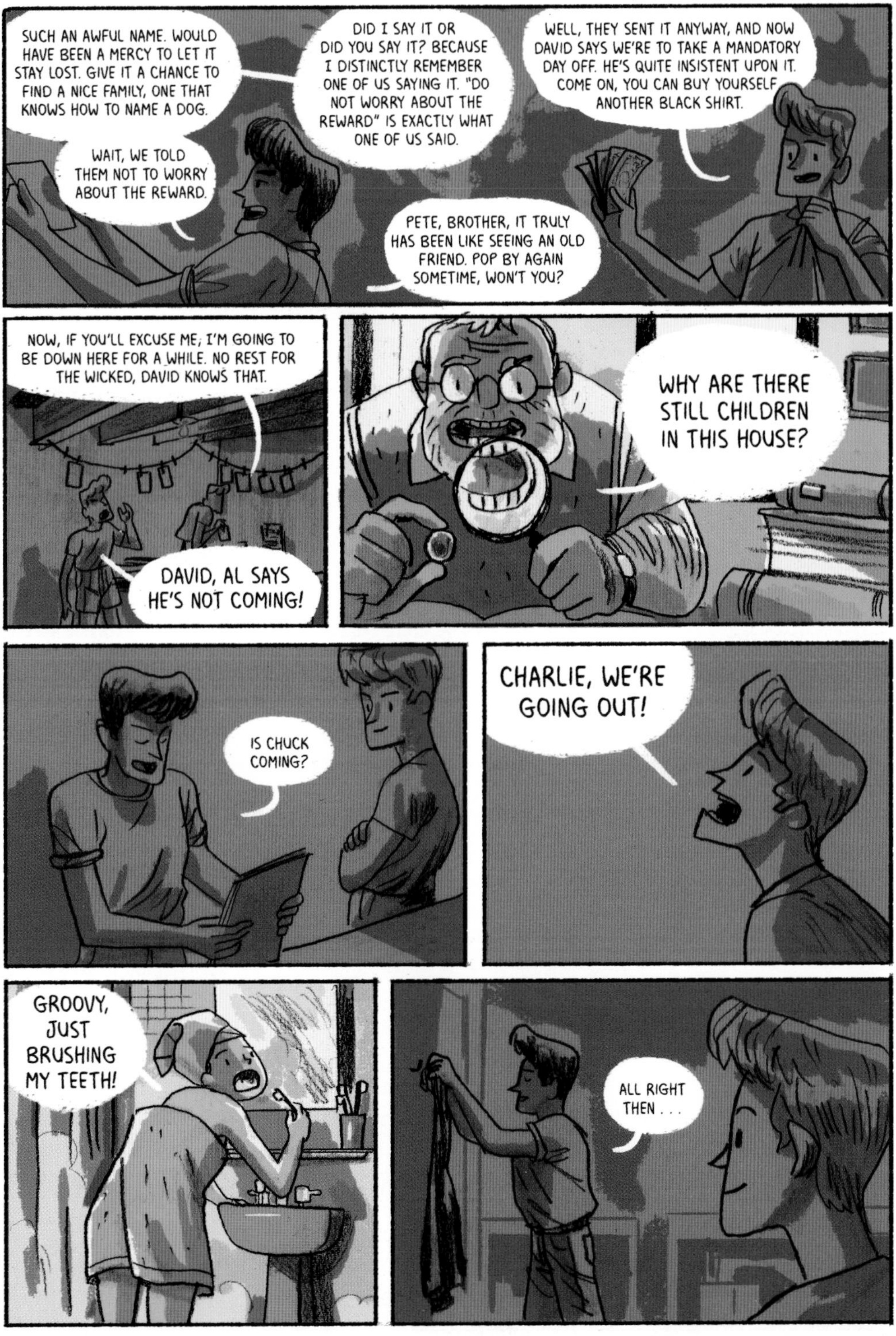
SUCH AN AWFUL NAME. WOULD HAVE BEEN A MERCY TO LET IT STAY LOST. GIVE IT A CHANCE TO FIND A NICE FAMILY, ONE THAT KNOWS HOW TO NAME A DOG.
WAIT, WE TOLD THEM NOT TO WORRY ABOUT THE REWARD.
DID I SAY IT OR DID YOU SAY IT? BECAUSE I DISTINCTLY REMEMBER ONE OF US SAYING IT. "DO NOT WORRY ABOUT THE REWARD" IS EXACTLY WHAT ONE OF US SAID.
PETE, BROTHER, IT TRULY HAS BEEN LIKE SEEING AN OLD FRIEND. POP BY AGAIN SOMETIME, WON'T YOU?
WELL, THEY SENT IT ANYWAY, AND NOW DAVID SAYS WE'RE TO TAKE A MANDATORY DAY OFF. HE'S QUITE INSISTENT UPON IT. COME ON, YOU CAN BUY YOURSELF ANOTHER BLACK SHIRT.
NOW, IF YOU'LL EXCUSE ME, I'M GOING TO BE DOWN HERE FOR A WHILE. NO REST FOR THE WICKED, DAVID KNOWS THAT.
DAVID, AL SAYS HE'S NOT COMING!
WHY ARE THERE STILL CHILDREN IN THIS HOUSE?
IS CHUCK COMING?
CHARLIE, WE'RE GOING OUT!
GROOVY, JUST BRUSHING MY TEETH!
ALL RIGHT THEN . . .

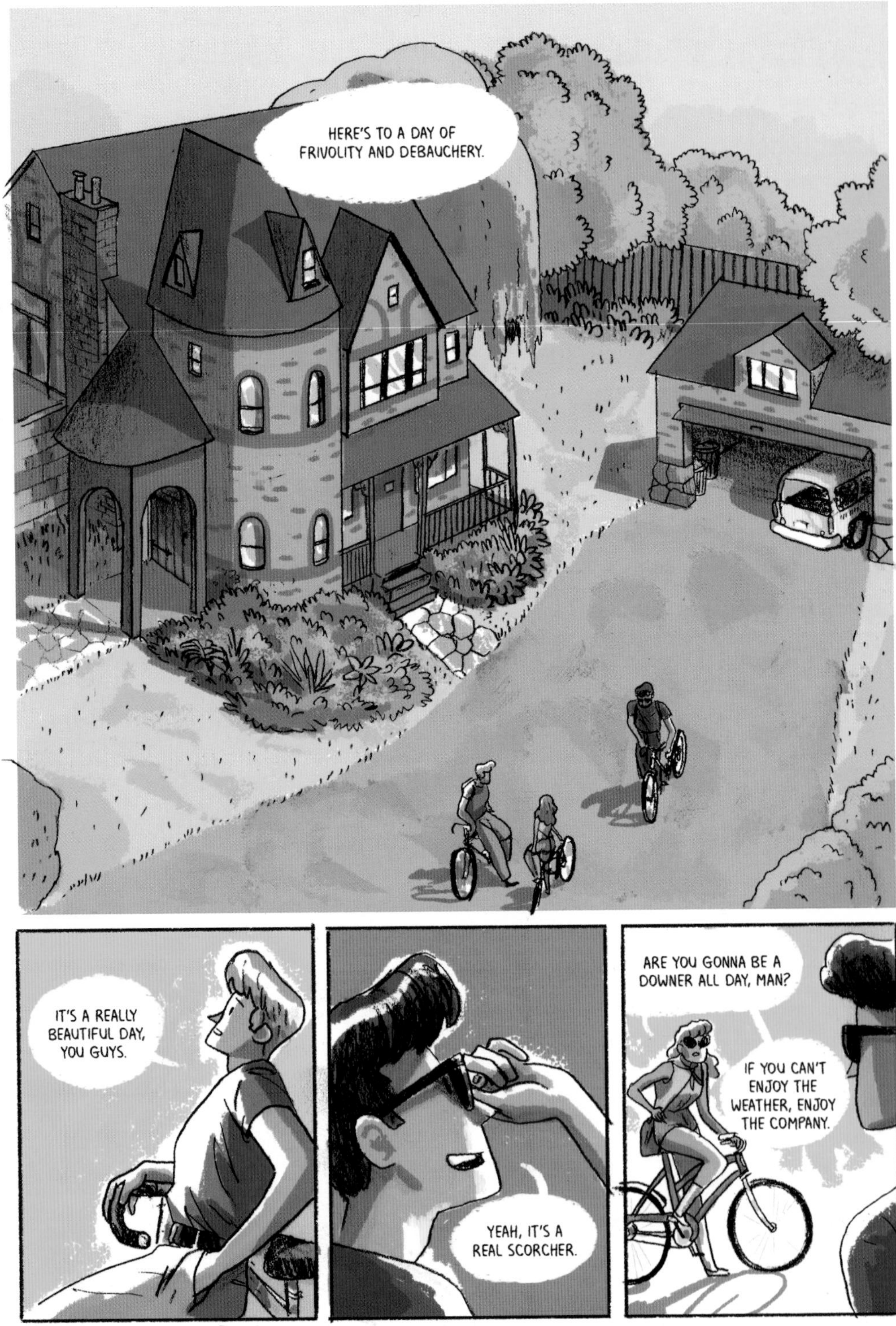
HERE'S TO A DAY OF FRIVOLITY AND DEBAUCHERY.
IT'S A REALLY BEAUTIFUL DAY, YOU GUYS.
YEAH, IT'S A REAL SCORCHER.
ARE YOU GONNA BE A DOWNER ALL DAY, MAN?
IF YOU CAN'T ENJOY THE WEATHER, ENJOY THE COMPANY.

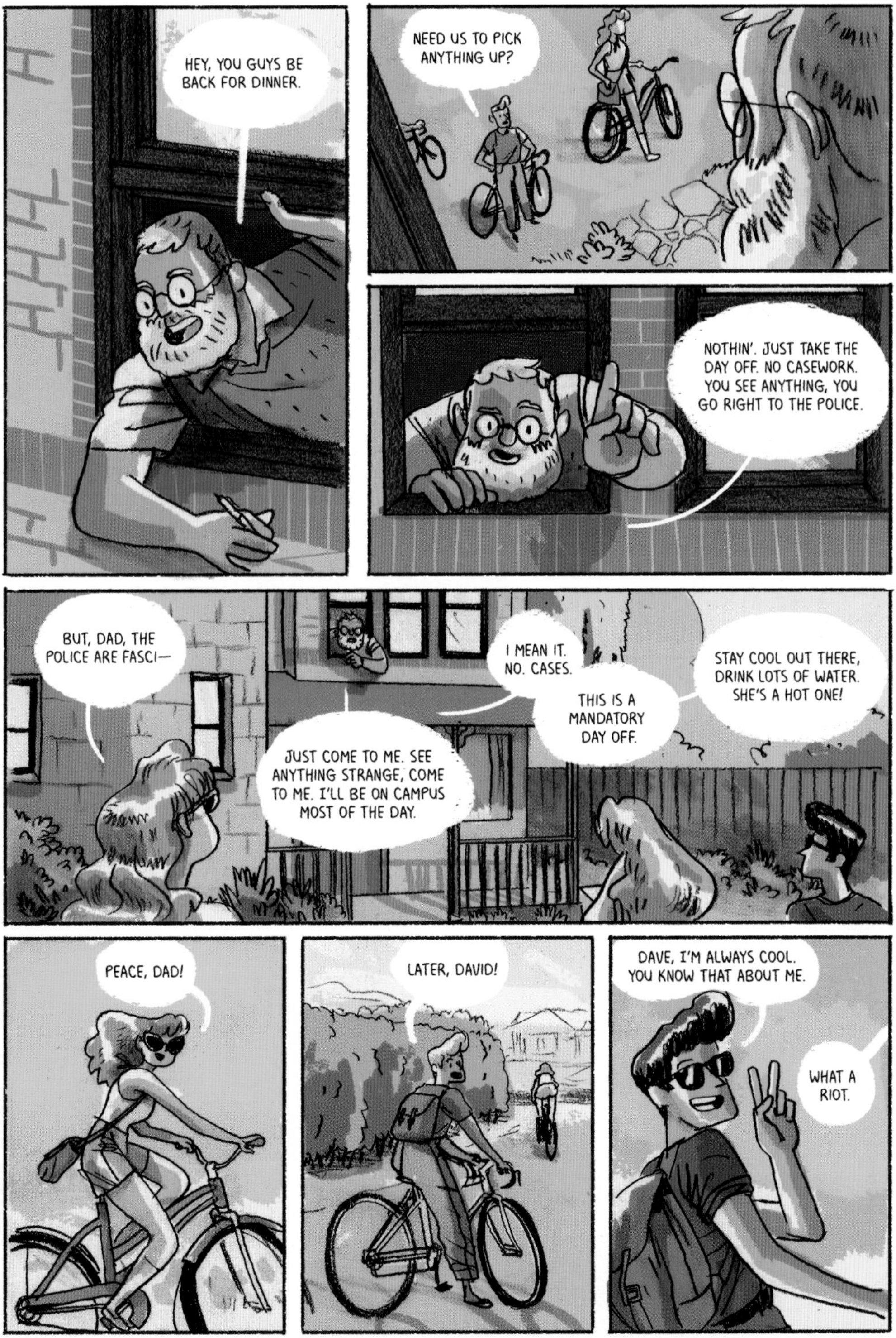
HEY, YOU GUYS BE BACK FOR DINNER.
NEED US TO PICK ANYTHING UP?
NOTHIN'. JUST TAKE THE DAY OFF. NO CASEWORK. YOU SEE ANYTHING, YOU GO RIGHT TO THE POLICE.
BUT, DAD, THE POLICE ARE FASCI—
JUST COME TO ME. SEE ANYTHING STRANGE, COME TO ME. I'LL BE ON CAMPUS MOST OF THE DAY.
I MEAN IT. NO. CASES.
THIS IS A MANDATORY DAY OFF.
STAY COOL OUT THERE, DRINK LOTS OF WATER. SHE'S A HOT ONE!
PEACE, DAD!
LATER, DAVID!
DAVE, I'M ALWAYS COOL. YOU KNOW THAT ABOUT ME.
WHAT A RIOT.

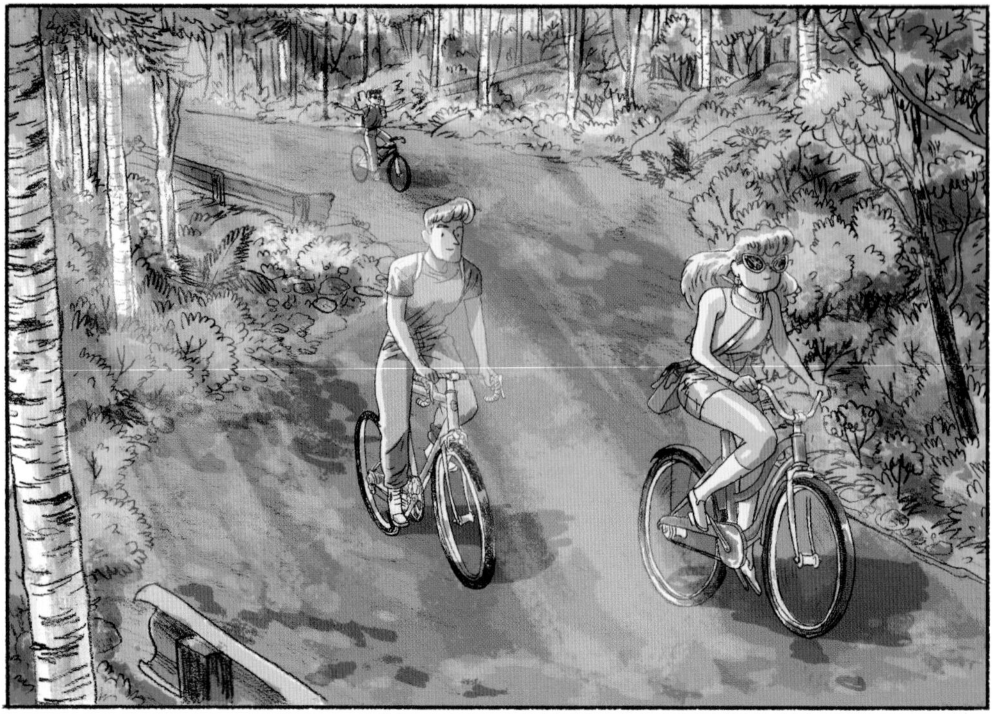

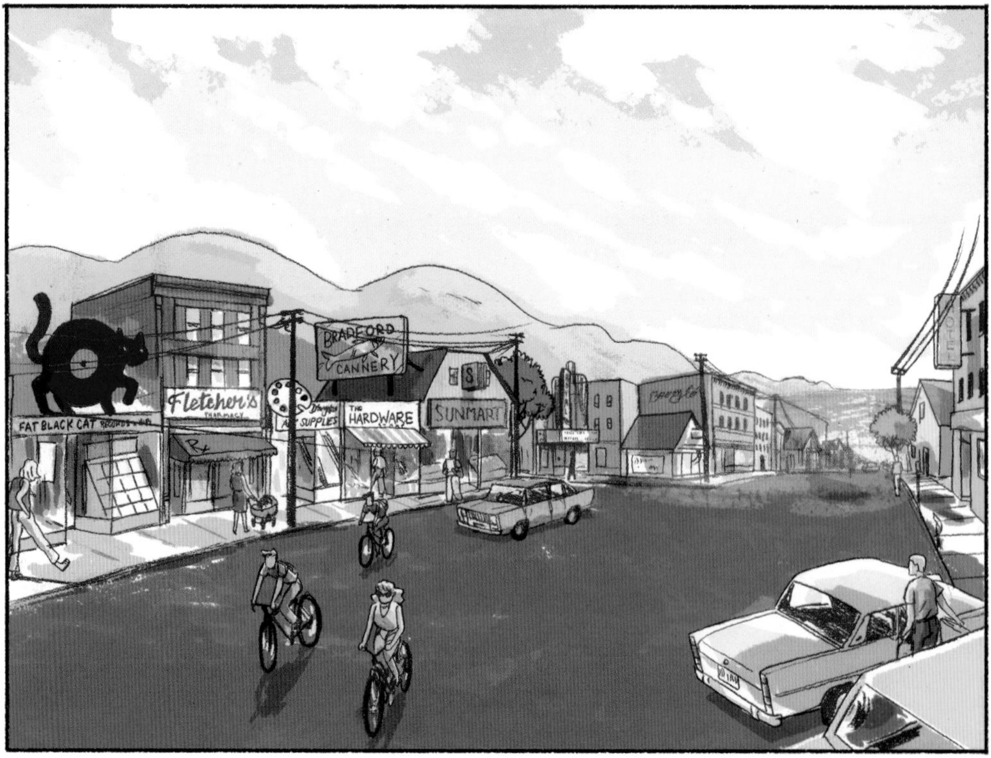
FAT BLACK CAT
Fletcher's
PHARMACY
BRADFORD
CANNERY
SUPPLIES
THE HARDWARE
SUNMART

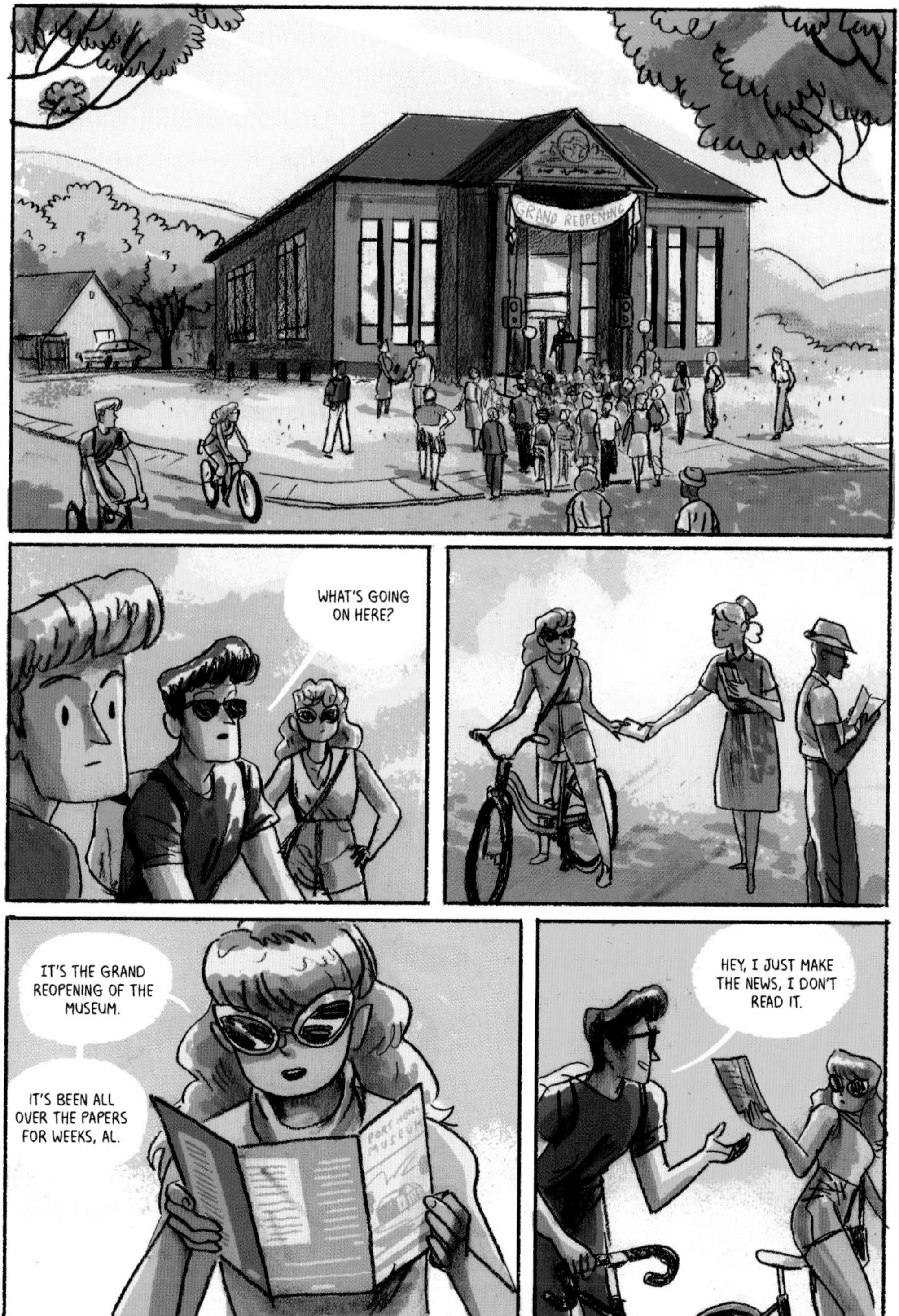
GRAND REOPENING
WHAT'S GOING ON HERE?
IT'S THE GRAND REOPENING OF THE MUSEUM.
IT'S BEEN ALL OVER THE PAPERS FOR WEEKS, AL.
HEY, I JUST MAKE THE NEWS, I DON'T READ IT.

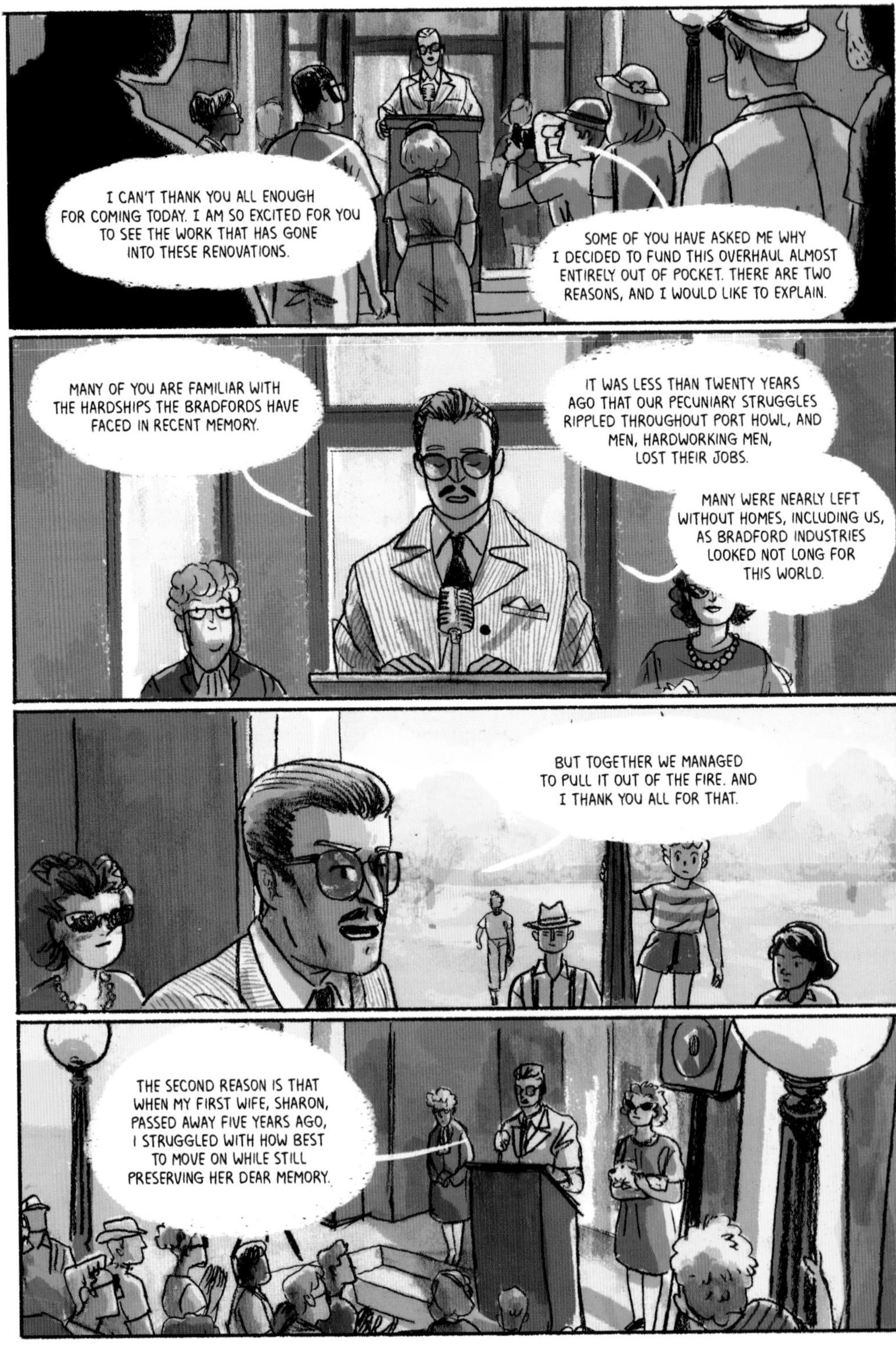

I CAN'T THANK YOU ALL ENOUGH FOR COMING TODAY. I AM SO EXCITED FOR YOU TO SEE THE WORK THAT HAS GONE INTO THESE RENOVATIONS.
SOME OF YOU HAVE ASKED ME WHY I DECIDED TO FUND THIS OVERHAUL ALMOST ENTIRELY OUT OF POCKET. THERE ARE TWO REASONS, AND I WOULD LIKE TO EXPLAIN.
MANY OF YOU ARE FAMILIAR WITH THE HARDSHIPS THE BRADFORDS HAVE FACED IN RECENT MEMORY.
IT WAS LESS THAN TWENTY YEARS AGO THAT OUR PECUNIARY STRUGGLES RIPPLED THROUGHOUT PORT HOWL, AND MEN, HARDWORKING MEN, LOST THEIR JOBS.
MANY WERE NEARLY LEFT WITHOUT HOMES, INCLUDING US, AS BRADFORD INDUSTRIES LOOKED NOT LONG FOR THIS WORLD.
BUT TOGETHER WE MANAGED TO PULL IT OUT OF THE FIRE. AND I THANK YOU ALL FOR THAT.
THE SECOND REASON IS THAT WHEN MY FIRST WIFE, SHARON, PASSED AWAY FIVE YEARS AGO, I STRUGGLED WITH HOW BEST TO MOVE ON WHILE STILL PRESERVING HER DEAR MEMORY.

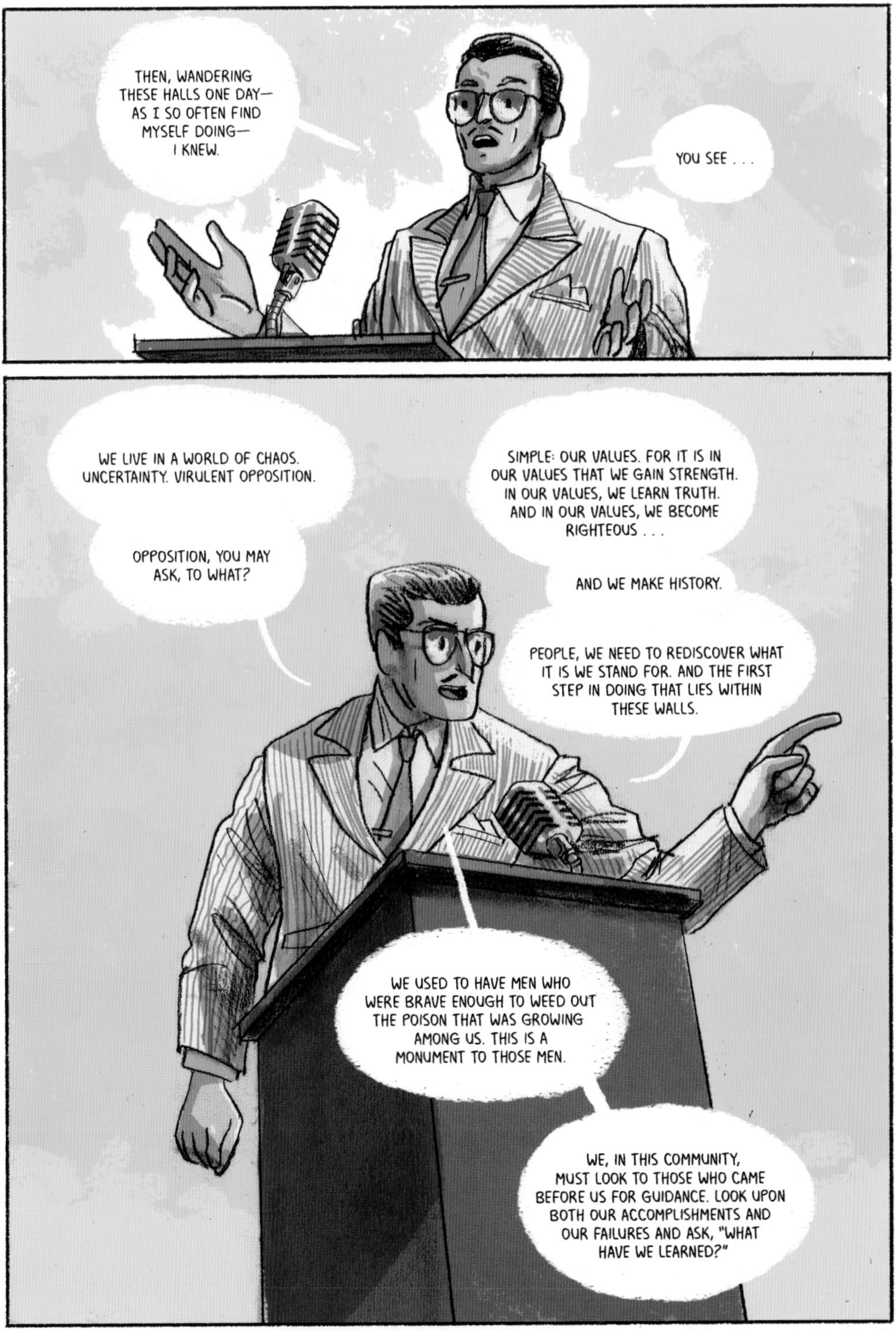
THEN, WANDERING THESE HALLS ONE DAY— AS I SO OFTEN FIND MYSELF DOING— I KNEW.
YOU SEE . . .
WE LIVE IN A WORLD OF CHAOS. UNCERTAINTY. VIRULENT OPPOSITION.
OPPOSITION, YOU MAY ASK, TO WHAT?
SIMPLE: OUR VALUES. FOR IT IS IN OUR VALUES THAT WE GAIN STRENGTH. IN OUR VALUES, WE LEARN TRUTH. AND IN OUR VALUES, WE BECOME RIGHTEOUS . . .
AND WE MAKE HISTORY.
PEOPLE, WE NEED TO REDISCOVER WHAT IT IS WE STAND FOR. AND THE FIRST STEP IN DOING THAT LIES WITHIN THESE WALLS.
WE USED TO HAVE MEN WHO WERE BRAVE ENOUGH TO WEED OUT THE POISON THAT WAS GROWING AMONG US. THIS IS A MONUMENT TO THOSE MEN.
WE, IN THIS COMMUNITY, MUST LOOK TO THOSE WHO CAME BEFORE US FOR GUIDANCE. LOOK UPON BOTH OUR ACCOMPLISHMENTS AND OUR FAILURES AND ASK, "WHAT HAVE WE LEARNED?"

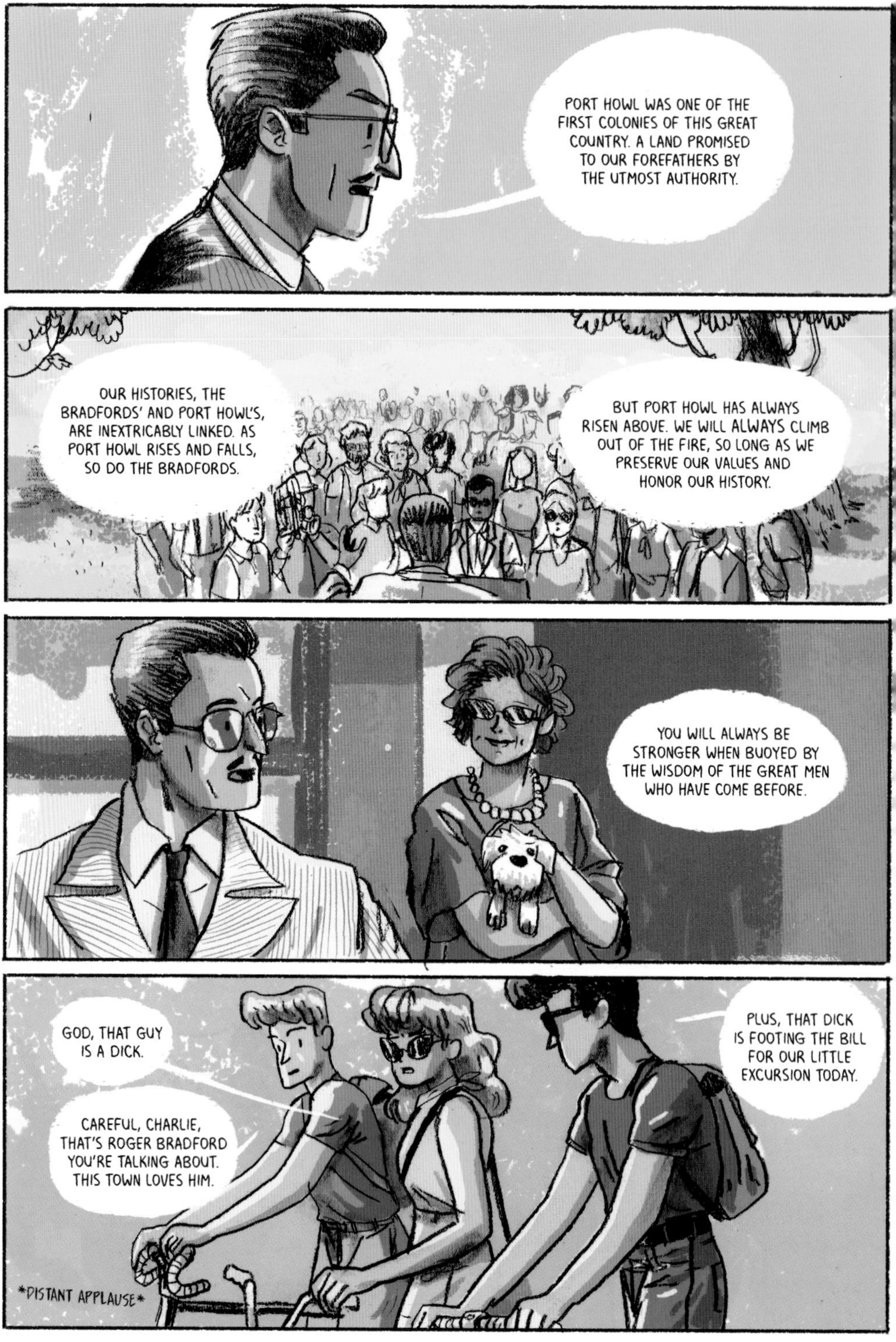
PORT HOWL WAS ONE OF THE FIRST COLONIES OF THIS GREAT COUNTRY. A LAND PROMISED TO OUR FOREFATHERS BY THE UTMOST AUTHORITY.
OUR HISTORIES, THE BRADFORDS' AND PORT HOWL'S, ARE INEXTRICABLY LINKED. AS PORT HOWL RISES AND FALLS, SO DO THE BRADFORDS.
BUT PORT HOWL HAS ALWAYS RISEN ABOVE. WE WILL ALWAYS CLIMB OUT OF THE FIRE, SO LONG AS WE PRESERVE OUR VALUES AND HONOR OUR HISTORY.
YOU WILL ALWAYS BE STRONGER WHEN BUOYED BY THE WISDOM OF THE GREAT MEN WHO HAVE COME BEFORE.
GOD, THAT GUY IS A DICK.
CAREFUL, CHARLIE, THAT'S ROGER BRADFORD YOU'RE TALKING ABOUT. THIS TOWN LOVES HIM.
PLUS, THAT DICK IS FOOTING THE BILL FOR OUR LITTLE EXCURSION TODAY.
DISTANT APPLAUSE

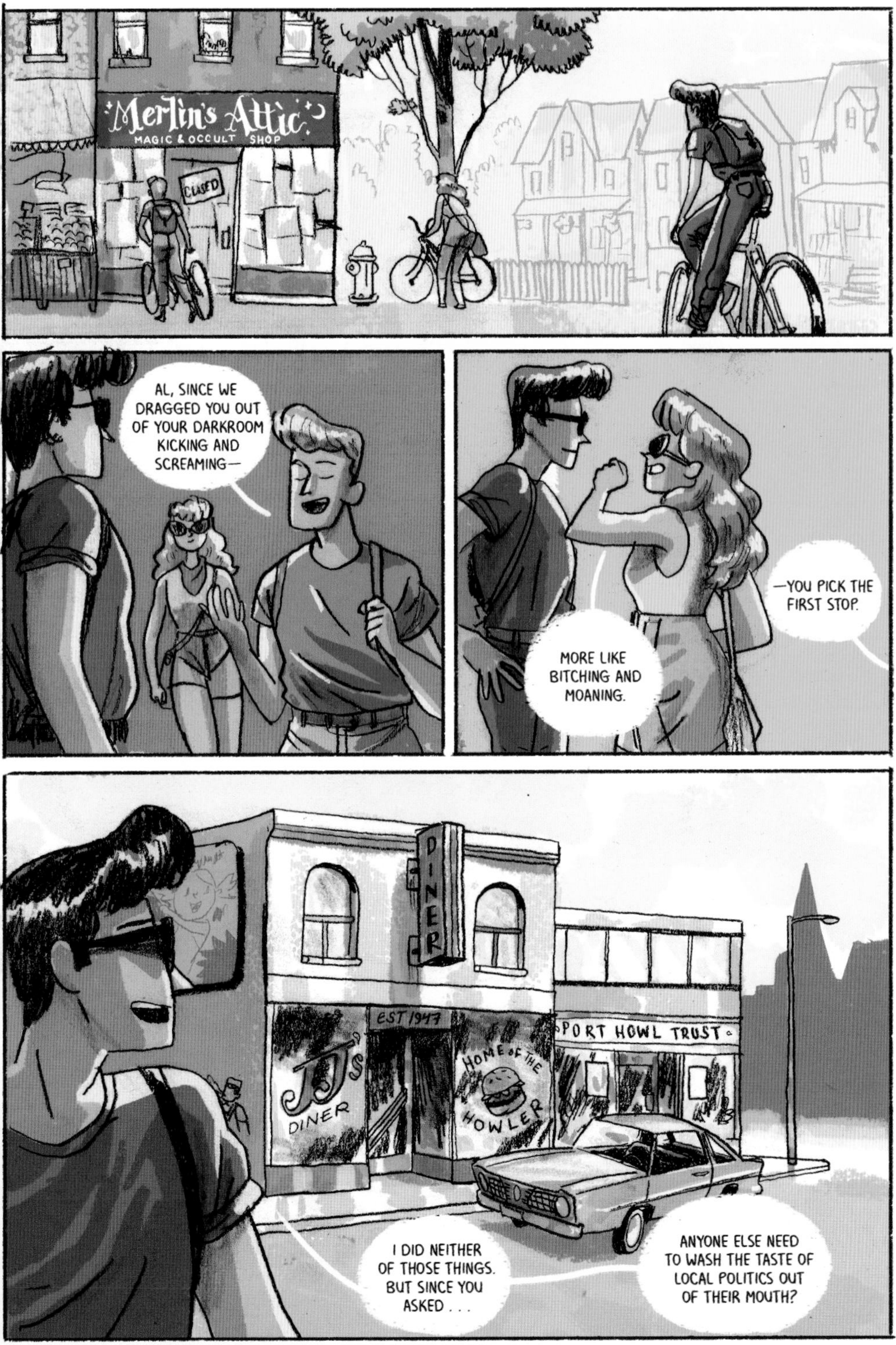
Merlin's Attic
MAGIC & OCCULT SHOP
CLOSED
AL, SINCE WE DRAGGED YOU OUT OF YOUR DARKROOM KICKING AND SCREAMING—
—YOU PICK THE FIRST STOP.
MORE LIKE BITCHING AND MOANING.
DINER
EST 1947
JJ's DINER
HOME OF THE HOWLER
PORT HOWL TRUST
I DID NEITHER OF THOSE THINGS. BUT SINCE YOU ASKED . . .
ANYONE ELSE NEED TO WASH THE TASTE OF LOCAL POLITICS OUT OF THEIR MOUTH?

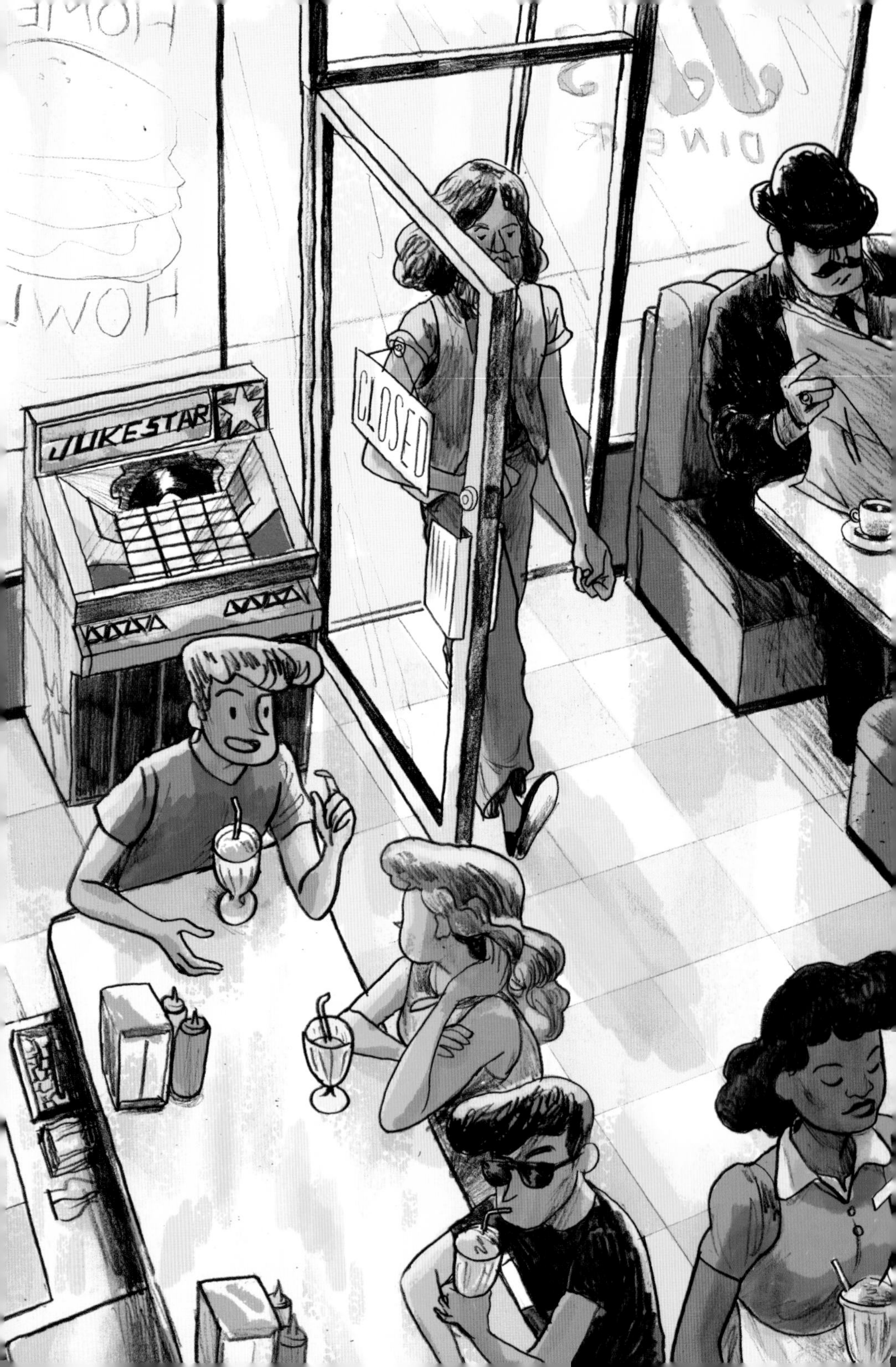
JUKESTAR
CLOSED

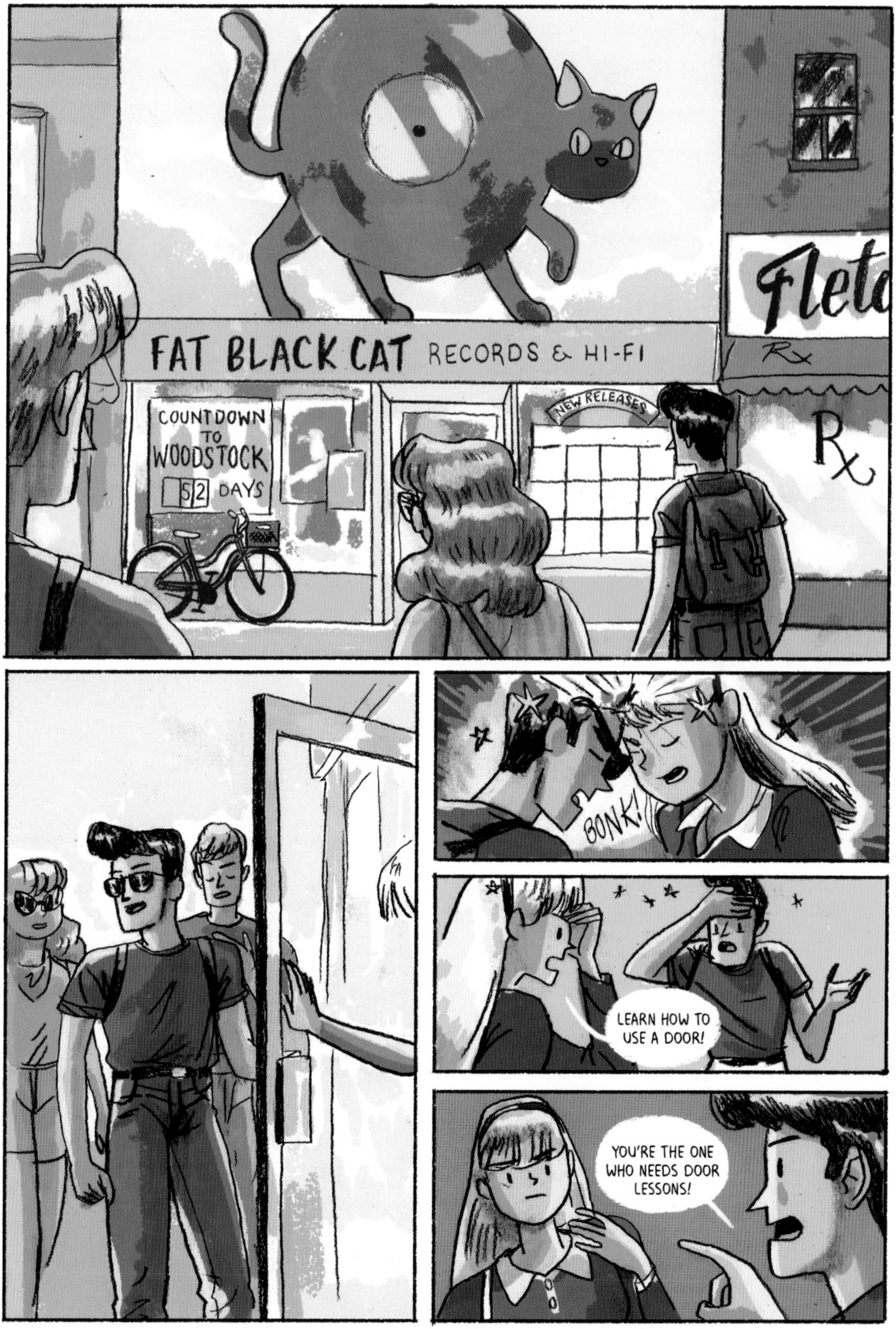
FAT BLACK CAT RECORDS & HI-FI
COUNTDOWN TO WOODSTOCK 52 DAYS
NEW RELEASES
Rx
BONK!
LEARN HOW TO USE A DOOR!
YOU'RE THE ONE WHO NEEDS DOOR LESSONS!

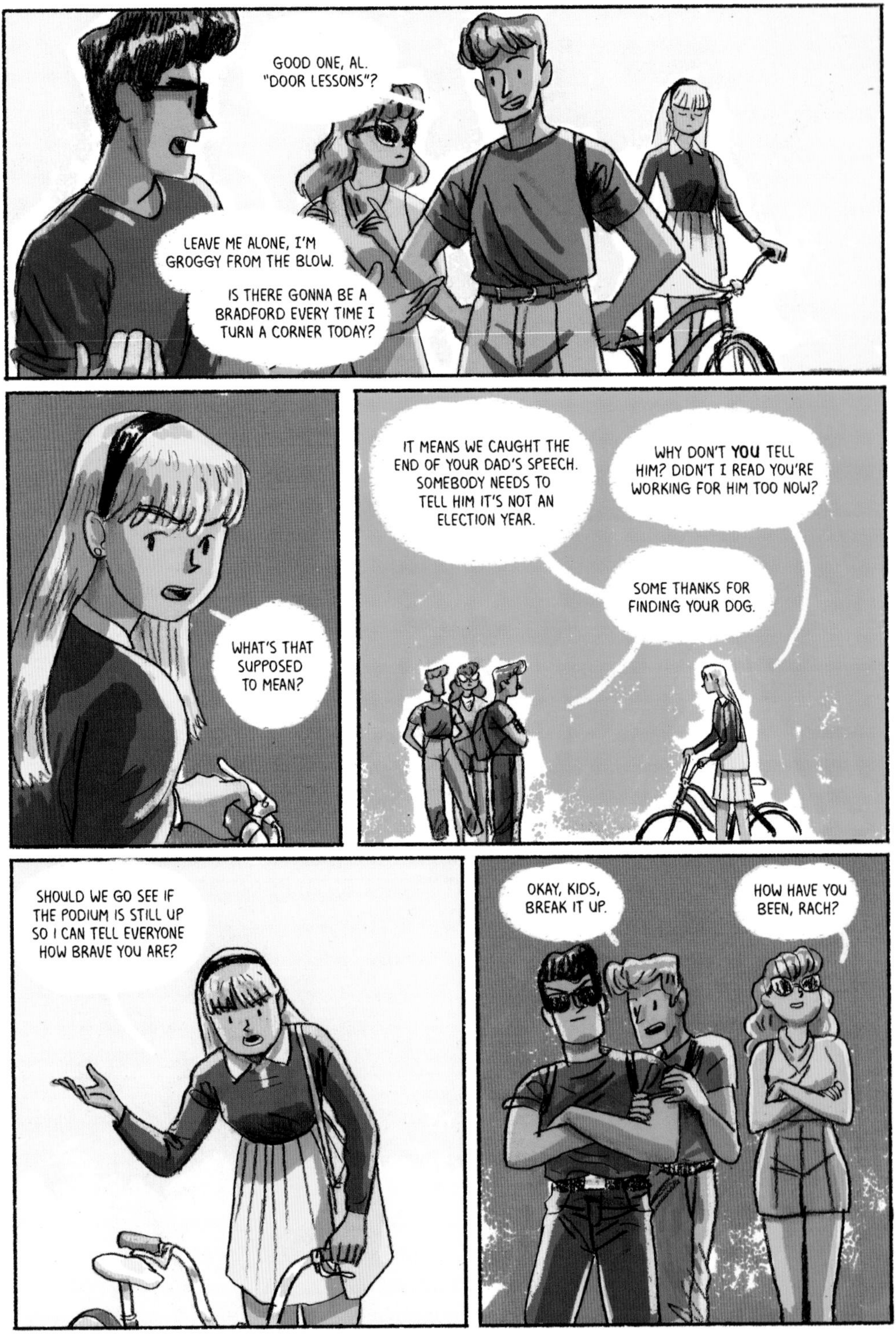
GOOD ONE, AL. "DOOR LESSONS"?
LEAVE ME ALONE, I'M GROGGY FROM THE BLOW.
IS THERE GONNA BE A BRADFORD EVERY TIME I TURN A CORNER TODAY?
WHAT'S THAT SUPPOSED TO MEAN?
IT MEANS WE CAUGHT THE END OF YOUR DAD'S SPEECH. SOMEBODY NEEDS TO TELL HIM IT'S NOT AN ELECTION YEAR.
WHY DON'T **YOU** TELL HIM? DIDN'T I READ YOU'RE WORKING FOR HIM TOO NOW?
SOME THANKS FOR FINDING YOUR DOG.
SHOULD WE GO SEE IF THE PODIUM IS STILL UP SO I CAN TELL EVERYONE HOW BRAVE YOU ARE?
OKAY, KIDS, BREAK IT UP.
HOW HAVE YOU BEEN, RACH?

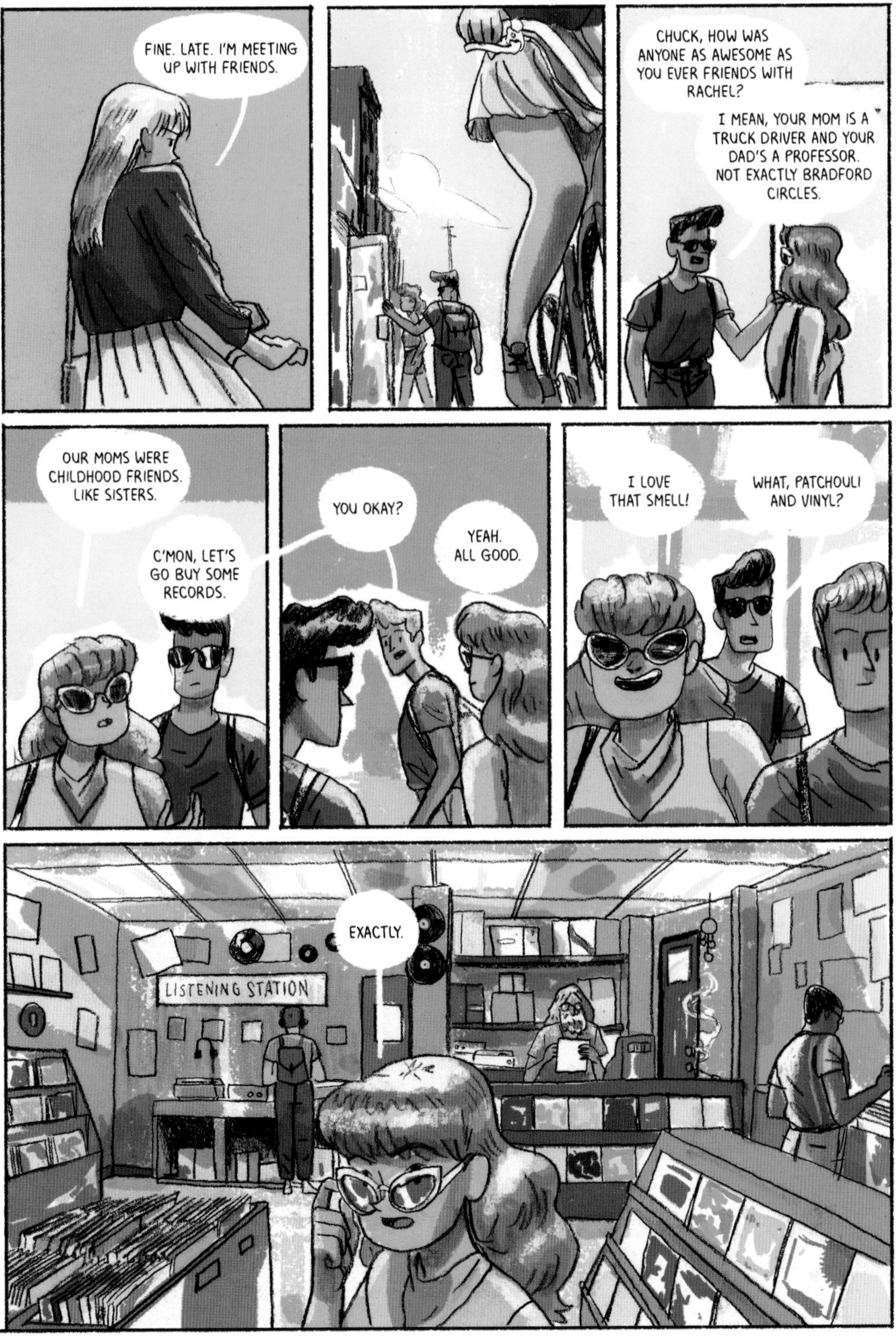
FINE. LATE. I'M MEETING UP WITH FRIENDS.
CHUCK, HOW WAS ANYONE AS AWESOME AS YOU EVER FRIENDS WITH RACHEL?
I MEAN, YOUR MOM IS A TRUCK DRIVER AND YOUR DAD'S A PROFESSOR. NOT EXACTLY BRADFORD CIRCLES.
OUR MOMS WERE CHILDHOOD FRIENDS. LIKE SISTERS.
C'MON, LET'S GO BUY SOME RECORDS.
YOU OKAY?
YEAH. ALL GOOD.
I LOVE THAT SMELL!
WHAT, PATCHOULI AND VINYL?
LISTENING STATION
EXACTLY.

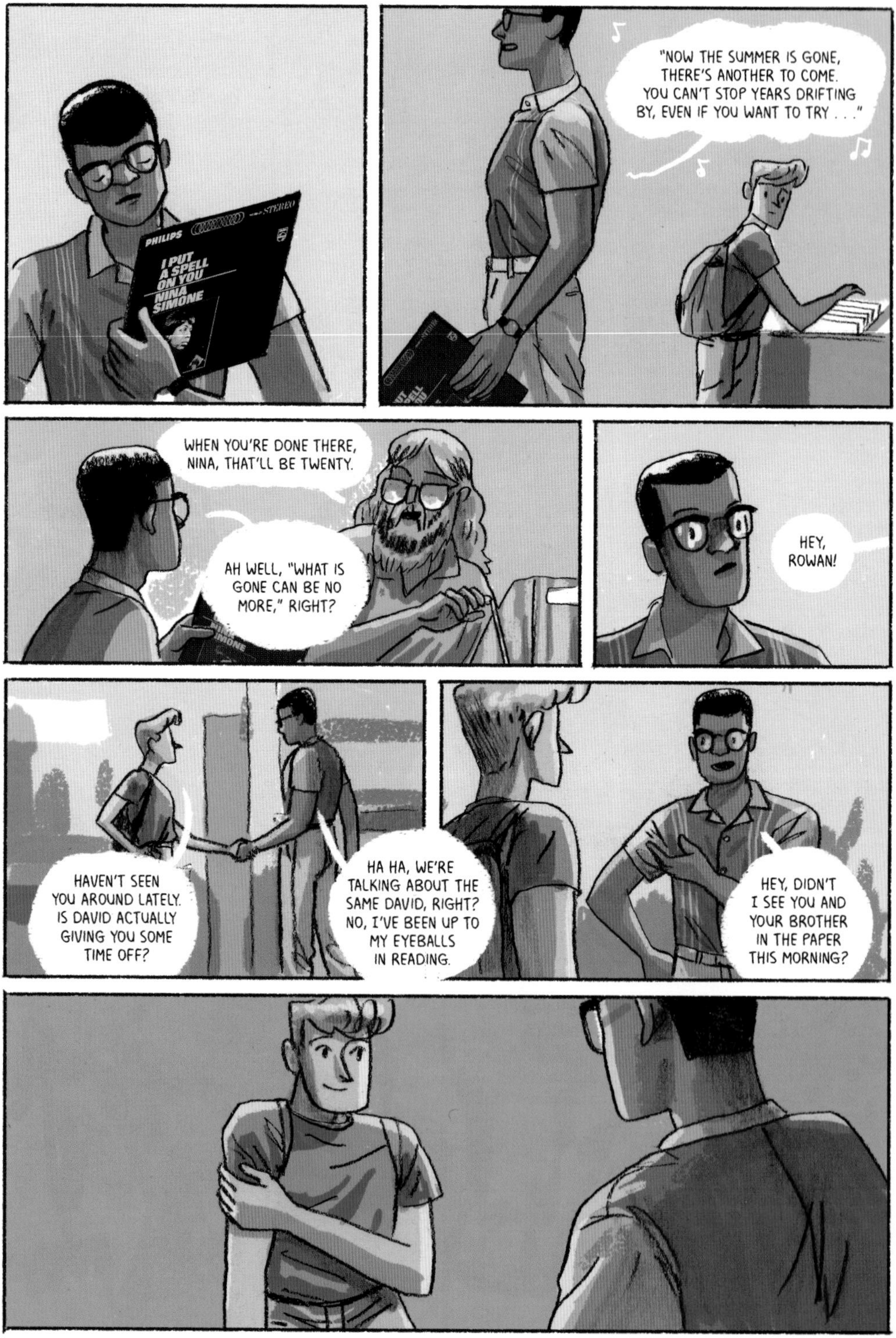
PHILIPS
STEREO
I PUT A SPELL ON YOU
NINA SIMONE
"NOW THE SUMMER IS GONE, THERE'S ANOTHER TO COME. YOU CAN'T STOP YEARS DRIFTING BY, EVEN IF YOU WANT TO TRY . . ."
WHEN YOU'RE DONE THERE, NINA, THAT'LL BE TWENTY.
AH WELL, "WHAT IS GONE CAN BE NO MORE," RIGHT?
HEY, ROWAN!
HAVEN'T SEEN YOU AROUND LATELY. IS DAVID ACTUALLY GIVING YOU SOME TIME OFF?
HA HA, WE'RE TALKING ABOUT THE SAME DAVID, RIGHT? NO, I'VE BEEN UP TO MY EYEBALLS IN READING.
HEY, DIDN'T I SEE YOU AND YOUR BROTHER IN THE PAPER THIS MORNING?

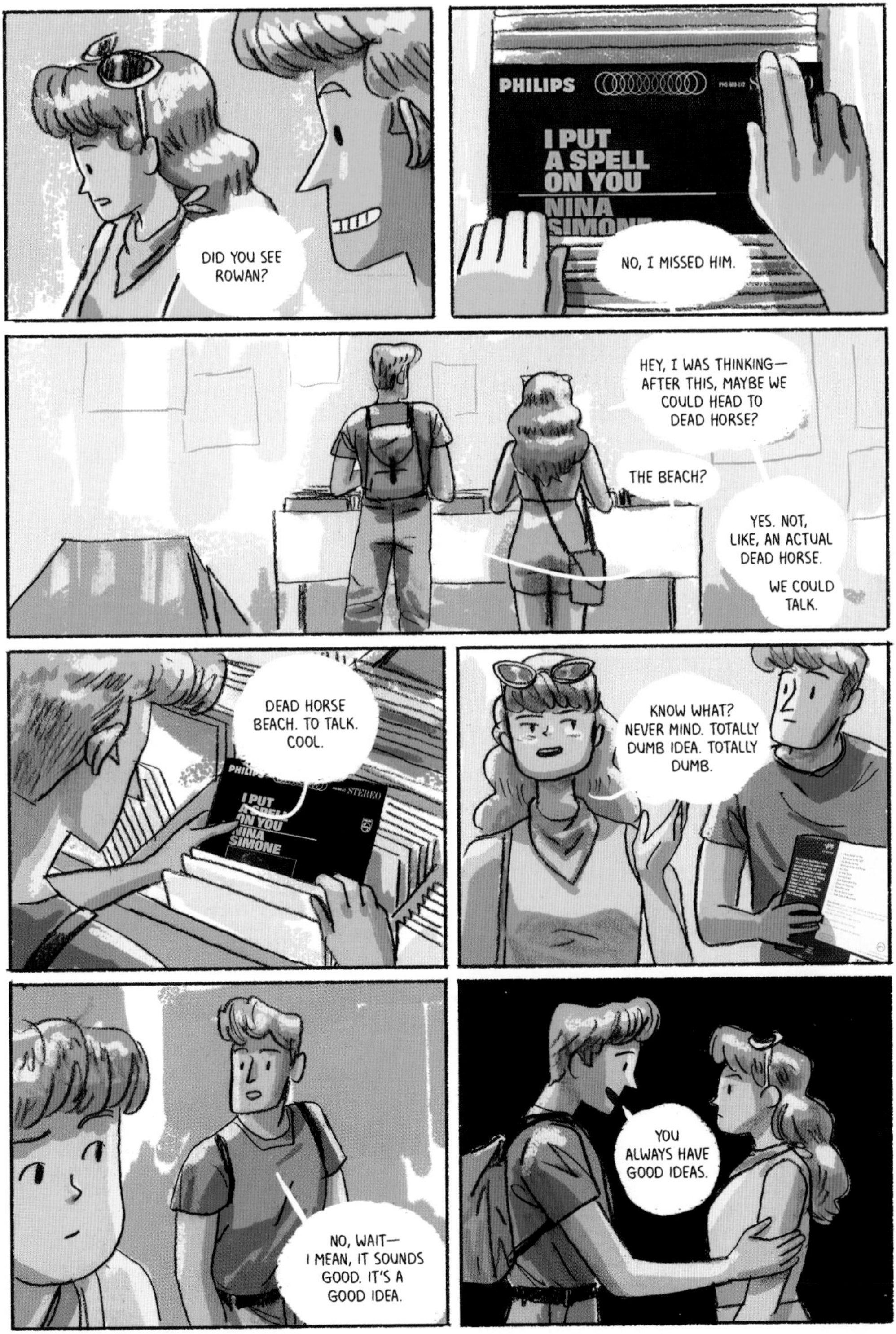

DID YOU SEE ROWAN?
PHILIPS
I PUT A SPELL ON YOU
NINA SIMONE
NO, I MISSED HIM.
HEY, I WAS THINKING— AFTER THIS, MAYBE WE COULD HEAD TO DEAD HORSE?
THE BEACH?
YES. NOT, LIKE, AN ACTUAL DEAD HORSE.
WE COULD TALK.
DEAD HORSE BEACH. TO TALK. COOL.
KNOW WHAT? NEVER MIND. TOTALLY DUMB IDEA. TOTALLY DUMB.
NO, WAIT— I MEAN, IT SOUNDS GOOD. IT'S A GOOD IDEA.
YOU ALWAYS HAVE GOOD IDEAS.

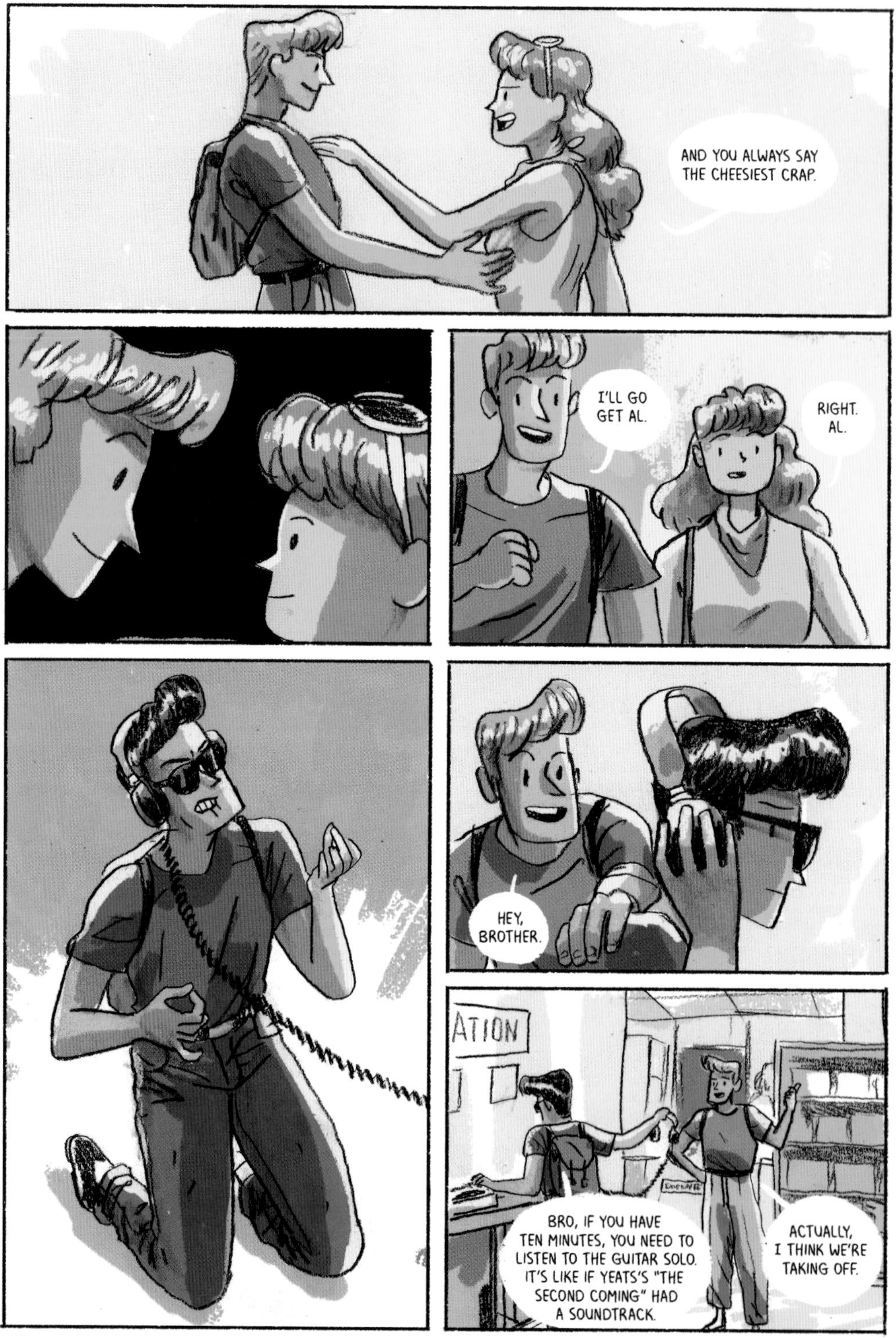
AND YOU ALWAYS SAY THE CHEESIEST CRAP.
I'LL GO GET AL.
RIGHT. AL.
HEY, BROTHER.
ATION
BRO, IF YOU HAVE TEN MINUTES, YOU NEED TO LISTEN TO THE GUITAR SOLO. IT'S LIKE IF YEATS'S "THE SECOND COMING" HAD A SOUNDTRACK.
ACTUALLY, I THINK WE'RE TAKING OFF.

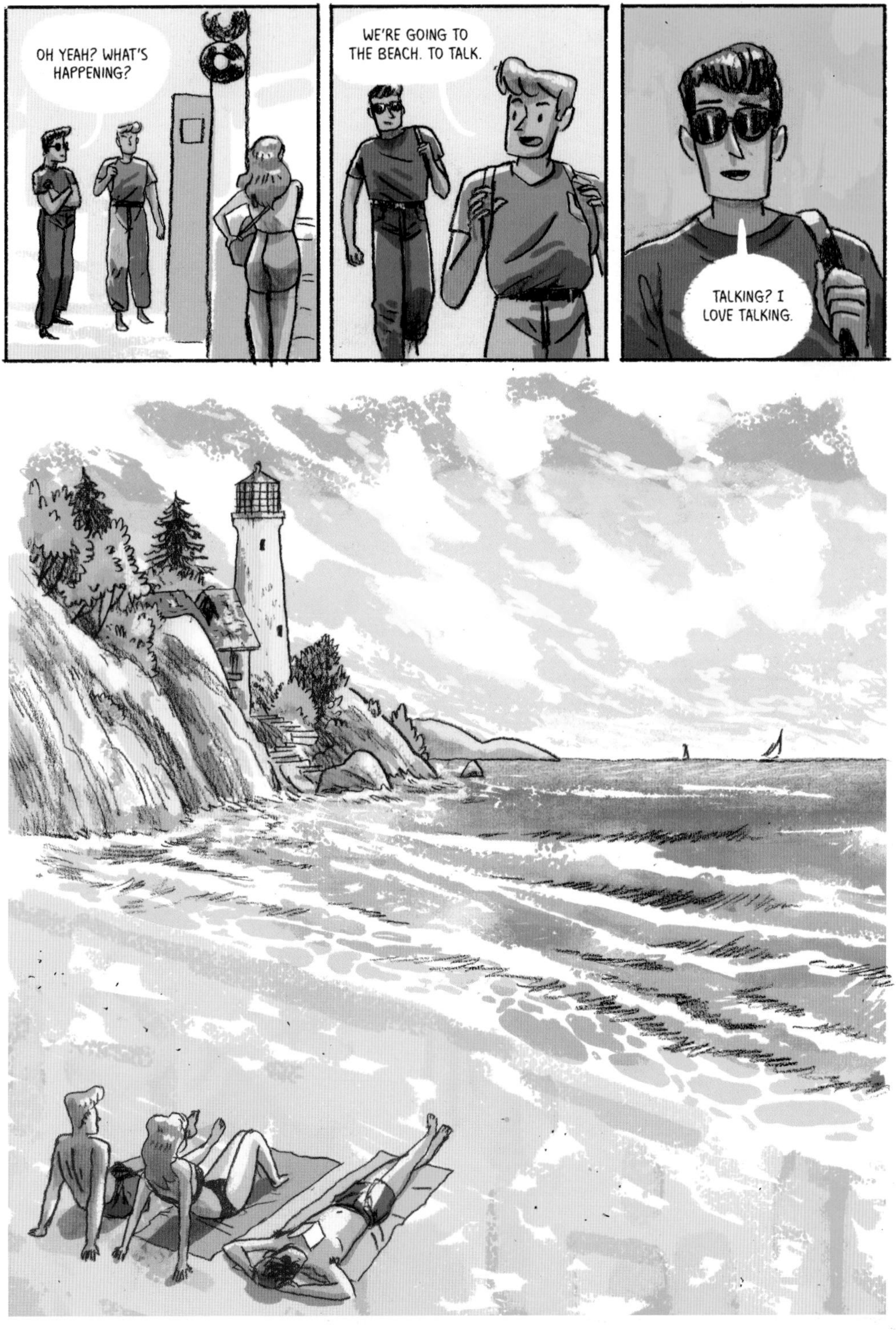
OH YEAH? WHAT'S HAPPENING?
WE'RE GOING TO THE BEACH. TO TALK.
TALKING? I LOVE TALKING.

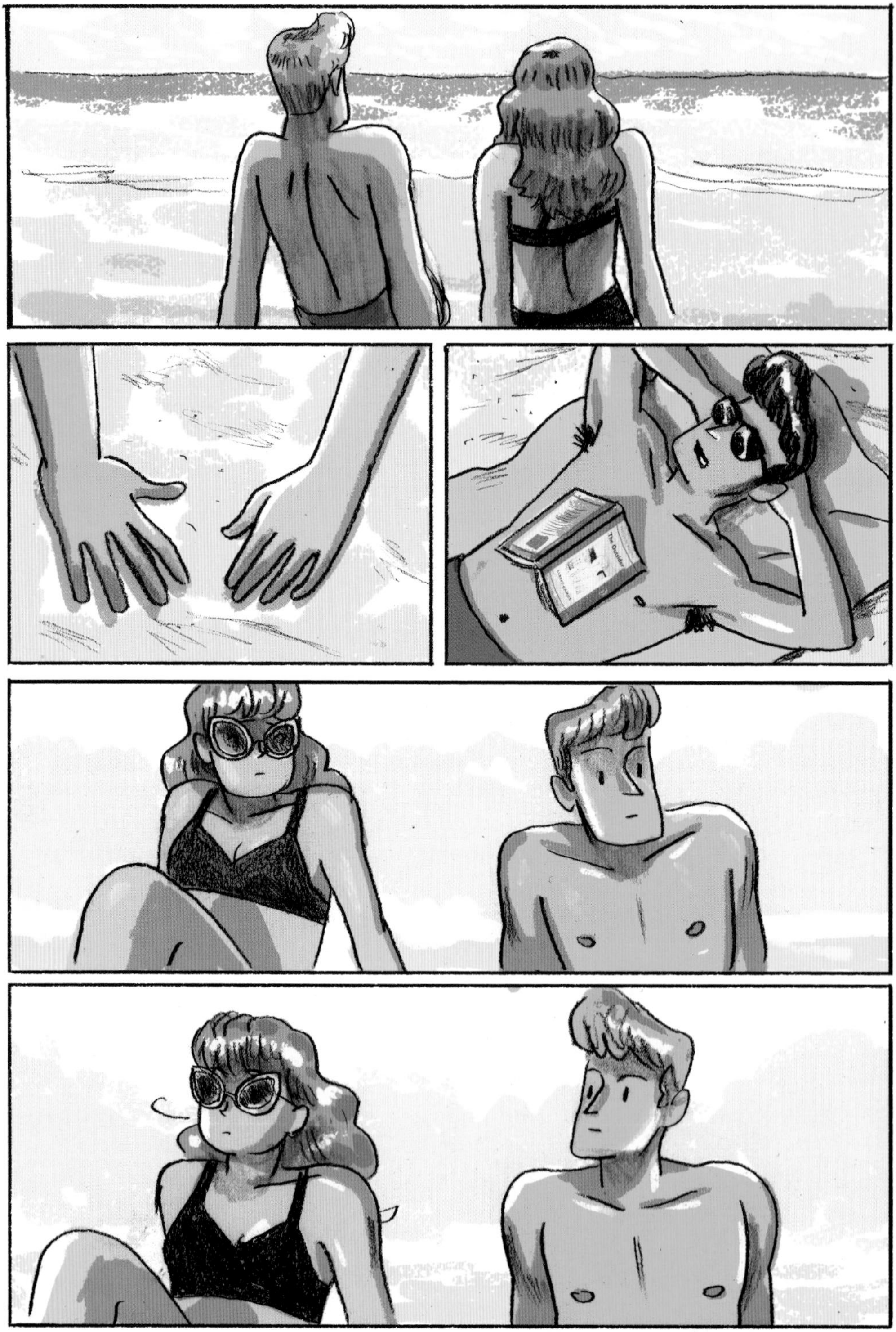
The Outsider

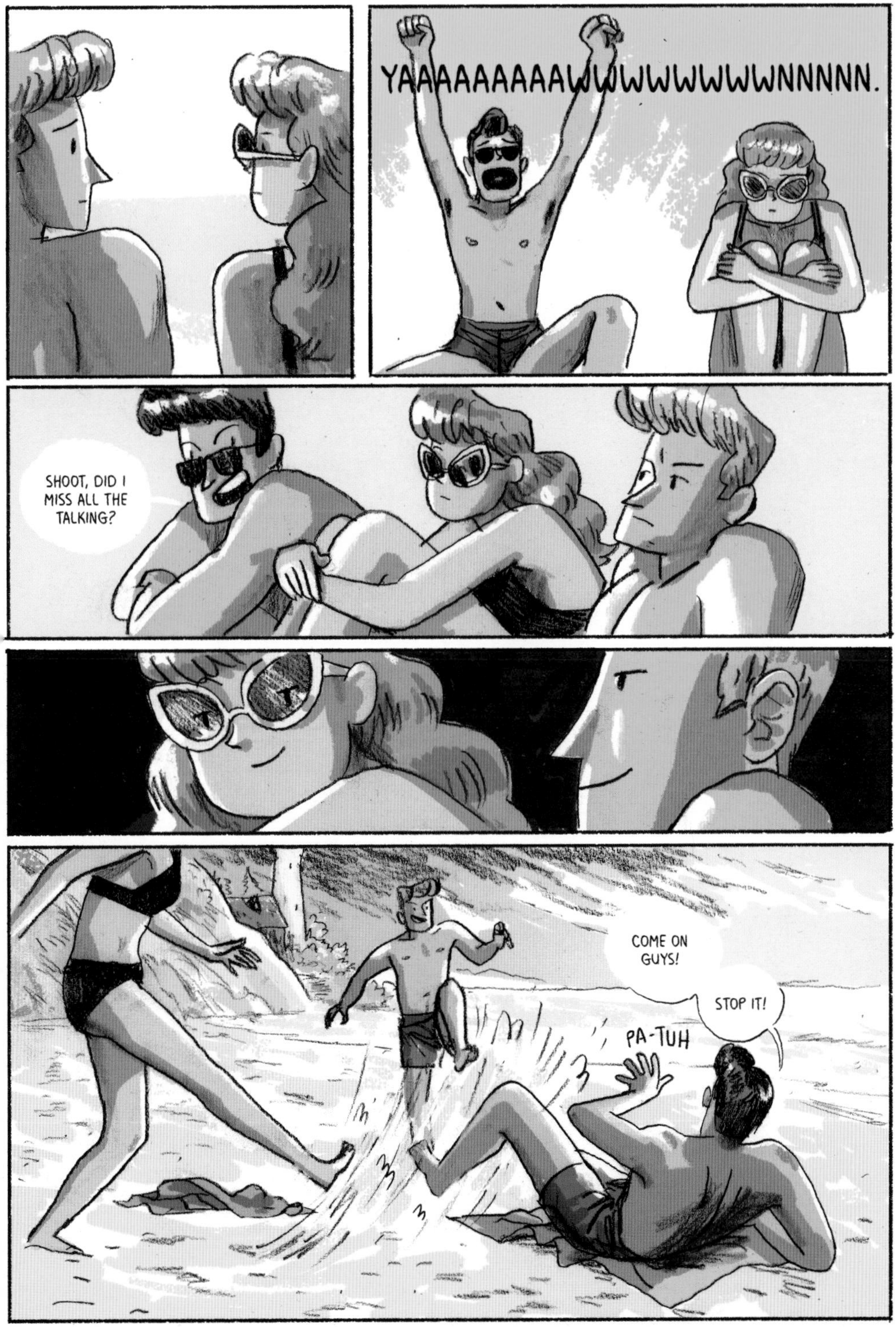
YAAAAAAAAWWWWWWWWNNNNN.
SHOOT, DID I MISS ALL THE TALKING?
COME ON GUYS!
STOP IT!
PA-TUH

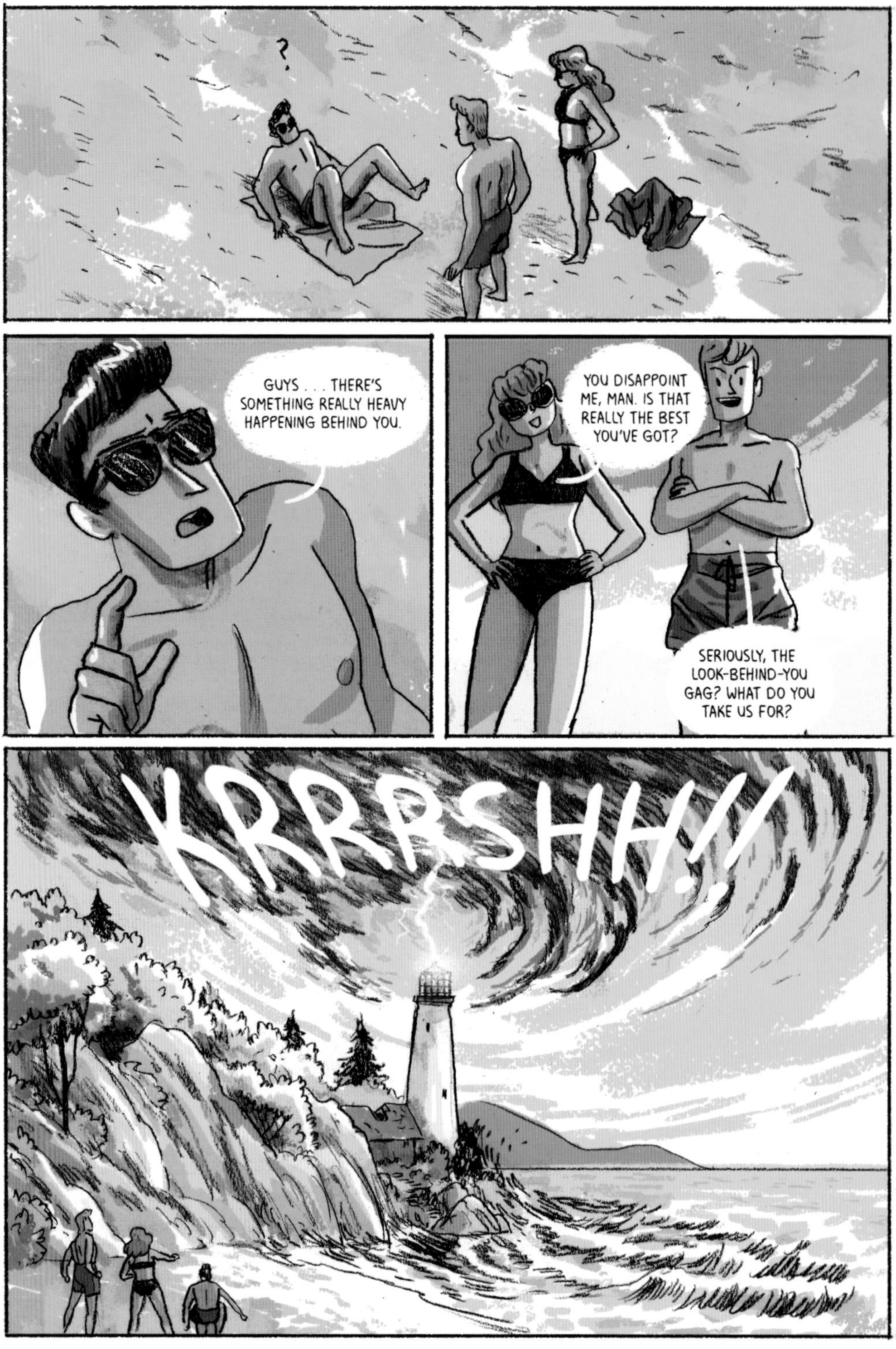
?
GUYS . . . THERE'S SOMETHING REALLY HEAVY HAPPENING BEHIND YOU.
YOU DISAPPOINT ME, MAN. IS THAT REALLY THE BEST YOU'VE GOT?
SERIOUSLY, THE LOOK-BEHIND-YOU GAG? WHAT DO YOU TAKE US FOR?
KRRRSHH!!

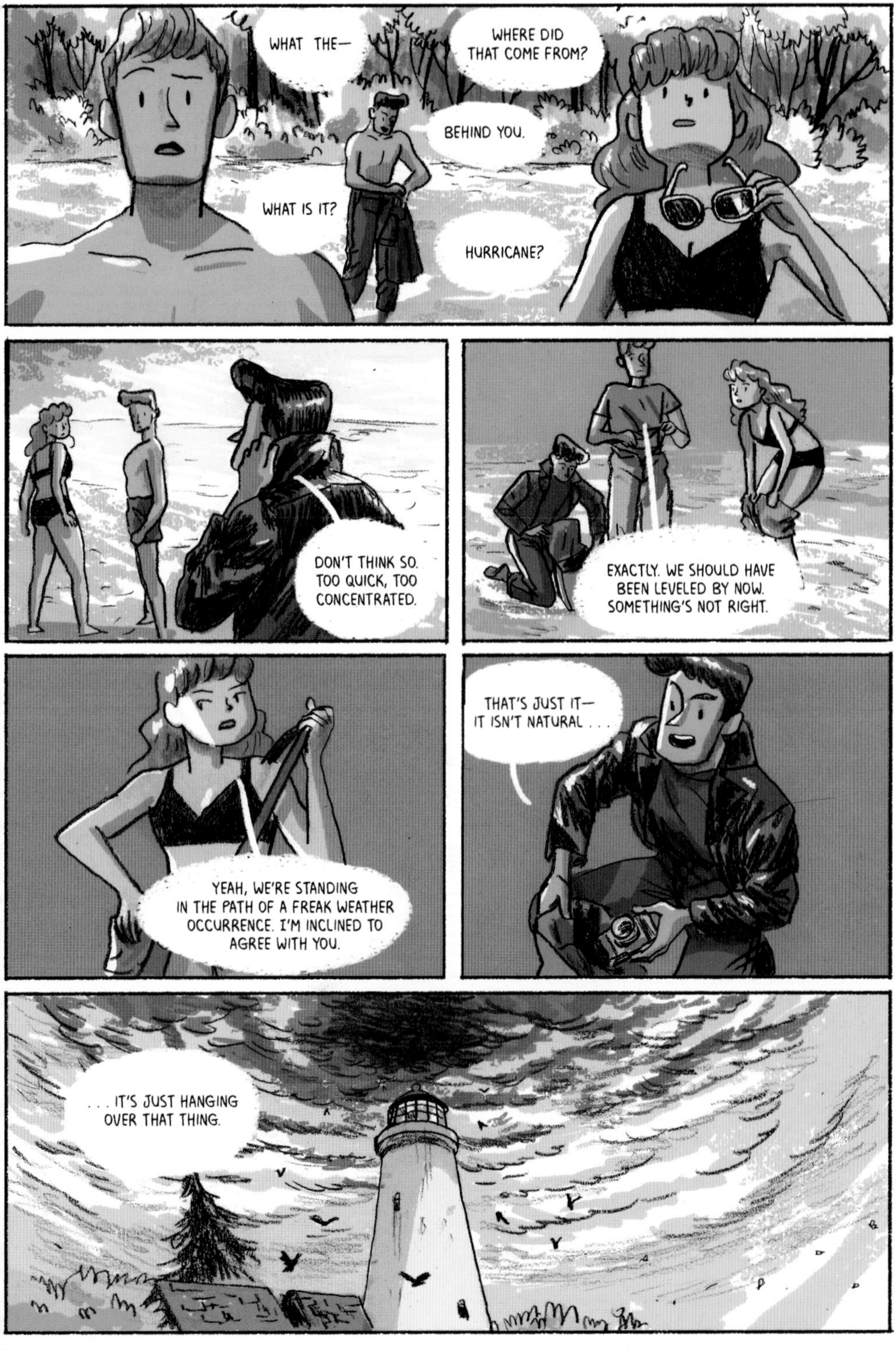
WHAT THE—
WHERE DID THAT COME FROM?
BEHIND YOU.
WHAT IS IT?
HURRICANE?
DON'T THINK SO. TOO QUICK, TOO CONCENTRATED.
EXACTLY. WE SHOULD HAVE BEEN LEVELED BY NOW. SOMETHING'S NOT RIGHT.
YEAH, WE'RE STANDING IN THE PATH OF A FREAK WEATHER OCCURRENCE. I'M INCLINED TO AGREE WITH YOU.
THAT'S JUST IT— IT ISN'T NATURAL . . .
. . . IT'S JUST HANGING OVER THAT THING.

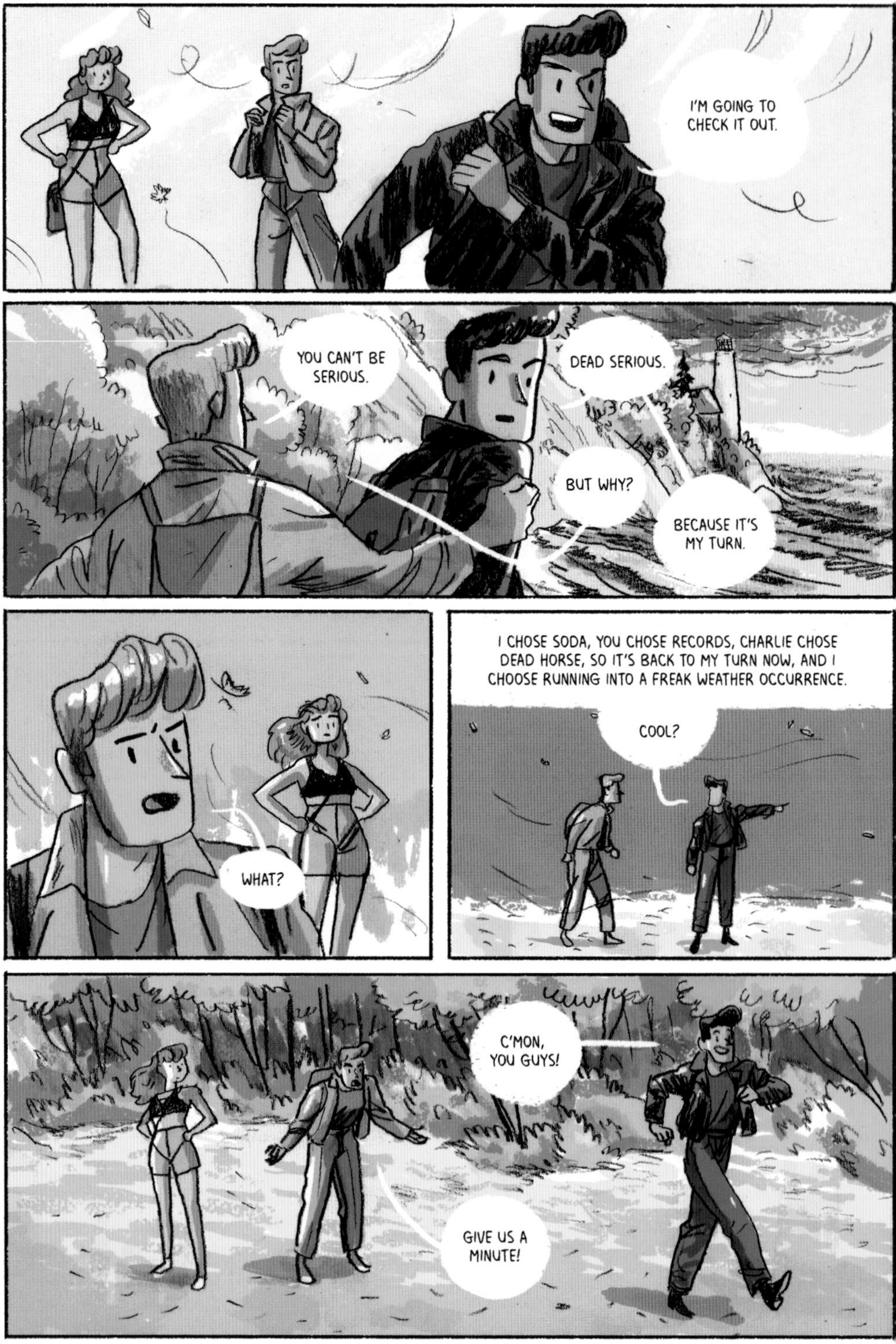
I'M GOING TO CHECK IT OUT.
YOU CAN'T BE SERIOUS.
DEAD SERIOUS.
BUT WHY?
BECAUSE IT'S MY TURN.
WHAT?
I CHOSE SODA, YOU CHOSE RECORDS, CHARLIE CHOSE DEAD HORSE, SO IT'S BACK TO MY TURN NOW, AND I CHOOSE RUNNING INTO A FREAK WEATHER OCCURRENCE.
COOL?
C'MON, YOU GUYS!
GIVE US A MINUTE!

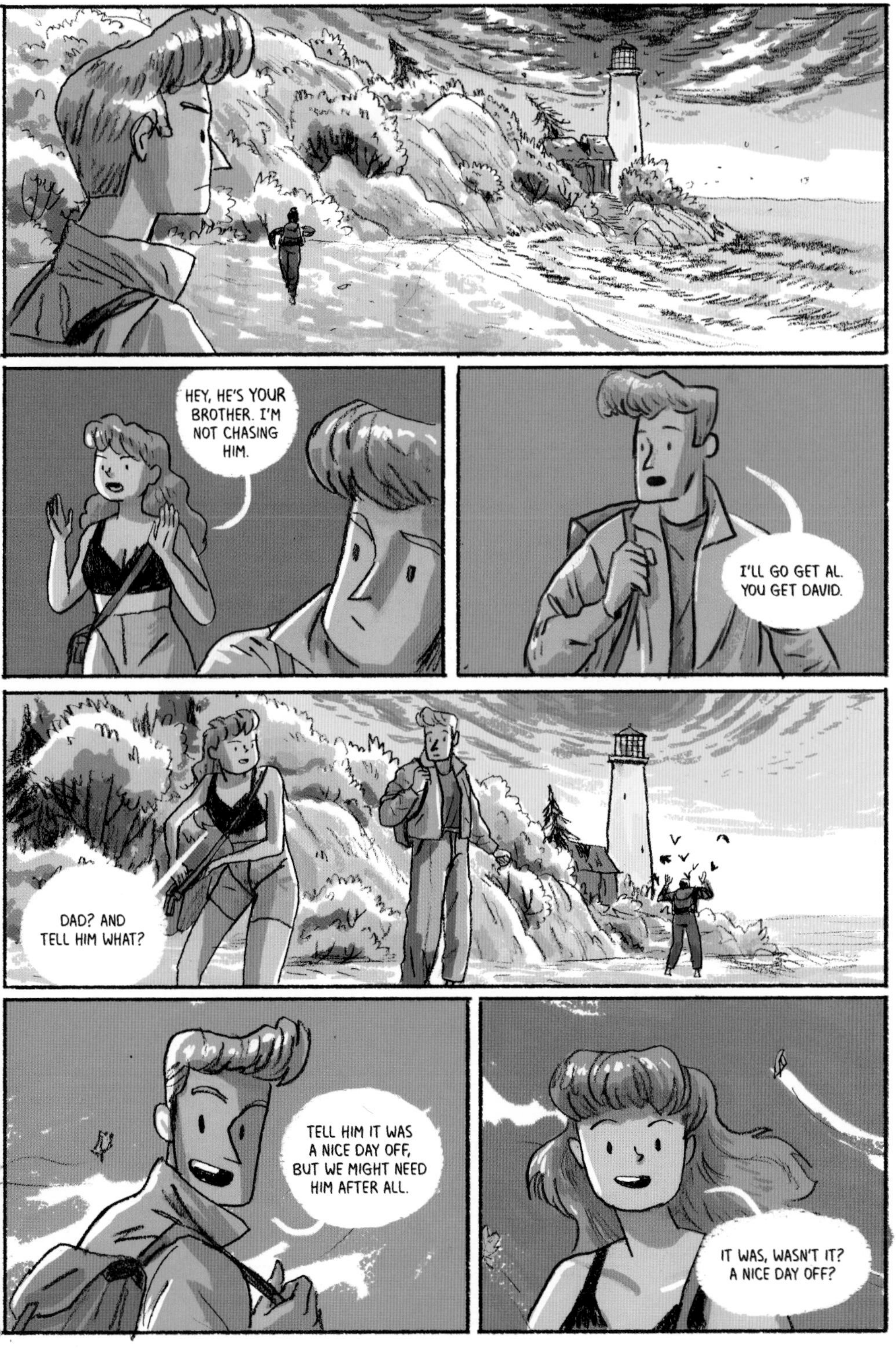
HEY, HE'S YOUR BROTHER. I'M NOT CHASING HIM.
I'LL GO GET AL. YOU GET DAVID.
DAD? AND TELL HIM WHAT?
TELL HIM IT WAS A NICE DAY OFF, BUT WE MIGHT NEED HIM AFTER ALL.
IT WAS, WASN'T IT? A NICE DAY OFF?

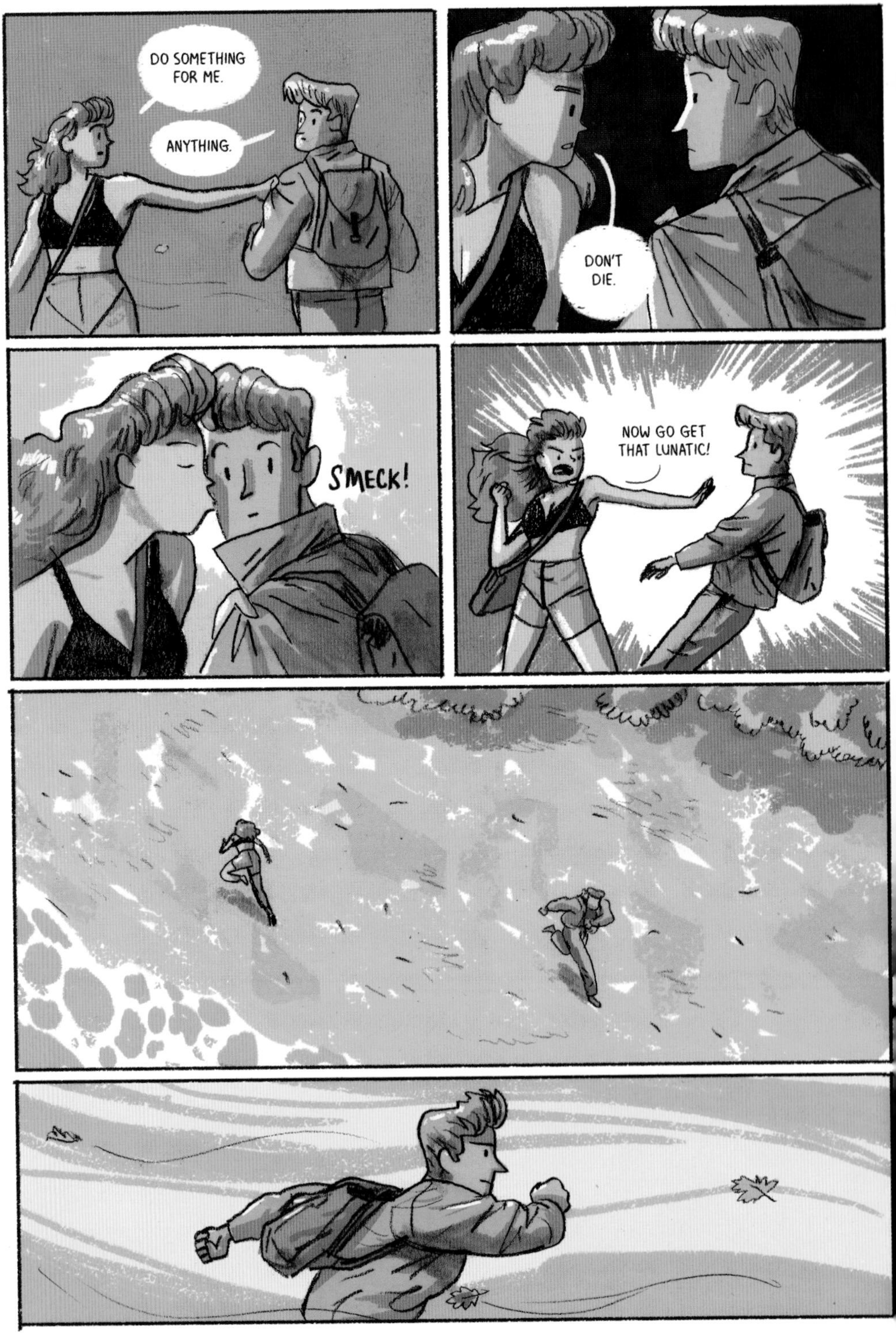
DO SOMETHING FOR ME.
ANYTHING.
DON'T DIE.
SMECK!
NOW GO GET THAT LUNATIC!

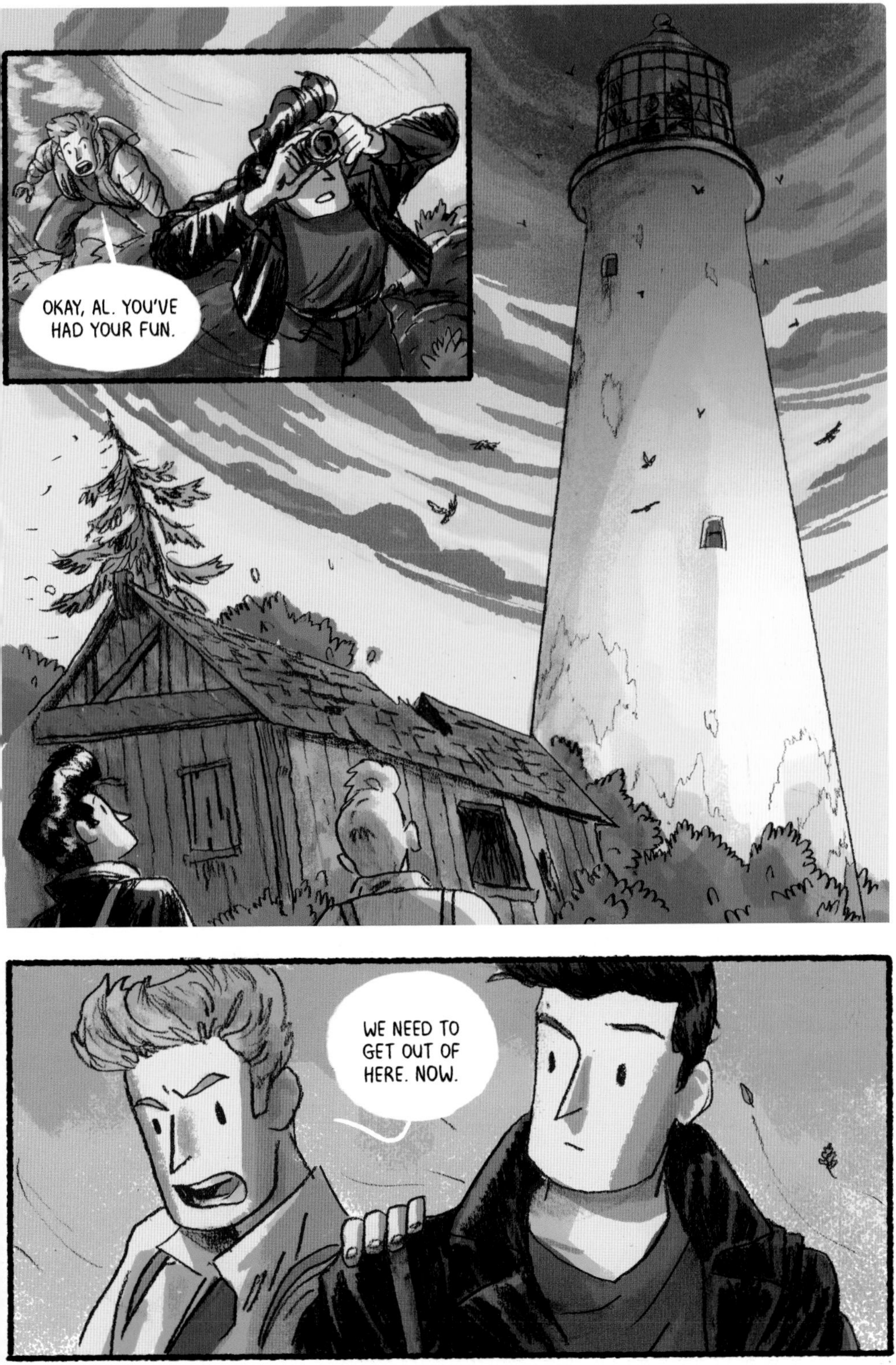
OKAY, AL. YOU'VE HAD YOUR FUN.
WE NEED TO GET OUT OF HERE. NOW.

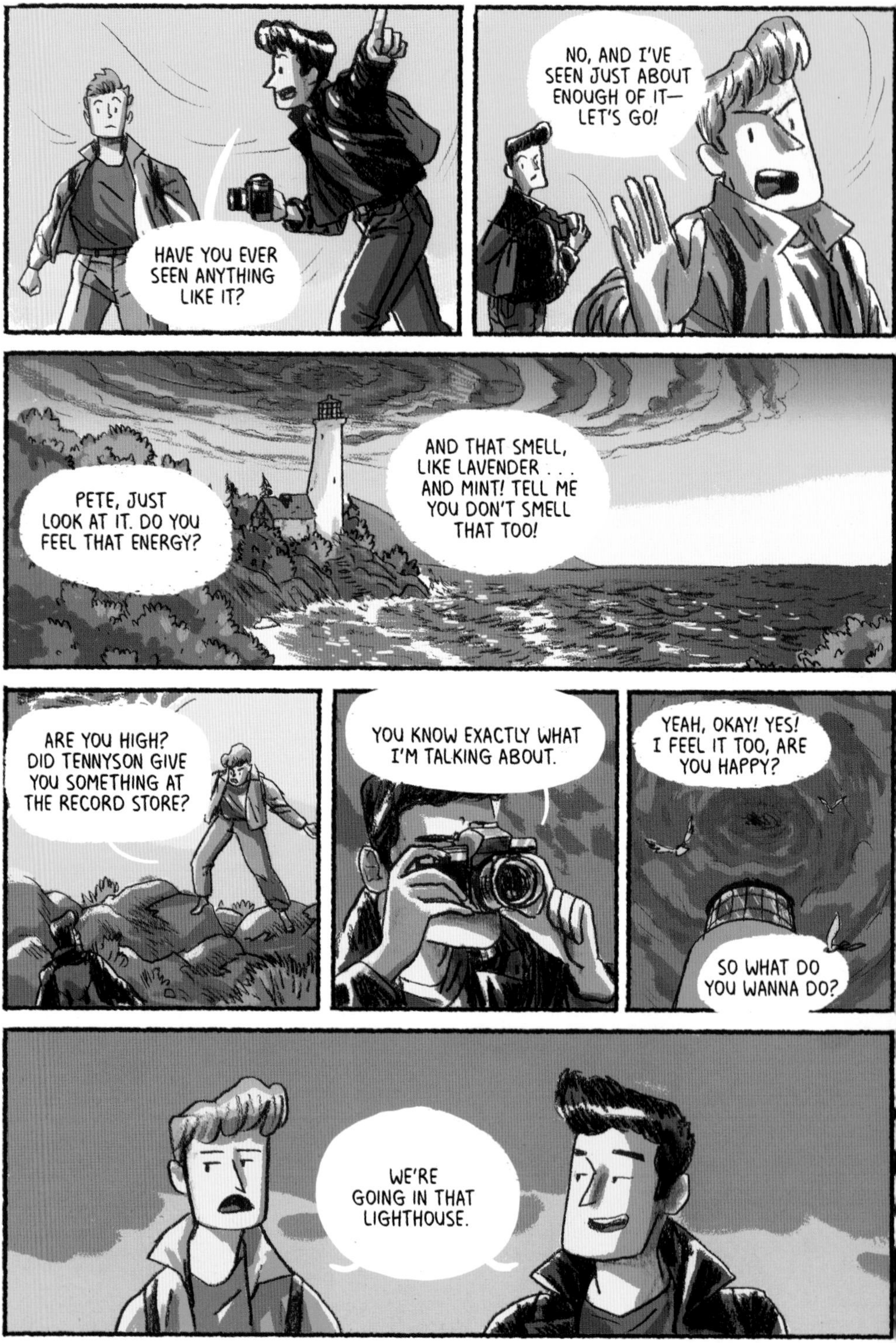
HAVE YOU EVER SEEN ANYTHING LIKE IT?
NO, AND I'VE SEEN JUST ABOUT ENOUGH OF IT—LET'S GO!
PETE, JUST LOOK AT IT. DO YOU FEEL THAT ENERGY?
AND THAT SMELL, LIKE LAVENDER . . . AND MINT! TELL ME YOU DON'T SMELL THAT TOO!
ARE YOU HIGH? DID TENNYSON GIVE YOU SOMETHING AT THE RECORD STORE?
YOU KNOW EXACTLY WHAT I'M TALKING ABOUT.
YEAH, OKAY! YES! I FEEL IT TOO, ARE YOU HAPPY?
SO WHAT DO YOU WANNA DO?
WE'RE GOING IN THAT LIGHTHOUSE.

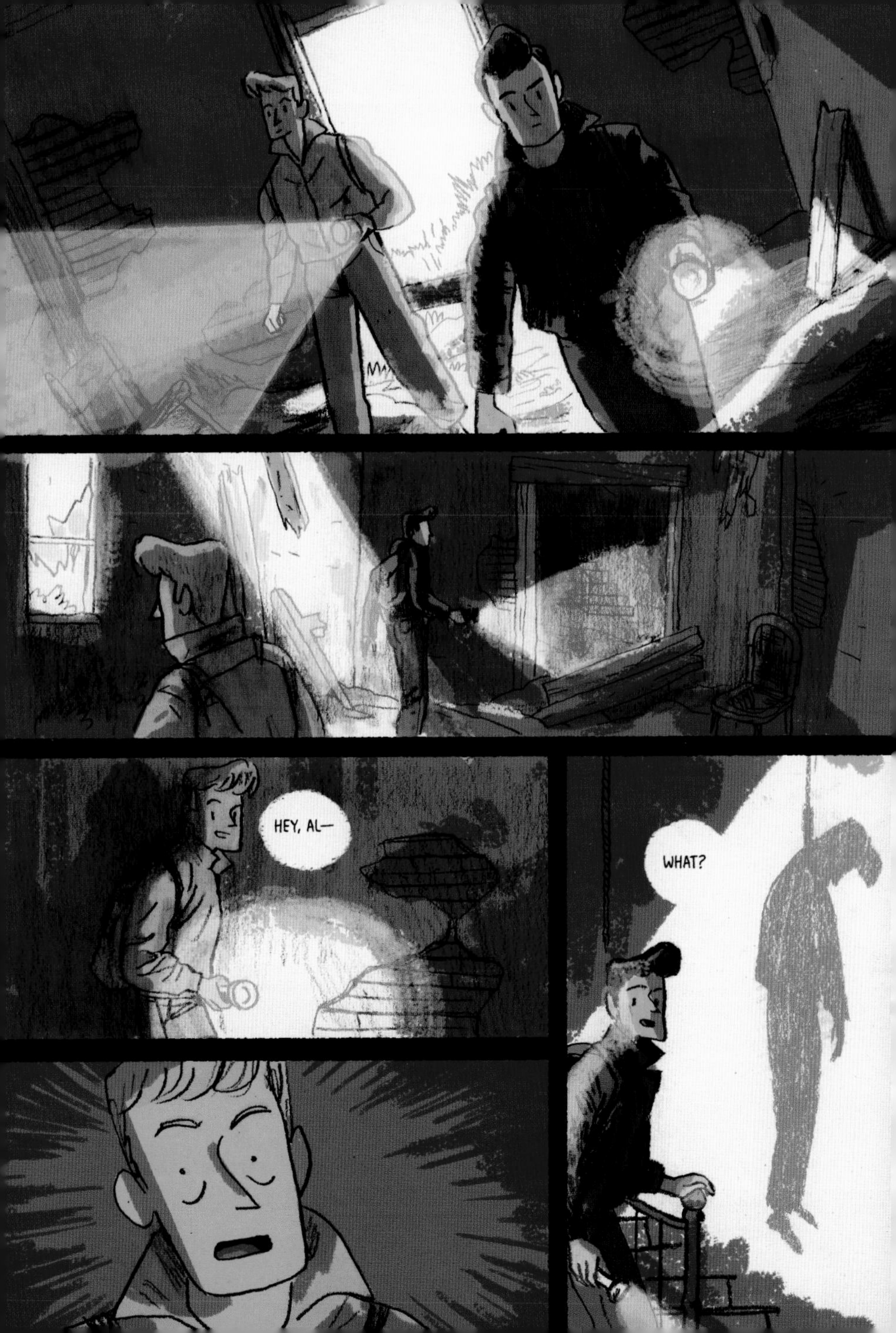
HEY, AL—
WHAT?

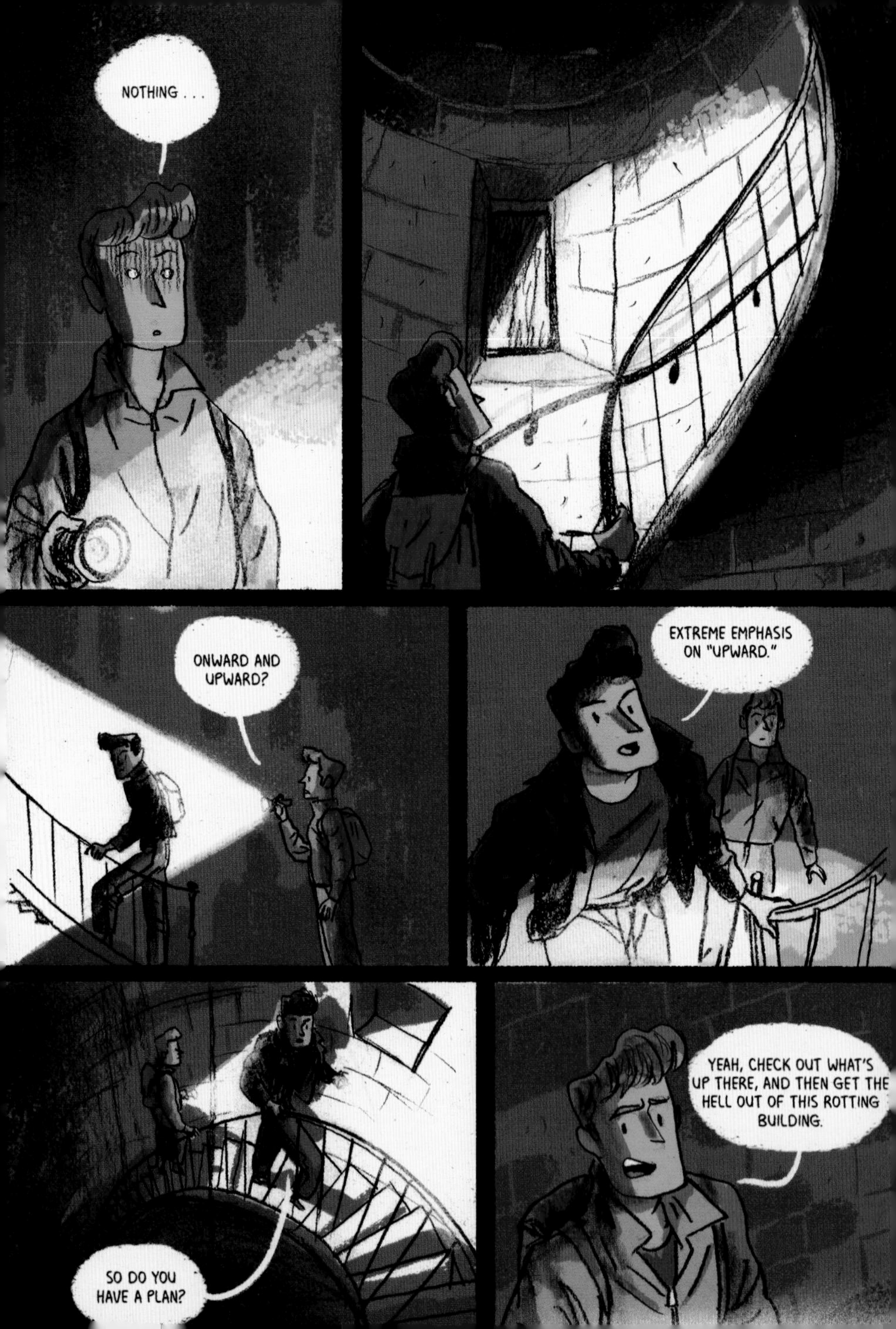
NOTHING . . .
ONWARD AND UPWARD?
EXTREME EMPHASIS ON "UPWARD."
SO DO YOU HAVE A PLAN?
YEAH, CHECK OUT WHAT'S UP THERE, AND THEN GET THE HELL OUT OF THIS ROTTING BUILDING.

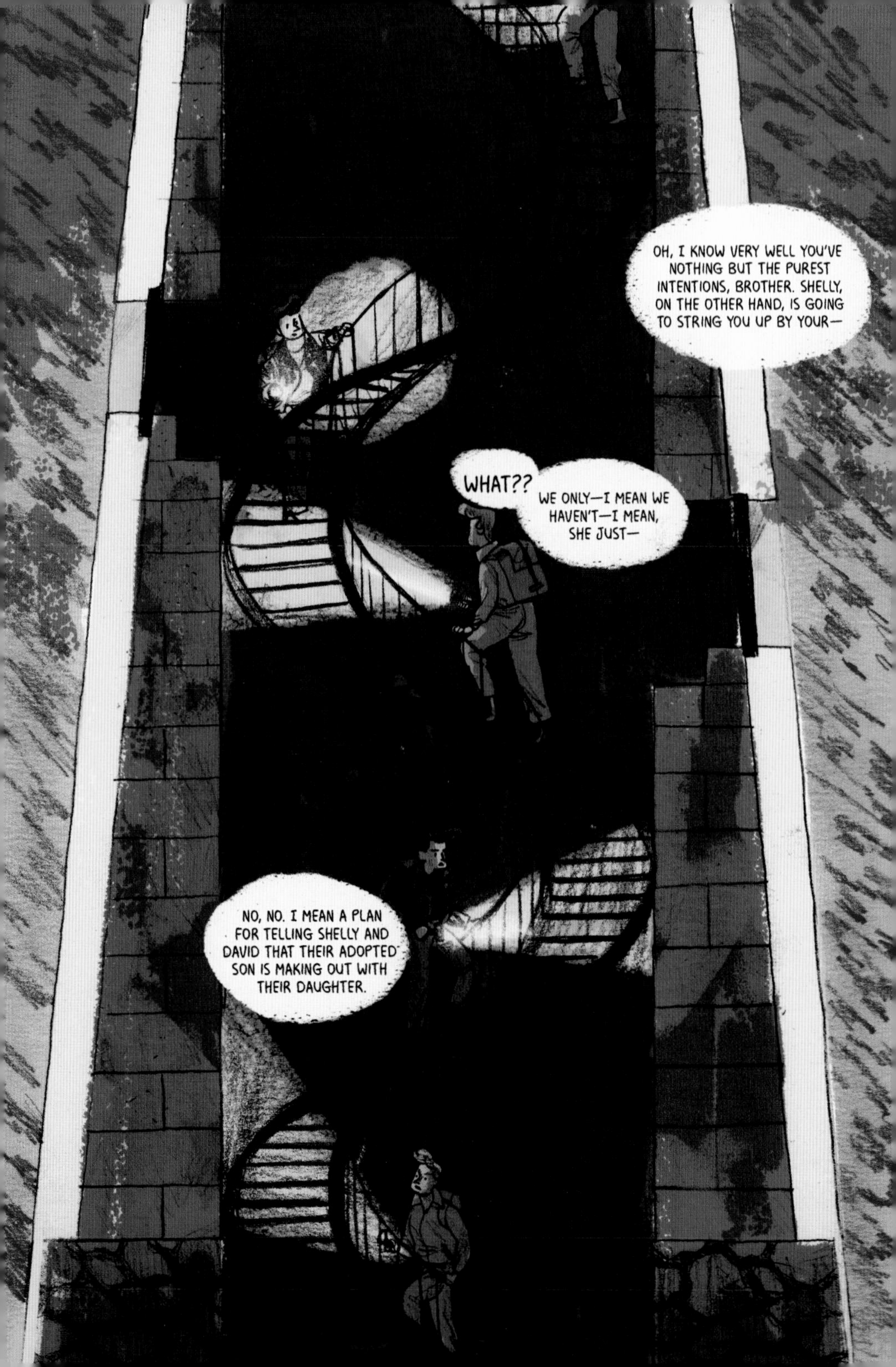

OH, I KNOW VERY WELL YOU'VE NOTHING BUT THE PUREST INTENTIONS, BROTHER. SHELLY, ON THE OTHER HAND, IS GOING TO STRING YOU UP BY YOUR—
WHAT??
WE ONLY—I MEAN WE HAVEN'T—I MEAN, SHE JUST—
NO, NO. I MEAN A PLAN FOR TELLING SHELLY AND DAVID THAT THEIR ADOPTED SON IS MAKING OUT WITH THEIR DAUGHTER.

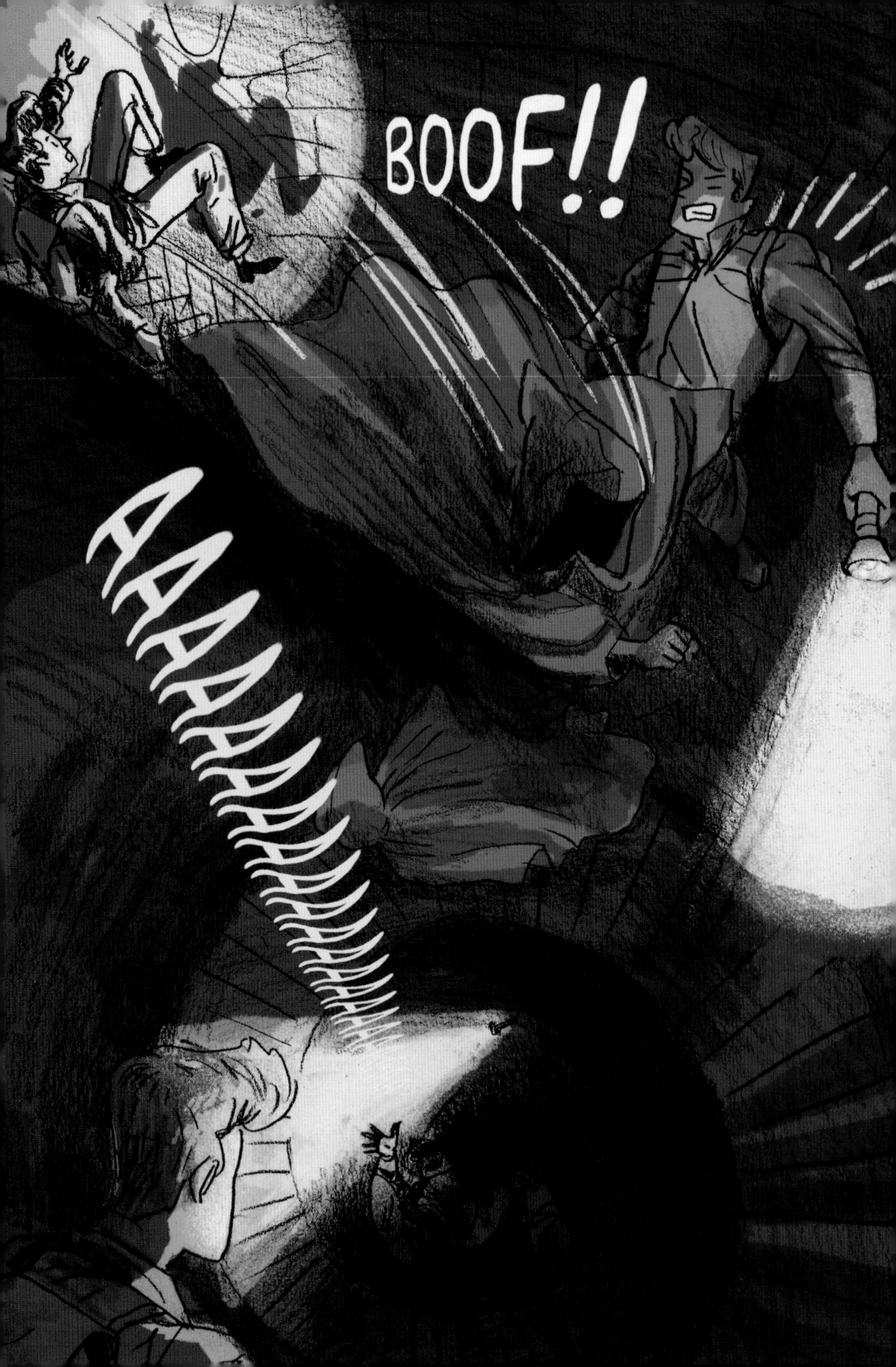
BOOF!!
AAAAAAAAAAAAAAAAAAAAAAA

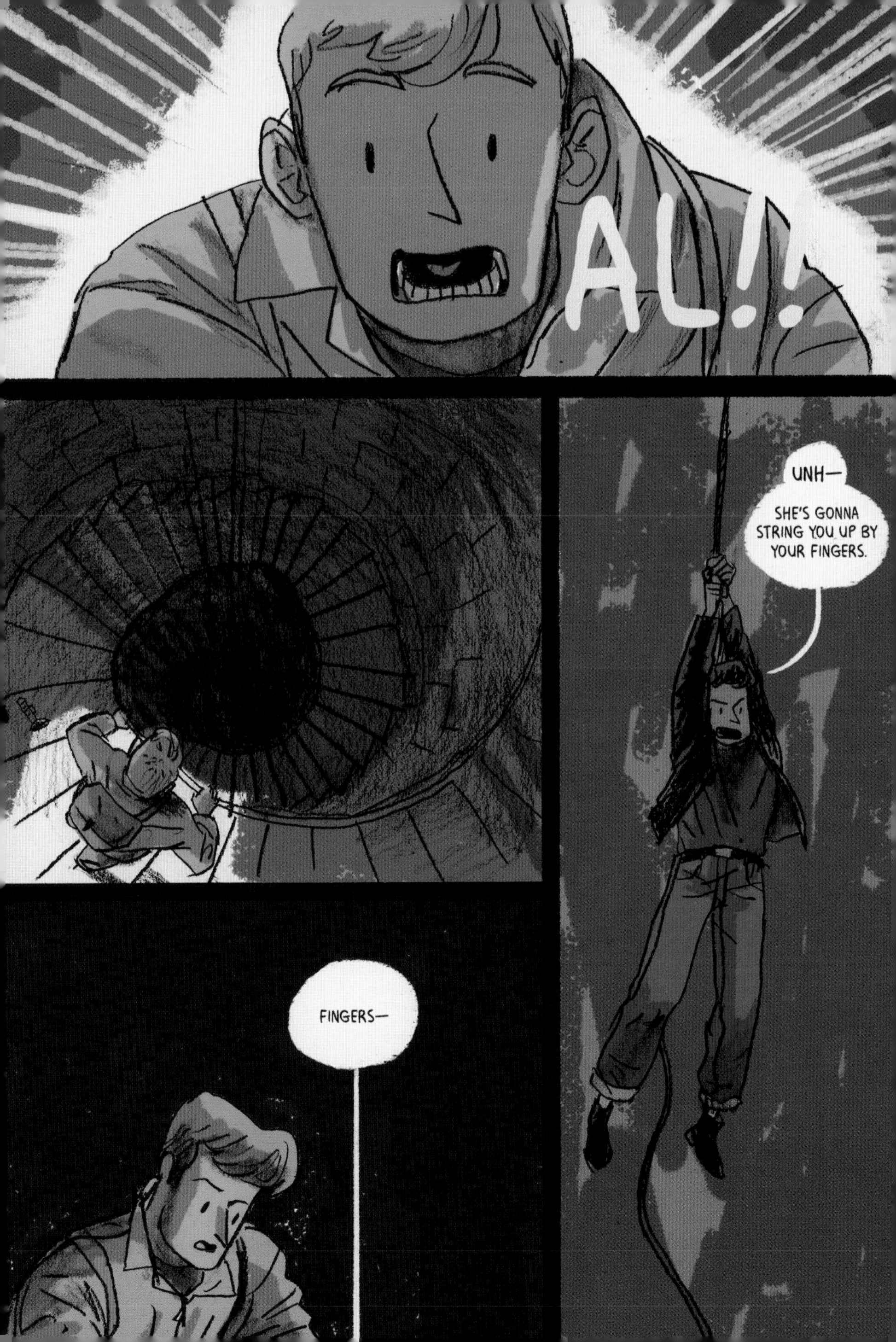
AL!!
UNH—
SHE'S GONNA STRING YOU UP BY YOUR FINGERS.
FINGERS—

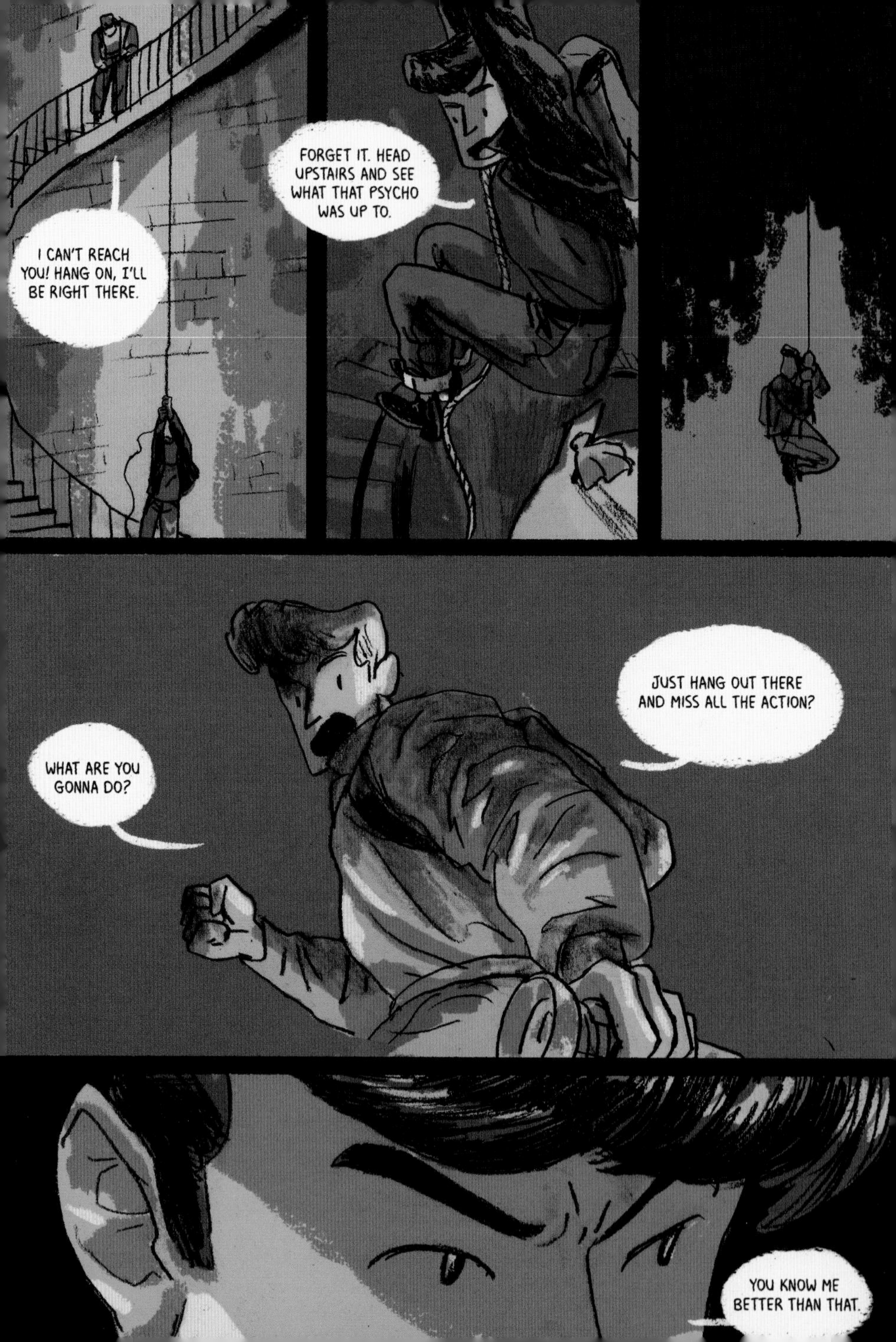
I CAN'T REACH YOU! HANG ON, I'LL BE RIGHT THERE.
FORGET IT. HEAD UPSTAIRS AND SEE WHAT THAT PSYCHO WAS UP TO.
WHAT ARE YOU GONNA DO?
JUST HANG OUT THERE AND MISS ALL THE ACTION?
YOU KNOW ME BETTER THAN THAT.

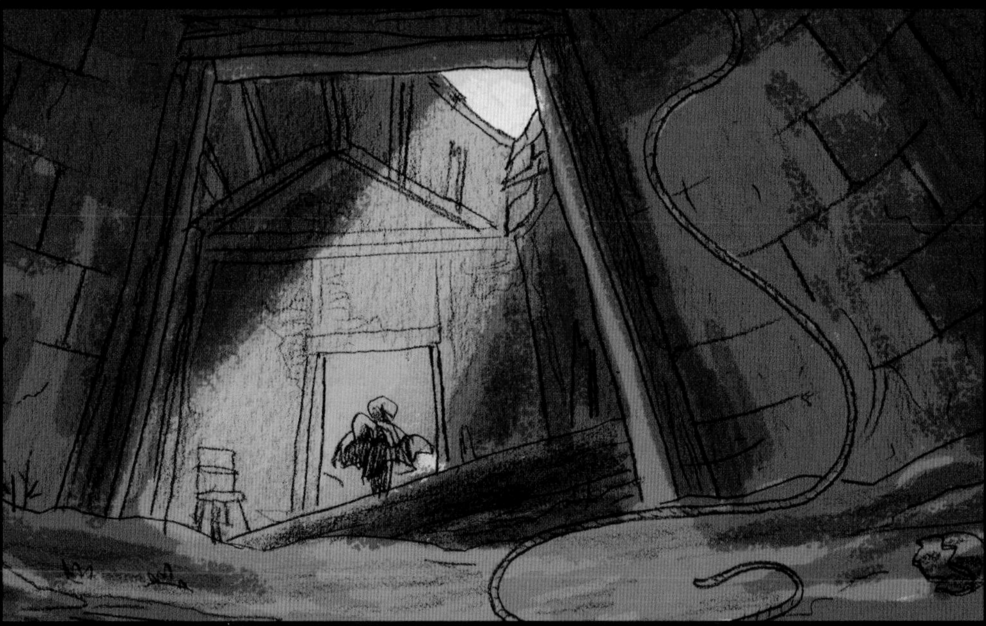

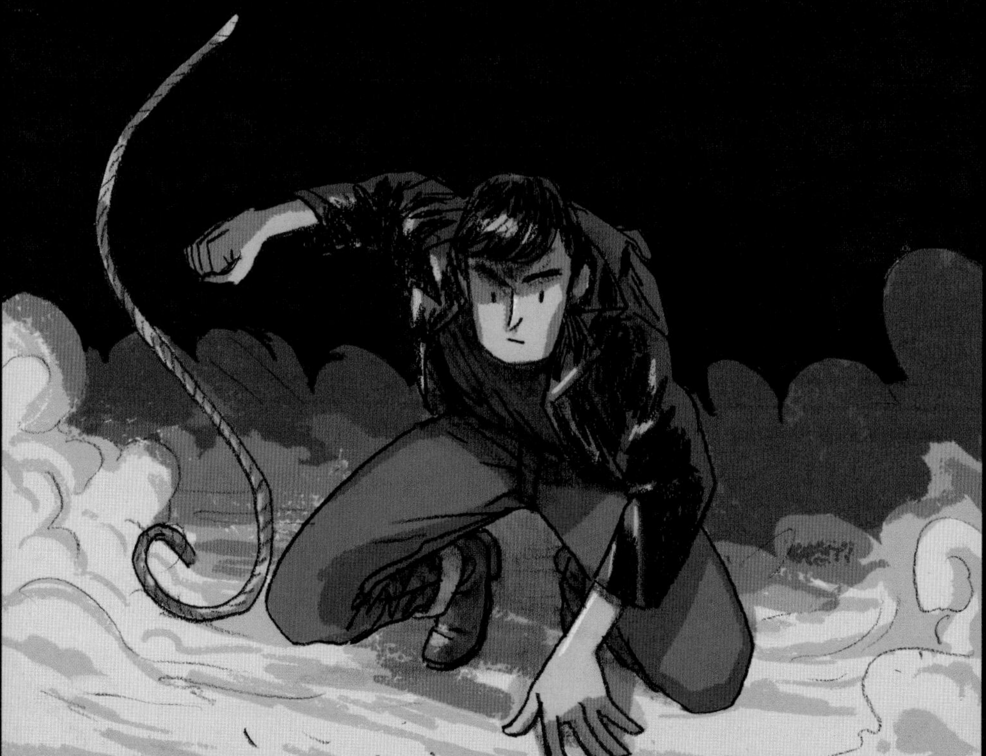

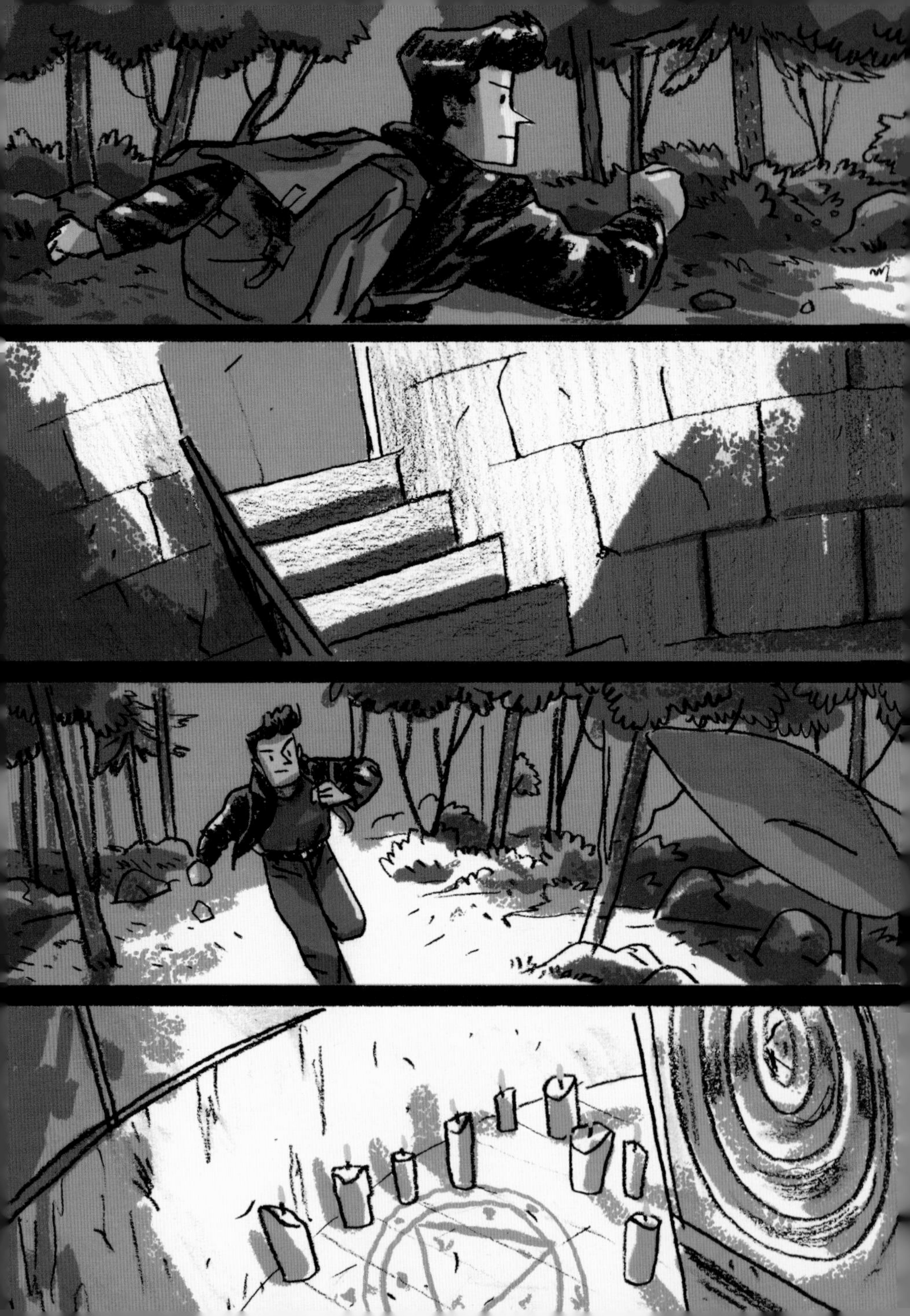

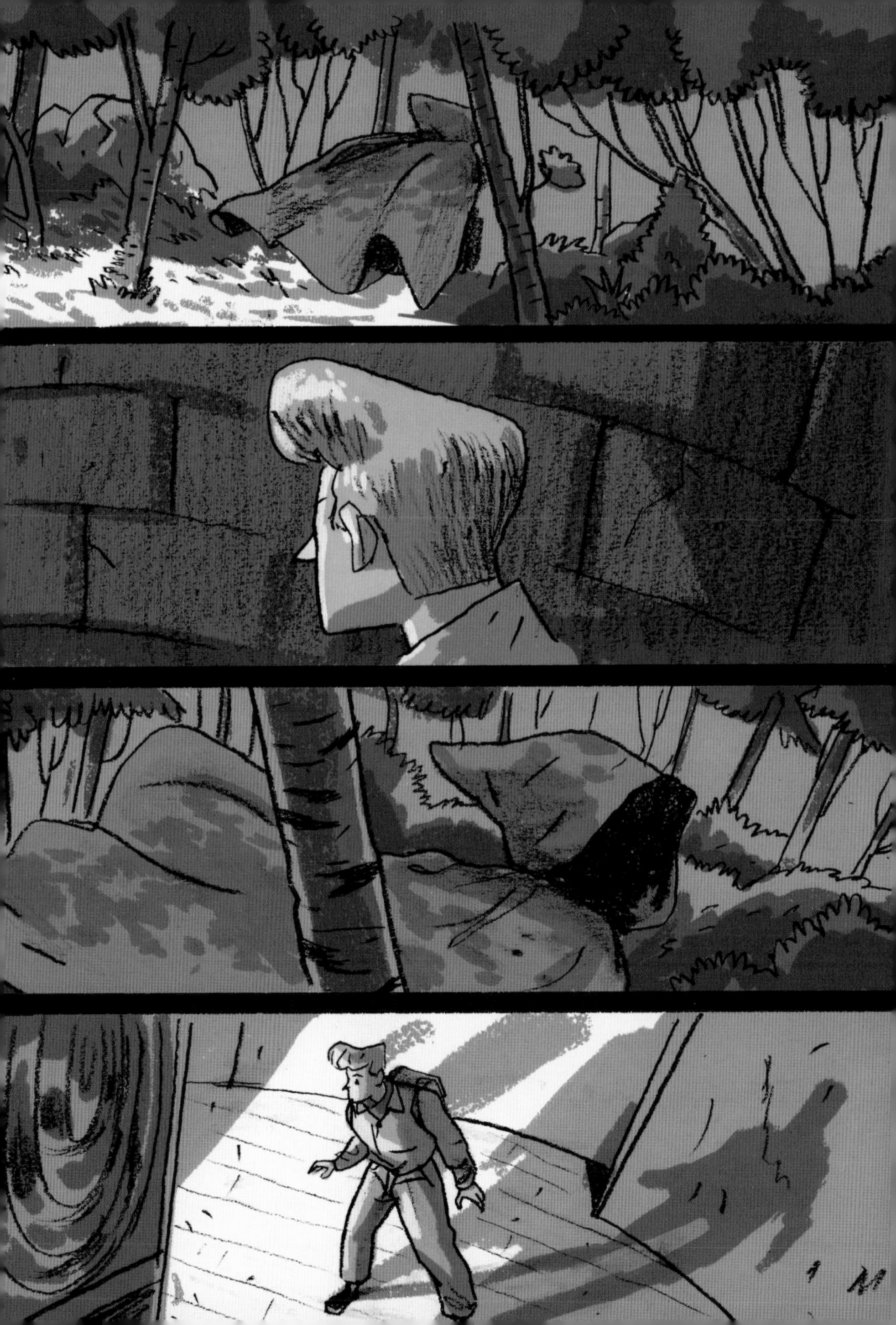

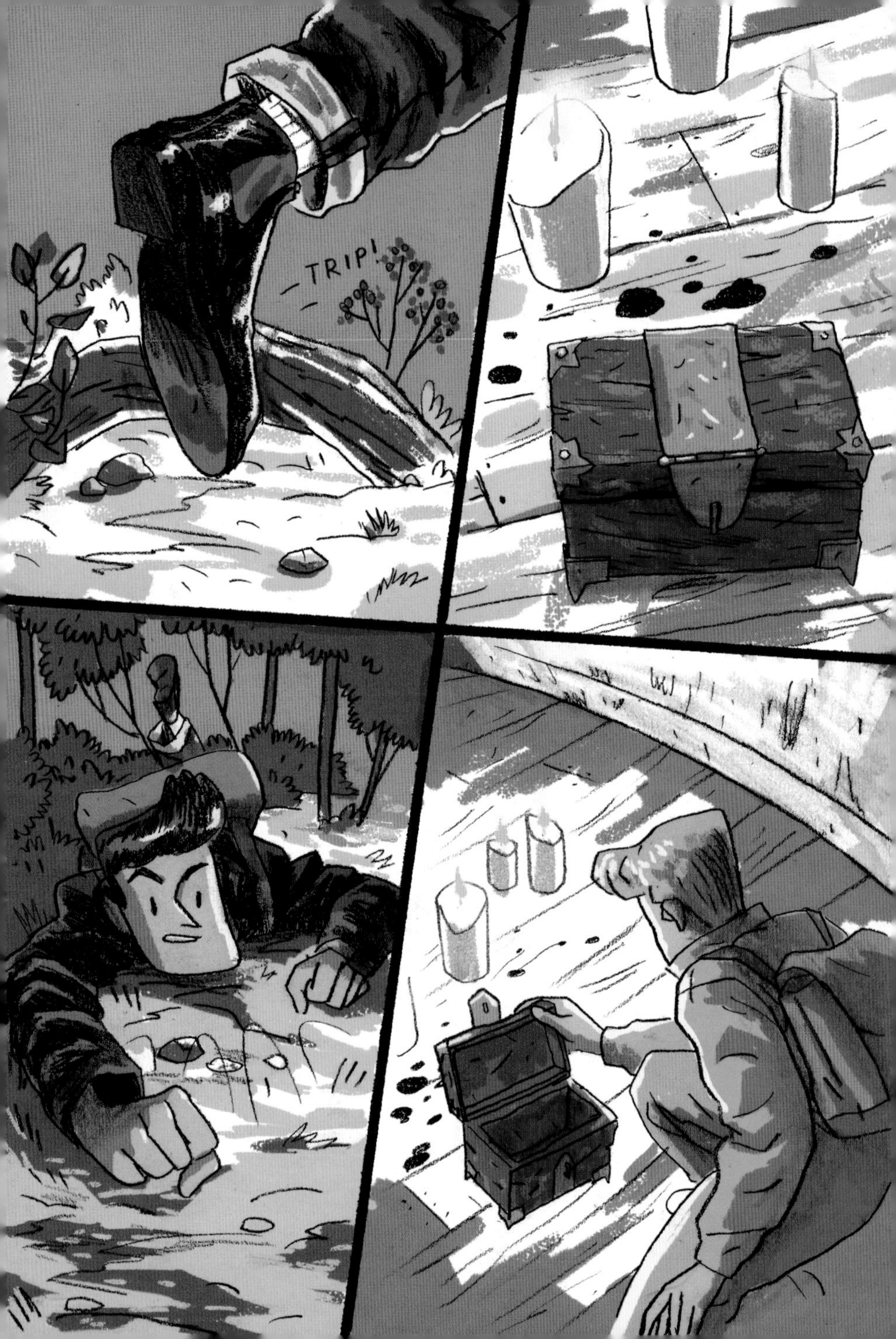
TRIP!

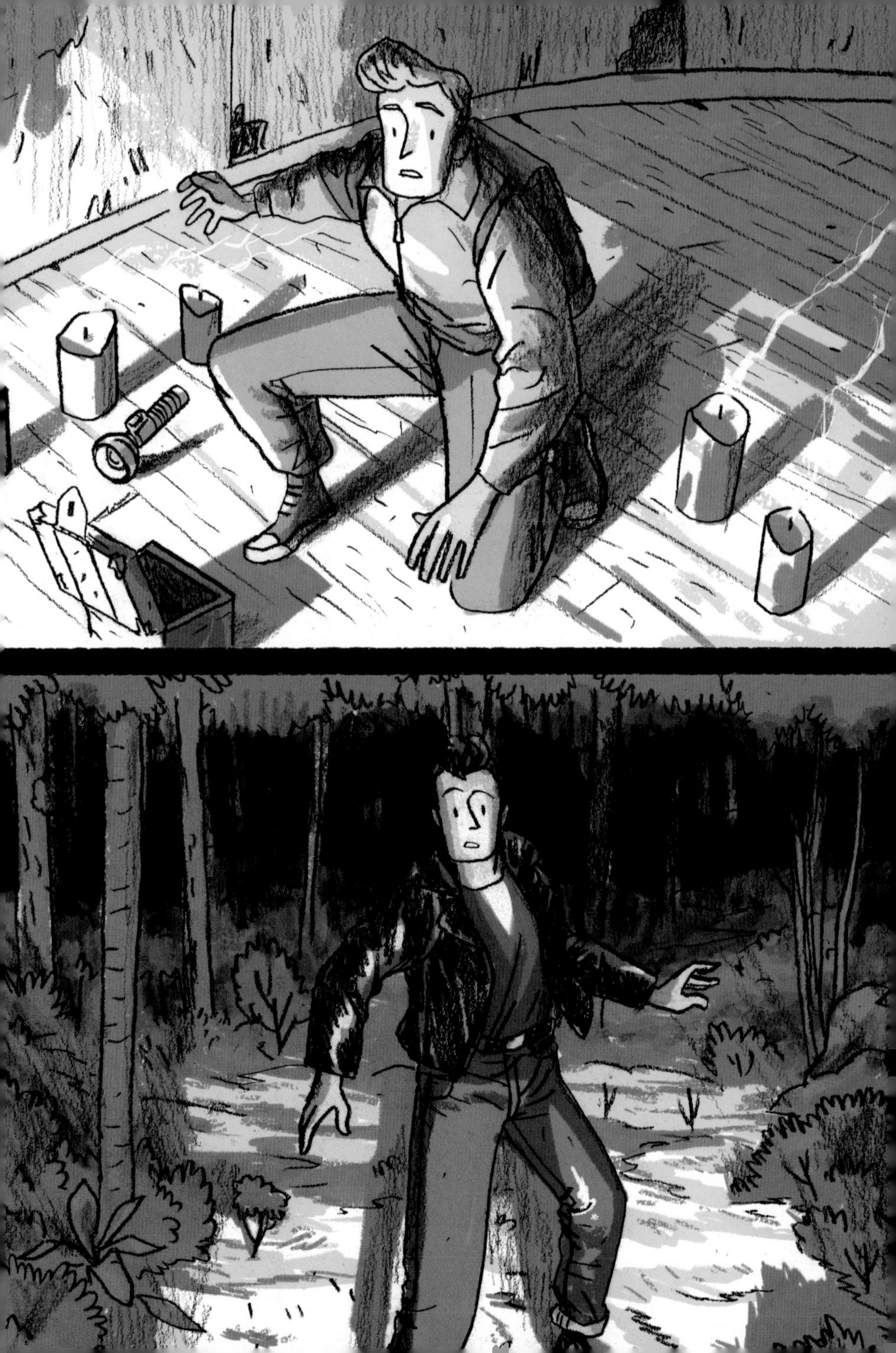

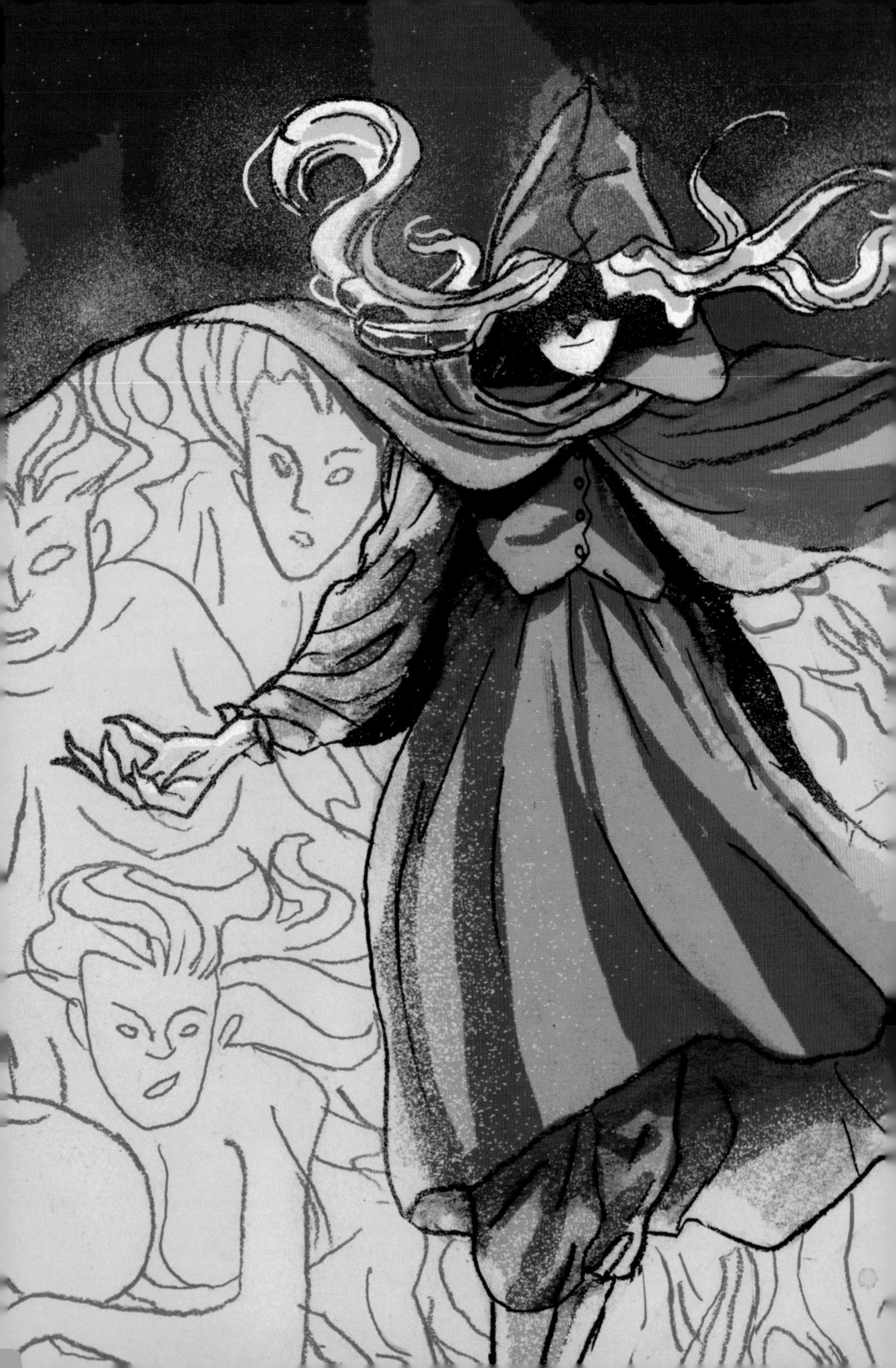

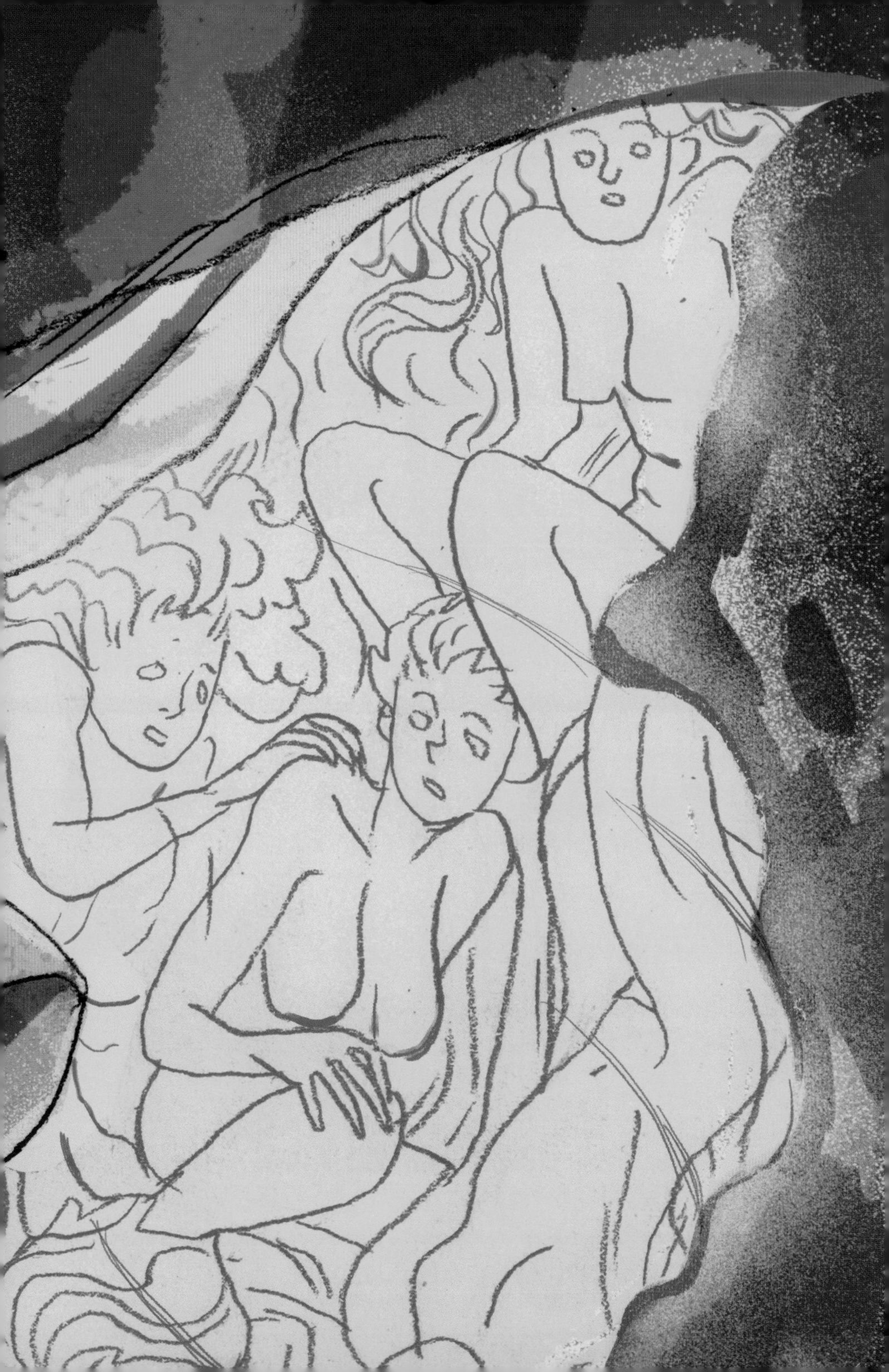

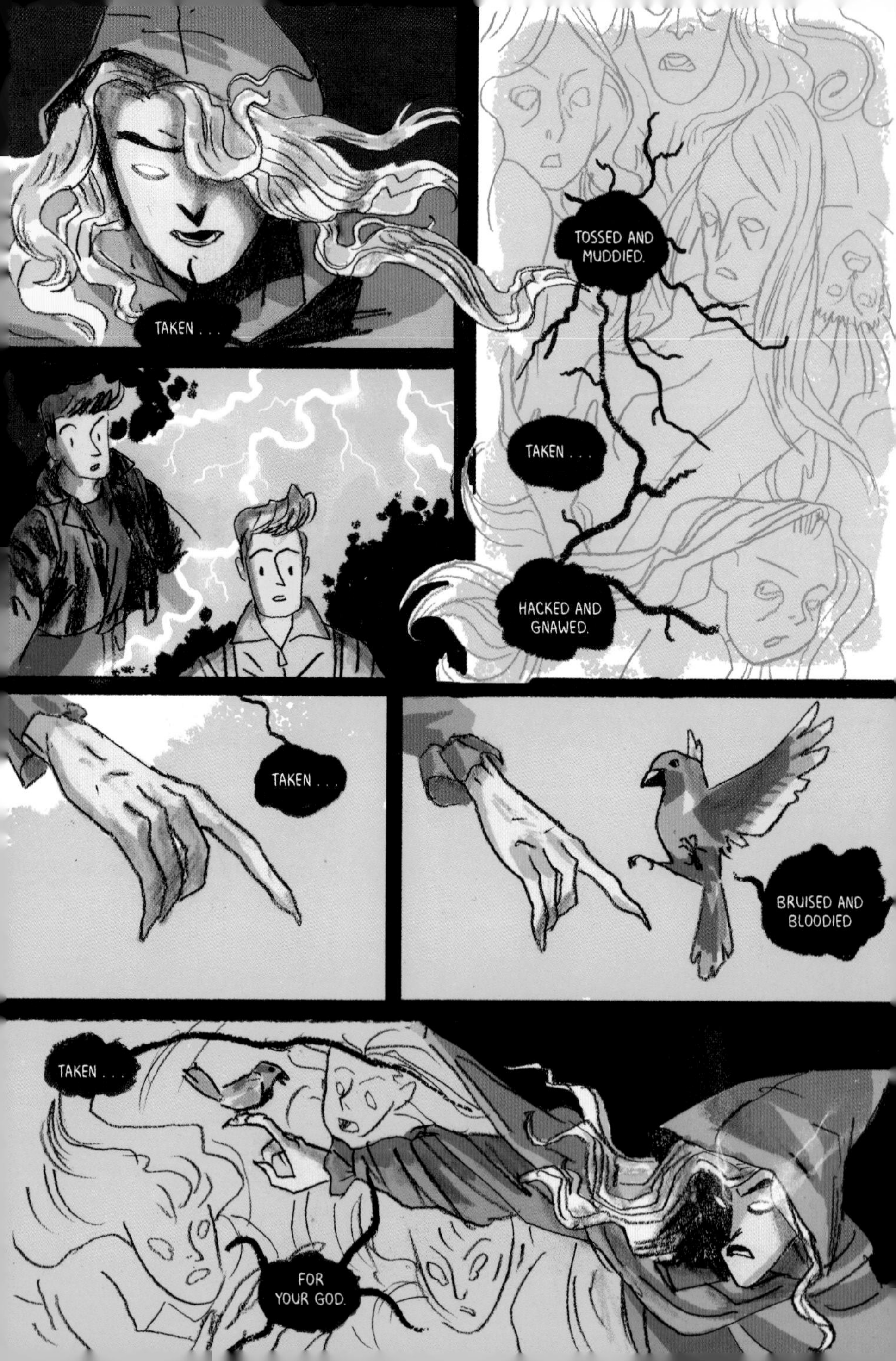
TAKEN . . .
TOSSED AND MUDDIED.
TAKEN . . .
HACKED AND GNAWED.
TAKEN . . .
BRUISED AND BLOODIED
TAKEN . . .
FOR YOUR GOD.

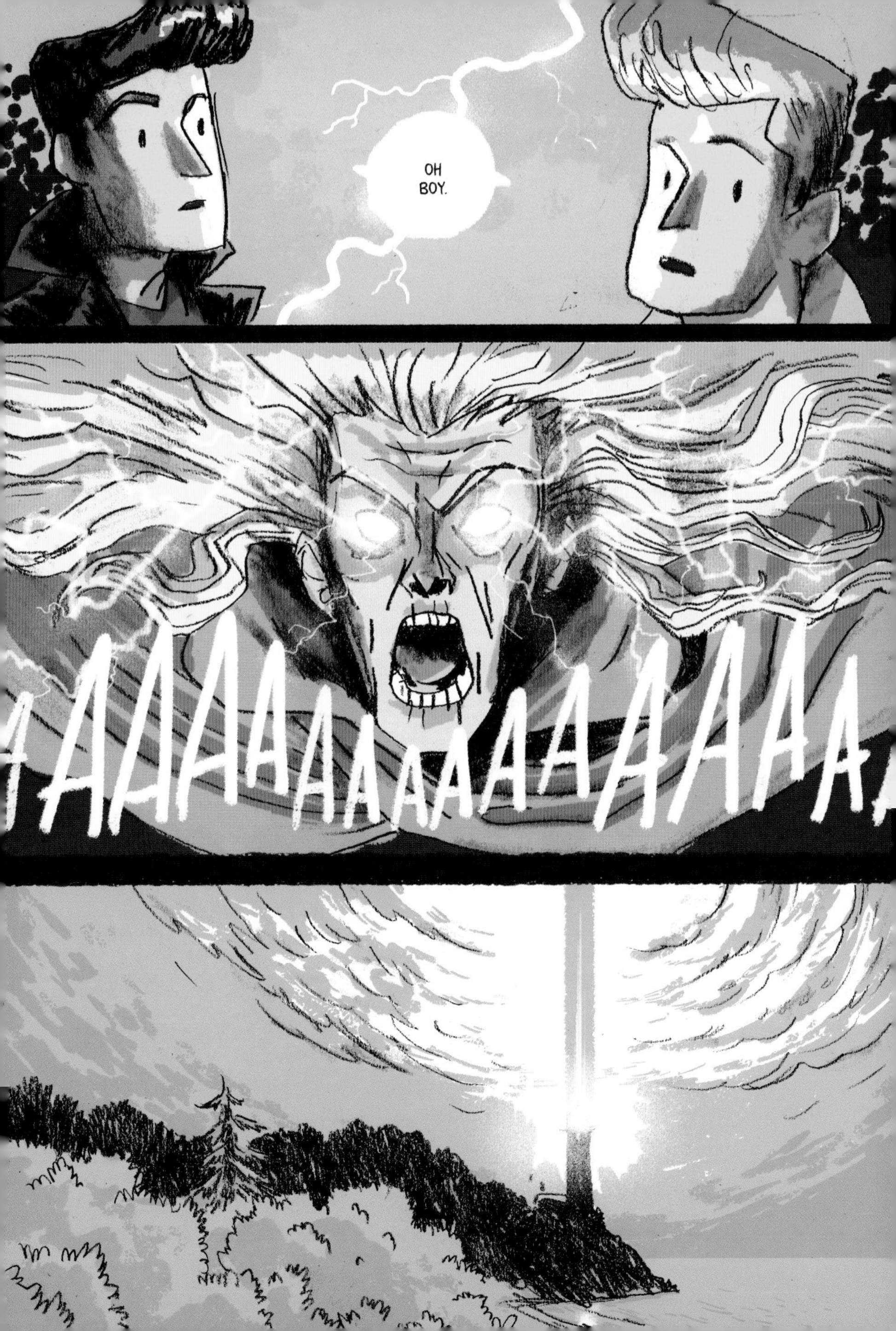
OH BOY.
AAAAAAAAAAAAAA

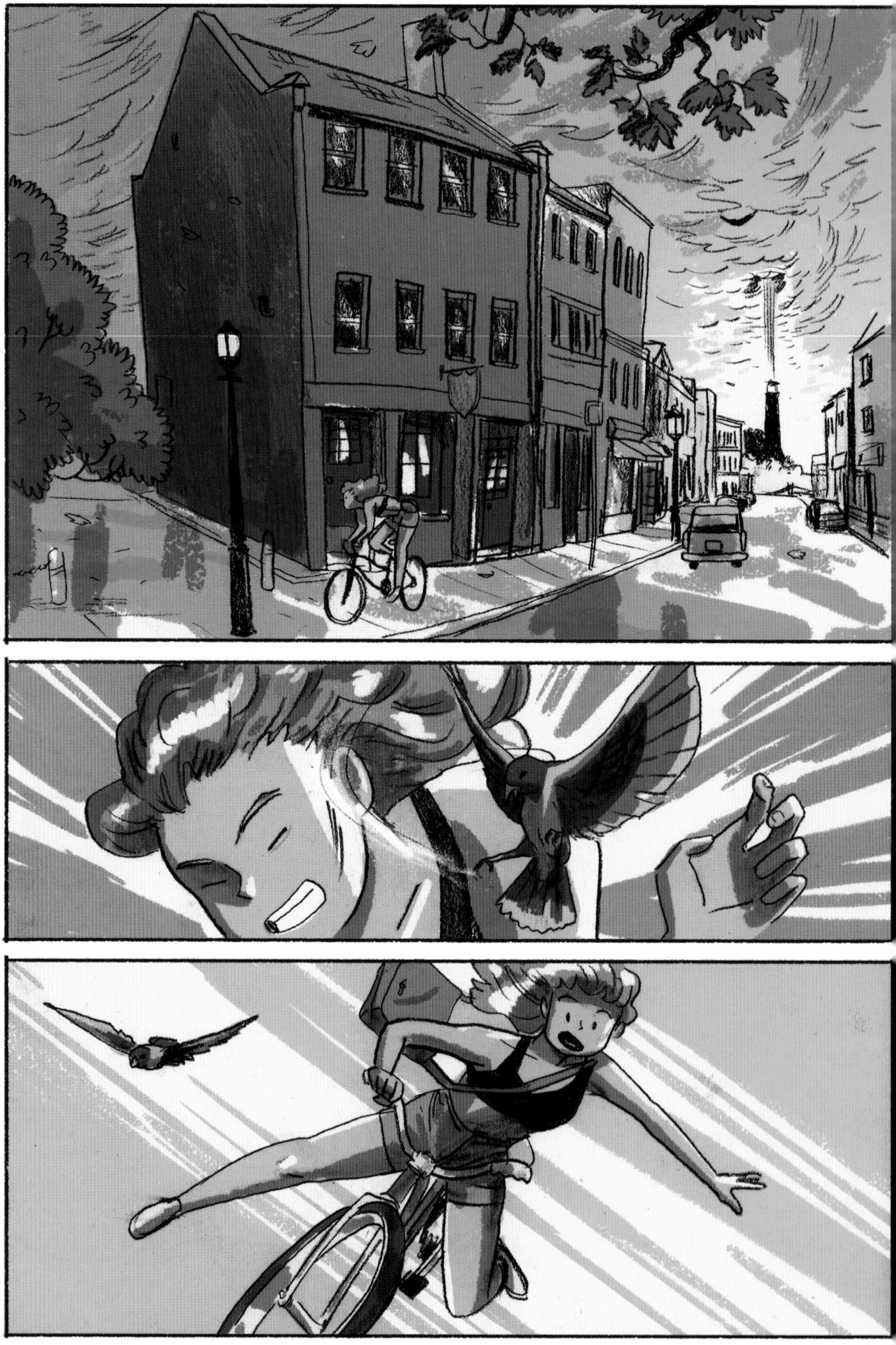

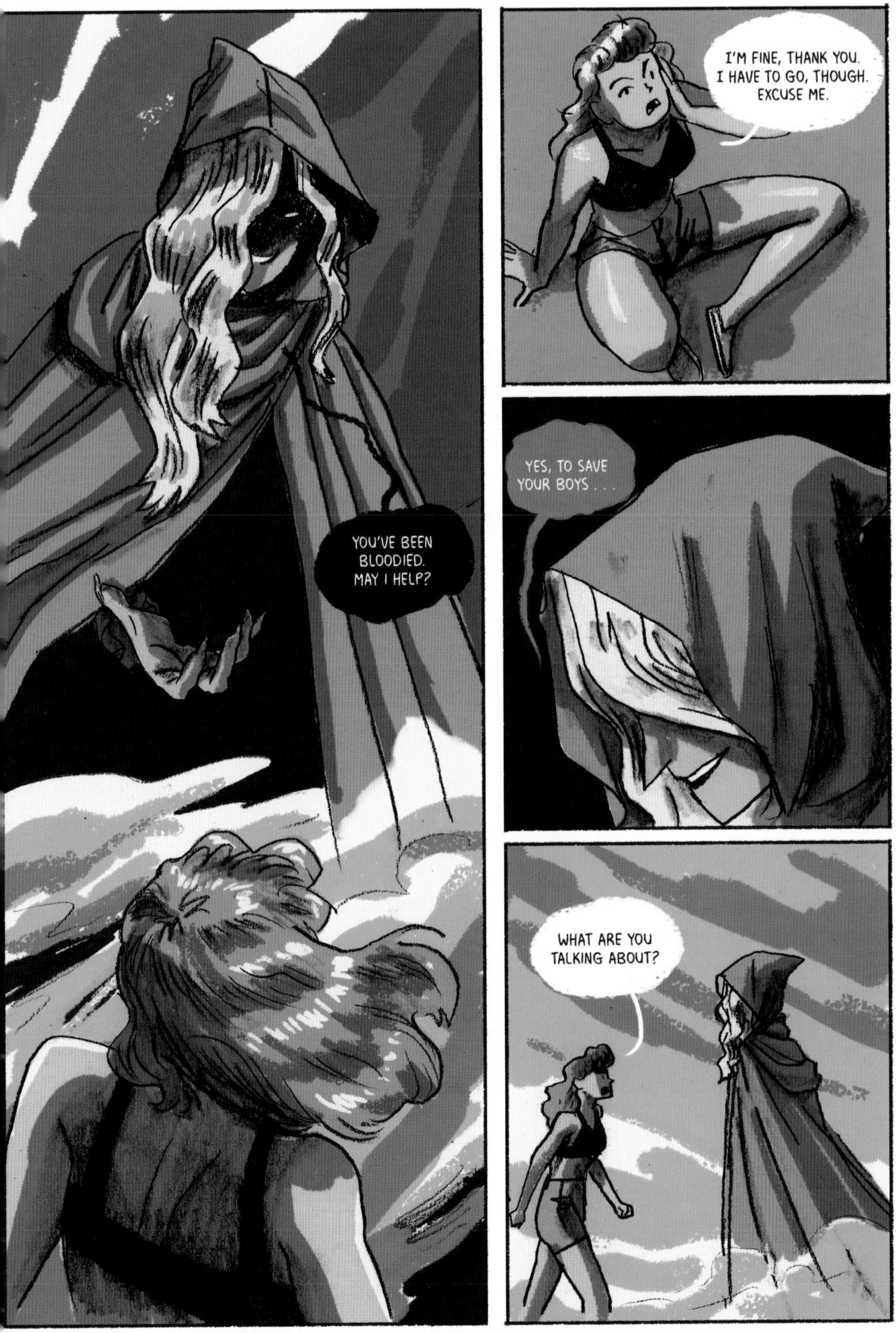
YOU'VE BEEN BLOODIED. MAY I HELP?
I'M FINE, THANK YOU. I HAVE TO GO, THOUGH. EXCUSE ME.
YES, TO SAVE YOUR BOYS . . .
WHAT ARE YOU TALKING ABOUT?

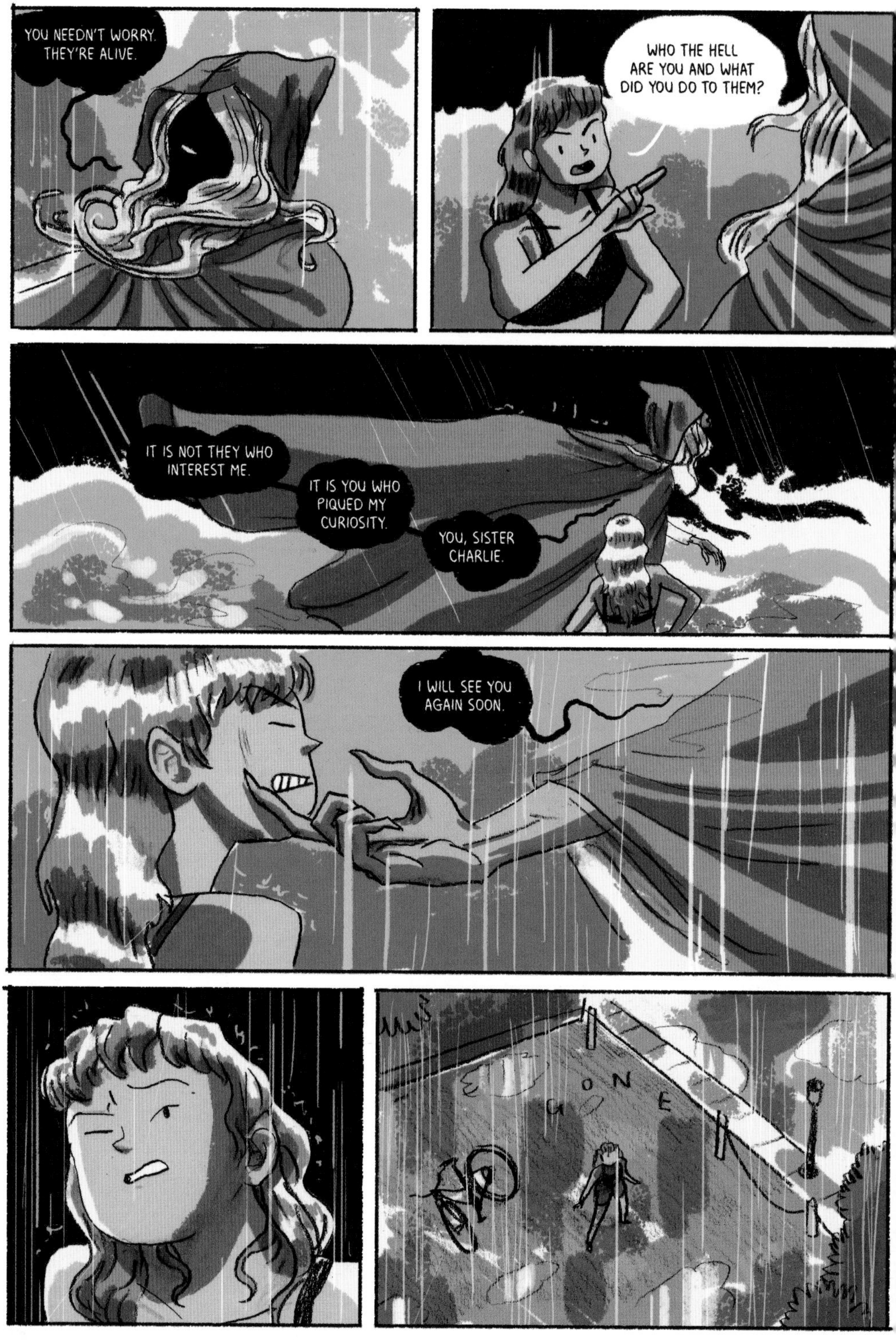
YOU NEEDN'T WORRY. THEY'RE ALIVE.
WHO THE HELL ARE YOU AND WHAT DID YOU DO TO THEM?
IT IS NOT THEY WHO INTEREST ME.
IT IS YOU WHO PIQUED MY CURIOSITY.
YOU, SISTER CHARLIE.
I WILL SEE YOU AGAIN SOON.
GONE

CHAPTER 2

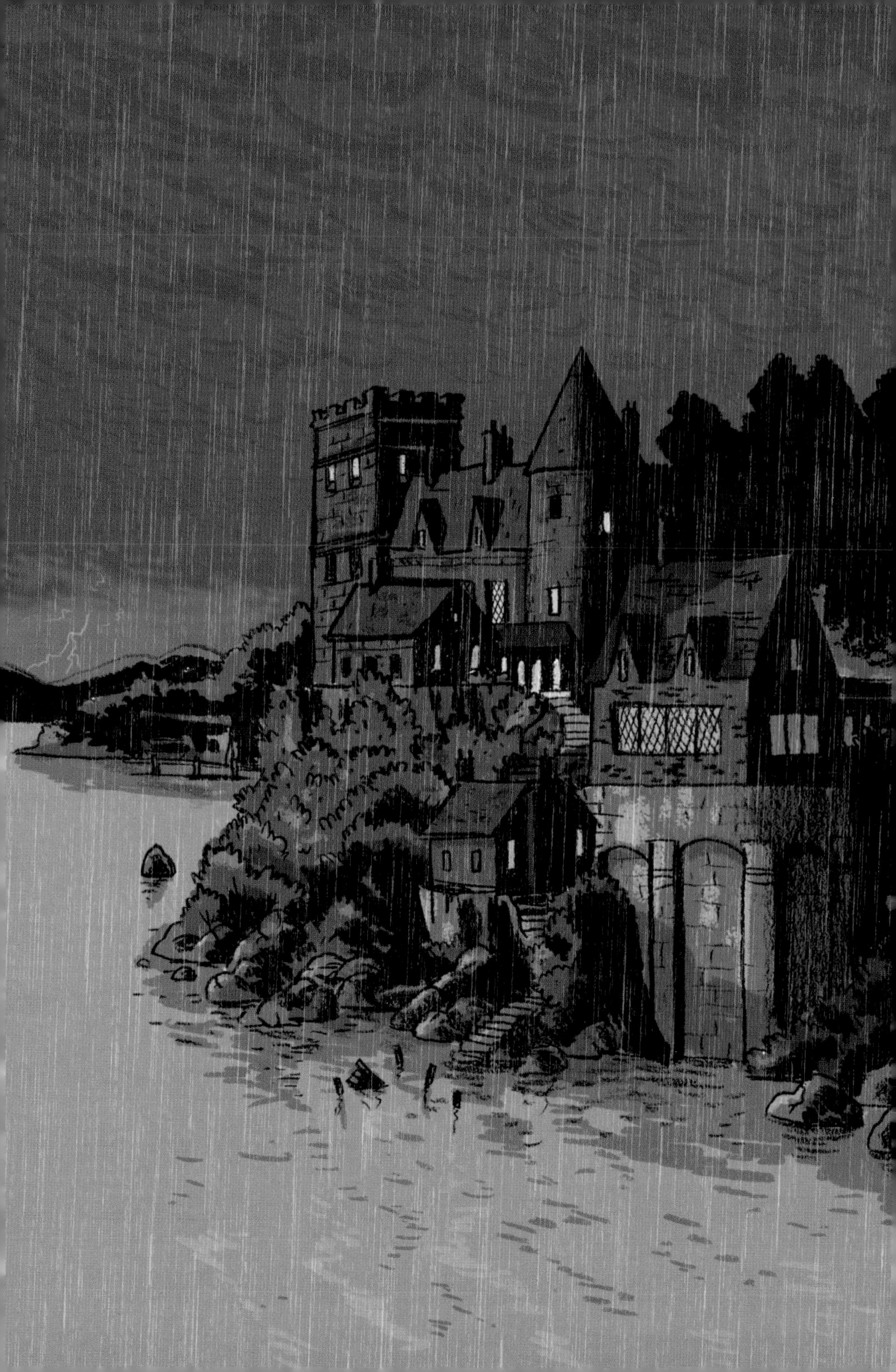

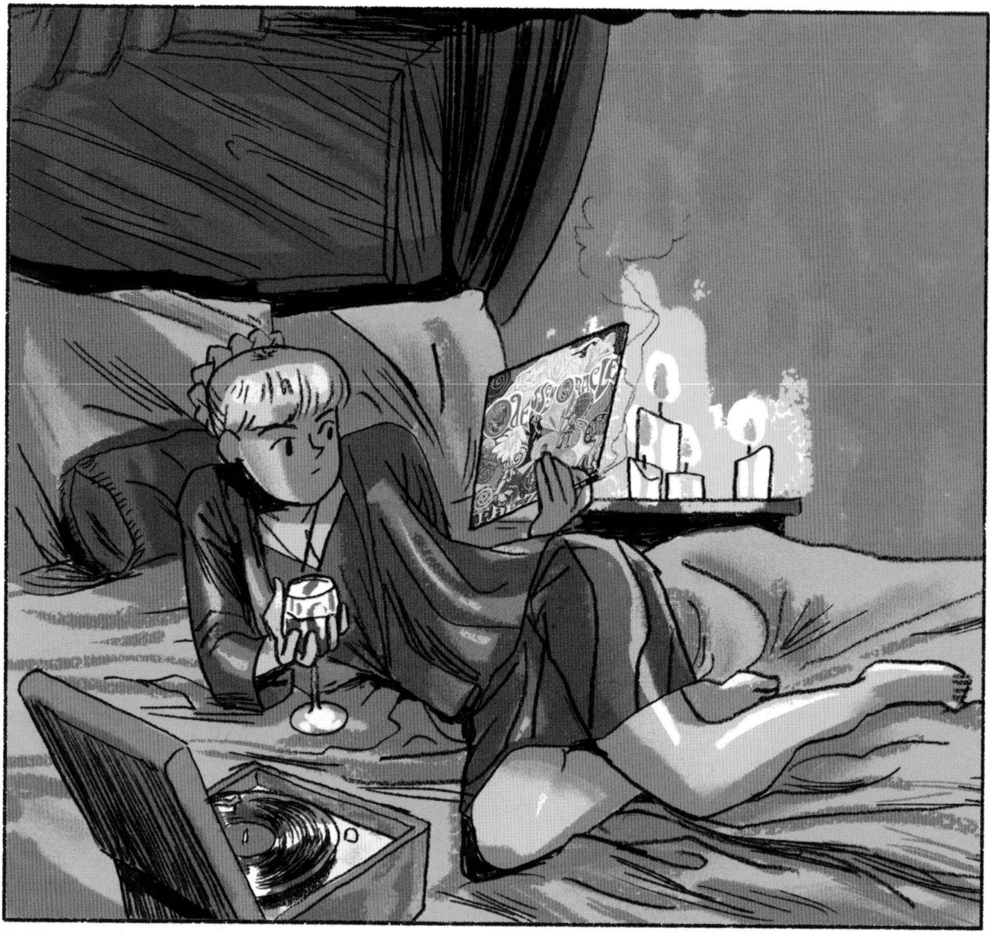

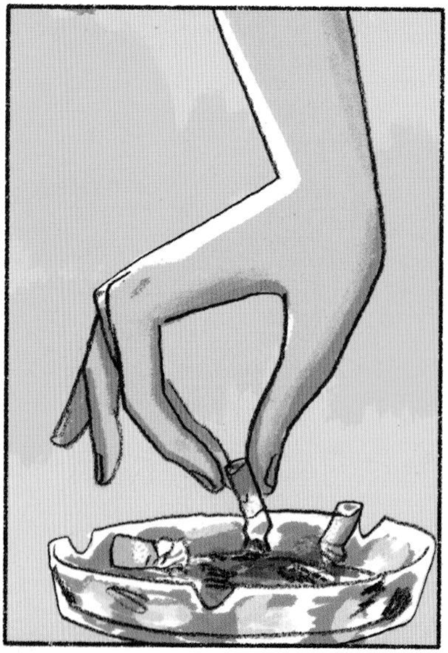

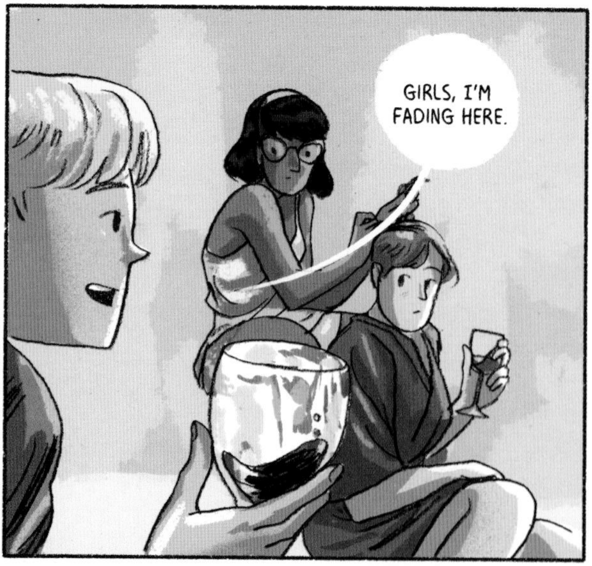
GIRLS, I'M FADING HERE.

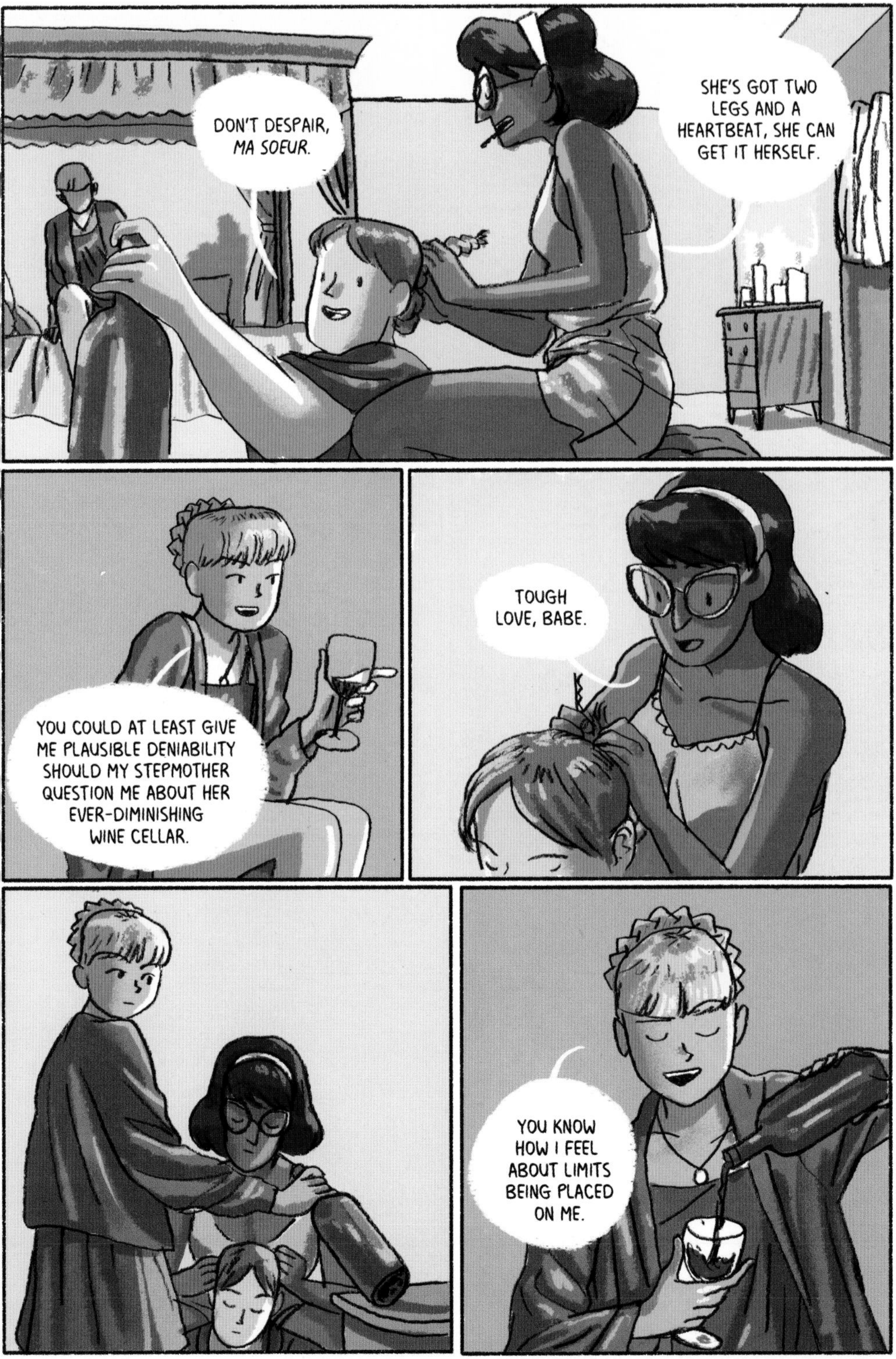
DON'T DESPAIR, MA SOEUR.
SHE'S GOT TWO LEGS AND A HEARTBEAT, SHE CAN GET IT HERSELF.
YOU COULD AT LEAST GIVE ME PLAUSIBLE DENIABILITY SHOULD MY STEPMOTHER QUESTION ME ABOUT HER EVER-DIMINISHING WINE CELLAR.
TOUGH LOVE, BABE.
YOU KNOW HOW I FEEL ABOUT LIMITS BEING PLACED ON ME.

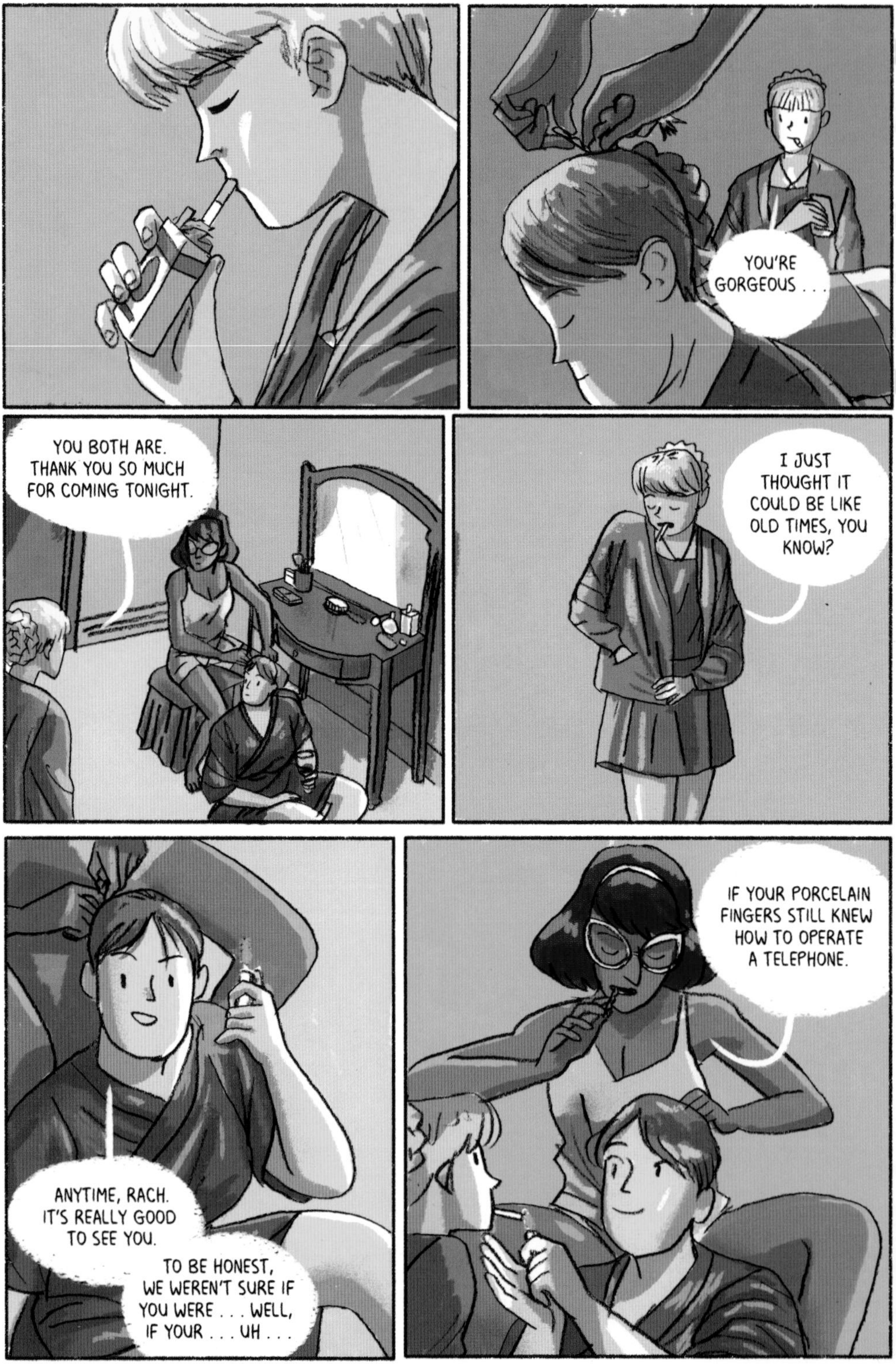
YOU'RE GORGEOUS . . .
YOU BOTH ARE. THANK YOU SO MUCH FOR COMING TONIGHT.
I JUST THOUGHT IT COULD BE LIKE OLD TIMES, YOU KNOW?
ANYTIME, RACH. IT'S REALLY GOOD TO SEE YOU.
TO BE HONEST, WE WEREN'T SURE IF YOU WERE . . . WELL, IF YOUR . . . UH . . .
IF YOUR PORCELAIN FINGERS STILL KNEW HOW TO OPERATE A TELEPHONE.

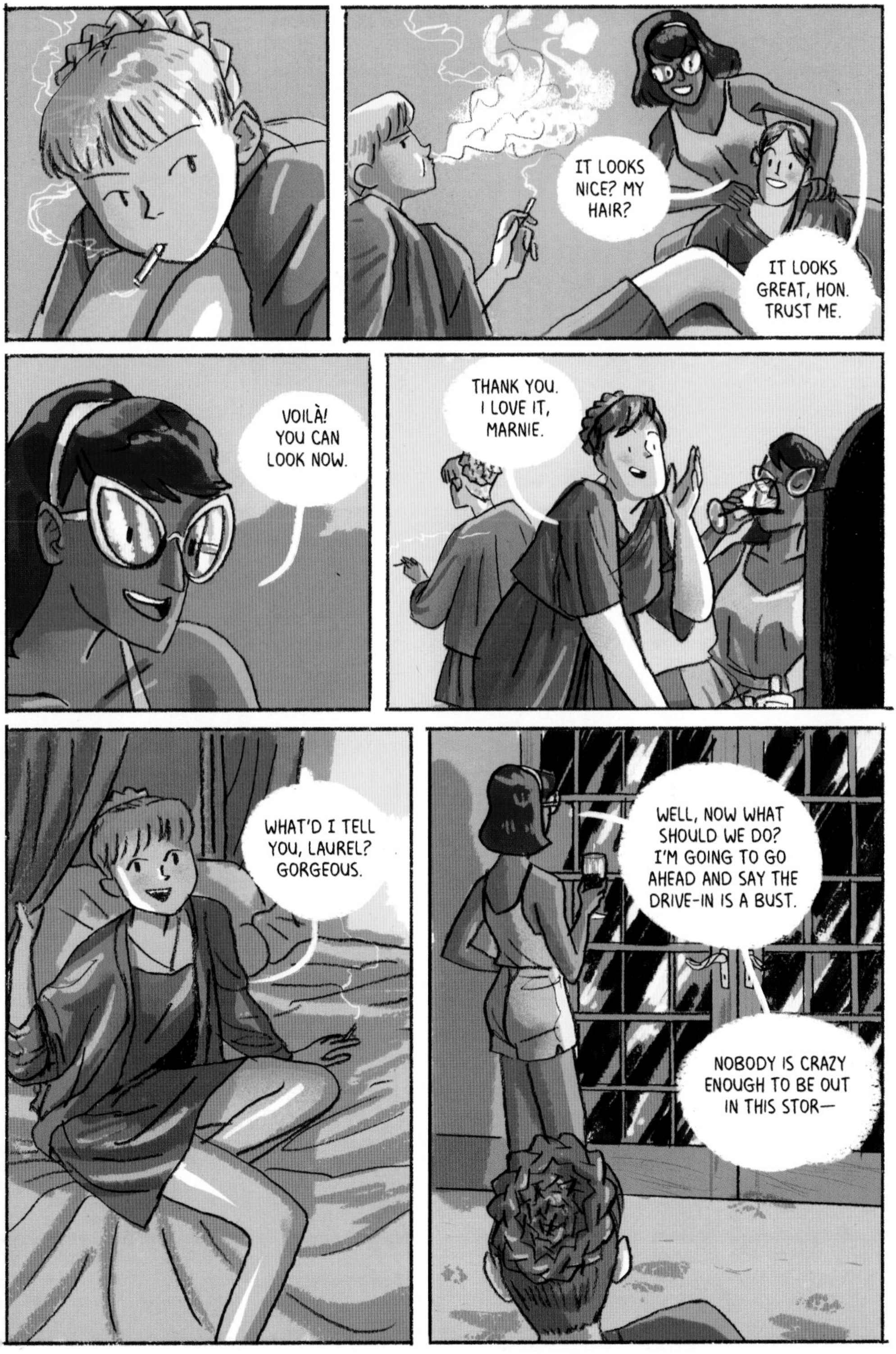
IT LOOKS NICE? MY HAIR?
IT LOOKS GREAT, HON. TRUST ME.
VOILÀ! YOU CAN LOOK NOW.
THANK YOU. I LOVE IT, MARNIE.
WHAT'D I TELL YOU, LAUREL? GORGEOUS.
WELL, NOW WHAT SHOULD WE DO? I'M GOING TO GO AHEAD AND SAY THE DRIVE-IN IS A BUST.
NOBODY IS CRAZY ENOUGH TO BE OUT IN THIS STOR—

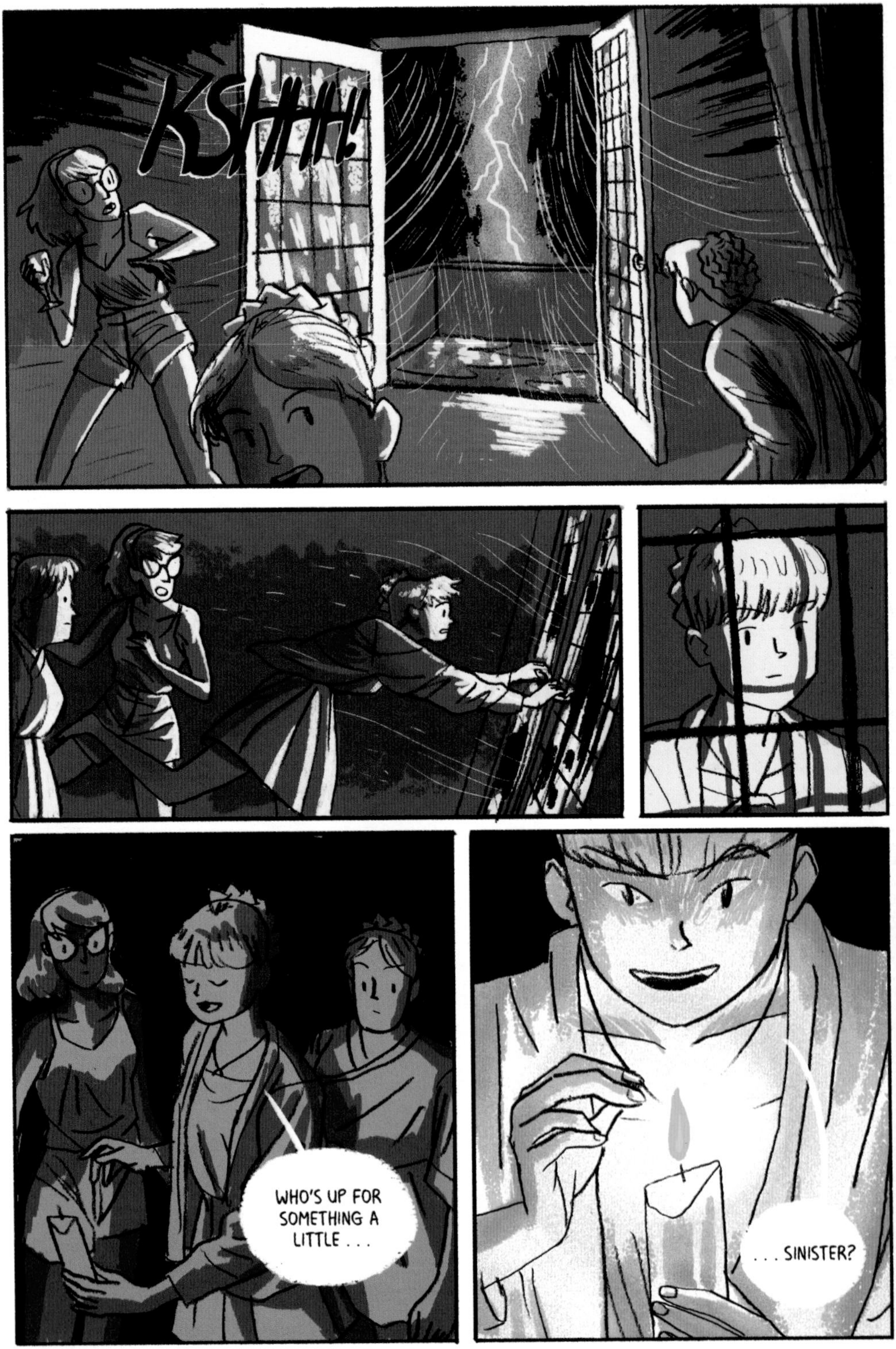
KSHHH!
WHO'S UP FOR SOMETHING A LITTLE . . .
. . . SINISTER?

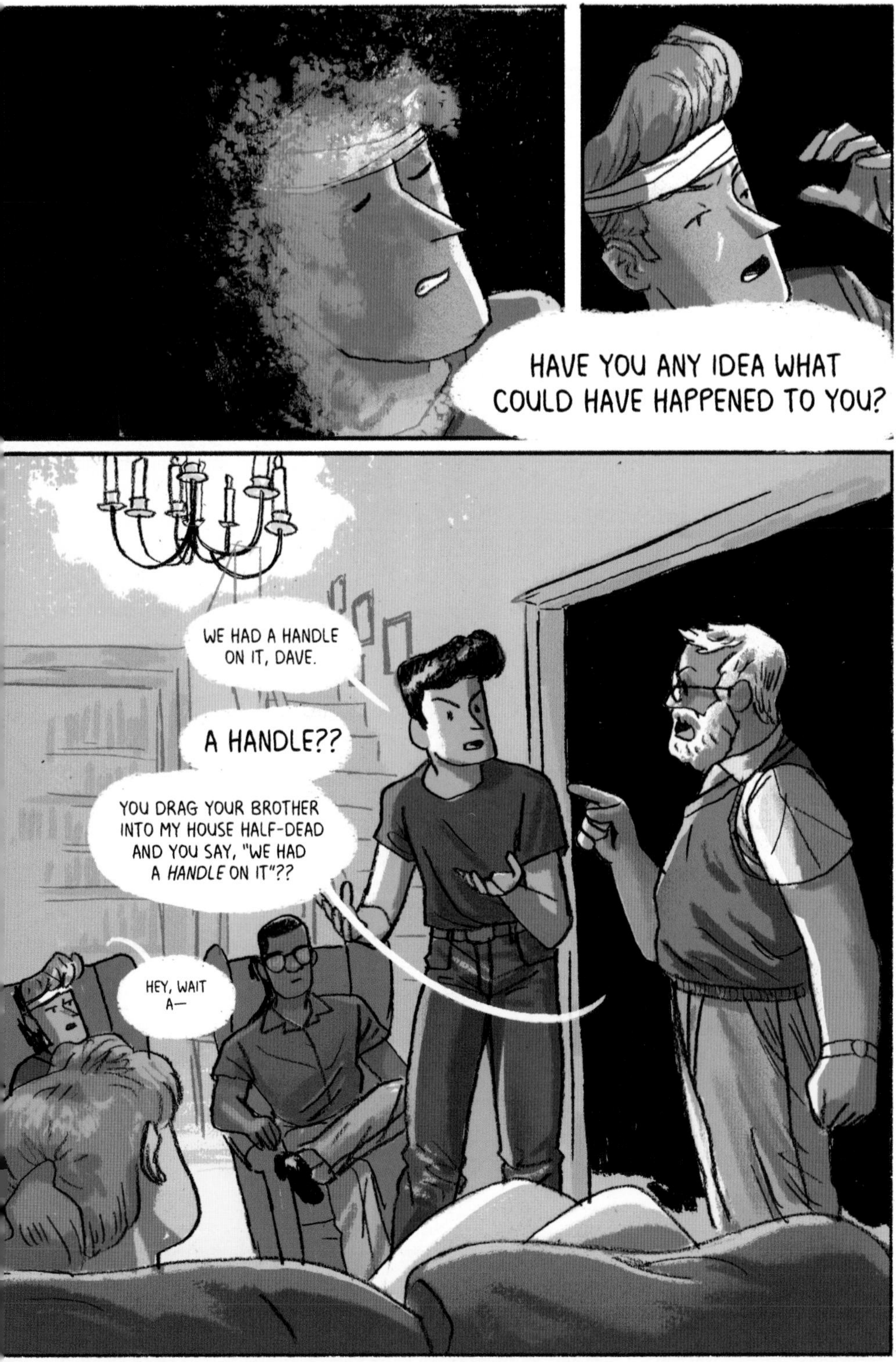
HAVE YOU ANY IDEA WHAT COULD HAVE HAPPENED TO YOU?
WE HAD A HANDLE ON IT, DAVE.
A HANDLE??
YOU DRAG YOUR BROTHER INTO MY HOUSE HALF-DEAD AND YOU SAY, "WE HAD A *HANDLE* ON IT"??
HEY, WAIT A—

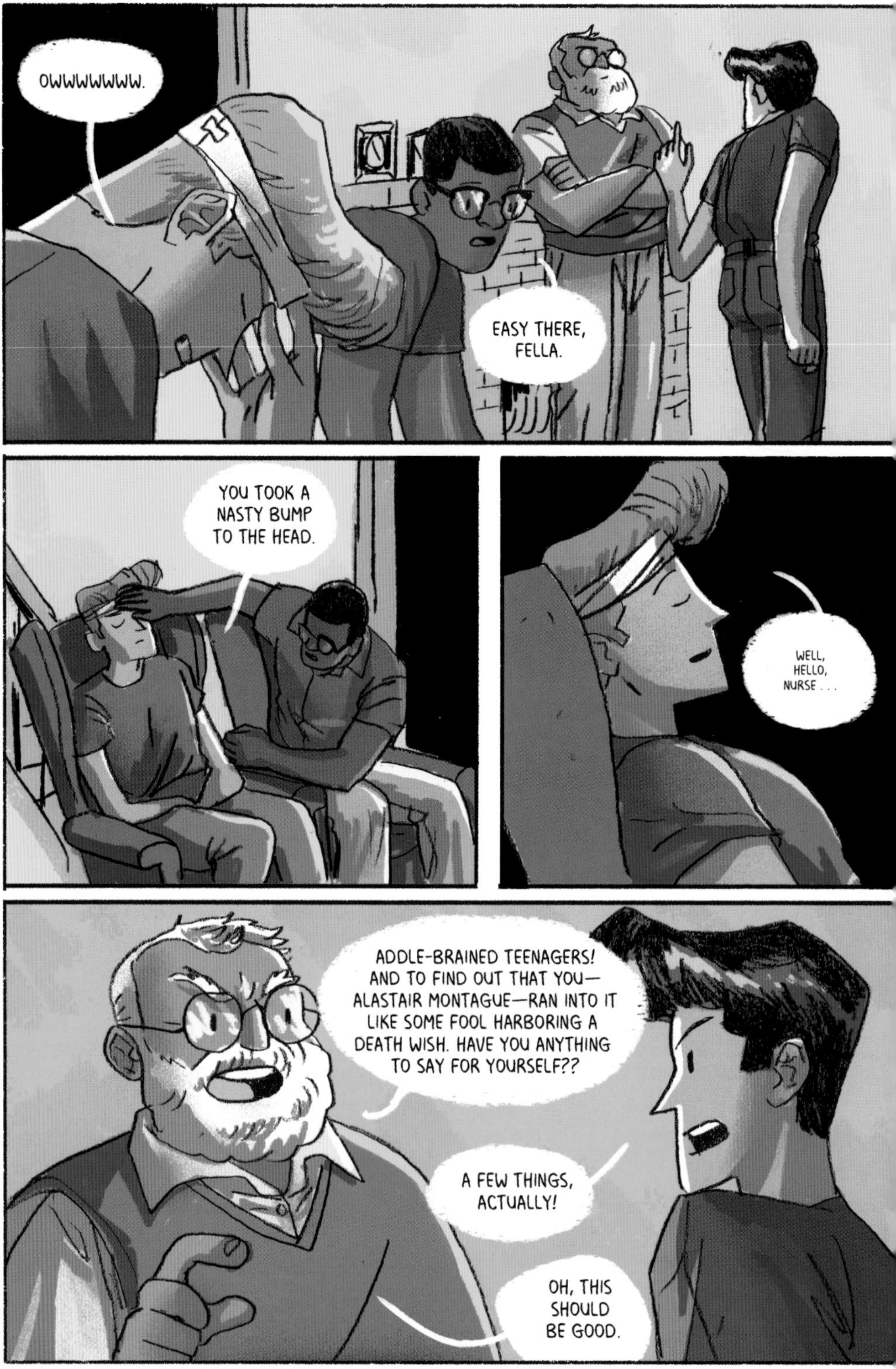
OWWWWWWW.
EASY THERE, FELLA.
YOU TOOK A NASTY BUMP TO THE HEAD.
WELL, HELLO, NURSE . . .
ADDLE-BRAINED TEENAGERS! AND TO FIND OUT THAT YOU—ALASTAIR MONTAGUE—RAN INTO IT LIKE SOME FOOL HARBORING A DEATH WISH. HAVE YOU ANYTHING TO SAY FOR YOURSELF??
A FEW THINGS, ACTUALLY!
OH, THIS SHOULD BE GOOD.

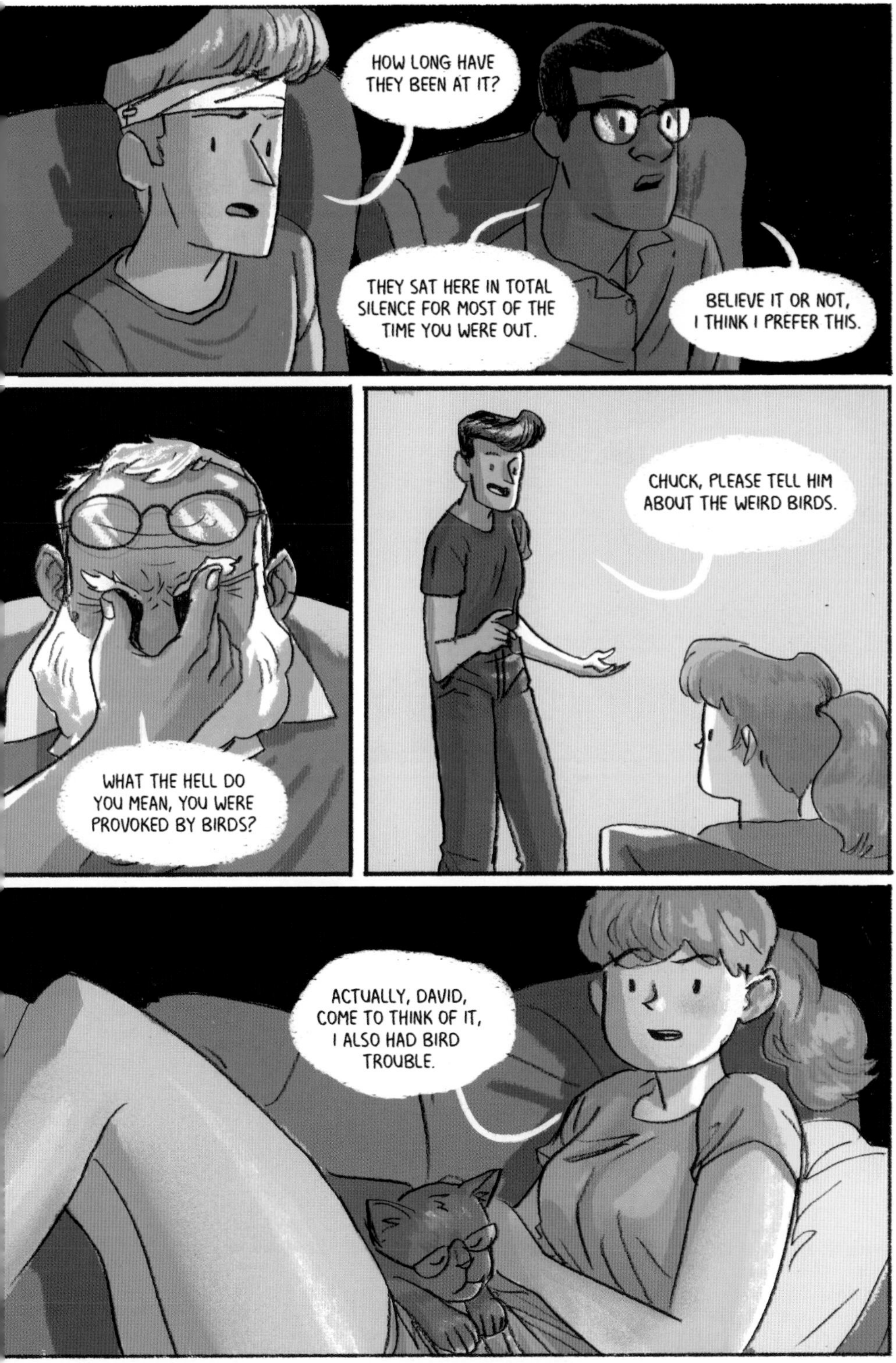
HOW LONG HAVE THEY BEEN AT IT?
THEY SAT HERE IN TOTAL SILENCE FOR MOST OF THE TIME YOU WERE OUT.
BELIEVE IT OR NOT, I THINK I PREFER THIS.
WHAT THE HELL DO YOU MEAN, YOU WERE PROVOKED BY BIRDS?
CHUCK, PLEASE TELL HIM ABOUT THE WEIRD BIRDS.
ACTUALLY, DAVID, COME TO THINK OF IT, I ALSO HAD BIRD TROUBLE.

OH, CHARLIE. DEAR, DEAR CHARLIE. PLEASE DON'T START WITH THIS BIRD NONSENSE TOO.

YOU WERE THE ONLY ONE WITH ENOUGH SENSE TO DO EXACTLY AS I SAID, AND THAT MAKES YOU MY FAVORITE RIGHT NOW. PLEASE DON'T RUIN THAT WITH BIRD TALK.

SORRY, MAURICE, I'M NOT DOWN WITH THE FALLOUT I'M GETTING ON THIS COUCH.

YOU KNOW, WHEN I SAID "DON'T DIE," I DIDN'T MEAN TO COME AS CLOSE AS HUMANLY POSSIBLE.

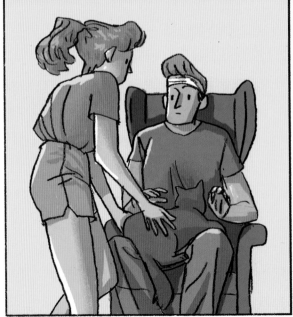

WELL, NOW YOU TELL ME.

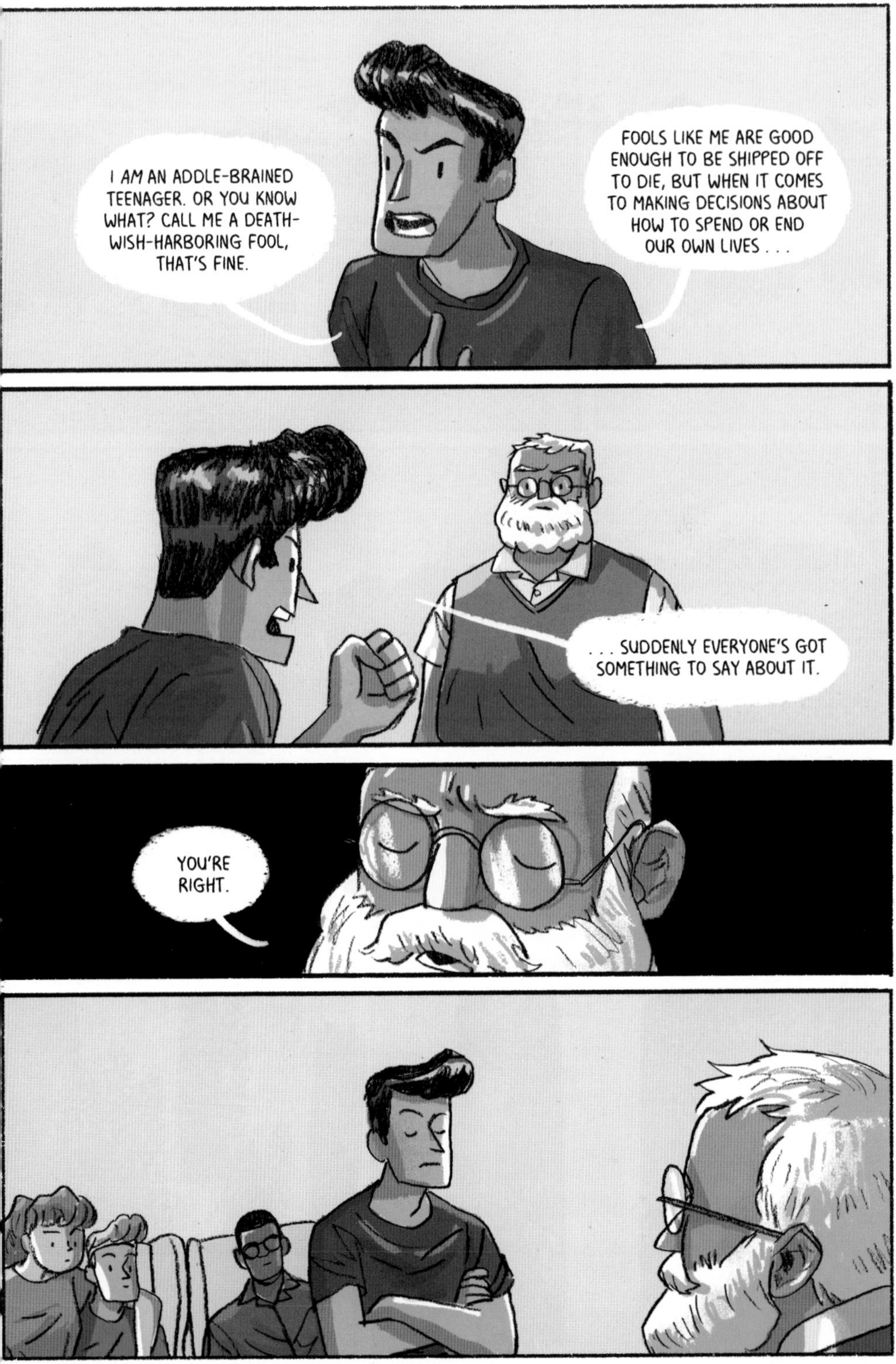
I *AM* AN ADDLE-BRAINED TEENAGER. OR YOU KNOW WHAT? CALL ME A DEATH-WISH-HARBORING FOOL, THAT'S FINE.
FOOLS LIKE ME ARE GOOD ENOUGH TO BE SHIPPED OFF TO DIE, BUT WHEN IT COMES TO MAKING DECISIONS ABOUT HOW TO SPEND OR END OUR OWN LIVES . . .
. . . SUDDENLY EVERYONE'S GOT SOMETHING TO SAY ABOUT IT.
YOU'RE RIGHT.

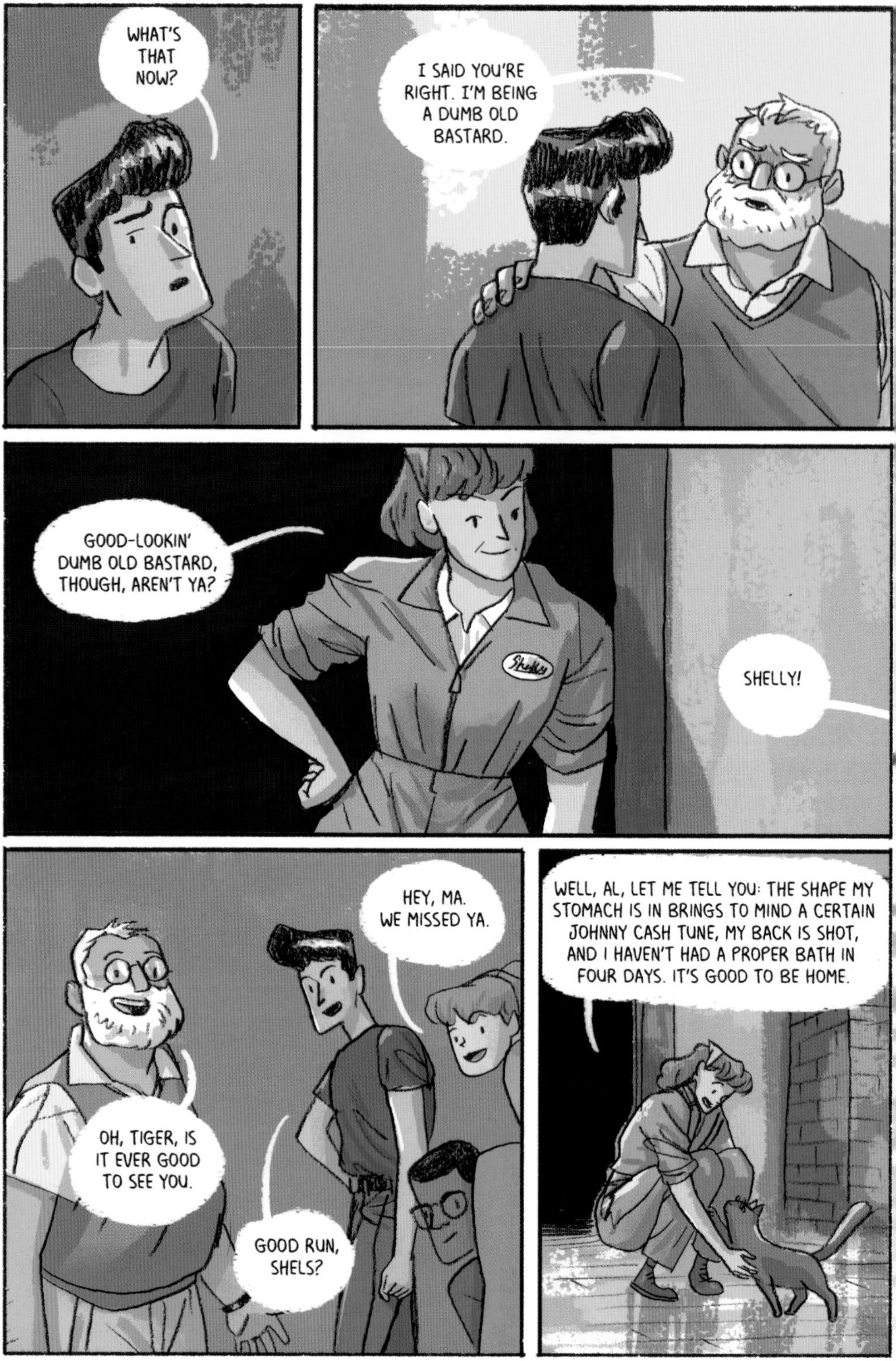
WHAT'S THAT NOW?
I SAID YOU'RE RIGHT. I'M BEING A DUMB OLD BASTARD.
GOOD-LOOKIN' DUMB OLD BASTARD, THOUGH, AREN'T YA?
SHELLY!
HEY, MA. WE MISSED YA.
OH, TIGER, IS IT EVER GOOD TO SEE YOU.
GOOD RUN, SHELS?
WELL, AL, LET ME TELL YOU: THE SHAPE MY STOMACH IS IN BRINGS TO MIND A CERTAIN JOHNNY CASH TUNE, MY BACK IS SHOT, AND I HAVEN'T HAD A PROPER BATH IN FOUR DAYS. IT'S GOOD TO BE HOME.

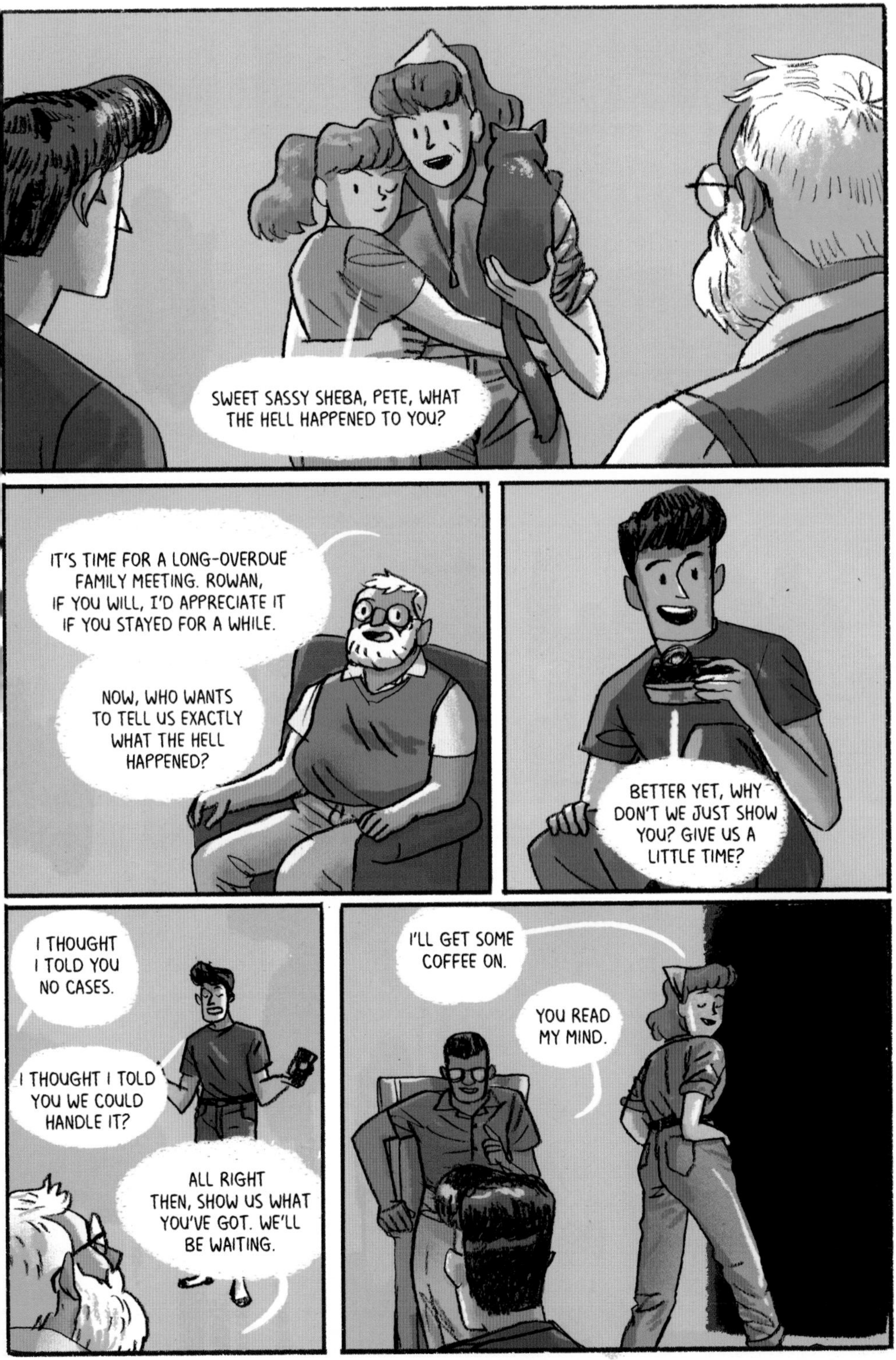
SWEET SASSY SHEBA, PETE, WHAT THE HELL HAPPENED TO YOU?
IT'S TIME FOR A LONG-OVERDUE FAMILY MEETING. ROWAN, IF YOU WILL, I'D APPRECIATE IT IF YOU STAYED FOR A WHILE.
NOW, WHO WANTS TO TELL US EXACTLY WHAT THE HELL HAPPENED?
BETTER YET, WHY DON'T WE JUST SHOW YOU? GIVE US A LITTLE TIME?
I THOUGHT I TOLD YOU NO CASES.
I THOUGHT I TOLD YOU WE COULD HANDLE IT?
ALL RIGHT THEN, SHOW US WHAT YOU'VE GOT. WE'LL BE WAITING.
I'LL GET SOME COFFEE ON.
YOU READ MY MIND.

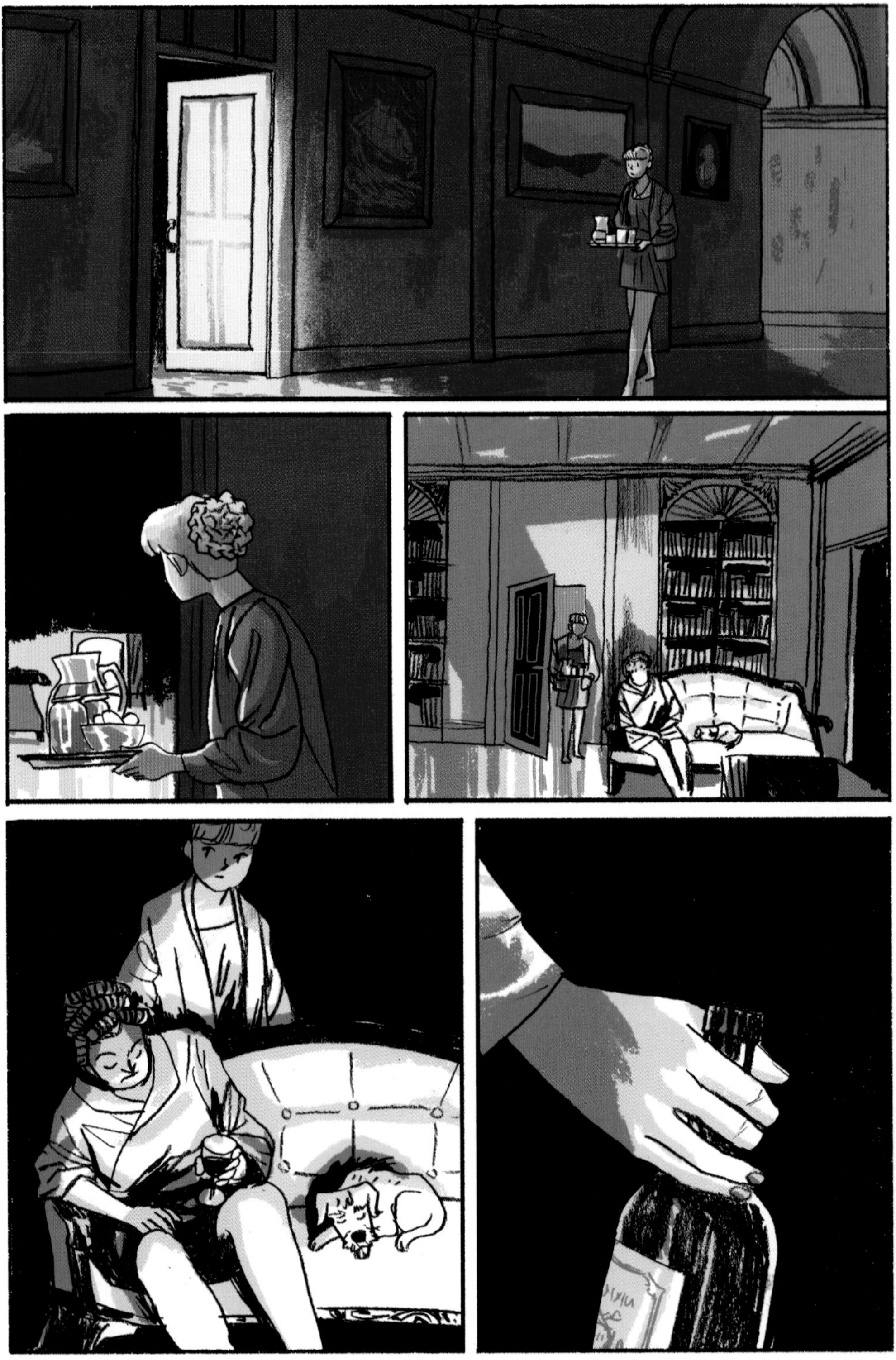

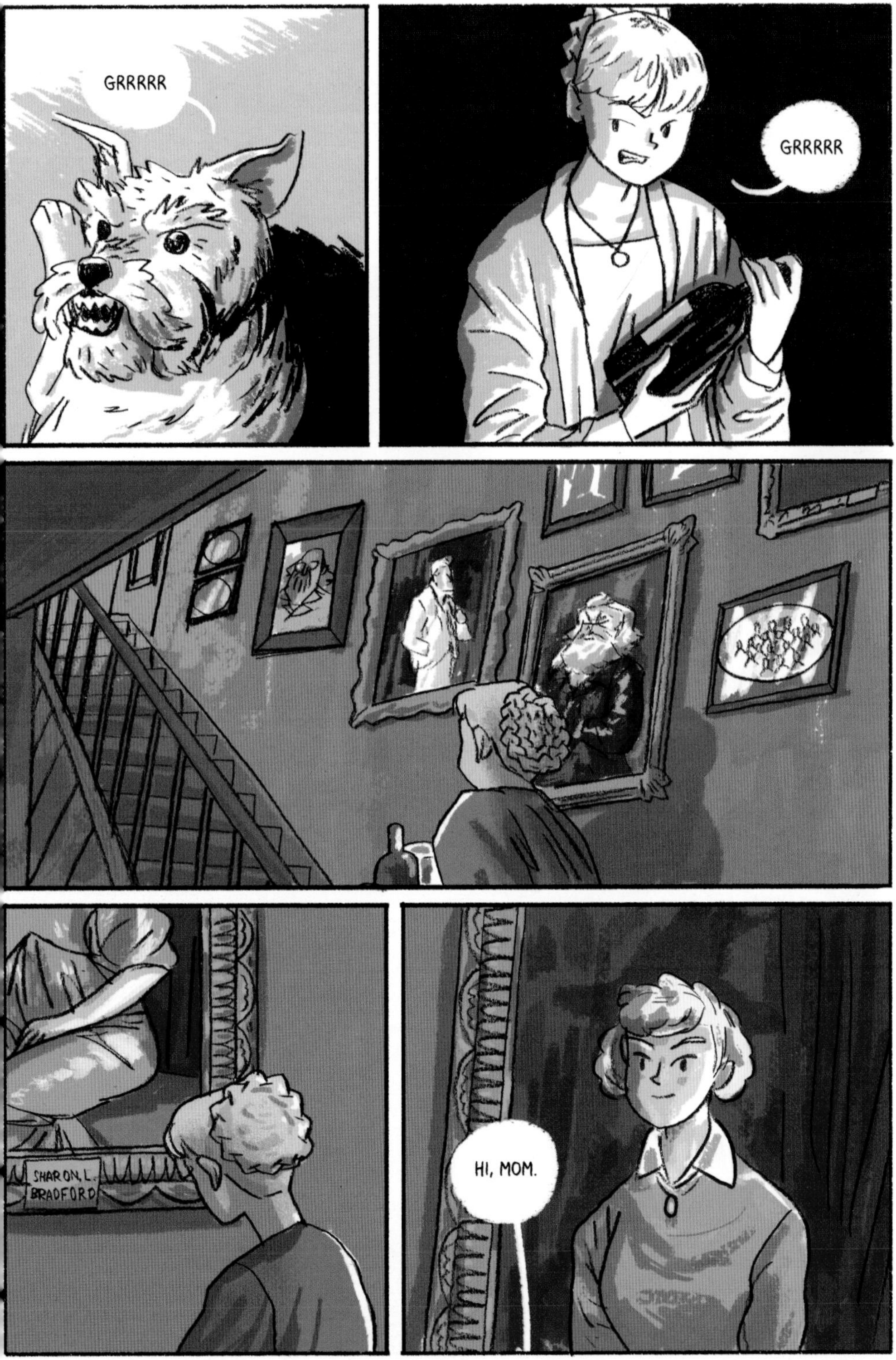
GRRRRR
GRRRRR
SHARON, L. BRADFORD
HI, MOM.

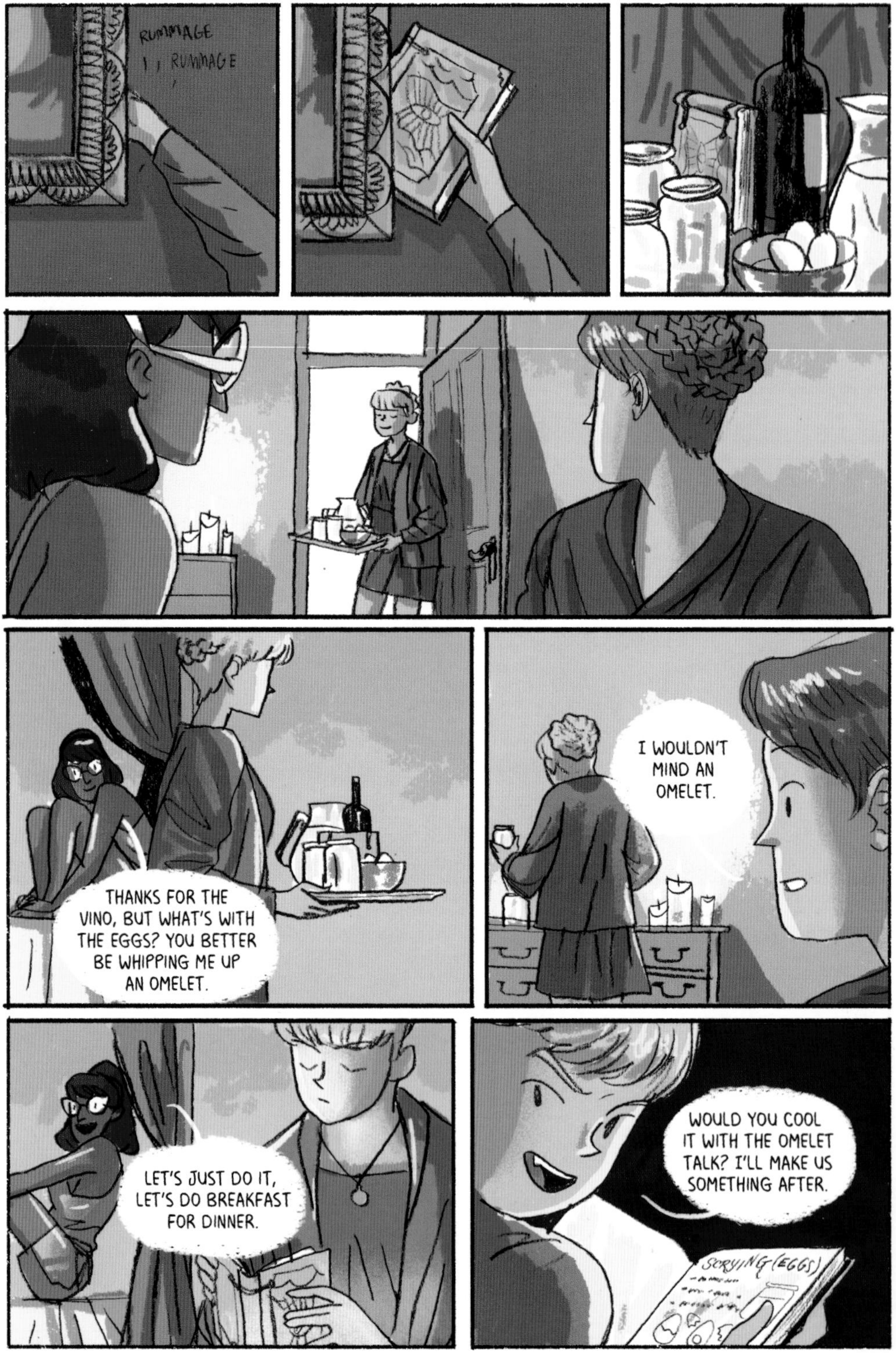
RUMMAGE
RUMMAGE
THANKS FOR THE VINO, BUT WHAT'S WITH THE EGGS? YOU BETTER BE WHIPPING ME UP AN OMELET.
I WOULDN'T MIND AN OMELET.
LET'S JUST DO IT, LET'S DO BREAKFAST FOR DINNER.
WOULD YOU COOL IT WITH THE OMELET TALK? I'LL MAKE US SOMETHING AFTER.
SCRYING (EGGS)

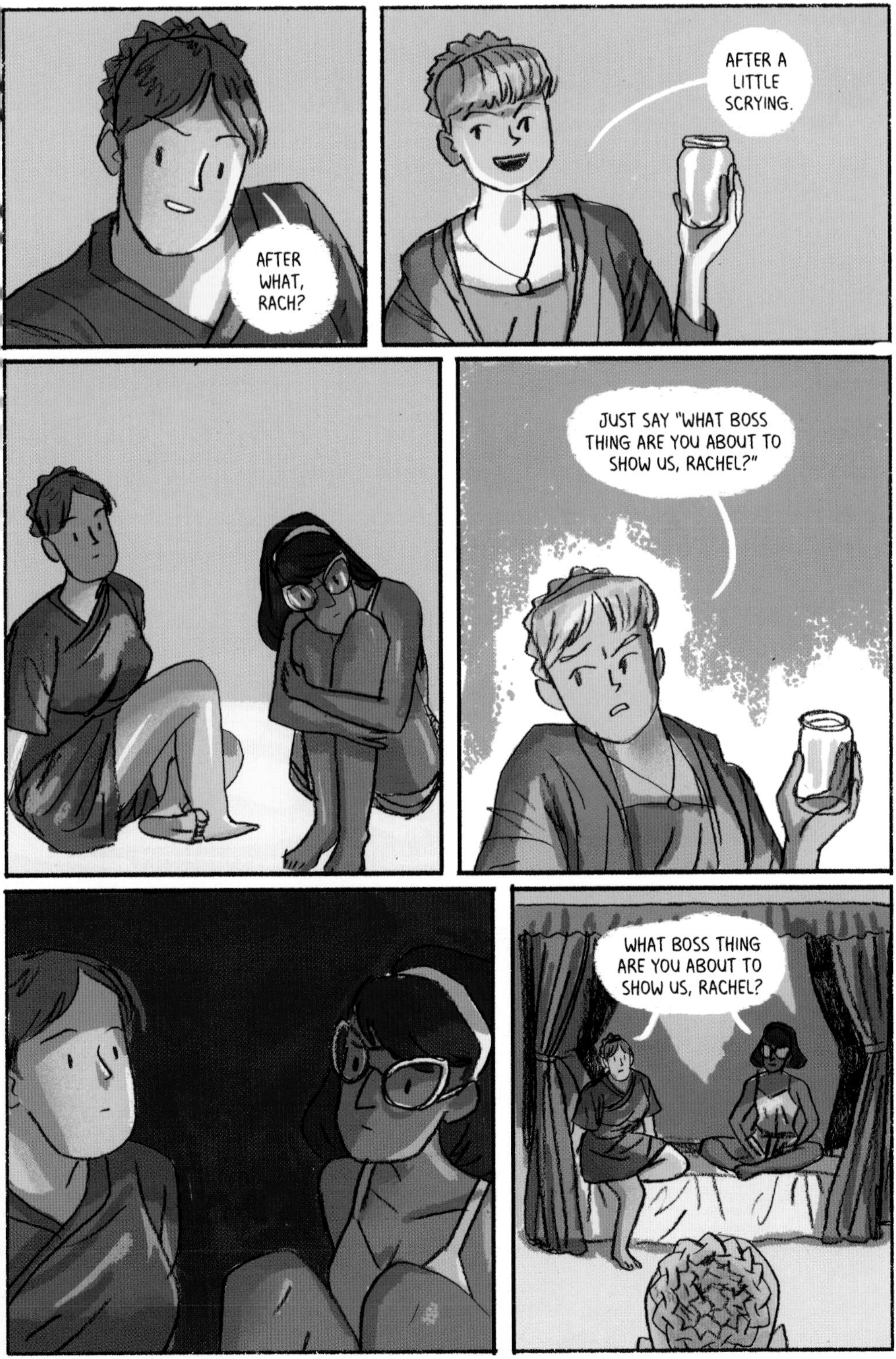
AFTER WHAT, RACH?
AFTER A LITTLE SCRYING.
JUST SAY "WHAT BOSS THING ARE YOU ABOUT TO SHOW US, RACHEL?"
WHAT BOSS THING ARE YOU ABOUT TO SHOW US, RACHEL?

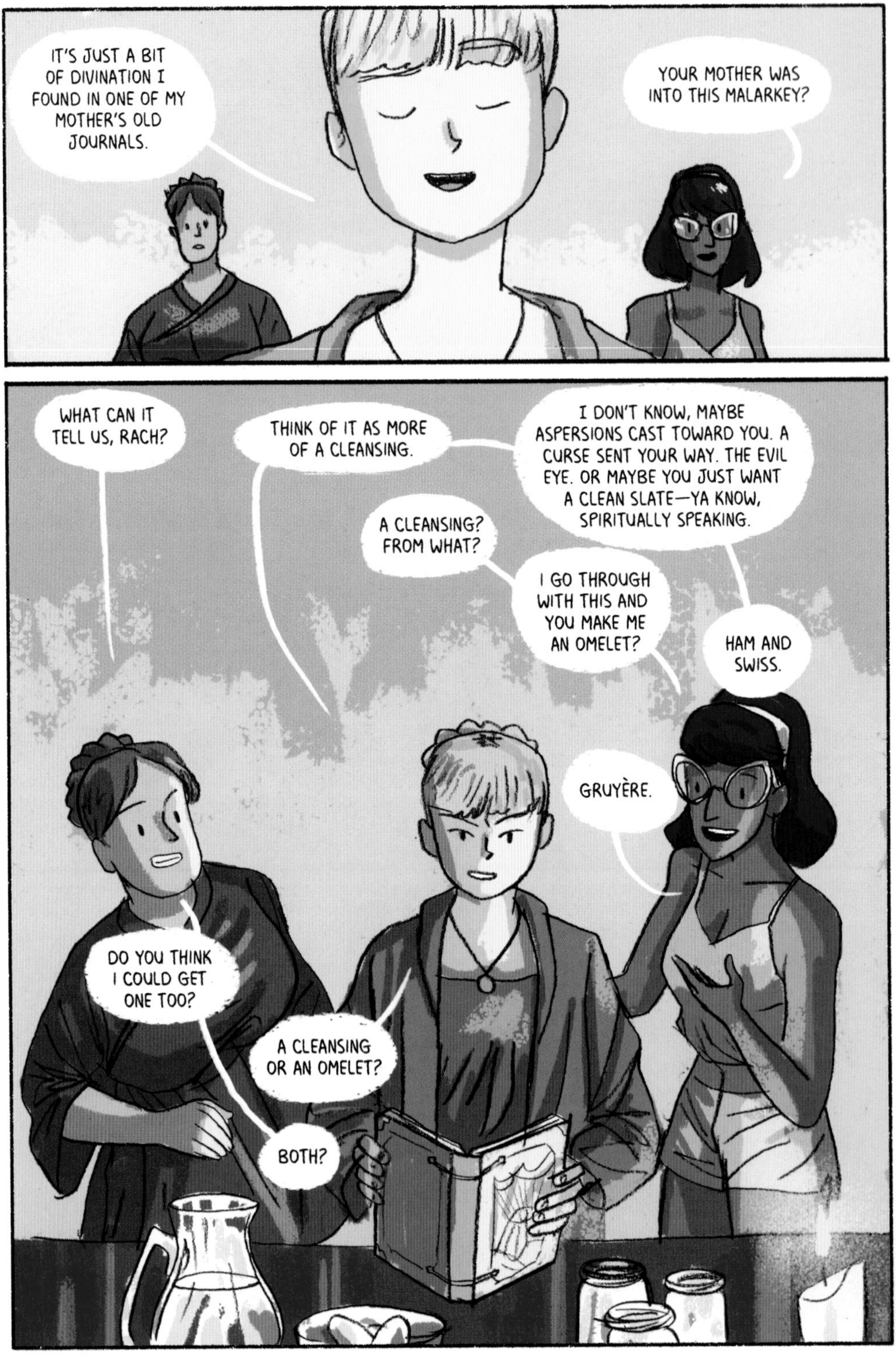
IT'S JUST A BIT OF DIVINATION I FOUND IN ONE OF MY MOTHER'S OLD JOURNALS.
YOUR MOTHER WAS INTO THIS MALARKEY?
WHAT CAN IT TELL US, RACH?
THINK OF IT AS MORE OF A CLEANSING.
I DON'T KNOW, MAYBE ASPERSIONS CAST TOWARD YOU. A CURSE SENT YOUR WAY. THE EVIL EYE. OR MAYBE YOU JUST WANT A CLEAN SLATE—YA KNOW, SPIRITUALLY SPEAKING.
A CLEANSING? FROM WHAT?
I GO THROUGH WITH THIS AND YOU MAKE ME AN OMELET?
HAM AND SWISS.
GRUYÈRE.
DO YOU THINK I COULD GET ONE TOO?
A CLEANSING OR AN OMELET?
BOTH?

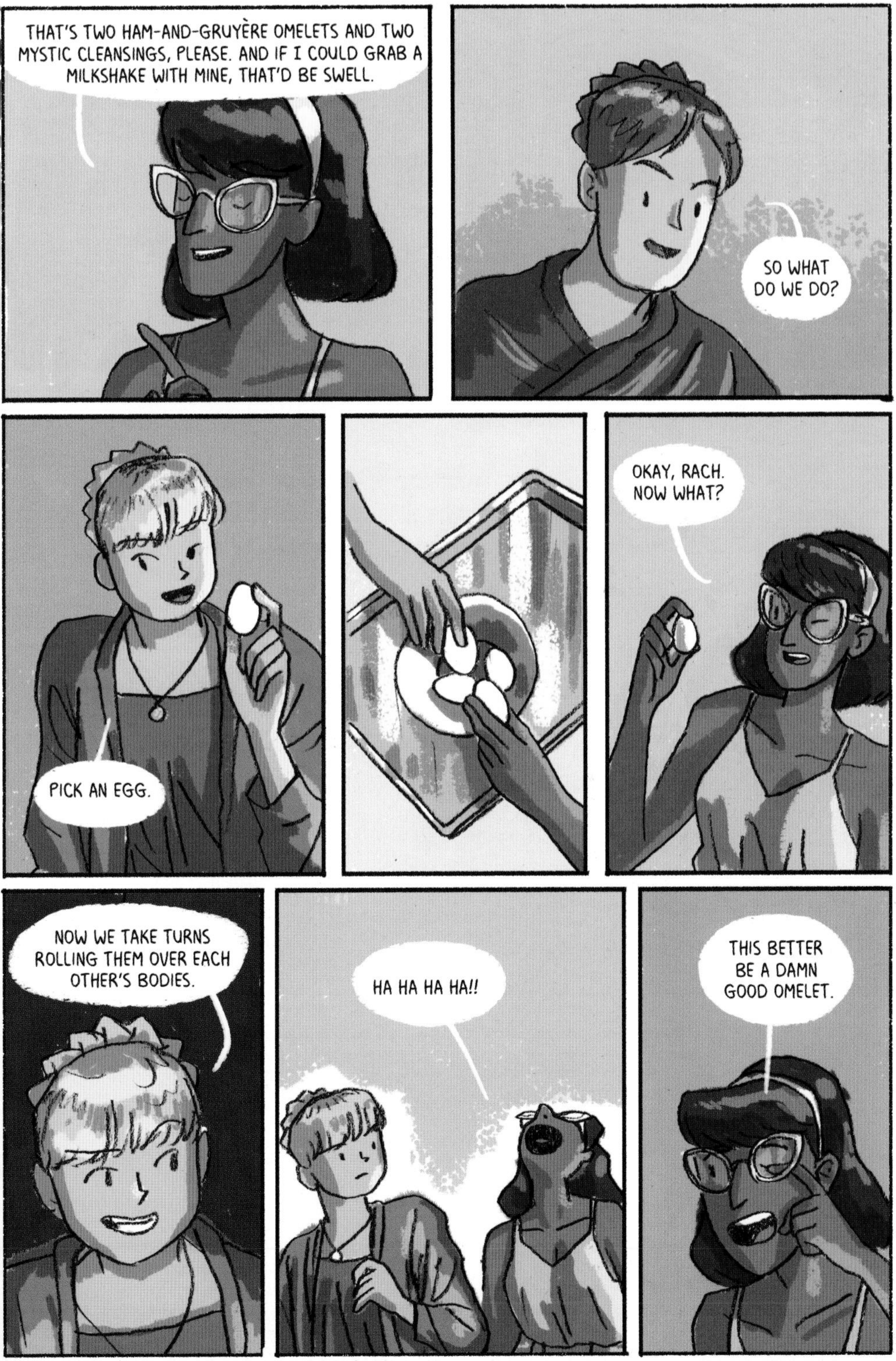
THAT'S TWO HAM-AND-GRUYÈRE OMELETS AND TWO MYSTIC CLEANSINGS, PLEASE. AND IF I COULD GRAB A MILKSHAKE WITH MINE, THAT'D BE SWELL.
SO WHAT DO WE DO?
PICK AN EGG.
OKAY, RACH. NOW WHAT?
NOW WE TAKE TURNS ROLLING THEM OVER EACH OTHER'S BODIES.
HA HA HA HA!!
THIS BETTER BE A DAMN GOOD OMELET.

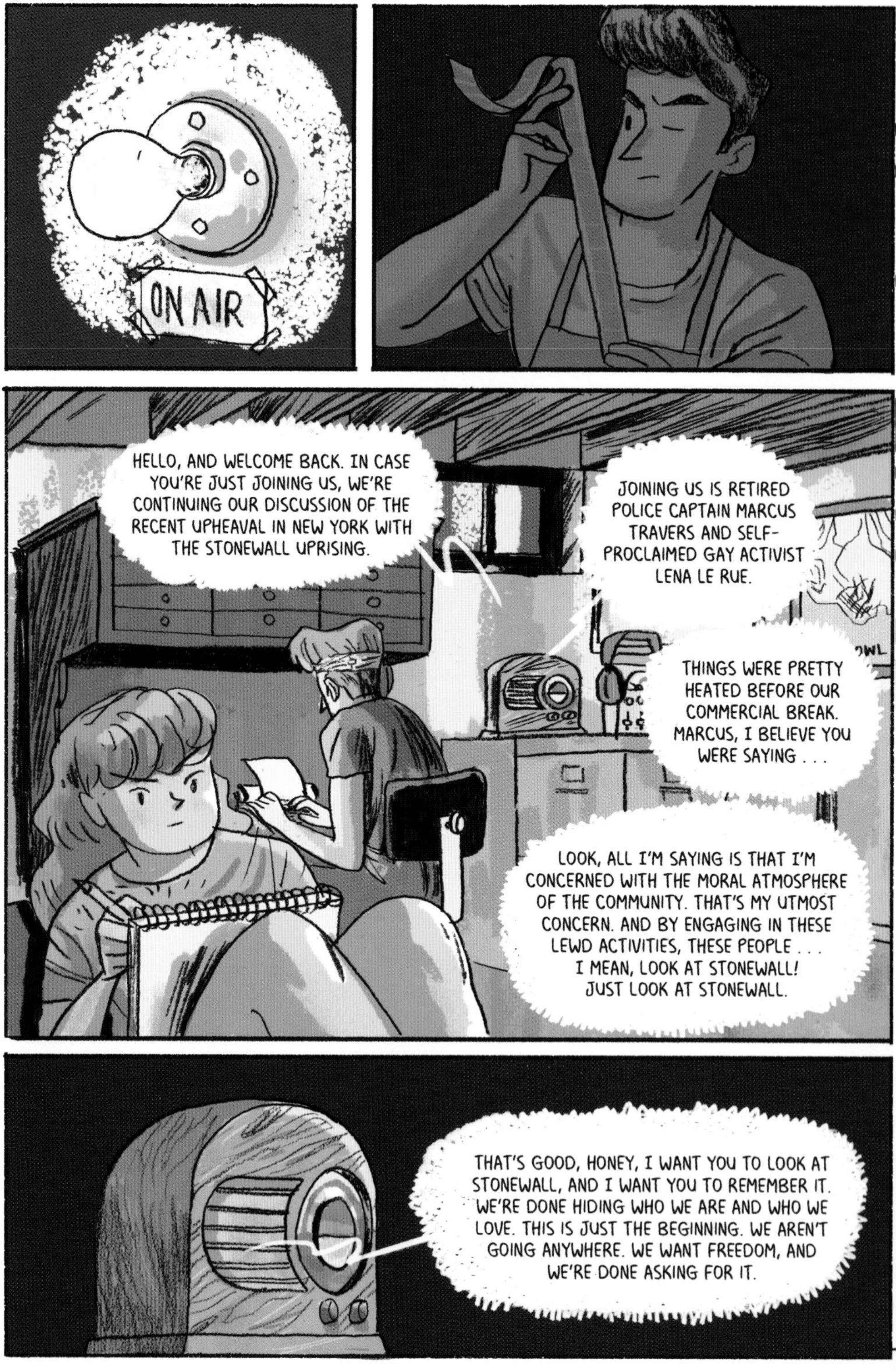
ON AIR
HELLO, AND WELCOME BACK. IN CASE YOU'RE JUST JOINING US, WE'RE CONTINUING OUR DISCUSSION OF THE RECENT UPHEAVAL IN NEW YORK WITH THE STONEWALL UPRISING.
JOINING US IS RETIRED POLICE CAPTAIN MARCUS TRAVERS AND SELF-PROCLAIMED GAY ACTIVIST LENA LE RUE.
THINGS WERE PRETTY HEATED BEFORE OUR COMMERCIAL BREAK. MARCUS, I BELIEVE YOU WERE SAYING . . .
LOOK, ALL I'M SAYING IS THAT I'M CONCERNED WITH THE MORAL ATMOSPHERE OF THE COMMUNITY. THAT'S MY UTMOST CONCERN. AND BY ENGAGING IN THESE LEWD ACTIVITIES, THESE PEOPLE . . . I MEAN, LOOK AT STONEWALL! JUST LOOK AT STONEWALL.
THAT'S GOOD, HONEY, I WANT YOU TO LOOK AT STONEWALL, AND I WANT YOU TO REMEMBER IT. WE'RE DONE HIDING WHO WE ARE AND WHO WE LOVE. THIS IS JUST THE BEGINNING. WE AREN'T GOING ANYWHERE. WE WANT FREEDOM, AND WE'RE DONE ASKING FOR IT.

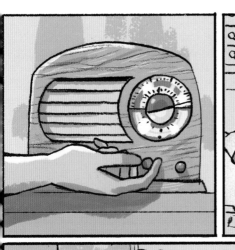

PETE.

RUB RUB RUB

ARE YOU ALL RIGHT?

YEAH. MY HEAD STILL HURTS A LITTLE BUT I'M FINE.

YOU KNOW WHAT I MEAN.

I'M GOOD. I'M . . . REALLY GOOD.

YOU GUYS HAVE GOT TO CHECK THESE OUT—

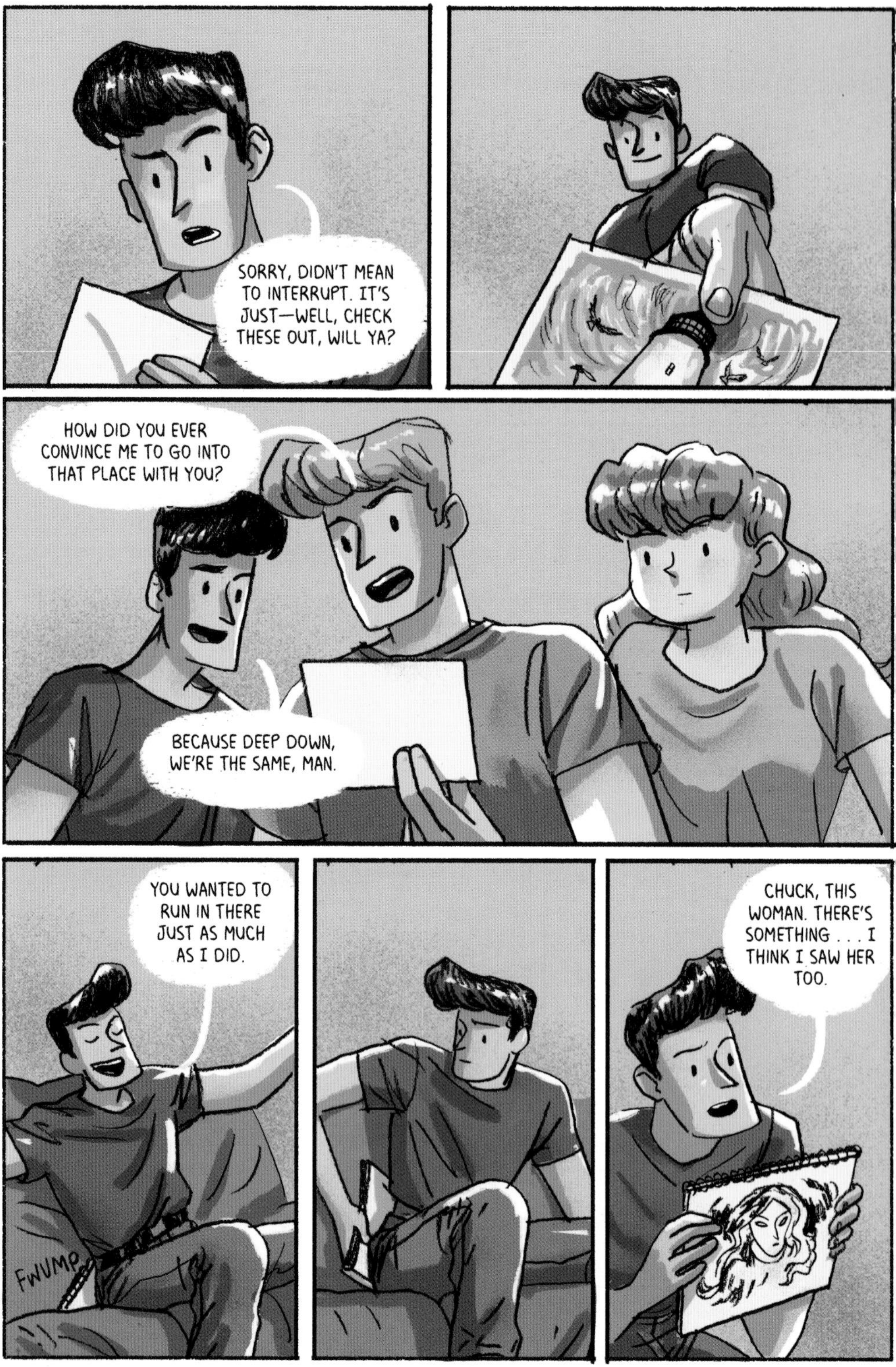
SORRY, DIDN'T MEAN TO INTERRUPT. IT'S JUST—WELL, CHECK THESE OUT, WILL YA?
HOW DID YOU EVER CONVINCE ME TO GO INTO THAT PLACE WITH YOU?
BECAUSE DEEP DOWN, WE'RE THE SAME, MAN.
YOU WANTED TO RUN IN THERE JUST AS MUCH AS I DID.
FWUMP
CHUCK, THIS WOMAN. THERE'S SOMETHING . . . I THINK I SAW HER TOO.

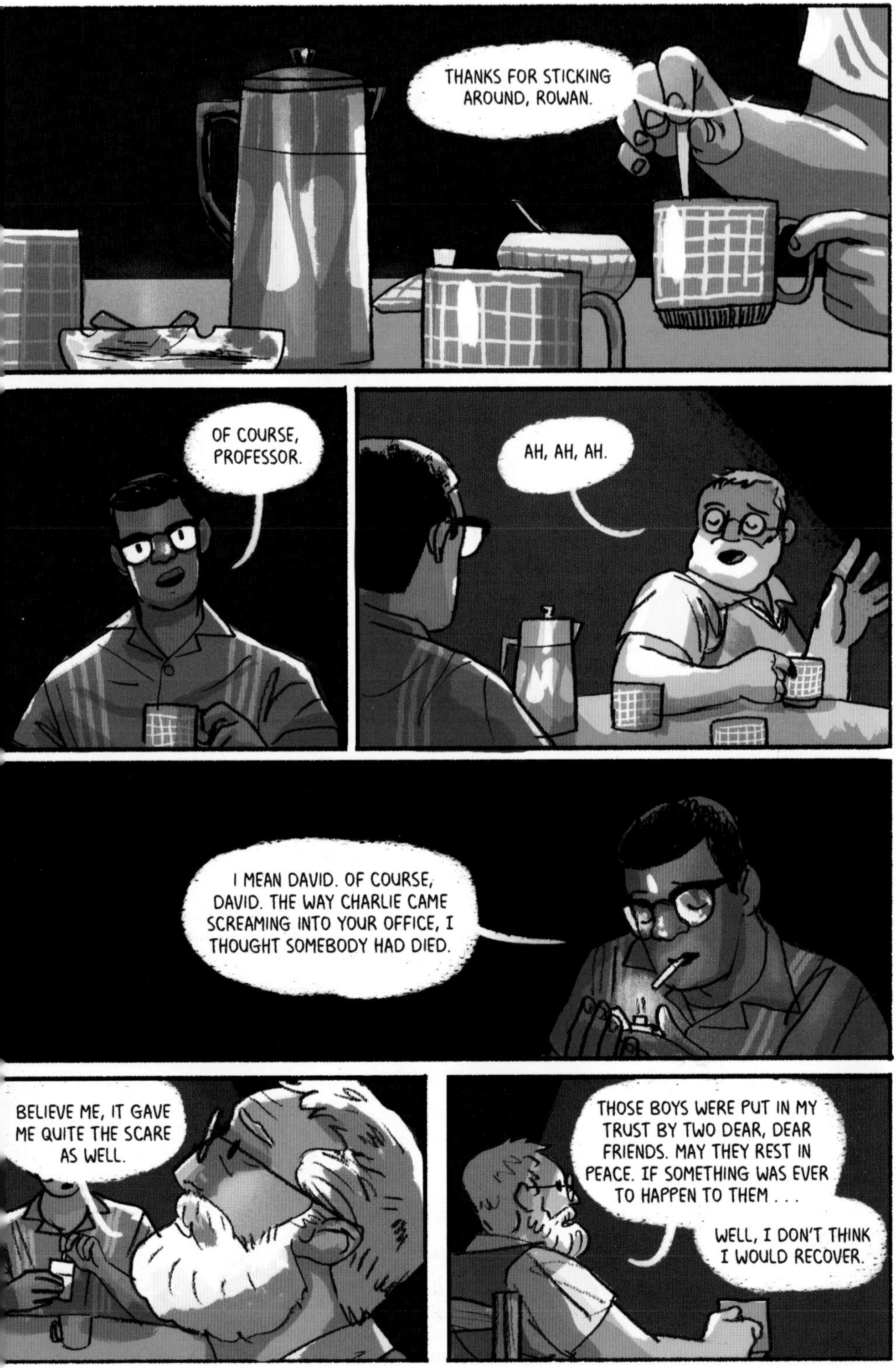
THANKS FOR STICKING AROUND, ROWAN.
OF COURSE, PROFESSOR.
AH, AH, AH.
I MEAN DAVID. OF COURSE, DAVID. THE WAY CHARLIE CAME SCREAMING INTO YOUR OFFICE, I THOUGHT SOMEBODY HAD DIED.
BELIEVE ME, IT GAVE ME QUITE THE SCARE AS WELL.
THOSE BOYS WERE PUT IN MY TRUST BY TWO DEAR, DEAR FRIENDS. MAY THEY REST IN PEACE. IF SOMETHING WAS EVER TO HAPPEN TO THEM . . .
WELL, I DON'T THINK I WOULD RECOVER.

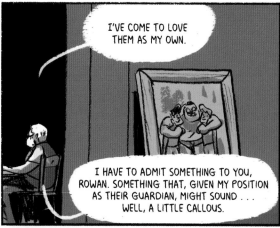

I'VE COME TO LOVE THEM AS MY OWN.

I HAVE TO ADMIT SOMETHING TO YOU, ROWAN. SOMETHING THAT, GIVEN MY POSITION AS THEIR GUARDIAN, MIGHT SOUND . . . WELL, A LITTLE CALLOUS.

I'VE BEEN WAITING FOR SOMETHING LIKE THIS TO HAPPEN.

ACCIDENTS HAPPEN, DAVID. BOYS WILL BE BOYS, RIGHT?

ROWAN, YOU'RE MY PROTÉGÉ. MY ASSISTANT. I'M VERY SELECTIVE ABOUT WHO I TAKE ON. IN OUR FIELD, YOU HAVE TO BE. THE STAKES ARE TOO HIGH. I KNOW YOU'RE NOT AN IDIOT. I KNOW YOU SENSE IT.

THEY REEK OF IT.

HA HA HA HA!

MAGIC, ROWAN. IT'S HOW THEY SOLVE THEIR CASES. THEY'VE MANAGED TO TEACH THEMSELVES A LITTLE BIT OF MAGIC.

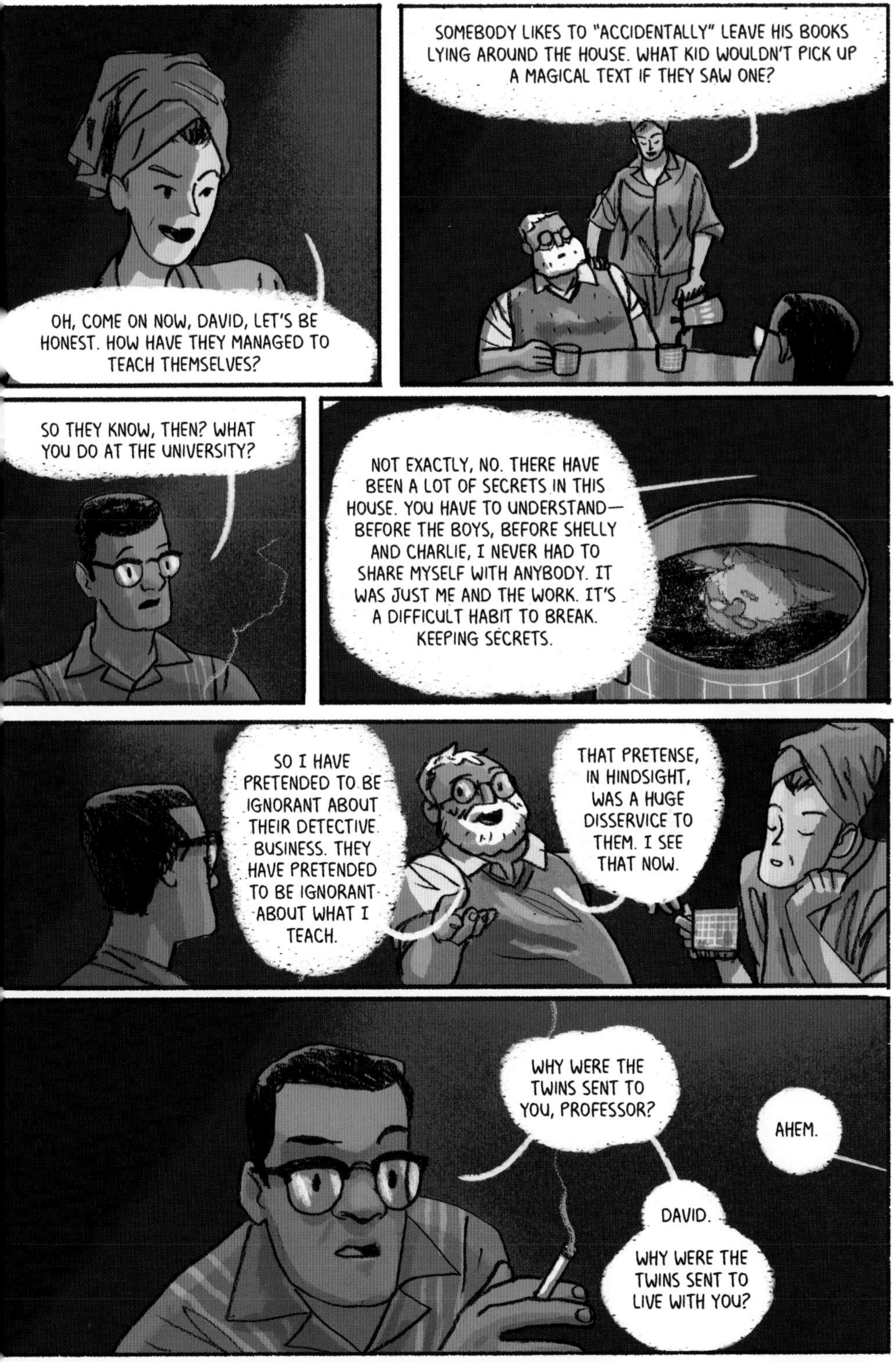
OH, COME ON NOW, DAVID, LET'S BE HONEST. HOW HAVE THEY MANAGED TO TEACH THEMSELVES?
SOMEBODY LIKES TO "ACCIDENTALLY" LEAVE HIS BOOKS LYING AROUND THE HOUSE. WHAT KID WOULDN'T PICK UP A MAGICAL TEXT IF THEY SAW ONE?
SO THEY KNOW, THEN? WHAT YOU DO AT THE UNIVERSITY?
NOT EXACTLY, NO. THERE HAVE BEEN A LOT OF SECRETS IN THIS HOUSE. YOU HAVE TO UNDERSTAND—BEFORE THE BOYS, BEFORE SHELLY AND CHARLIE, I NEVER HAD TO SHARE MYSELF WITH ANYBODY. IT WAS JUST ME AND THE WORK. IT'S A DIFFICULT HABIT TO BREAK. KEEPING SECRETS.
SO I HAVE PRETENDED TO BE IGNORANT ABOUT THEIR DETECTIVE BUSINESS. THEY HAVE PRETENDED TO BE IGNORANT ABOUT WHAT I TEACH.
THAT PRETENSE, IN HINDSIGHT, WAS A HUGE DISSERVICE TO THEM. I SEE THAT NOW.
WHY WERE THE TWINS SENT TO YOU, PROFESSOR?
AHEM.
DAVID.
WHY WERE THE TWINS SENT TO LIVE WITH YOU?

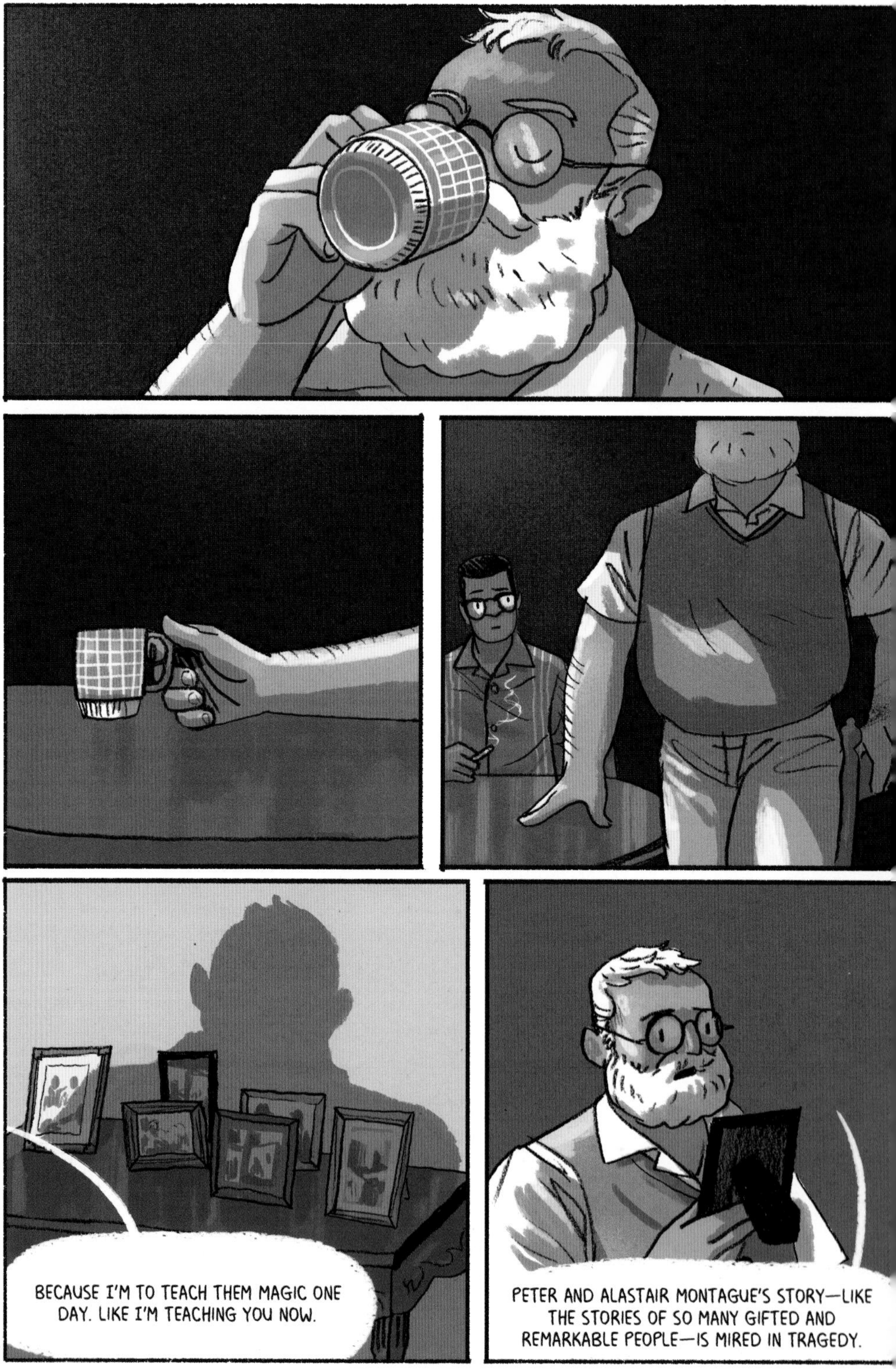
BECAUSE I'M TO TEACH THEM MAGIC ONE DAY. LIKE I'M TEACHING YOU NOW.
PETER AND ALASTAIR MONTAGUE'S STORY—LIKE THE STORIES OF SO MANY GIFTED AND REMARKABLE PEOPLE—IS MIRED IN TRAGEDY.

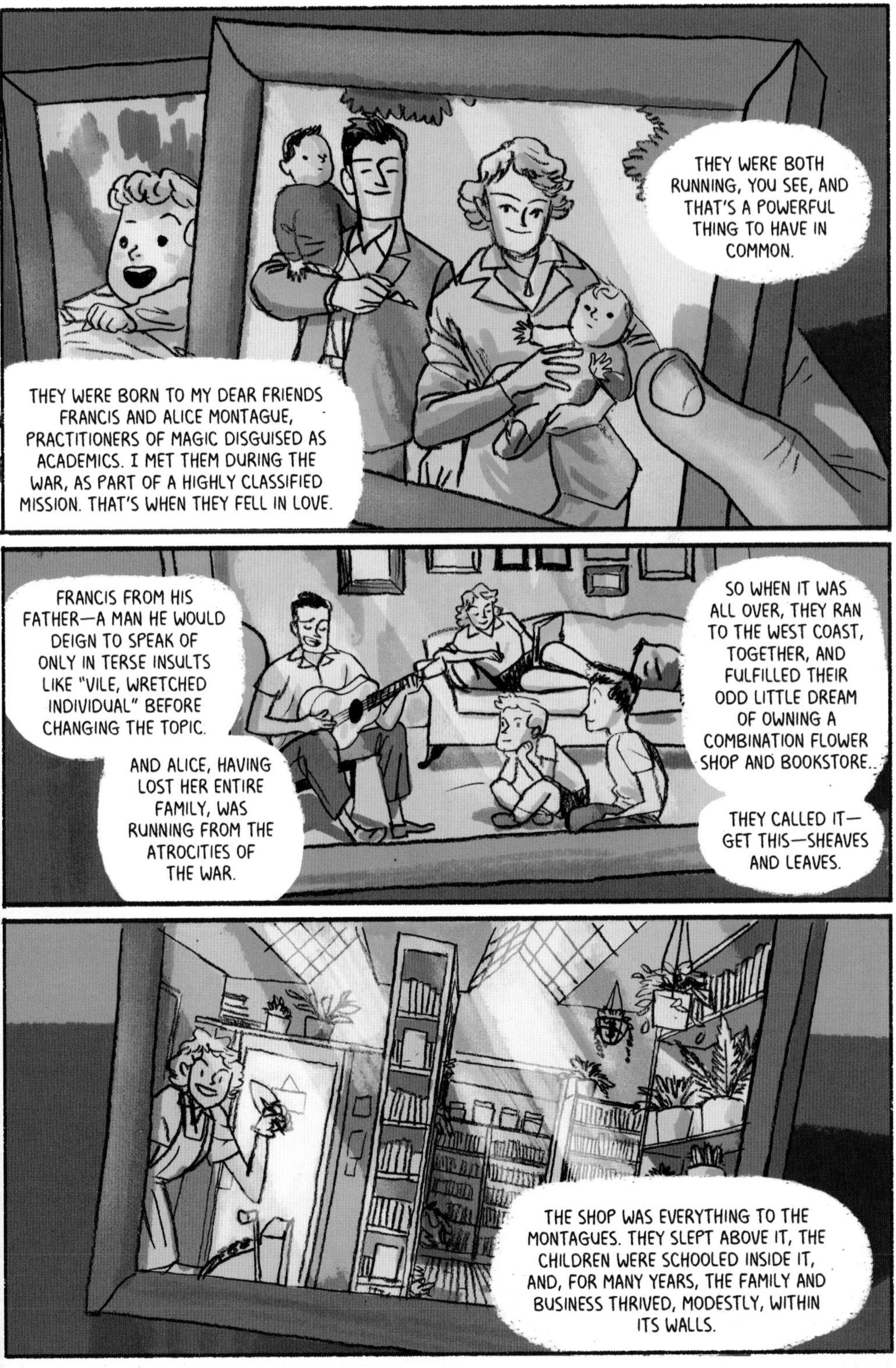
THEY WERE BOTH RUNNING, YOU SEE, AND THAT'S A POWERFUL THING TO HAVE IN COMMON.
THEY WERE BORN TO MY DEAR FRIENDS FRANCIS AND ALICE MONTAGUE, PRACTITIONERS OF MAGIC DISGUISED AS ACADEMICS. I MET THEM DURING THE WAR, AS PART OF A HIGHLY CLASSIFIED MISSION. THAT'S WHEN THEY FELL IN LOVE.
FRANCIS FROM HIS FATHER—A MAN HE WOULD DEIGN TO SPEAK OF ONLY IN TERSE INSULTS LIKE "VILE, WRETCHED INDIVIDUAL" BEFORE CHANGING THE TOPIC.
AND ALICE, HAVING LOST HER ENTIRE FAMILY, WAS RUNNING FROM THE ATROCITIES OF THE WAR.
SO WHEN IT WAS ALL OVER, THEY RAN TO THE WEST COAST, TOGETHER, AND FULFILLED THEIR ODD LITTLE DREAM OF OWNING A COMBINATION FLOWER SHOP AND BOOKSTORE.
THEY CALLED IT—GET THIS—SHEAVES AND LEAVES.
THE SHOP WAS EVERYTHING TO THE MONTAGUES. THEY SLEPT ABOVE IT, THE CHILDREN WERE SCHOOLED INSIDE IT, AND, FOR MANY YEARS, THE FAMILY AND BUSINESS THRIVED, MODESTLY, WITHIN ITS WALLS.

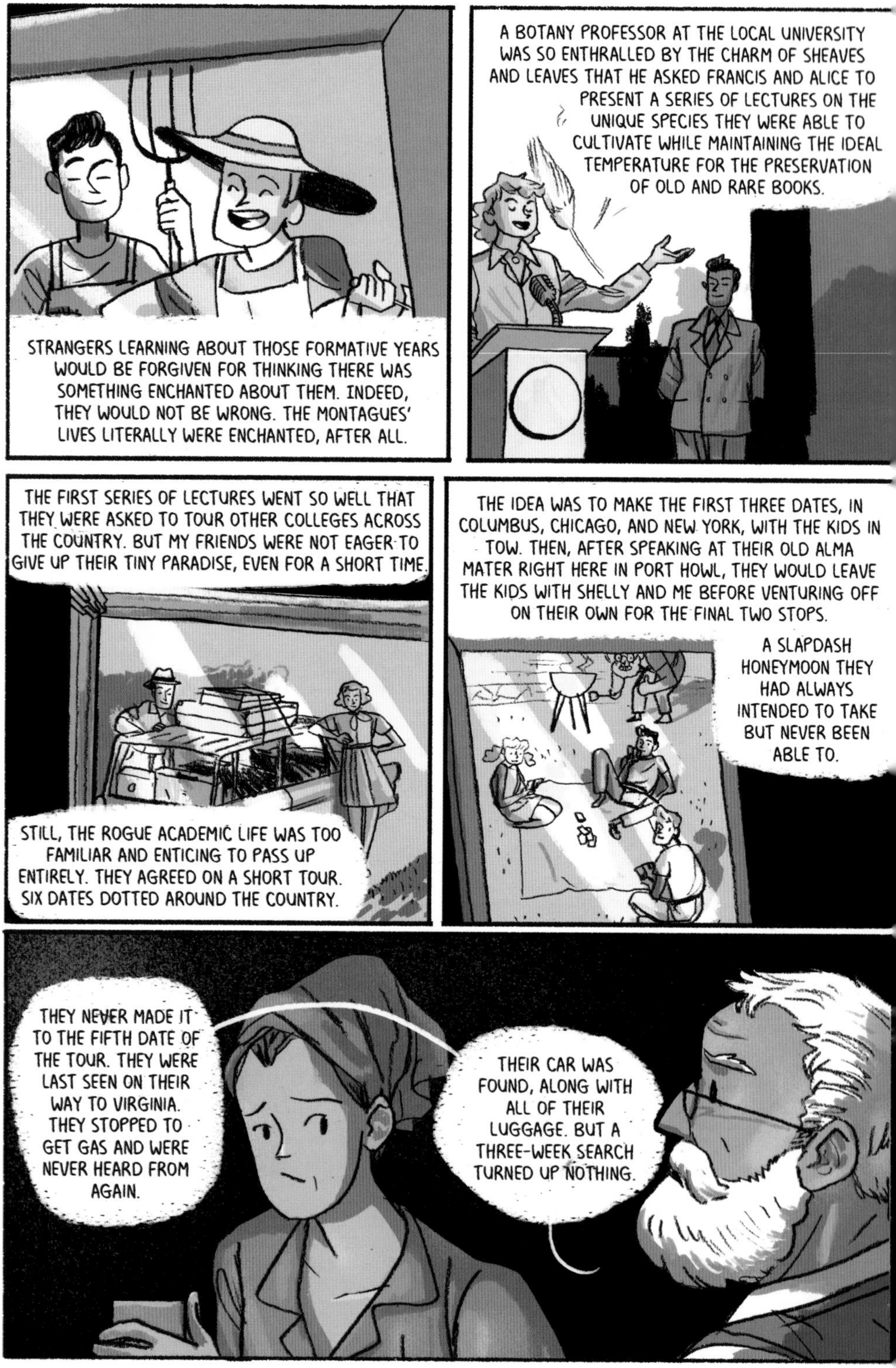
STRANGERS LEARNING ABOUT THOSE FORMATIVE YEARS WOULD BE FORGIVEN FOR THINKING THERE WAS SOMETHING ENCHANTED ABOUT THEM. INDEED, THEY WOULD NOT BE WRONG. THE MONTAGUES' LIVES LITERALLY WERE ENCHANTED, AFTER ALL.
A BOTANY PROFESSOR AT THE LOCAL UNIVERSITY WAS SO ENTHRALLED BY THE CHARM OF SHEAVES AND LEAVES THAT HE ASKED FRANCIS AND ALICE TO PRESENT A SERIES OF LECTURES ON THE UNIQUE SPECIES THEY WERE ABLE TO CULTIVATE WHILE MAINTAINING THE IDEAL TEMPERATURE FOR THE PRESERVATION OF OLD AND RARE BOOKS.
THE FIRST SERIES OF LECTURES WENT SO WELL THAT THEY WERE ASKED TO TOUR OTHER COLLEGES ACROSS THE COUNTRY. BUT MY FRIENDS WERE NOT EAGER TO GIVE UP THEIR TINY PARADISE, EVEN FOR A SHORT TIME.
STILL, THE ROGUE ACADEMIC LIFE WAS TOO FAMILIAR AND ENTICING TO PASS UP ENTIRELY. THEY AGREED ON A SHORT TOUR. SIX DATES DOTTED AROUND THE COUNTRY.
THE IDEA WAS TO MAKE THE FIRST THREE DATES, IN COLUMBUS, CHICAGO, AND NEW YORK, WITH THE KIDS IN TOW. THEN, AFTER SPEAKING AT THEIR OLD ALMA MATER RIGHT HERE IN PORT HOWL, THEY WOULD LEAVE THE KIDS WITH SHELLY AND ME BEFORE VENTURING OFF ON THEIR OWN FOR THE FINAL TWO STOPS.
A SLAPDASH HONEYMOON THEY HAD ALWAYS INTENDED TO TAKE BUT NEVER BEEN ABLE TO.
THEY NEVER MADE IT TO THE FIFTH DATE OF THE TOUR. THEY WERE LAST SEEN ON THEIR WAY TO VIRGINIA. THEY STOPPED TO GET GAS AND WERE NEVER HEARD FROM AGAIN.
THEIR CAR WAS FOUND, ALONG WITH ALL OF THEIR LUGGAGE. BUT A THREE-WEEK SEARCH TURNED UP NOTHING.

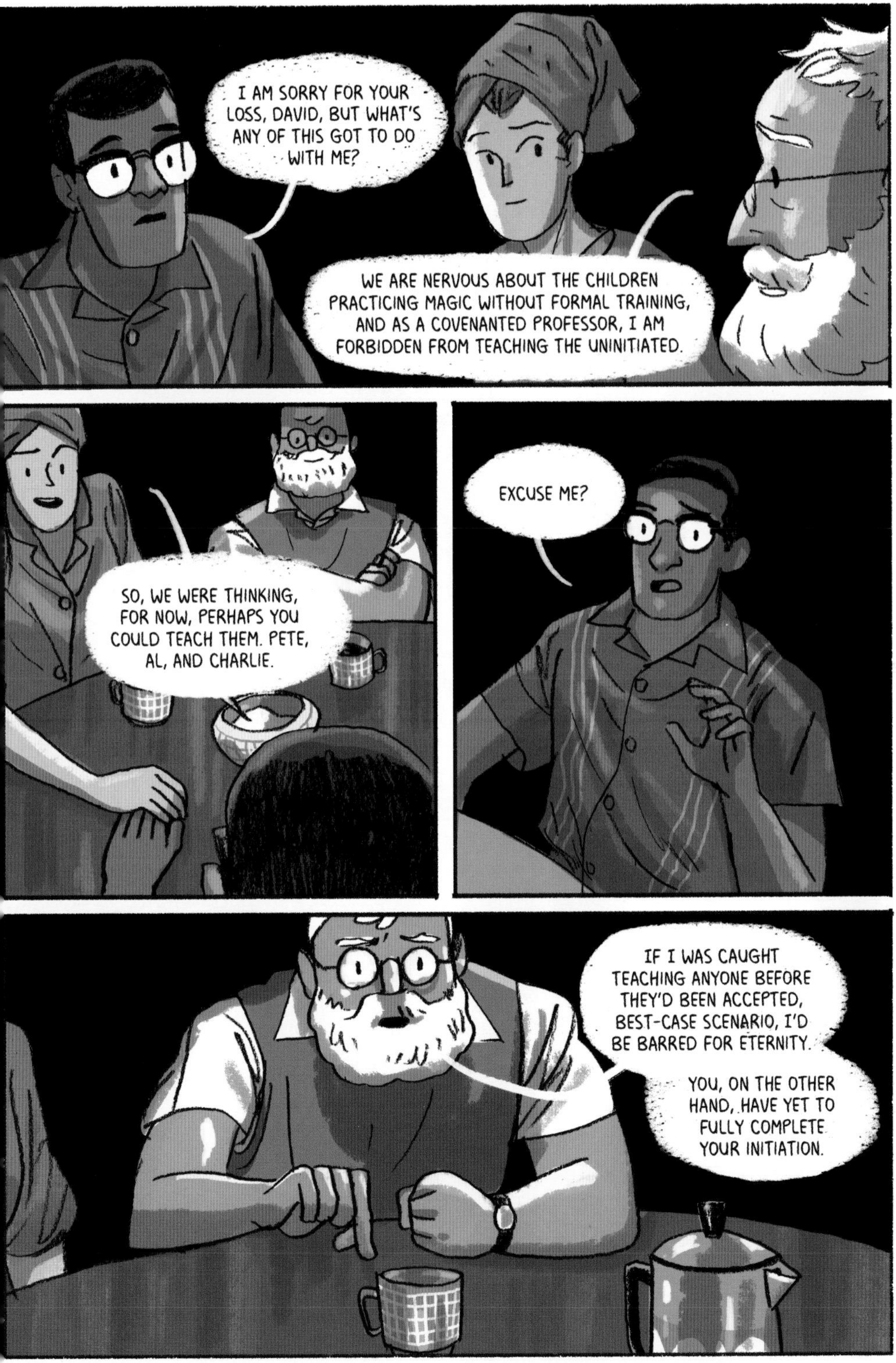
I AM SORRY FOR YOUR LOSS, DAVID, BUT WHAT'S ANY OF THIS GOT TO DO WITH ME?
WE ARE NERVOUS ABOUT THE CHILDREN PRACTICING MAGIC WITHOUT FORMAL TRAINING, AND AS A COVENANTED PROFESSOR, I AM FORBIDDEN FROM TEACHING THE UNINITIATED.
SO, WE WERE THINKING, FOR NOW, PERHAPS YOU COULD TEACH THEM. PETE, AL, AND CHARLIE.
EXCUSE ME?
IF I WAS CAUGHT TEACHING ANYONE BEFORE THEY'D BEEN ACCEPTED, BEST-CASE SCENARIO, I'D BE BARRED FOR ETERNITY.
YOU, ON THE OTHER HAND, HAVE YET TO FULLY COMPLETE YOUR INITIATION.

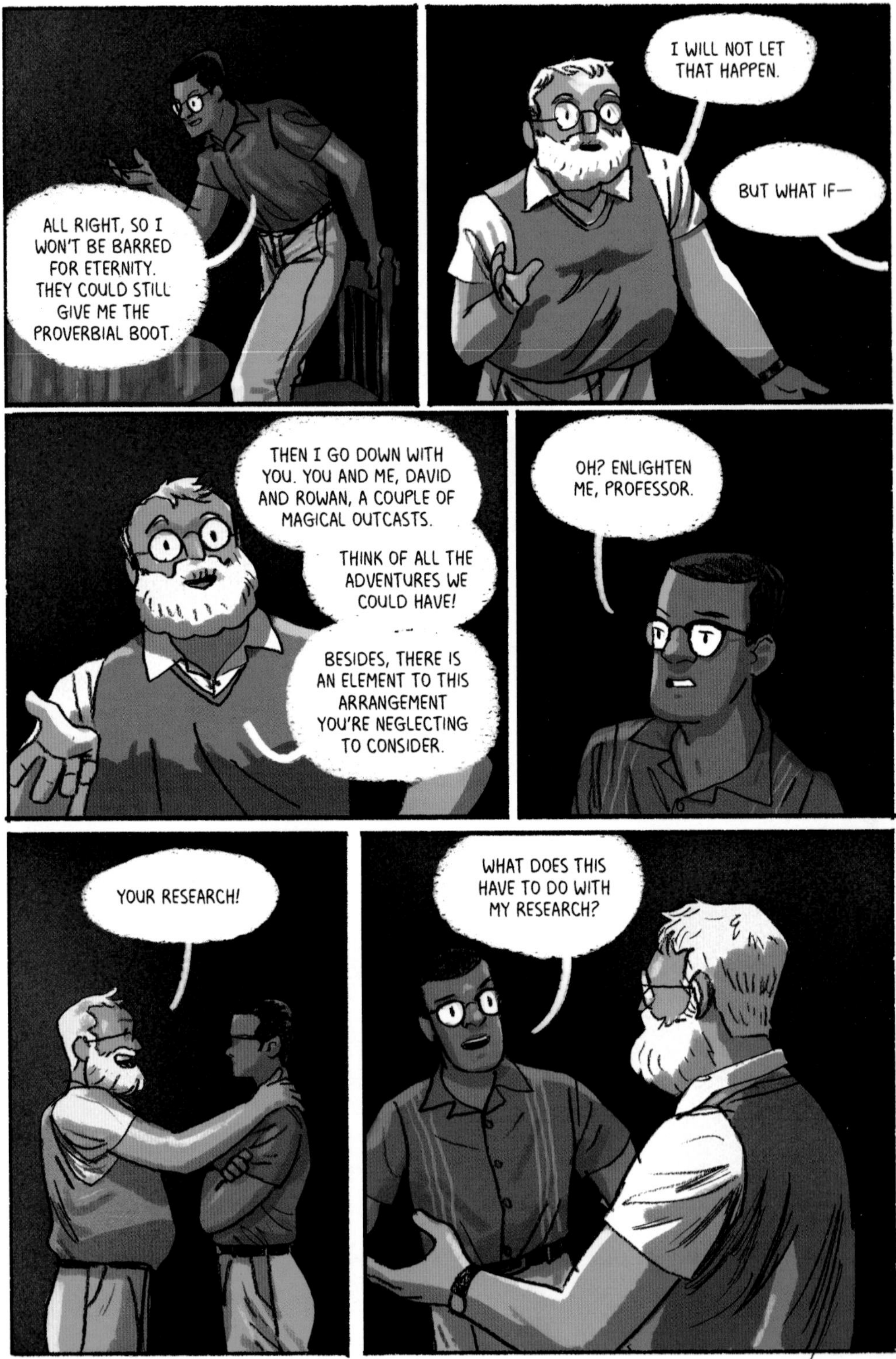
ALL RIGHT, SO I WON'T BE BARRED FOR ETERNITY. THEY COULD STILL GIVE ME THE PROVERBIAL BOOT.
I WILL NOT LET THAT HAPPEN.
BUT WHAT IF—
THEN I GO DOWN WITH YOU. YOU AND ME, DAVID AND ROWAN, A COUPLE OF MAGICAL OUTCASTS.
THINK OF ALL THE ADVENTURES WE COULD HAVE!
BESIDES, THERE IS AN ELEMENT TO THIS ARRANGEMENT YOU'RE NEGLECTING TO CONSIDER.
OH? ENLIGHTEN ME, PROFESSOR.
YOUR RESEARCH!
WHAT DOES THIS HAVE TO DO WITH MY RESEARCH?

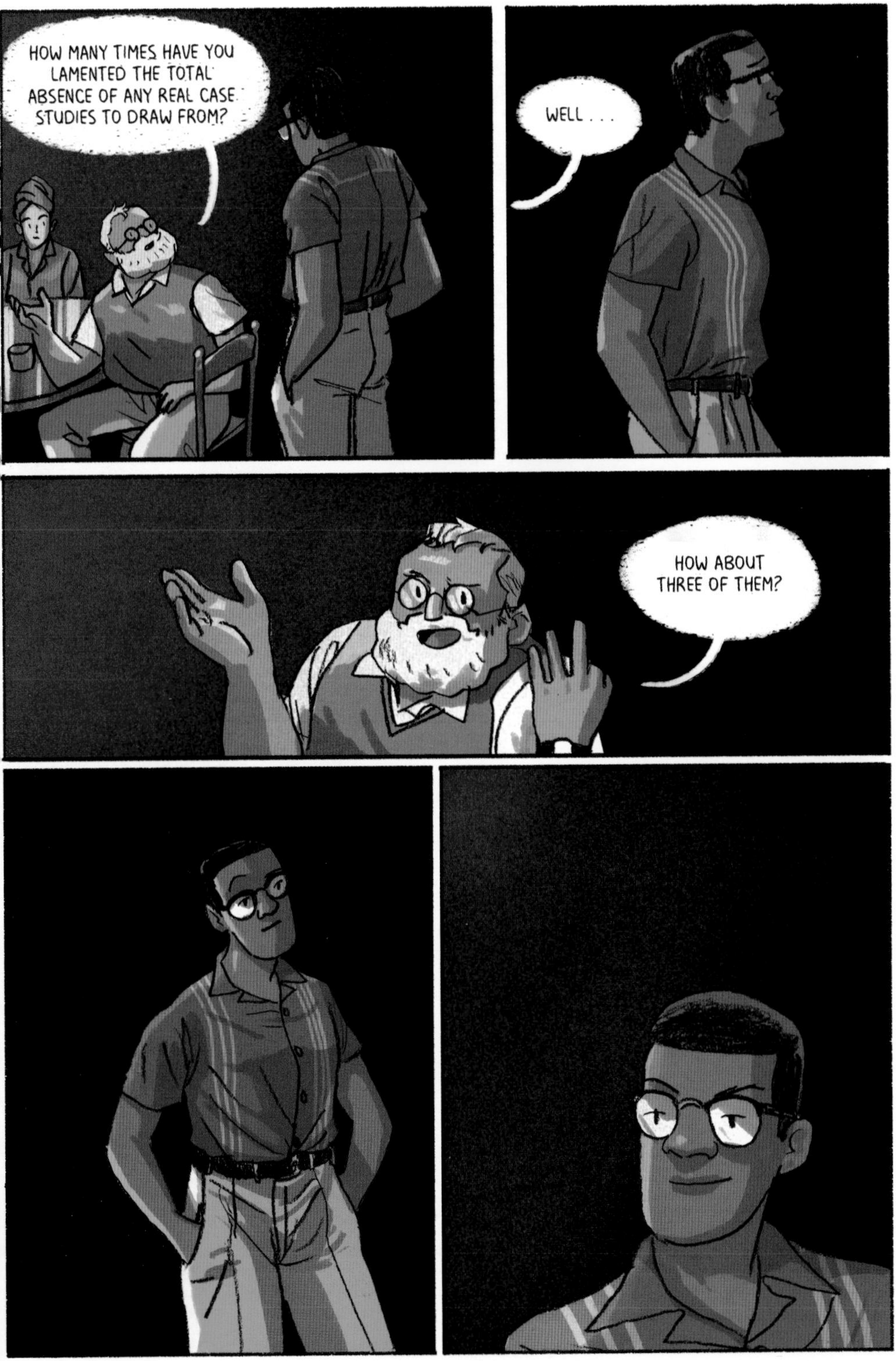
HOW MANY TIMES HAVE YOU LAMENTED THE TOTAL ABSENCE OF ANY REAL CASE STUDIES TO DRAW FROM?
WELL . . .
HOW ABOUT THREE OF THEM?

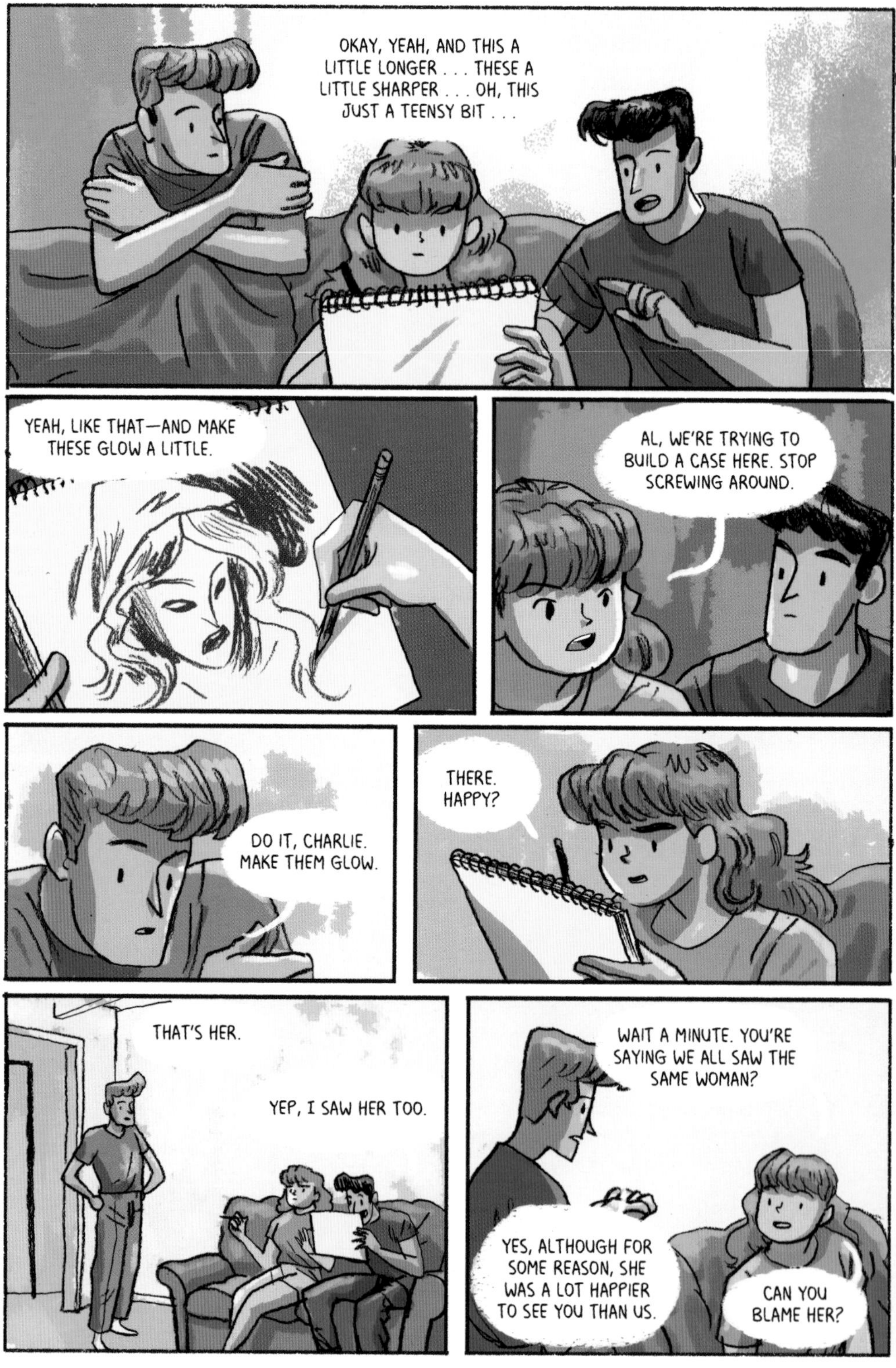
OKAY, YEAH, AND THIS A LITTLE LONGER . . . THESE A LITTLE SHARPER . . . OH, THIS JUST A TEENSY BIT . . .
YEAH, LIKE THAT—AND MAKE THESE GLOW A LITTLE.
AL, WE'RE TRYING TO BUILD A CASE HERE. STOP SCREWING AROUND.
DO IT, CHARLIE. MAKE THEM GLOW.
THERE. HAPPY?
THAT'S HER.
YEP, I SAW HER TOO.
WAIT A MINUTE. YOU'RE SAYING WE ALL SAW THE SAME WOMAN?
YES, ALTHOUGH FOR SOME REASON, SHE WAS A LOT HAPPIER TO SEE YOU THAN US.
CAN YOU BLAME HER?

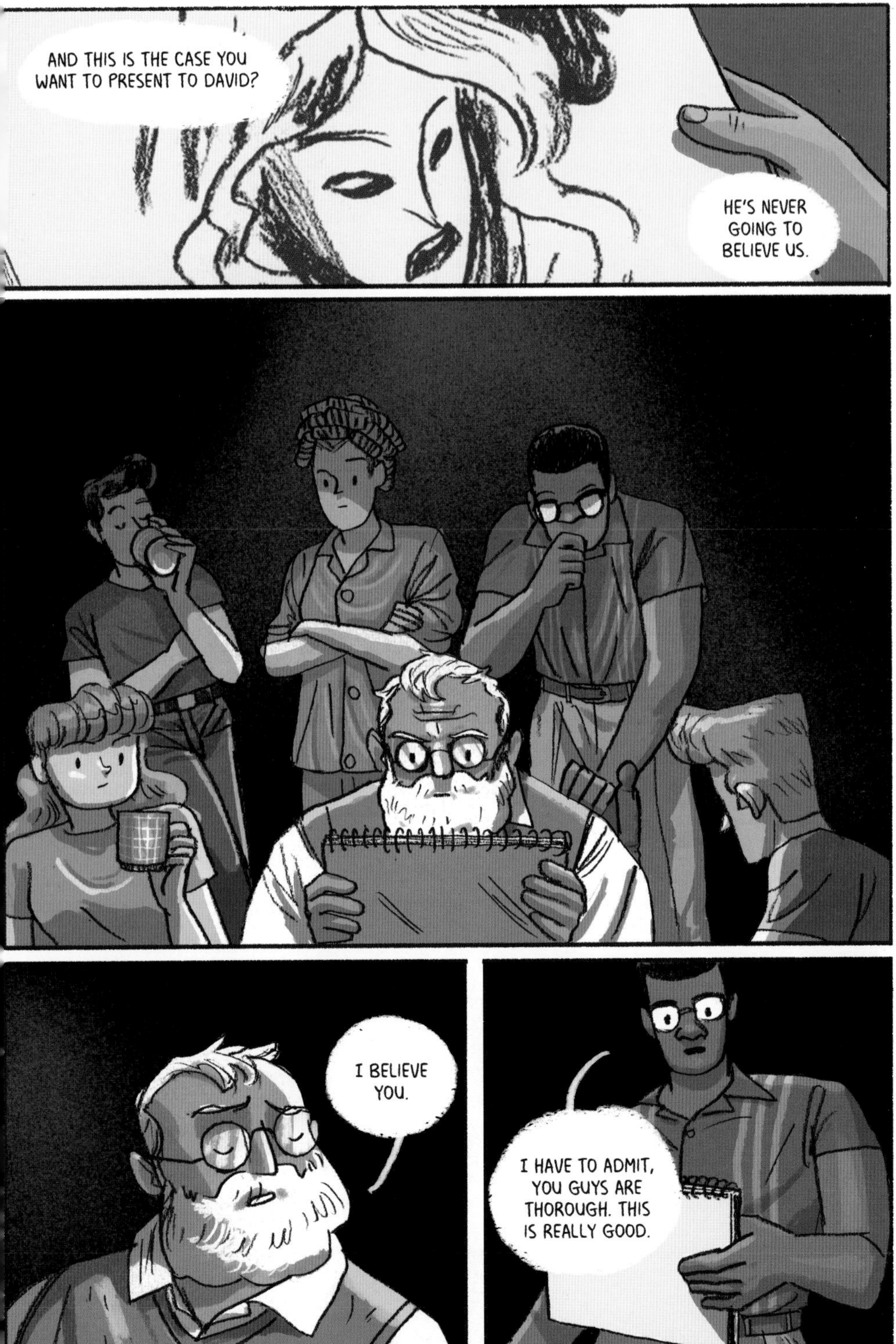
AND THIS IS THE CASE YOU WANT TO PRESENT TO DAVID?
HE'S NEVER GOING TO BELIEVE US.
I BELIEVE YOU.
I HAVE TO ADMIT, YOU GUYS ARE THOROUGH. THIS IS REALLY GOOD.

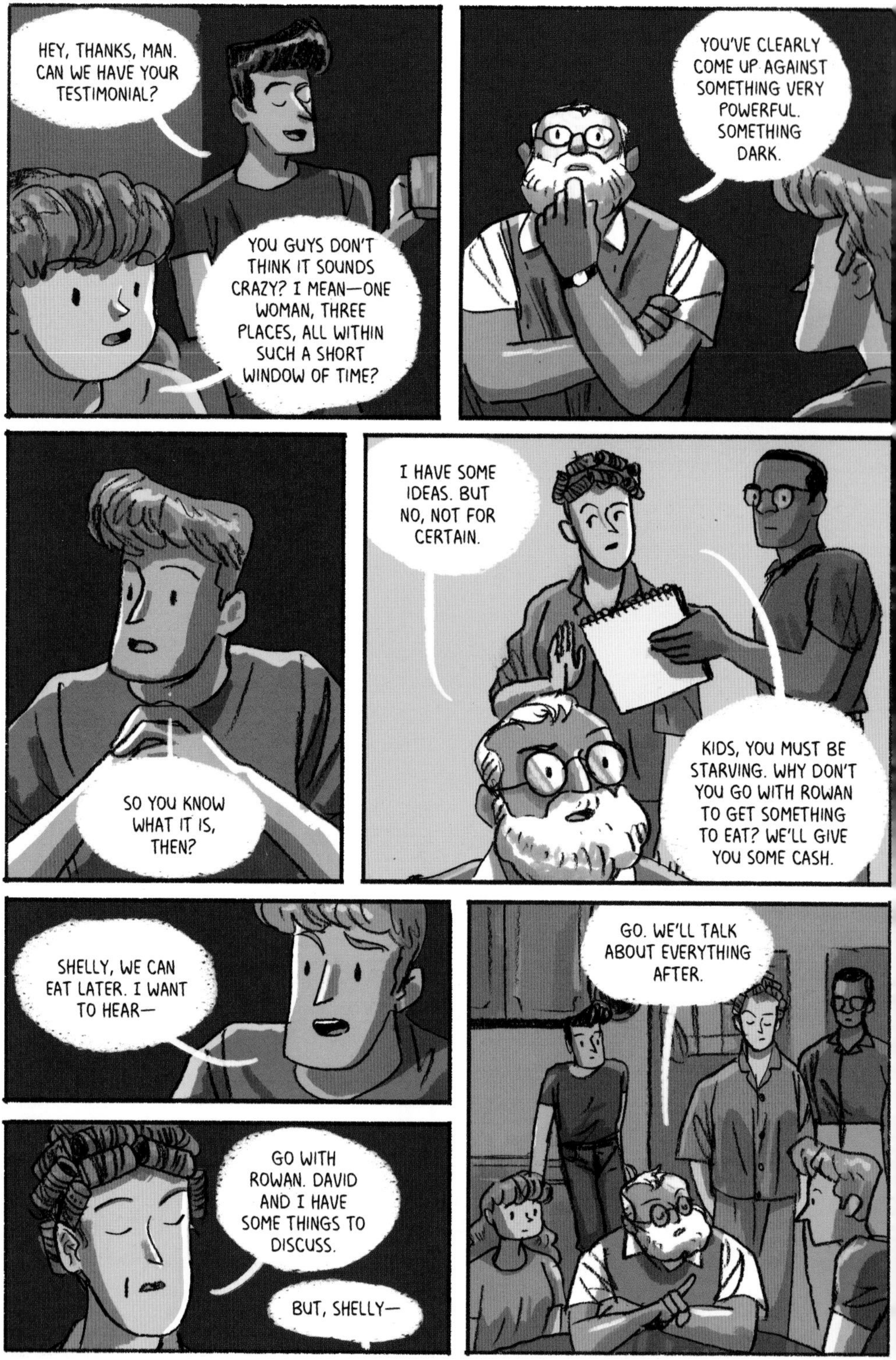
HEY, THANKS, MAN. CAN WE HAVE YOUR TESTIMONIAL?
YOU GUYS DON'T THINK IT SOUNDS CRAZY? I MEAN—ONE WOMAN, THREE PLACES, ALL WITHIN SUCH A SHORT WINDOW OF TIME?
YOU'VE CLEARLY COME UP AGAINST SOMETHING VERY POWERFUL. SOMETHING DARK.
SO YOU KNOW WHAT IT IS, THEN?
I HAVE SOME IDEAS. BUT NO, NOT FOR CERTAIN.
KIDS, YOU MUST BE STARVING. WHY DON'T YOU GO WITH ROWAN TO GET SOMETHING TO EAT? WE'LL GIVE YOU SOME CASH.
SHELLY, WE CAN EAT LATER. I WANT TO HEAR—
GO WITH ROWAN. DAVID AND I HAVE SOME THINGS TO DISCUSS.
BUT, SHELLY—
GO. WE'LL TALK ABOUT EVERYTHING AFTER.

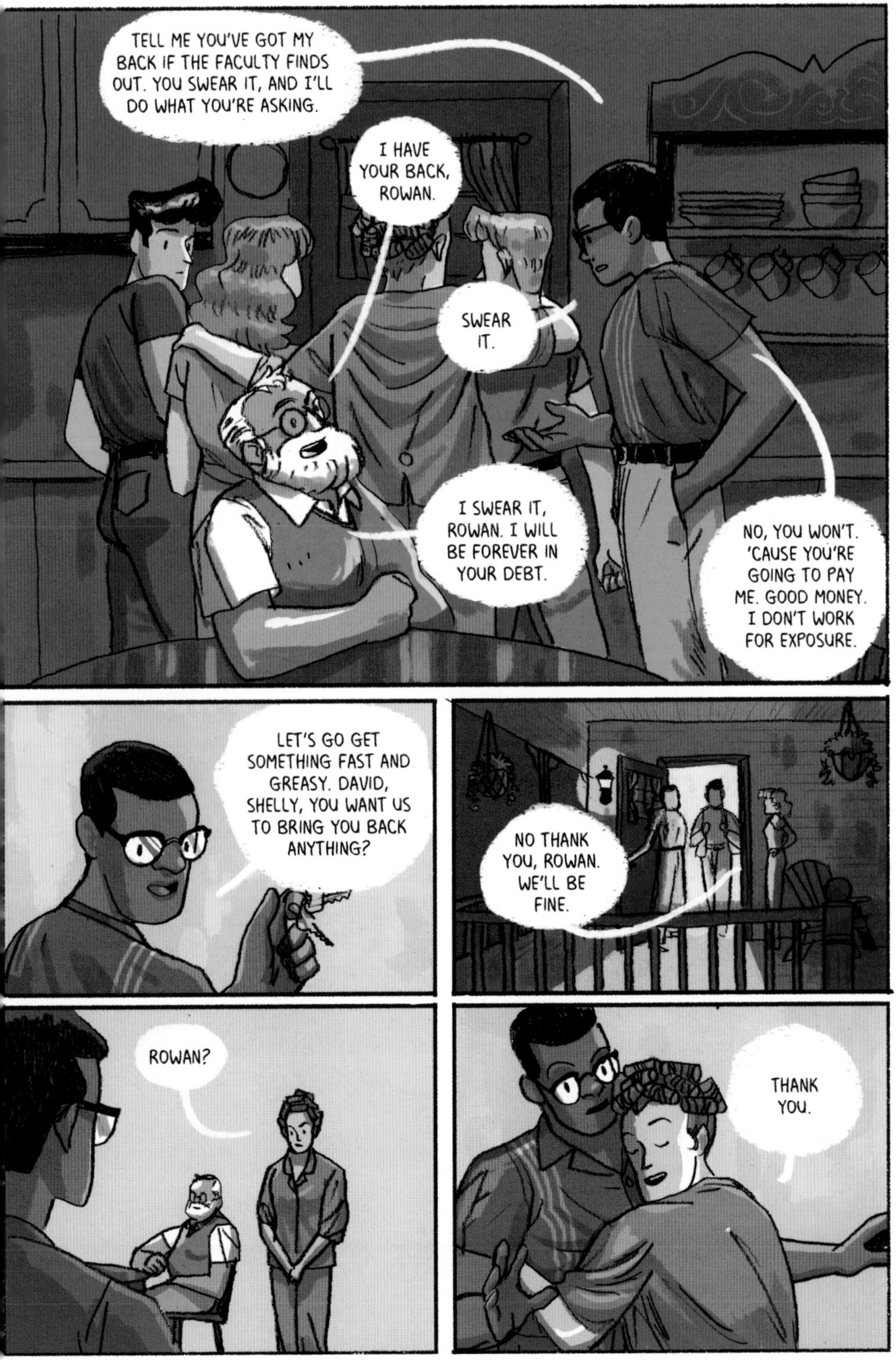
TELL ME YOU'VE GOT MY BACK IF THE FACULTY FINDS OUT. YOU SWEAR IT, AND I'LL DO WHAT YOU'RE ASKING.
I HAVE YOUR BACK, ROWAN.
SWEAR IT.
I SWEAR IT, ROWAN. I WILL BE FOREVER IN YOUR DEBT.
NO, YOU WON'T. 'CAUSE YOU'RE GOING TO PAY ME. GOOD MONEY. I DON'T WORK FOR EXPOSURE.
LET'S GO GET SOMETHING FAST AND GREASY. DAVID, SHELLY, YOU WANT US TO BRING YOU BACK ANYTHING?
NO THANK YOU, ROWAN. WE'LL BE FINE.
ROWAN?
THANK YOU.

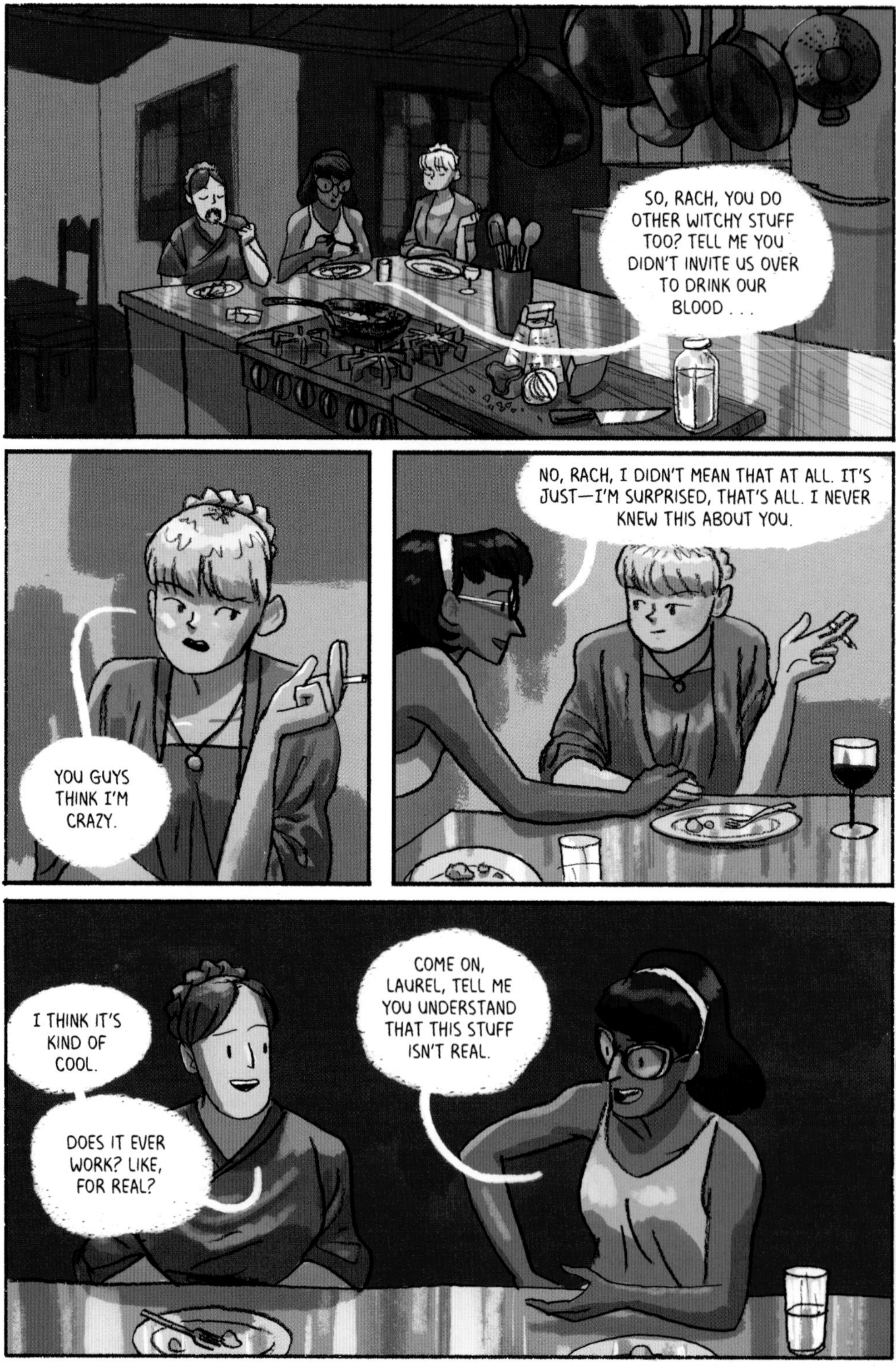
SO, RACH, YOU DO OTHER WITCHY STUFF TOO? TELL ME YOU DIDN'T INVITE US OVER TO DRINK OUR BLOOD . . .
YOU GUYS THINK I'M CRAZY.
NO, RACH, I DIDN'T MEAN THAT AT ALL. IT'S JUST—I'M SURPRISED, THAT'S ALL. I NEVER KNEW THIS ABOUT YOU.
I THINK IT'S KIND OF COOL.
DOES IT EVER WORK? LIKE, FOR REAL?
COME ON, LAUREL, TELL ME YOU UNDERSTAND THAT THIS STUFF ISN'T REAL.

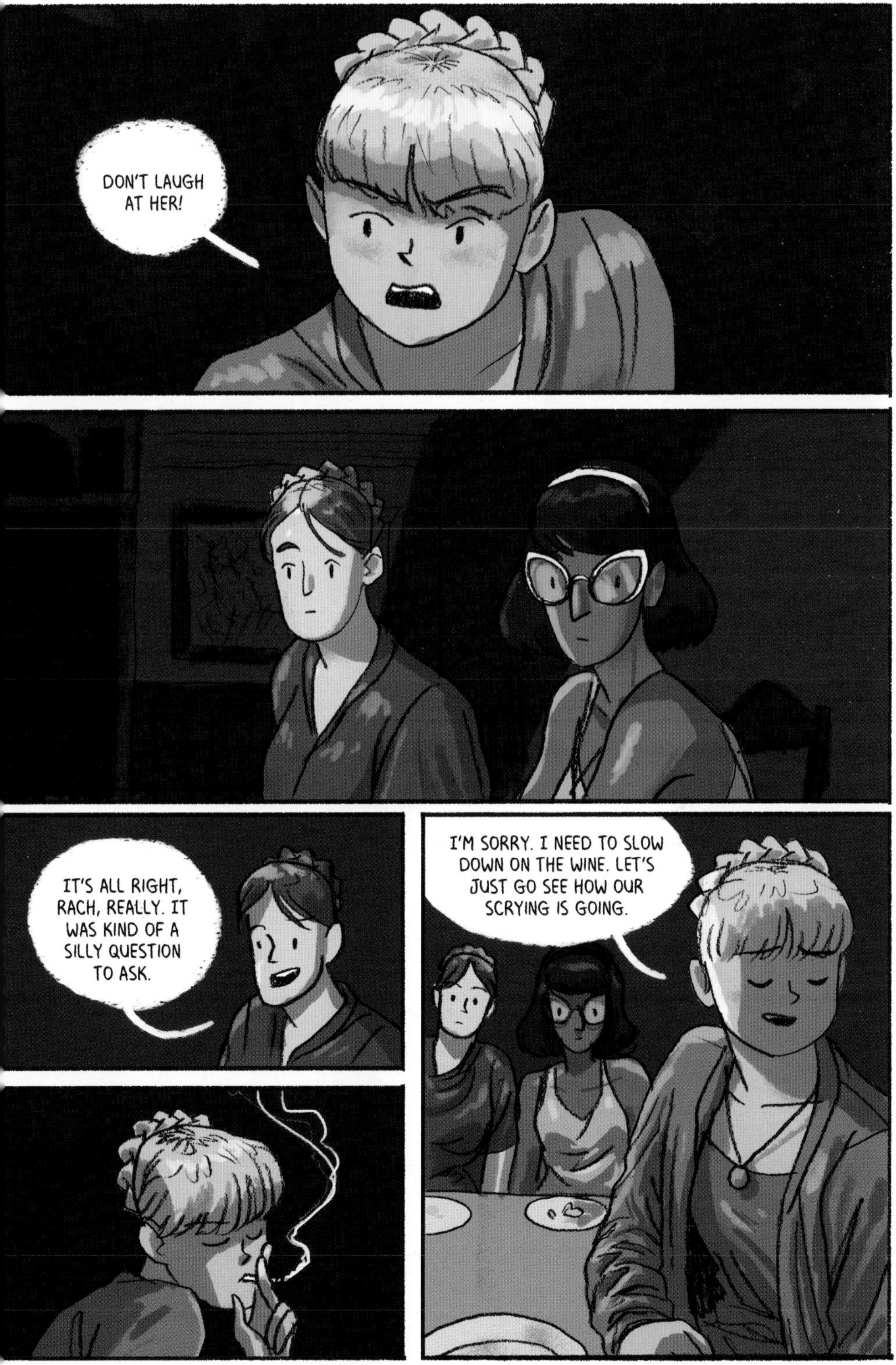
DON'T LAUGH AT HER!
IT'S ALL RIGHT, RACH, REALLY. IT WAS KIND OF A SILLY QUESTION TO ASK.
I'M SORRY. I NEED TO SLOW DOWN ON THE WINE. LET'S JUST GO SEE HOW OUR SCRYING IS GOING.

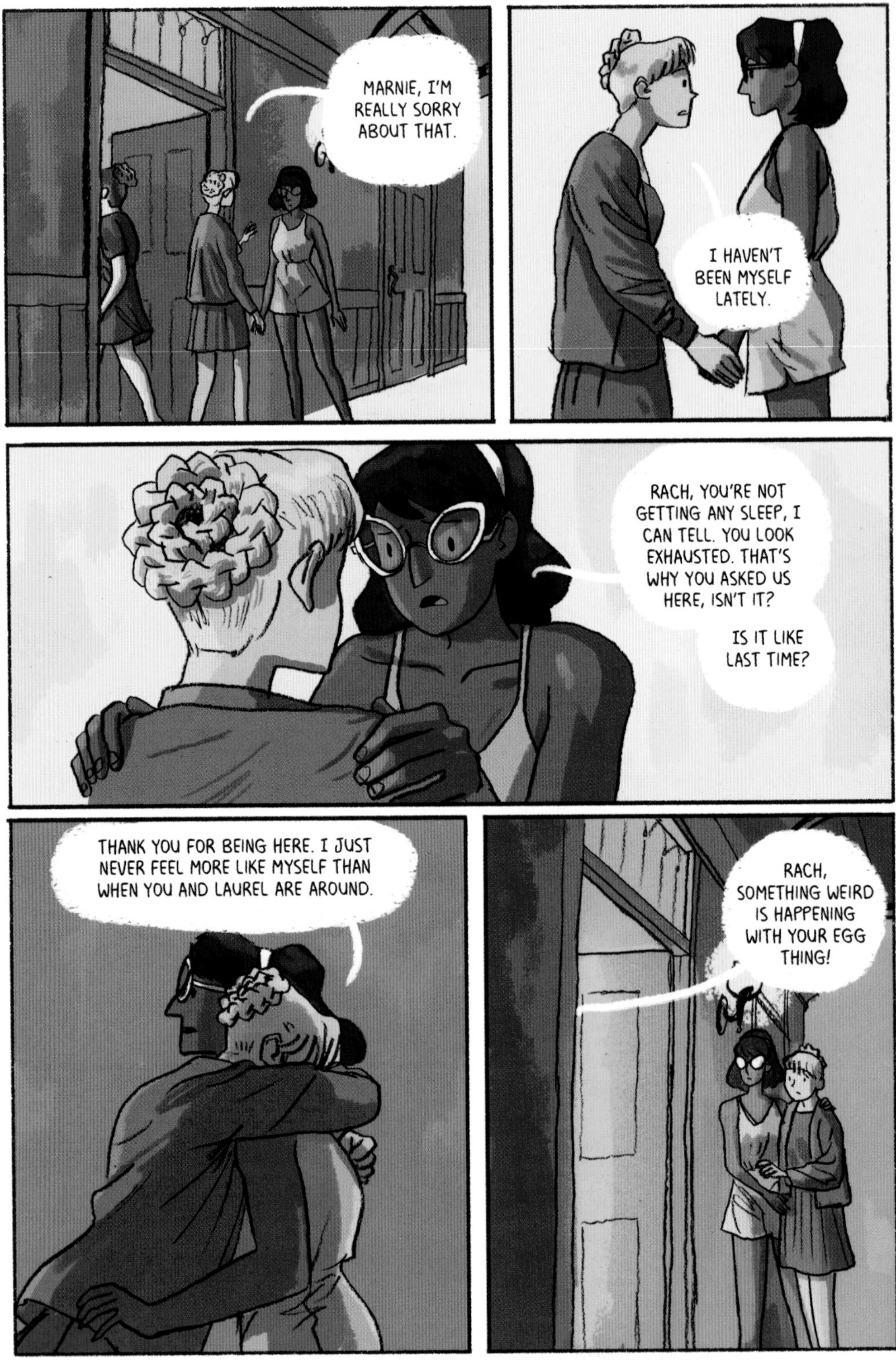
MARNIE, I'M REALLY SORRY ABOUT THAT.
I HAVEN'T BEEN MYSELF LATELY.
RACH, YOU'RE NOT GETTING ANY SLEEP, I CAN TELL. YOU LOOK EXHAUSTED. THAT'S WHY YOU ASKED US HERE, ISN'T IT?
IS IT LIKE LAST TIME?
THANK YOU FOR BEING HERE. I JUST NEVER FEEL MORE LIKE MYSELF THAN WHEN YOU AND LAUREL ARE AROUND.
RACH, SOMETHING WEIRD IS HAPPENING WITH YOUR EGG THING!

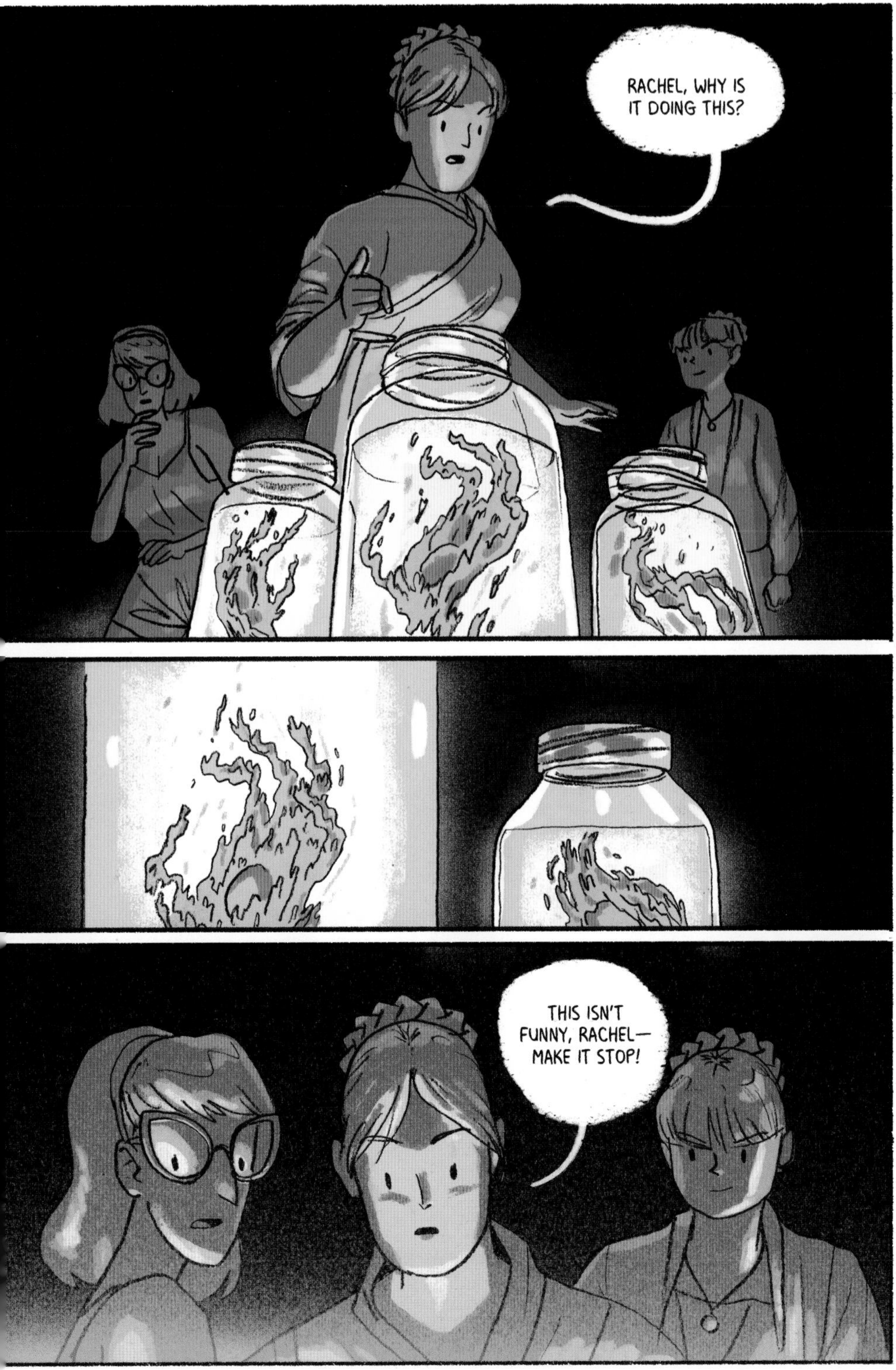
RACHEL, WHY IS IT DOING THIS?
THIS ISN'T FUNNY, RACHEL—MAKE IT STOP!

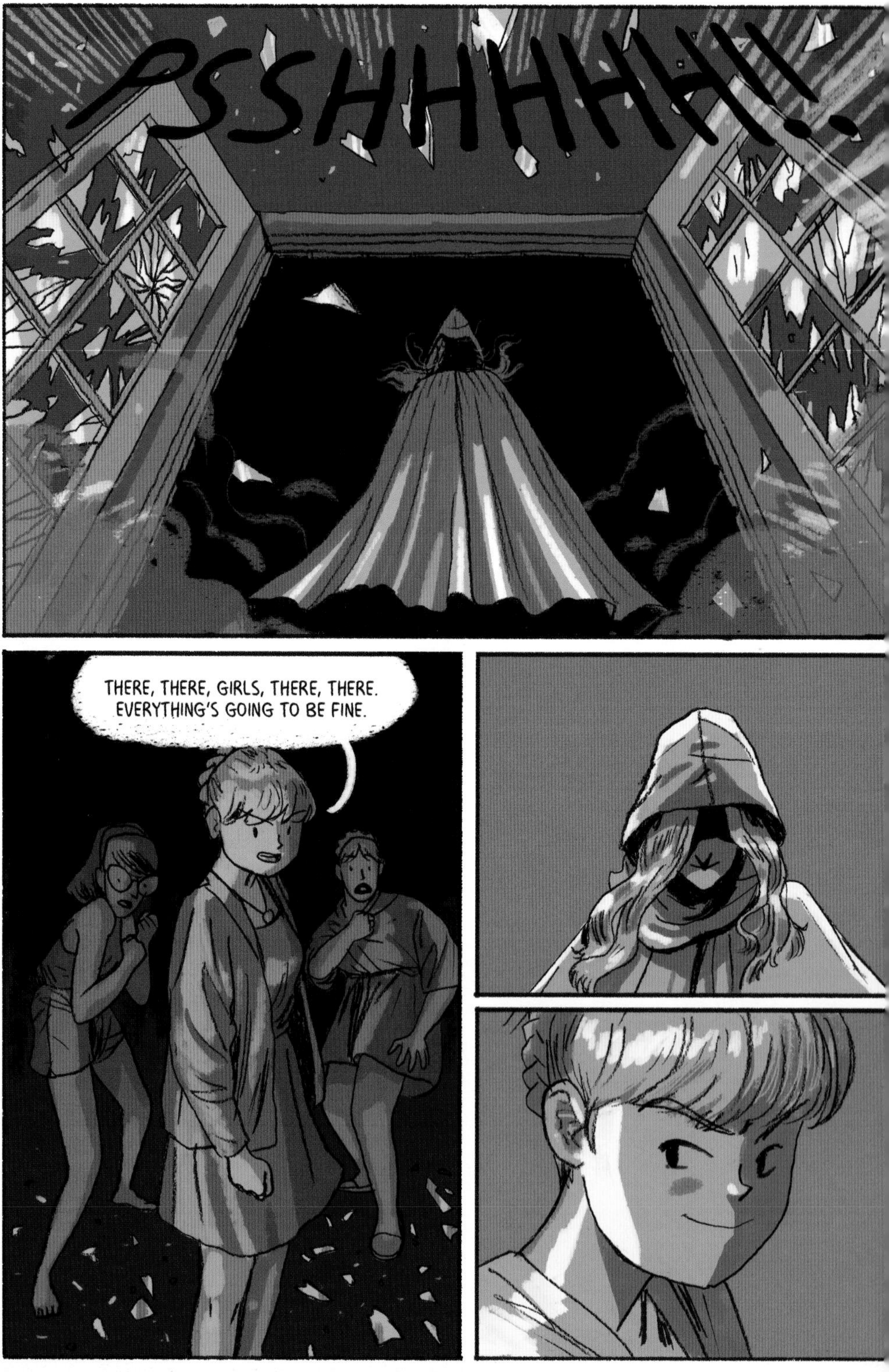
PSSHHHHH!!
THERE, THERE, GIRLS, THERE, THERE. EVERYTHING'S GOING TO BE FINE.

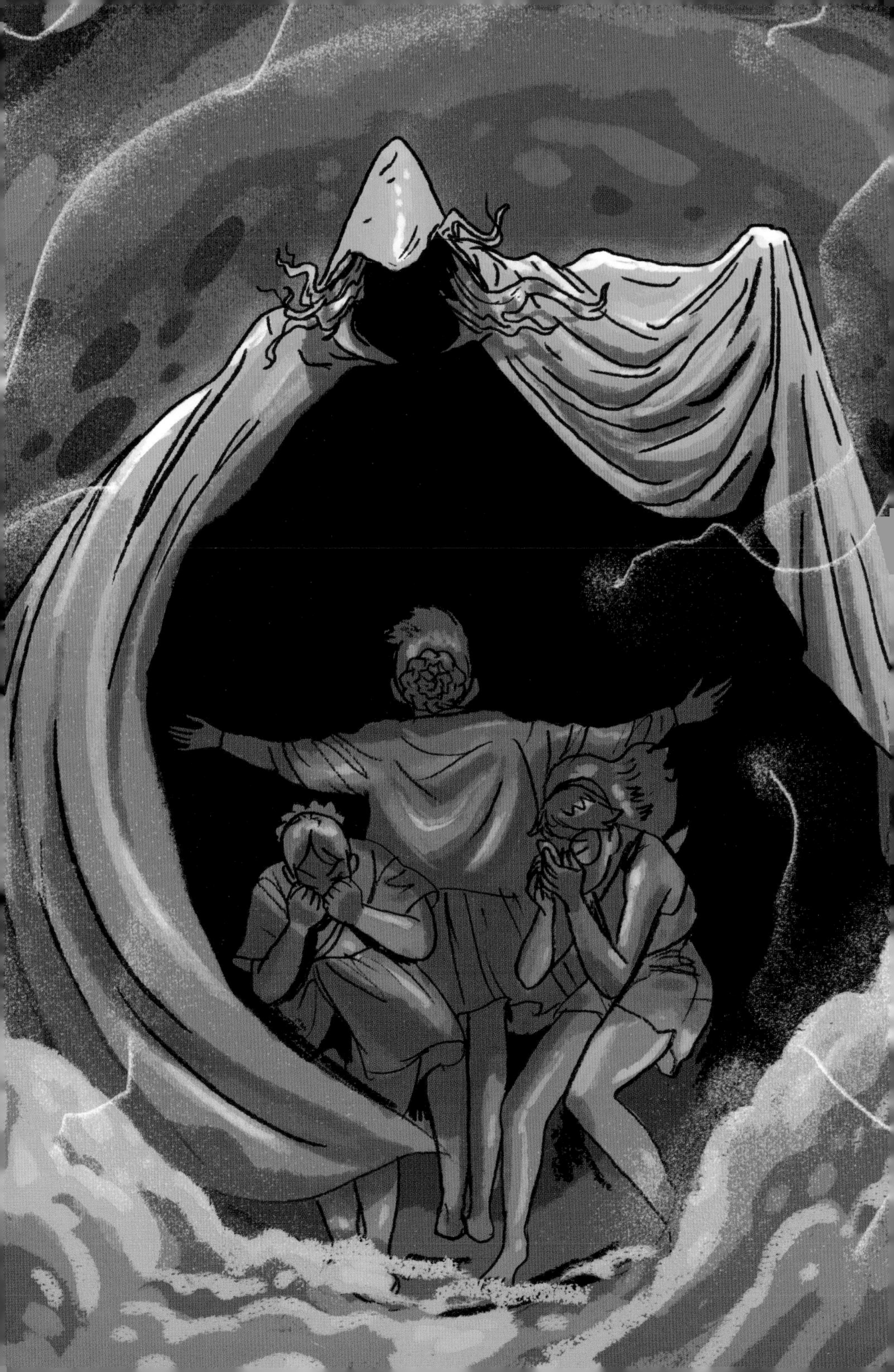

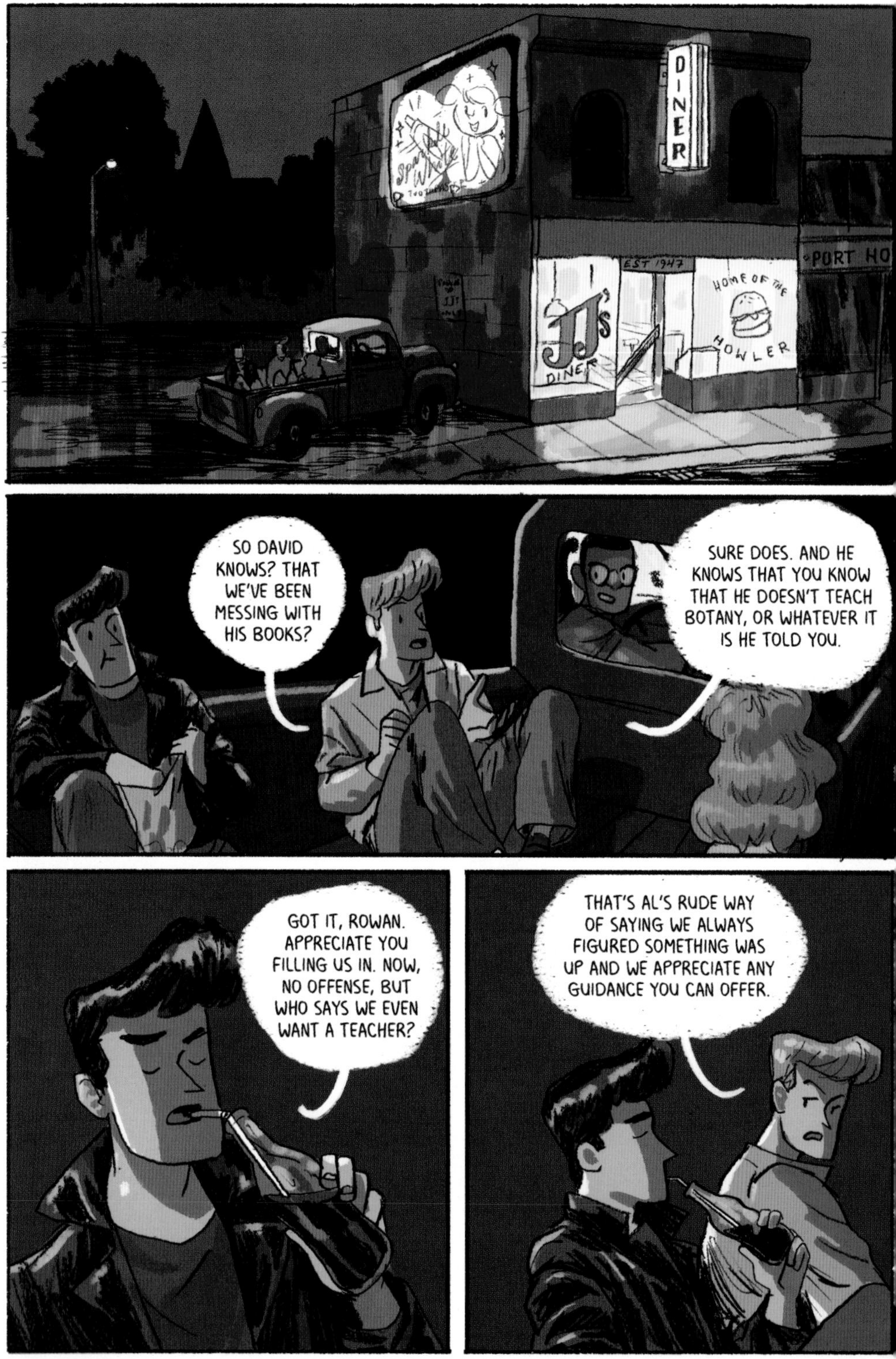
DINER
EST 1947
JJ's DINER
HOME OF THE HOWLER
PORT HO
SO DAVID KNOWS? THAT WE'VE BEEN MESSING WITH HIS BOOKS?
SURE DOES. AND HE KNOWS THAT YOU KNOW THAT HE DOESN'T TEACH BOTANY, OR WHATEVER IT IS HE TOLD YOU.
GOT IT, ROWAN. APPRECIATE YOU FILLING US IN. NOW, NO OFFENSE, BUT WHO SAYS WE EVEN WANT A TEACHER?
THAT'S AL'S RUDE WAY OF SAYING WE ALWAYS FIGURED SOMETHING WAS UP AND WE APPRECIATE ANY GUIDANCE YOU CAN OFFER.

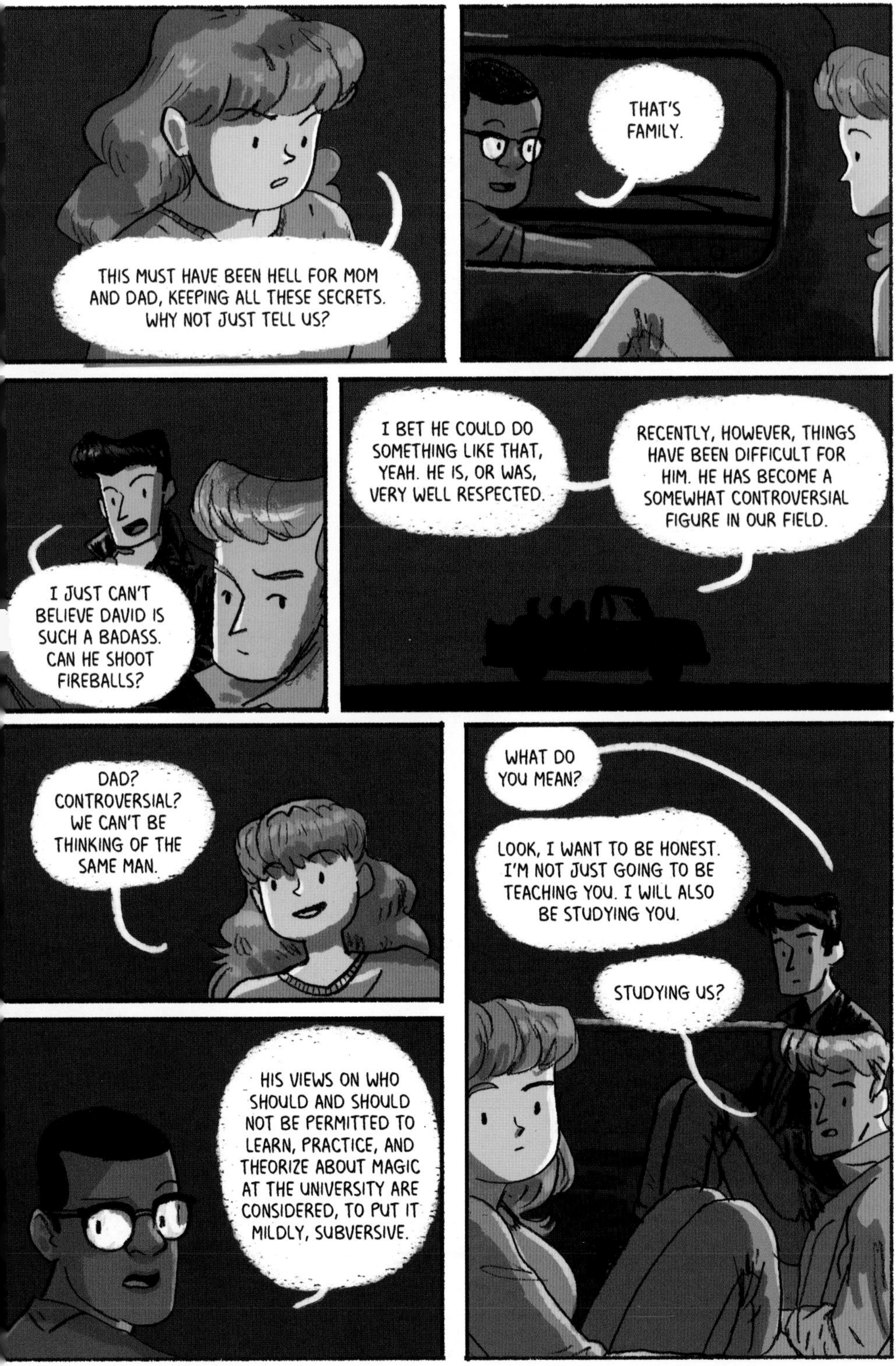
THIS MUST HAVE BEEN HELL FOR MOM AND DAD, KEEPING ALL THESE SECRETS. WHY NOT JUST TELL US?
THAT'S FAMILY.
I JUST CAN'T BELIEVE DAVID IS SUCH A BADASS. CAN HE SHOOT FIREBALLS?
I BET HE COULD DO SOMETHING LIKE THAT, YEAH. HE IS, OR WAS, VERY WELL RESPECTED.
RECENTLY, HOWEVER, THINGS HAVE BEEN DIFFICULT FOR HIM. HE HAS BECOME A SOMEWHAT CONTROVERSIAL FIGURE IN OUR FIELD.
DAD? CONTROVERSIAL? WE CAN'T BE THINKING OF THE SAME MAN.
HIS VIEWS ON WHO SHOULD AND SHOULD NOT BE PERMITTED TO LEARN, PRACTICE, AND THEORIZE ABOUT MAGIC AT THE UNIVERSITY ARE CONSIDERED, TO PUT IT MILDLY, SUBVERSIVE.
WHAT DO YOU MEAN?
LOOK, I WANT TO BE HONEST. I'M NOT JUST GOING TO BE TEACHING YOU. I WILL ALSO BE STUDYING YOU.
STUDYING US?

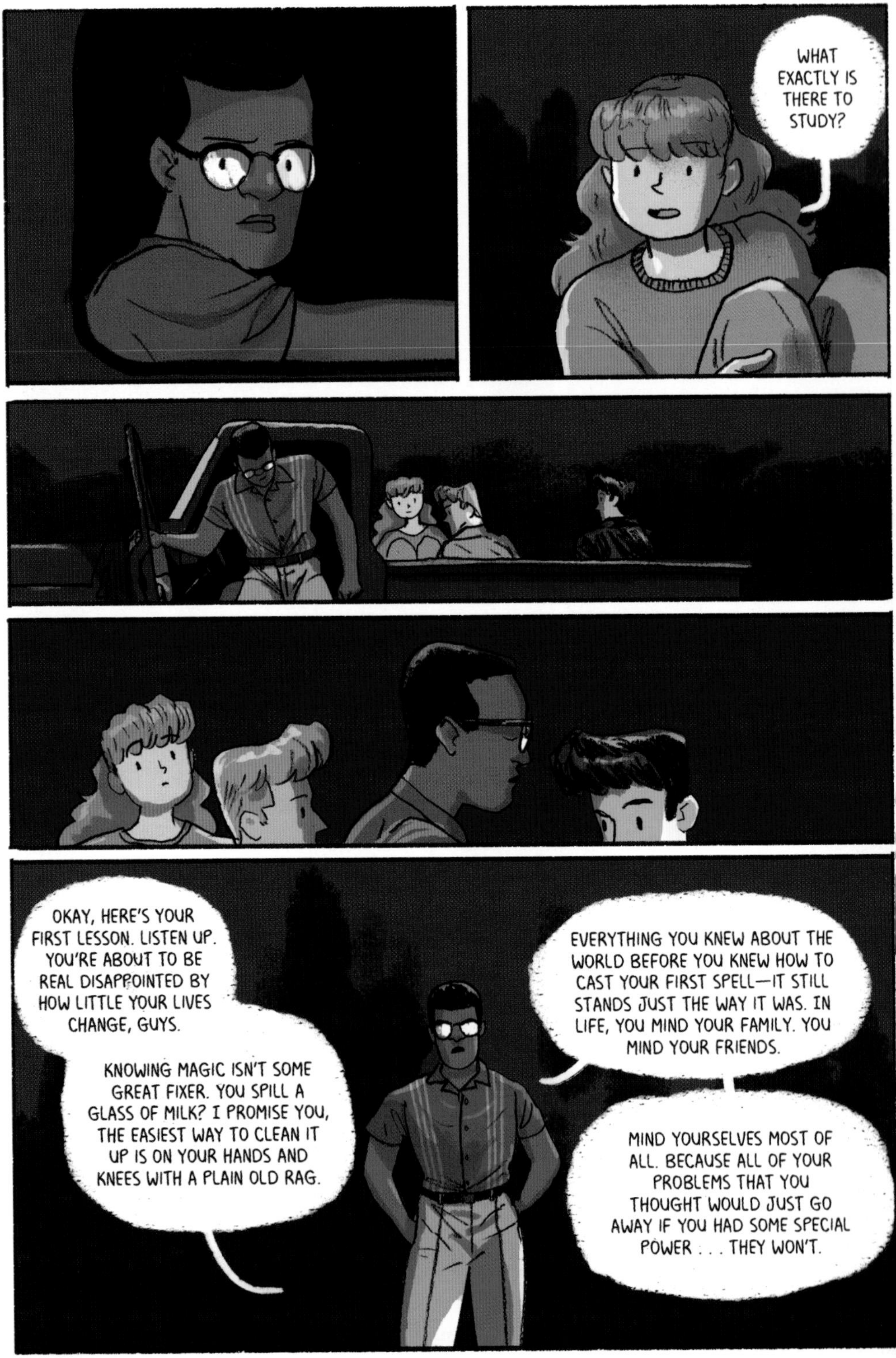
WHAT EXACTLY IS THERE TO STUDY?
OKAY, HERE'S YOUR FIRST LESSON. LISTEN UP. YOU'RE ABOUT TO BE REAL DISAPPOINTED BY HOW LITTLE YOUR LIVES CHANGE, GUYS.
KNOWING MAGIC ISN'T SOME GREAT FIXER. YOU SPILL A GLASS OF MILK? I PROMISE YOU, THE EASIEST WAY TO CLEAN IT UP IS ON YOUR HANDS AND KNEES WITH A PLAIN OLD RAG.
EVERYTHING YOU KNEW ABOUT THE WORLD BEFORE YOU KNEW HOW TO CAST YOUR FIRST SPELL—IT STILL STANDS JUST THE WAY IT WAS. IN LIFE, YOU MIND YOUR FAMILY. YOU MIND YOUR FRIENDS.
MIND YOURSELVES MOST OF ALL. BECAUSE ALL OF YOUR PROBLEMS THAT YOU THOUGHT WOULD JUST GO AWAY IF YOU HAD SOME SPECIAL POWER . . . THEY WON'T.

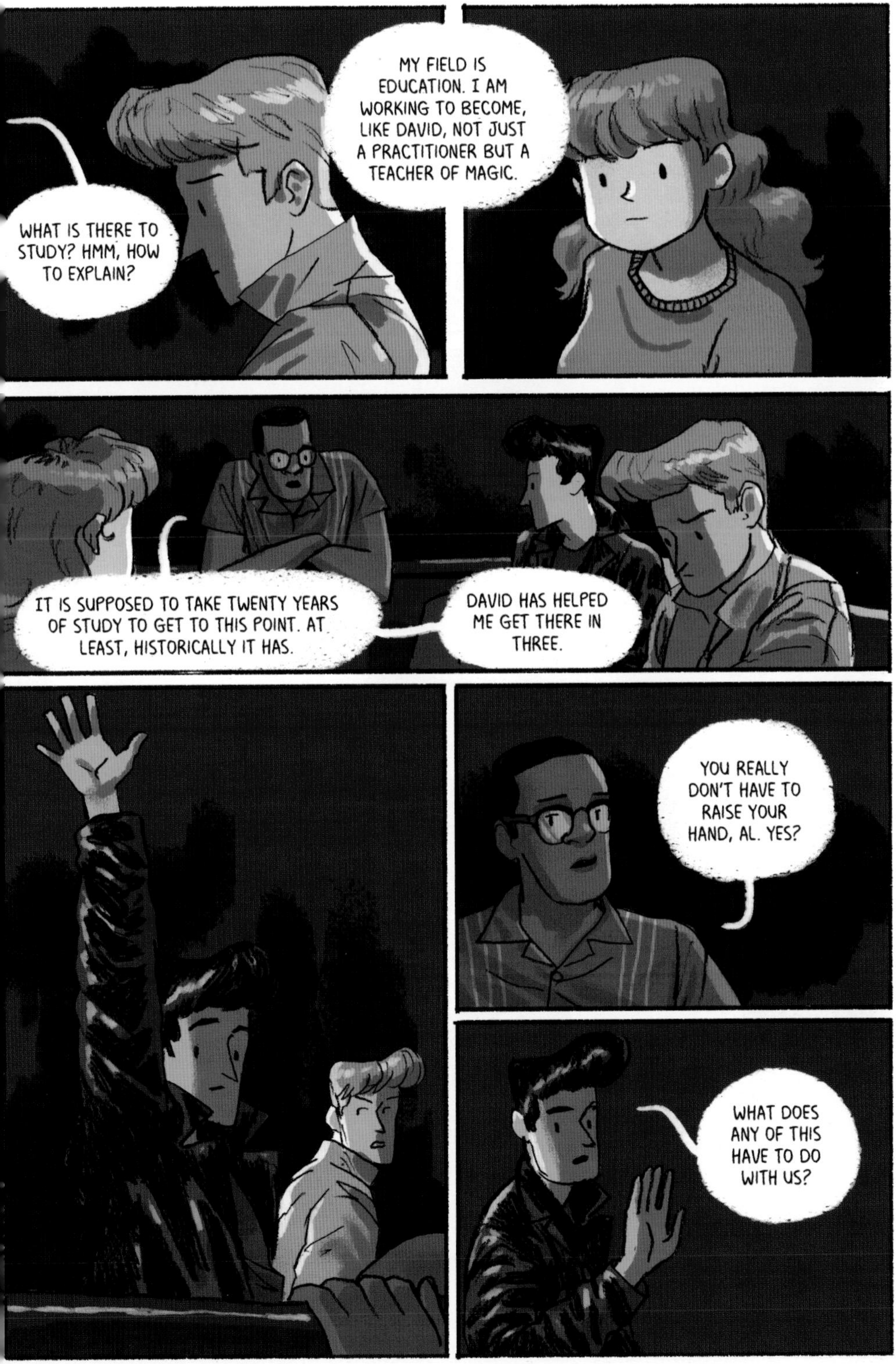
WHAT IS THERE TO STUDY? HMM, HOW TO EXPLAIN?
MY FIELD IS EDUCATION. I AM WORKING TO BECOME, LIKE DAVID, NOT JUST A PRACTITIONER BUT A TEACHER OF MAGIC.
IT IS SUPPOSED TO TAKE TWENTY YEARS OF STUDY TO GET TO THIS POINT. AT LEAST, HISTORICALLY IT HAS.
DAVID HAS HELPED ME GET THERE IN THREE.
YOU REALLY DON'T HAVE TO RAISE YOUR HAND, AL. YES?
WHAT DOES ANY OF THIS HAVE TO DO WITH US?

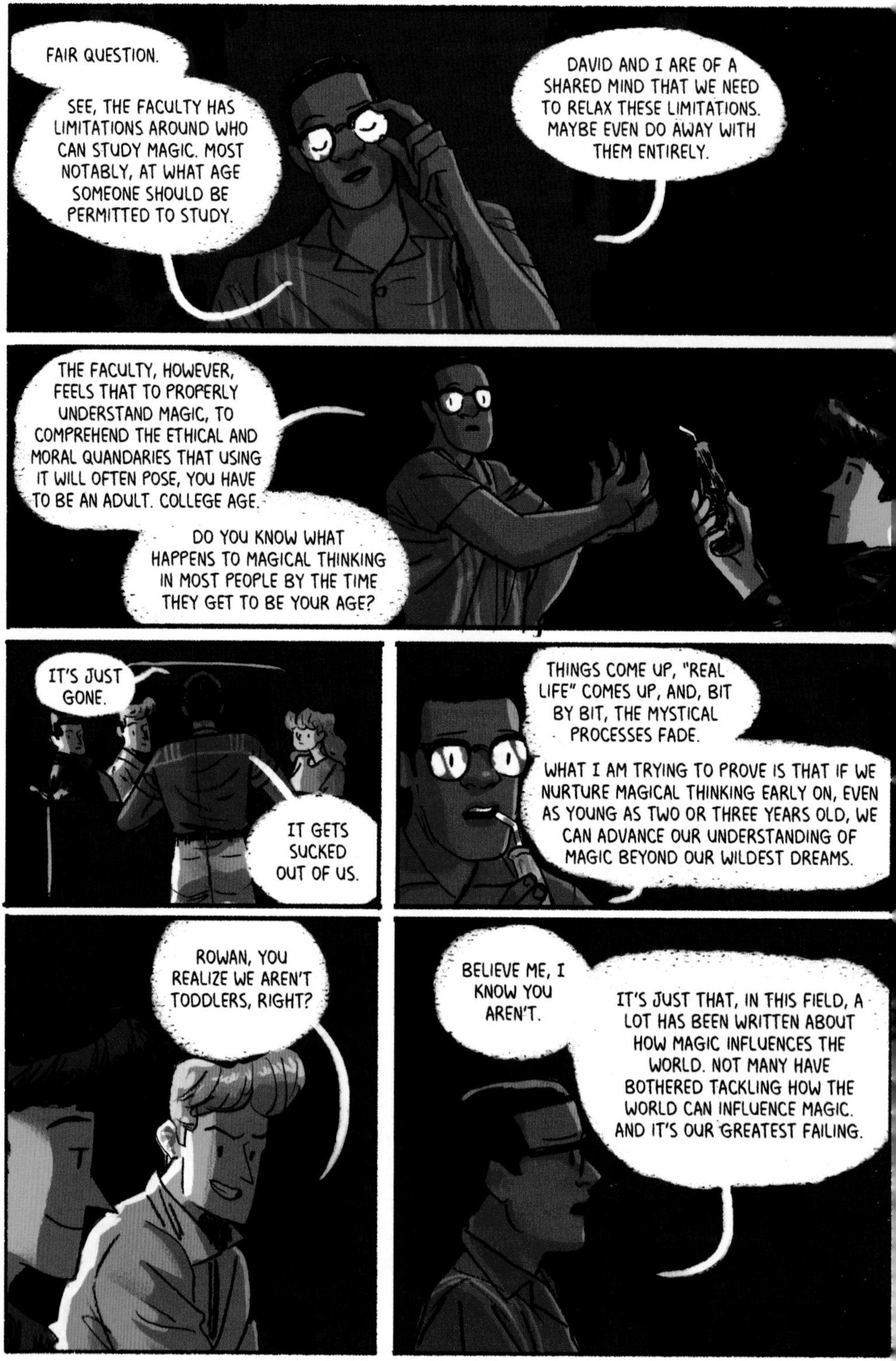
FAIR QUESTION.
SEE, THE FACULTY HAS LIMITATIONS AROUND WHO CAN STUDY MAGIC. MOST NOTABLY, AT WHAT AGE SOMEONE SHOULD BE PERMITTED TO STUDY.
DAVID AND I ARE OF A SHARED MIND THAT WE NEED TO RELAX THESE LIMITATIONS. MAYBE EVEN DO AWAY WITH THEM ENTIRELY.
THE FACULTY, HOWEVER, FEELS THAT TO PROPERLY UNDERSTAND MAGIC, TO COMPREHEND THE ETHICAL AND MORAL QUANDARIES THAT USING IT WILL OFTEN POSE, YOU HAVE TO BE AN ADULT. COLLEGE AGE.
DO YOU KNOW WHAT HAPPENS TO MAGICAL THINKING IN MOST PEOPLE BY THE TIME THEY GET TO BE YOUR AGE?
IT'S JUST GONE.
IT GETS SUCKED OUT OF US.
THINGS COME UP, "REAL LIFE" COMES UP, AND, BIT BY BIT, THE MYSTICAL PROCESSES FADE.
WHAT I AM TRYING TO PROVE IS THAT IF WE NURTURE MAGICAL THINKING EARLY ON, EVEN AS YOUNG AS TWO OR THREE YEARS OLD, WE CAN ADVANCE OUR UNDERSTANDING OF MAGIC BEYOND OUR WILDEST DREAMS.
ROWAN, YOU REALIZE WE AREN'T TODDLERS, RIGHT?
BELIEVE ME, I KNOW YOU AREN'T.
IT'S JUST THAT, IN THIS FIELD, A LOT HAS BEEN WRITTEN ABOUT HOW MAGIC INFLUENCES THE WORLD. NOT MANY HAVE BOTHERED TACKLING HOW THE WORLD CAN INFLUENCE MAGIC. AND IT'S OUR GREATEST FAILING.

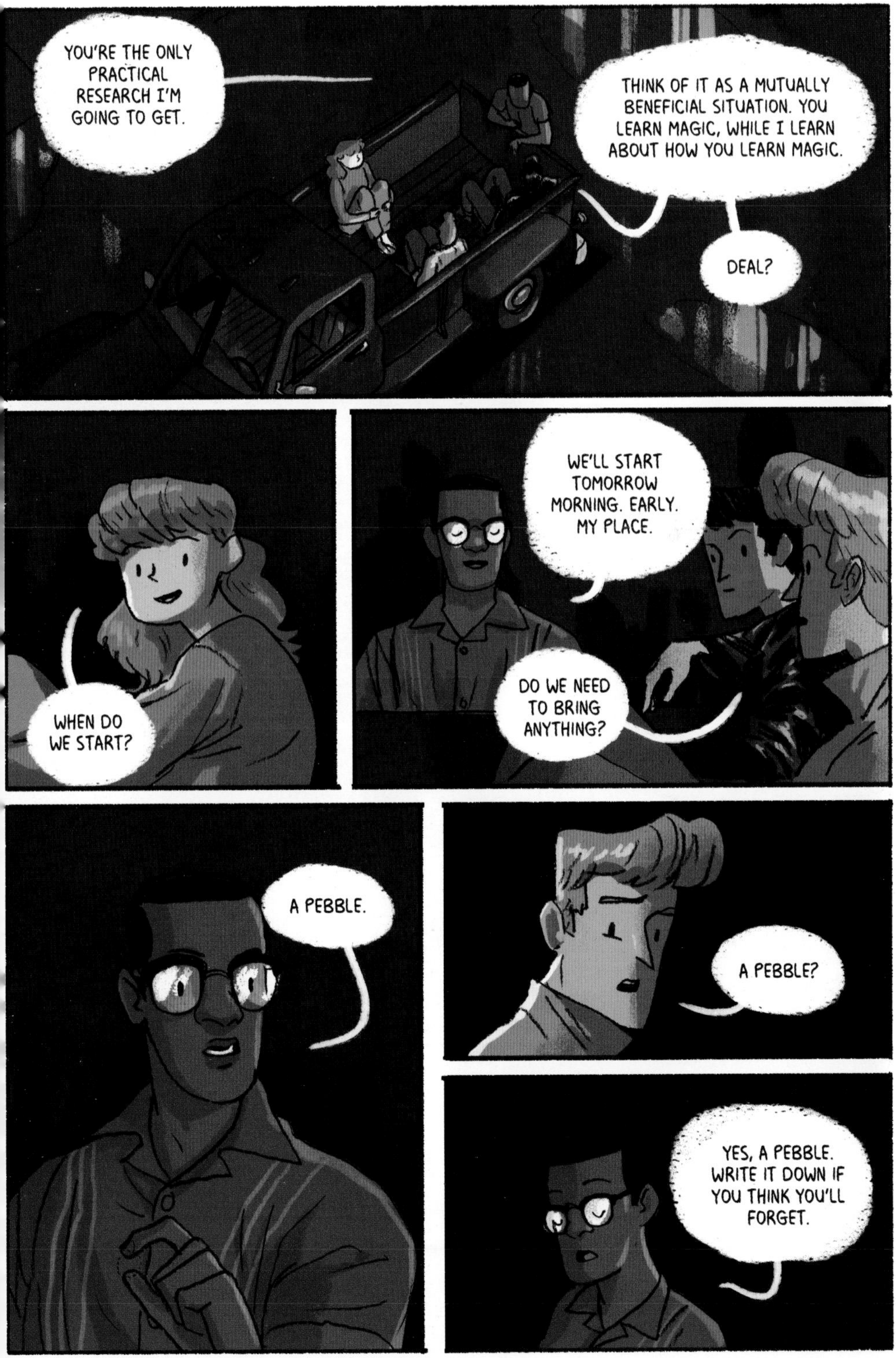
YOU'RE THE ONLY PRACTICAL RESEARCH I'M GOING TO GET.
THINK OF IT AS A MUTUALLY BENEFICIAL SITUATION. YOU LEARN MAGIC, WHILE I LEARN ABOUT HOW YOU LEARN MAGIC.
DEAL?
WHEN DO WE START?
WE'LL START TOMORROW MORNING. EARLY. MY PLACE.
DO WE NEED TO BRING ANYTHING?
A PEBBLE.
A PEBBLE?
YES, A PEBBLE. WRITE IT DOWN IF YOU THINK YOU'LL FORGET.

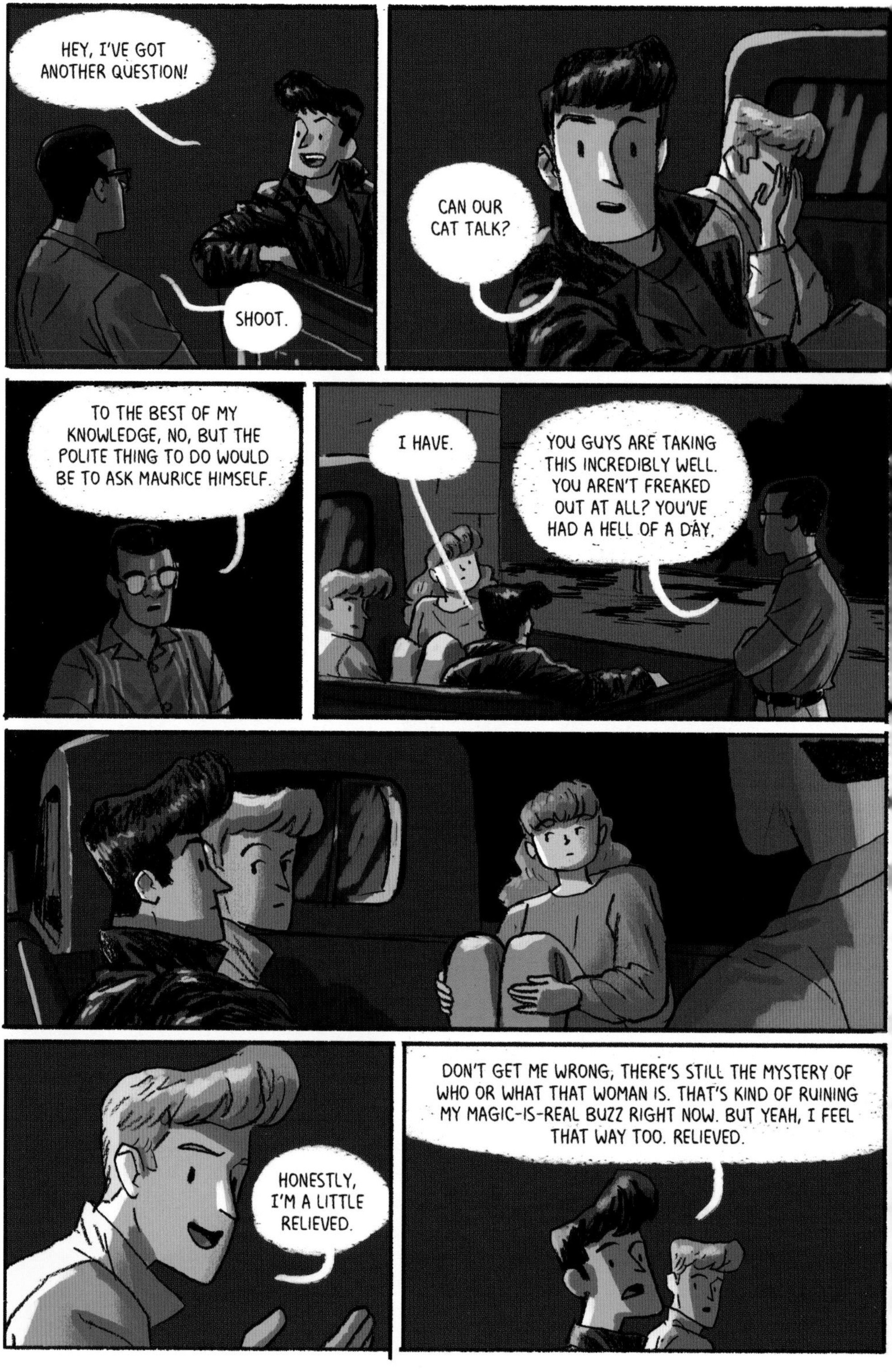
HEY, I'VE GOT ANOTHER QUESTION!
SHOOT.
CAN OUR CAT TALK?
TO THE BEST OF MY KNOWLEDGE, NO, BUT THE POLITE THING TO DO WOULD BE TO ASK MAURICE HIMSELF.
I HAVE.
YOU GUYS ARE TAKING THIS INCREDIBLY WELL. YOU AREN'T FREAKED OUT AT ALL? YOU'VE HAD A HELL OF A DAY.
HONESTLY, I'M A LITTLE RELIEVED.
DON'T GET ME WRONG, THERE'S STILL THE MYSTERY OF WHO OR WHAT THAT WOMAN IS. THAT'S KIND OF RUINING MY MAGIC-IS-REAL BUZZ RIGHT NOW. BUT YEAH, I FEEL THAT WAY TOO. RELIEVED.

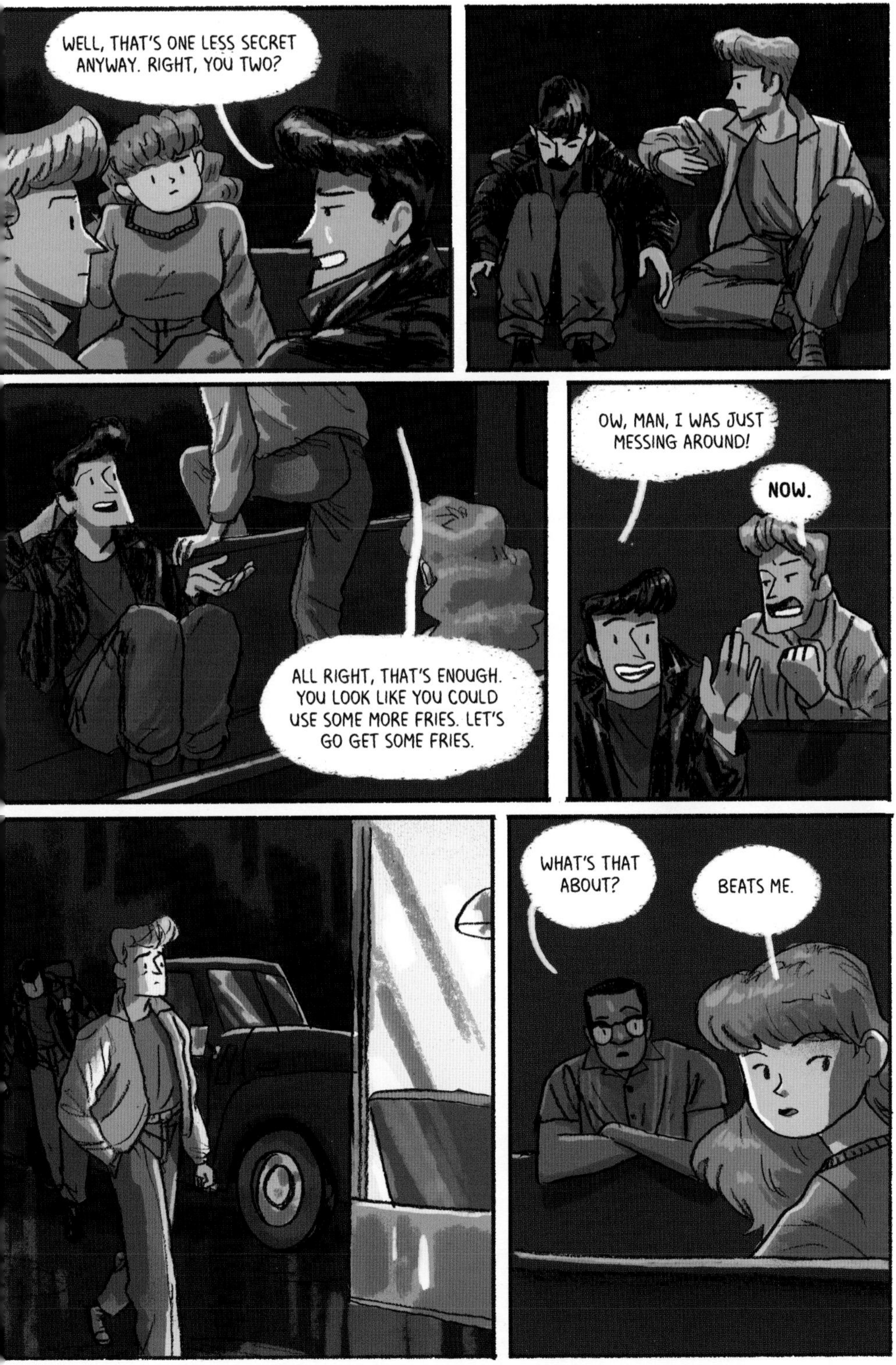
WELL, THAT'S ONE LESS SECRET ANYWAY. RIGHT, YOU TWO?
ALL RIGHT, THAT'S ENOUGH. YOU LOOK LIKE YOU COULD USE SOME MORE FRIES. LET'S GO GET SOME FRIES.
OW, MAN, I WAS JUST MESSING AROUND!
NOW.
WHAT'S THAT ABOUT?
BEATS ME.

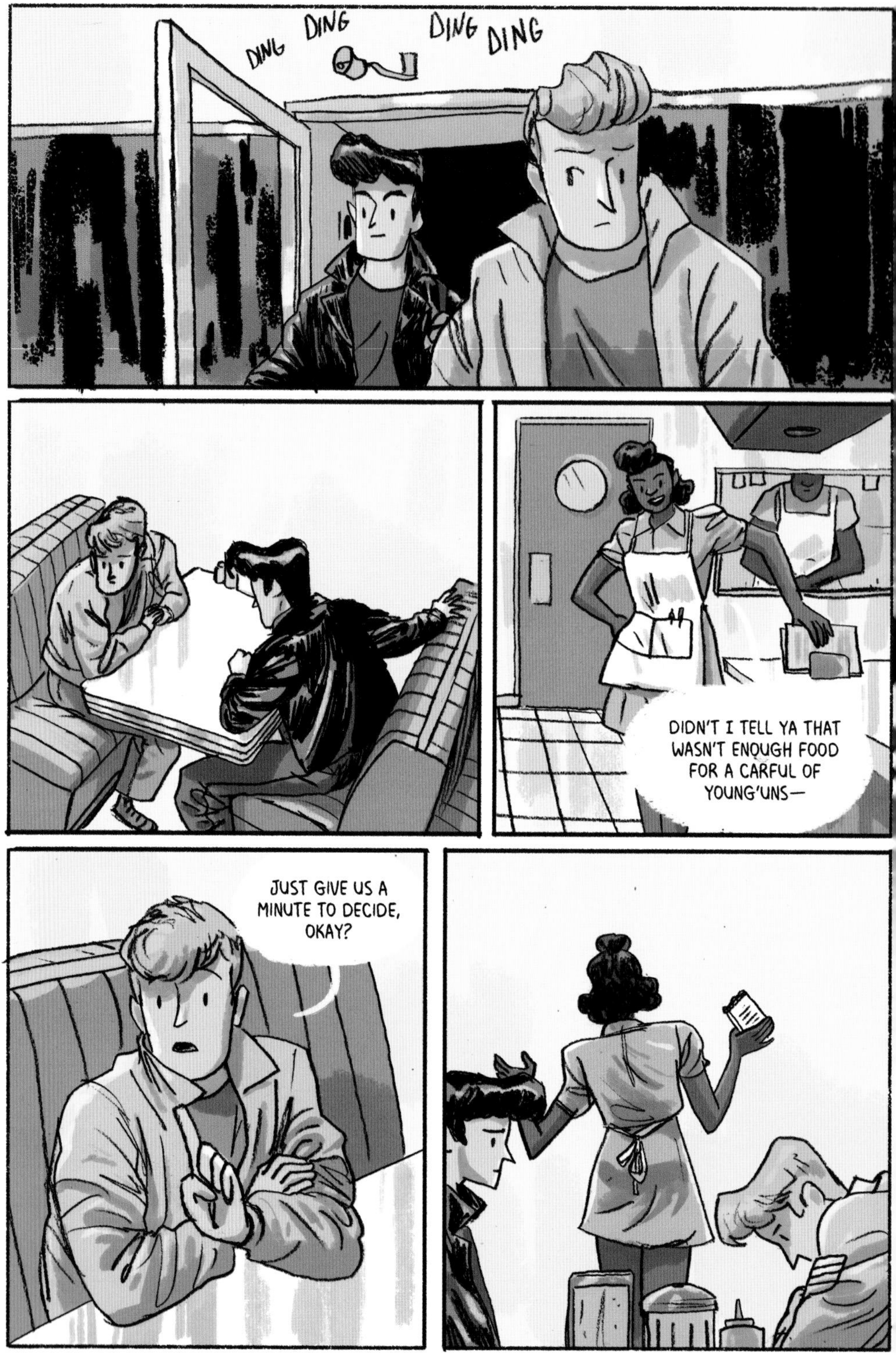
DING DING
DING DING
DIDN'T I TELL YA THAT WASN'T ENOUGH FOOD FOR A CARFUL OF YOUNG'UNS—
JUST GIVE US A MINUTE TO DECIDE, OKAY?

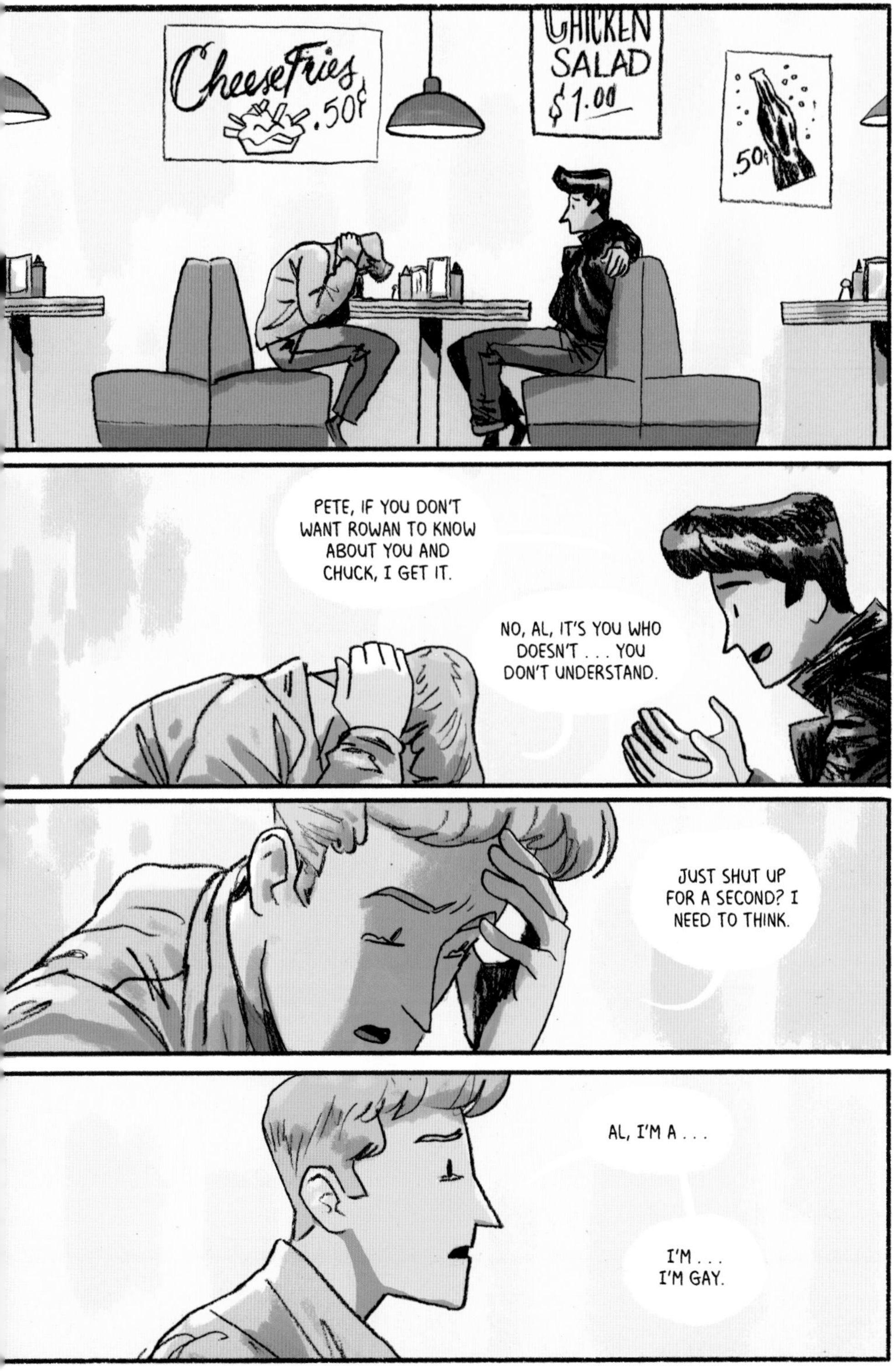
CheeseFries .50¢
CHICKEN SALAD $1.00
.50¢
PETE, IF YOU DON'T WANT ROWAN TO KNOW ABOUT YOU AND CHUCK, I GET IT.
NO, AL, IT'S YOU WHO DOESN'T . . . YOU DON'T UNDERSTAND.
JUST SHUT UP FOR A SECOND? I NEED TO THINK.
AL, I'M A . . .
I'M . . . I'M GAY.

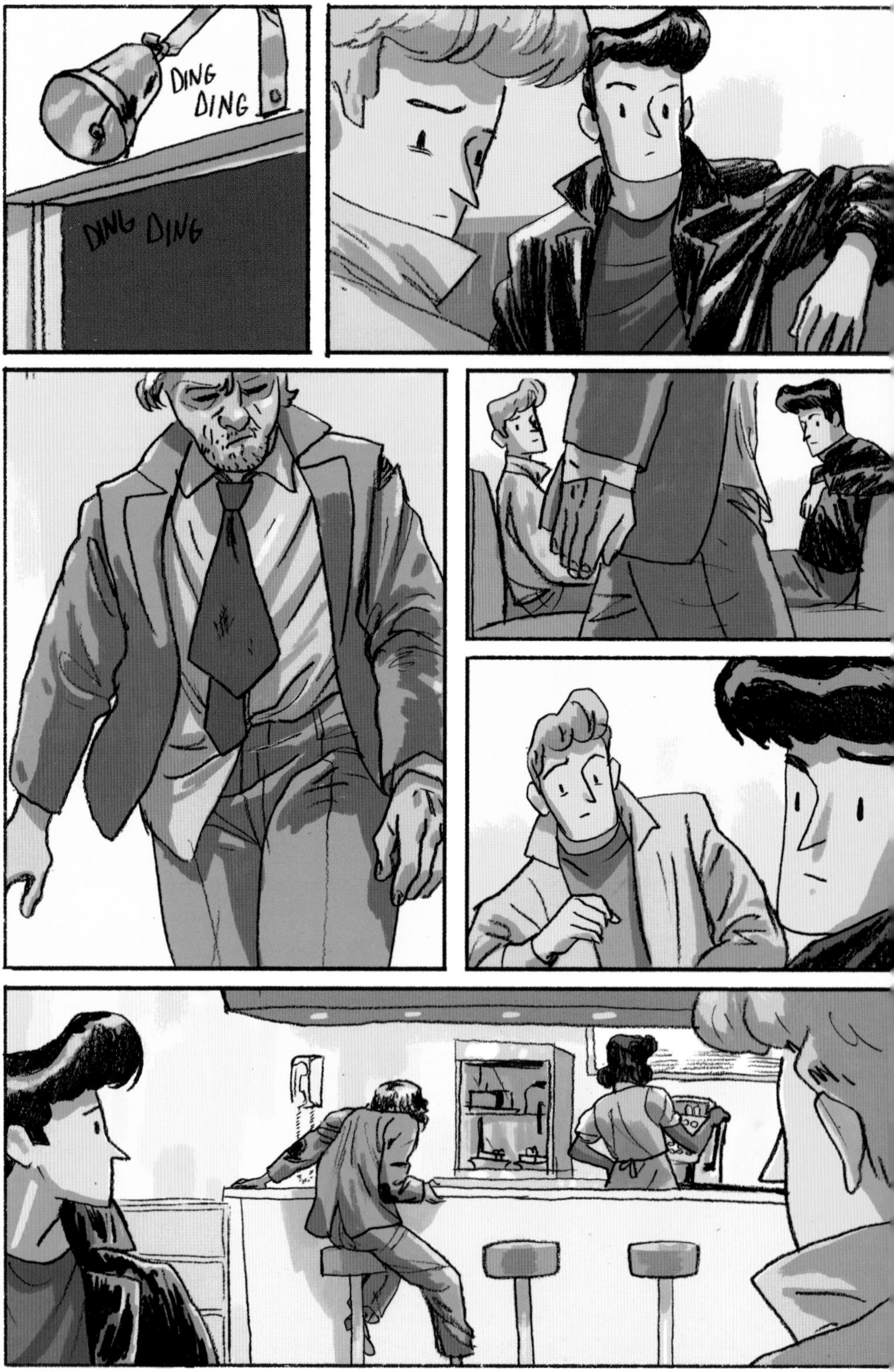
DING
DING
DING DING

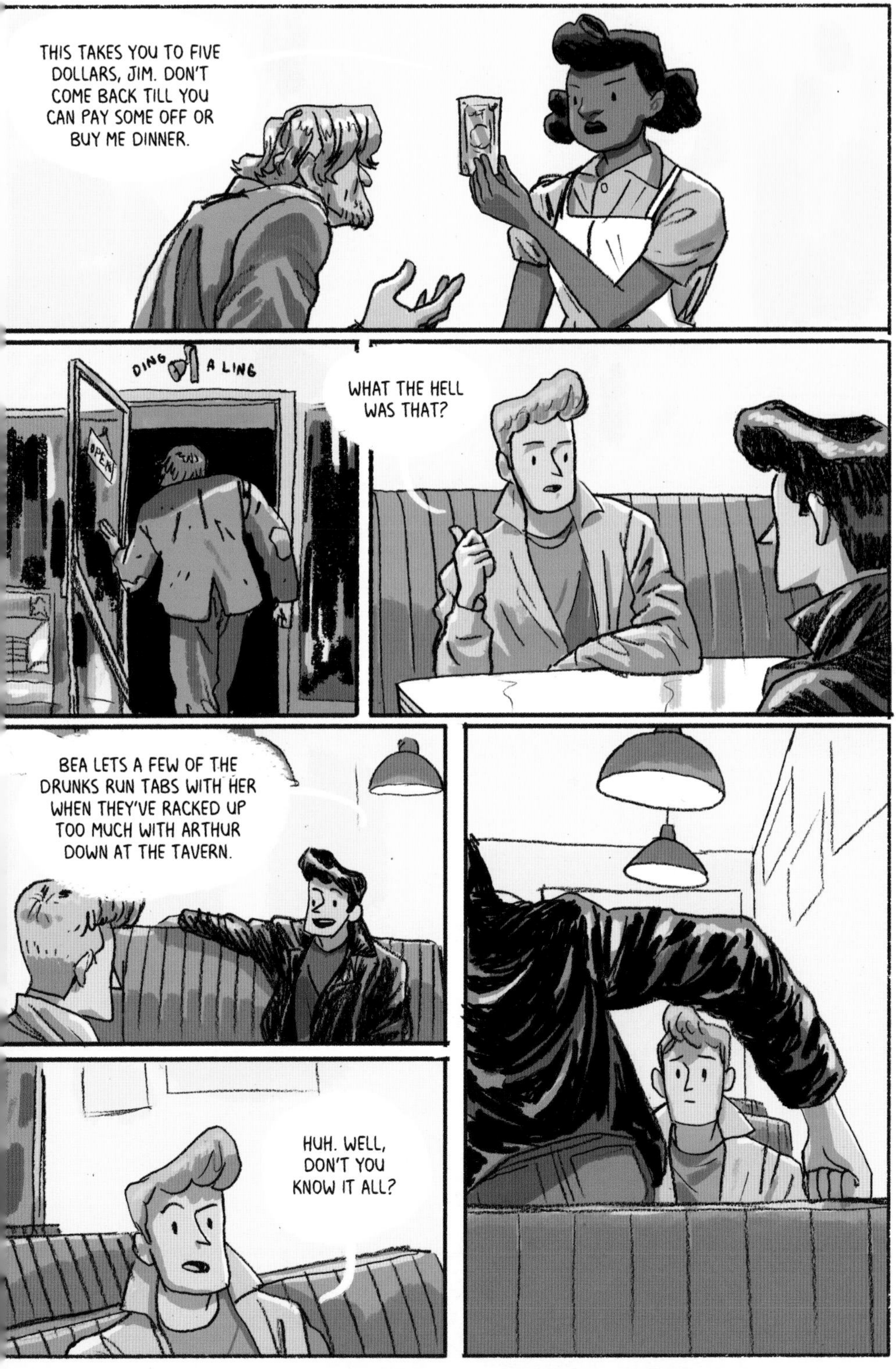
THIS TAKES YOU TO FIVE DOLLARS, JIM. DON'T COME BACK TILL YOU CAN PAY SOME OFF OR BUY ME DINNER.
DING A LING
OPEN
WHAT THE HELL WAS THAT?
BEA LETS A FEW OF THE DRUNKS RUN TABS WITH HER WHEN THEY'VE RACKED UP TOO MUCH WITH ARTHUR DOWN AT THE TAVERN.
HUH. WELL, DON'T YOU KNOW IT ALL?

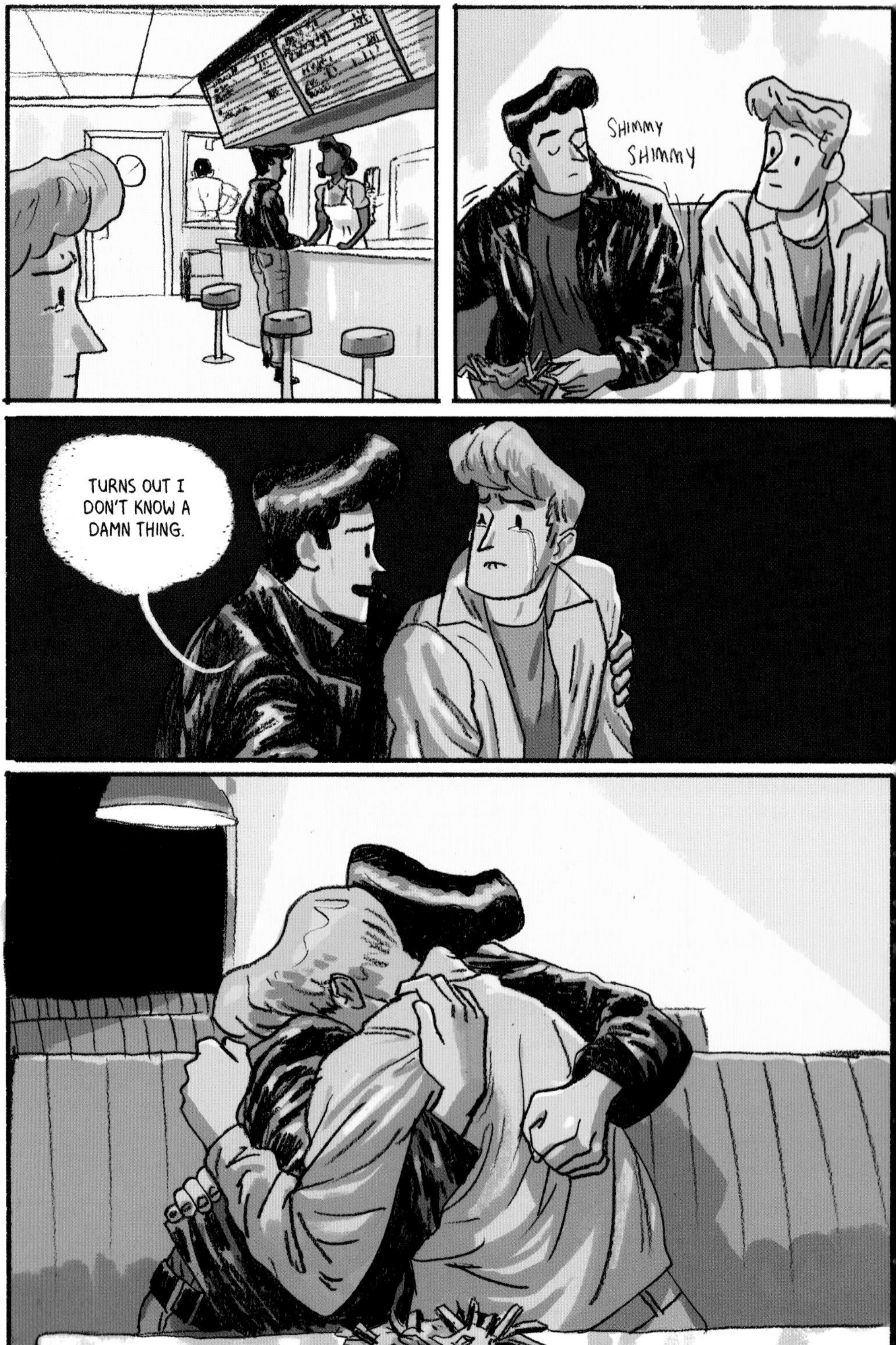
SHIMMY
SHIMMY
TURNS OUT I DON'T KNOW A DAMN THING.

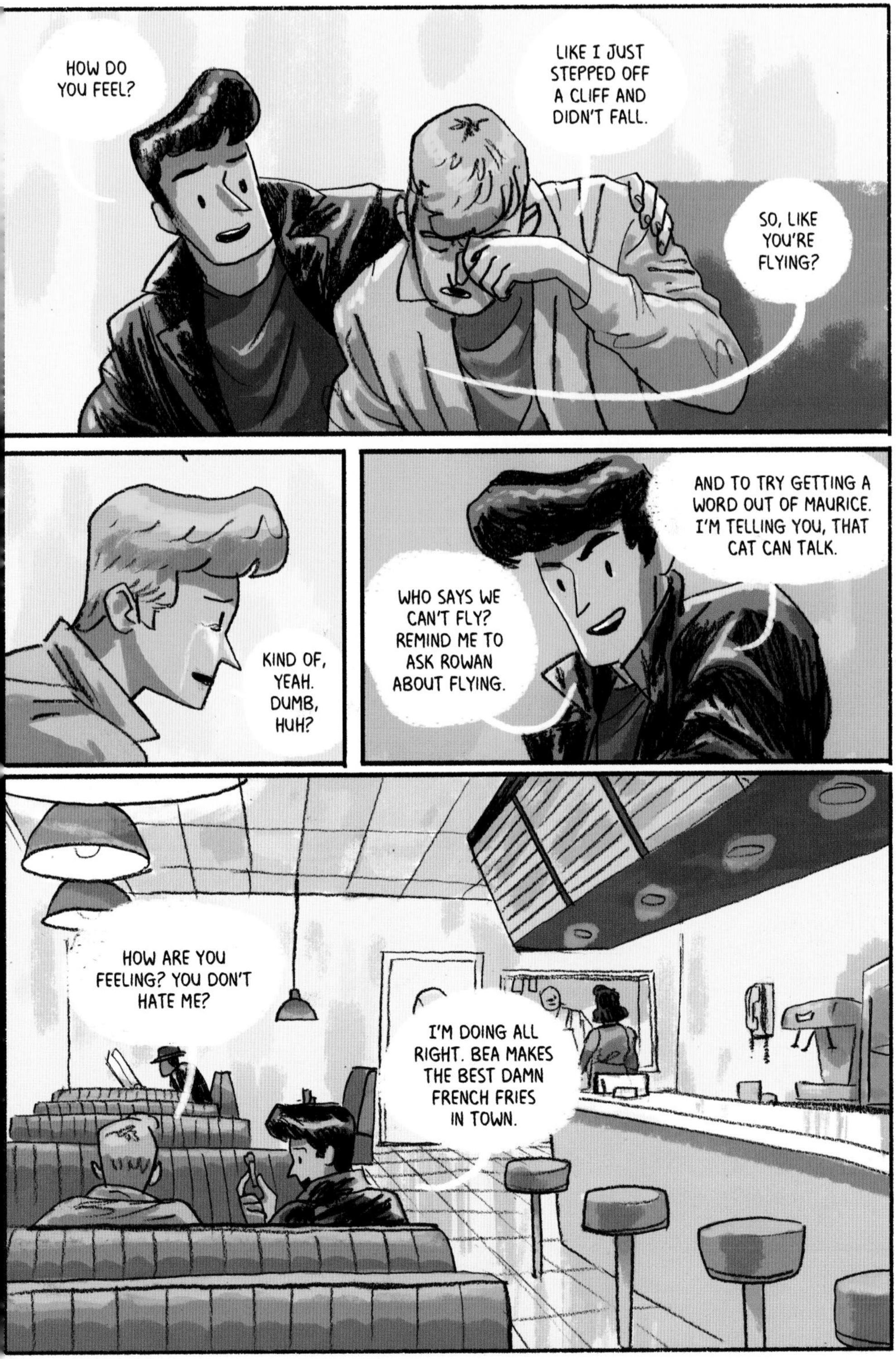
HOW DO YOU FEEL?
LIKE I JUST STEPPED OFF A CLIFF AND DIDN'T FALL.
SO, LIKE YOU'RE FLYING?
KIND OF, YEAH. DUMB, HUH?
WHO SAYS WE CAN'T FLY? REMIND ME TO ASK ROWAN ABOUT FLYING.
AND TO TRY GETTING A WORD OUT OF MAURICE. I'M TELLING YOU, THAT CAT CAN TALK.
HOW ARE YOU FEELING? YOU DON'T HATE ME?
I'M DOING ALL RIGHT. BEA MAKES THE BEST DAMN FRENCH FRIES IN TOWN.

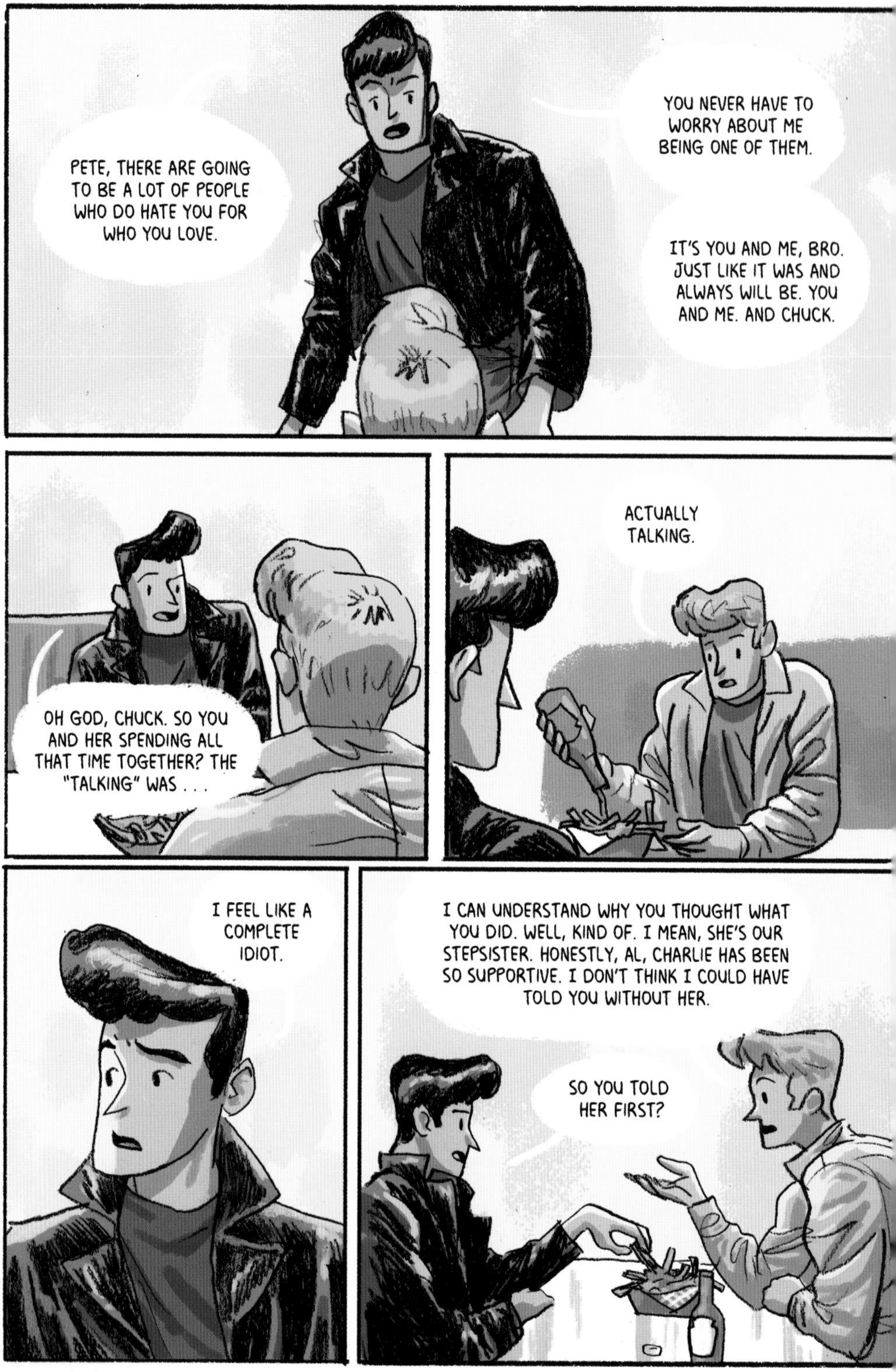
PETE, THERE ARE GOING TO BE A LOT OF PEOPLE WHO DO HATE YOU FOR WHO YOU LOVE.
YOU NEVER HAVE TO WORRY ABOUT ME BEING ONE OF THEM.
IT'S YOU AND ME, BRO. JUST LIKE IT WAS AND ALWAYS WILL BE. YOU AND ME. AND CHUCK.
OH GOD, CHUCK. SO YOU AND HER SPENDING ALL THAT TIME TOGETHER? THE "TALKING" WAS . . .
ACTUALLY TALKING.
I FEEL LIKE A COMPLETE IDIOT.
I CAN UNDERSTAND WHY YOU THOUGHT WHAT YOU DID. WELL, KIND OF. I MEAN, SHE'S OUR STEPSISTER. HONESTLY, AL, CHARLIE HAS BEEN SO SUPPORTIVE. I DON'T THINK I COULD HAVE TOLD YOU WITHOUT HER.
SO YOU TOLD HER FIRST?

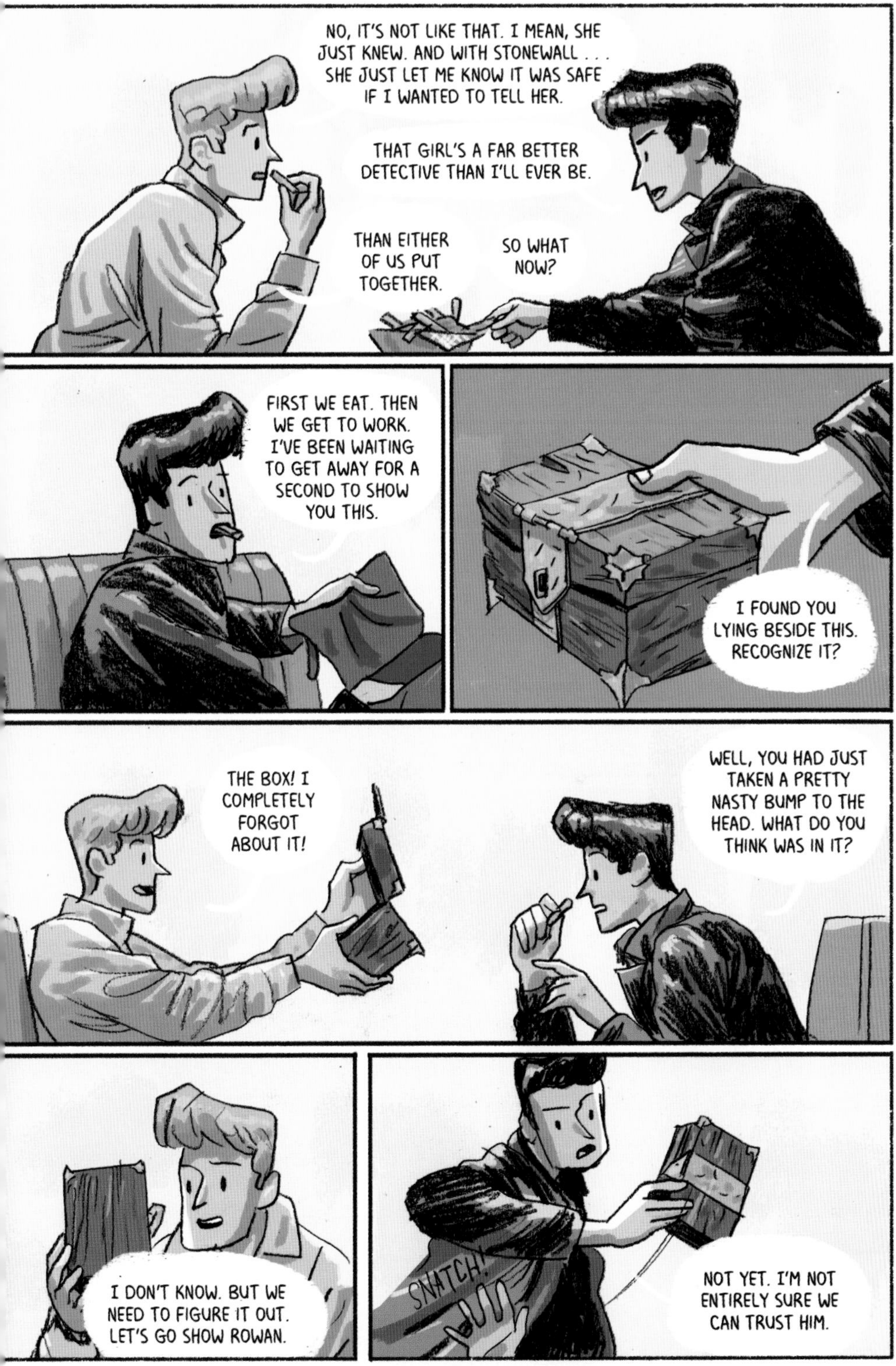
NO, IT'S NOT LIKE THAT. I MEAN, SHE JUST KNEW. AND WITH STONEWALL . . . SHE JUST LET ME KNOW IT WAS SAFE IF I WANTED TO TELL HER.
THAT GIRL'S A FAR BETTER DETECTIVE THAN I'LL EVER BE.
THAN EITHER OF US PUT TOGETHER.
SO WHAT NOW?
FIRST WE EAT. THEN WE GET TO WORK. I'VE BEEN WAITING TO GET AWAY FOR A SECOND TO SHOW YOU THIS.
I FOUND YOU LYING BESIDE THIS. RECOGNIZE IT?
THE BOX! I COMPLETELY FORGOT ABOUT IT!
WELL, YOU HAD JUST TAKEN A PRETTY NASTY BUMP TO THE HEAD. WHAT DO YOU THINK WAS IN IT?
I DON'T KNOW. BUT WE NEED TO FIGURE IT OUT. LET'S GO SHOW ROWAN.
SNATCH!
NOT YET. I'M NOT ENTIRELY SURE WE CAN TRUST HIM.

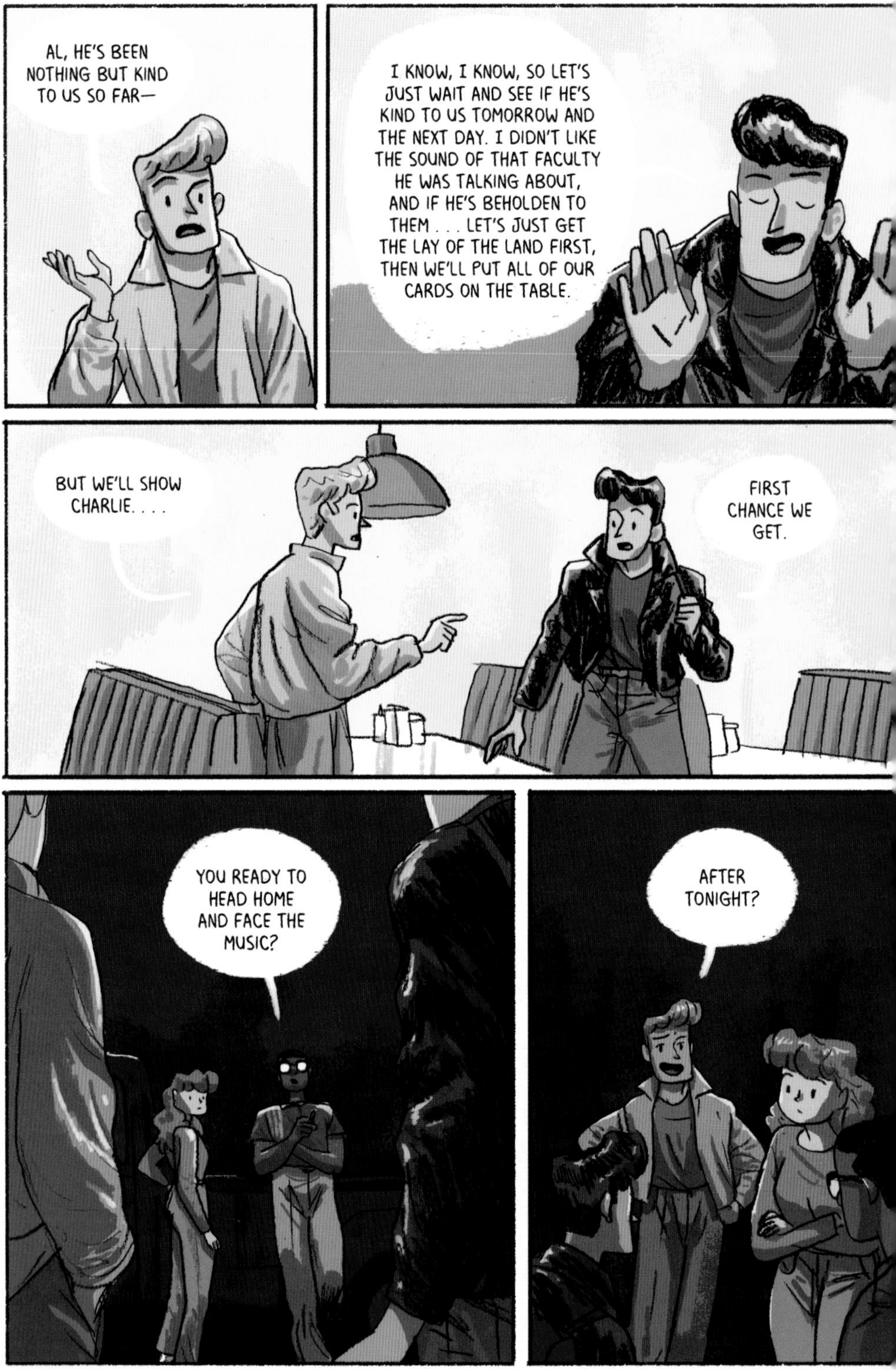
AL, HE'S BEEN NOTHING BUT KIND TO US SO FAR—
I KNOW, I KNOW, SO LET'S JUST WAIT AND SEE IF HE'S KIND TO US TOMORROW AND THE NEXT DAY. I DIDN'T LIKE THE SOUND OF THAT FACULTY HE WAS TALKING ABOUT, AND IF HE'S BEHOLDEN TO THEM . . . LET'S JUST GET THE LAY OF THE LAND FIRST, THEN WE'LL PUT ALL OF OUR CARDS ON THE TABLE.
BUT WE'LL SHOW CHARLIE. . . .
FIRST CHANCE WE GET.
YOU READY TO HEAD HOME AND FACE THE MUSIC?
AFTER TONIGHT?

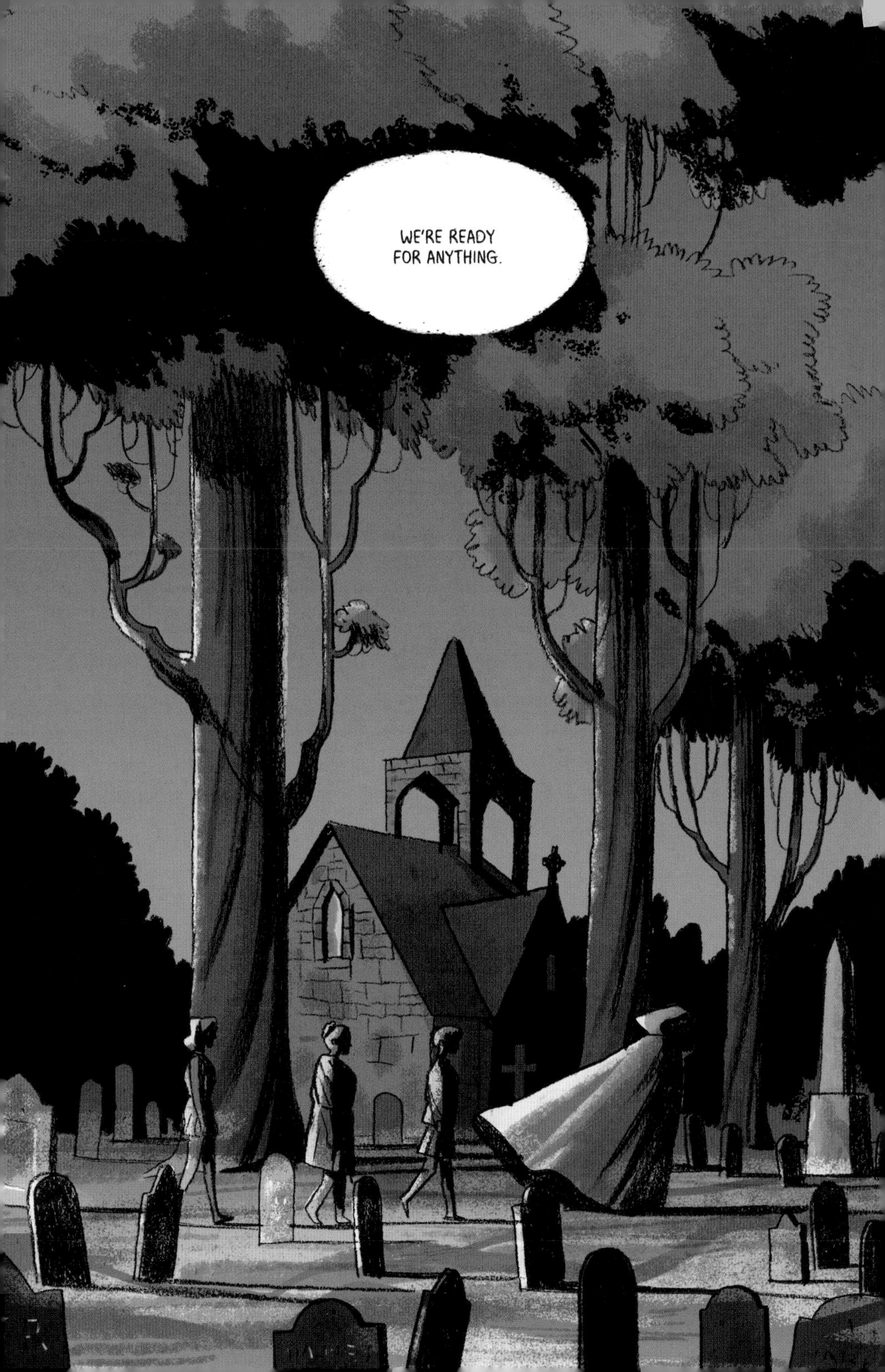
WE'RE READY
FOR ANYTHING.

CHAPTER 3

THEY'RE WITH ROWAN. THEY'RE FINE.

OH, I KNOW THAT.

THEN WHY HAVEN'T YOU STOPPED PACING SINCE THEY LEFT?

THEY'RE GOING TO HAVE QUESTIONS.

ABOUT FRANCIS AND ALICE, YOU MEAN.

ABOUT EVERYTHING.

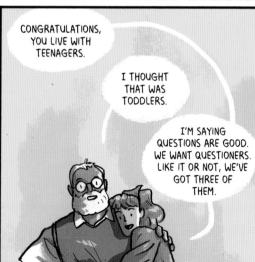

CONGRATULATIONS, YOU LIVE WITH TEENAGERS.

I THOUGHT THAT WAS TODDLERS.

I'M SAYING QUESTIONS ARE GOOD. WE WANT QUESTIONERS. LIKE IT OR NOT, WE'VE GOT THREE OF THEM.

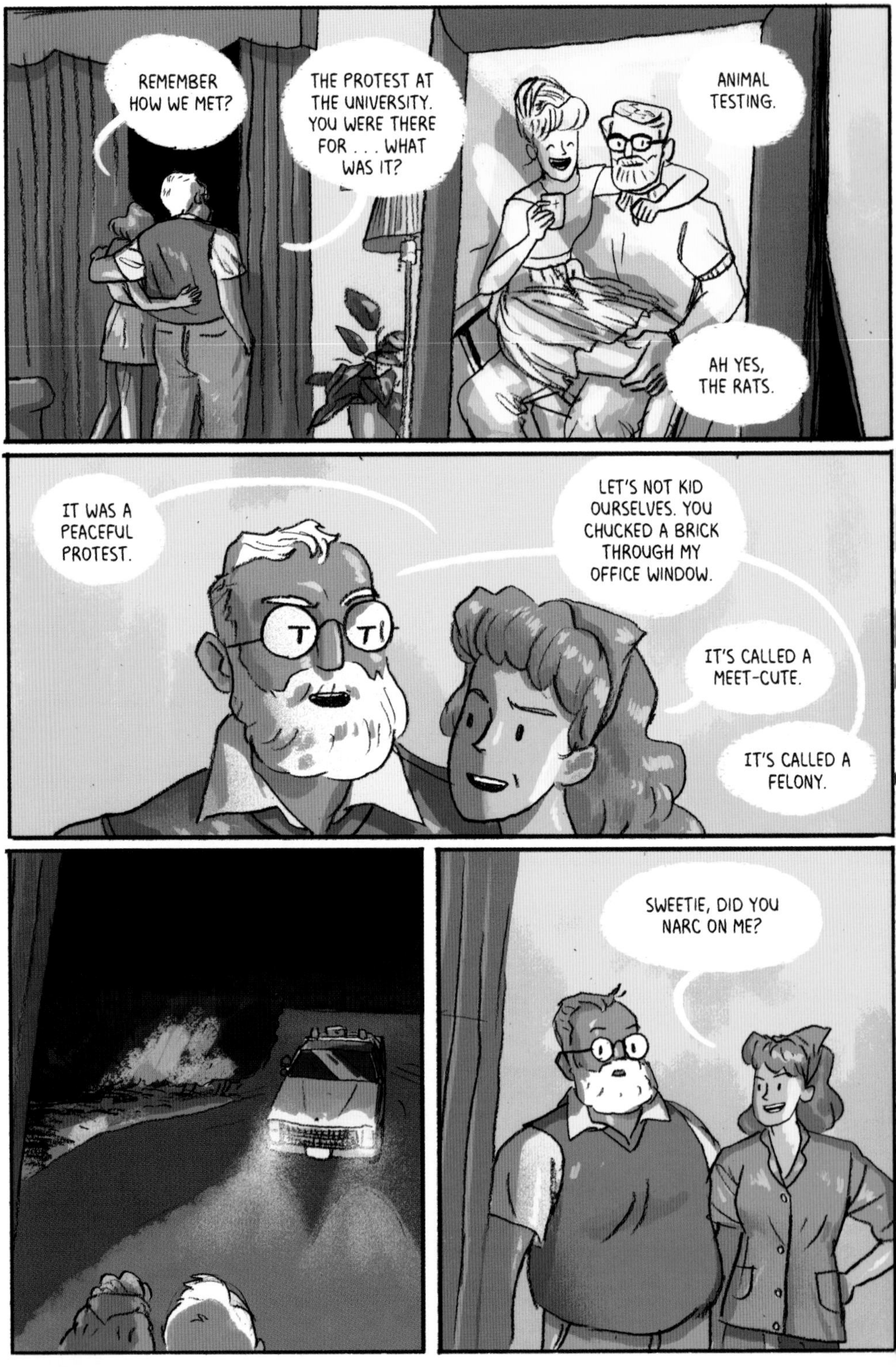
REMEMBER HOW WE MET?
THE PROTEST AT THE UNIVERSITY. YOU WERE THERE FOR . . . WHAT WAS IT?
ANIMAL TESTING.
AH YES, THE RATS.
IT WAS A PEACEFUL PROTEST.
LET'S NOT KID OURSELVES. YOU CHUCKED A BRICK THROUGH MY OFFICE WINDOW.
IT'S CALLED A MEET-CUTE.
IT'S CALLED A FELONY.
SWEETIE, DID YOU NARC ON ME?

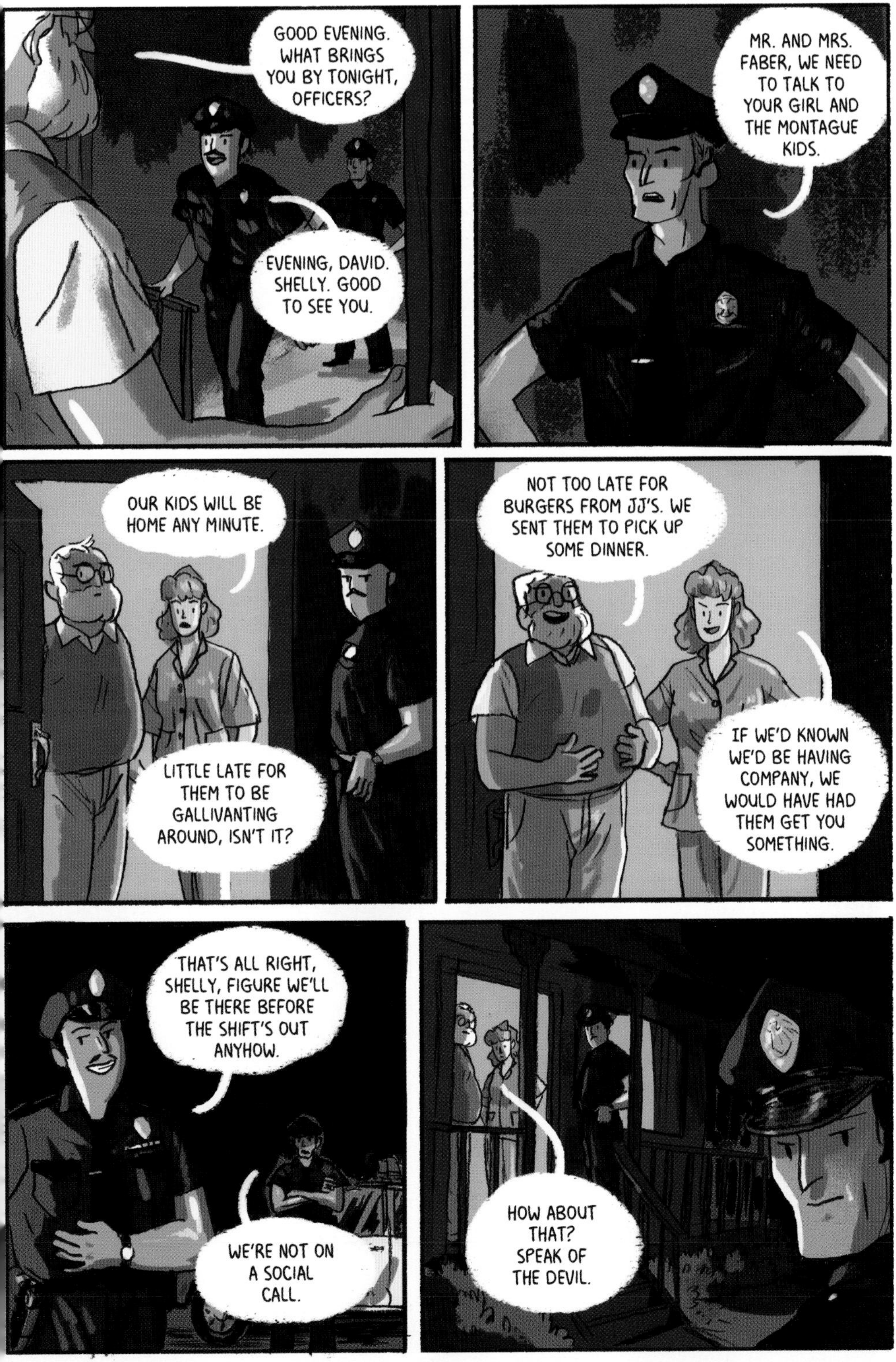
GOOD EVENING. WHAT BRINGS YOU BY TONIGHT, OFFICERS?
EVENING, DAVID. SHELLY. GOOD TO SEE YOU.
MR. AND MRS. FABER, WE NEED TO TALK TO YOUR GIRL AND THE MONTAGUE KIDS.
OUR KIDS WILL BE HOME ANY MINUTE.
LITTLE LATE FOR THEM TO BE GALLIVANTING AROUND, ISN'T IT?
NOT TOO LATE FOR BURGERS FROM JJ'S. WE SENT THEM TO PICK UP SOME DINNER.
IF WE'D KNOWN WE'D BE HAVING COMPANY, WE WOULD HAVE HAD THEM GET YOU SOMETHING.
THAT'S ALL RIGHT, SHELLY, FIGURE WE'LL BE THERE BEFORE THE SHIFT'S OUT ANYHOW.
WE'RE NOT ON A SOCIAL CALL.
HOW ABOUT THAT? SPEAK OF THE DEVIL.

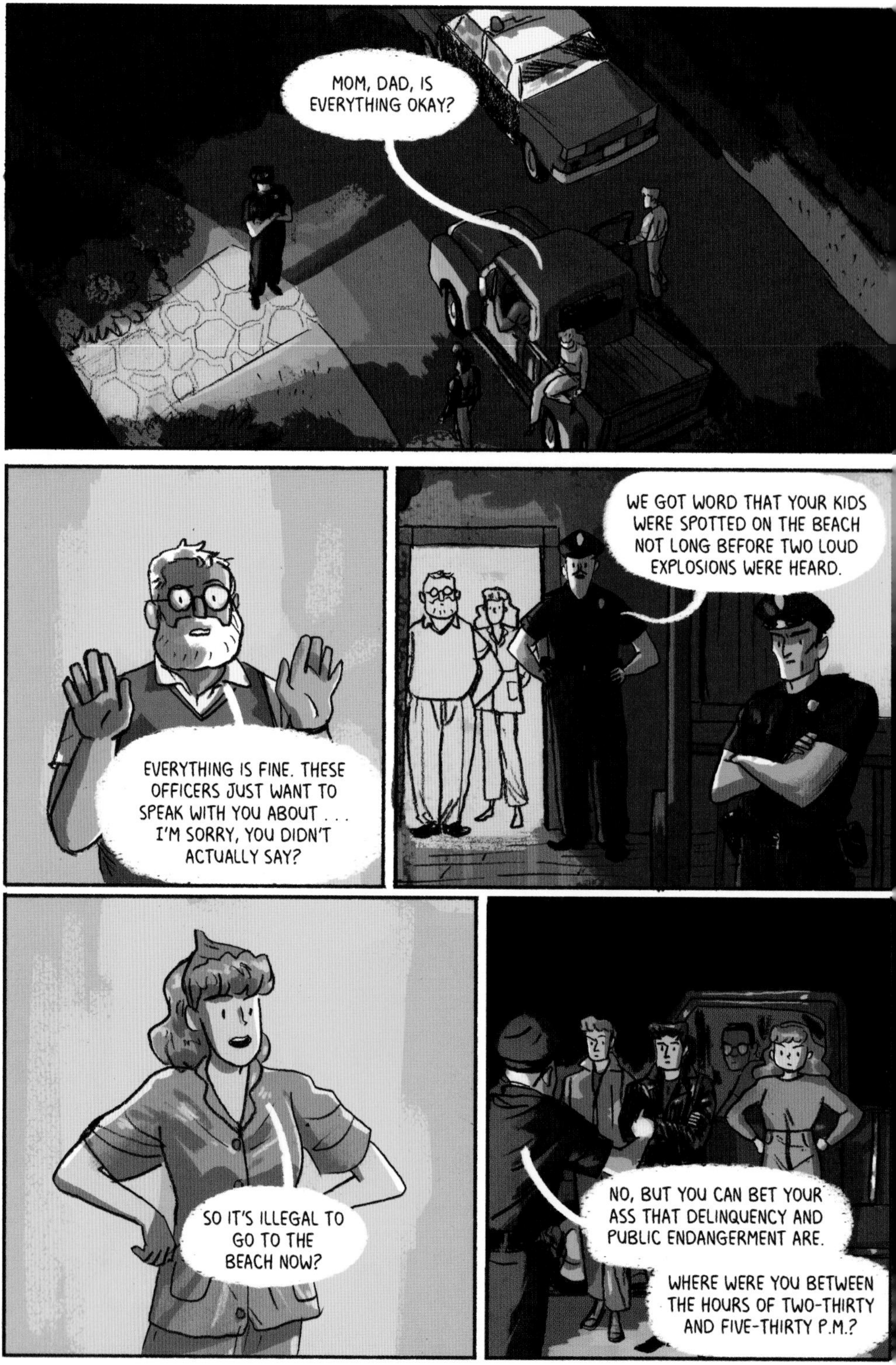
MOM, DAD, IS EVERYTHING OKAY?
EVERYTHING IS FINE. THESE OFFICERS JUST WANT TO SPEAK WITH YOU ABOUT . . . I'M SORRY, YOU DIDN'T ACTUALLY SAY?
WE GOT WORD THAT YOUR KIDS WERE SPOTTED ON THE BEACH NOT LONG BEFORE TWO LOUD EXPLOSIONS WERE HEARD.
SO IT'S ILLEGAL TO GO TO THE BEACH NOW?
NO, BUT YOU CAN BET YOUR ASS THAT DELINQUENCY AND PUBLIC ENDANGERMENT ARE.
WHERE WERE YOU BETWEEN THE HOURS OF TWO-THIRTY AND FIVE-THIRTY P.M.?

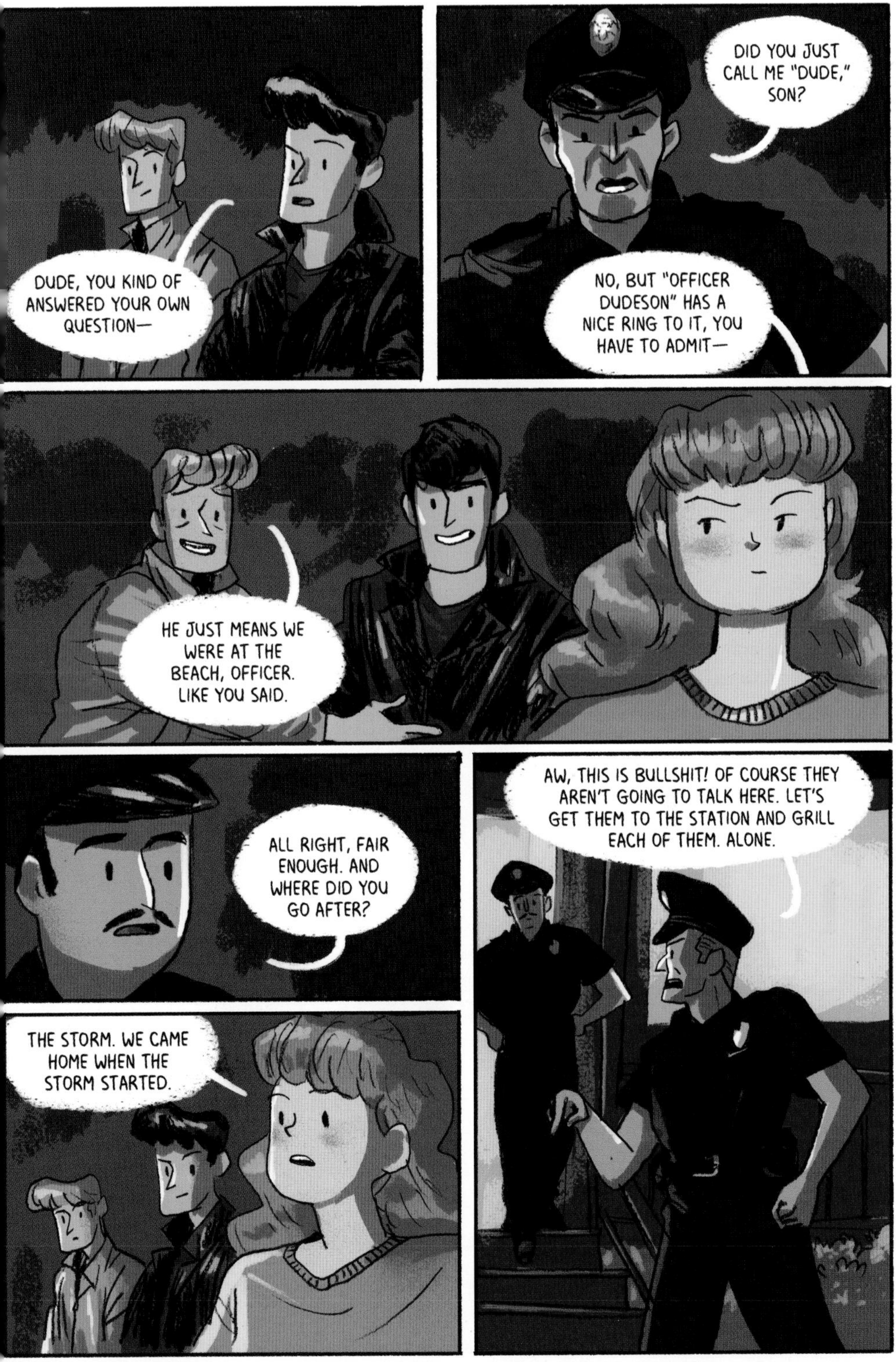
DUDE, YOU KIND OF ANSWERED YOUR OWN QUESTION—
DID YOU JUST CALL ME "DUDE," SON?
NO, BUT "OFFICER DUDESON" HAS A NICE RING TO IT, YOU HAVE TO ADMIT—
HE JUST MEANS WE WERE AT THE BEACH, OFFICER. LIKE YOU SAID.
ALL RIGHT, FAIR ENOUGH. AND WHERE DID YOU GO AFTER?
THE STORM. WE CAME HOME WHEN THE STORM STARTED.
AW, THIS IS BULLSHIT! OF COURSE THEY AREN'T GOING TO TALK HERE. LET'S GET THEM TO THE STATION AND GRILL EACH OF THEM. ALONE.

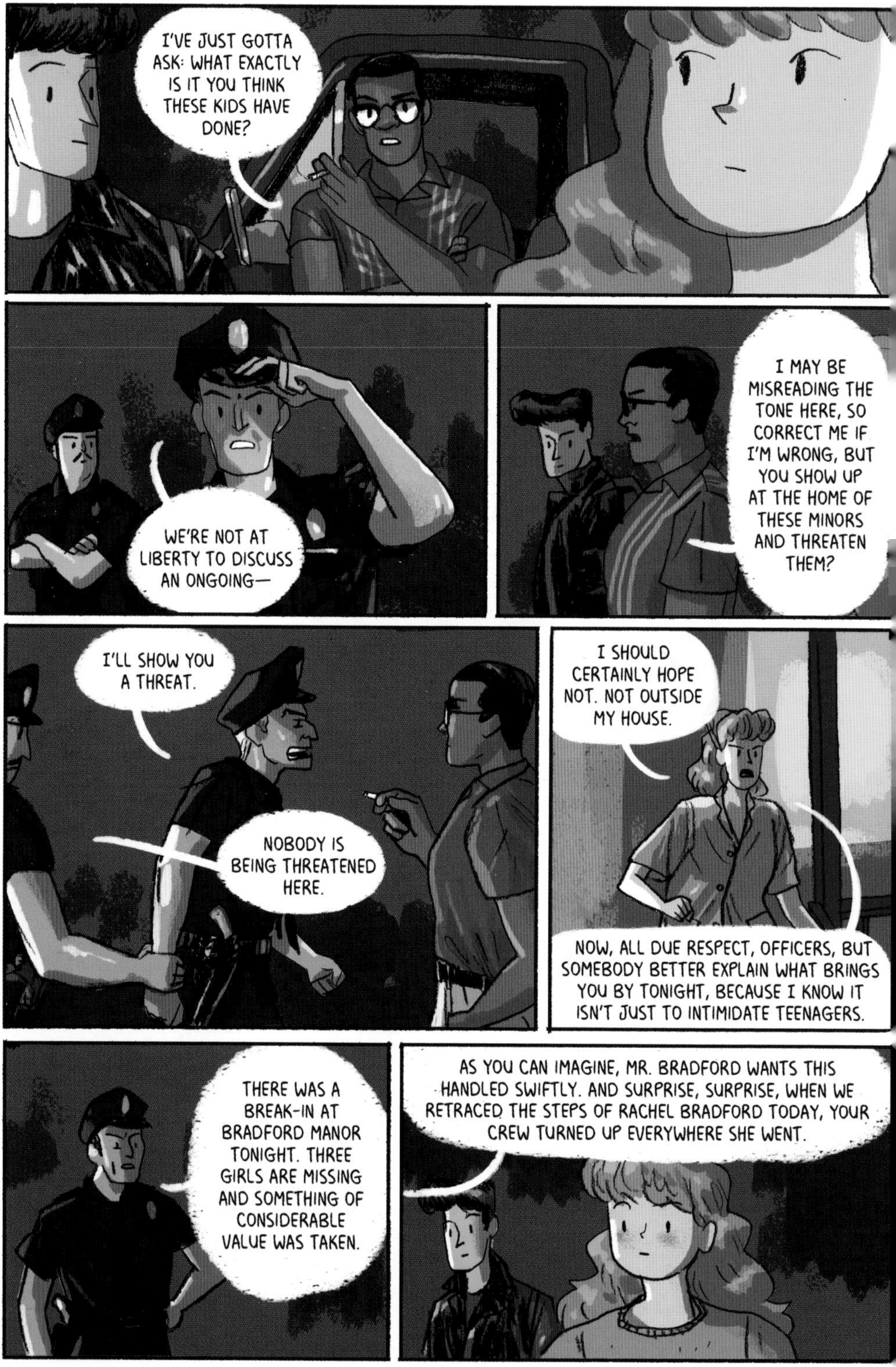
I'VE JUST GOTTA ASK: WHAT EXACTLY IS IT YOU THINK THESE KIDS HAVE DONE?
WE'RE NOT AT LIBERTY TO DISCUSS AN ONGOING—
I MAY BE MISREADING THE TONE HERE, SO CORRECT ME IF I'M WRONG, BUT YOU SHOW UP AT THE HOME OF THESE MINORS AND THREATEN THEM?
I'LL SHOW YOU A THREAT.
NOBODY IS BEING THREATENED HERE.
I SHOULD CERTAINLY HOPE NOT. NOT OUTSIDE MY HOUSE.
NOW, ALL DUE RESPECT, OFFICERS, BUT SOMEBODY BETTER EXPLAIN WHAT BRINGS YOU BY TONIGHT, BECAUSE I KNOW IT ISN'T JUST TO INTIMIDATE TEENAGERS.
THERE WAS A BREAK-IN AT BRADFORD MANOR TONIGHT. THREE GIRLS ARE MISSING AND SOMETHING OF CONSIDERABLE VALUE WAS TAKEN.
AS YOU CAN IMAGINE, MR. BRADFORD WANTS THIS HANDLED SWIFTLY. AND SURPRISE, SURPRISE, WHEN WE RETRACED THE STEPS OF RACHEL BRADFORD TODAY, YOUR CREW TURNED UP EVERYWHERE SHE WENT.

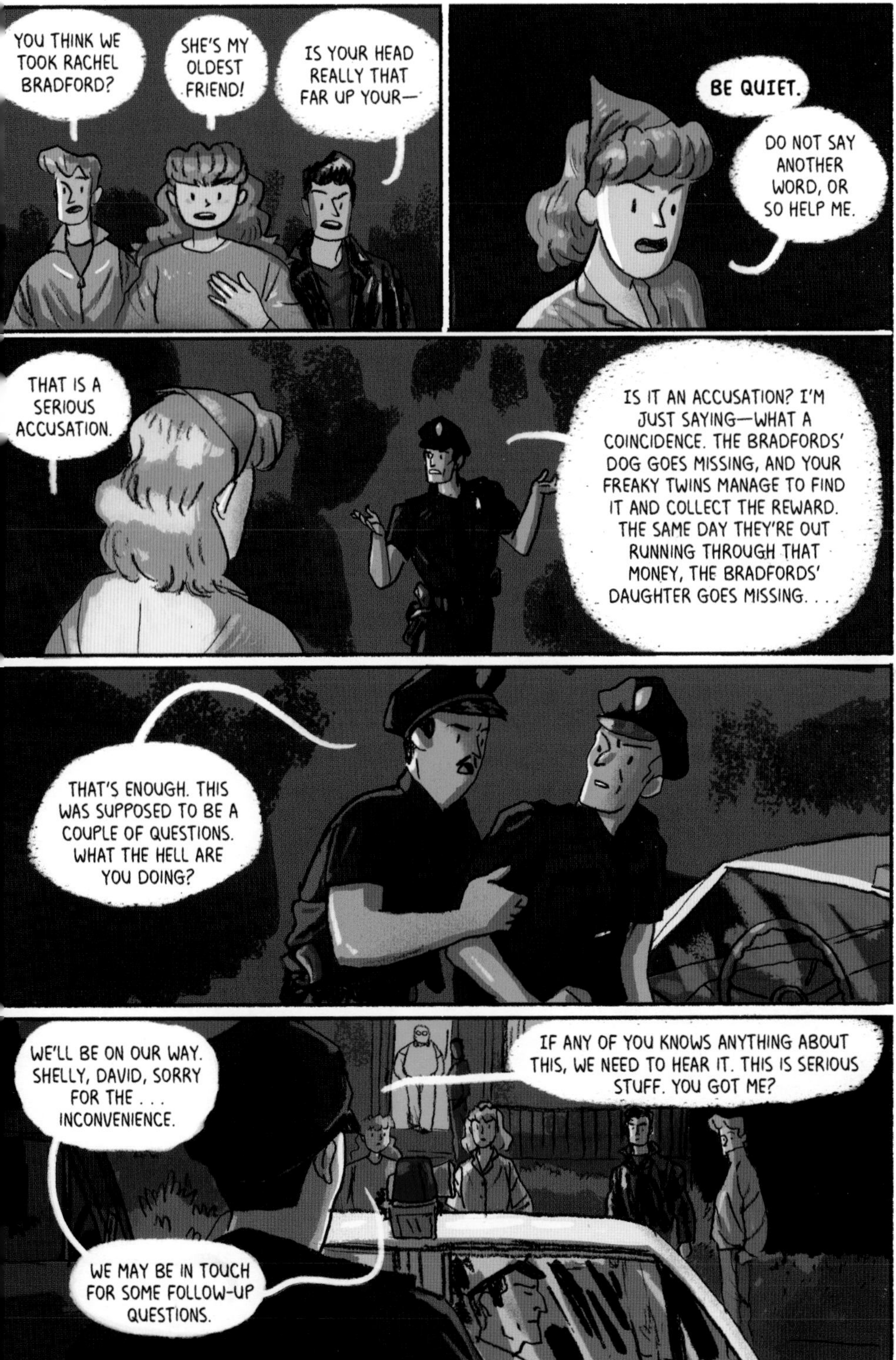
YOU THINK WE TOOK RACHEL BRADFORD?
SHE'S MY OLDEST FRIEND!
IS YOUR HEAD REALLY THAT FAR UP YOUR—
BE QUIET.
DO NOT SAY ANOTHER WORD, OR SO HELP ME.
THAT IS A SERIOUS ACCUSATION.
IS IT AN ACCUSATION? I'M JUST SAYING—WHAT A COINCIDENCE. THE BRADFORDS' DOG GOES MISSING, AND YOUR FREAKY TWINS MANAGE TO FIND IT AND COLLECT THE REWARD. THE SAME DAY THEY'RE OUT RUNNING THROUGH THAT MONEY, THE BRADFORDS' DAUGHTER GOES MISSING. . . .
THAT'S ENOUGH. THIS WAS SUPPOSED TO BE A COUPLE OF QUESTIONS. WHAT THE HELL ARE YOU DOING?
WE'LL BE ON OUR WAY. SHELLY, DAVID, SORRY FOR THE . . . INCONVENIENCE.
IF ANY OF YOU KNOWS ANYTHING ABOUT THIS, WE NEED TO HEAR IT. THIS IS SERIOUS STUFF. YOU GOT ME?
WE MAY BE IN TOUCH FOR SOME FOLLOW-UP QUESTIONS.

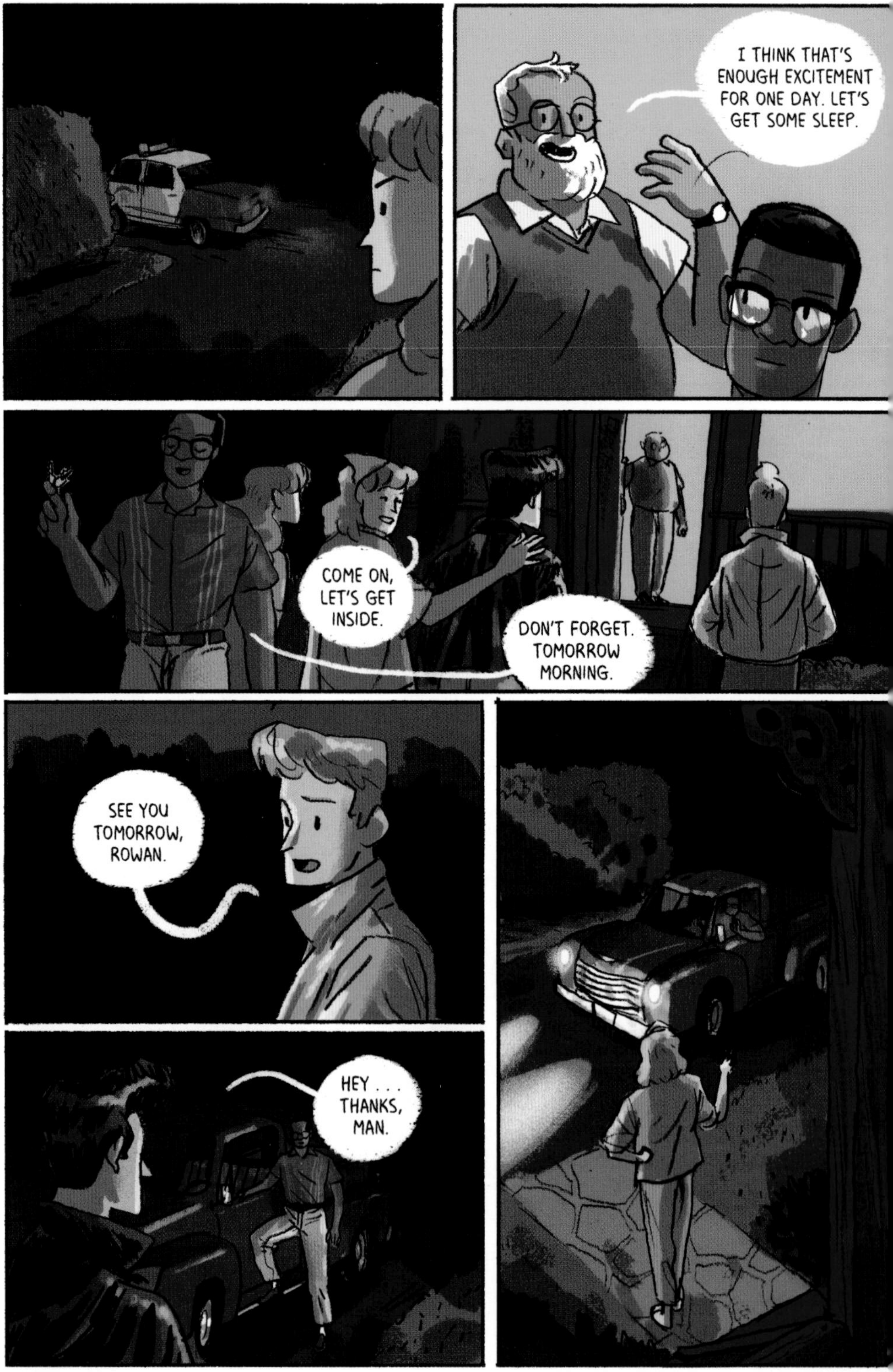
I THINK THAT'S ENOUGH EXCITEMENT FOR ONE DAY. LET'S GET SOME SLEEP.
COME ON, LET'S GET INSIDE.
DON'T FORGET. TOMORROW MORNING.
SEE YOU TOMORROW, ROWAN.
HEY . . . THANKS, MAN.

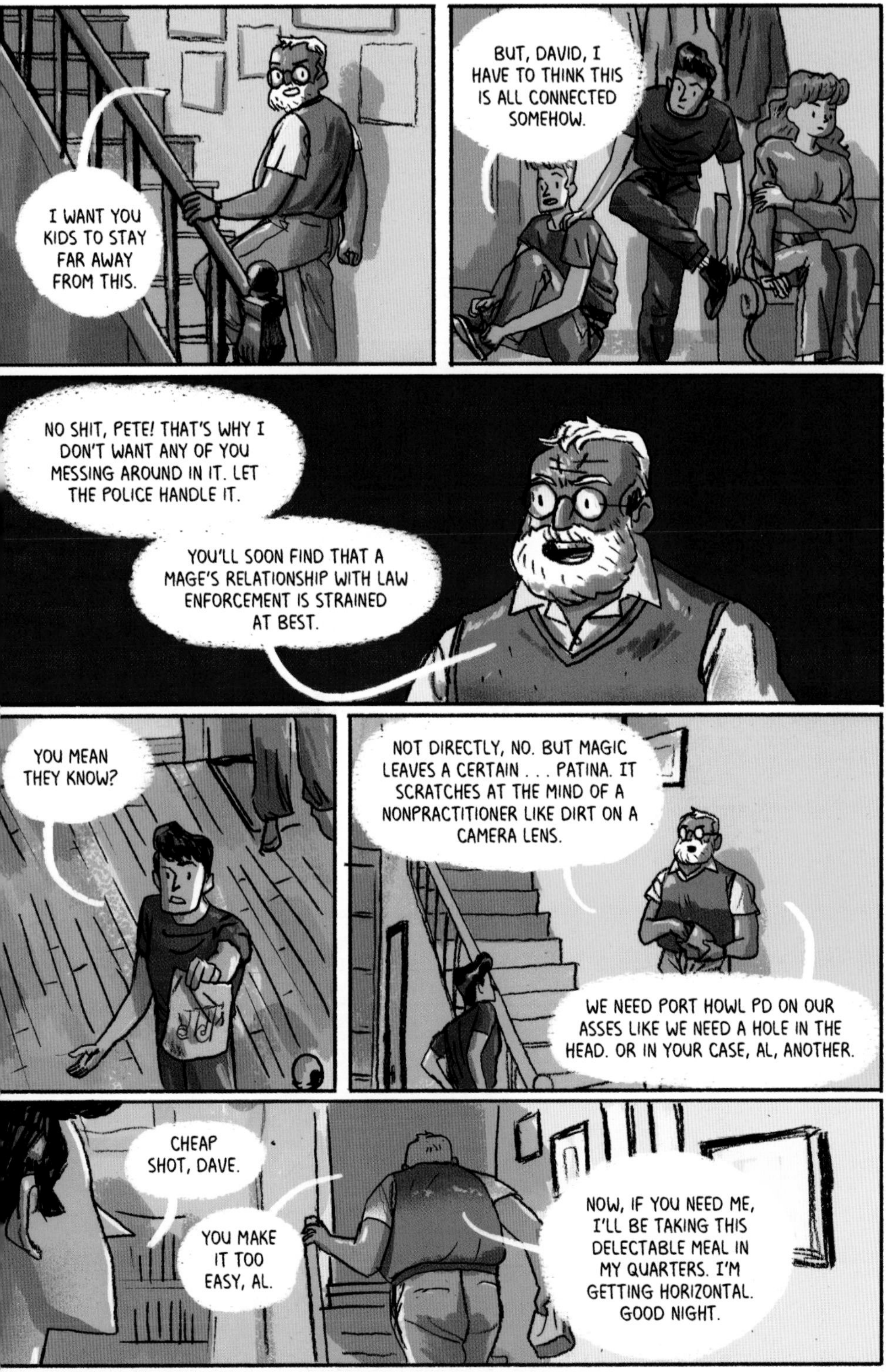
I WANT YOU KIDS TO STAY FAR AWAY FROM THIS.
BUT, DAVID, I HAVE TO THINK THIS IS ALL CONNECTED SOMEHOW.
NO SHIT, PETE! THAT'S WHY I DON'T WANT ANY OF YOU MESSING AROUND IN IT. LET THE POLICE HANDLE IT.
YOU'LL SOON FIND THAT A MAGE'S RELATIONSHIP WITH LAW ENFORCEMENT IS STRAINED AT BEST.
YOU MEAN THEY KNOW?
NOT DIRECTLY, NO. BUT MAGIC LEAVES A CERTAIN . . . PATINA. IT SCRATCHES AT THE MIND OF A NONPRACTITIONER LIKE DIRT ON A CAMERA LENS.
WE NEED PORT HOWL PD ON OUR ASSES LIKE WE NEED A HOLE IN THE HEAD. OR IN YOUR CASE, AL, ANOTHER.
CHEAP SHOT, DAVE.
YOU MAKE IT TOO EASY, AL.
NOW, IF YOU NEED ME, I'LL BE TAKING THIS DELECTABLE MEAL IN MY QUARTERS. I'M GETTING HORIZONTAL. GOOD NIGHT.

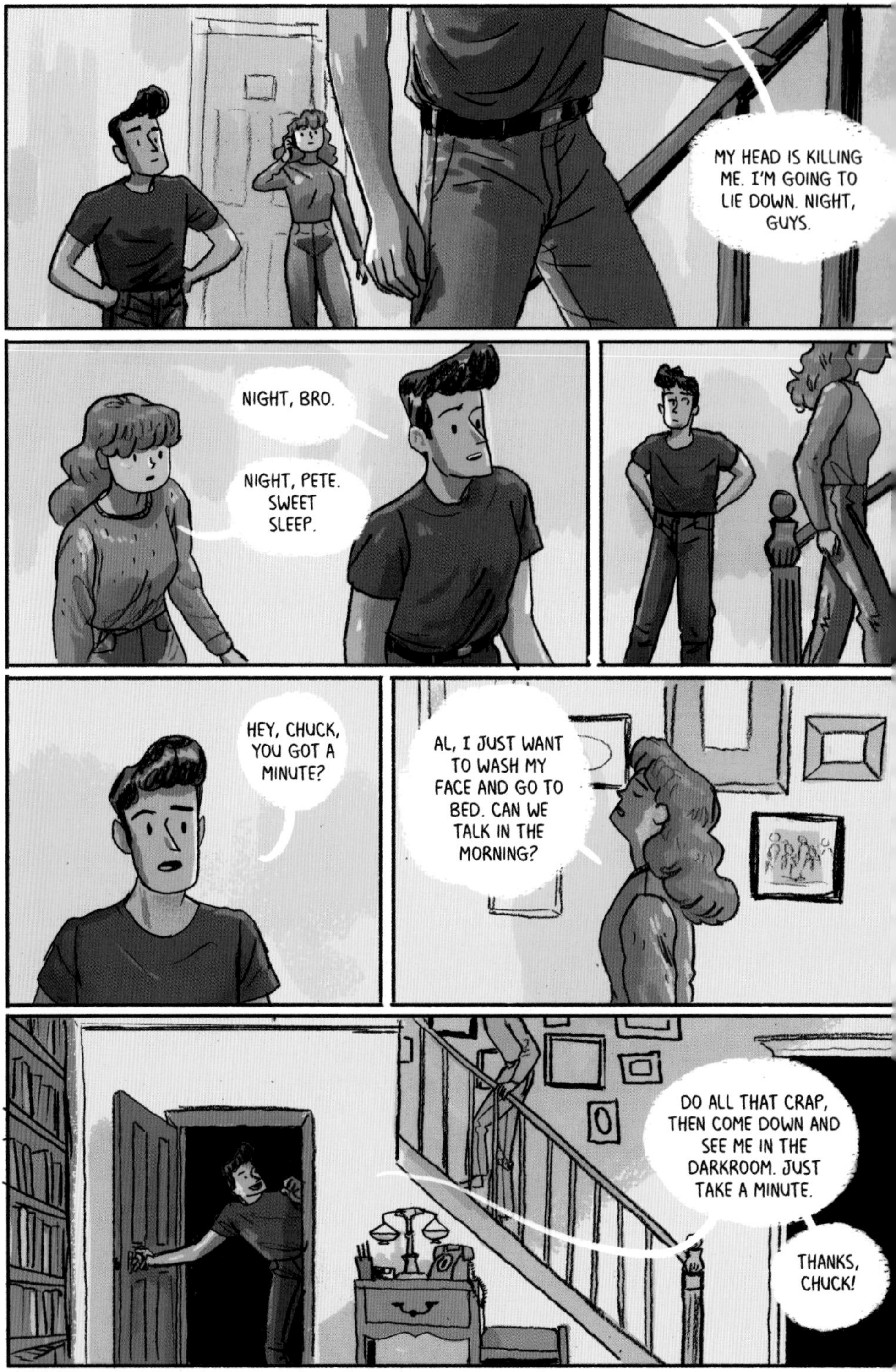
MY HEAD IS KILLING ME. I'M GOING TO LIE DOWN. NIGHT, GUYS.
NIGHT, BRO.
NIGHT, PETE. SWEET SLEEP.
HEY, CHUCK, YOU GOT A MINUTE?
AL, I JUST WANT TO WASH MY FACE AND GO TO BED. CAN WE TALK IN THE MORNING?
DO ALL THAT CRAP, THEN COME DOWN AND SEE ME IN THE DARKROOM. JUST TAKE A MINUTE.
THANKS, CHUCK!

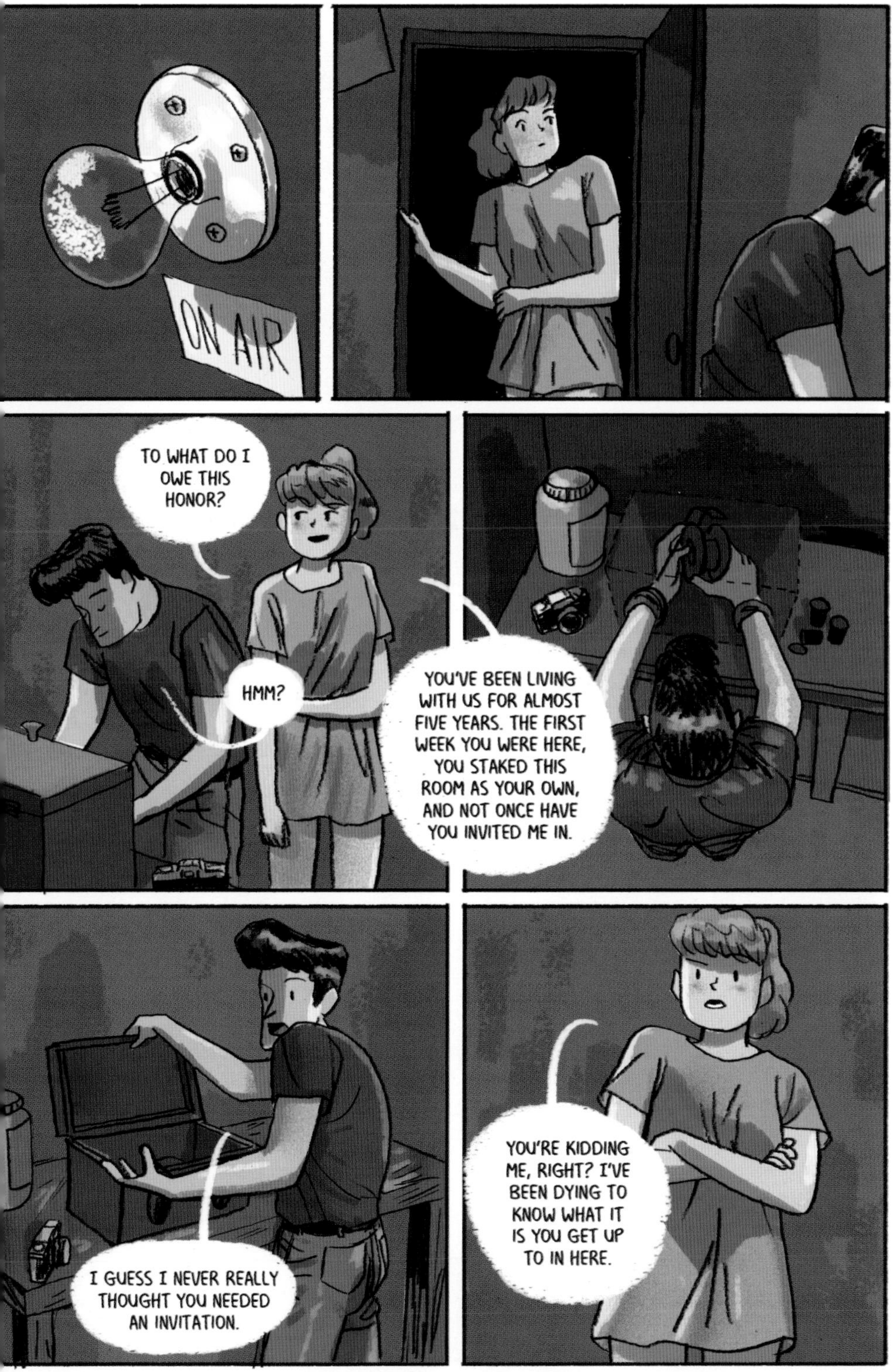
ON AIR
TO WHAT DO I OWE THIS HONOR?
HMM?
YOU'VE BEEN LIVING WITH US FOR ALMOST FIVE YEARS. THE FIRST WEEK YOU WERE HERE, YOU STAKED THIS ROOM AS YOUR OWN, AND NOT ONCE HAVE YOU INVITED ME IN.
I GUESS I NEVER REALLY THOUGHT YOU NEEDED AN INVITATION.
YOU'RE KIDDING ME, RIGHT? I'VE BEEN DYING TO KNOW WHAT IT IS YOU GET UP TO IN HERE.

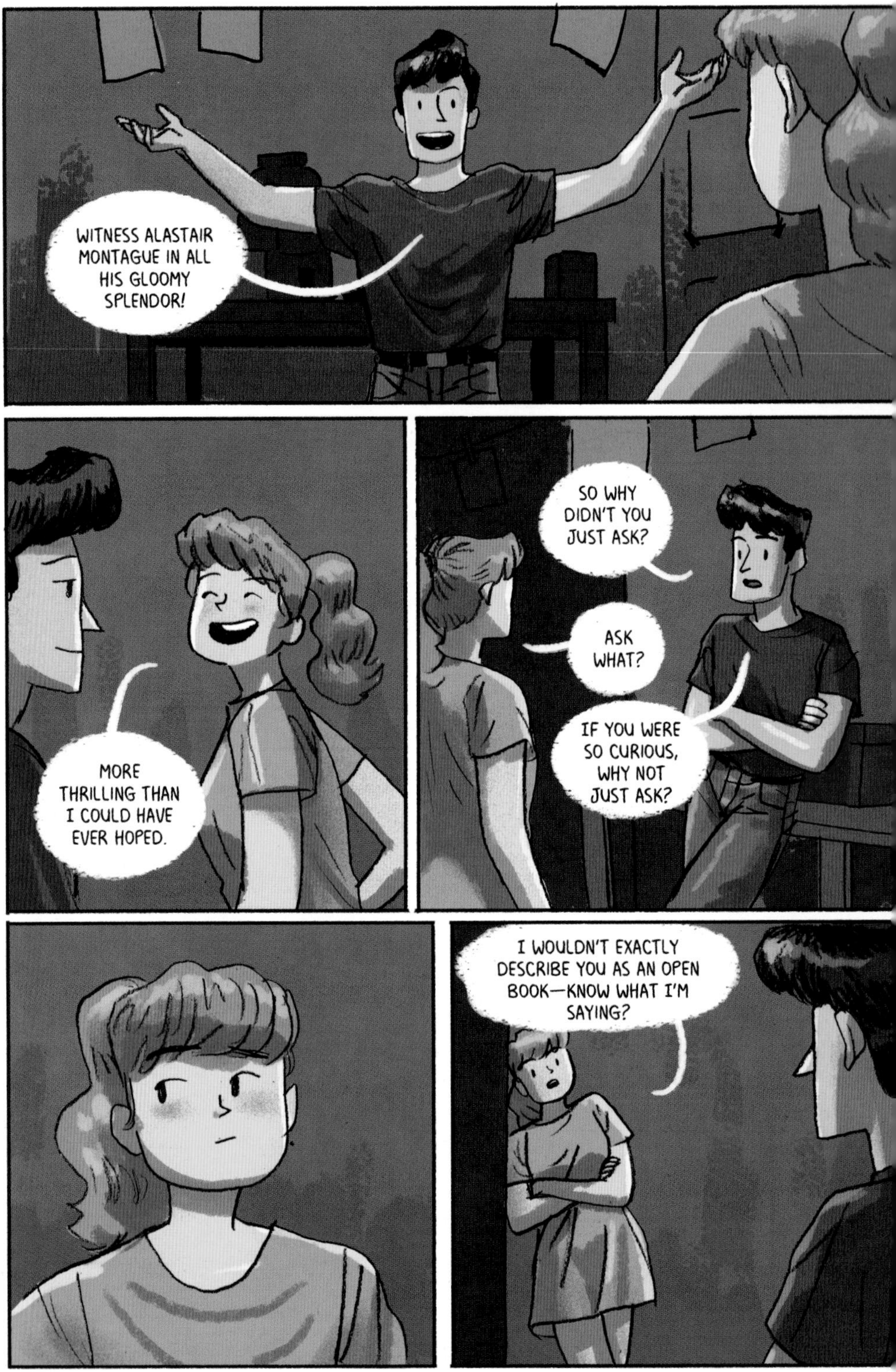
WITNESS ALASTAIR MONTAGUE IN ALL HIS GLOOMY SPLENDOR!
MORE THRILLING THAN I COULD HAVE EVER HOPED.
SO WHY DIDN'T YOU JUST ASK?
ASK WHAT?
IF YOU WERE SO CURIOUS, WHY NOT JUST ASK?
I WOULDN'T EXACTLY DESCRIBE YOU AS AN OPEN BOOK—KNOW WHAT I'M SAYING?

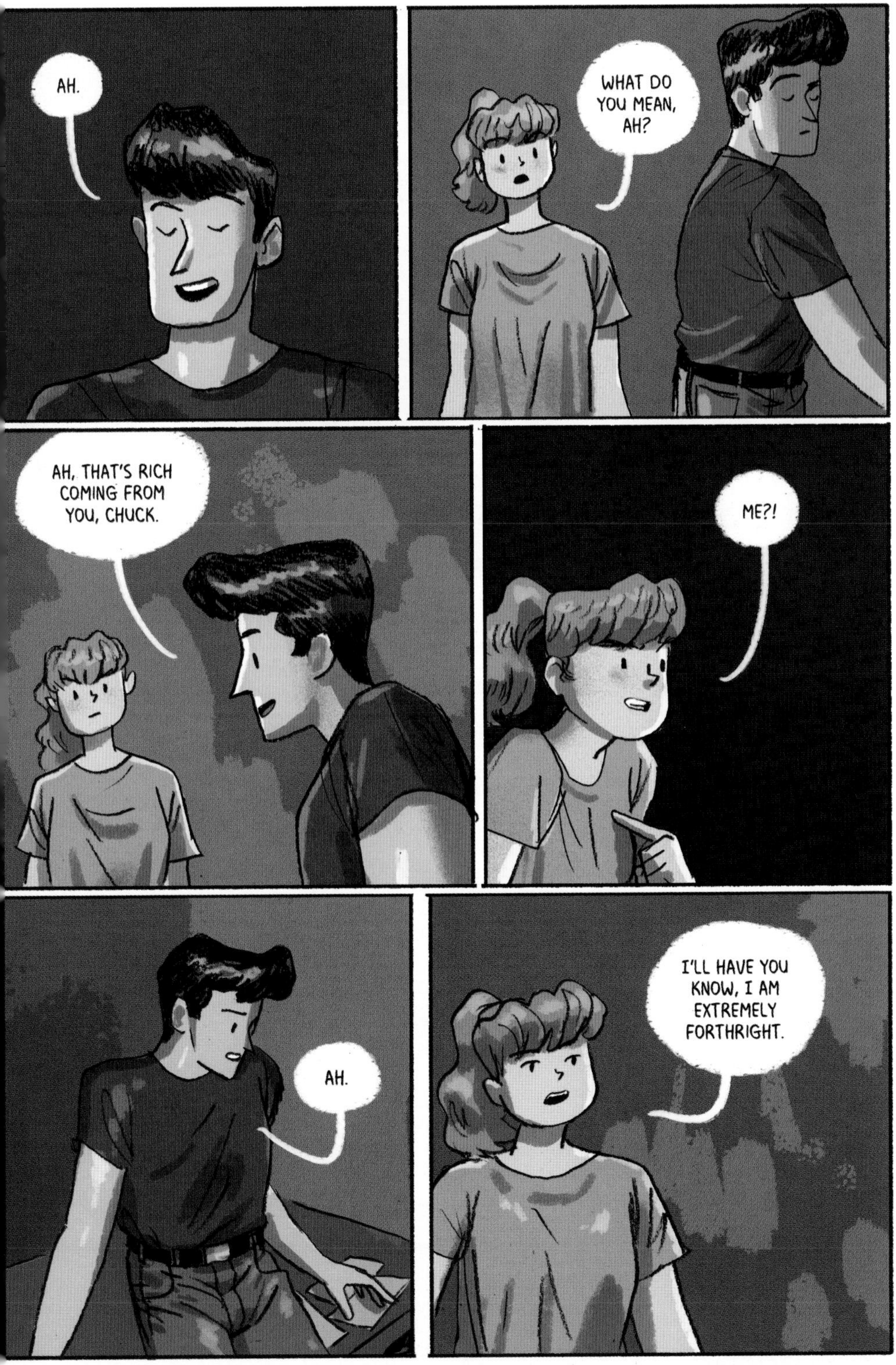
AH.
WHAT DO YOU MEAN, AH?
AH, THAT'S RICH COMING FROM YOU, CHUCK.
ME?!
AH.
I'LL HAVE YOU KNOW, I AM EXTREMELY FORTHRIGHT.

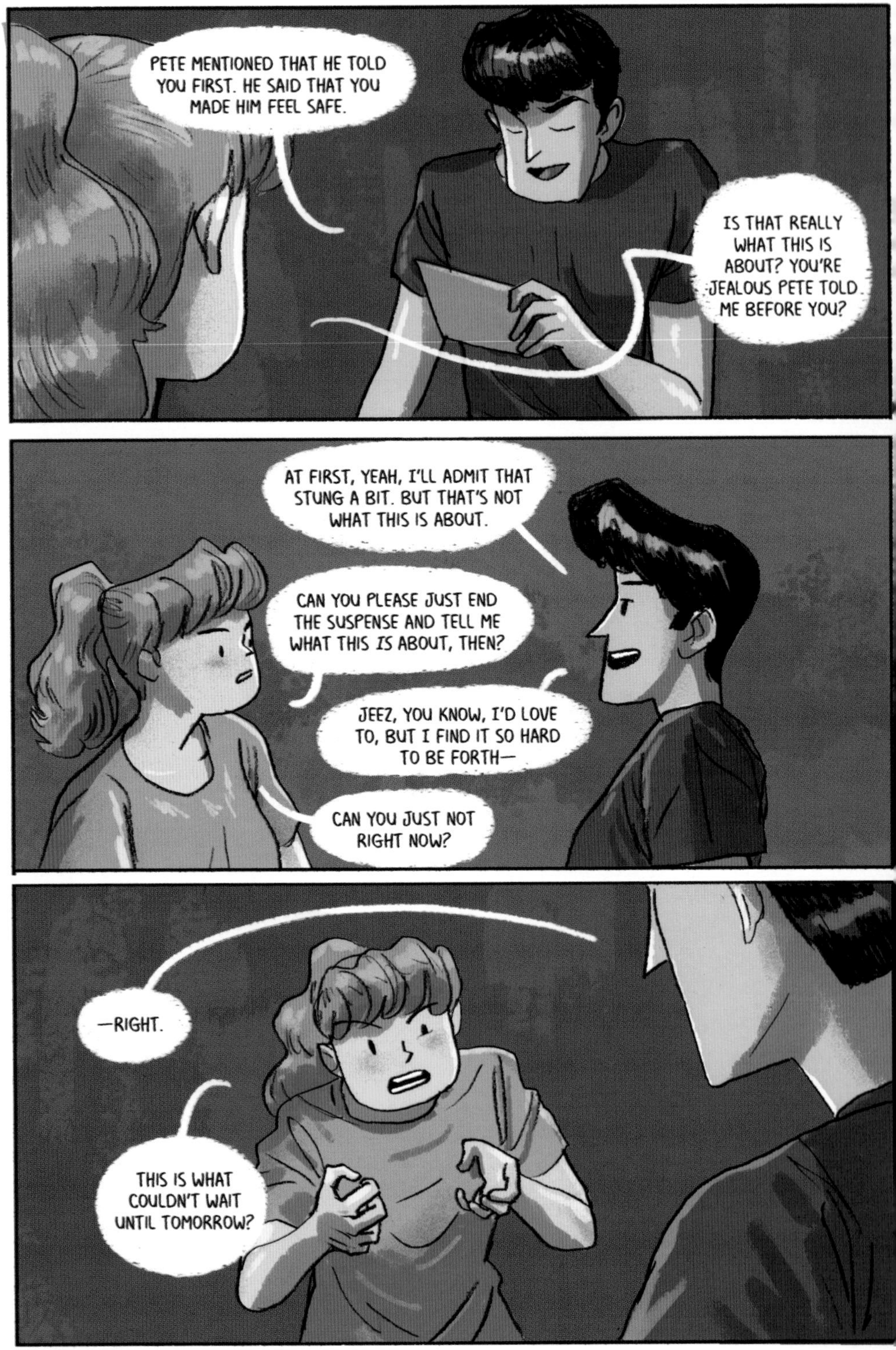
PETE MENTIONED THAT HE TOLD YOU FIRST. HE SAID THAT YOU MADE HIM FEEL SAFE.
IS THAT REALLY WHAT THIS IS ABOUT? YOU'RE JEALOUS PETE TOLD ME BEFORE YOU?
AT FIRST, YEAH, I'LL ADMIT THAT STUNG A BIT. BUT THAT'S NOT WHAT THIS IS ABOUT.
CAN YOU PLEASE JUST END THE SUSPENSE AND TELL ME WHAT THIS *IS* ABOUT, THEN?
JEEZ, YOU KNOW, I'D LOVE TO, BUT I FIND IT SO HARD TO BE FORTH—
CAN YOU JUST NOT RIGHT NOW?
—RIGHT.
THIS IS WHAT COULDN'T WAIT UNTIL TOMORROW?

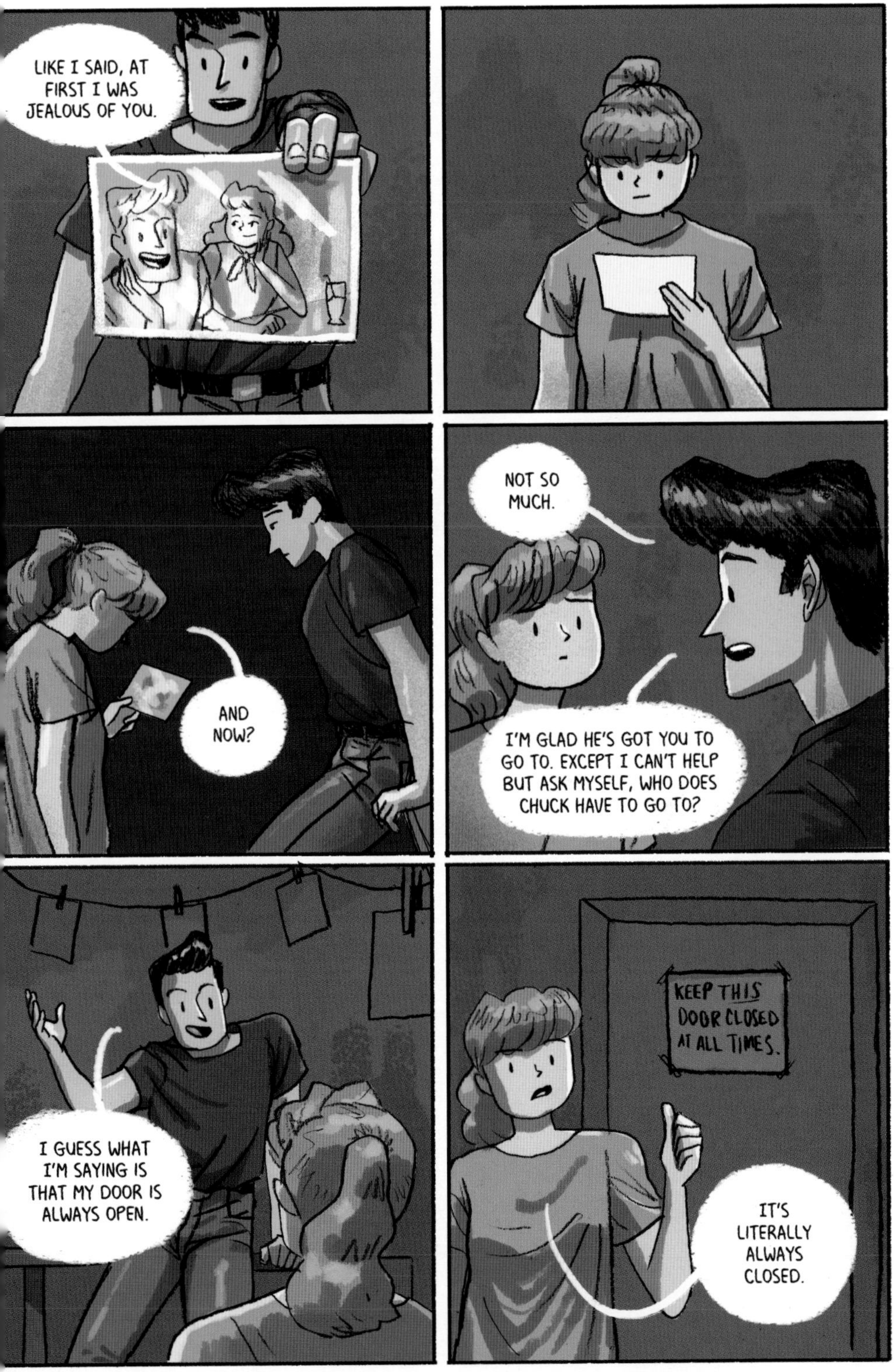
LIKE I SAID, AT FIRST I WAS JEALOUS OF YOU.
AND NOW?
NOT SO MUCH.
I'M GLAD HE'S GOT YOU TO GO TO. EXCEPT I CAN'T HELP BUT ASK MYSELF, WHO DOES CHUCK HAVE TO GO TO?
I GUESS WHAT I'M SAYING IS THAT MY DOOR IS ALWAYS OPEN.
KEEP THIS DOOR CLOSED AT ALL TIMES.
IT'S LITERALLY ALWAYS CLOSED.

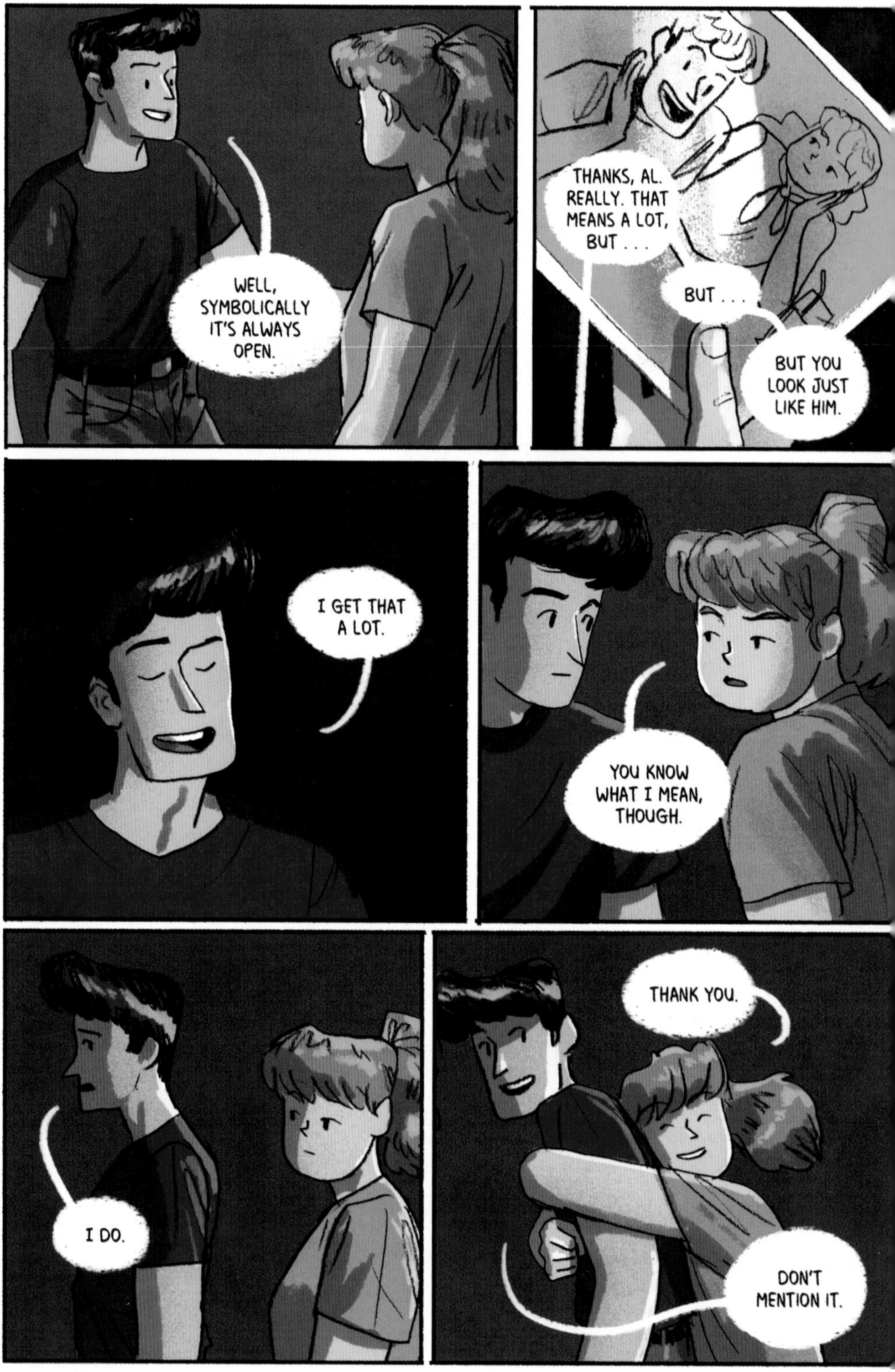
WELL, SYMBOLICALLY IT'S ALWAYS OPEN.
THANKS, AL. REALLY. THAT MEANS A LOT, BUT . . .
BUT . . .
BUT YOU LOOK JUST LIKE HIM.
I GET THAT A LOT.
YOU KNOW WHAT I MEAN, THOUGH.
I DO.
THANK YOU.
DON'T MENTION IT.

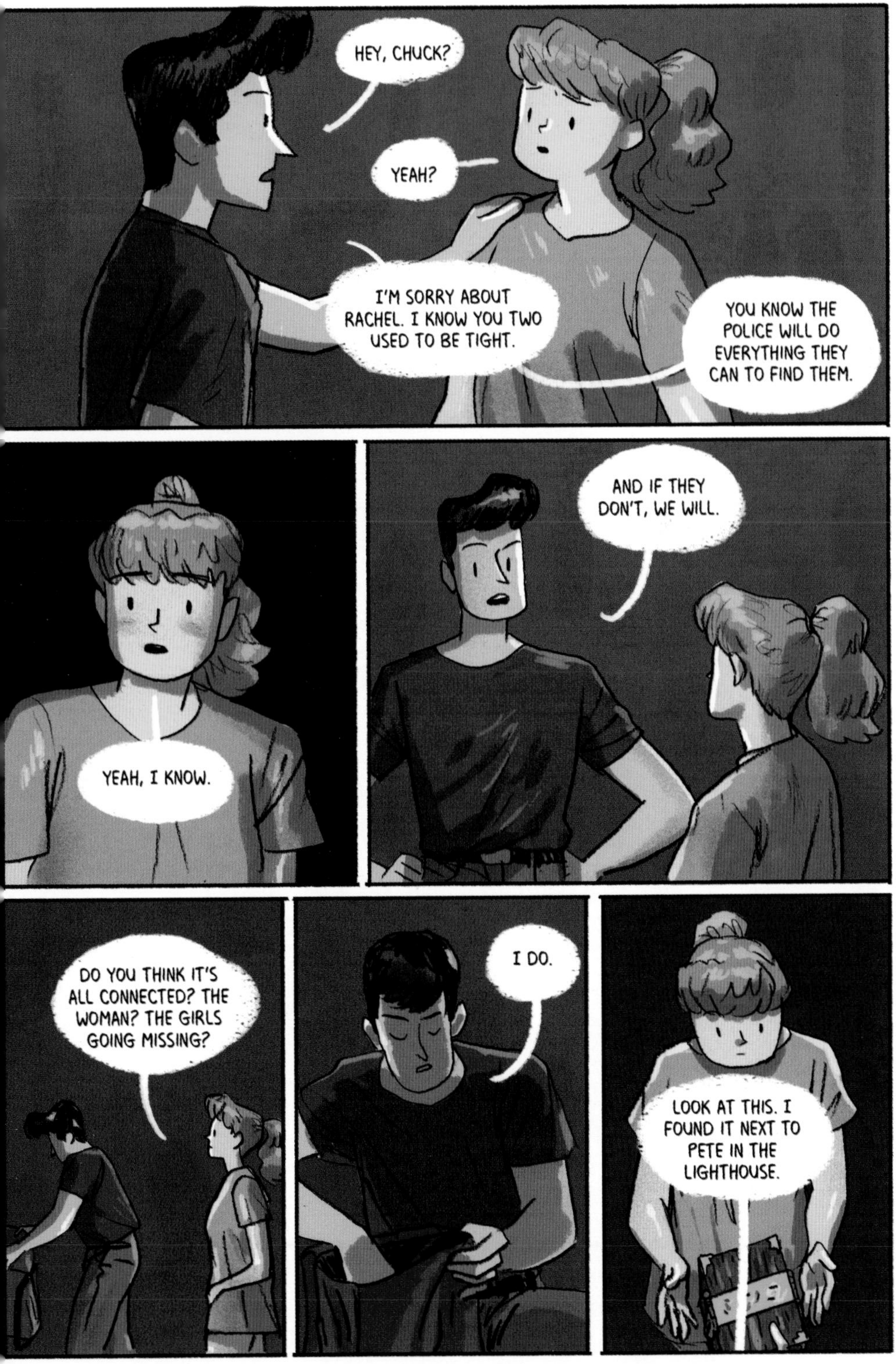
HEY, CHUCK?
YEAH?
I'M SORRY ABOUT RACHEL. I KNOW YOU TWO USED TO BE TIGHT.
YOU KNOW THE POLICE WILL DO EVERYTHING THEY CAN TO FIND THEM.
YEAH, I KNOW.
AND IF THEY DON'T, WE WILL.
DO YOU THINK IT'S ALL CONNECTED? THE WOMAN? THE GIRLS GOING MISSING?
I DO.
LOOK AT THIS. I FOUND IT NEXT TO PETE IN THE LIGHTHOUSE.

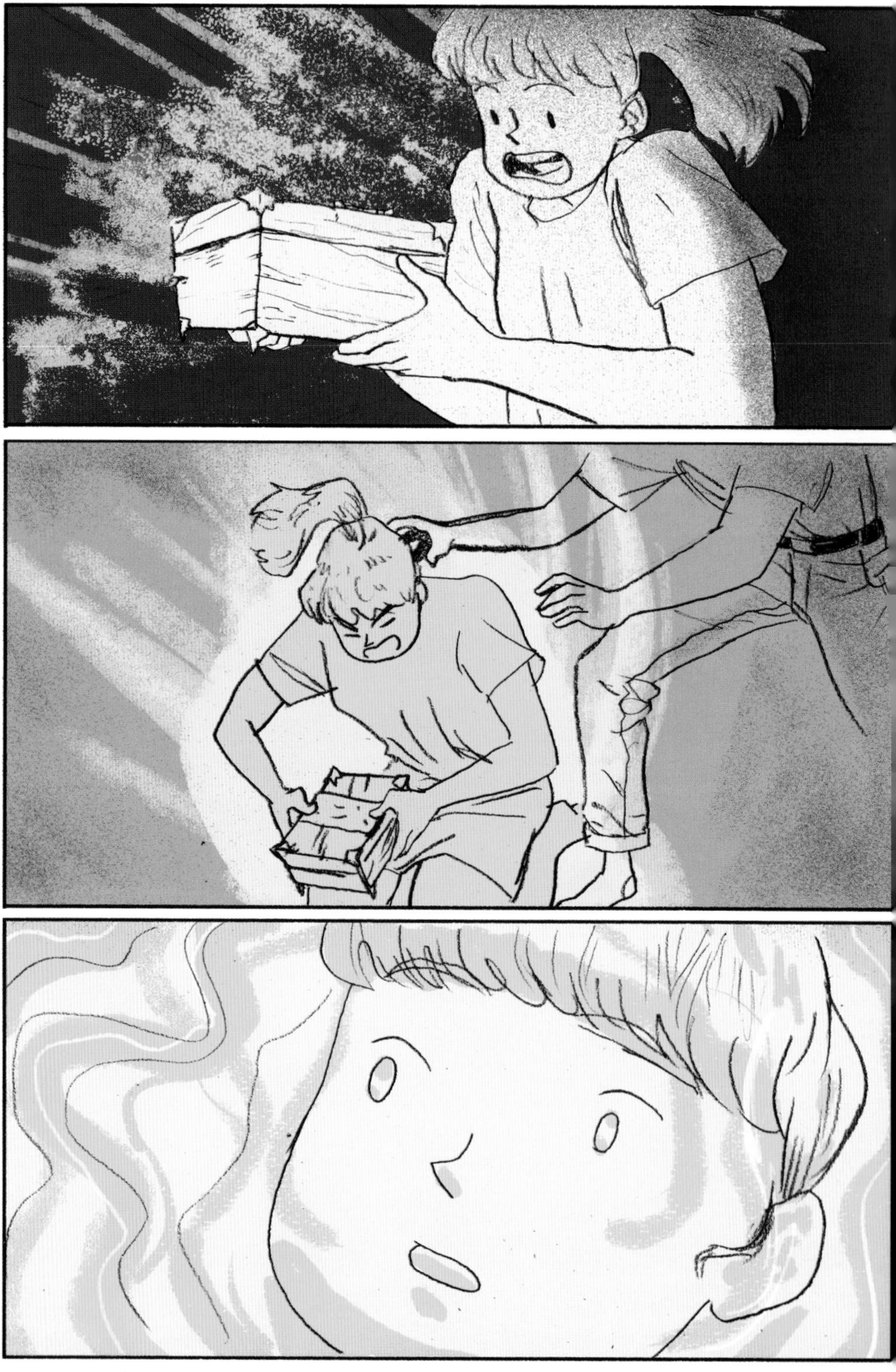

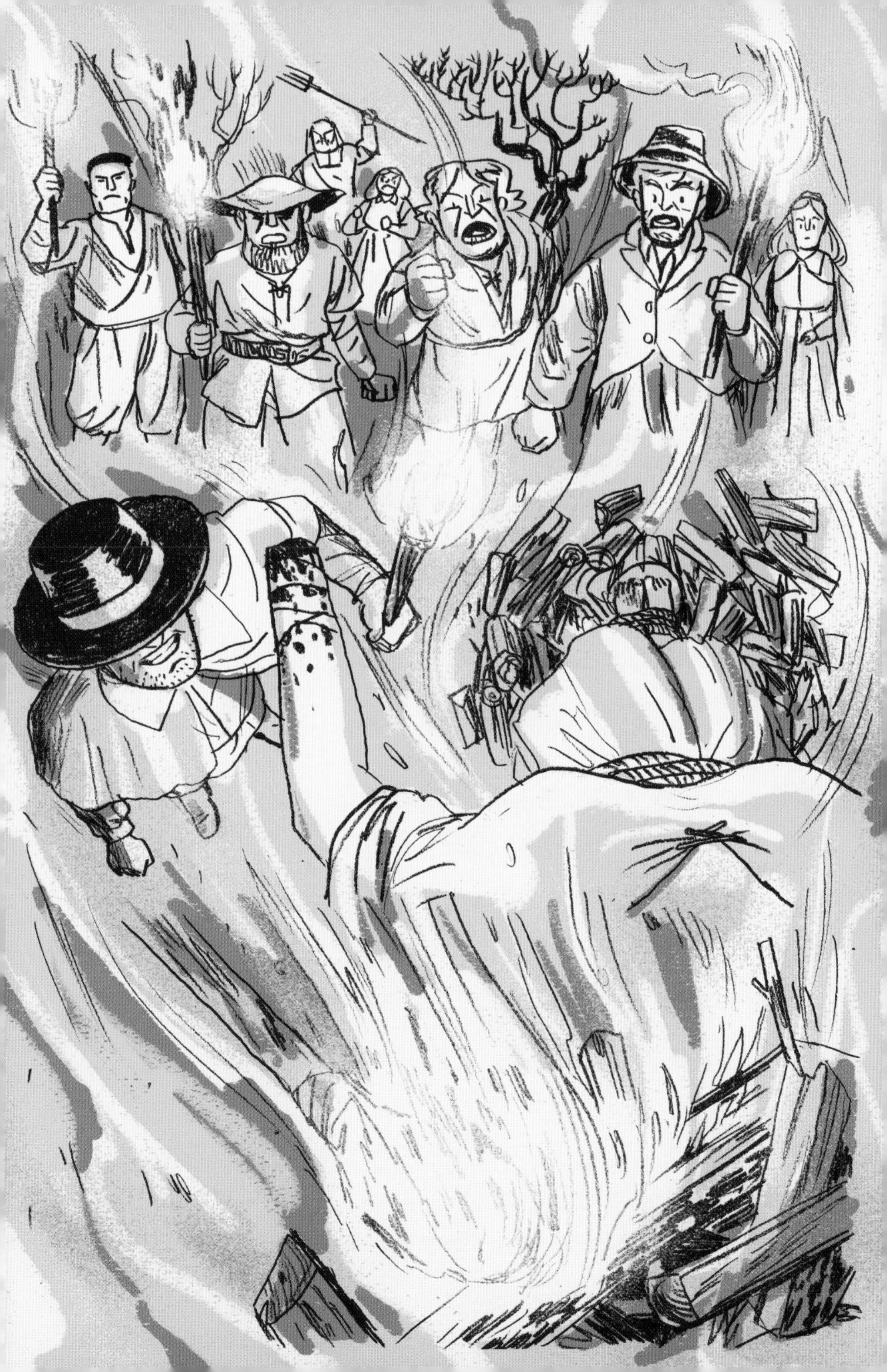

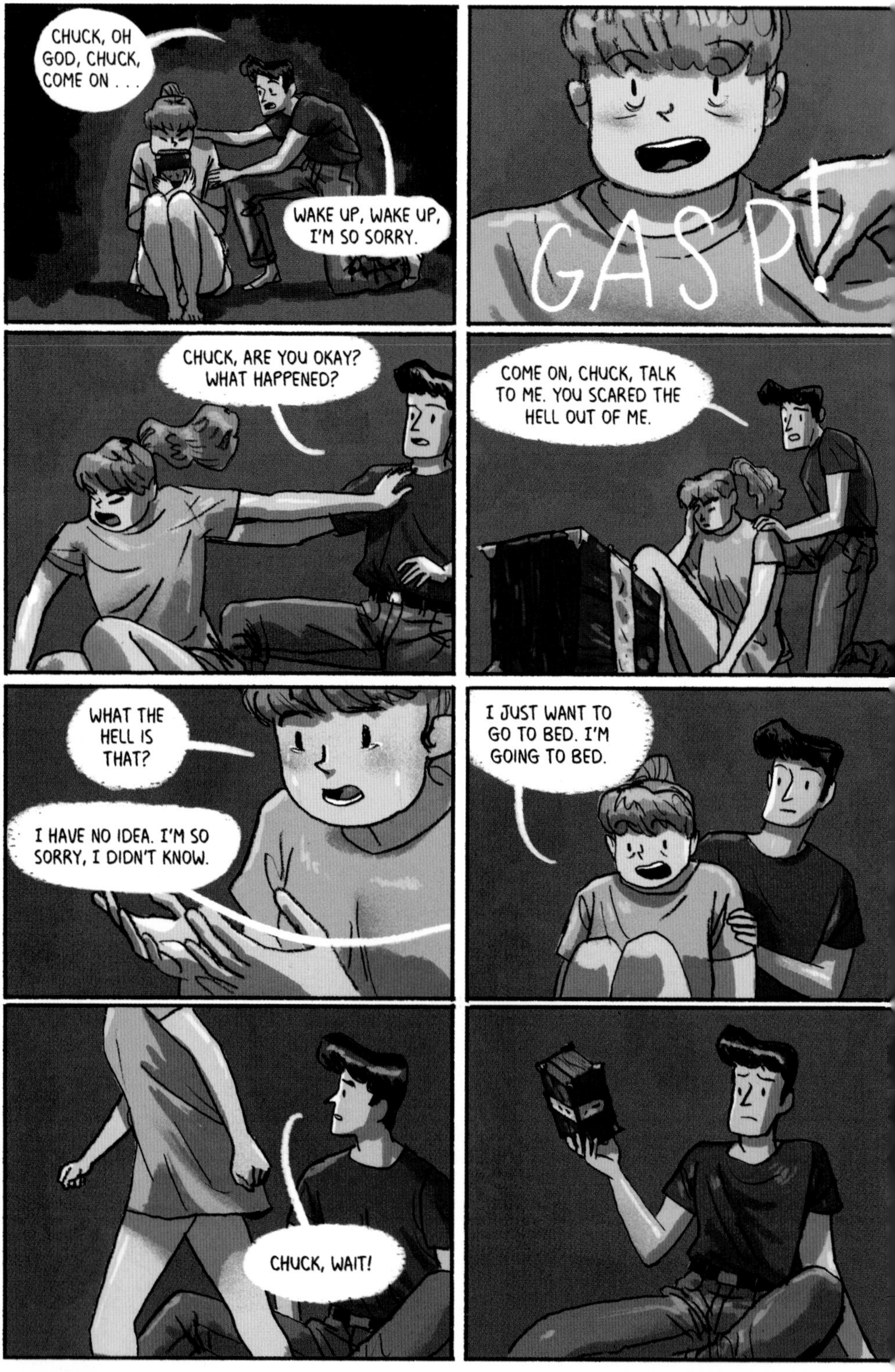

CHUCK, OH GOD, CHUCK, COME ON . . .
WAKE UP, WAKE UP, I'M SO SORRY.
GASP!
CHUCK, ARE YOU OKAY? WHAT HAPPENED?
COME ON, CHUCK, TALK TO ME. YOU SCARED THE HELL OUT OF ME.
WHAT THE HELL IS THAT?
I HAVE NO IDEA. I'M SO SORRY, I DIDN'T KNOW.
I JUST WANT TO GO TO BED. I'M GOING TO BED.
CHUCK, WAIT!

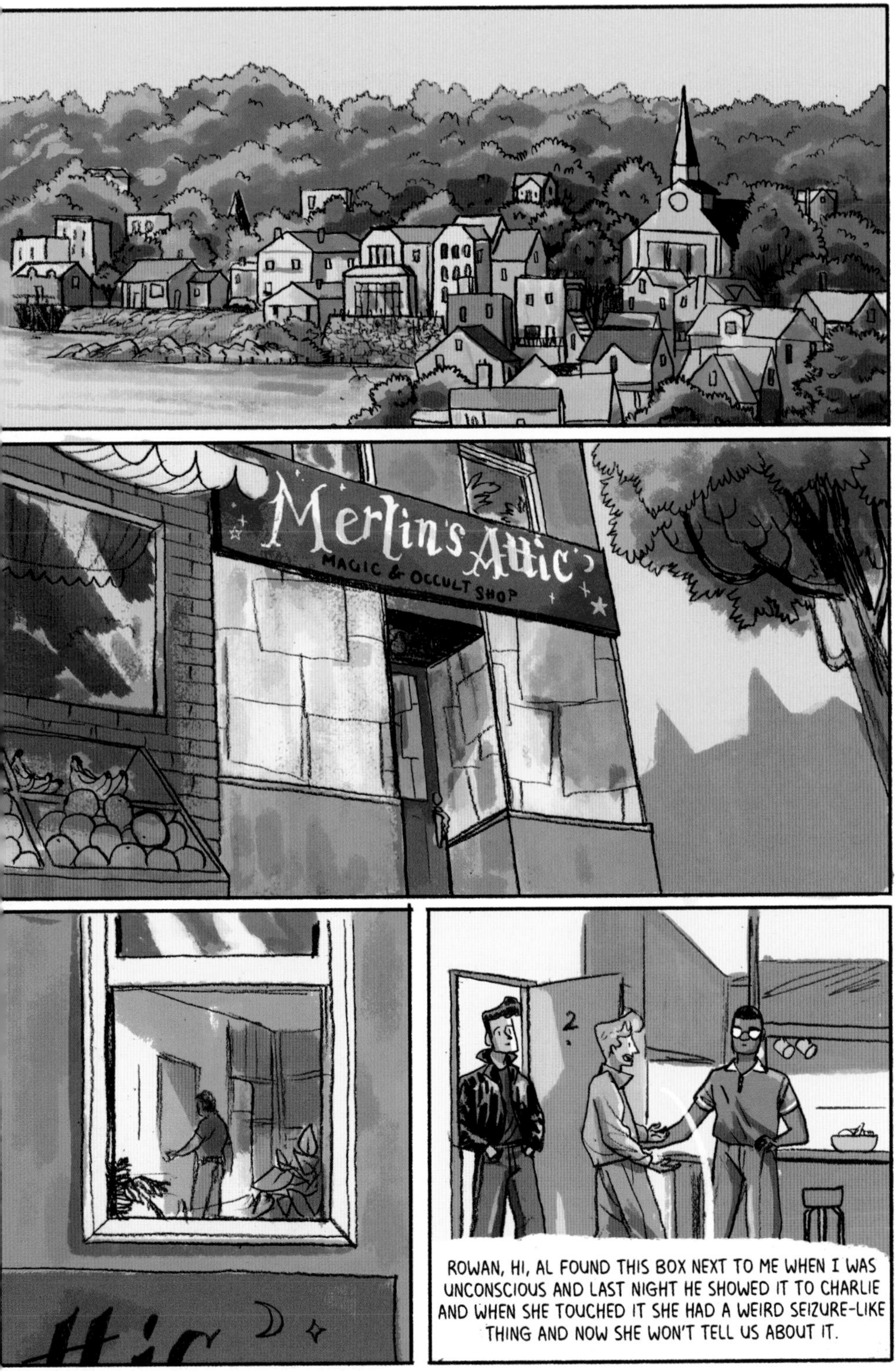
Merlin's Attic
MAGIC & OCCULT SHOP
ROWAN, HI, AL FOUND THIS BOX NEXT TO ME WHEN I WAS UNCONSCIOUS AND LAST NIGHT HE SHOWED IT TO CHARLIE AND WHEN SHE TOUCHED IT SHE HAD A WEIRD SEIZURE-LIKE THING AND NOW SHE WON'T TELL US ABOUT IT.

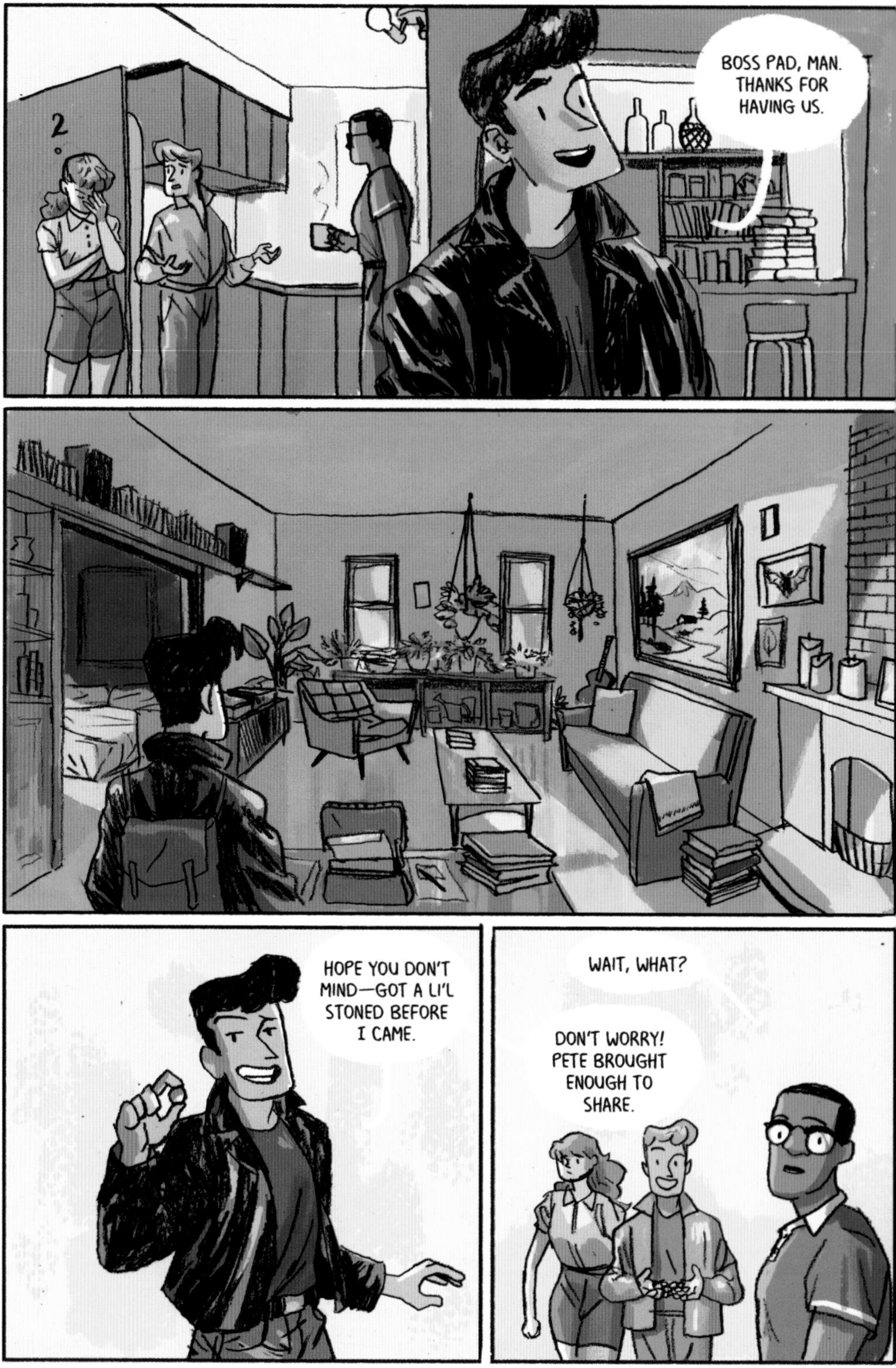
BOSS PAD, MAN. THANKS FOR HAVING US.
HOPE YOU DON'T MIND—GOT A LI'L STONED BEFORE I CAME.
WAIT, WHAT?
DON'T WORRY! PETE BROUGHT ENOUGH TO SHARE.

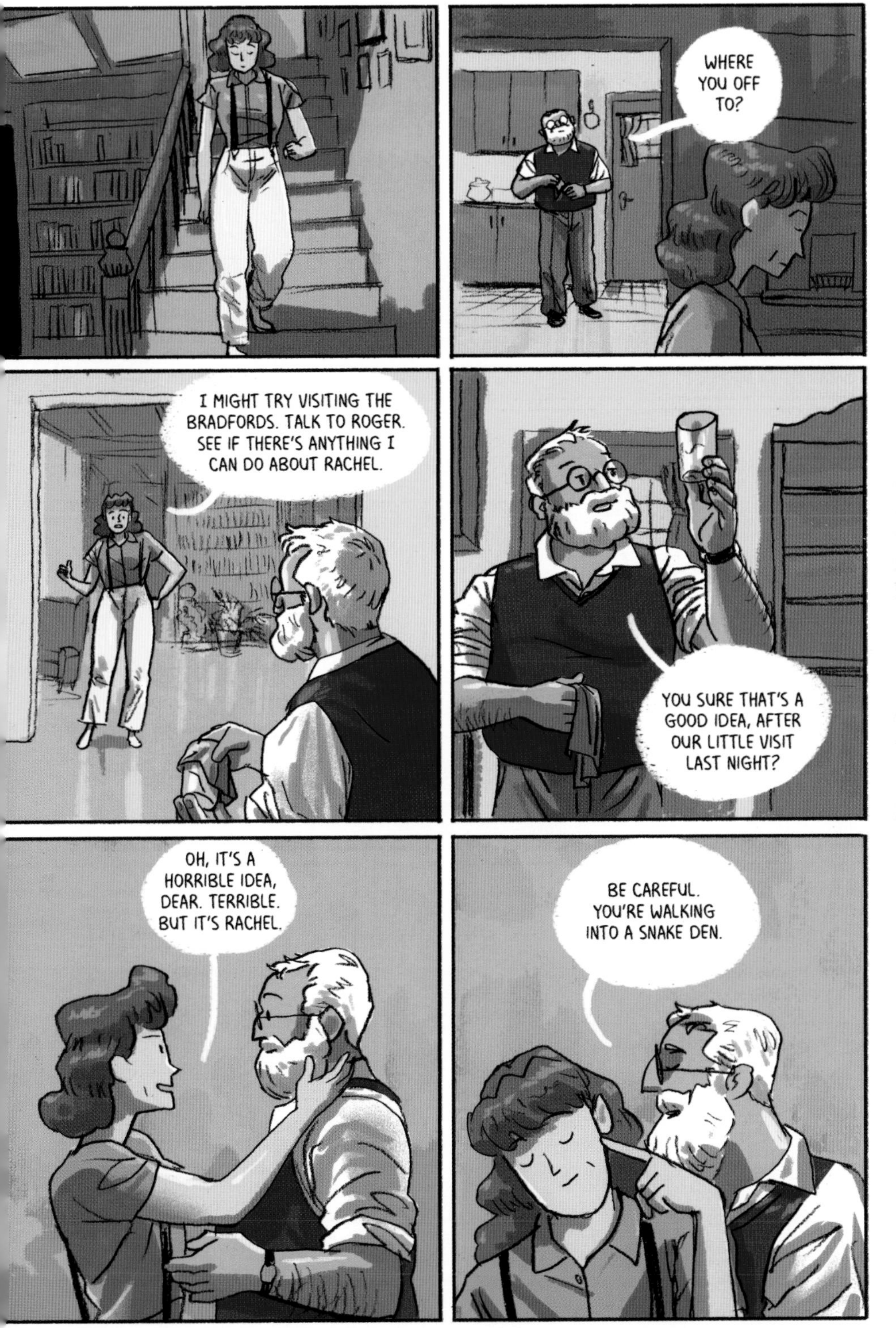
WHERE YOU OFF TO?
I MIGHT TRY VISITING THE BRADFORDS. TALK TO ROGER. SEE IF THERE'S ANYTHING I CAN DO ABOUT RACHEL.
YOU SURE THAT'S A GOOD IDEA, AFTER OUR LITTLE VISIT LAST NIGHT?
OH, IT'S A HORRIBLE IDEA, DEAR. TERRIBLE. BUT IT'S RACHEL.
BE CAREFUL. YOU'RE WALKING INTO A SNAKE DEN.

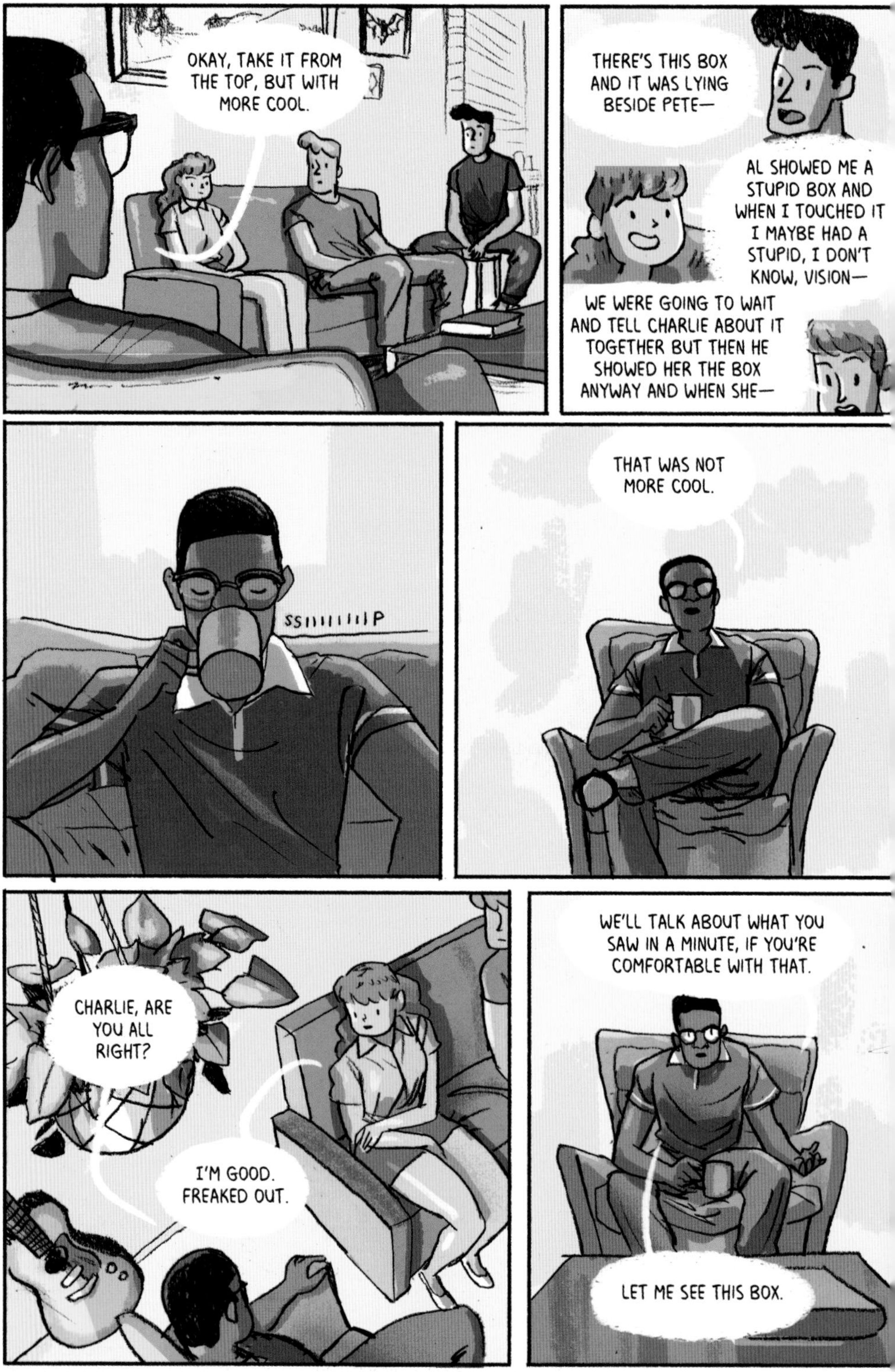
OKAY, TAKE IT FROM THE TOP, BUT WITH MORE COOL.
THERE'S THIS BOX AND IT WAS LYING BESIDE PETE—
AL SHOWED ME A STUPID BOX AND WHEN I TOUCHED IT I MAYBE HAD A STUPID, I DON'T KNOW, VISION—
WE WERE GOING TO WAIT AND TELL CHARLIE ABOUT IT TOGETHER BUT THEN HE SHOWED HER THE BOX ANYWAY AND WHEN SHE—
SSIIIIIIIP
THAT WAS NOT MORE COOL.
CHARLIE, ARE YOU ALL RIGHT?
I'M GOOD. FREAKED OUT.
WE'LL TALK ABOUT WHAT YOU SAW IN A MINUTE, IF YOU'RE COMFORTABLE WITH THAT.
LET ME SEE THIS BOX.

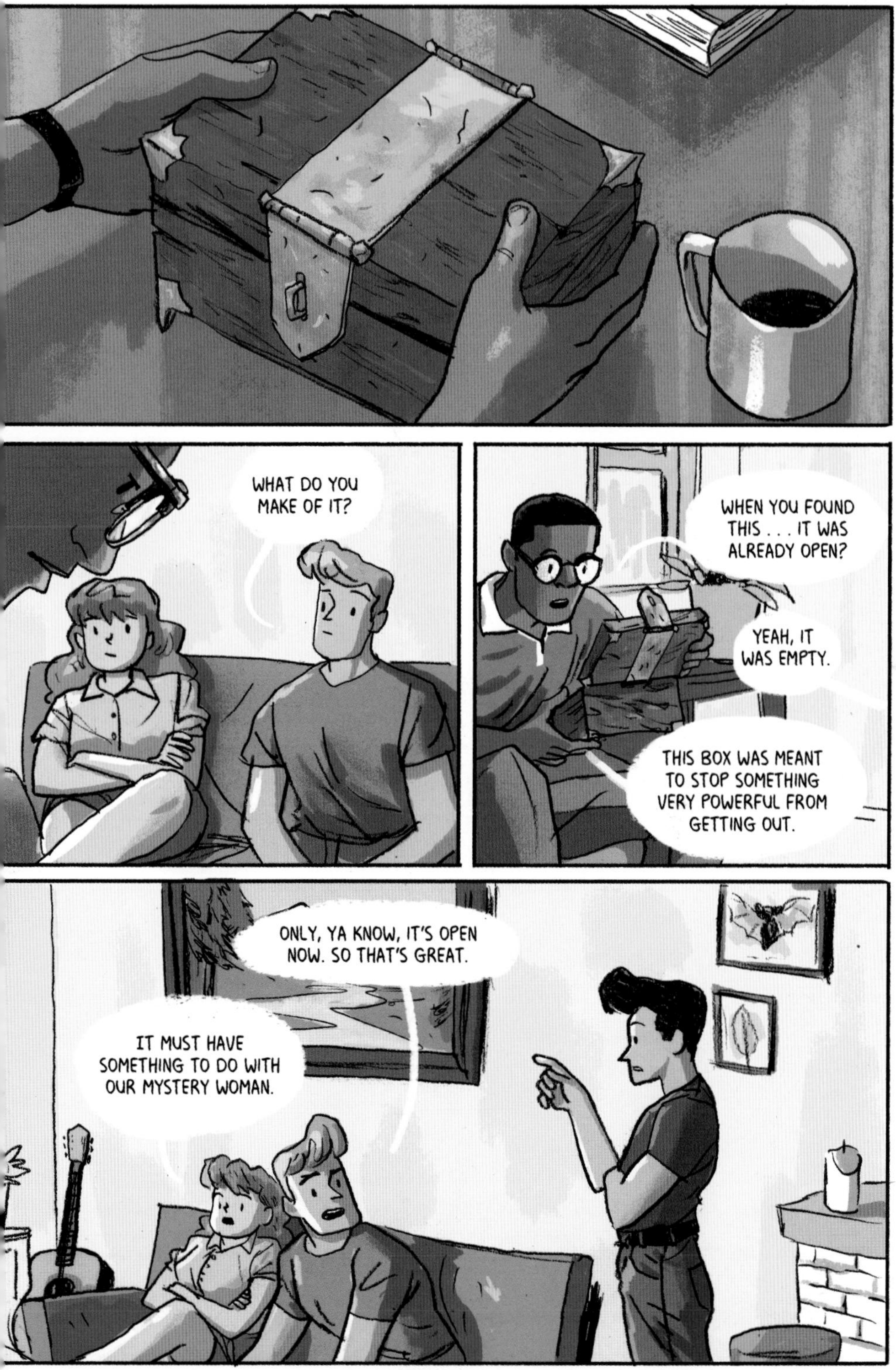
WHAT DO YOU MAKE OF IT?
WHEN YOU FOUND THIS . . . IT WAS ALREADY OPEN?
YEAH, IT WAS EMPTY.
THIS BOX WAS MEANT TO STOP SOMETHING VERY POWERFUL FROM GETTING OUT.
ONLY, YA KNOW, IT'S OPEN NOW. SO THAT'S GREAT.
IT MUST HAVE SOMETHING TO DO WITH OUR MYSTERY WOMAN.

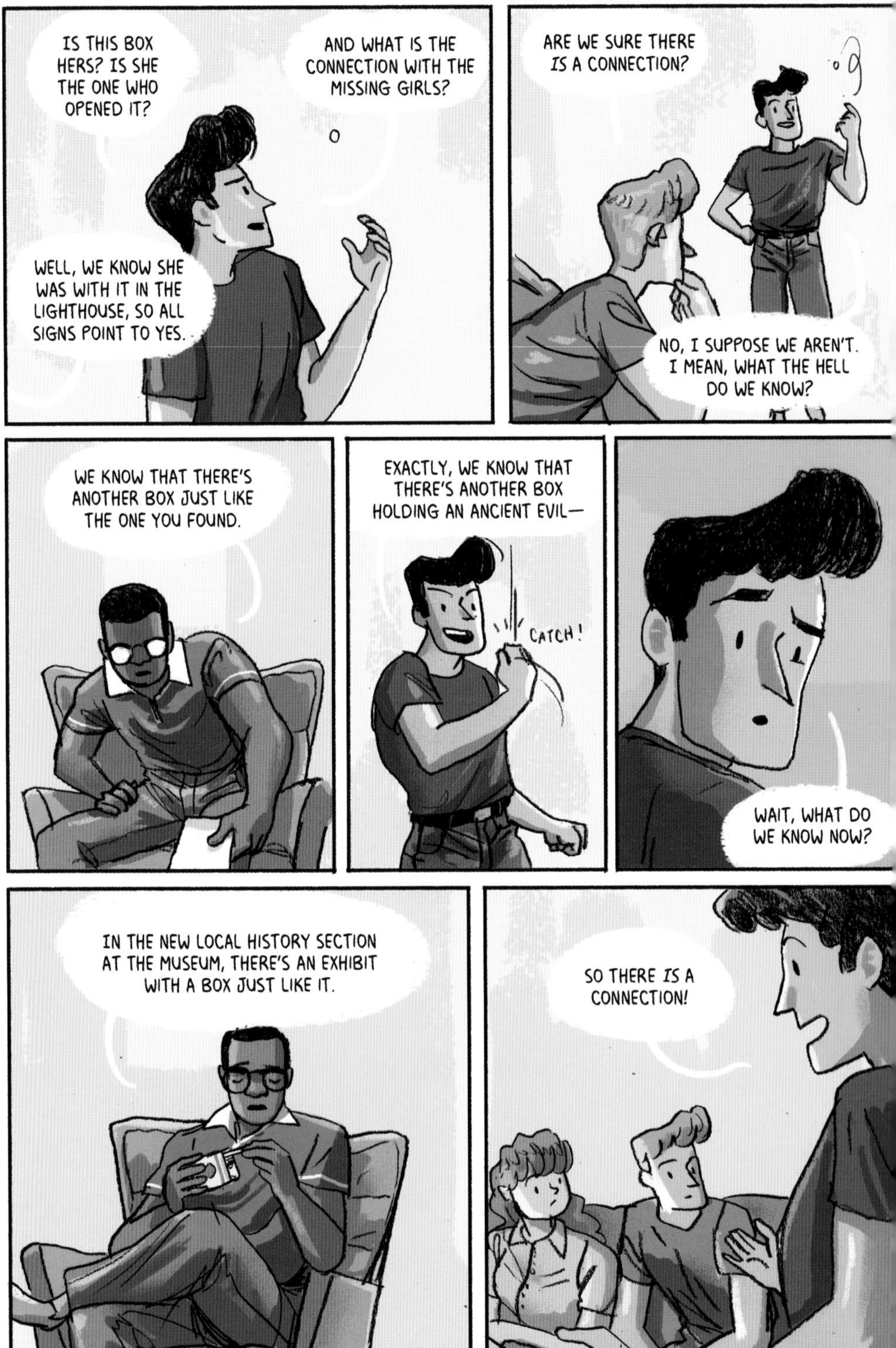
IS THIS BOX HERS? IS SHE THE ONE WHO OPENED IT?
AND WHAT IS THE CONNECTION WITH THE MISSING GIRLS?
WELL, WE KNOW SHE WAS WITH IT IN THE LIGHTHOUSE, SO ALL SIGNS POINT TO YES.
ARE WE SURE THERE *IS* A CONNECTION?
NO, I SUPPOSE WE AREN'T. I MEAN, WHAT THE HELL DO WE KNOW?
WE KNOW THAT THERE'S ANOTHER BOX JUST LIKE THE ONE YOU FOUND.
EXACTLY, WE KNOW THAT THERE'S ANOTHER BOX HOLDING AN ANCIENT EVIL—
CATCH!
WAIT, WHAT DO WE KNOW NOW?
IN THE NEW LOCAL HISTORY SECTION AT THE MUSEUM, THERE'S AN EXHIBIT WITH A BOX JUST LIKE IT.
SO THERE *IS* A CONNECTION!

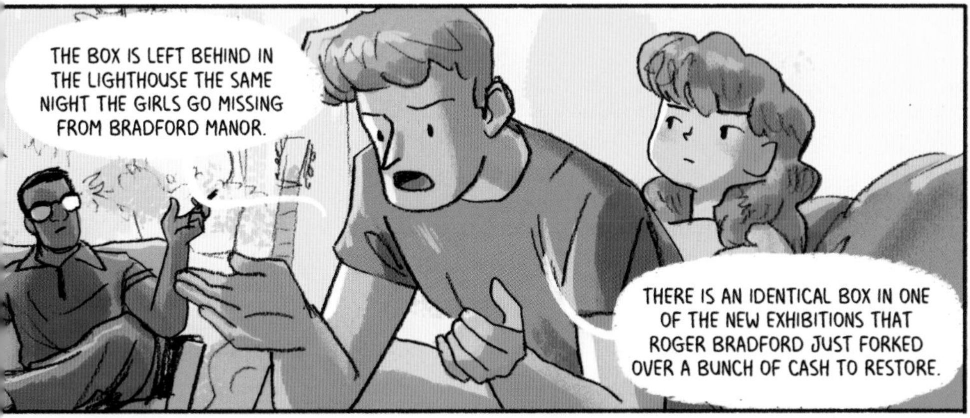
THE BOX IS LEFT BEHIND IN THE LIGHTHOUSE THE SAME NIGHT THE GIRLS GO MISSING FROM BRADFORD MANOR.
THERE IS AN IDENTICAL BOX IN ONE OF THE NEW EXHIBITIONS THAT ROGER BRADFORD JUST FORKED OVER A BUNCH OF CASH TO RESTORE.

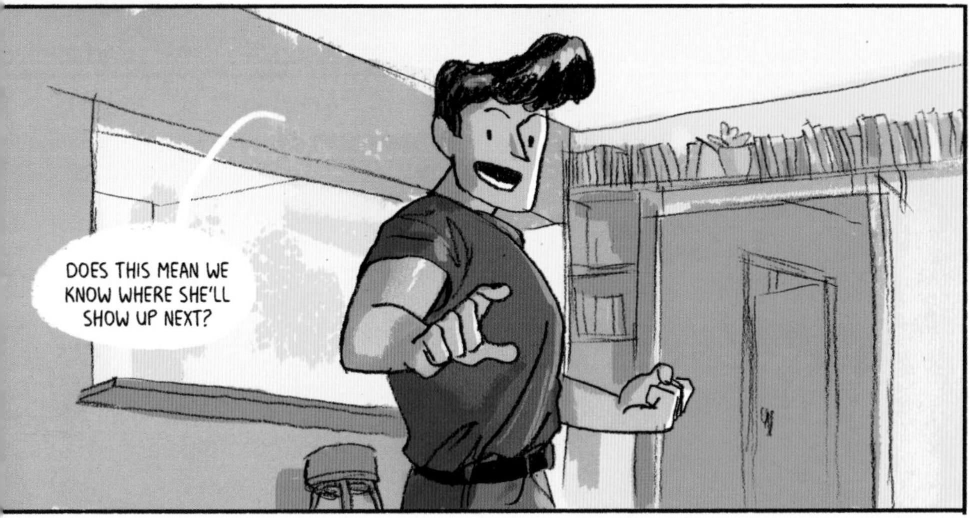
DOES THIS MEAN WE KNOW WHERE SHE'LL SHOW UP NEXT?

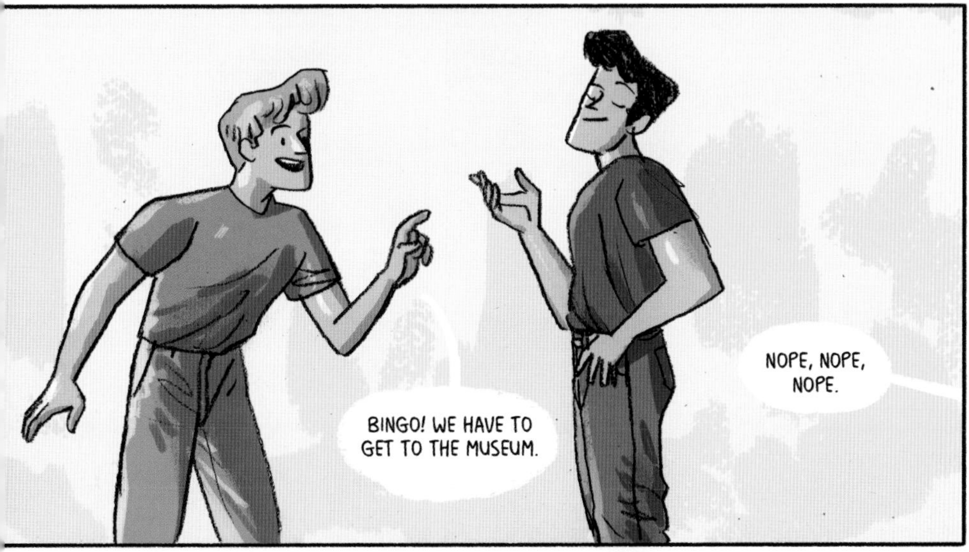
BINGO! WE HAVE TO GET TO THE MUSEUM.
NOPE, NOPE, NOPE.

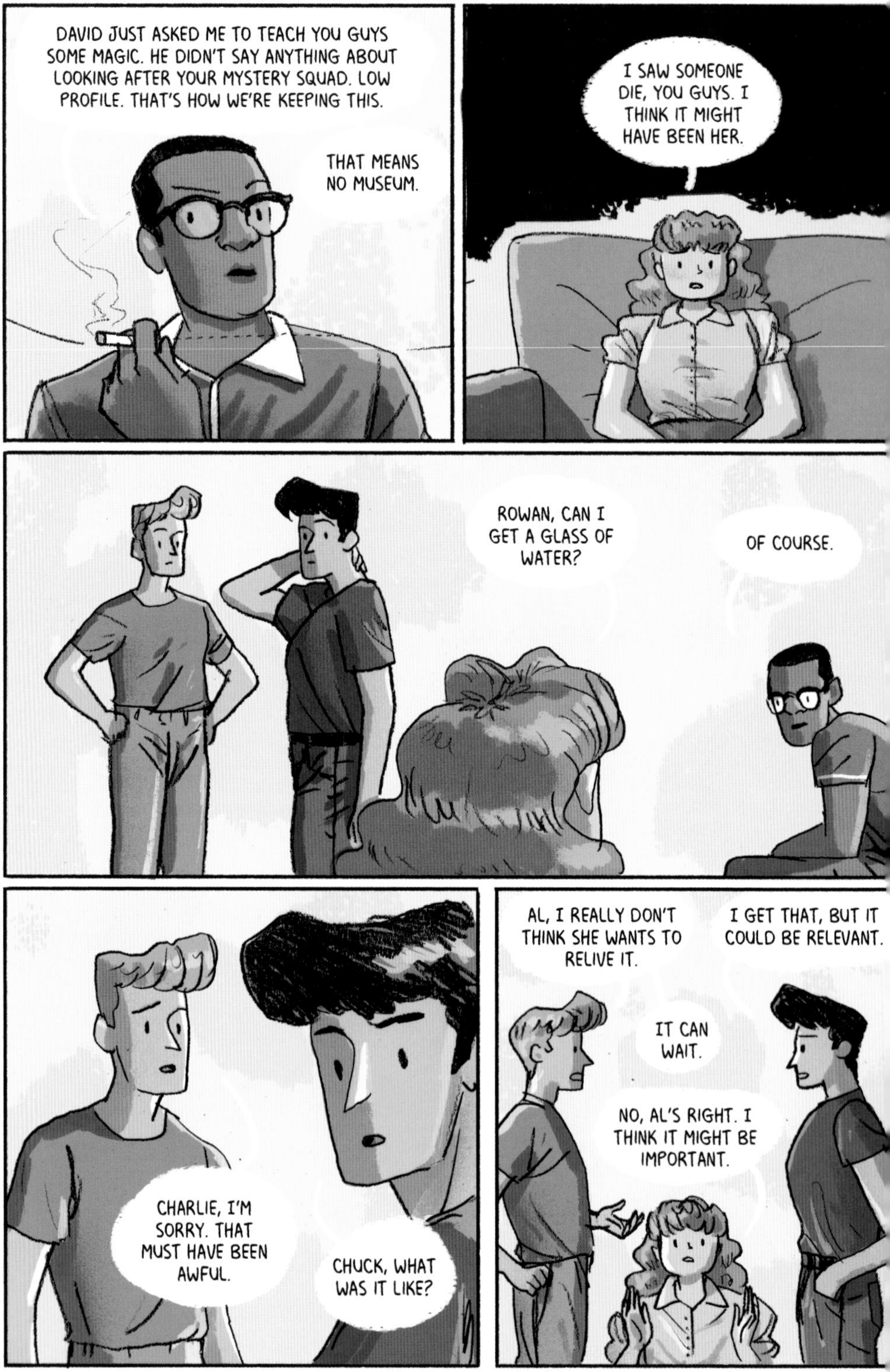
DAVID JUST ASKED ME TO TEACH YOU GUYS SOME MAGIC. HE DIDN'T SAY ANYTHING ABOUT LOOKING AFTER YOUR MYSTERY SQUAD. LOW PROFILE. THAT'S HOW WE'RE KEEPING THIS.
THAT MEANS NO MUSEUM.
I SAW SOMEONE DIE, YOU GUYS. I THINK IT MIGHT HAVE BEEN HER.
ROWAN, CAN I GET A GLASS OF WATER?
OF COURSE.
CHARLIE, I'M SORRY. THAT MUST HAVE BEEN AWFUL.
CHUCK, WHAT WAS IT LIKE?
AL, I REALLY DON'T THINK SHE WANTS TO RELIVE IT.
I GET THAT, BUT IT COULD BE RELEVANT.
IT CAN WAIT.
NO, AL'S RIGHT. I THINK IT MIGHT BE IMPORTANT.

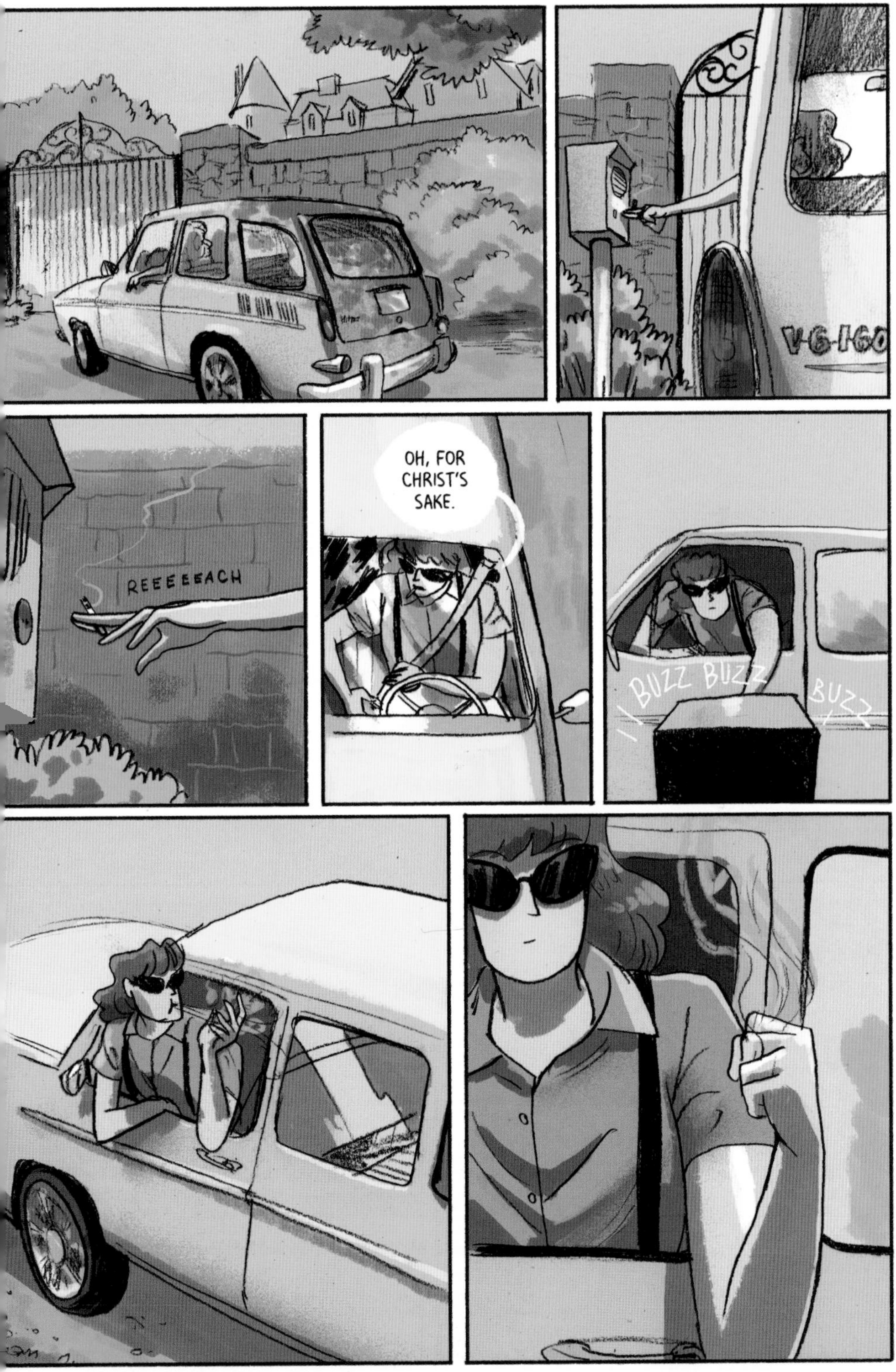

V-G-160
REEEEEACH
OH, FOR CHRIST'S SAKE.
BUZZ BUZZ BUZZ

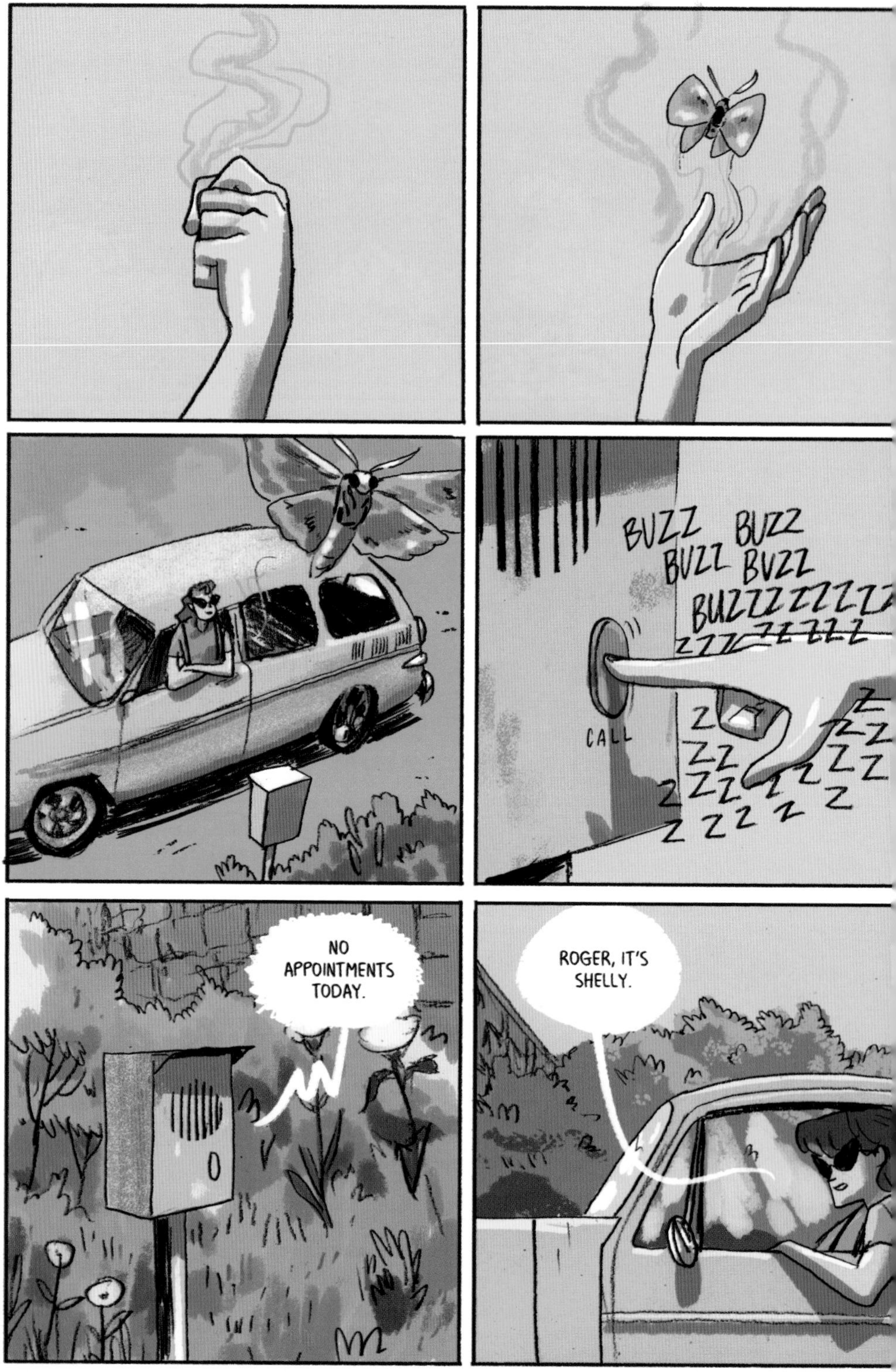
BUZZ BUZZ
BUZZ BUZZ
BUZZZZZZZZ
CALL
NO APPOINTMENTS TODAY.
ROGER, IT'S SHELLY.

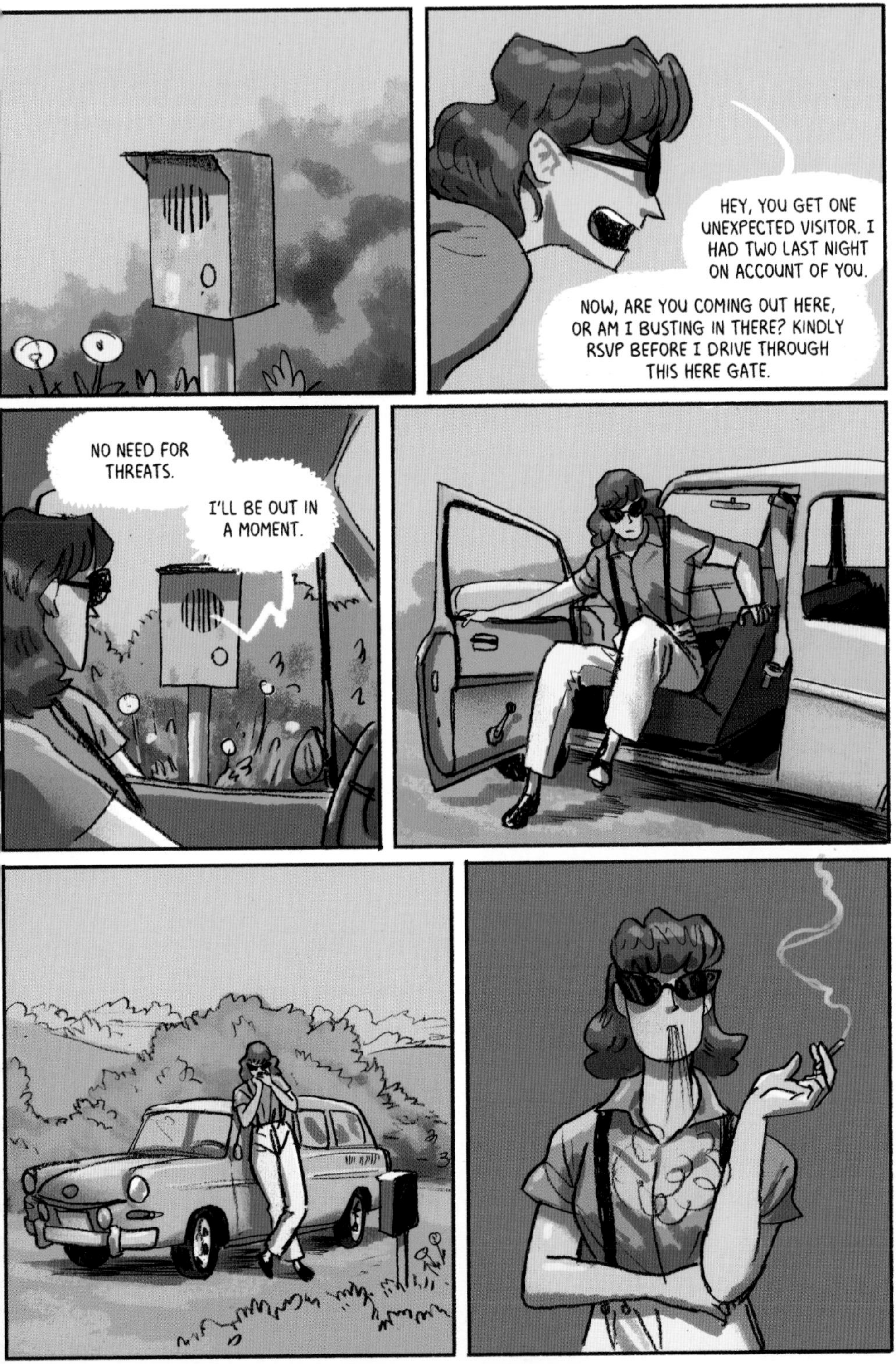
HEY, YOU GET ONE UNEXPECTED VISITOR. I HAD TWO LAST NIGHT ON ACCOUNT OF YOU.
NOW, ARE YOU COMING OUT HERE, OR AM I BUSTING IN THERE? KINDLY RSVP BEFORE I DRIVE THROUGH THIS HERE GATE.
NO NEED FOR THREATS.
I'LL BE OUT IN A MOMENT.

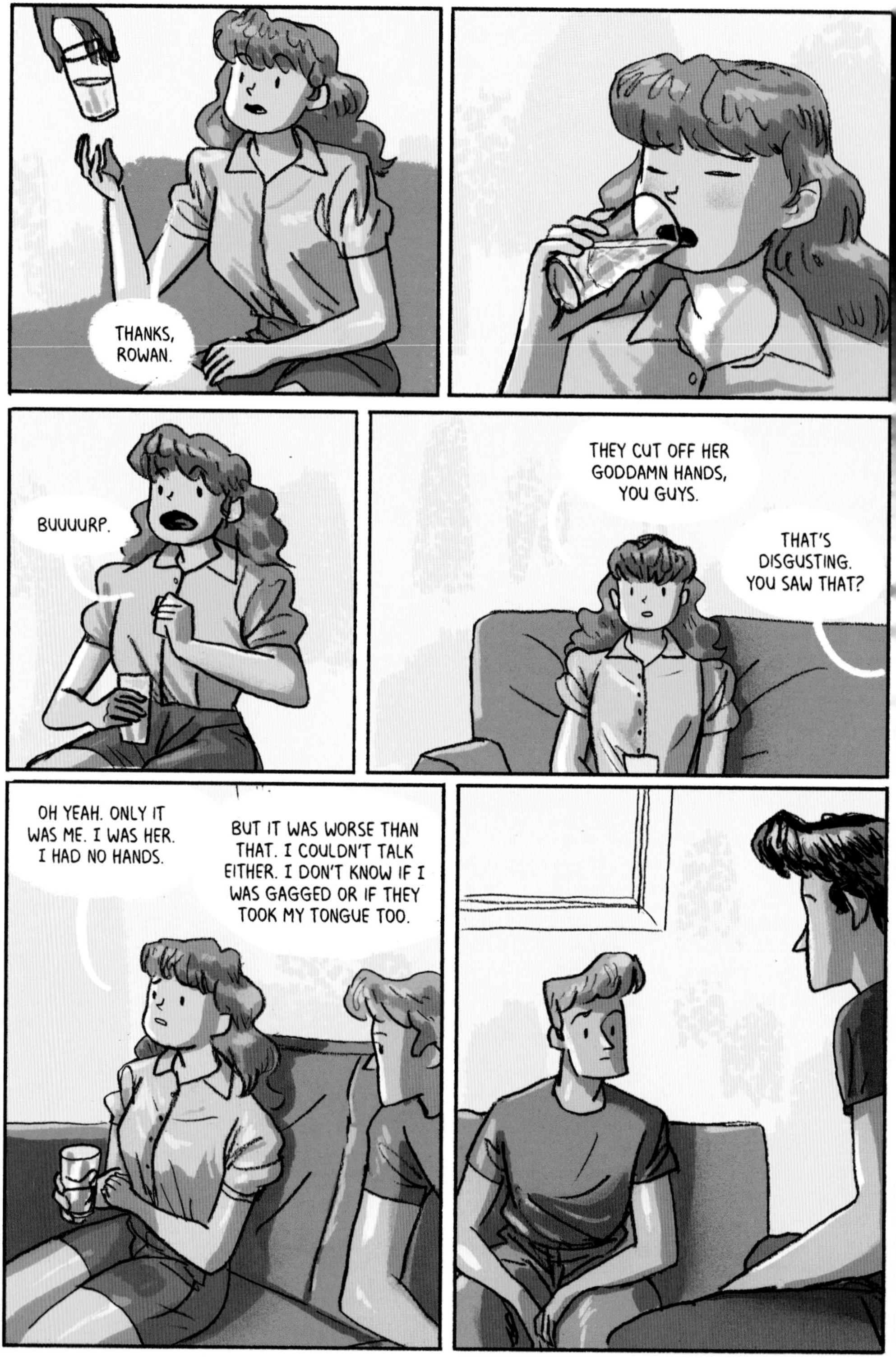
THANKS, ROWAN.
BUUUURP.
THEY CUT OFF HER GODDAMN HANDS, YOU GUYS.
THAT'S DISGUSTING. YOU SAW THAT?
OH YEAH. ONLY IT WAS ME. I WAS HER. I HAD NO HANDS.
BUT IT WAS WORSE THAN THAT. I COULDN'T TALK EITHER. I DON'T KNOW IF I WAS GAGGED OR IF THEY TOOK MY TONGUE TOO.

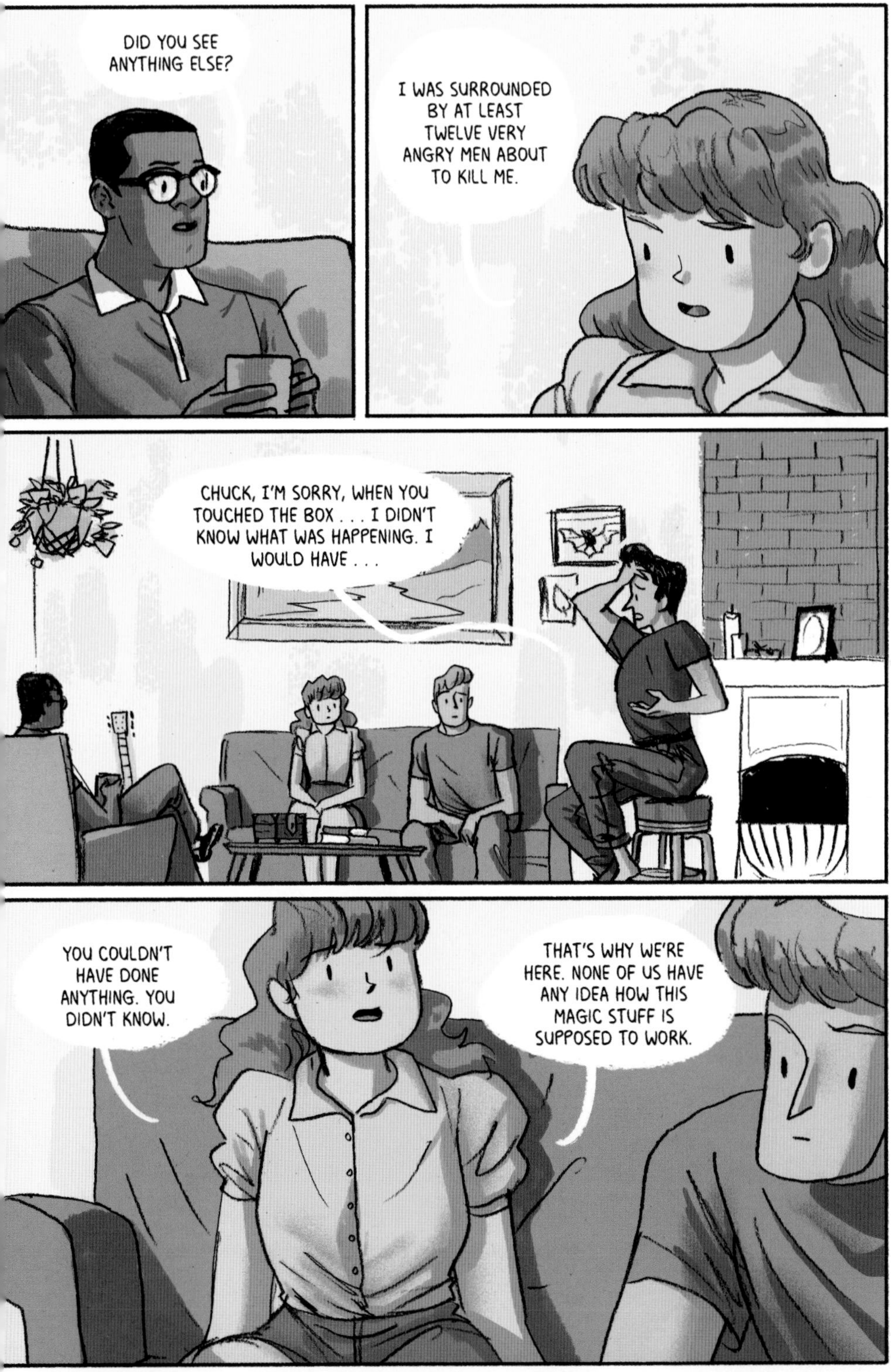
DID YOU SEE ANYTHING ELSE?
I WAS SURROUNDED BY AT LEAST TWELVE VERY ANGRY MEN ABOUT TO KILL ME.
CHUCK, I'M SORRY, WHEN YOU TOUCHED THE BOX . . . I DIDN'T KNOW WHAT WAS HAPPENING. I WOULD HAVE . . .
YOU COULDN'T HAVE DONE ANYTHING. YOU DIDN'T KNOW.
THAT'S WHY WE'RE HERE. NONE OF US HAVE ANY IDEA HOW THIS MAGIC STUFF IS SUPPOSED TO WORK.

RIGHT, THE LESSONS! OKAY, LET'S LEARN TO THROW SOME FIREBALLS AND SHIT.

THEN WE'LL GO TO THE MUSEUM AND CHECK OUT THIS BOX. DEAL?

FIREBALLS? THAT'S YOUR FIRST PULL? YOU WANT TO LEARN HOW TO THROW A FIREBALL?

YEAH, TEACH US SOMETHING WE DON'T KNOW.

I THINK YOU MIGHT BE SURPRISED BY HOW MUCH WE CAN DO ALREADY.

I'VE ALREADY GIVEN THE FIRST LESSON.

LOOK AT YOUR STONES.

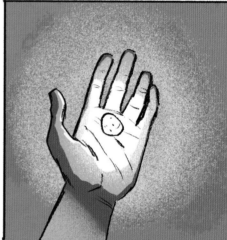

OKAY, THAT'S COOL.

HUH. IT'S PEBBLE NUMBER SEVEN— WHO WOULD HAVE THOUGHT?

ANYONE HAVE NUMBER SEVEN IN THE PEBBLE POOL? BIG MONEY, NUMBER SEVEN? NO?

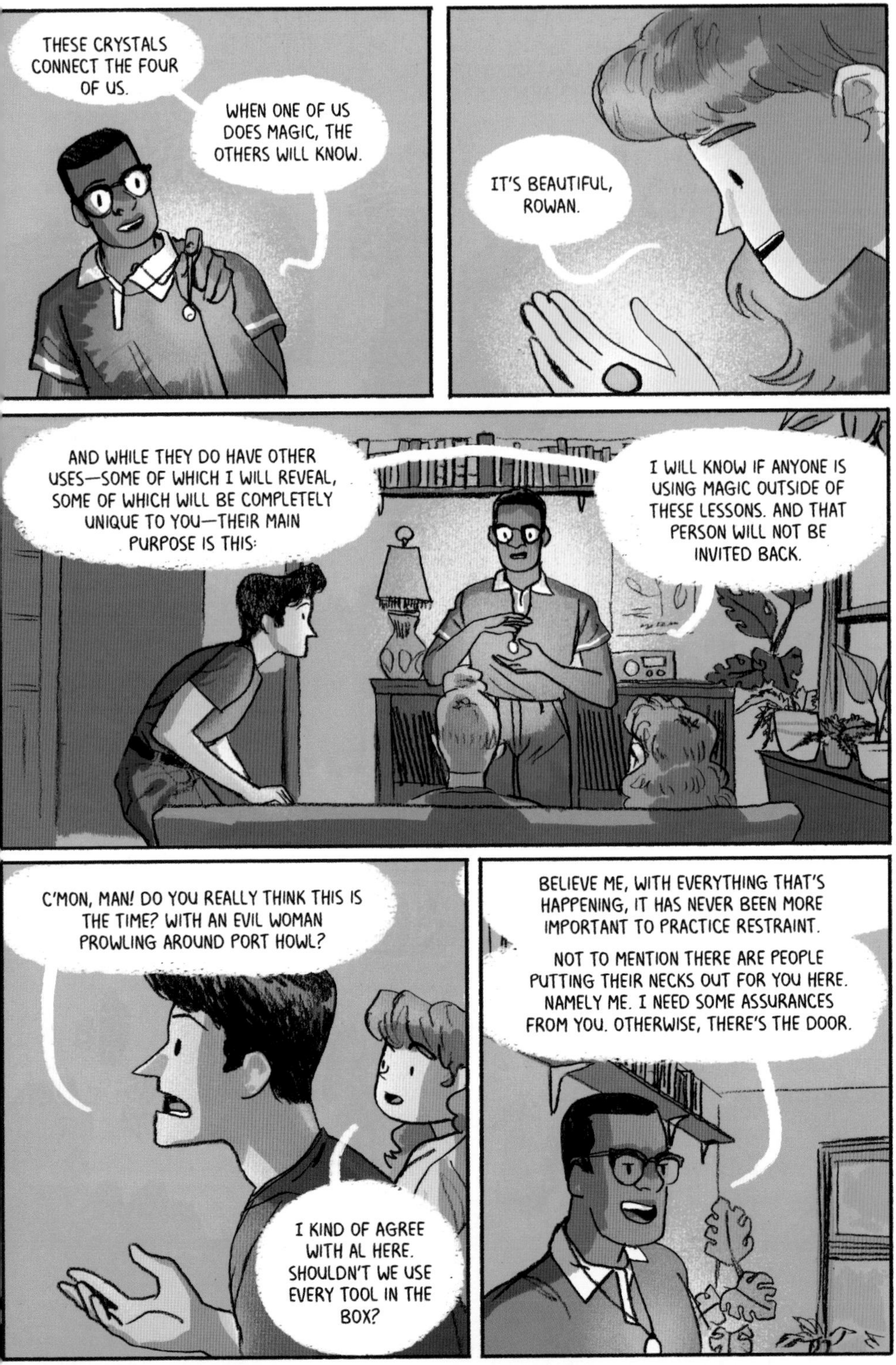
THESE CRYSTALS CONNECT THE FOUR OF US.
WHEN ONE OF US DOES MAGIC, THE OTHERS WILL KNOW.
IT'S BEAUTIFUL, ROWAN.
AND WHILE THEY DO HAVE OTHER USES—SOME OF WHICH I WILL REVEAL, SOME OF WHICH WILL BE COMPLETELY UNIQUE TO YOU—THEIR MAIN PURPOSE IS THIS:
I WILL KNOW IF ANYONE IS USING MAGIC OUTSIDE OF THESE LESSONS. AND THAT PERSON WILL NOT BE INVITED BACK.
C'MON, MAN! DO YOU REALLY THINK THIS IS THE TIME? WITH AN EVIL WOMAN PROWLING AROUND PORT HOWL?
I KIND OF AGREE WITH AL HERE. SHOULDN'T WE USE EVERY TOOL IN THE BOX?
BELIEVE ME, WITH EVERYTHING THAT'S HAPPENING, IT HAS NEVER BEEN MORE IMPORTANT TO PRACTICE RESTRAINT.
NOT TO MENTION THERE ARE PEOPLE PUTTING THEIR NECKS OUT FOR YOU HERE. NAMELY ME. I NEED SOME ASSURANCES FROM YOU. OTHERWISE, THERE'S THE DOOR.

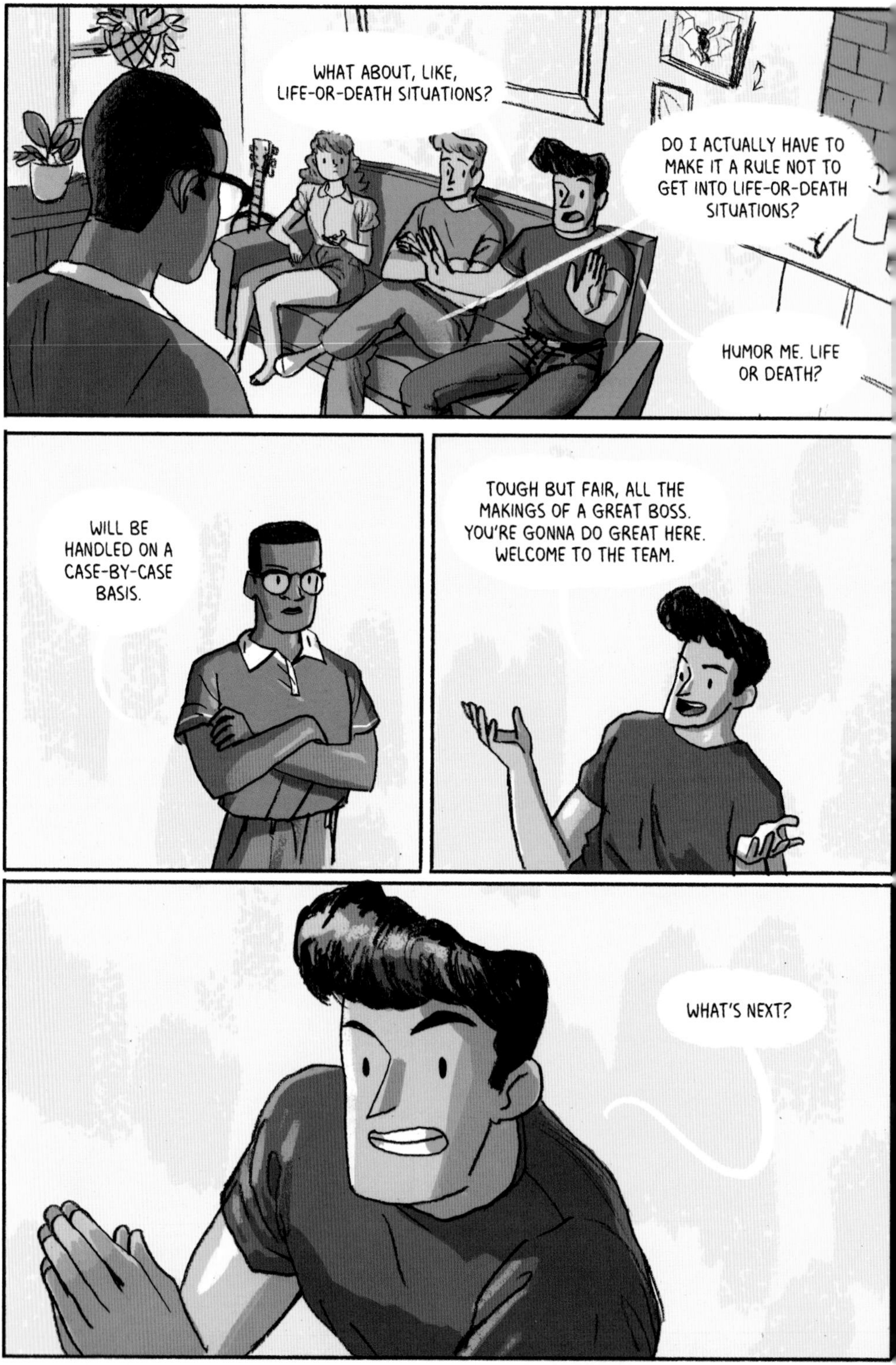
WHAT ABOUT, LIKE, LIFE-OR-DEATH SITUATIONS?
DO I ACTUALLY HAVE TO MAKE IT A RULE NOT TO GET INTO LIFE-OR-DEATH SITUATIONS?
HUMOR ME. LIFE OR DEATH?
WILL BE HANDLED ON A CASE-BY-CASE BASIS.
TOUGH BUT FAIR, ALL THE MAKINGS OF A GREAT BOSS. YOU'RE GONNA DO GREAT HERE. WELCOME TO THE TEAM.
WHAT'S NEXT?

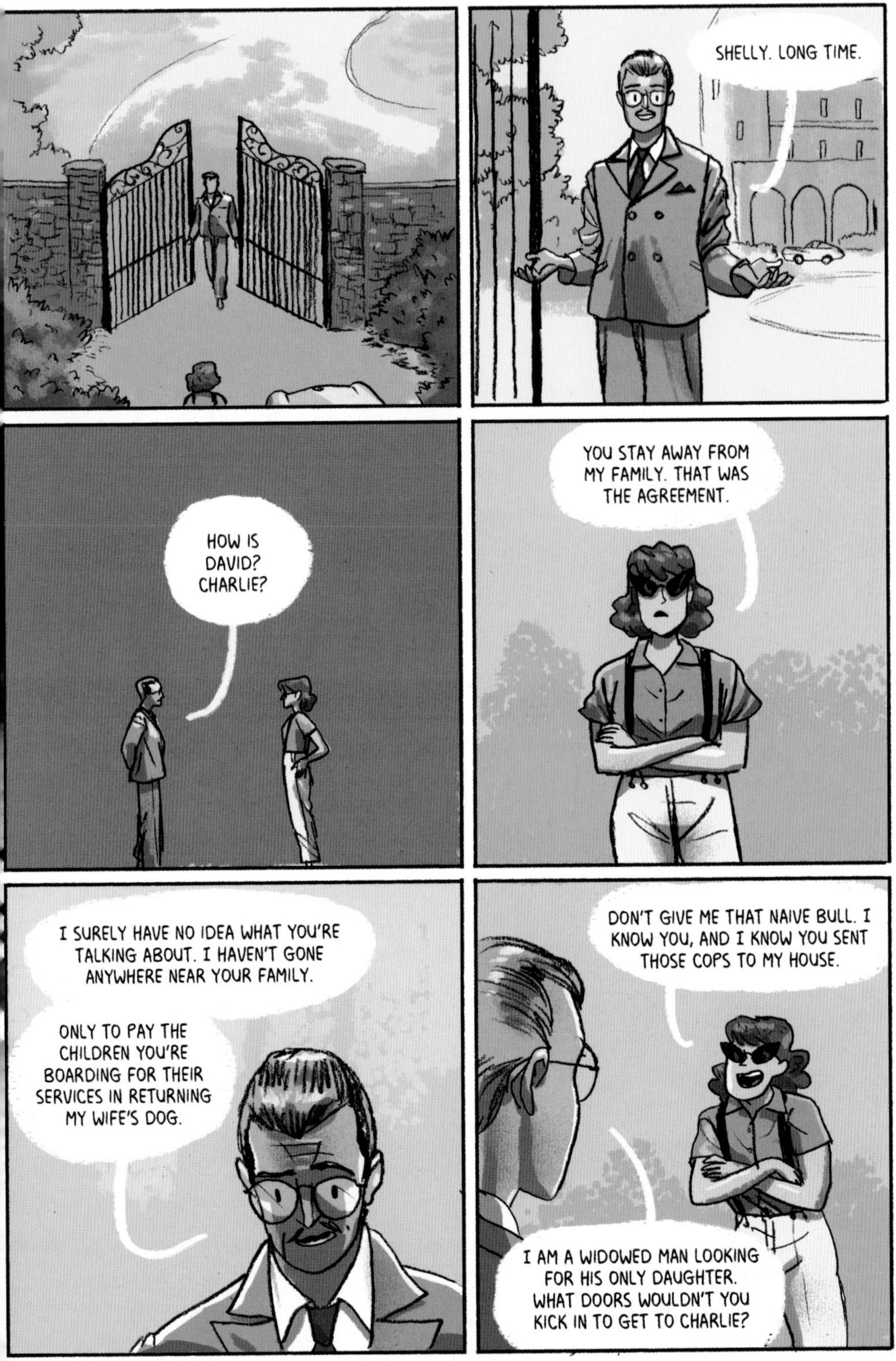
SHELLY. LONG TIME.
HOW IS DAVID? CHARLIE?
YOU STAY AWAY FROM MY FAMILY. THAT WAS THE AGREEMENT.
I SURELY HAVE NO IDEA WHAT YOU'RE TALKING ABOUT. I HAVEN'T GONE ANYWHERE NEAR YOUR FAMILY.
ONLY TO PAY THE CHILDREN YOU'RE BOARDING FOR THEIR SERVICES IN RETURNING MY WIFE'S DOG.
DON'T GIVE ME THAT NAIVE BULL. I KNOW YOU, AND I KNOW YOU SENT THOSE COPS TO MY HOUSE.
I AM A WIDOWED MAN LOOKING FOR HIS ONLY DAUGHTER. WHAT DOORS WOULDN'T YOU KICK IN TO GET TO CHARLIE?

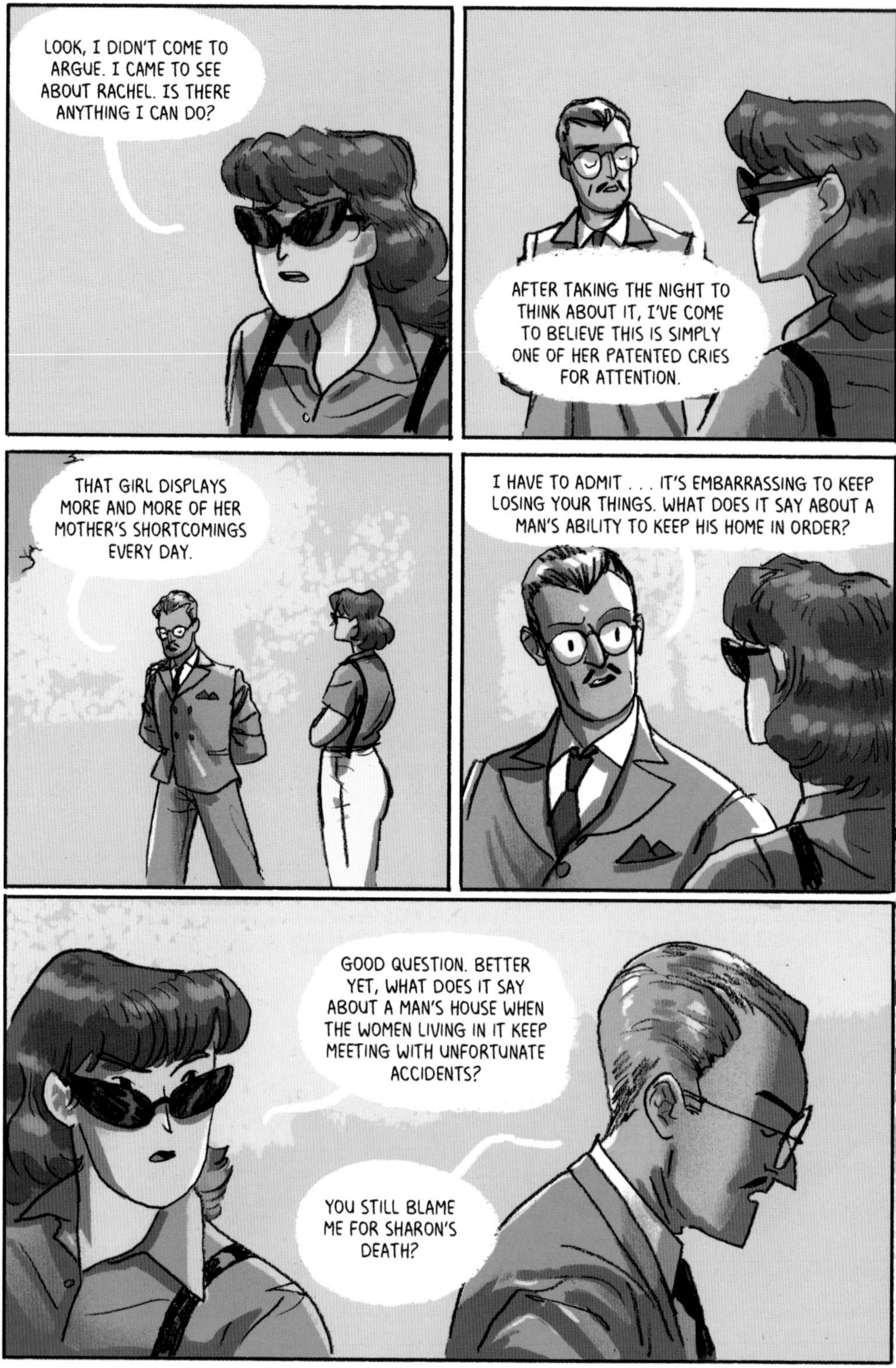
LOOK, I DIDN'T COME TO ARGUE. I CAME TO SEE ABOUT RACHEL. IS THERE ANYTHING I CAN DO?
AFTER TAKING THE NIGHT TO THINK ABOUT IT, I'VE COME TO BELIEVE THIS IS SIMPLY ONE OF HER PATENTED CRIES FOR ATTENTION.
THAT GIRL DISPLAYS MORE AND MORE OF HER MOTHER'S SHORTCOMINGS EVERY DAY.
I HAVE TO ADMIT . . . IT'S EMBARRASSING TO KEEP LOSING YOUR THINGS. WHAT DOES IT SAY ABOUT A MAN'S ABILITY TO KEEP HIS HOME IN ORDER?
GOOD QUESTION. BETTER YET, WHAT DOES IT SAY ABOUT A MAN'S HOUSE WHEN THE WOMEN LIVING IN IT KEEP MEETING WITH UNFORTUNATE ACCIDENTS?
YOU STILL BLAME ME FOR SHARON'S DEATH?

HAVEN'T WE BEEN DOWN THIS ROAD? AS I RECALL, YOU TRIED TO HAVE MY DAUGHTER TAKEN AWAY FROM ME.

I DO.

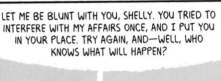

LET ME BE BLUNT WITH YOU, SHELLY. YOU TRIED TO INTERFERE WITH MY AFFAIRS ONCE, AND I PUT YOU IN YOUR PLACE. TRY AGAIN, AND—WELL, WHO KNOWS WHAT WILL HAPPEN?

YOU WANT TO HELP RACHEL? CAN YOU GO BACK IN TIME SO THAT I HAVE THE SENSE TO CHOOSE A BETTER WOMAN AS MY FIRST WIFE? THEN I WOULDN'T HAVE THAT EVIL IN MY HOME TO BEGIN WITH.

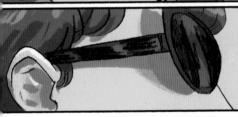

NO, YOU CAN DO NOTHING. EXCEPT STAY AWAY. YOU AND YOUR LOT.

THEN TELL YOUR FRIENDS TO STAY AWAY FROM MY HOME.

GOODBYE, SHELLY. AS ALWAYS, A PLEASURE.

HEY, ROGER?

HOW DIGNIFIED. DAVID REALLY IS A LUCKY MAN.

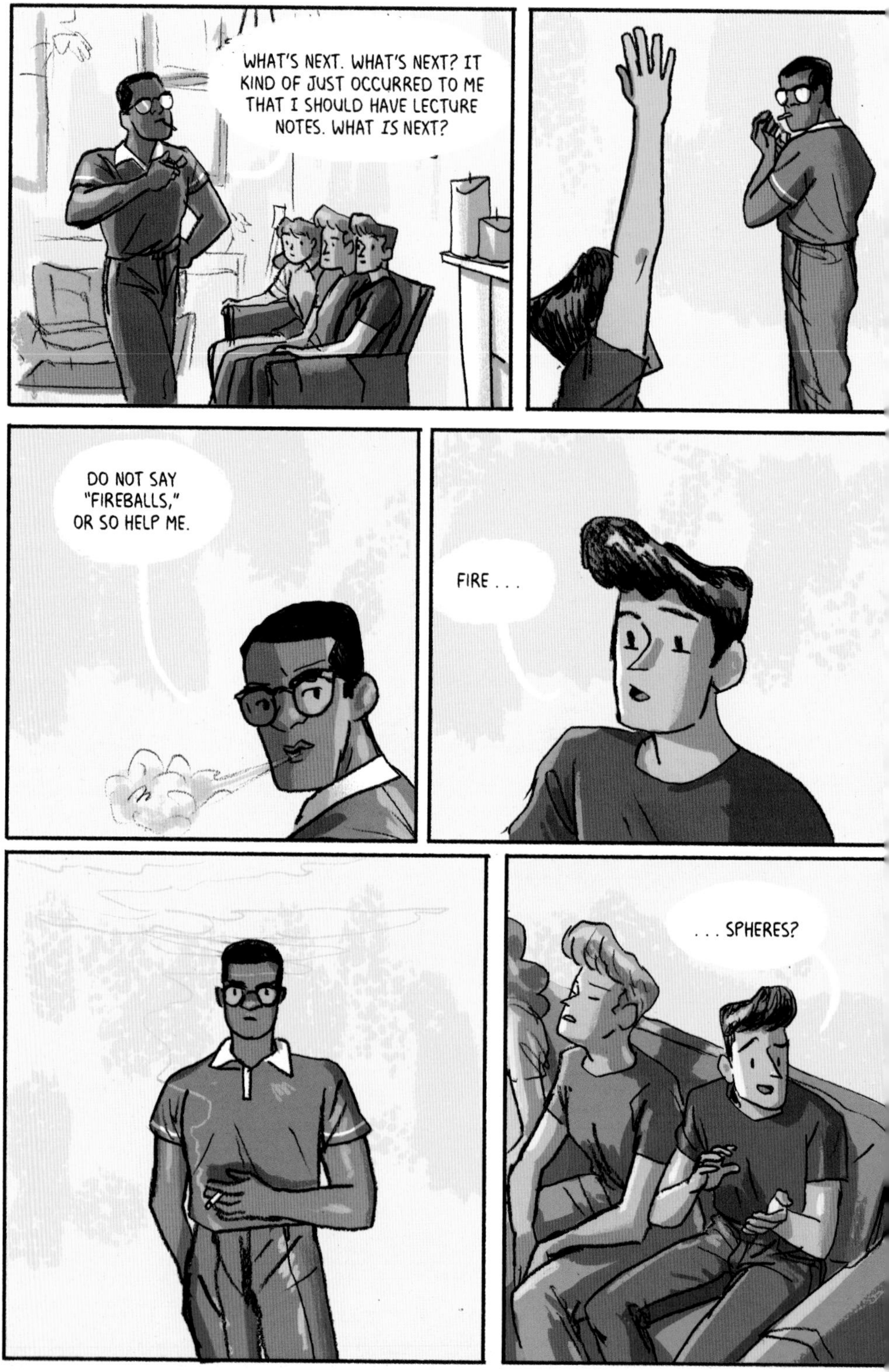
WHAT'S NEXT. WHAT'S NEXT? IT KIND OF JUST OCCURRED TO ME THAT I SHOULD HAVE LECTURE NOTES. WHAT *IS* NEXT?
DO NOT SAY "FIREBALLS," OR SO HELP ME.
FIRE . . .
. . . SPHERES?

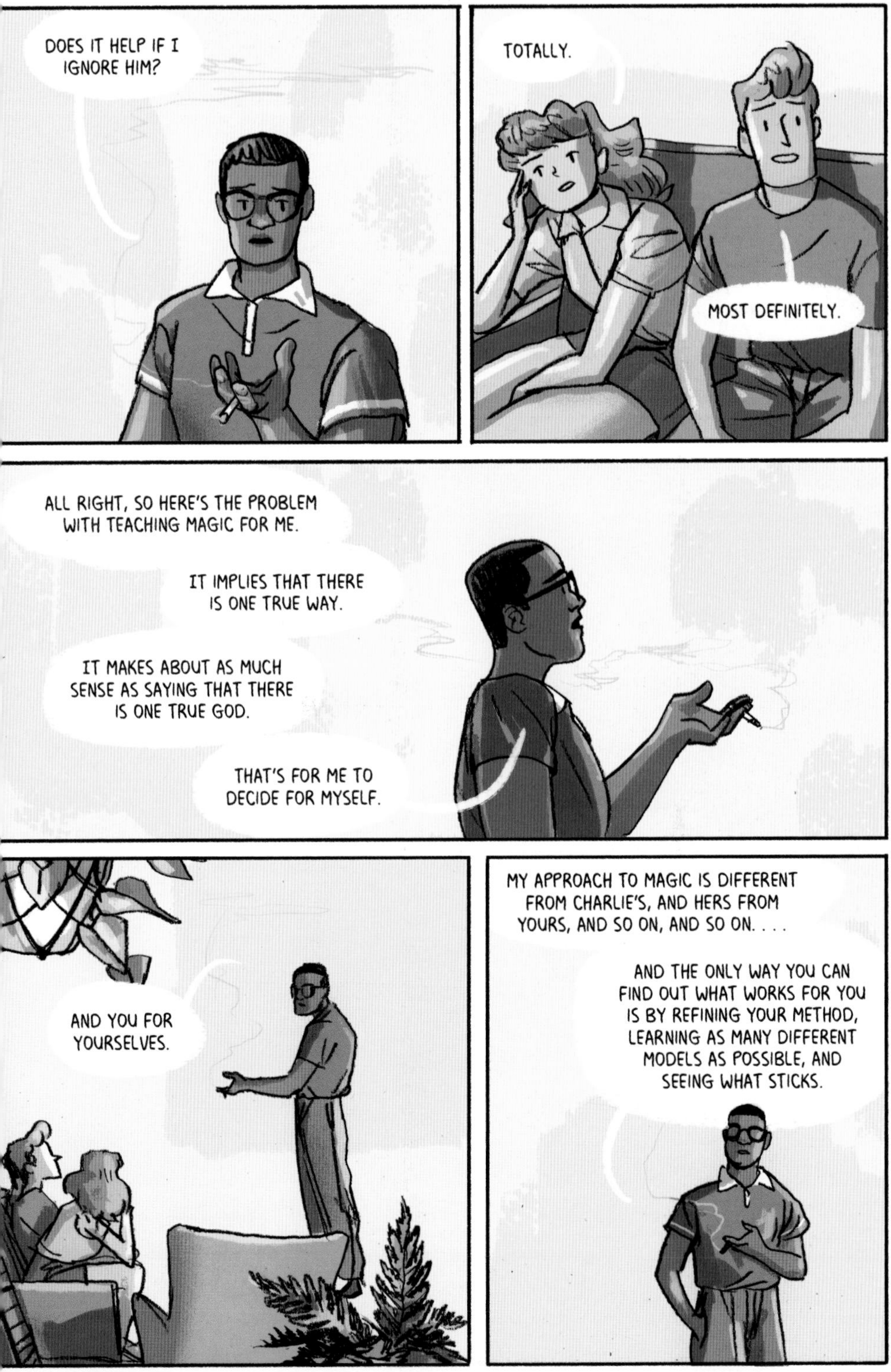
DOES IT HELP IF I IGNORE HIM?
TOTALLY.
MOST DEFINITELY.
ALL RIGHT, SO HERE'S THE PROBLEM WITH TEACHING MAGIC FOR ME.
IT IMPLIES THAT THERE IS ONE TRUE WAY.
IT MAKES ABOUT AS MUCH SENSE AS SAYING THAT THERE IS ONE TRUE GOD.
THAT'S FOR ME TO DECIDE FOR MYSELF.
AND YOU FOR YOURSELVES.
MY APPROACH TO MAGIC IS DIFFERENT FROM CHARLIE'S, AND HERS FROM YOURS, AND SO ON, AND SO ON. . . .
AND THE ONLY WAY YOU CAN FIND OUT WHAT WORKS FOR YOU IS BY REFINING YOUR METHOD, LEARNING AS MANY DIFFERENT MODELS AS POSSIBLE, AND SEEING WHAT STICKS.

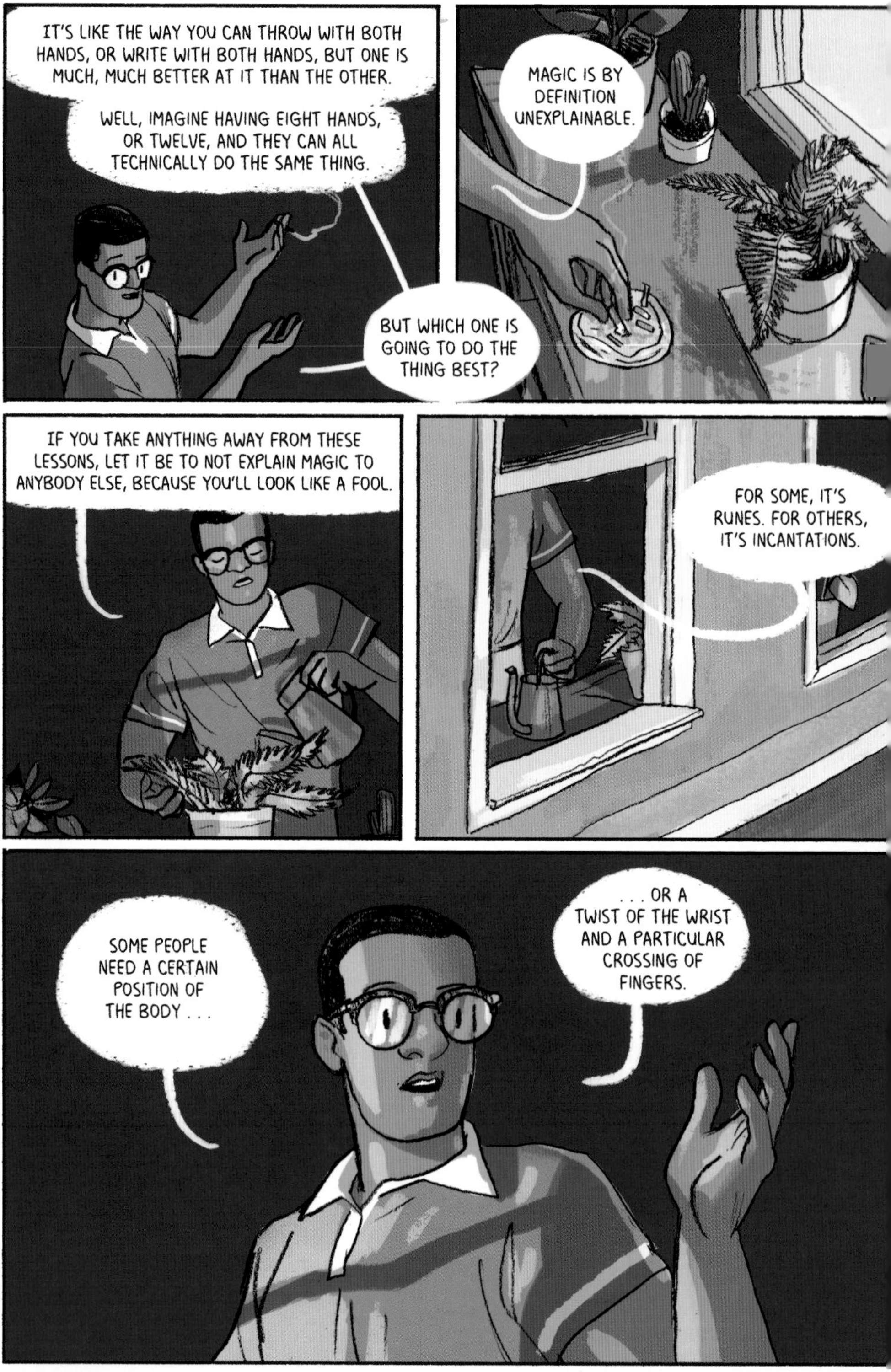
IT'S LIKE THE WAY YOU CAN THROW WITH BOTH HANDS, OR WRITE WITH BOTH HANDS, BUT ONE IS MUCH, MUCH BETTER AT IT THAN THE OTHER.
WELL, IMAGINE HAVING EIGHT HANDS, OR TWELVE, AND THEY CAN ALL TECHNICALLY DO THE SAME THING.
BUT WHICH ONE IS GOING TO DO THE THING BEST?
MAGIC IS BY DEFINITION UNEXPLAINABLE.
IF YOU TAKE ANYTHING AWAY FROM THESE LESSONS, LET IT BE TO NOT EXPLAIN MAGIC TO ANYBODY ELSE, BECAUSE YOU'LL LOOK LIKE A FOOL.
FOR SOME, IT'S RUNES. FOR OTHERS, IT'S INCANTATIONS.
SOME PEOPLE NEED A CERTAIN POSITION OF THE BODY . . .
. . . OR A TWIST OF THE WRIST AND A PARTICULAR CROSSING OF FINGERS.

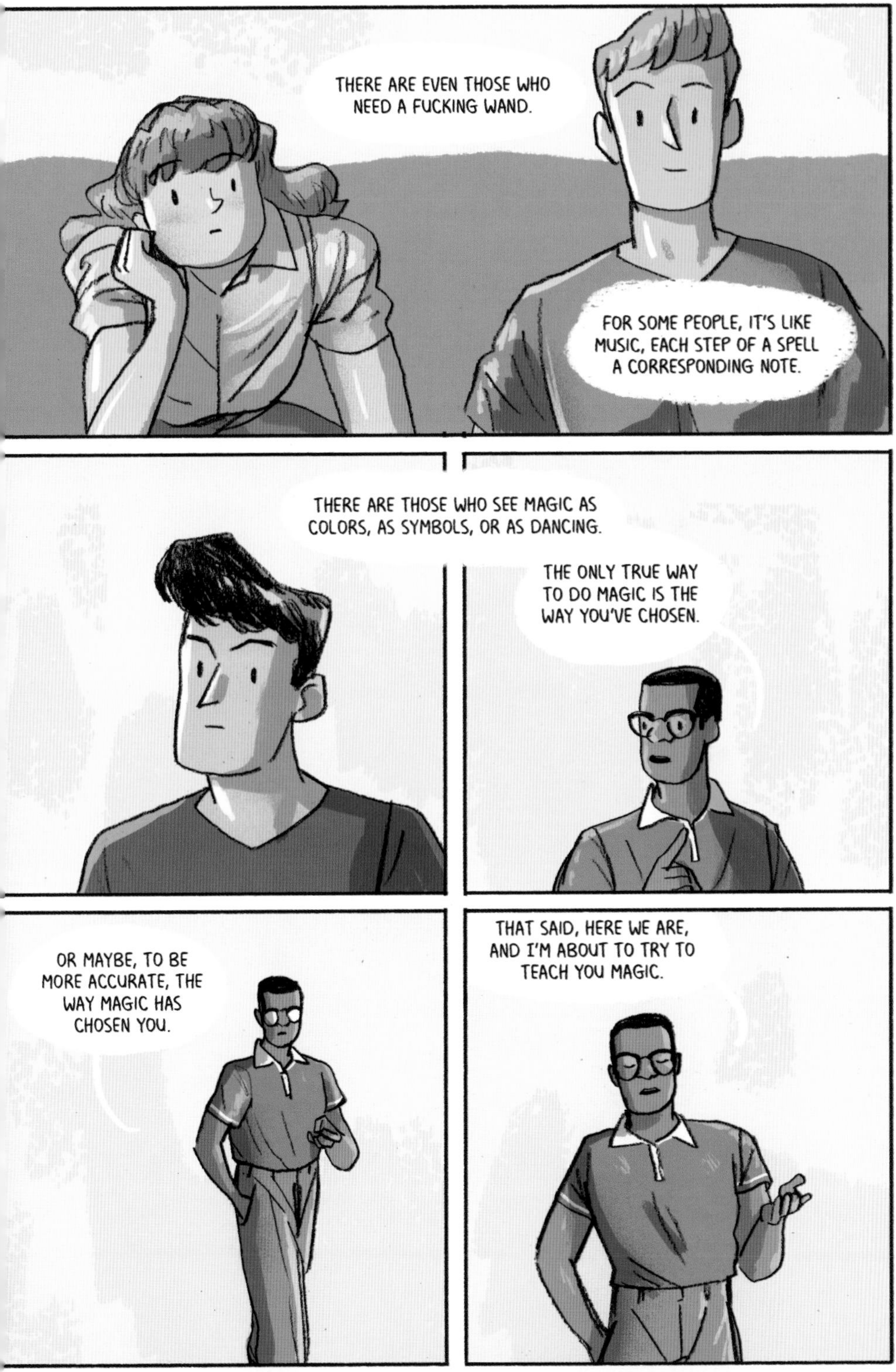
THERE ARE EVEN THOSE WHO NEED A FUCKING WAND.
FOR SOME PEOPLE, IT'S LIKE MUSIC, EACH STEP OF A SPELL A CORRESPONDING NOTE.
THERE ARE THOSE WHO SEE MAGIC AS COLORS, AS SYMBOLS, OR AS DANCING.
THE ONLY TRUE WAY TO DO MAGIC IS THE WAY YOU'VE CHOSEN.
OR MAYBE, TO BE MORE ACCURATE, THE WAY MAGIC HAS CHOSEN YOU.
THAT SAID, HERE WE ARE, AND I'M ABOUT TO TRY TO TEACH YOU MAGIC.

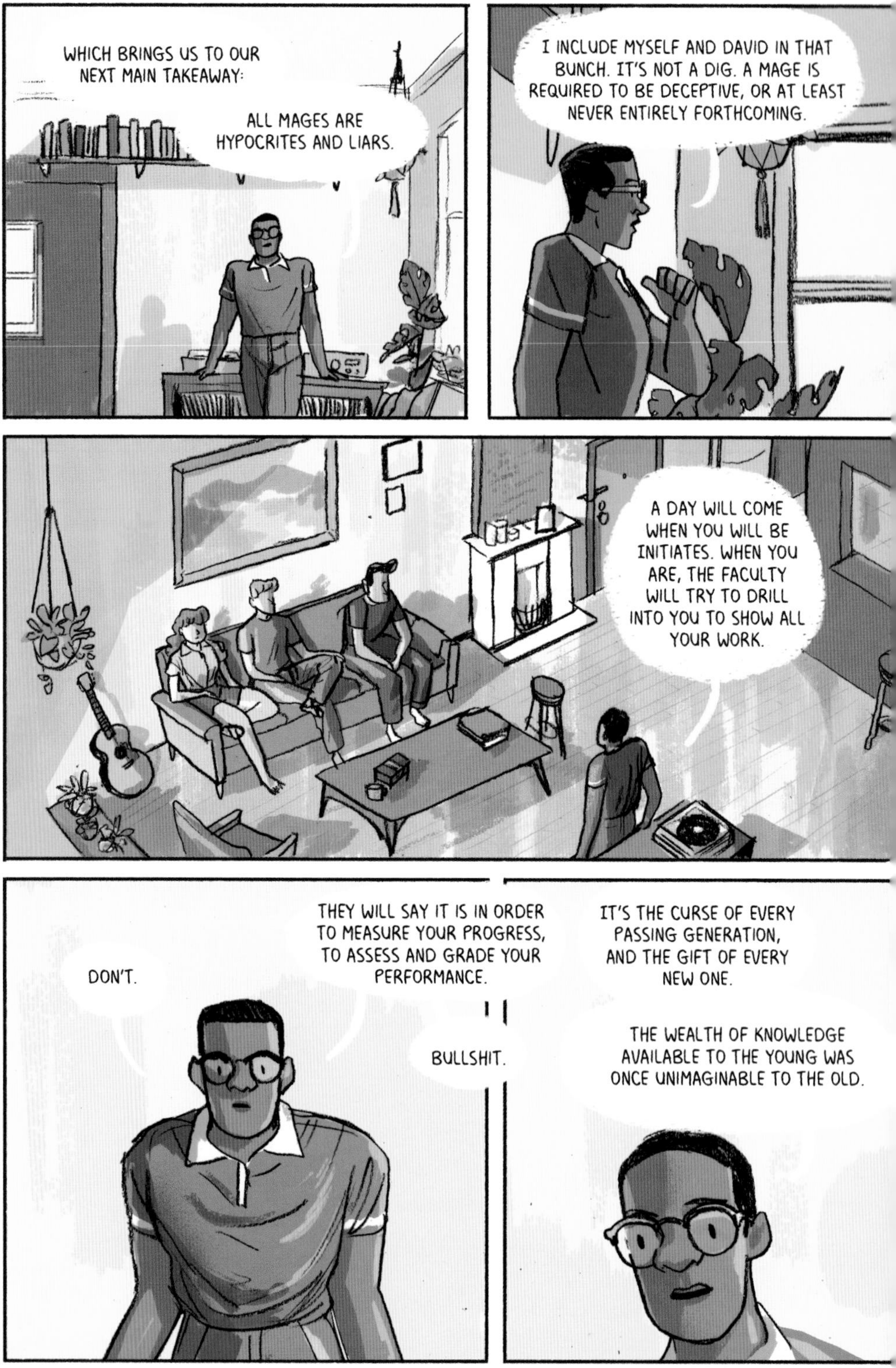
WHICH BRINGS US TO OUR NEXT MAIN TAKEAWAY:
ALL MAGES ARE HYPOCRITES AND LIARS.
I INCLUDE MYSELF AND DAVID IN THAT BUNCH. IT'S NOT A DIG. A MAGE IS REQUIRED TO BE DECEPTIVE, OR AT LEAST NEVER ENTIRELY FORTHCOMING.
A DAY WILL COME WHEN YOU WILL BE INITIATES. WHEN YOU ARE, THE FACULTY WILL TRY TO DRILL INTO YOU TO SHOW ALL YOUR WORK.
THEY WILL SAY IT IS IN ORDER TO MEASURE YOUR PROGRESS, TO ASSESS AND GRADE YOUR PERFORMANCE.
DON'T.
BULLSHIT.
IT'S THE CURSE OF EVERY PASSING GENERATION, AND THE GIFT OF EVERY NEW ONE.
THE WEALTH OF KNOWLEDGE AVAILABLE TO THE YOUNG WAS ONCE UNIMAGINABLE TO THE OLD.

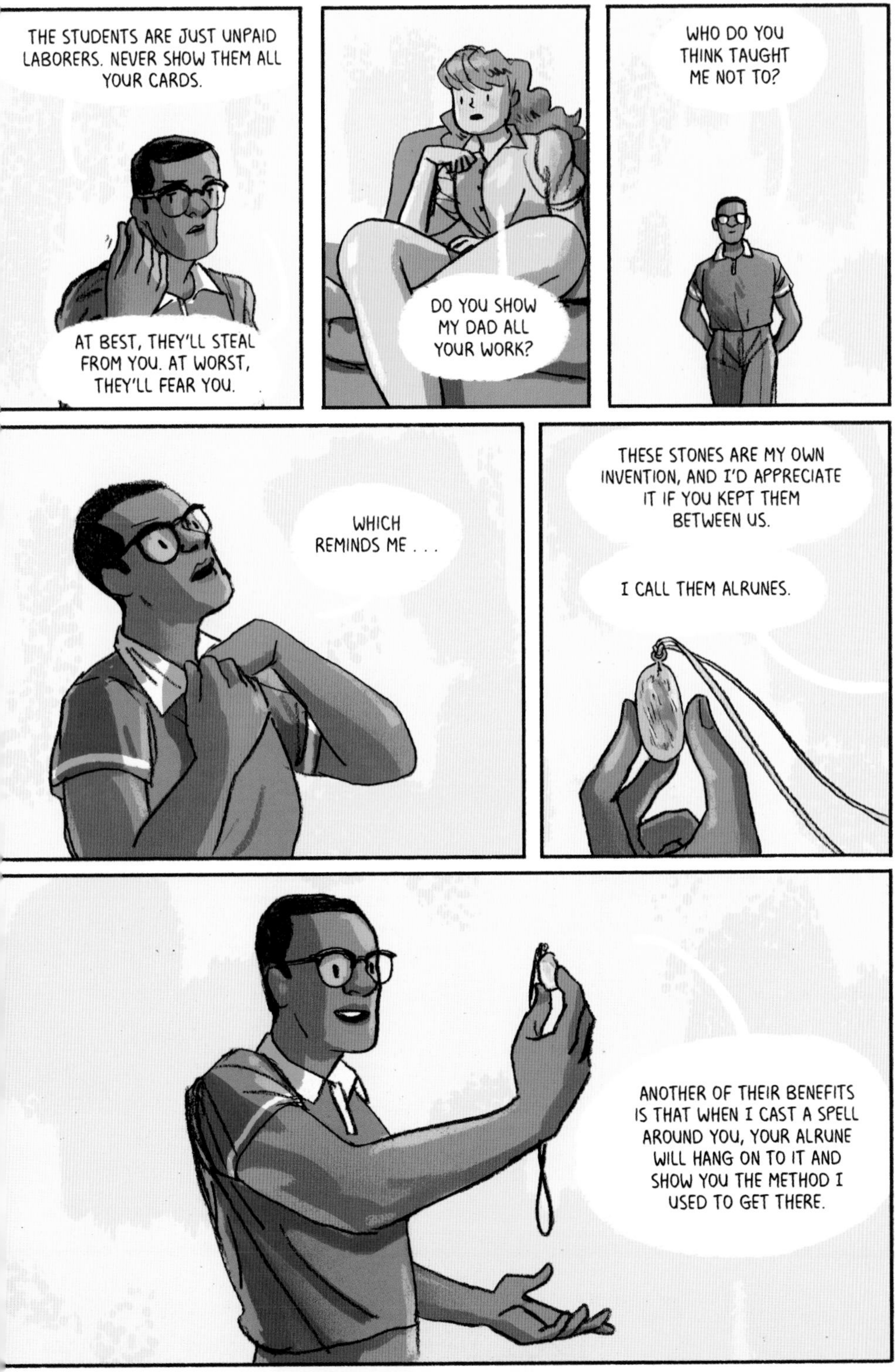
THE STUDENTS ARE JUST UNPAID LABORERS. NEVER SHOW THEM ALL YOUR CARDS.
AT BEST, THEY'LL STEAL FROM YOU. AT WORST, THEY'LL FEAR YOU.
DO YOU SHOW MY DAD ALL YOUR WORK?
WHO DO YOU THINK TAUGHT ME NOT TO?
WHICH REMINDS ME . . .
THESE STONES ARE MY OWN INVENTION, AND I'D APPRECIATE IT IF YOU KEPT THEM BETWEEN US.
I CALL THEM ALRUNES.
ANOTHER OF THEIR BENEFITS IS THAT WHEN I CAST A SPELL AROUND YOU, YOUR ALRUNE WILL HANG ON TO IT AND SHOW YOU THE METHOD I USED TO GET THERE.

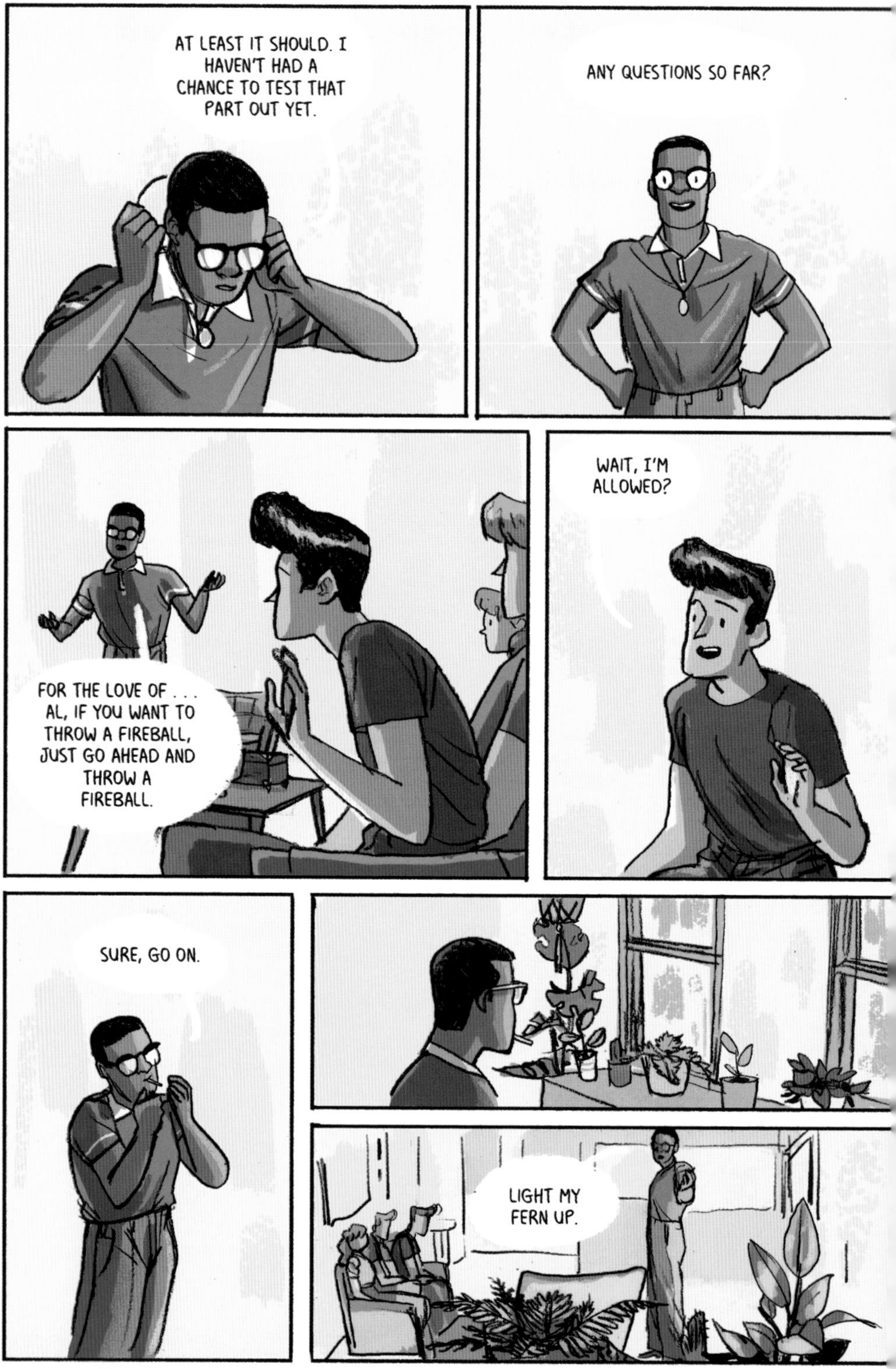

AT LEAST IT SHOULD. I HAVEN'T HAD A CHANCE TO TEST THAT PART OUT YET.
ANY QUESTIONS SO FAR?
FOR THE LOVE OF . . . AL, IF YOU WANT TO THROW A FIREBALL, JUST GO AHEAD AND THROW A FIREBALL.
WAIT, I'M ALLOWED?
SURE, GO ON.
LIGHT MY FERN UP.

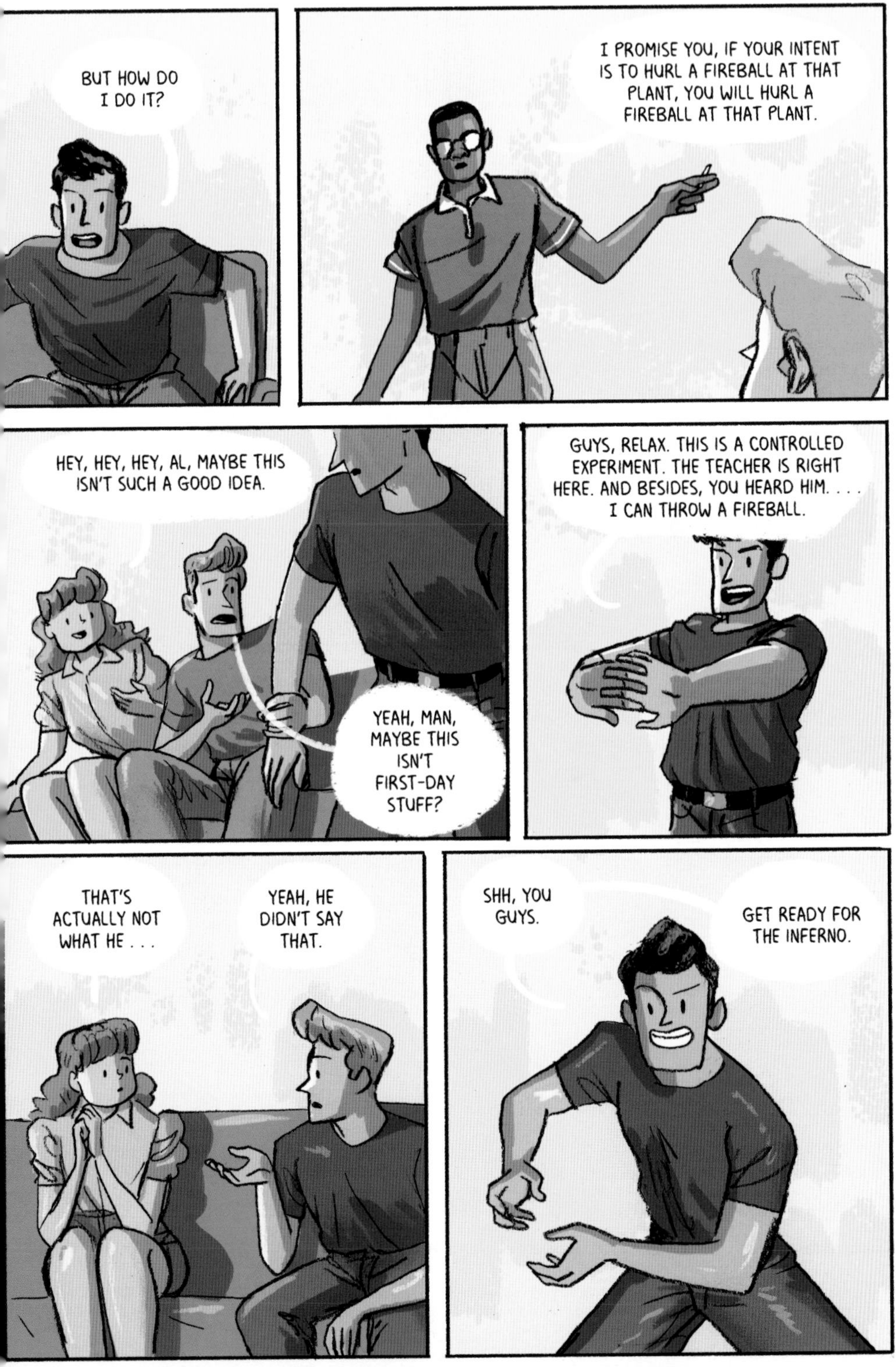
BUT HOW DO I DO IT?
I PROMISE YOU, IF YOUR INTENT IS TO HURL A FIREBALL AT THAT PLANT, YOU WILL HURL A FIREBALL AT THAT PLANT.
HEY, HEY, HEY, AL, MAYBE THIS ISN'T SUCH A GOOD IDEA.
YEAH, MAN, MAYBE THIS ISN'T FIRST-DAY STUFF?
GUYS, RELAX. THIS IS A CONTROLLED EXPERIMENT. THE TEACHER IS RIGHT HERE. AND BESIDES, YOU HEARD HIM. . . . I CAN THROW A FIREBALL.
THAT'S ACTUALLY NOT WHAT HE . . .
YEAH, HE DIDN'T SAY THAT.
SHH, YOU GUYS.
GET READY FOR THE INFERNO.

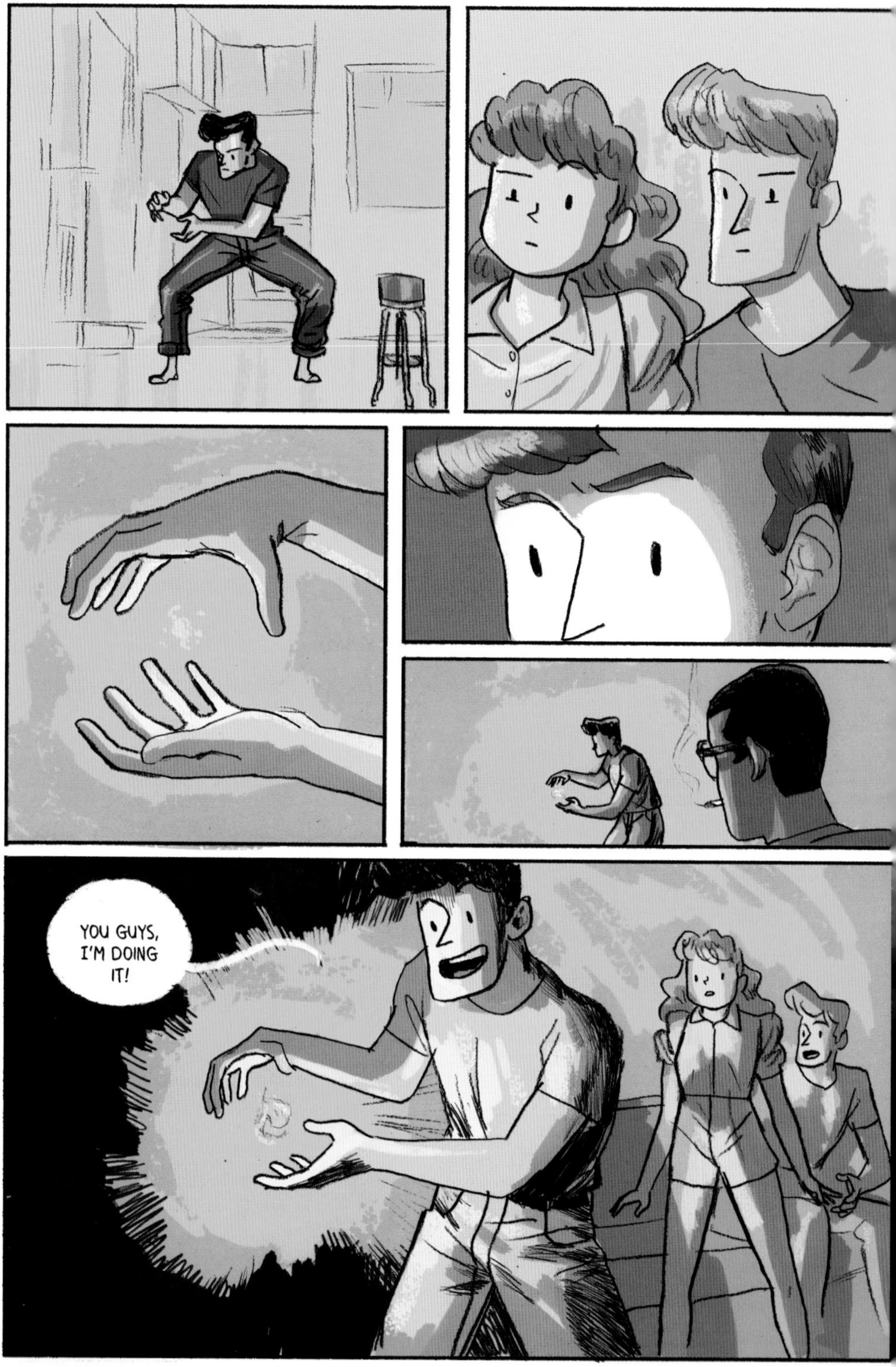
YOU GUYS, I'M DOING IT!

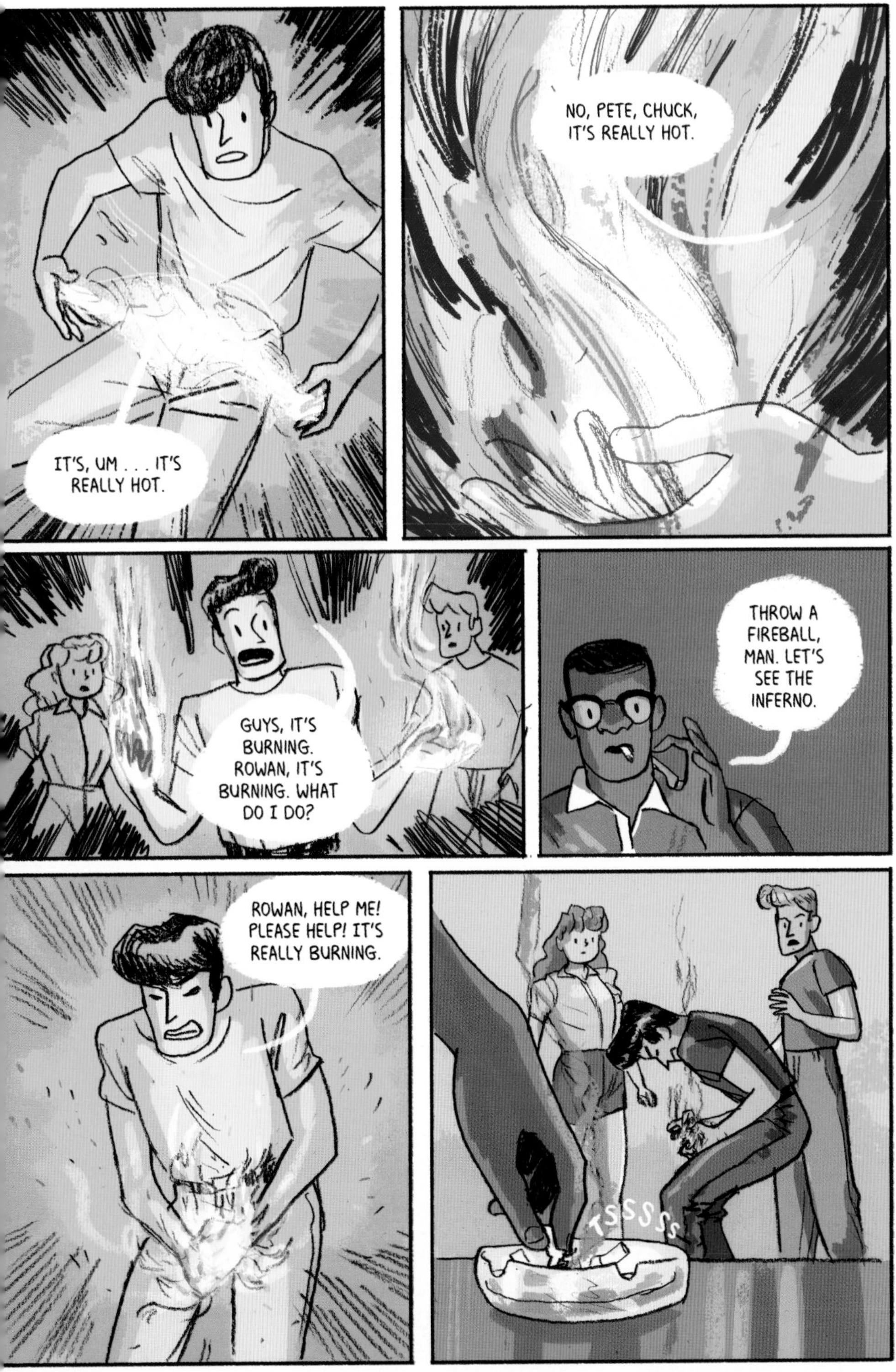
IT'S, UM . . . IT'S REALLY HOT.
NO, PETE, CHUCK, IT'S REALLY HOT.
GUYS, IT'S BURNING. ROWAN, IT'S BURNING. WHAT DO I DO?
THROW A FIREBALL, MAN. LET'S SEE THE INFERNO.
ROWAN, HELP ME! PLEASE HELP! IT'S REALLY BURNING.
TSSSSS

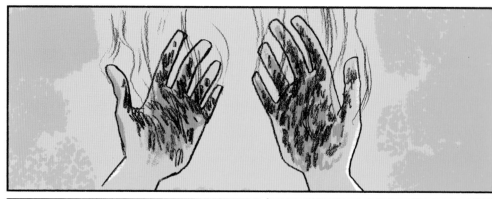

VERY FUNNY.

YOU HAVE SOME MAGIC TO HEAL THEM, RIGHT?

AS A MATTER OF FACT, I DO. . . .

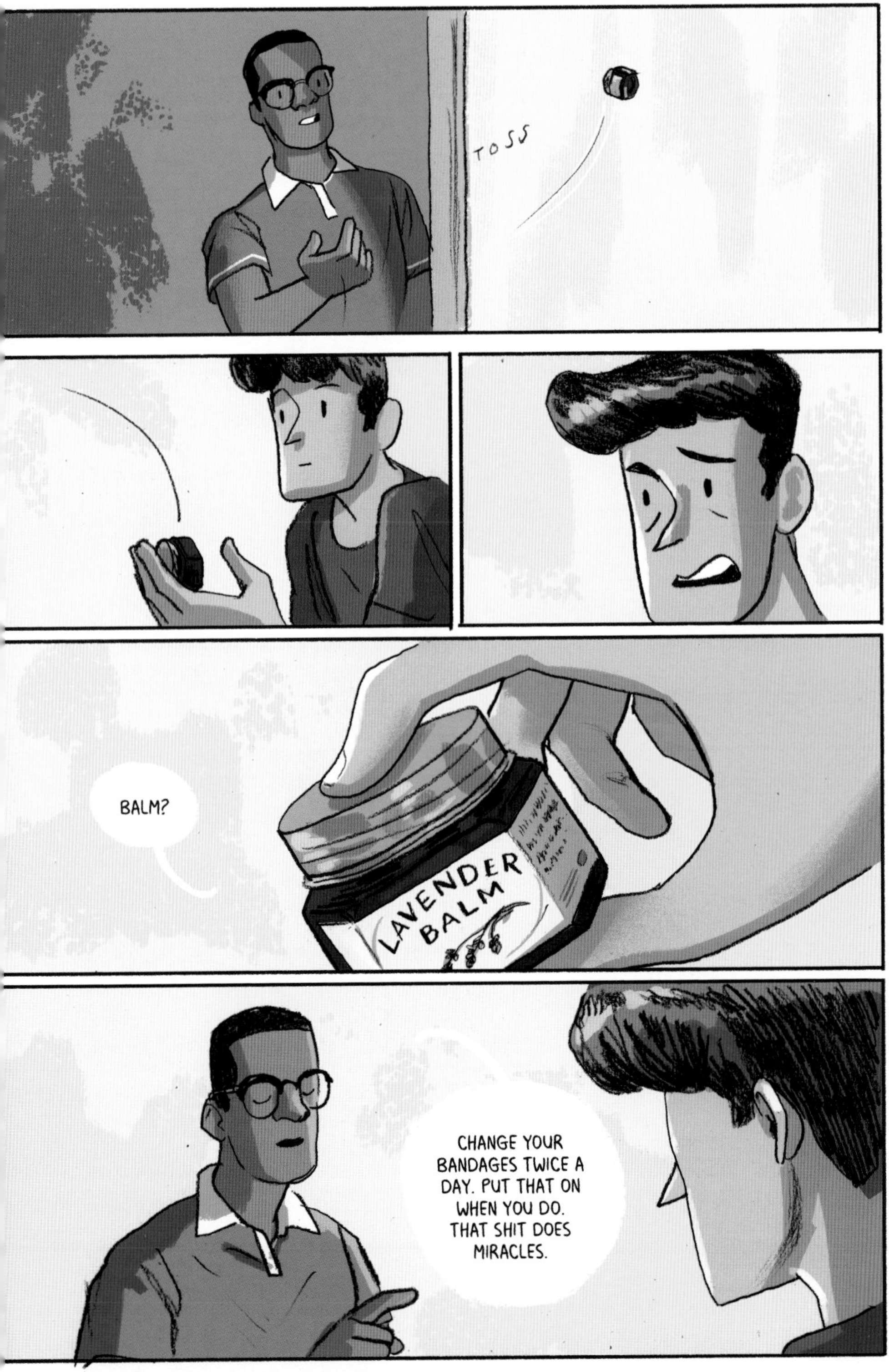
TOSS
BALM?
LAVENDER BALM
CHANGE YOUR BANDAGES TWICE A DAY. PUT THAT ON WHEN YOU DO. THAT SHIT DOES MIRACLES.

CAN ANYONE TELL ME WHAT WENT WRONG WITH AL'S . . . FIREBALL?

YOU MENTIONED HIS INTENT.

YES, PRECISELY.

BUT THE PROBLEM, AL, ISN'T WHETHER OR NOT YOU INTENDED TO THROW FIRE.

THE PROBLEM IS THAT YOU DIDN'T THINK OF WHAT THAT ACTUALLY MEANS.

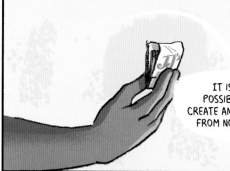

IT ISN'T POSSIBLE TO CREATE AN ELEMENT FROM NOTHING.

WHAT YOU CAN CONTROL, IF YOU ARE EXTREMELY DELIBERATE—

—WHICH, I MEAN, WITH FIRE, WHO WOULDN'T BE?

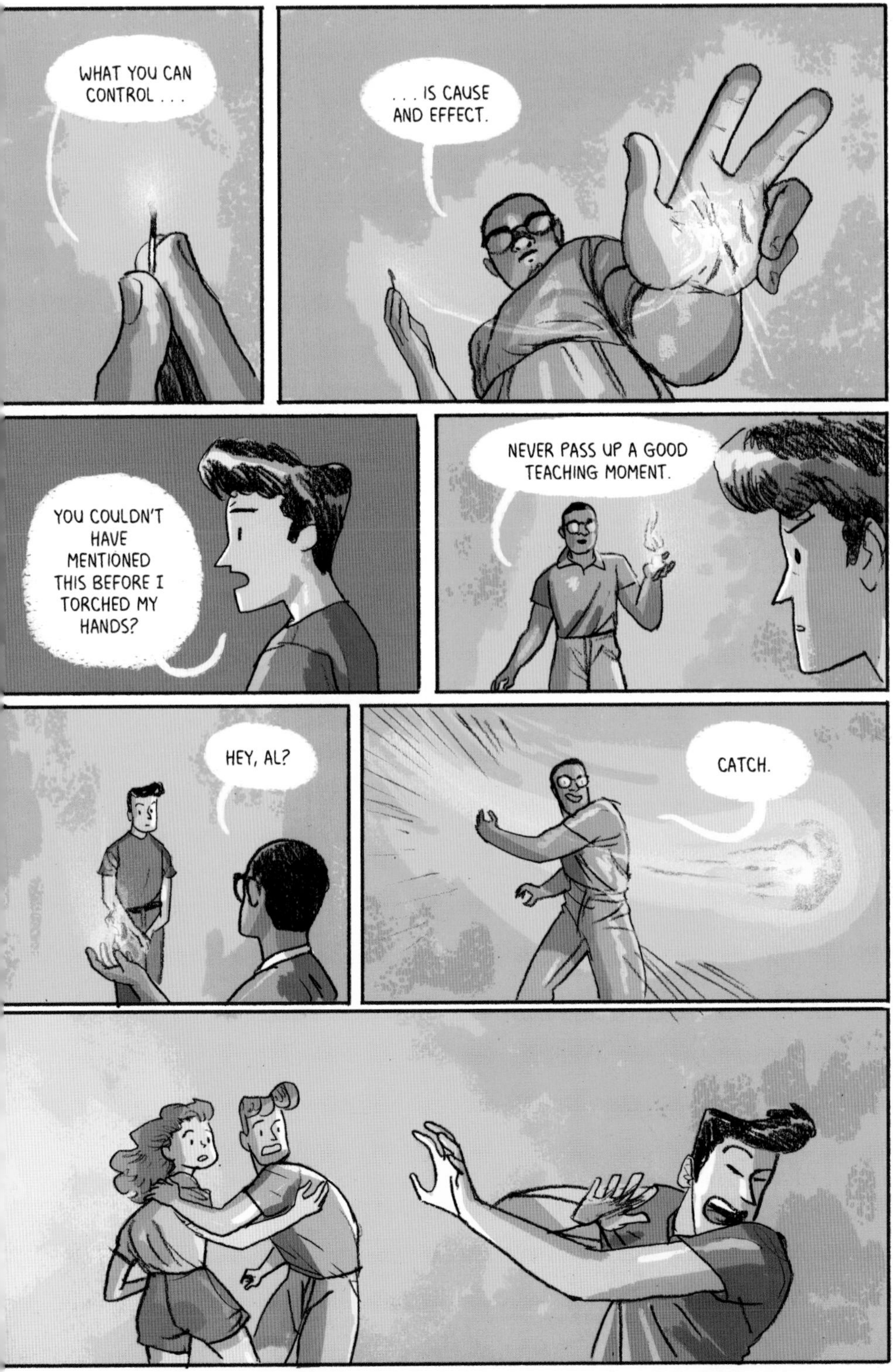
WHAT YOU CAN CONTROL . . .
. . . IS CAUSE AND EFFECT.
YOU COULDN'T HAVE MENTIONED THIS BEFORE I TORCHED MY HANDS?
NEVER PASS UP A GOOD TEACHING MOMENT.
HEY, AL?
CATCH.

PARDON THE THEATRICS, BUT TELL ME THIS:

HOW CAN YOU CONTROL FIRE IF YOU DON'T EVEN KNOW WHERE IT CAME FROM?

OKAY, I GET IT, MAN.

I'M NOT TRYING TO SINGLE YOU OUT, AL. IT'S A MISTAKE EVERY YOUNG MAGE MAKES AT LEAST ONCE. MYSELF INCLUDED.

THAT'S WHY WE'RE HERE. TO LEARN.

YOU ALL REALLY DON'T NEED TO RAISE YOUR HANDS. IT MAKES ME KIND OF UNCOMFORTABLE.

YOU MENTIONED A MISTAKE EVERY YOUNG MAGE MAKES. ARE THERE ANY OTHERS? LIKE, THAT EVERYONE DOES?

EXCELLENT QUESTION! AND YES, THERE ARE.

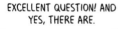

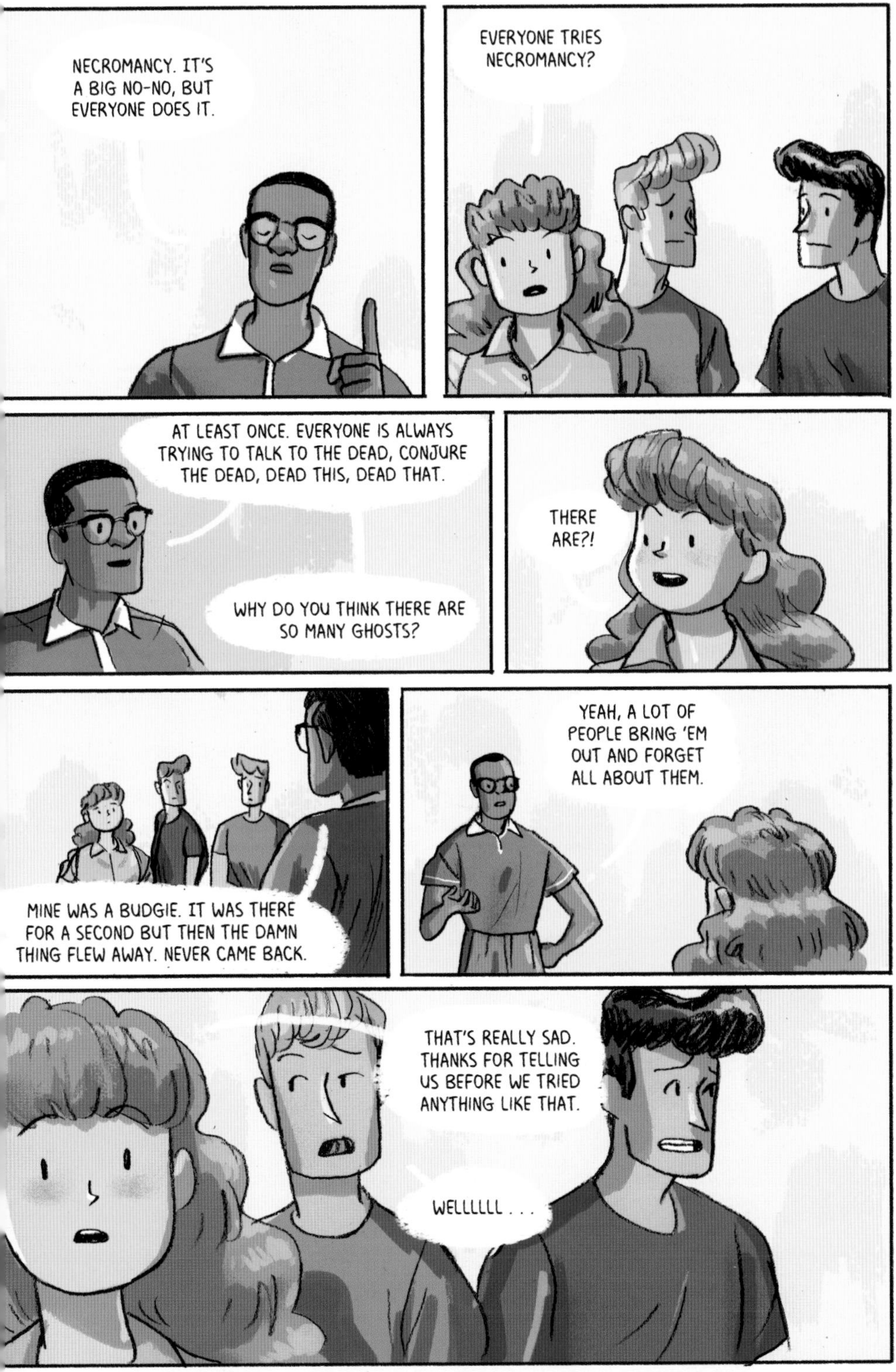
NECROMANCY. IT'S A BIG NO-NO, BUT EVERYONE DOES IT.
EVERYONE TRIES NECROMANCY?
AT LEAST ONCE. EVERYONE IS ALWAYS TRYING TO TALK TO THE DEAD, CONJURE THE DEAD, DEAD THIS, DEAD THAT.
WHY DO YOU THINK THERE ARE SO MANY GHOSTS?
THERE ARE?!
YEAH, A LOT OF PEOPLE BRING 'EM OUT AND FORGET ALL ABOUT THEM.
MINE WAS A BUDGIE. IT WAS THERE FOR A SECOND BUT THEN THE DAMN THING FLEW AWAY. NEVER CAME BACK.
THAT'S REALLY SAD. THANKS FOR TELLING US BEFORE WE TRIED ANYTHING LIKE THAT.
WELLLLLL . . .

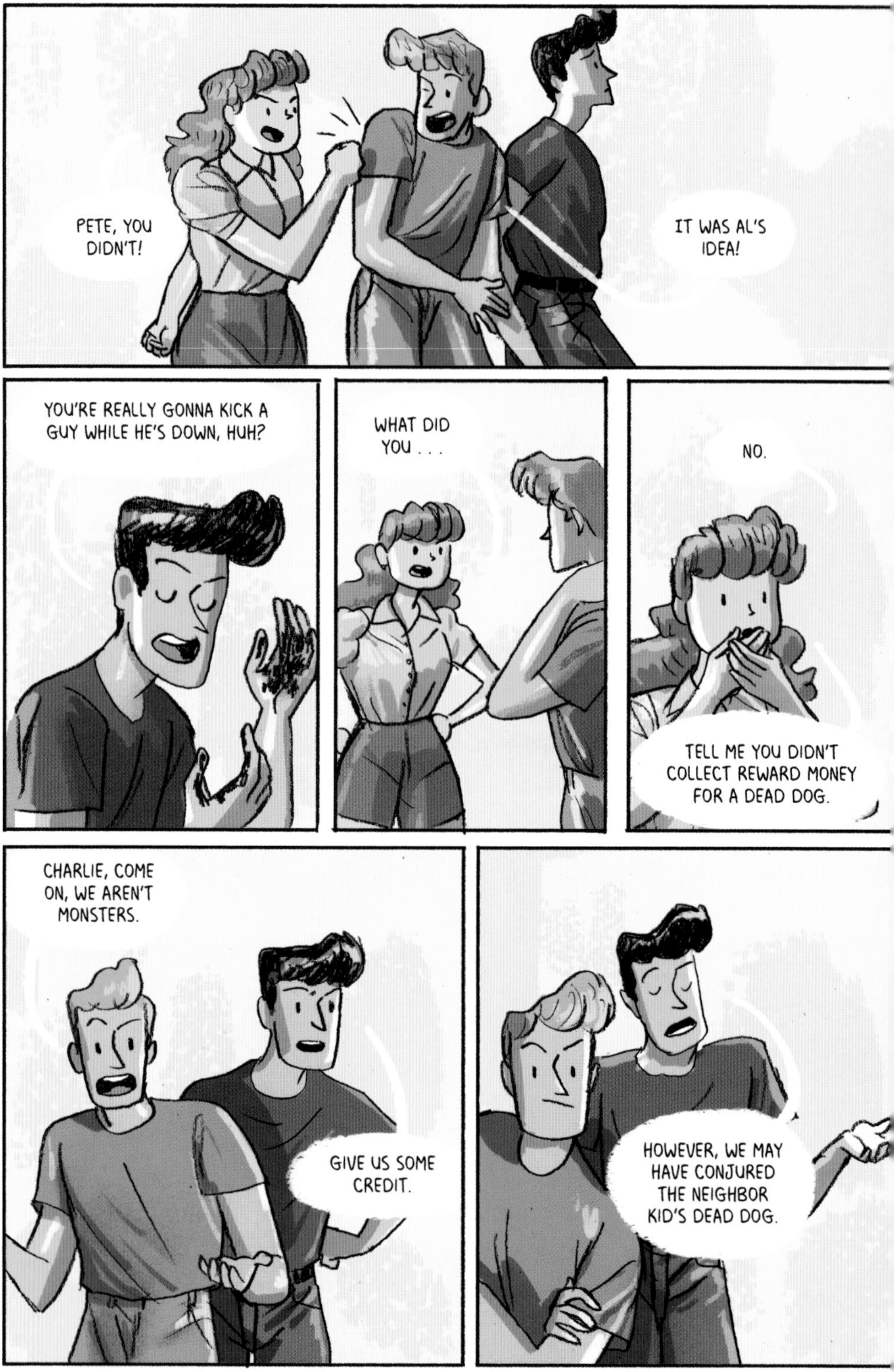
PETE, YOU DIDN'T!
IT WAS AL'S IDEA!
YOU'RE REALLY GONNA KICK A GUY WHILE HE'S DOWN, HUH?
WHAT DID YOU . . .
NO.
TELL ME YOU DIDN'T COLLECT REWARD MONEY FOR A DEAD DOG.
CHARLIE, COME ON, WE AREN'T MONSTERS.
GIVE US SOME CREDIT.
HOWEVER, WE MAY HAVE CONJURED THE NEIGHBOR KID'S DEAD DOG.

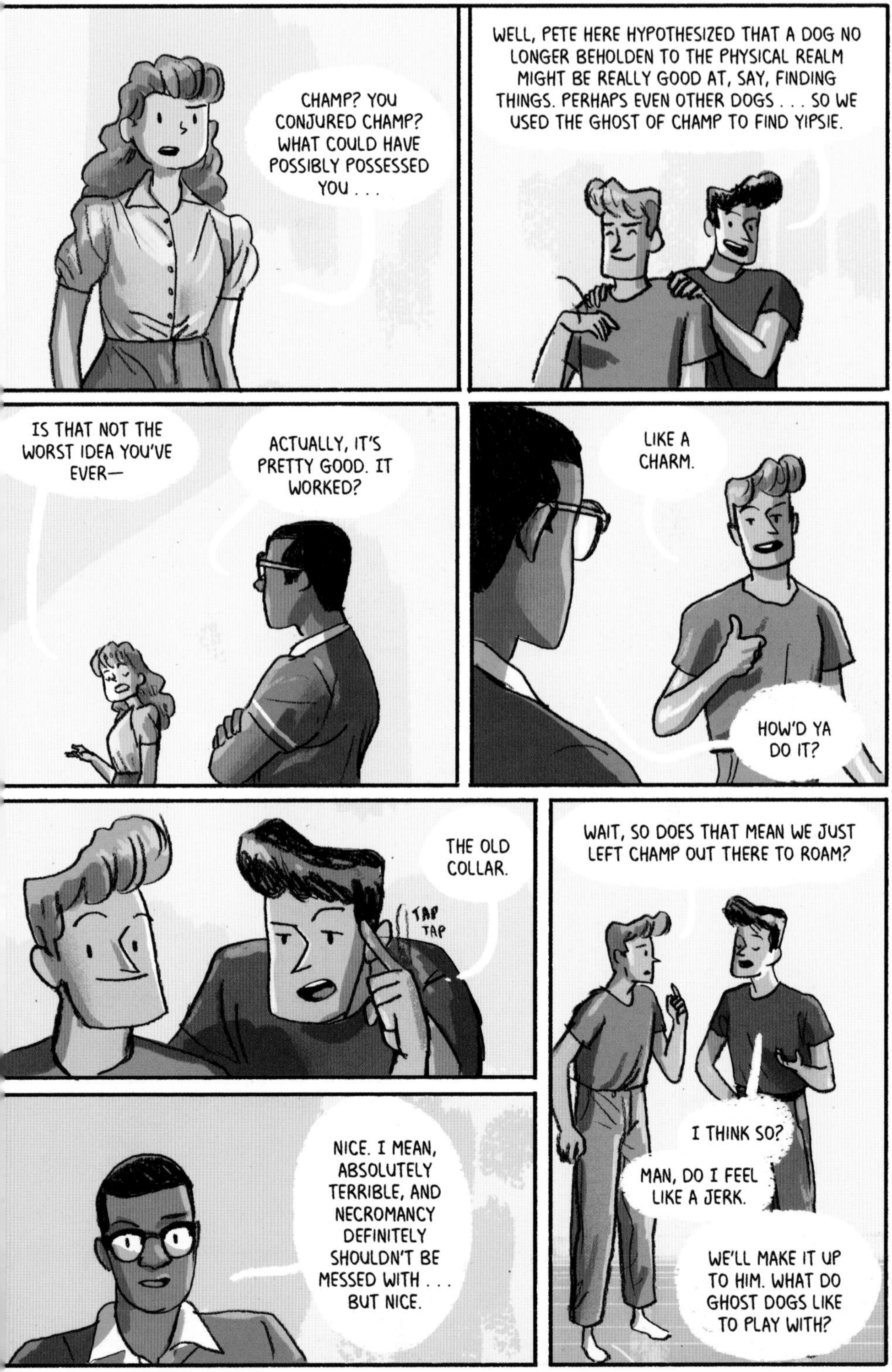
CHAMP? YOU CONJURED CHAMP? WHAT COULD HAVE POSSIBLY POSSESSED YOU . . .
WELL, PETE HERE HYPOTHESIZED THAT A DOG NO LONGER BEHOLDEN TO THE PHYSICAL REALM MIGHT BE REALLY GOOD AT, SAY, FINDING THINGS. PERHAPS EVEN OTHER DOGS . . . SO WE USED THE GHOST OF CHAMP TO FIND YIPSIE.
IS THAT NOT THE WORST IDEA YOU'VE EVER—
ACTUALLY, IT'S PRETTY GOOD. IT WORKED?
LIKE A CHARM.
HOW'D YA DO IT?
THE OLD COLLAR.
TAP TAP
NICE. I MEAN, ABSOLUTELY TERRIBLE, AND NECROMANCY DEFINITELY SHOULDN'T BE MESSED WITH . . . BUT NICE.
WAIT, SO DOES THAT MEAN WE JUST LEFT CHAMP OUT THERE TO ROAM?
I THINK SO?
MAN, DO I FEEL LIKE A JERK.
WE'LL MAKE IT UP TO HIM. WHAT DO GHOST DOGS LIKE TO PLAY WITH?

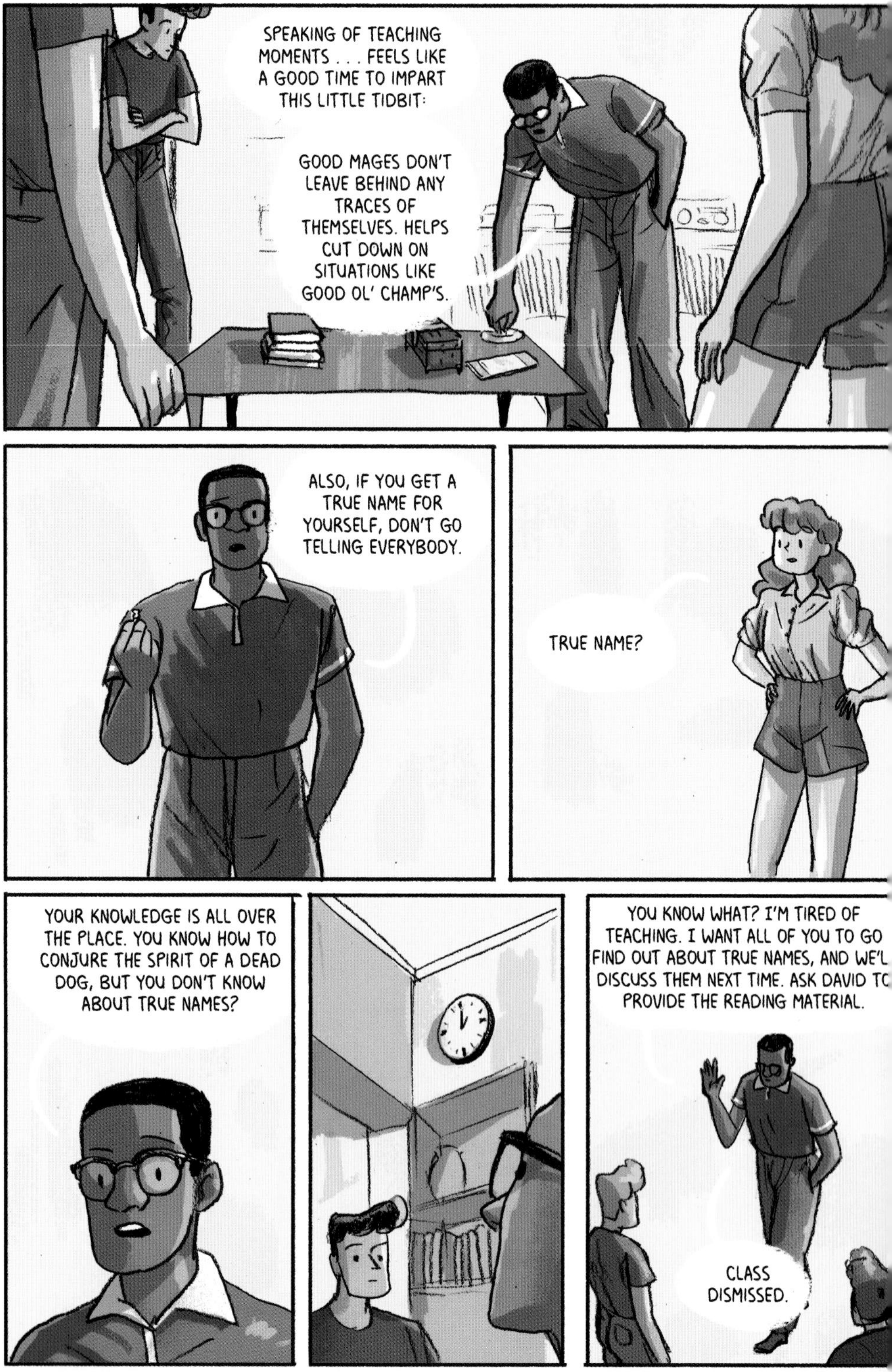
SPEAKING OF TEACHING MOMENTS . . . FEELS LIKE A GOOD TIME TO IMPART THIS LITTLE TIDBIT:
GOOD MAGES DON'T LEAVE BEHIND ANY TRACES OF THEMSELVES. HELPS CUT DOWN ON SITUATIONS LIKE GOOD OL' CHAMP'S.
ALSO, IF YOU GET A TRUE NAME FOR YOURSELF, DON'T GO TELLING EVERYBODY.
TRUE NAME?
YOUR KNOWLEDGE IS ALL OVER THE PLACE. YOU KNOW HOW TO CONJURE THE SPIRIT OF A DEAD DOG, BUT YOU DON'T KNOW ABOUT TRUE NAMES?
YOU KNOW WHAT? I'M TIRED OF TEACHING. I WANT ALL OF YOU TO GO FIND OUT ABOUT TRUE NAMES, AND WE'L DISCUSS THEM NEXT TIME. ASK DAVID TC PROVIDE THE READING MATERIAL.
CLASS DISMISSED.

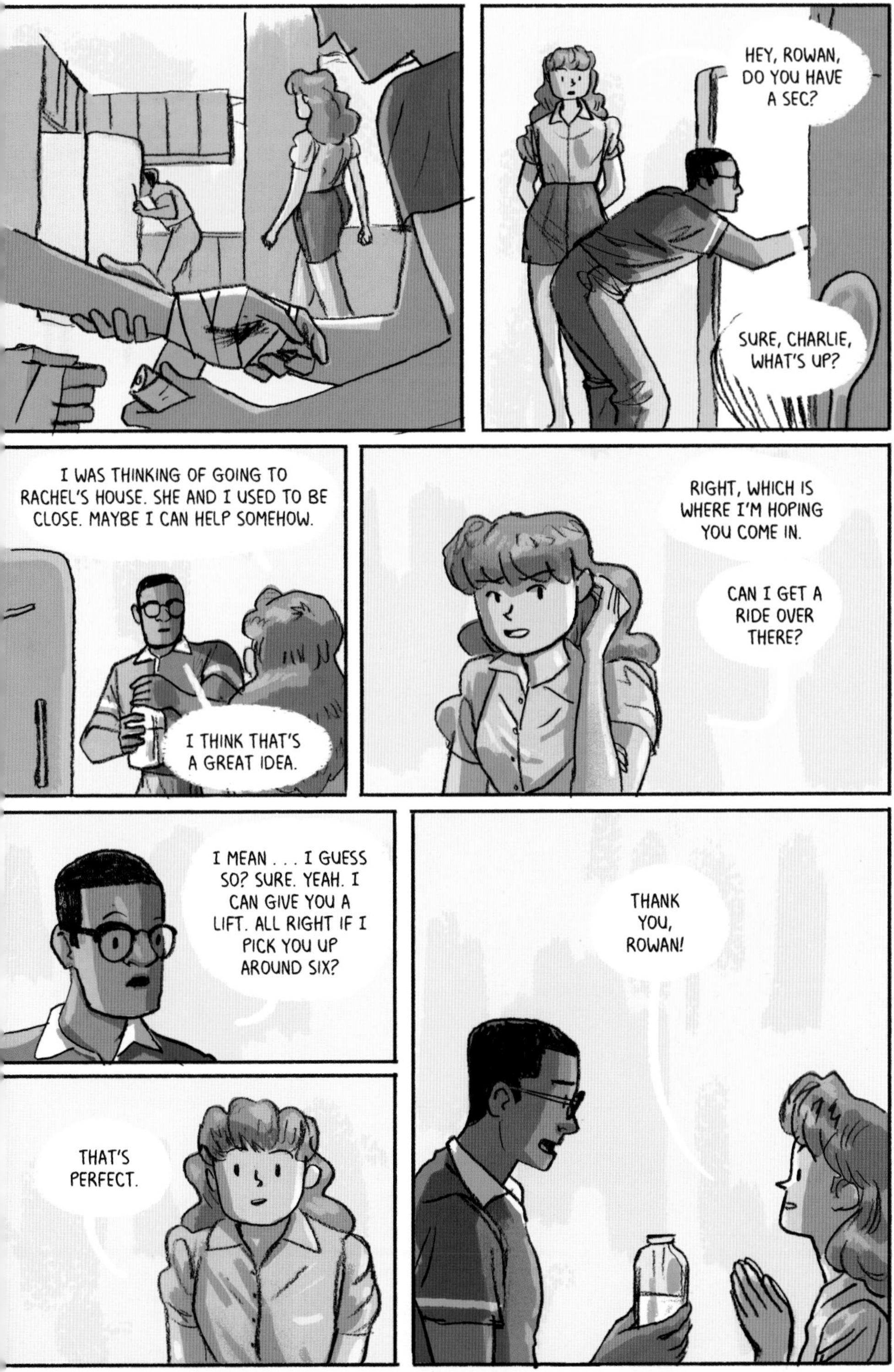
HEY, ROWAN, DO YOU HAVE A SEC?
SURE, CHARLIE, WHAT'S UP?
I WAS THINKING OF GOING TO RACHEL'S HOUSE. SHE AND I USED TO BE CLOSE. MAYBE I CAN HELP SOMEHOW.
I THINK THAT'S A GREAT IDEA.
RIGHT, WHICH IS WHERE I'M HOPING YOU COME IN.
CAN I GET A RIDE OVER THERE?
I MEAN . . . I GUESS SO? SURE. YEAH. I CAN GIVE YOU A LIFT. ALL RIGHT IF I PICK YOU UP AROUND SIX?
THAT'S PERFECT.
THANK YOU, ROWAN!

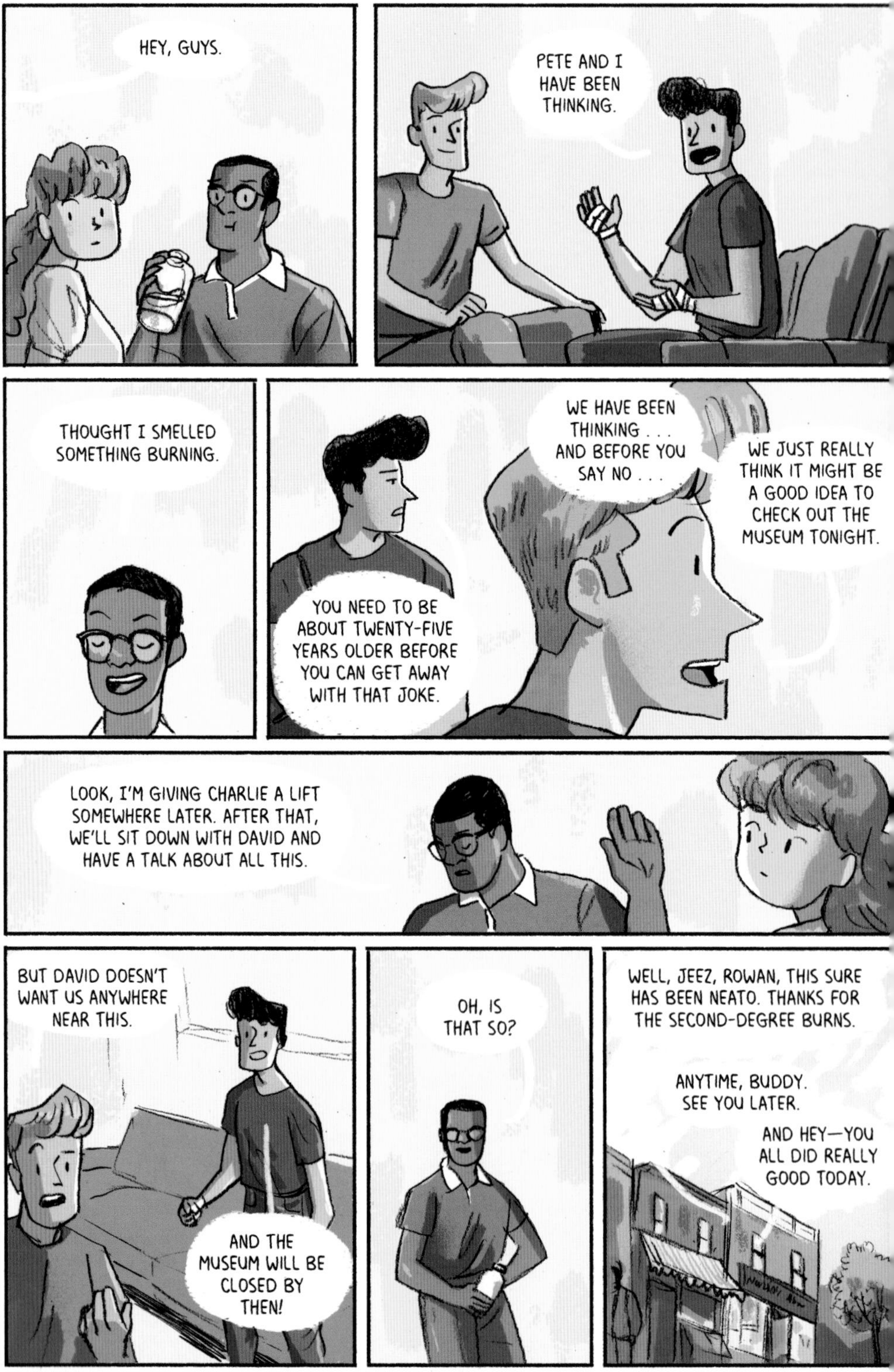
HEY, GUYS.
PETE AND I HAVE BEEN THINKING.
THOUGHT I SMELLED SOMETHING BURNING.
WE HAVE BEEN THINKING . . . AND BEFORE YOU SAY NO . . .
WE JUST REALLY THINK IT MIGHT BE A GOOD IDEA TO CHECK OUT THE MUSEUM TONIGHT.
YOU NEED TO BE ABOUT TWENTY-FIVE YEARS OLDER BEFORE YOU CAN GET AWAY WITH THAT JOKE.
LOOK, I'M GIVING CHARLIE A LIFT SOMEWHERE LATER. AFTER THAT, WE'LL SIT DOWN WITH DAVID AND HAVE A TALK ABOUT ALL THIS.
BUT DAVID DOESN'T WANT US ANYWHERE NEAR THIS.
AND THE MUSEUM WILL BE CLOSED BY THEN!
OH, IS THAT SO?
WELL, JEEZ, ROWAN, THIS SURE HAS BEEN NEATO. THANKS FOR THE SECOND-DEGREE BURNS.
ANYTIME, BUDDY. SEE YOU LATER.
AND HEY—YOU ALL DID REALLY GOOD TODAY.

CHAPTER 4

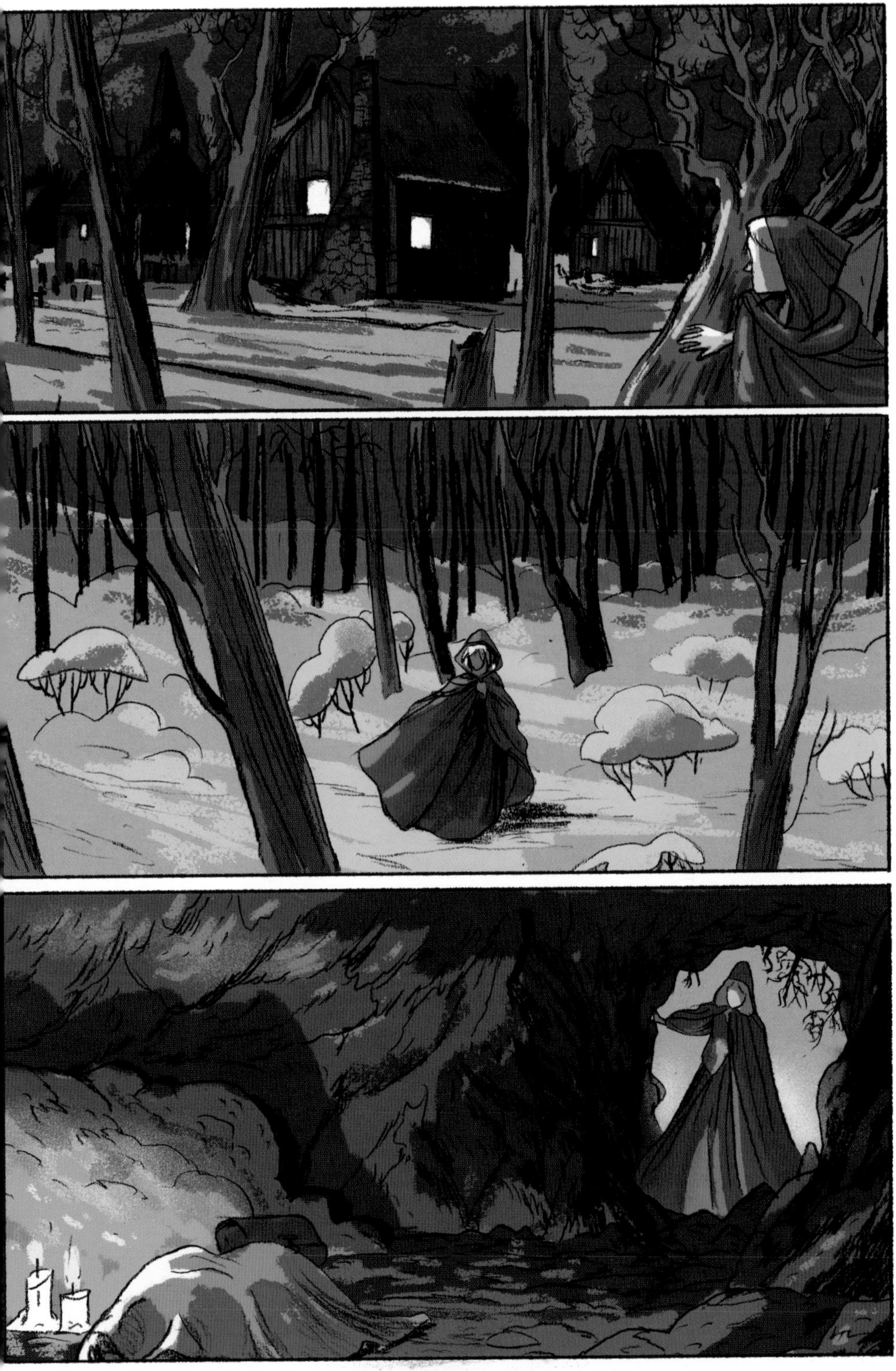

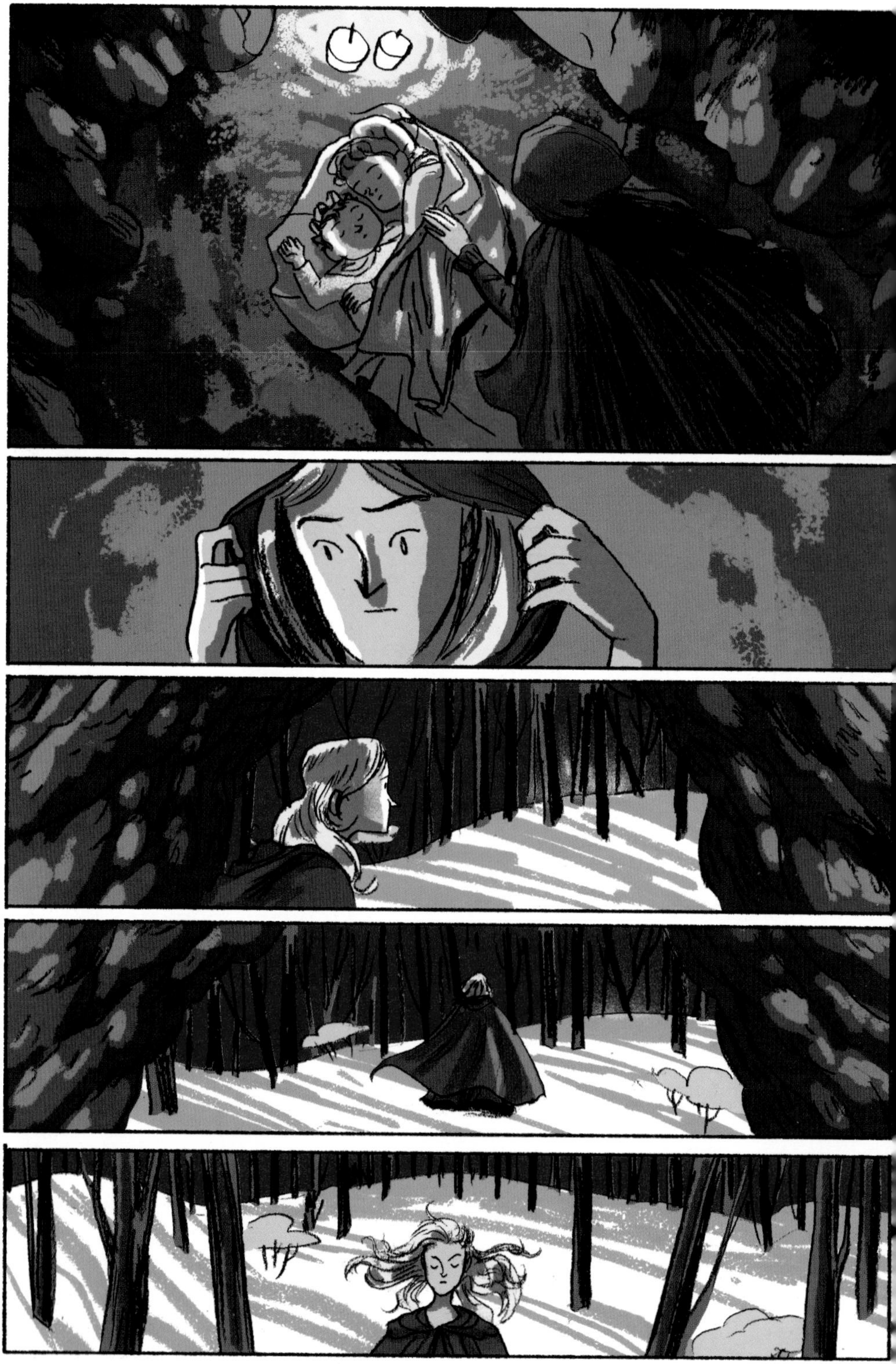

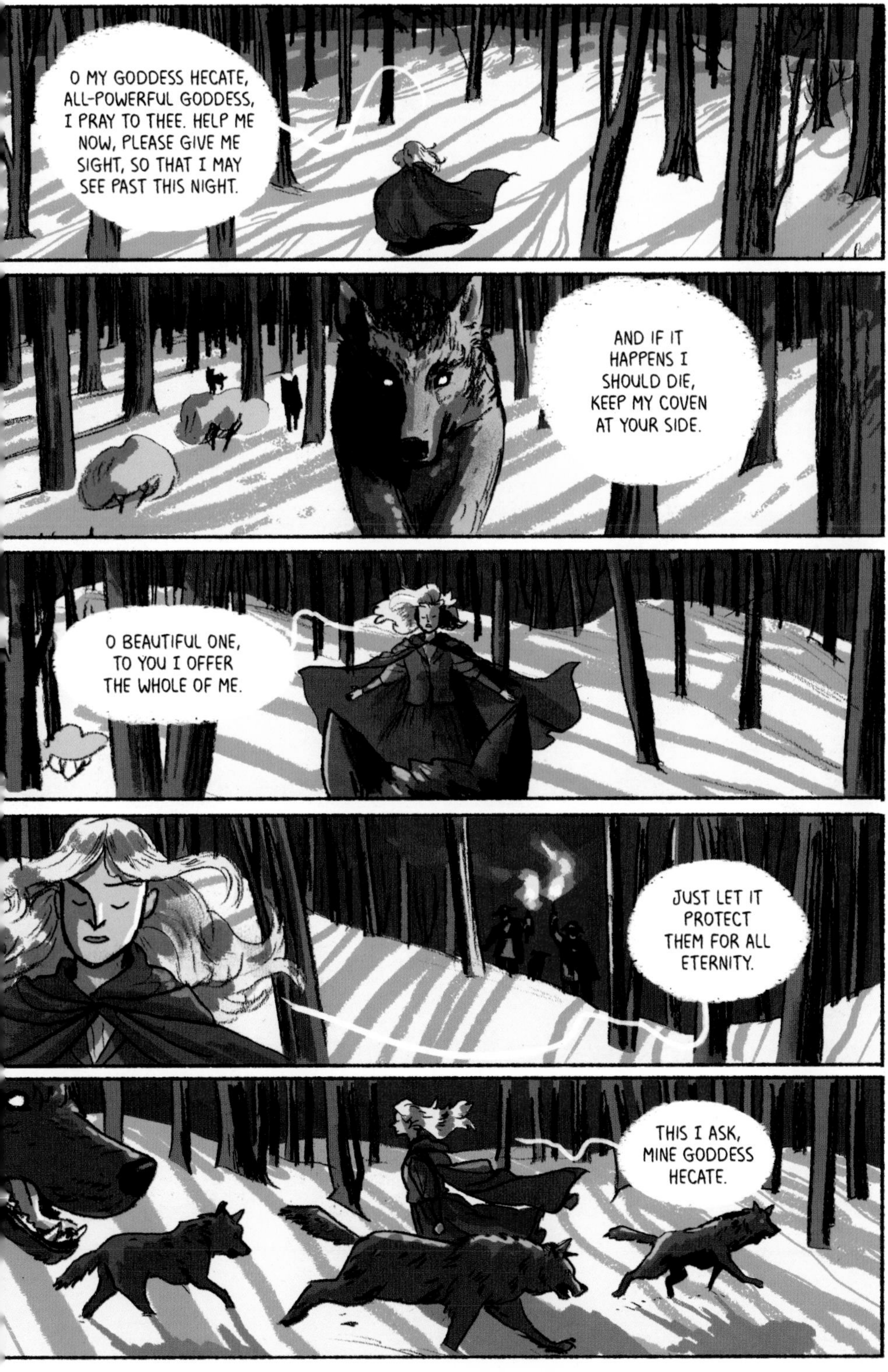
O MY GODDESS HECATE, ALL-POWERFUL GODDESS, I PRAY TO THEE. HELP ME NOW, PLEASE GIVE ME SIGHT, SO THAT I MAY SEE PAST THIS NIGHT.
AND IF IT HAPPENS I SHOULD DIE, KEEP MY COVEN AT YOUR SIDE.
O BEAUTIFUL ONE, TO YOU I OFFER THE WHOLE OF ME.
JUST LET IT PROTECT THEM FOR ALL ETERNITY.
THIS I ASK, MINE GODDESS HECATE.

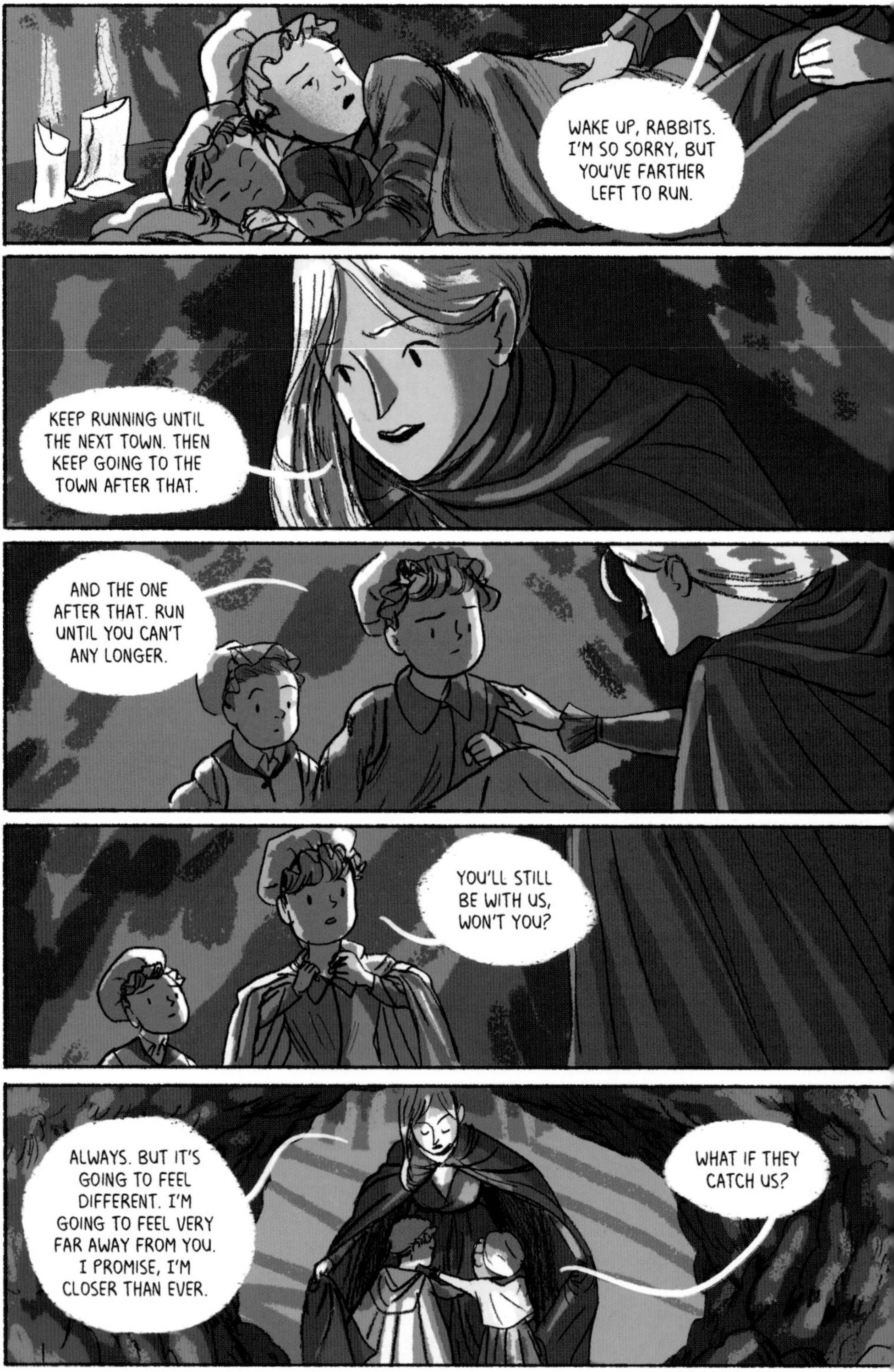
WAKE UP, RABBITS. I'M SO SORRY, BUT YOU'VE FARTHER LEFT TO RUN.
KEEP RUNNING UNTIL THE NEXT TOWN. THEN KEEP GOING TO THE TOWN AFTER THAT.
AND THE ONE AFTER THAT. RUN UNTIL YOU CAN'T ANY LONGER.
YOU'LL STILL BE WITH US, WON'T YOU?
ALWAYS. BUT IT'S GOING TO FEEL DIFFERENT. I'M GOING TO FEEL VERY FAR AWAY FROM YOU. I PROMISE, I'M CLOSER THAN EVER.
WHAT IF THEY CATCH US?

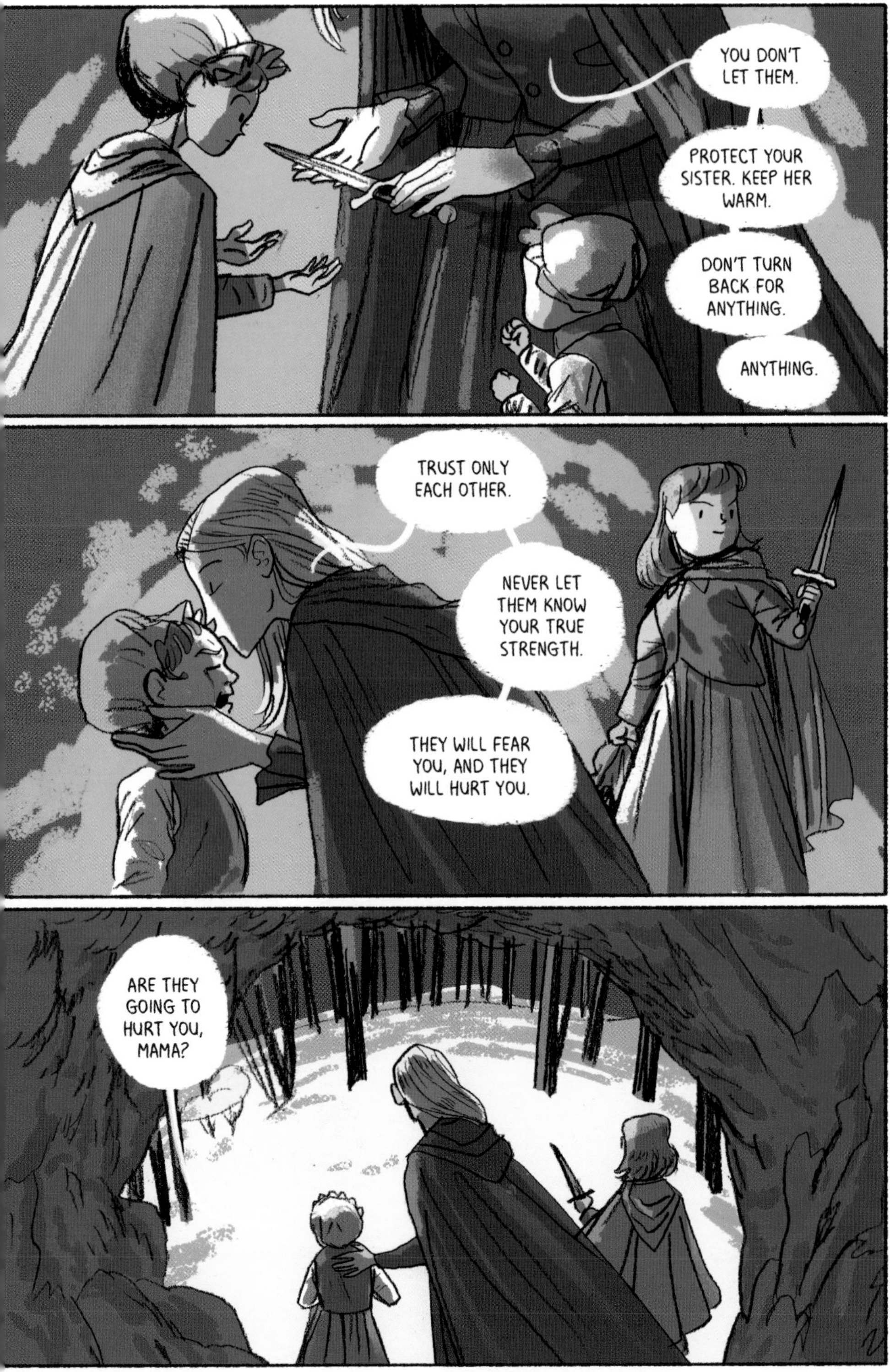
YOU DON'T LET THEM.
PROTECT YOUR SISTER. KEEP HER WARM.
DON'T TURN BACK FOR ANYTHING.
ANYTHING.
TRUST ONLY EACH OTHER.
NEVER LET THEM KNOW YOUR TRUE STRENGTH.
THEY WILL FEAR YOU, AND THEY WILL HURT YOU.
ARE THEY GOING TO HURT YOU, MAMA?

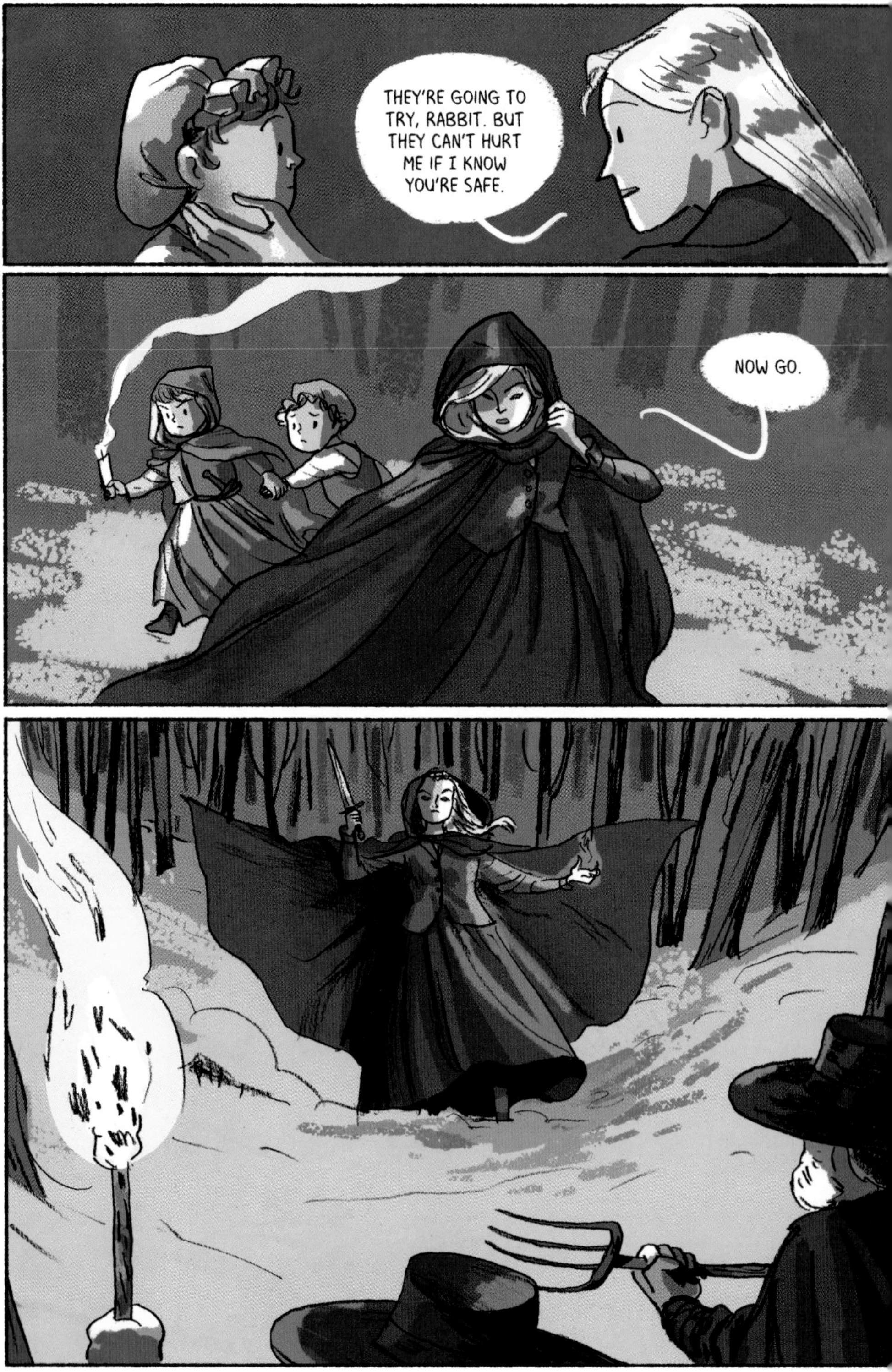
THEY'RE GOING TO TRY, RABBIT. BUT THEY CAN'T HURT ME IF I KNOW YOU'RE SAFE.
NOW GO.

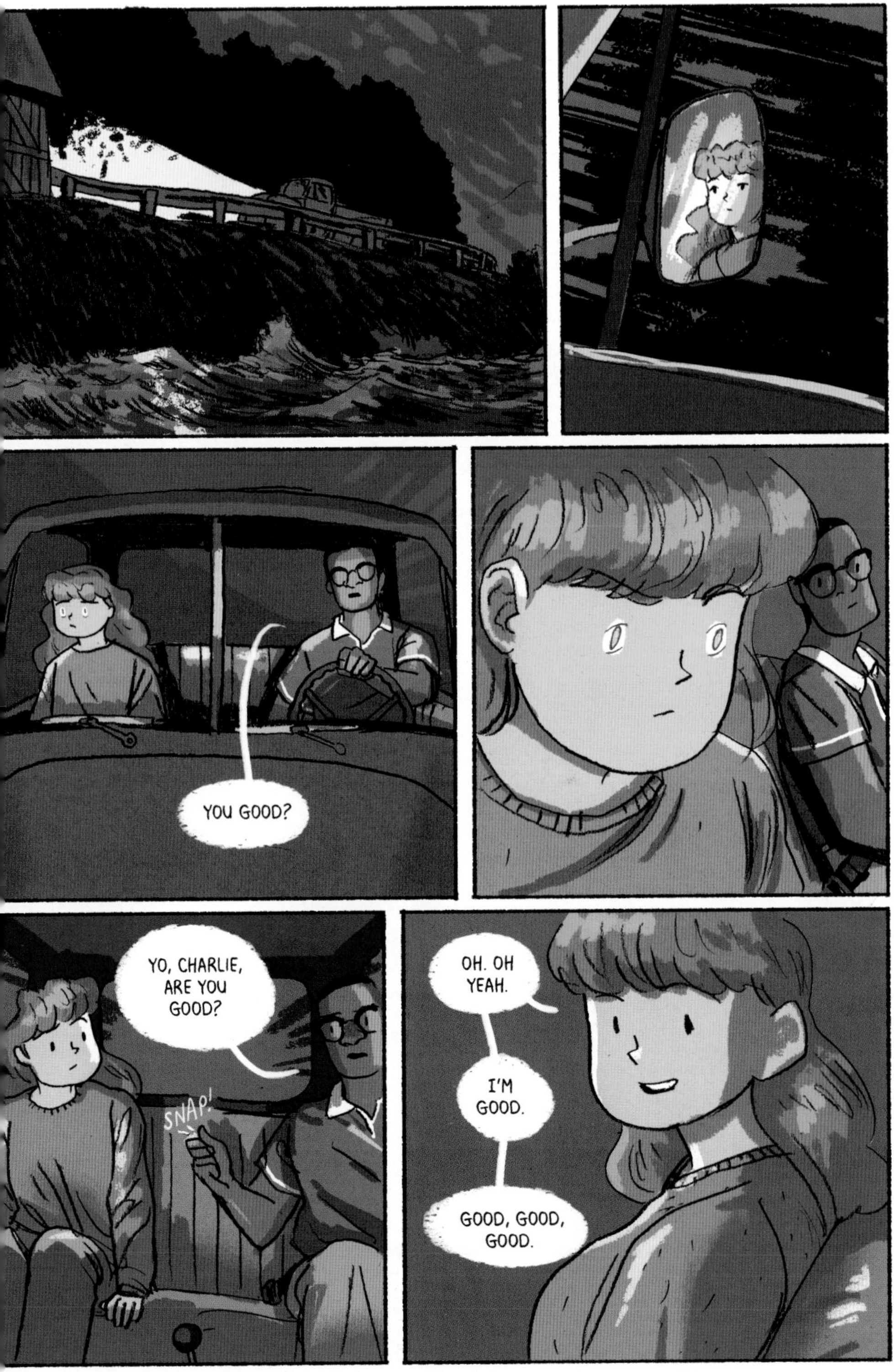
YOU GOOD?
YO, CHARLIE, ARE YOU GOOD?
SNAP!
OH. OH YEAH.
I'M GOOD.
GOOD, GOOD, GOOD.

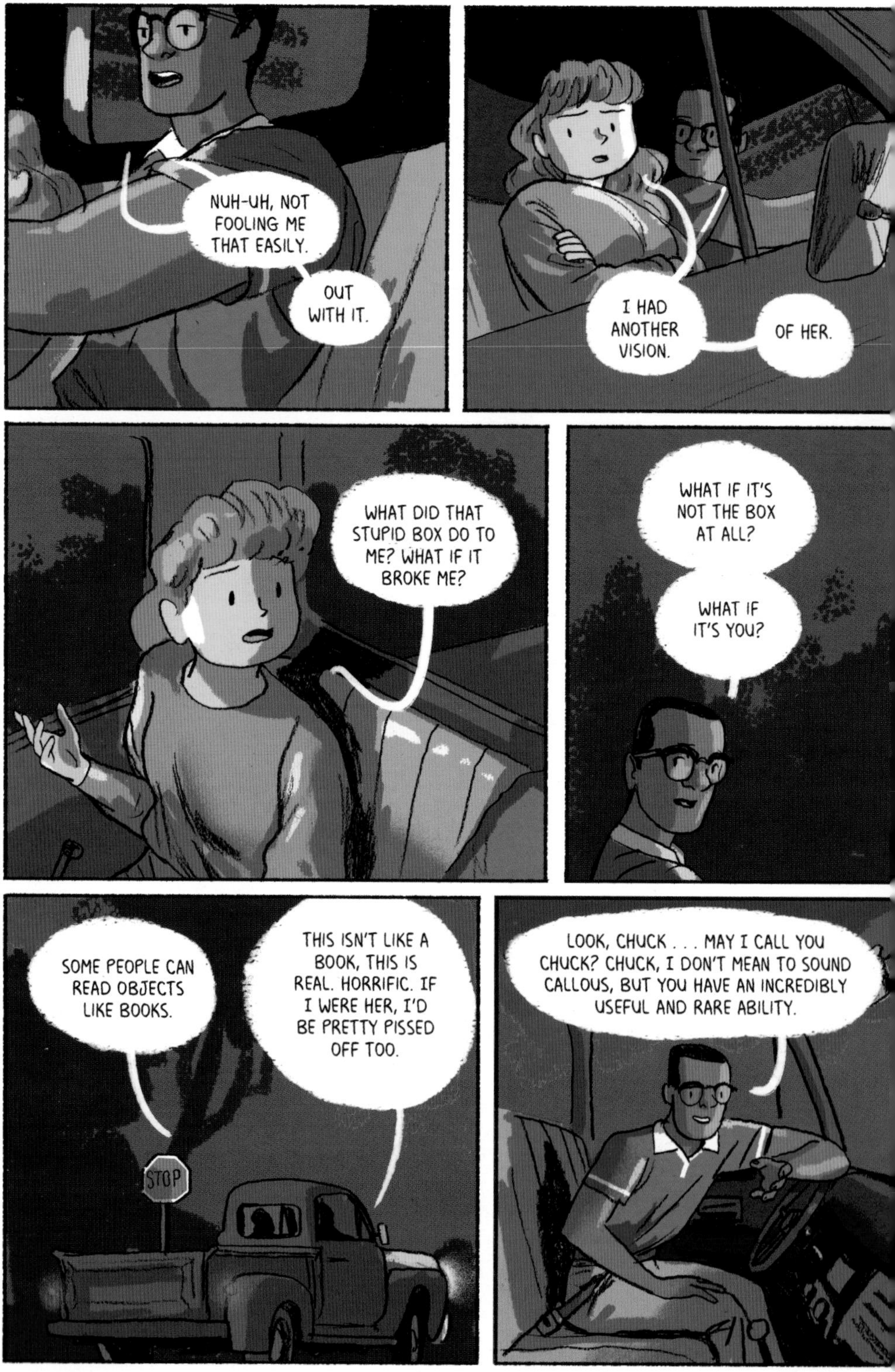
NUH-UH, NOT FOOLING ME THAT EASILY.
OUT WITH IT.
I HAD ANOTHER VISION.
OF HER.
WHAT DID THAT STUPID BOX DO TO ME? WHAT IF IT BROKE ME?
WHAT IF IT'S NOT THE BOX AT ALL?
WHAT IF IT'S YOU?
SOME PEOPLE CAN READ OBJECTS LIKE BOOKS.
THIS ISN'T LIKE A BOOK, THIS IS REAL. HORRIFIC. IF I WERE HER, I'D BE PRETTY PISSED OFF TOO.
STOP
LOOK, CHUCK . . . MAY I CALL YOU CHUCK? CHUCK, I DON'T MEAN TO SOUND CALLOUS, BUT YOU HAVE AN INCREDIBLY USEFUL AND RARE ABILITY.

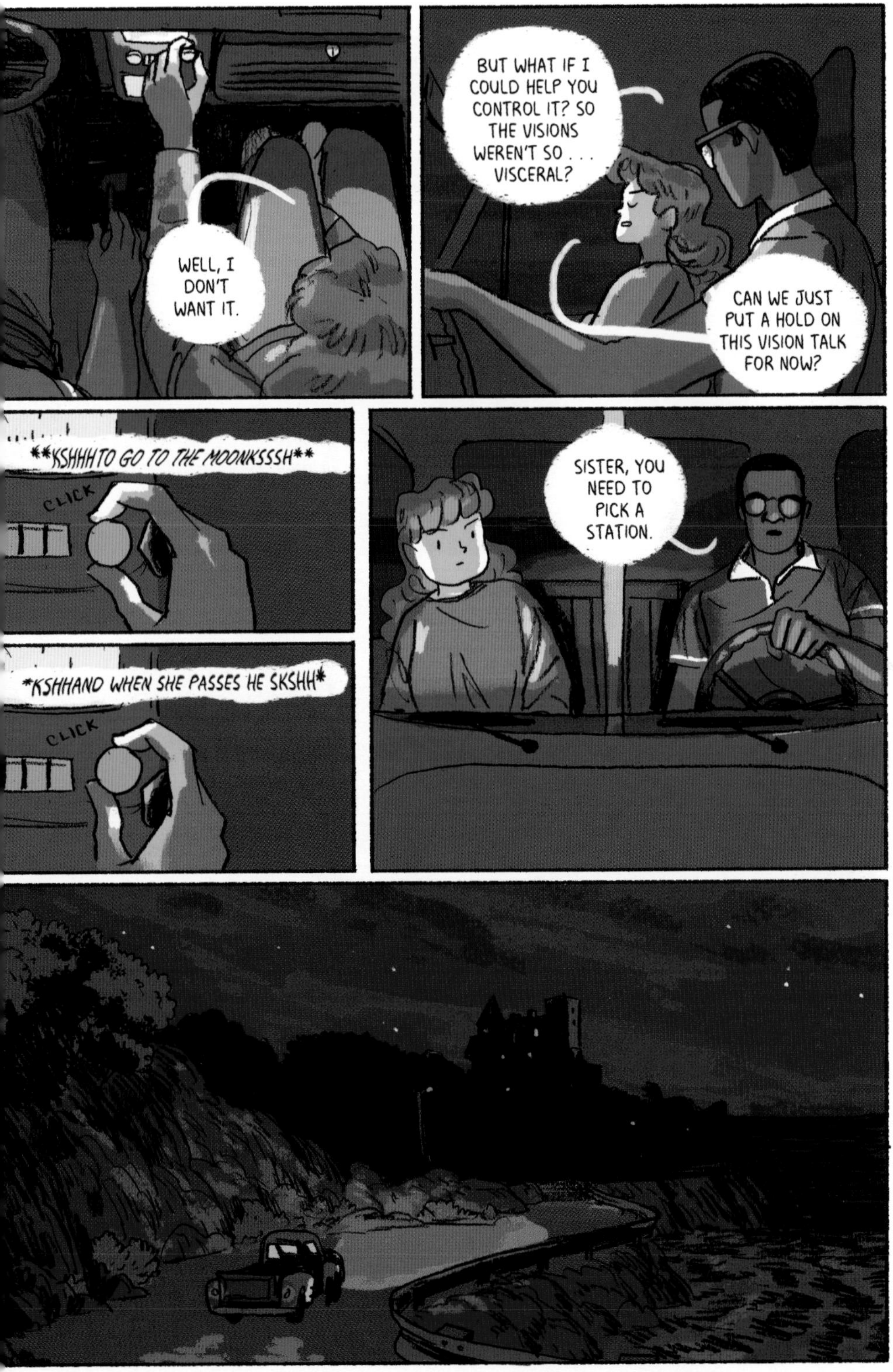
WELL, I DON'T WANT IT.
BUT WHAT IF I COULD HELP YOU CONTROL IT? SO THE VISIONS WEREN'T SO . . . VISCERAL?
CAN WE JUST PUT A HOLD ON THIS VISION TALK FOR NOW?
KSHHHTO GO TO THE MOONKSSSH
CLICK
KSHHAND WHEN SHE PASSES HE SKSHH
CLICK
SISTER, YOU NEED TO PICK A STATION.

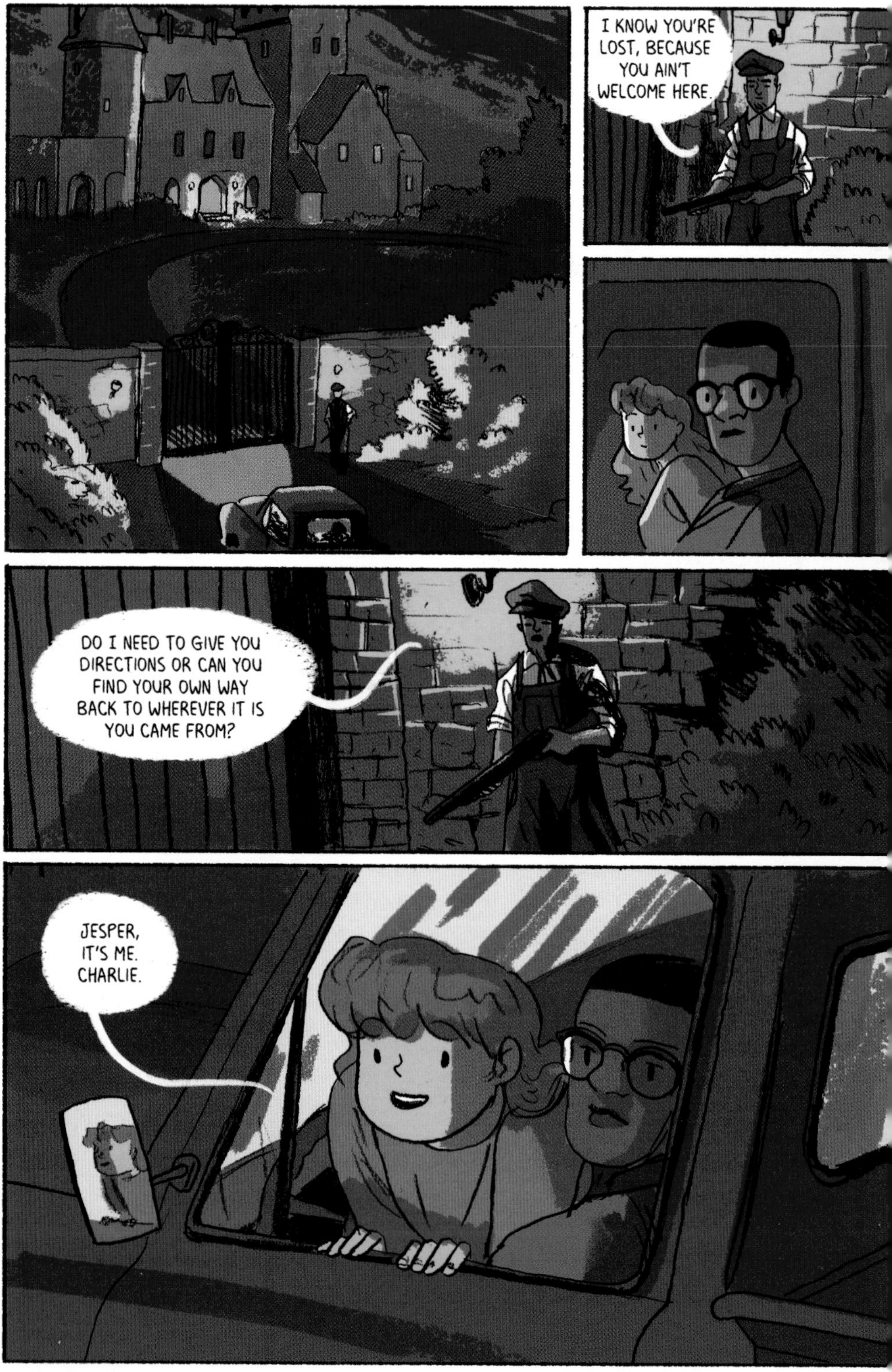
I KNOW YOU'RE LOST, BECAUSE YOU AIN'T WELCOME HERE.
DO I NEED TO GIVE YOU DIRECTIONS OR CAN YOU FIND YOUR OWN WAY BACK TO WHEREVER IT IS YOU CAME FROM?
JESPER, IT'S ME. CHARLIE.

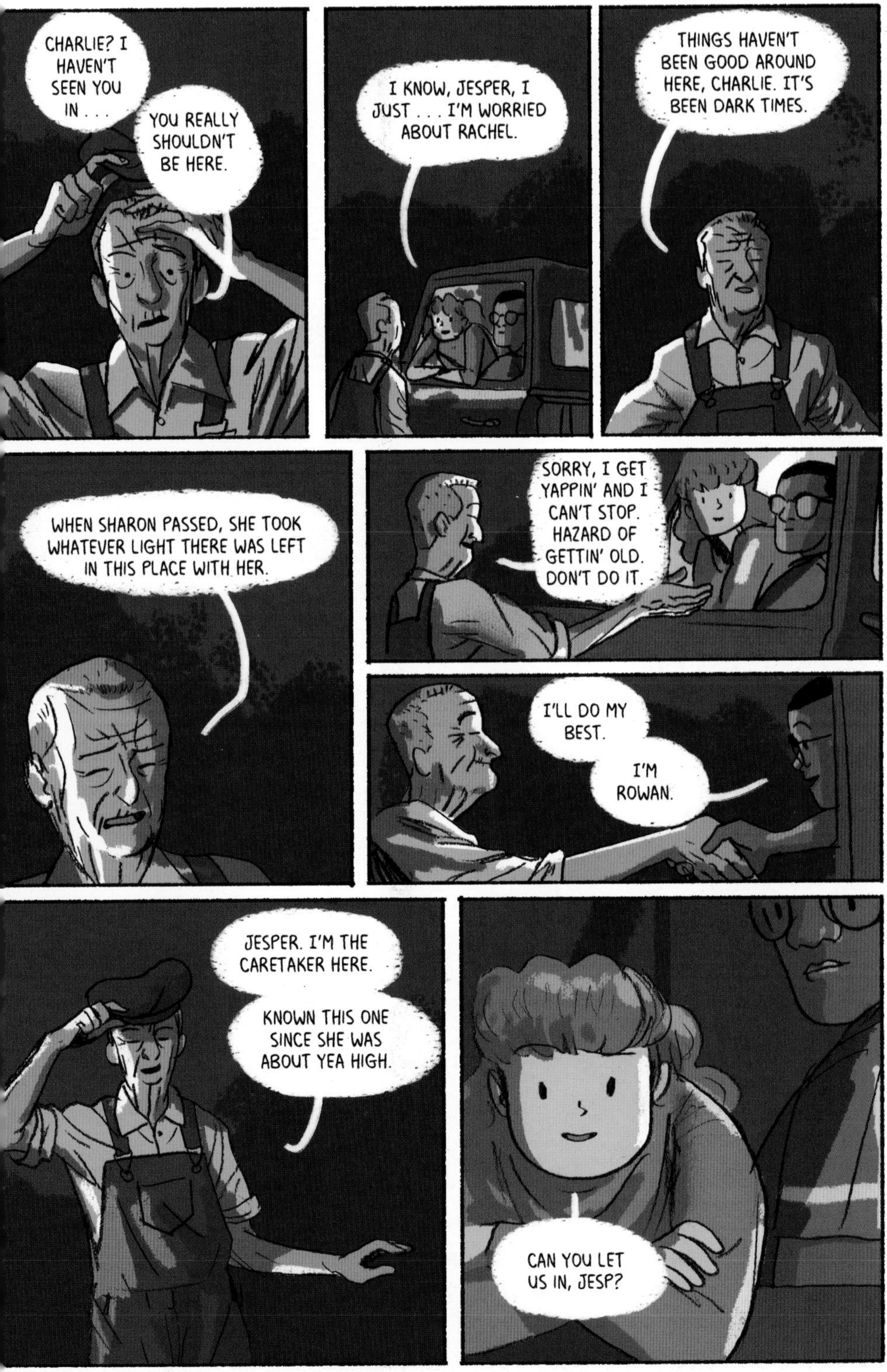
CHARLIE? I HAVEN'T SEEN YOU IN . . .
YOU REALLY SHOULDN'T BE HERE.
I KNOW, JESPER, I JUST . . . I'M WORRIED ABOUT RACHEL.
THINGS HAVEN'T BEEN GOOD AROUND HERE, CHARLIE. IT'S BEEN DARK TIMES.
WHEN SHARON PASSED, SHE TOOK WHATEVER LIGHT THERE WAS LEFT IN THIS PLACE WITH HER.
SORRY, I GET YAPPIN' AND I CAN'T STOP. HAZARD OF GETTIN' OLD. DON'T DO IT.
I'LL DO MY BEST.
I'M ROWAN.
JESPER. I'M THE CARETAKER HERE.
KNOWN THIS ONE SINCE SHE WAS ABOUT YEA HIGH.
CAN YOU LET US IN, JESP?

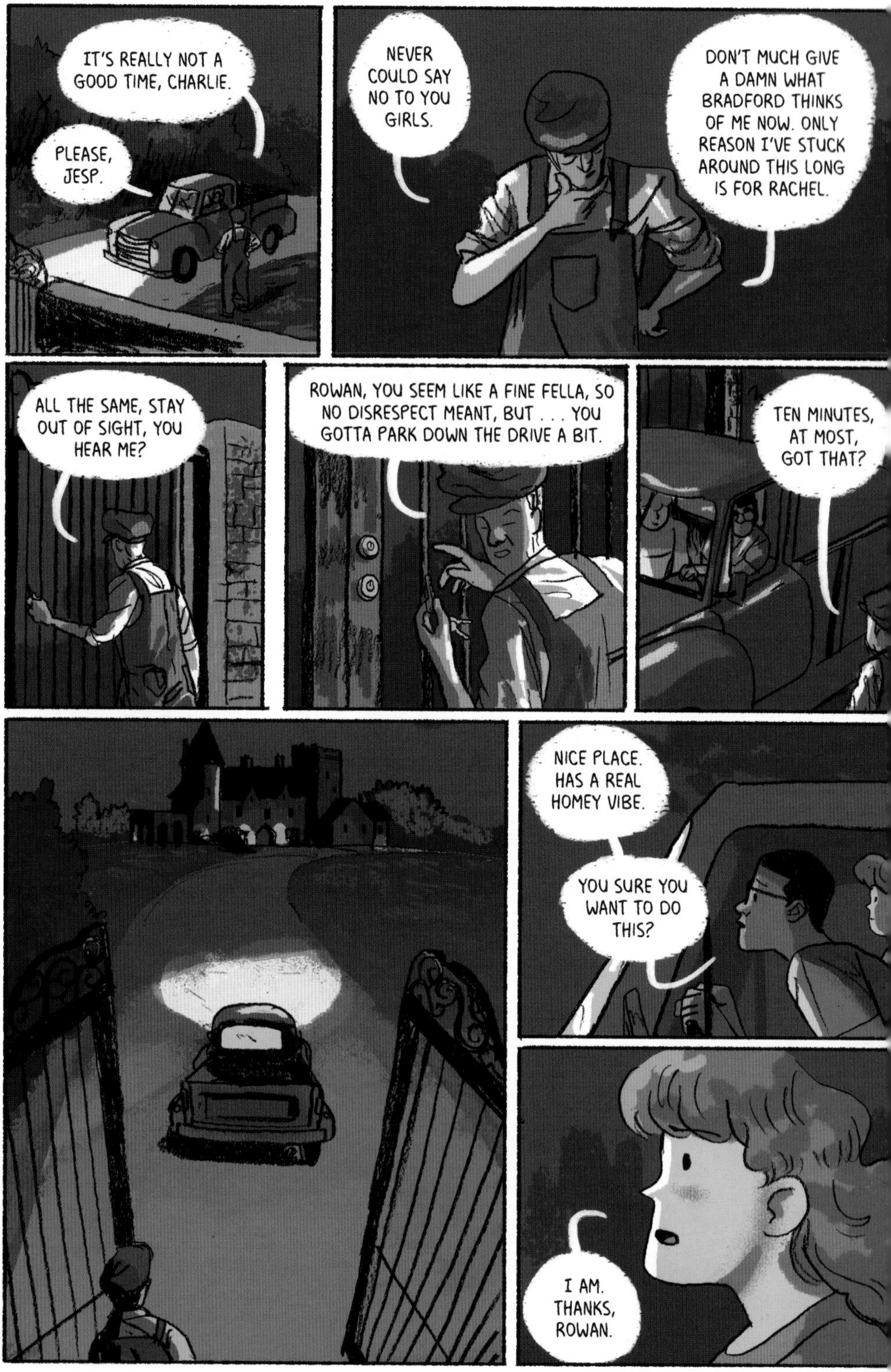
IT'S REALLY NOT A GOOD TIME, CHARLIE.
PLEASE, JESP.
NEVER COULD SAY NO TO YOU GIRLS.
DON'T MUCH GIVE A DAMN WHAT BRADFORD THINKS OF ME NOW. ONLY REASON I'VE STUCK AROUND THIS LONG IS FOR RACHEL.
ALL THE SAME, STAY OUT OF SIGHT, YOU HEAR ME?
ROWAN, YOU SEEM LIKE A FINE FELLA, SO NO DISRESPECT MEANT, BUT . . . YOU GOTTA PARK DOWN THE DRIVE A BIT.
TEN MINUTES, AT MOST, GOT THAT?
NICE PLACE. HAS A REAL HOMEY VIBE.
YOU SURE YOU WANT TO DO THIS?
I AM. THANKS, ROWAN.

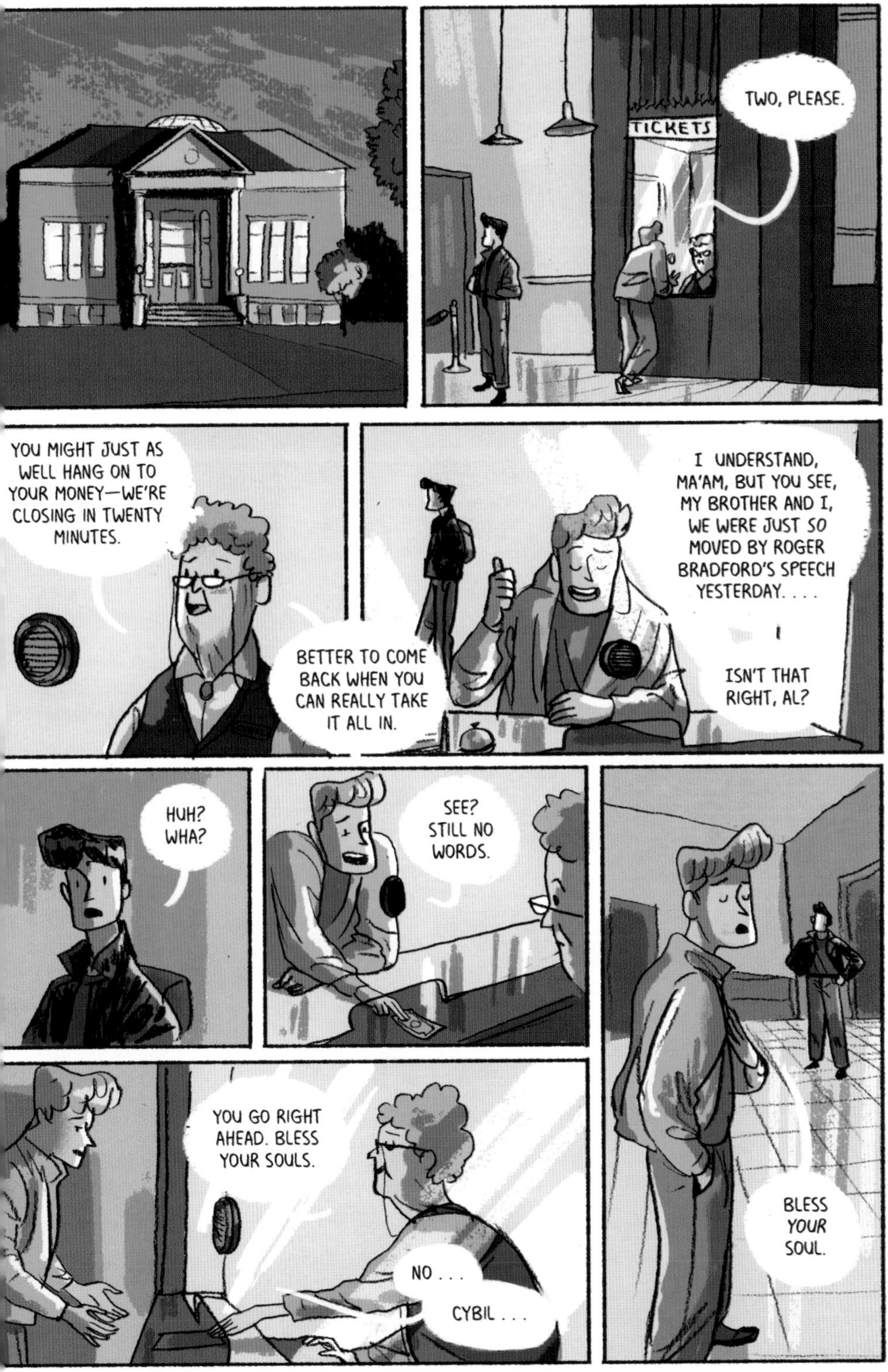
TWO, PLEASE.
TICKETS
YOU MIGHT JUST AS WELL HANG ON TO YOUR MONEY—WE'RE CLOSING IN TWENTY MINUTES.
BETTER TO COME BACK WHEN YOU CAN REALLY TAKE IT ALL IN.
I UNDERSTAND, MA'AM, BUT YOU SEE, MY BROTHER AND I, WE WERE JUST SO MOVED BY ROGER BRADFORD'S SPEECH YESTERDAY. . . .
ISN'T THAT RIGHT, AL?
HUH? WHA?
SEE? STILL NO WORDS.
BLESS *YOUR* SOUL.
YOU GO RIGHT AHEAD. BLESS YOUR SOULS.
NO . . .
CYBIL . . .

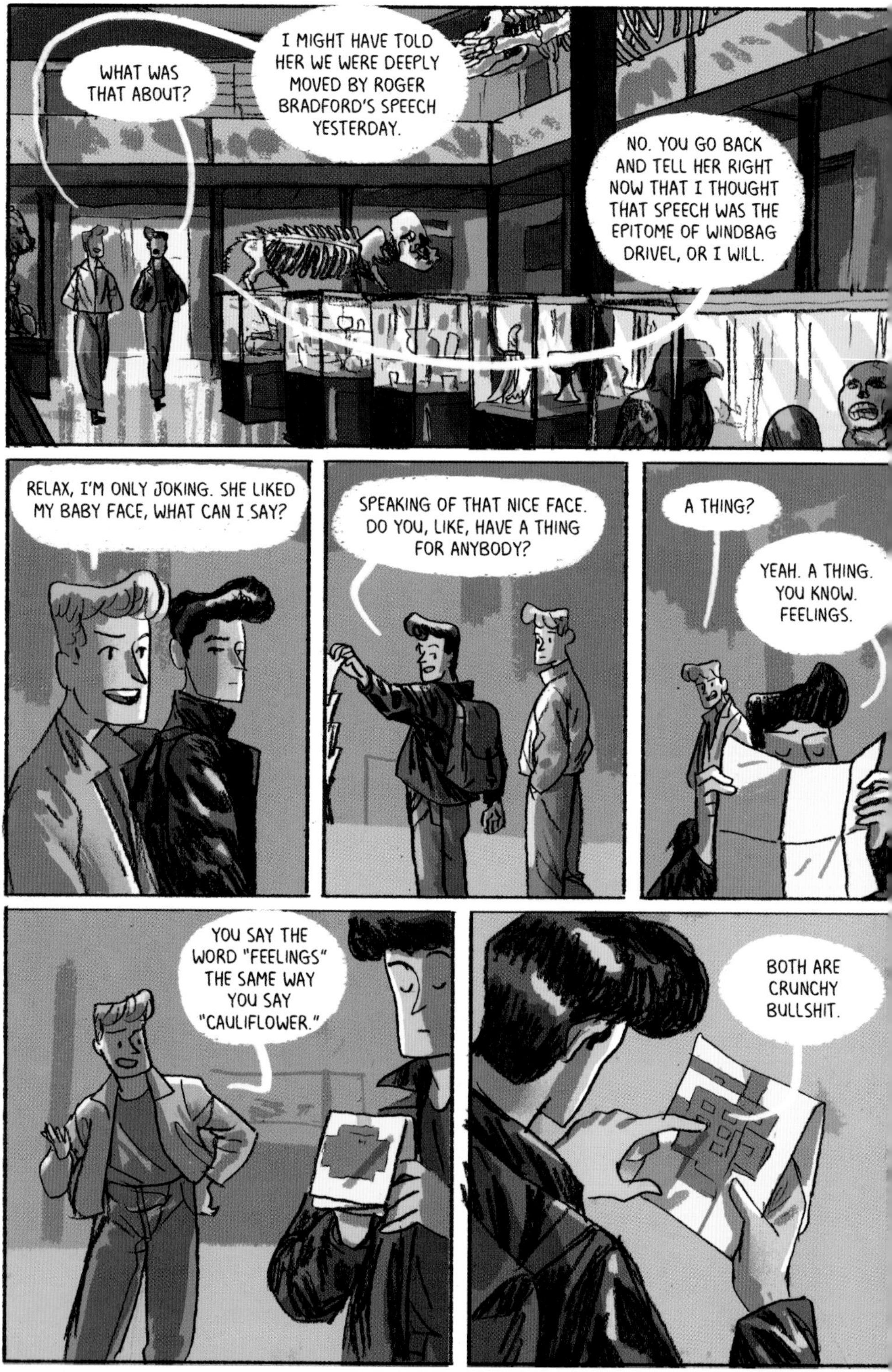
WHAT WAS THAT ABOUT?
I MIGHT HAVE TOLD HER WE WERE DEEPLY MOVED BY ROGER BRADFORD'S SPEECH YESTERDAY.
NO. YOU GO BACK AND TELL HER RIGHT NOW THAT I THOUGHT THAT SPEECH WAS THE EPITOME OF WINDBAG DRIVEL, OR I WILL.
RELAX, I'M ONLY JOKING. SHE LIKED MY BABY FACE, WHAT CAN I SAY?
SPEAKING OF THAT NICE FACE. DO YOU, LIKE, HAVE A THING FOR ANYBODY?
A THING?
YEAH. A THING. YOU KNOW. FEELINGS.
YOU SAY THE WORD "FEELINGS" THE SAME WAY YOU SAY "CAULIFLOWER."
BOTH ARE CRUNCHY BULLSHIT.

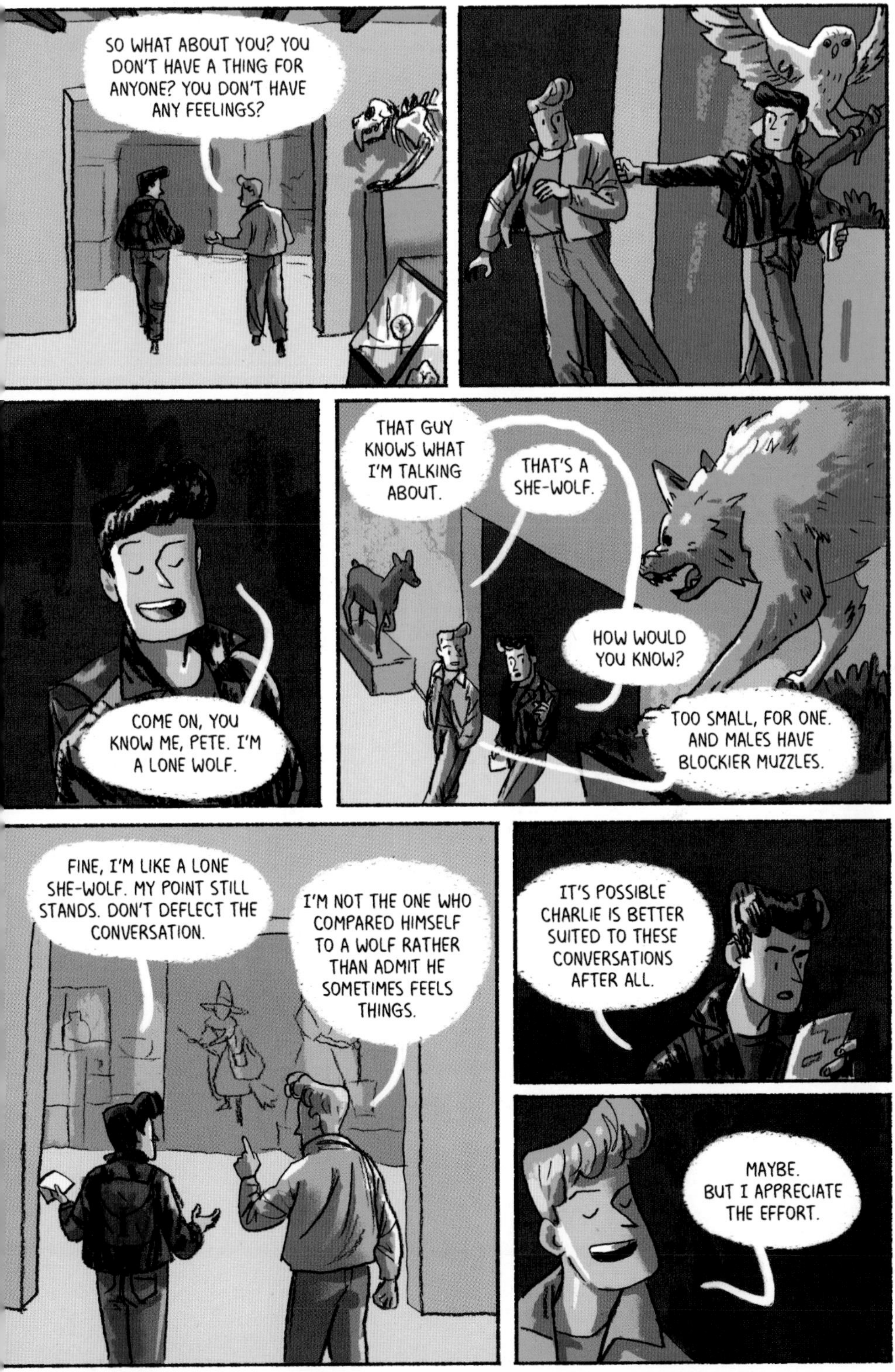
SO WHAT ABOUT YOU? YOU DON'T HAVE A THING FOR ANYONE? YOU DON'T HAVE ANY FEELINGS?
COME ON, YOU KNOW ME, PETE. I'M A LONE WOLF.
THAT GUY KNOWS WHAT I'M TALKING ABOUT.
THAT'S A SHE-WOLF.
HOW WOULD YOU KNOW?
TOO SMALL, FOR ONE. AND MALES HAVE BLOCKIER MUZZLES.
FINE, I'M LIKE A LONE SHE-WOLF. MY POINT STILL STANDS. DON'T DEFLECT THE CONVERSATION.
I'M NOT THE ONE WHO COMPARED HIMSELF TO A WOLF RATHER THAN ADMIT HE SOMETIMES FEELS THINGS.
IT'S POSSIBLE CHARLIE IS BETTER SUITED TO THESE CONVERSATIONS AFTER ALL.
MAYBE. BUT I APPRECIATE THE EFFORT.

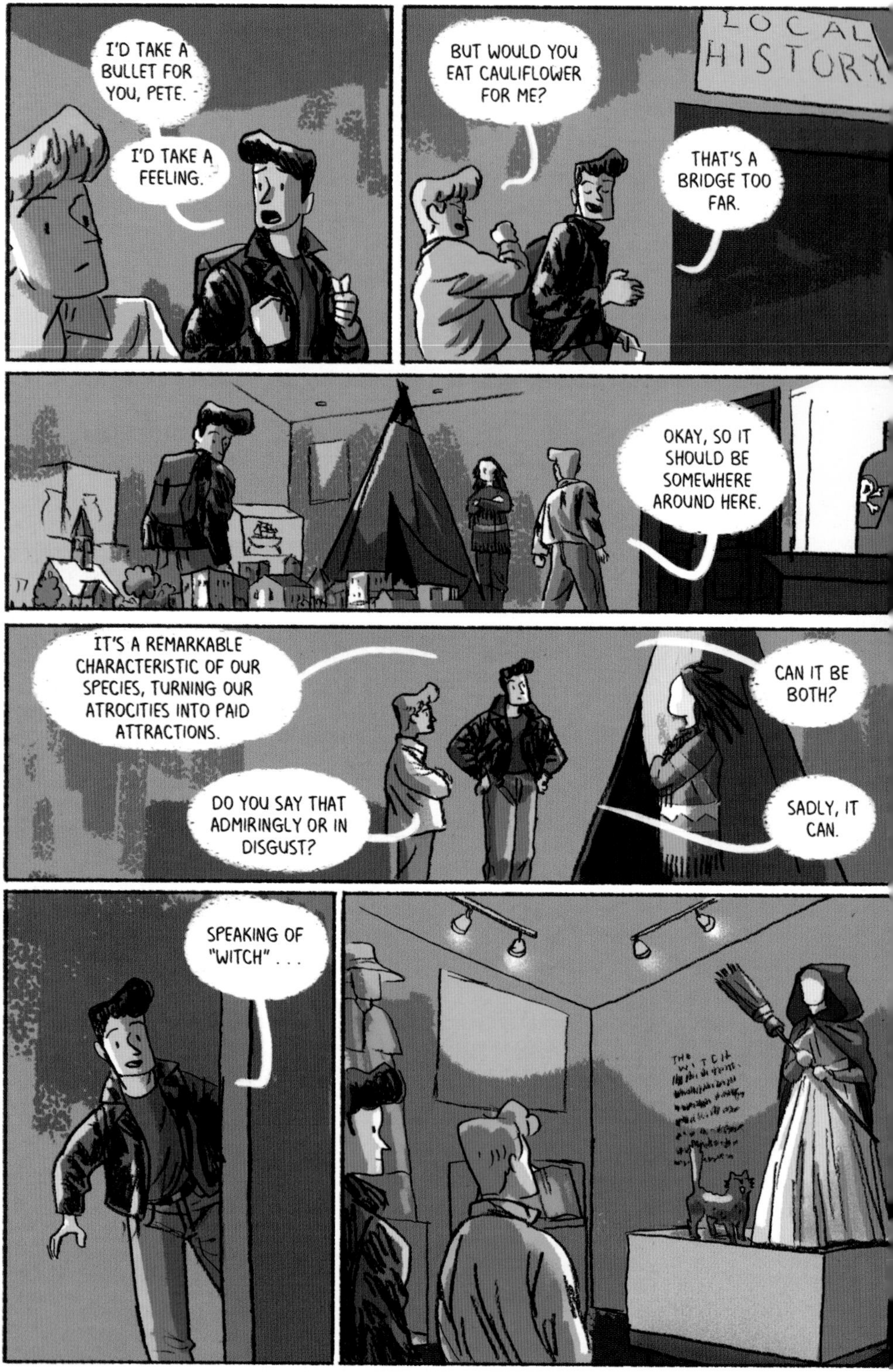
I'D TAKE A BULLET FOR YOU, PETE.
I'D TAKE A FEELING.
BUT WOULD YOU EAT CAULIFLOWER FOR ME?
LOCAL HISTORY
THAT'S A BRIDGE TOO FAR.
OKAY, SO IT SHOULD BE SOMEWHERE AROUND HERE.
IT'S A REMARKABLE CHARACTERISTIC OF OUR SPECIES, TURNING OUR ATROCITIES INTO PAID ATTRACTIONS.
DO YOU SAY THAT ADMIRINGLY OR IN DISGUST?
CAN IT BE BOTH?
SADLY, IT CAN.
SPEAKING OF "WITCH" . . .

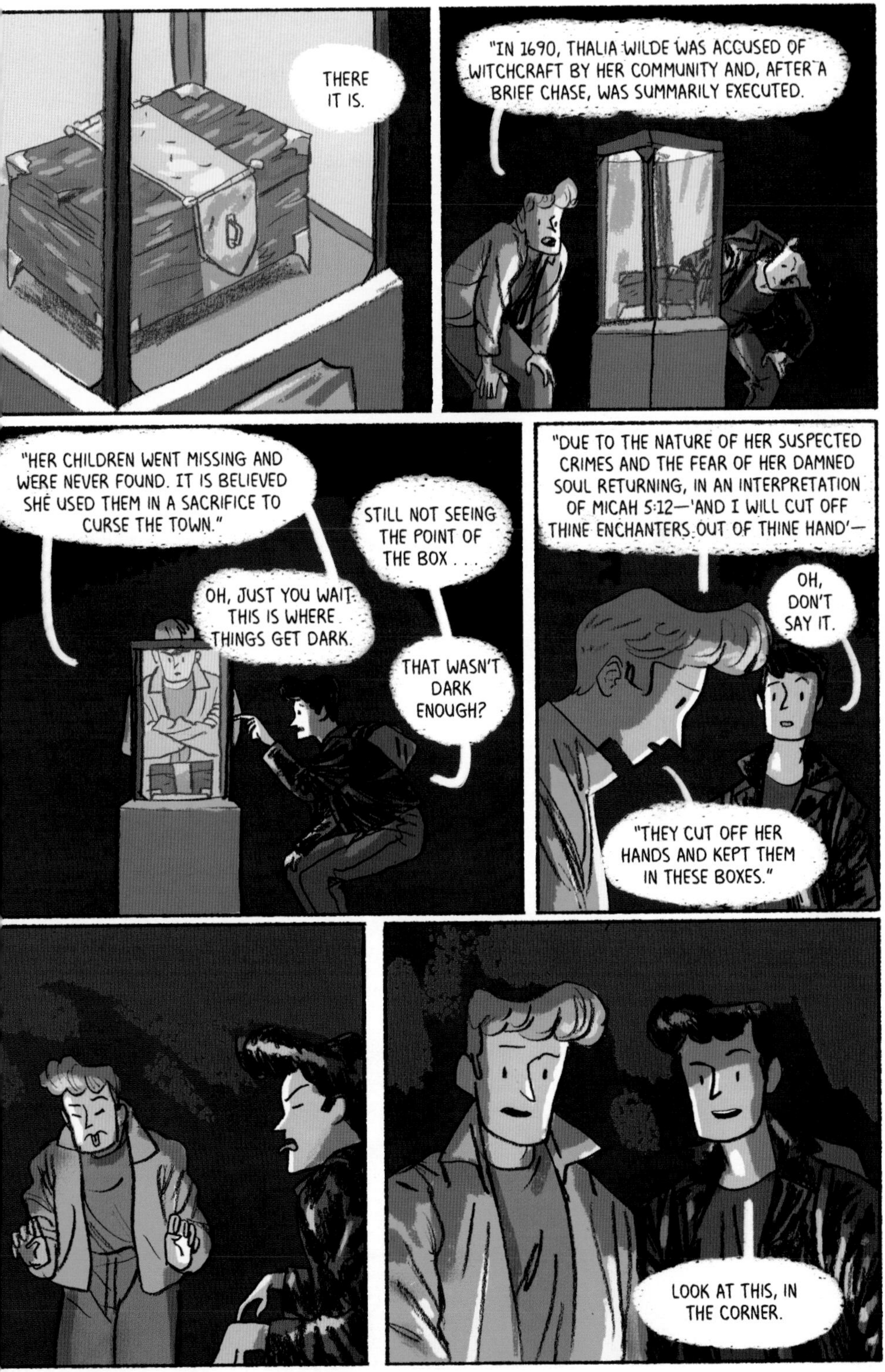
THERE IT IS.
"IN 1690, THALIA WILDE WAS ACCUSED OF WITCHCRAFT BY HER COMMUNITY AND, AFTER A BRIEF CHASE, WAS SUMMARILY EXECUTED.
"HER CHILDREN WENT MISSING AND WERE NEVER FOUND. IT IS BELIEVED SHE USED THEM IN A SACRIFICE TO CURSE THE TOWN."
STILL NOT SEEING THE POINT OF THE BOX . . .
OH, JUST YOU WAIT. THIS IS WHERE THINGS GET DARK.
THAT WASN'T DARK ENOUGH?
"DUE TO THE NATURE OF HER SUSPECTED CRIMES AND THE FEAR OF HER DAMNED SOUL RETURNING, IN AN INTERPRETATION OF MICAH 5:12—'AND I WILL CUT OFF THINE ENCHANTERS OUT OF THINE HAND'—
OH, DON'T SAY IT.
"THEY CUT OFF HER HANDS AND KEPT THEM IN THESE BOXES."
LOOK AT THIS, IN THE CORNER.

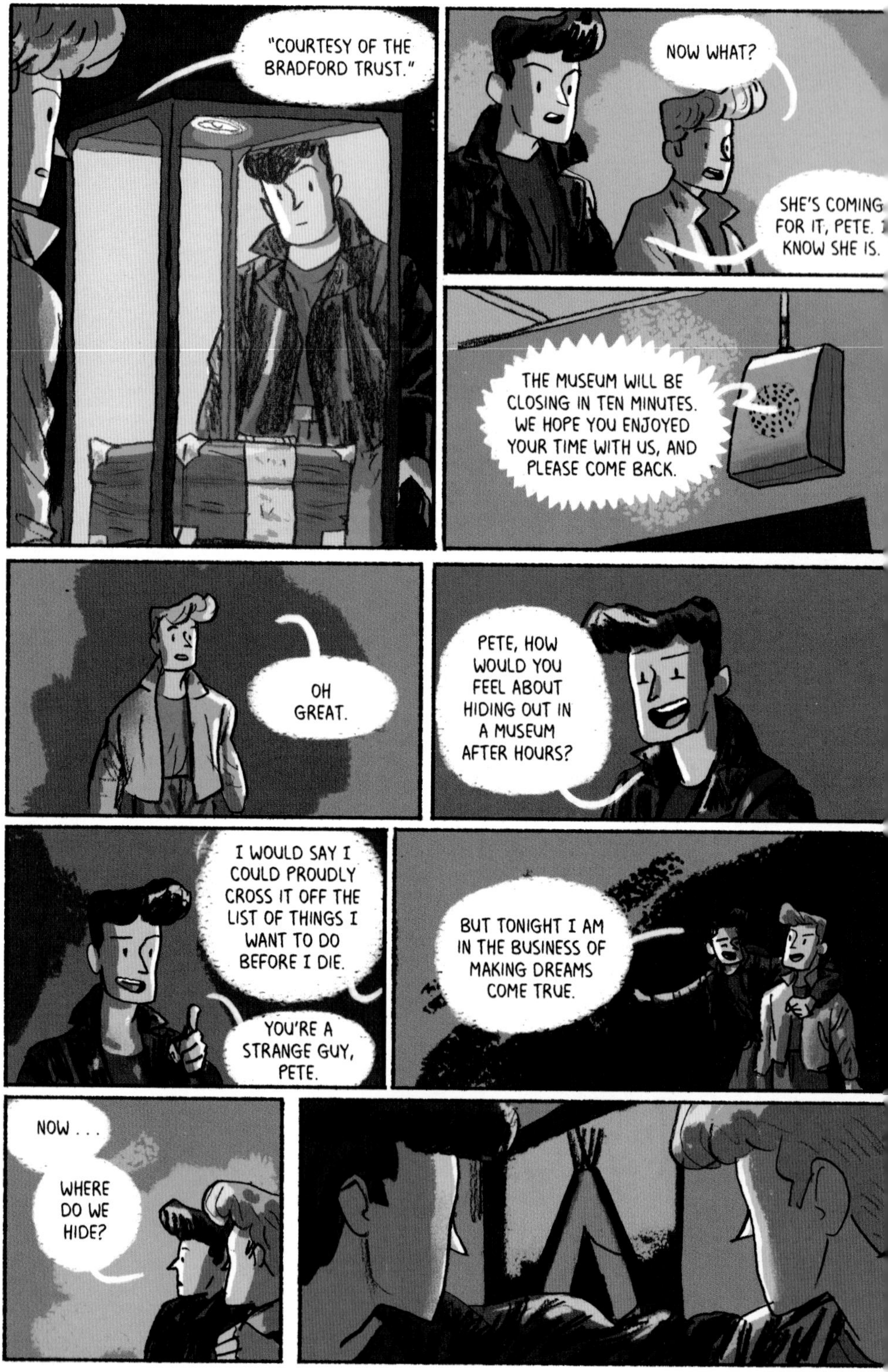
"COURTESY OF THE BRADFORD TRUST."
NOW WHAT?
SHE'S COMING FOR IT, PETE. I KNOW SHE IS.
THE MUSEUM WILL BE CLOSING IN TEN MINUTES. WE HOPE YOU ENJOYED YOUR TIME WITH US, AND PLEASE COME BACK.
OH GREAT.
PETE, HOW WOULD YOU FEEL ABOUT HIDING OUT IN A MUSEUM AFTER HOURS?
I WOULD SAY I COULD PROUDLY CROSS IT OFF THE LIST OF THINGS I WANT TO DO BEFORE I DIE.
YOU'RE A STRANGE GUY, PETE.
BUT TONIGHT I AM IN THE BUSINESS OF MAKING DREAMS COME TRUE.
NOW . . .
WHERE DO WE HIDE?

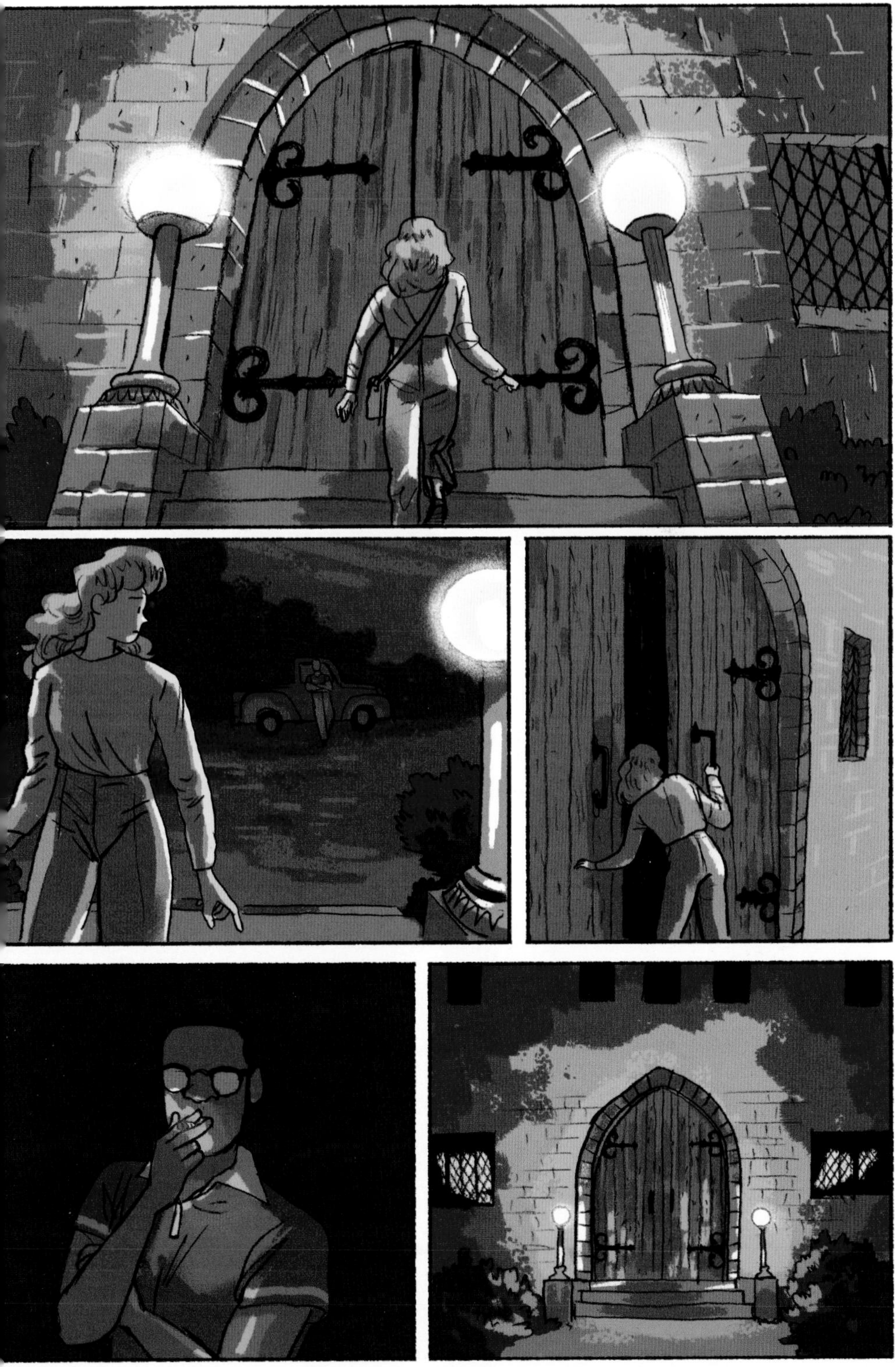

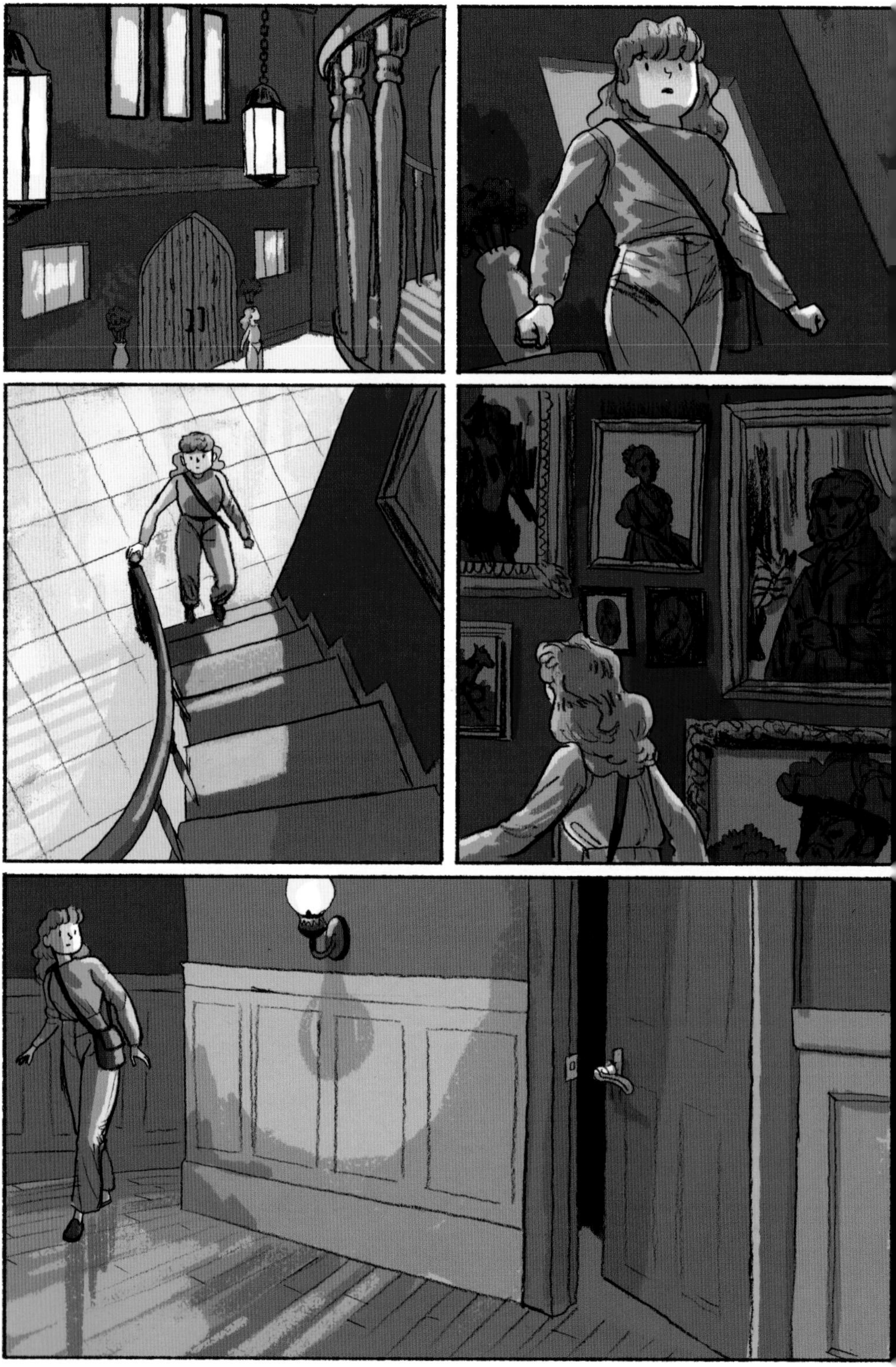

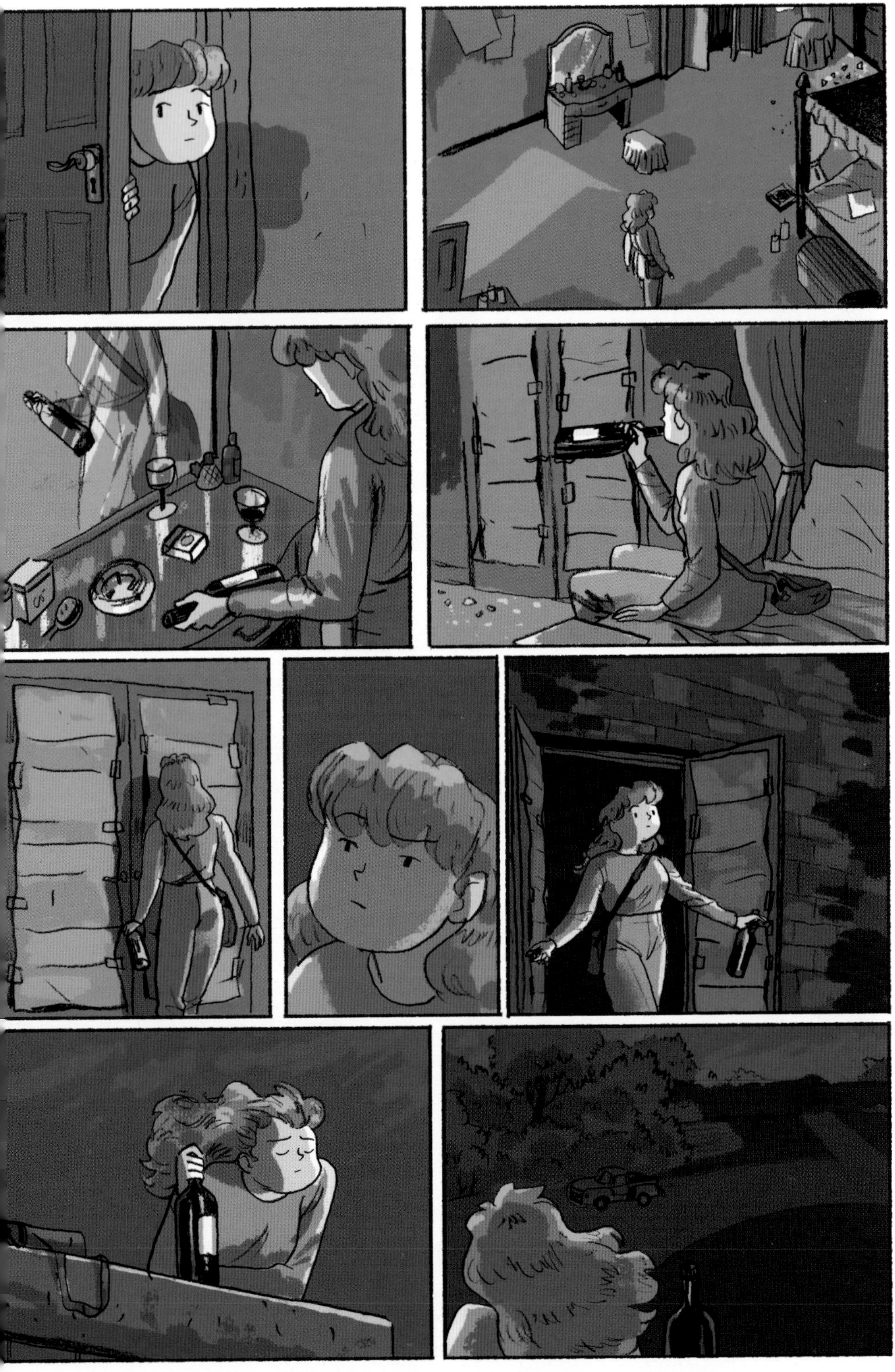

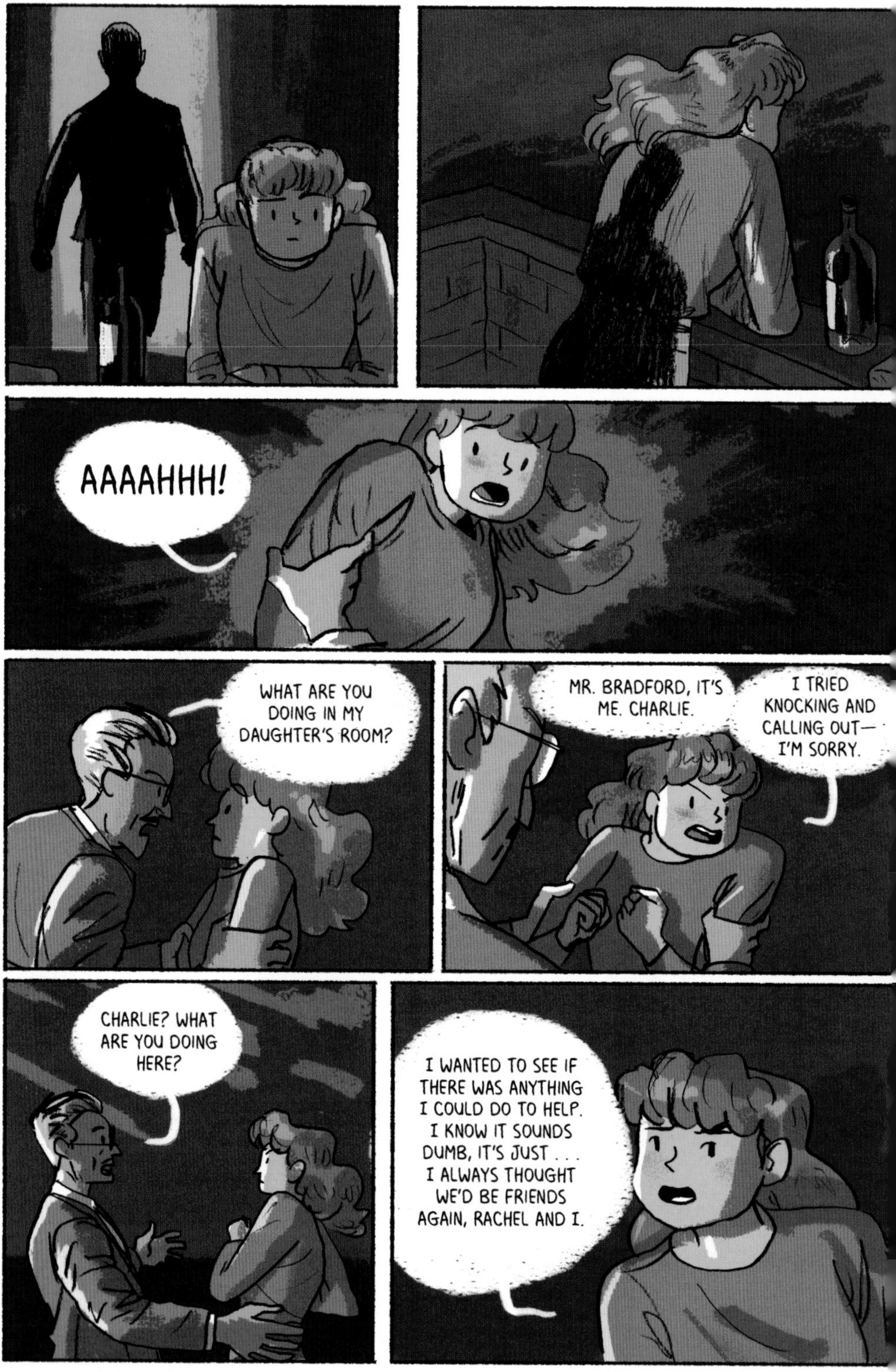
AAAAHHH!
WHAT ARE YOU DOING IN MY DAUGHTER'S ROOM?
MR. BRADFORD, IT'S ME. CHARLIE.
I TRIED KNOCKING AND CALLING OUT— I'M SORRY.
CHARLIE? WHAT ARE YOU DOING HERE?
I WANTED TO SEE IF THERE WAS ANYTHING I COULD DO TO HELP. I KNOW IT SOUNDS DUMB, IT'S JUST . . . I ALWAYS THOUGHT WE'D BE FRIENDS AGAIN, RACHEL AND I.

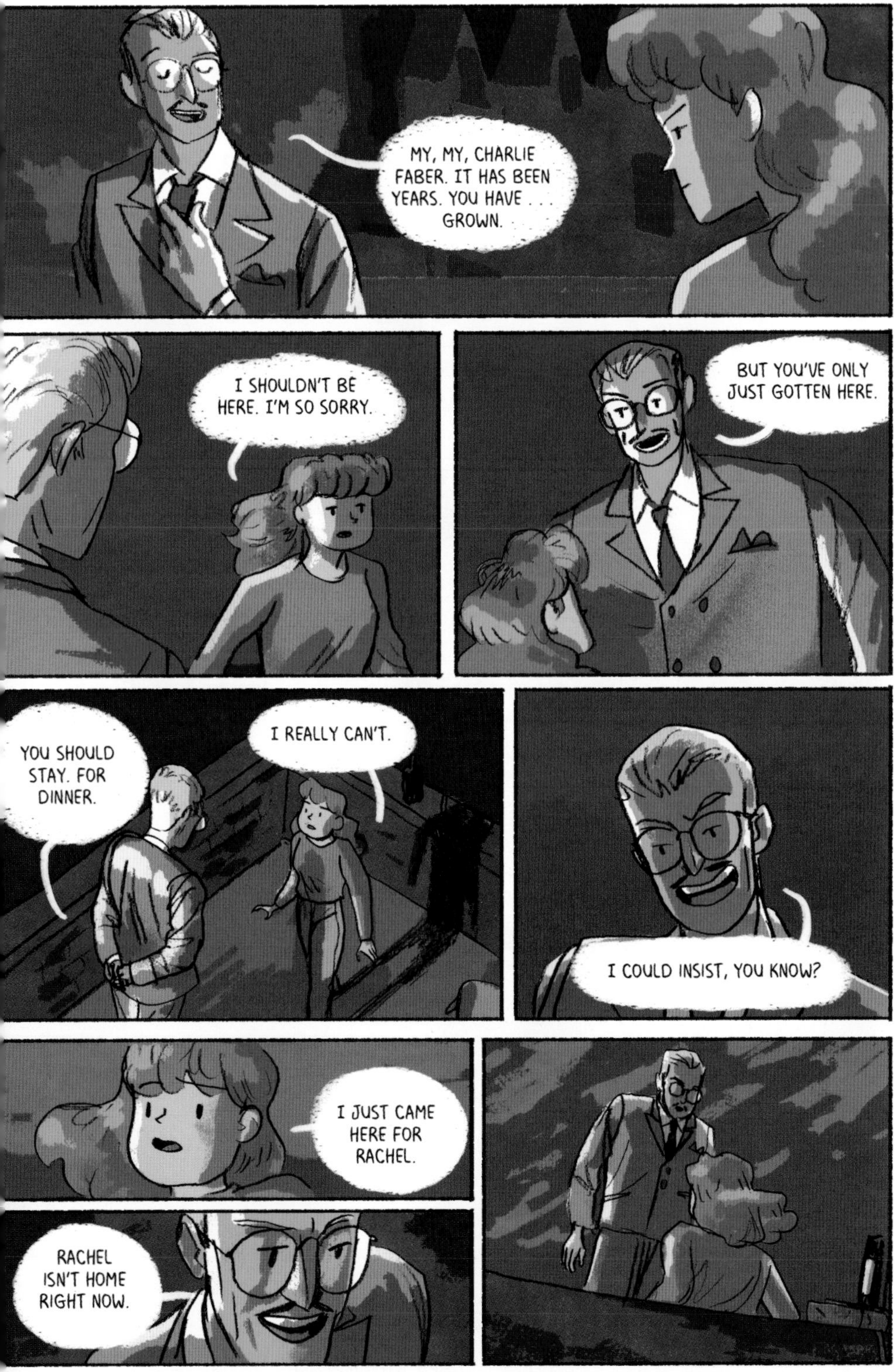
MY, MY, CHARLIE FABER. IT HAS BEEN YEARS. YOU HAVE . . . GROWN.
I SHOULDN'T BE HERE. I'M SO SORRY.
BUT YOU'VE ONLY JUST GOTTEN HERE.
YOU SHOULD STAY. FOR DINNER.
I REALLY CAN'T.
I COULD INSIST, YOU KNOW?
I JUST CAME HERE FOR RACHEL.
RACHEL ISN'T HOME RIGHT NOW.

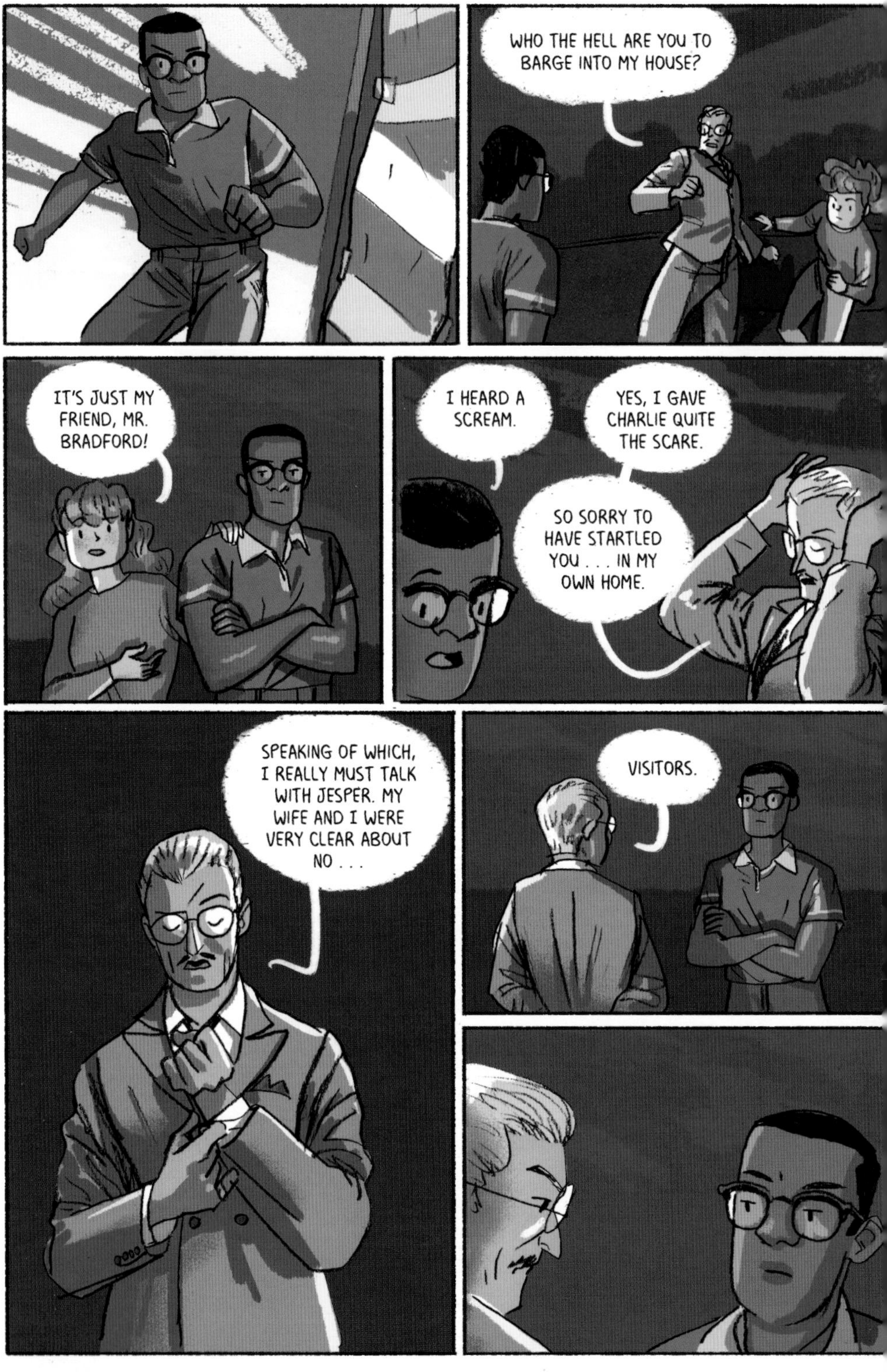
WHO THE HELL ARE YOU TO BARGE INTO MY HOUSE?
IT'S JUST MY FRIEND, MR. BRADFORD!
I HEARD A SCREAM.
YES, I GAVE CHARLIE QUITE THE SCARE.
SO SORRY TO HAVE STARTLED YOU . . . IN MY OWN HOME.
SPEAKING OF WHICH, I REALLY MUST TALK WITH JESPER. MY WIFE AND I WERE VERY CLEAR ABOUT NO . . .
VISITORS.

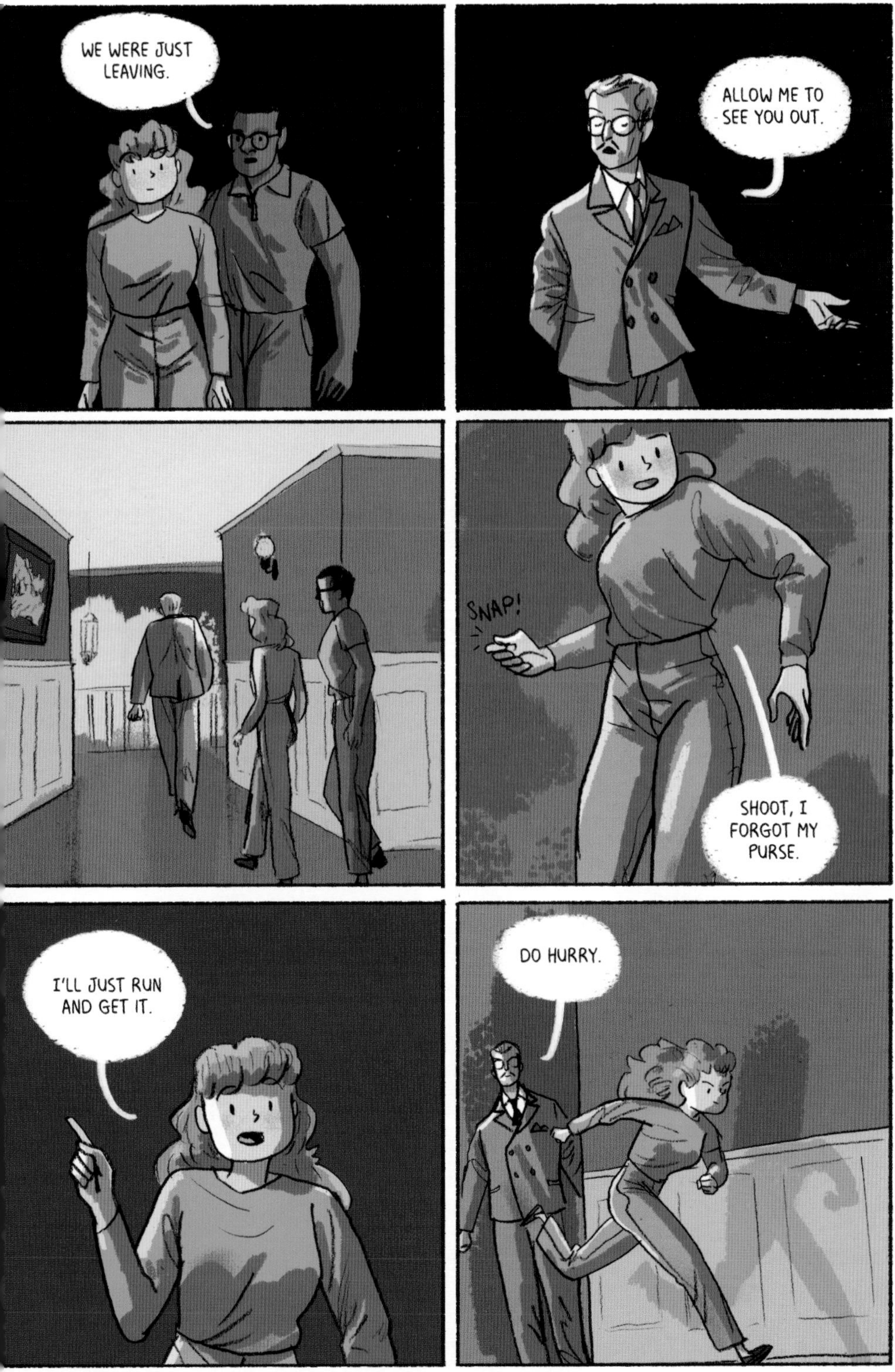
WE WERE JUST LEAVING.
ALLOW ME TO SEE YOU OUT.
SNAP!
SHOOT, I FORGOT MY PURSE.
I'LL JUST RUN AND GET IT.
DO HURRY.

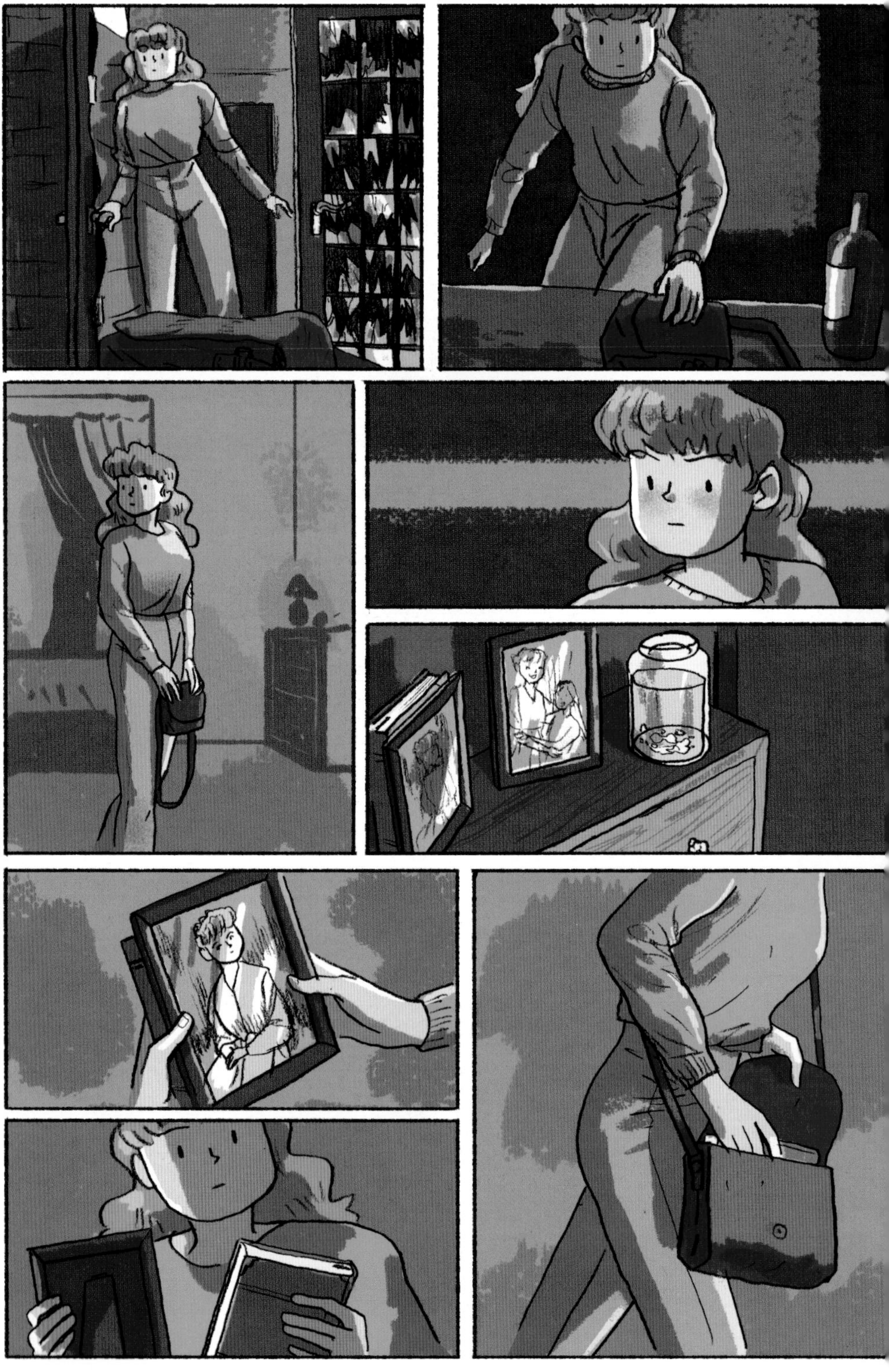

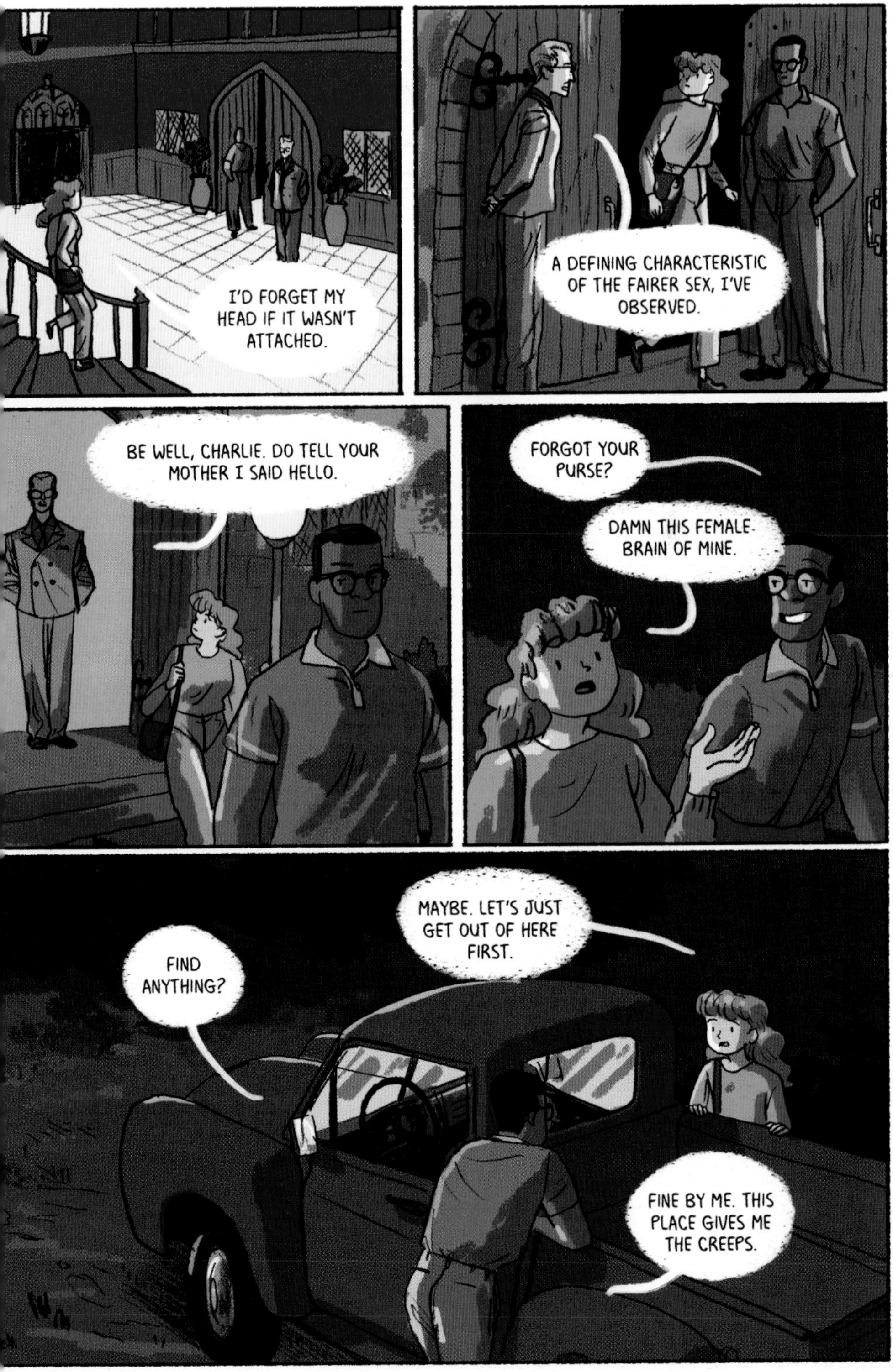
I'D FORGET MY HEAD IF IT WASN'T ATTACHED.
A DEFINING CHARACTERISTIC OF THE FAIRER SEX, I'VE OBSERVED.
BE WELL, CHARLIE. DO TELL YOUR MOTHER I SAID HELLO.
FORGOT YOUR PURSE?
DAMN THIS FEMALE BRAIN OF MINE.
FIND ANYTHING?
MAYBE. LET'S JUST GET OUT OF HERE FIRST.
FINE BY ME. THIS PLACE GIVES ME THE CREEPS.

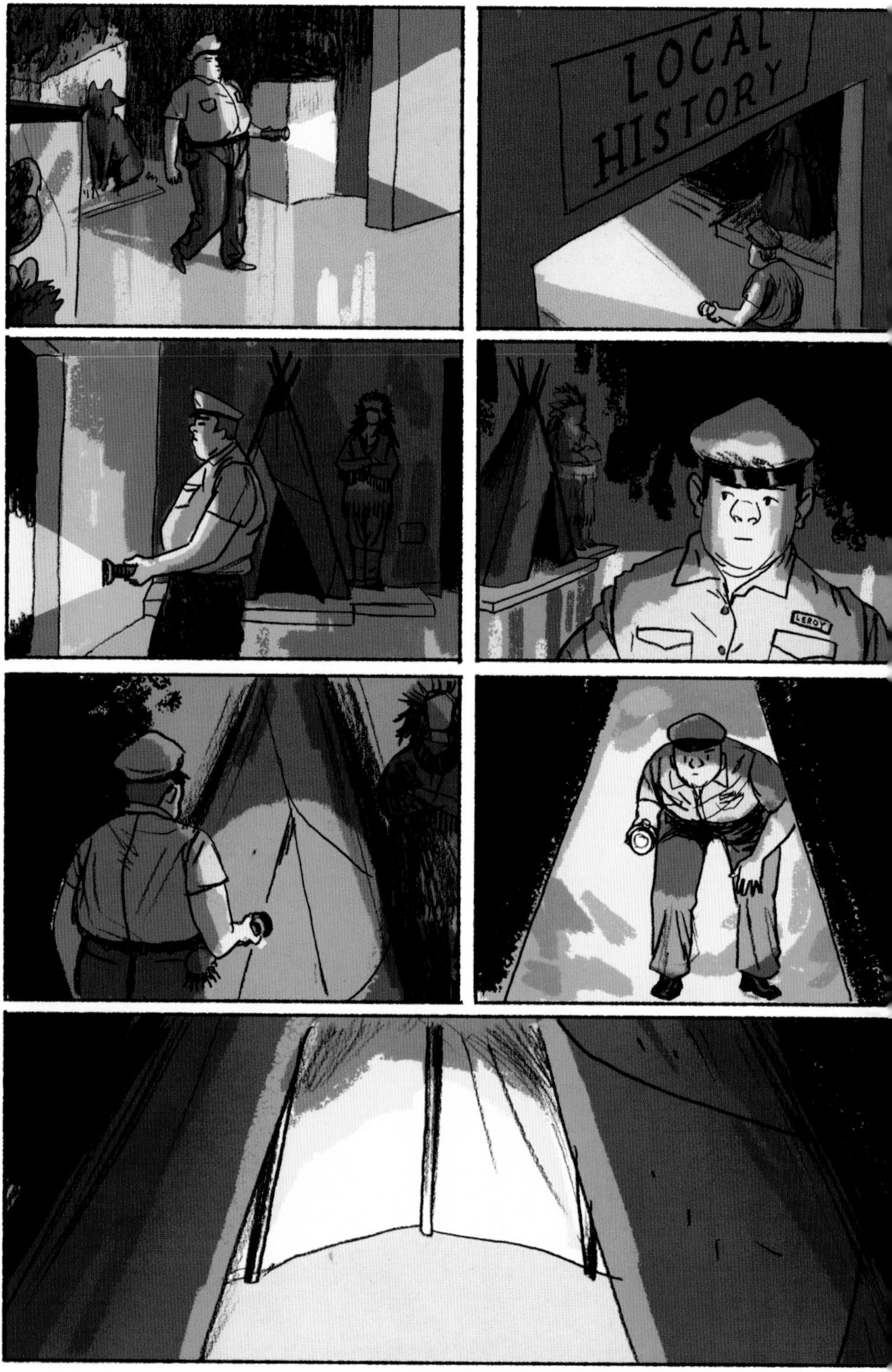
LOCAL HISTORY
LEROY

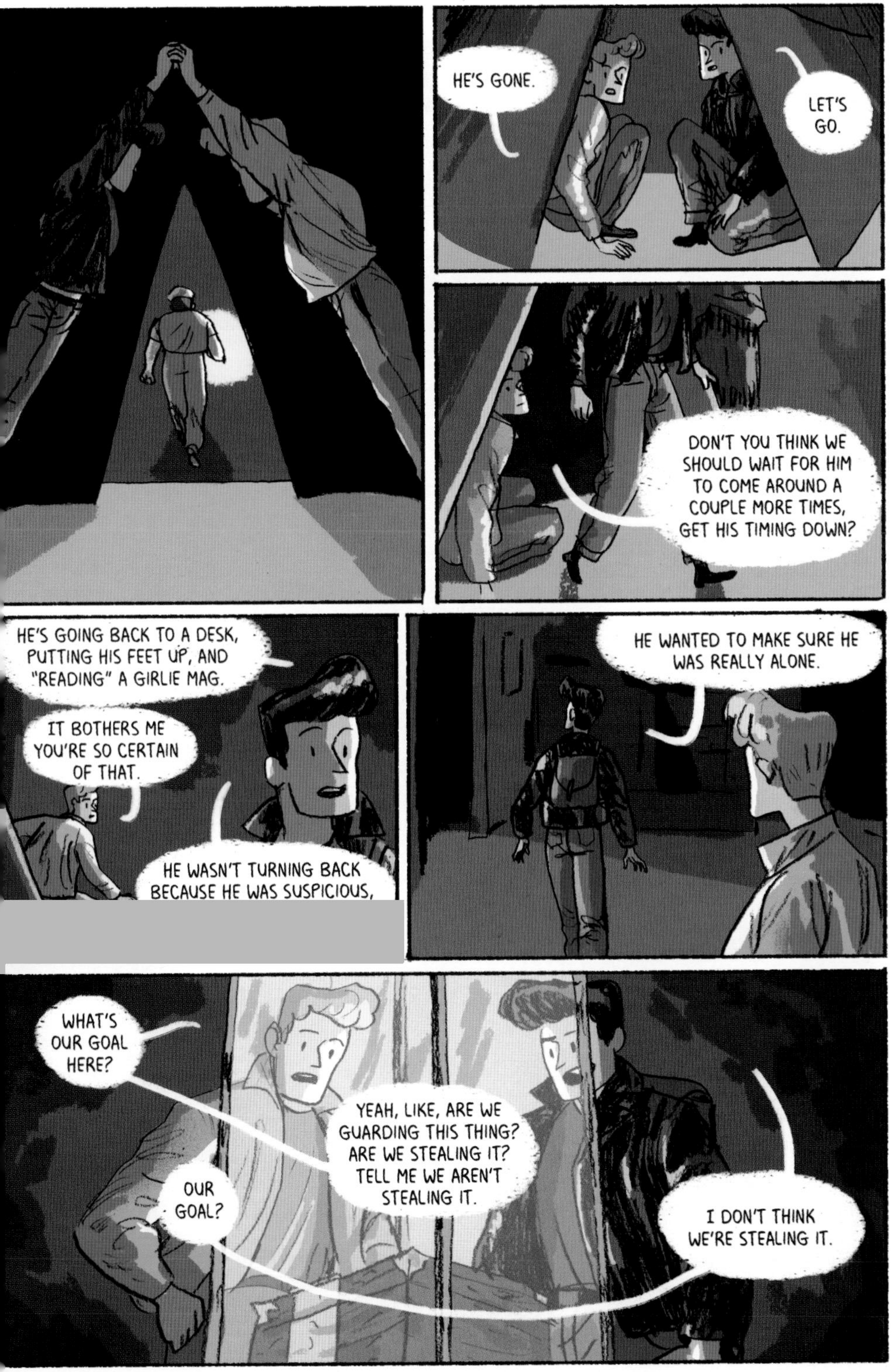
HE'S GONE.
LET'S GO.
DON'T YOU THINK WE SHOULD WAIT FOR HIM TO COME AROUND A COUPLE MORE TIMES, GET HIS TIMING DOWN?
HE'S GOING BACK TO A DESK, PUTTING HIS FEET UP, AND "READING" A GIRLIE MAG.
IT BOTHERS ME YOU'RE SO CERTAIN OF THAT.
HE WASN'T TURNING BACK BECAUSE HE WAS SUSPICIOUS,
HE WANTED TO MAKE SURE HE WAS REALLY ALONE.
WHAT'S OUR GOAL HERE?
OUR GOAL?
YEAH, LIKE, ARE WE GUARDING THIS THING? ARE WE STEALING IT? TELL ME WE AREN'T STEALING IT.
I DON'T THINK WE'RE STEALING IT.

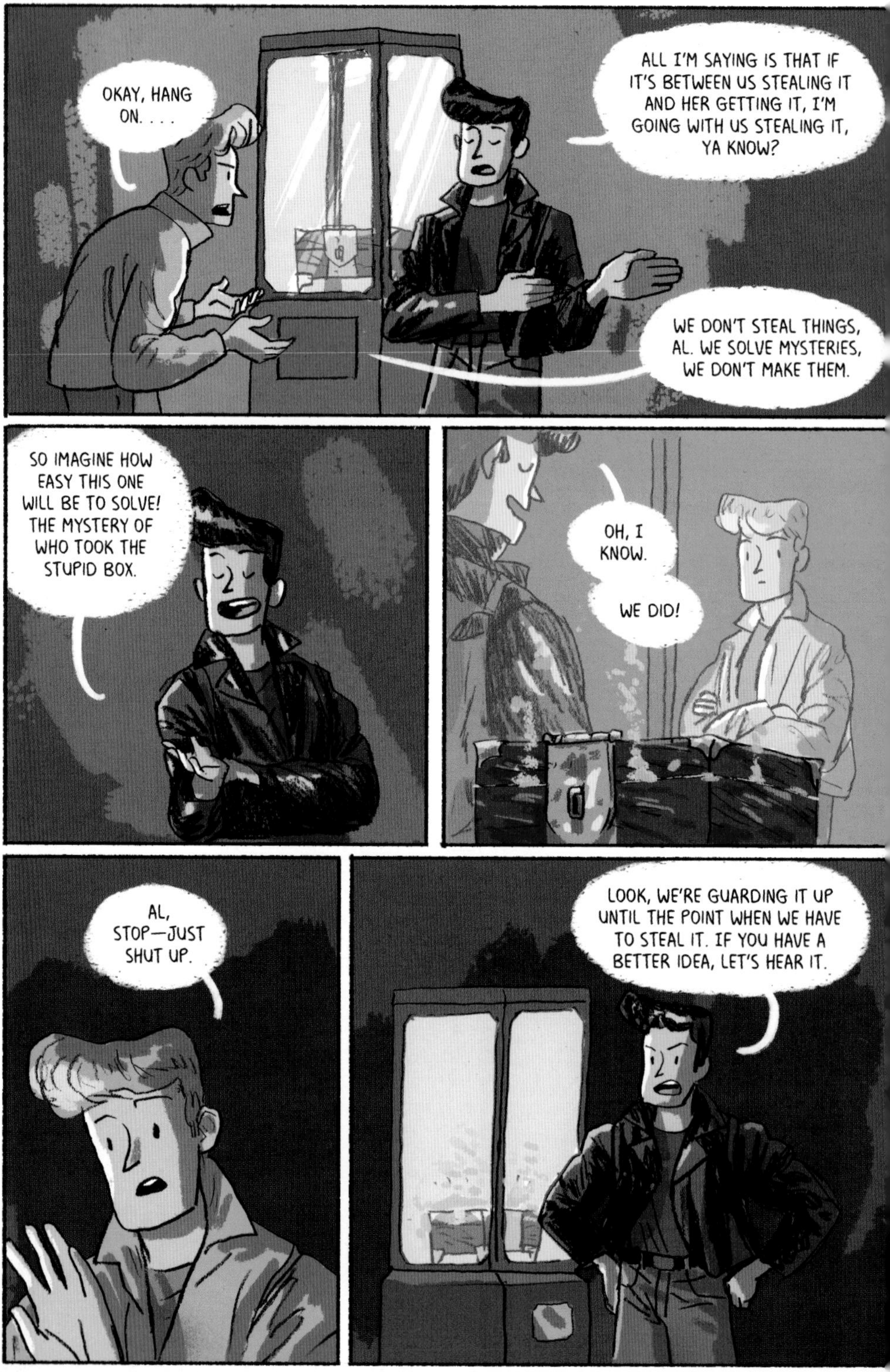
OKAY, HANG ON. . . .
ALL I'M SAYING IS THAT IF IT'S BETWEEN US STEALING IT AND HER GETTING IT, I'M GOING WITH US STEALING IT, YA KNOW?
WE DON'T STEAL THINGS, AL. WE SOLVE MYSTERIES, WE DON'T MAKE THEM.
SO IMAGINE HOW EASY THIS ONE WILL BE TO SOLVE! THE MYSTERY OF WHO TOOK THE STUPID BOX.
OH, I KNOW.
WE DID!
AL, STOP—JUST SHUT UP.
LOOK, WE'RE GUARDING IT UP UNTIL THE POINT WHEN WE HAVE TO STEAL IT. IF YOU HAVE A BETTER IDEA, LET'S HEAR IT.

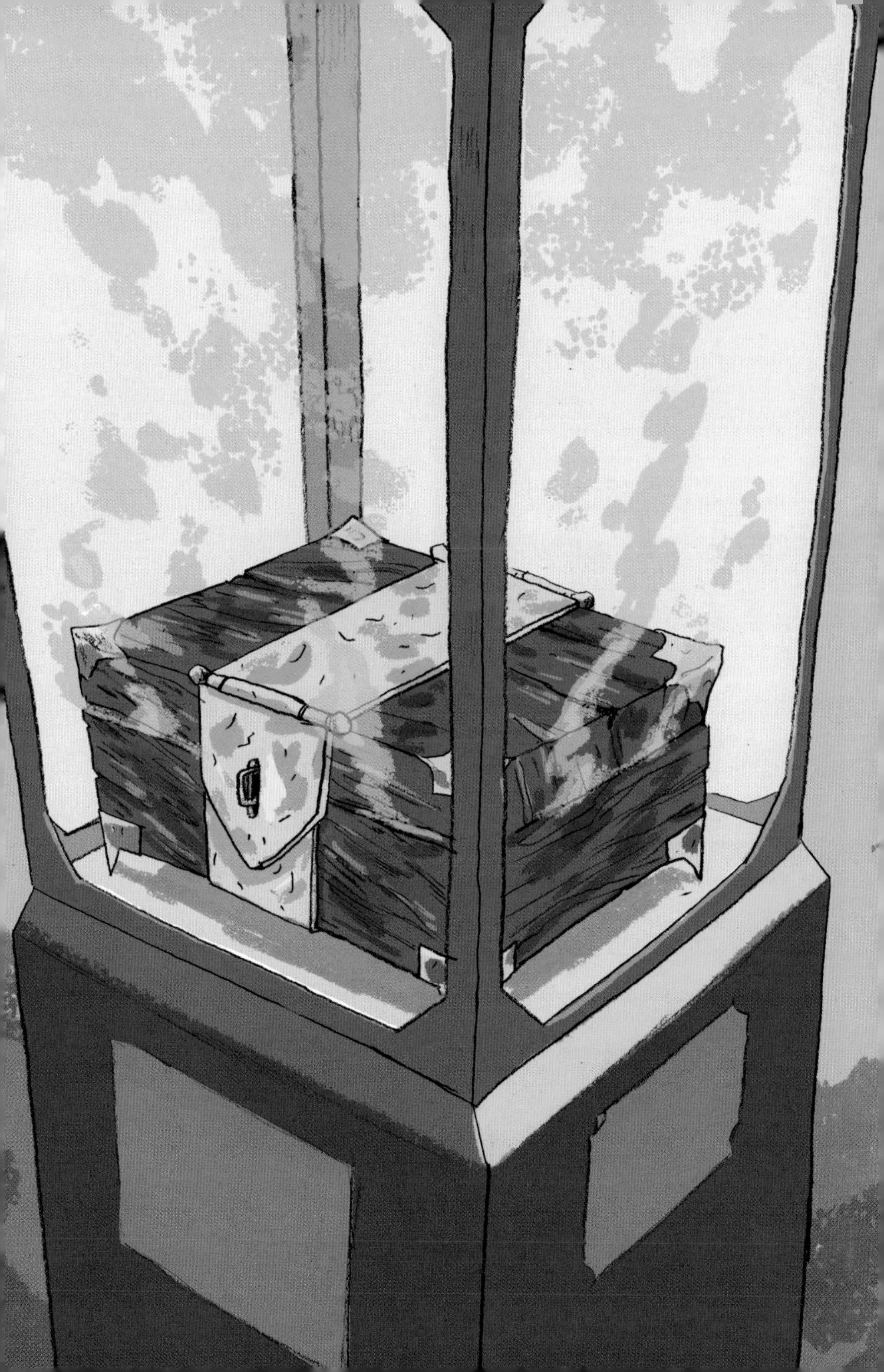

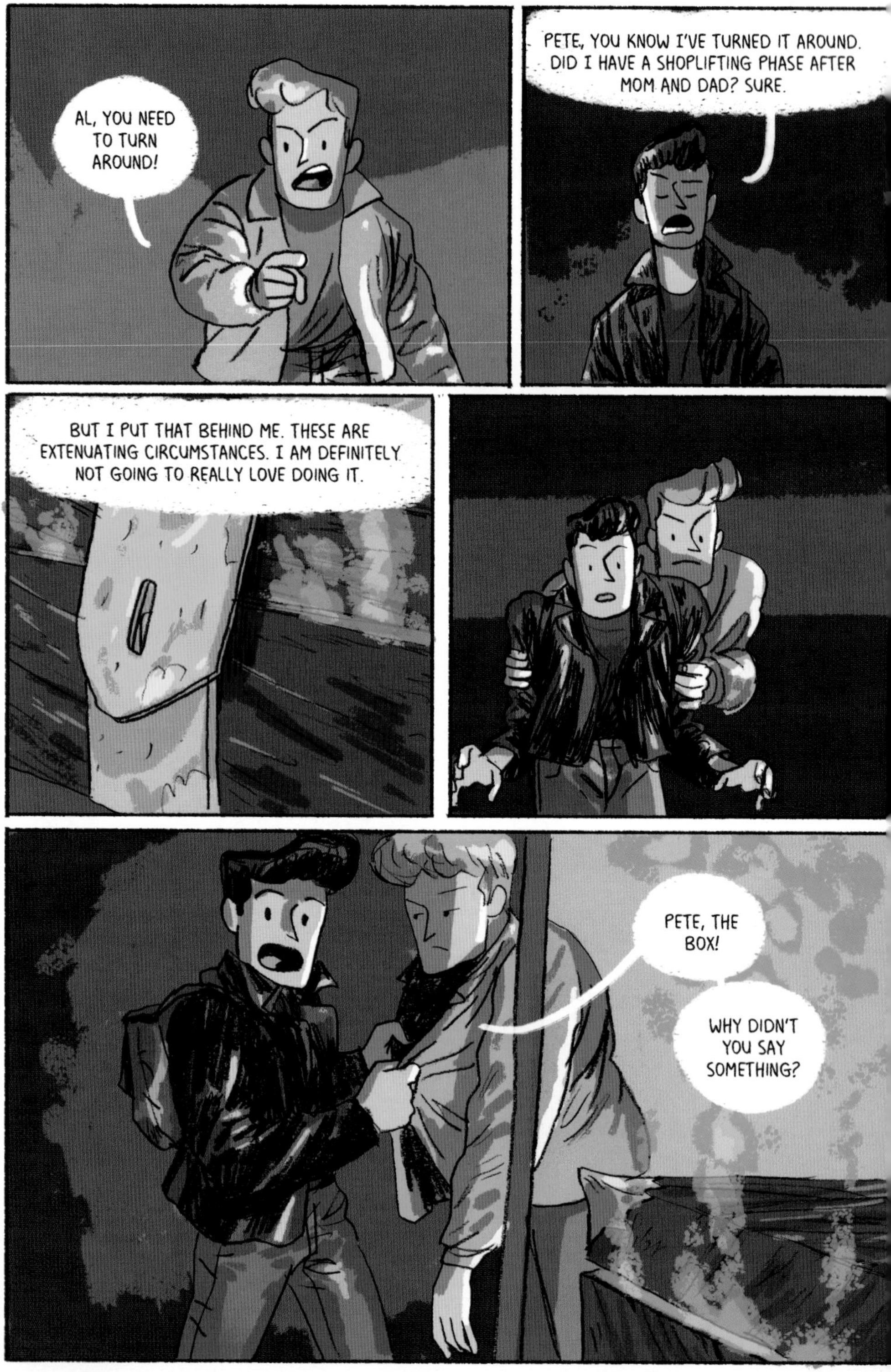
AL, YOU NEED TO TURN AROUND!
PETE, YOU KNOW I'VE TURNED IT AROUND. DID I HAVE A SHOPLIFTING PHASE AFTER MOM AND DAD? SURE.
BUT I PUT THAT BEHIND ME. THESE ARE EXTENUATING CIRCUMSTANCES. I AM DEFINITELY NOT GOING TO REALLY LOVE DOING IT.
PETE, THE BOX!
WHY DIDN'T YOU SAY SOMETHING?

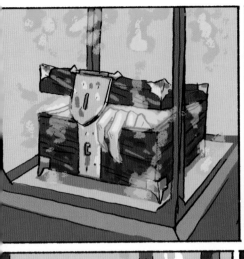

IT'S KIND OF . . .

AWESOME?

RIGHT?!

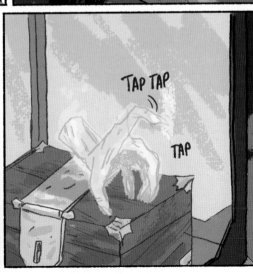

TAP TAP

TAP

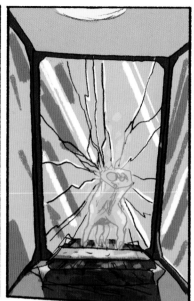

WE'VE GOT OURSELVES A CASE OF GOOD NEWS/BAD NEWS.

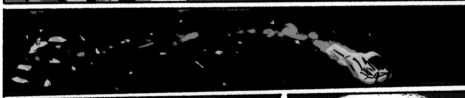

WE TECHNICALLY AREN'T GOING TO BE STEALING THE HAND.

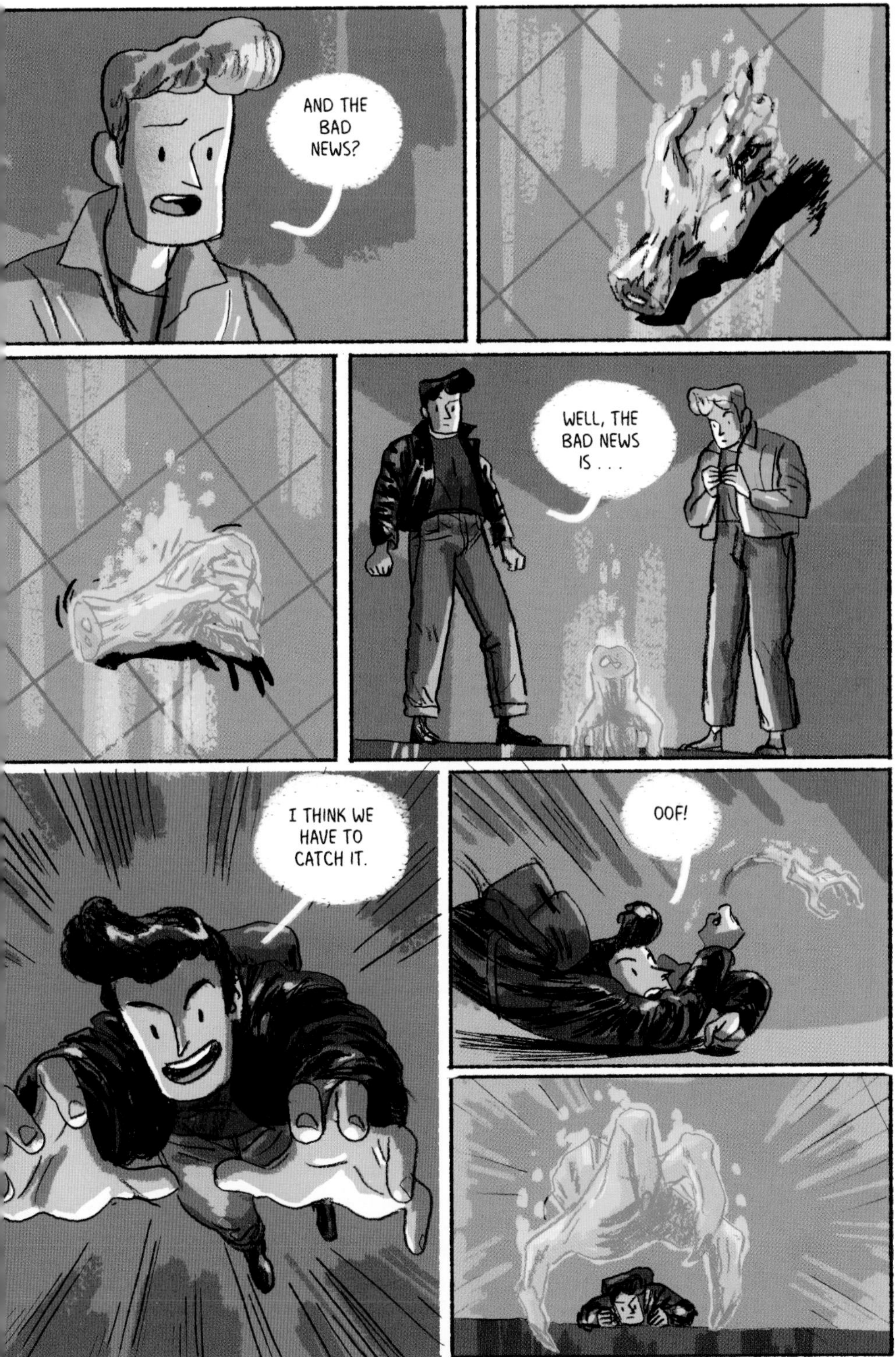
AND THE BAD NEWS?
WELL, THE BAD NEWS IS . . .
I THINK WE HAVE TO CATCH IT.
OOF!

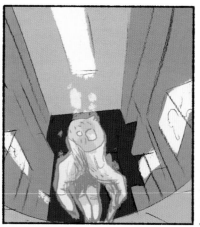

GOOD IDEA! YOU DO THE RUNNING THIS TIME.

GET THE BOX AND COME ON!

SURE, PETE. I'LL JUST STICK MY HANDS THROUGH A TRILLION TINY PIECES OF GLASS AND GET THE BOX. SURE THING, PETE. NO PROBLEM.

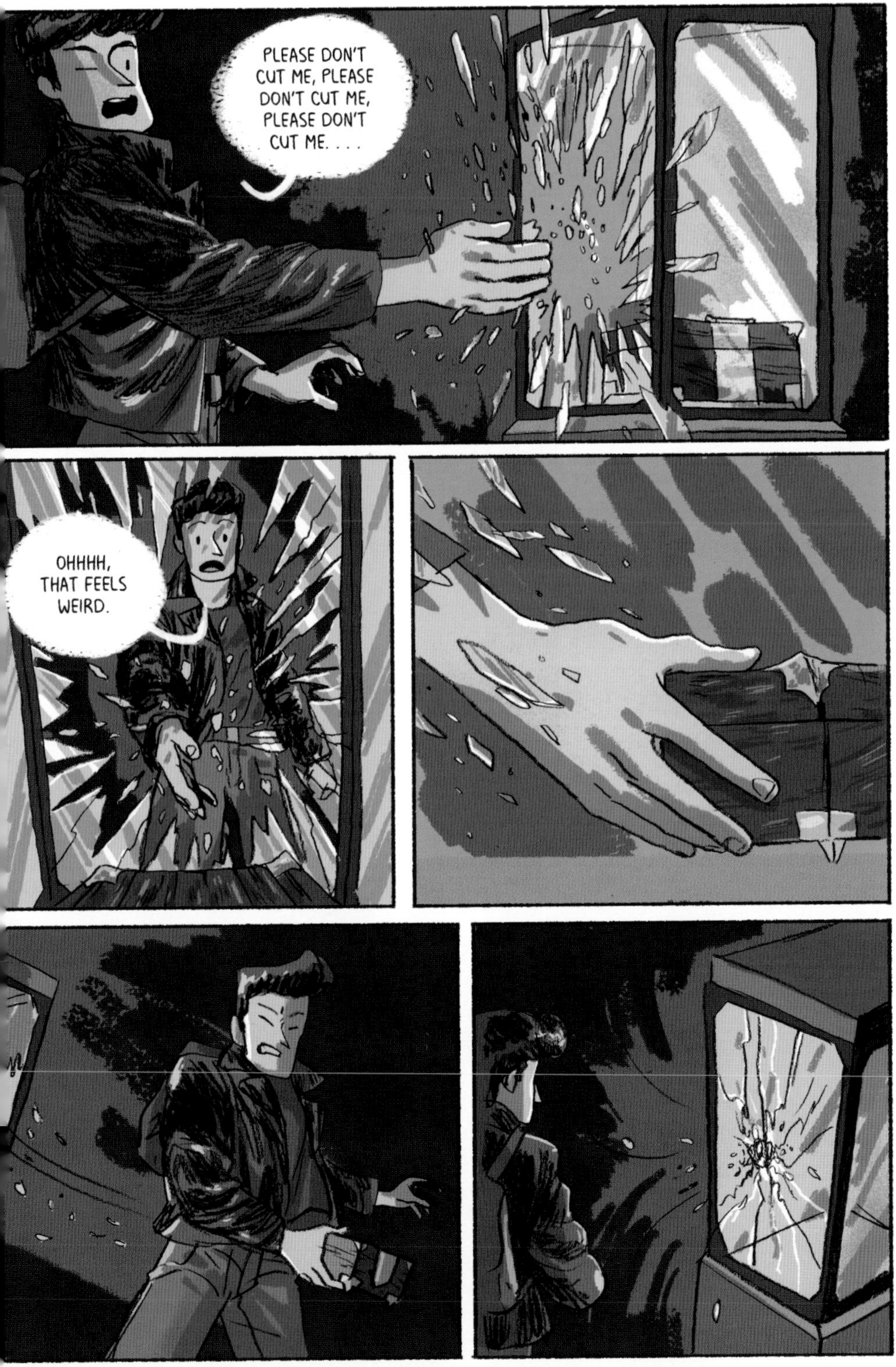
PLEASE DON'T CUT ME, PLEASE DON'T CUT ME, PLEASE DON'T CUT ME. . . .
OHHHH, THAT FEELS WEIRD.

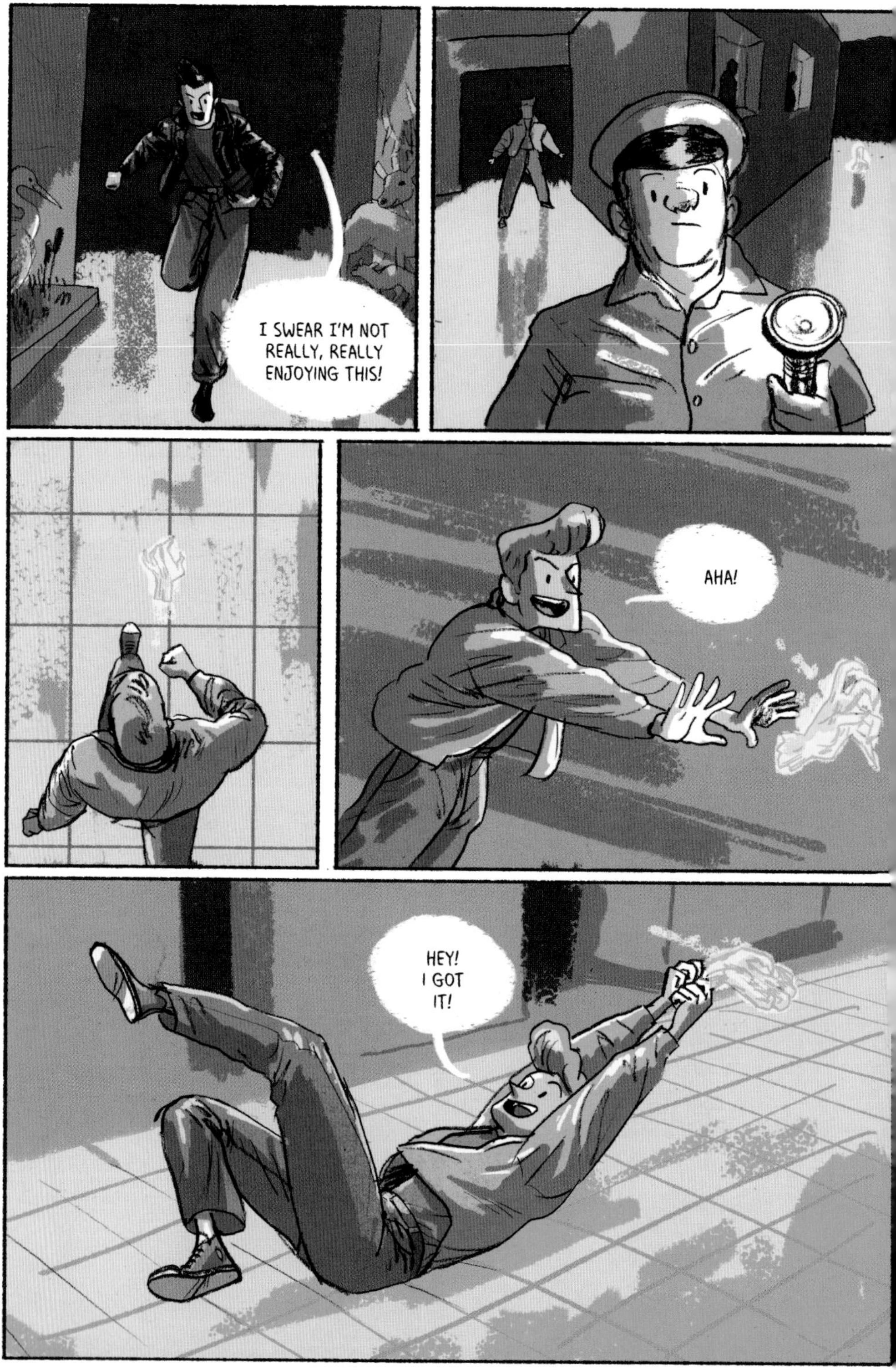
I SWEAR I'M NOT REALLY, REALLY ENJOYING THIS!
AHA!
HEY! I GOT IT!

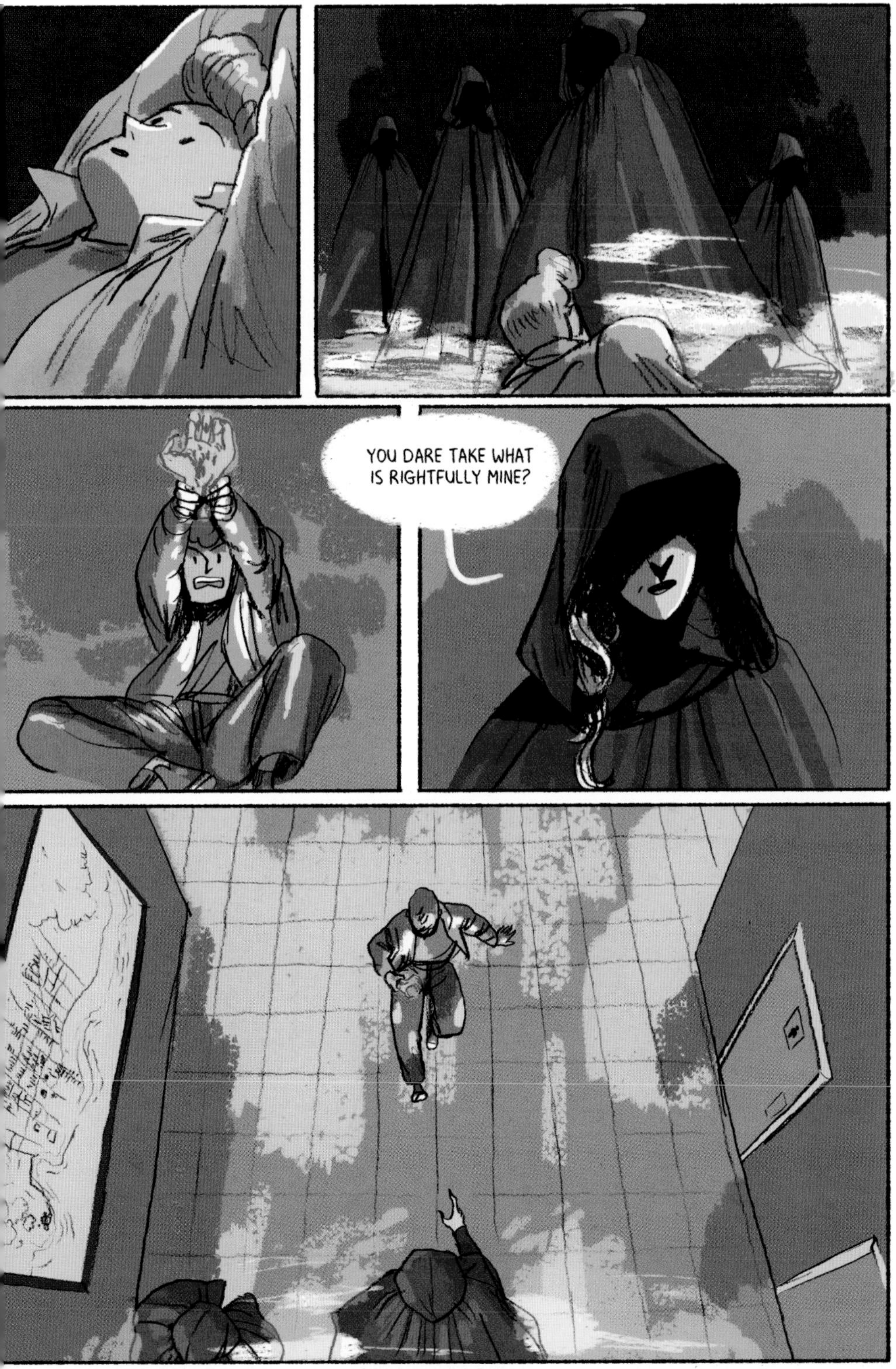
YOU DARE TAKE WHAT IS RIGHTFULLY MINE?

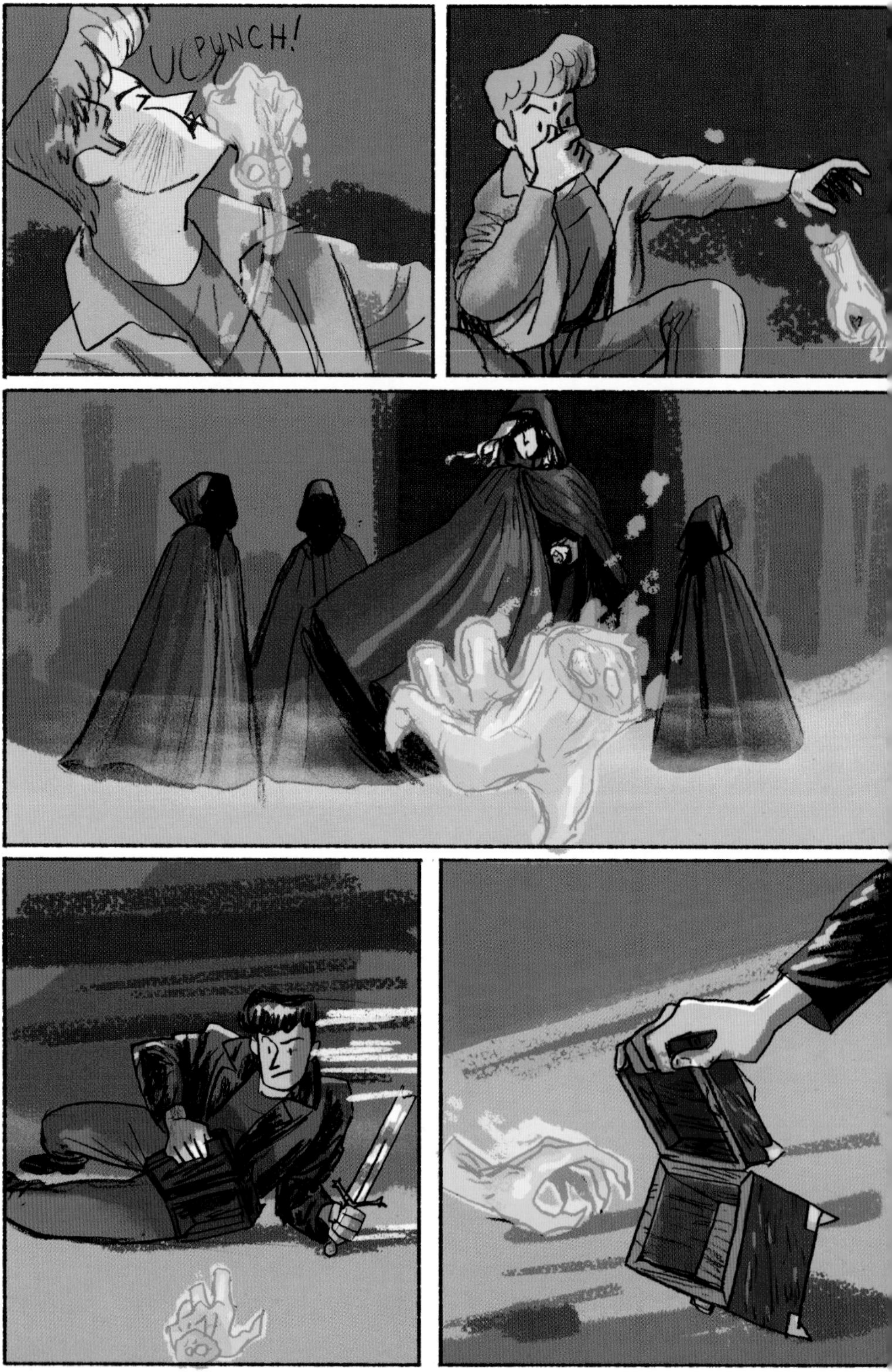
PUNCH!

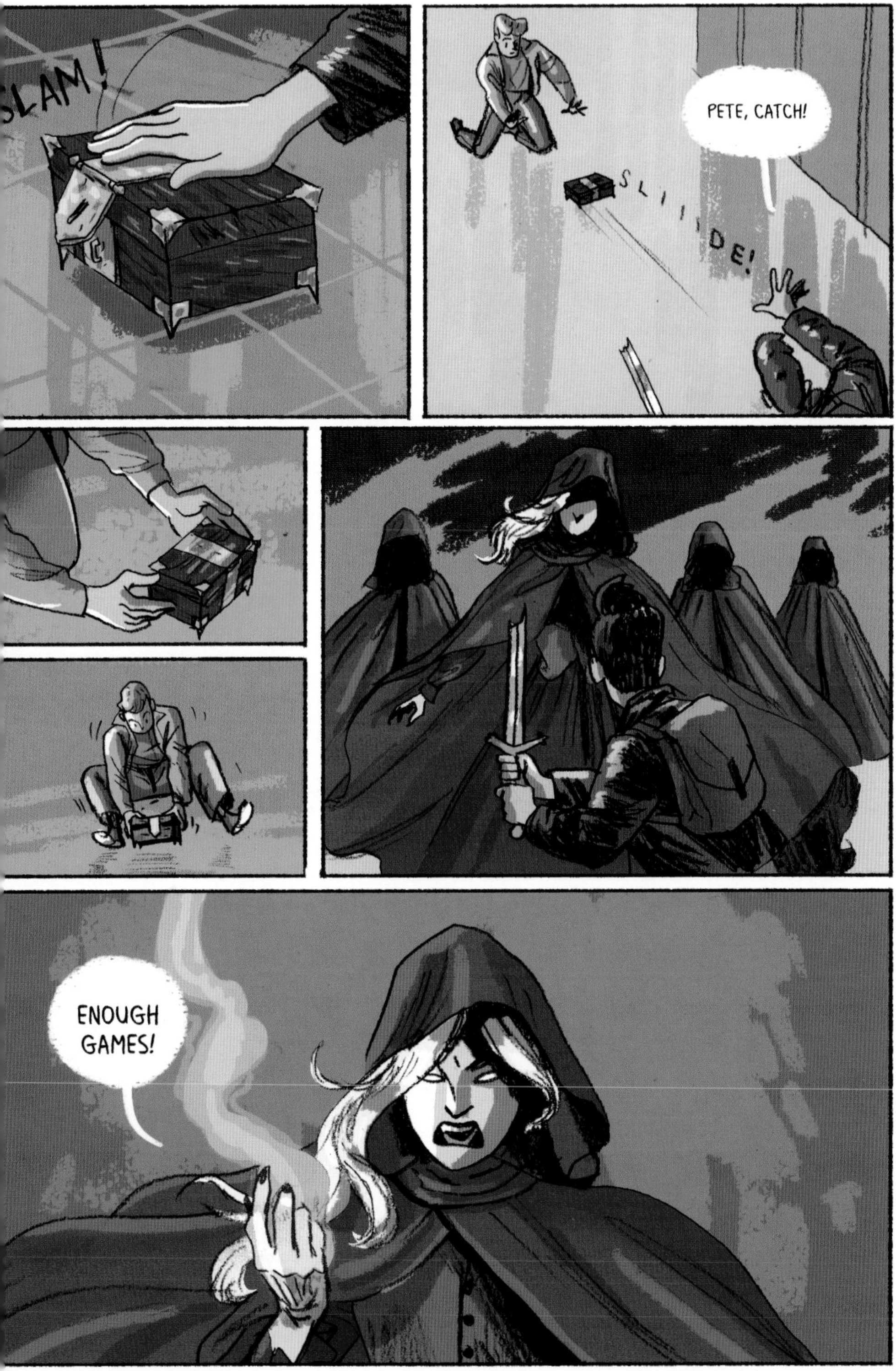
SLAM!
PETE, CATCH!
SLIIIIDE!
ENOUGH GAMES!

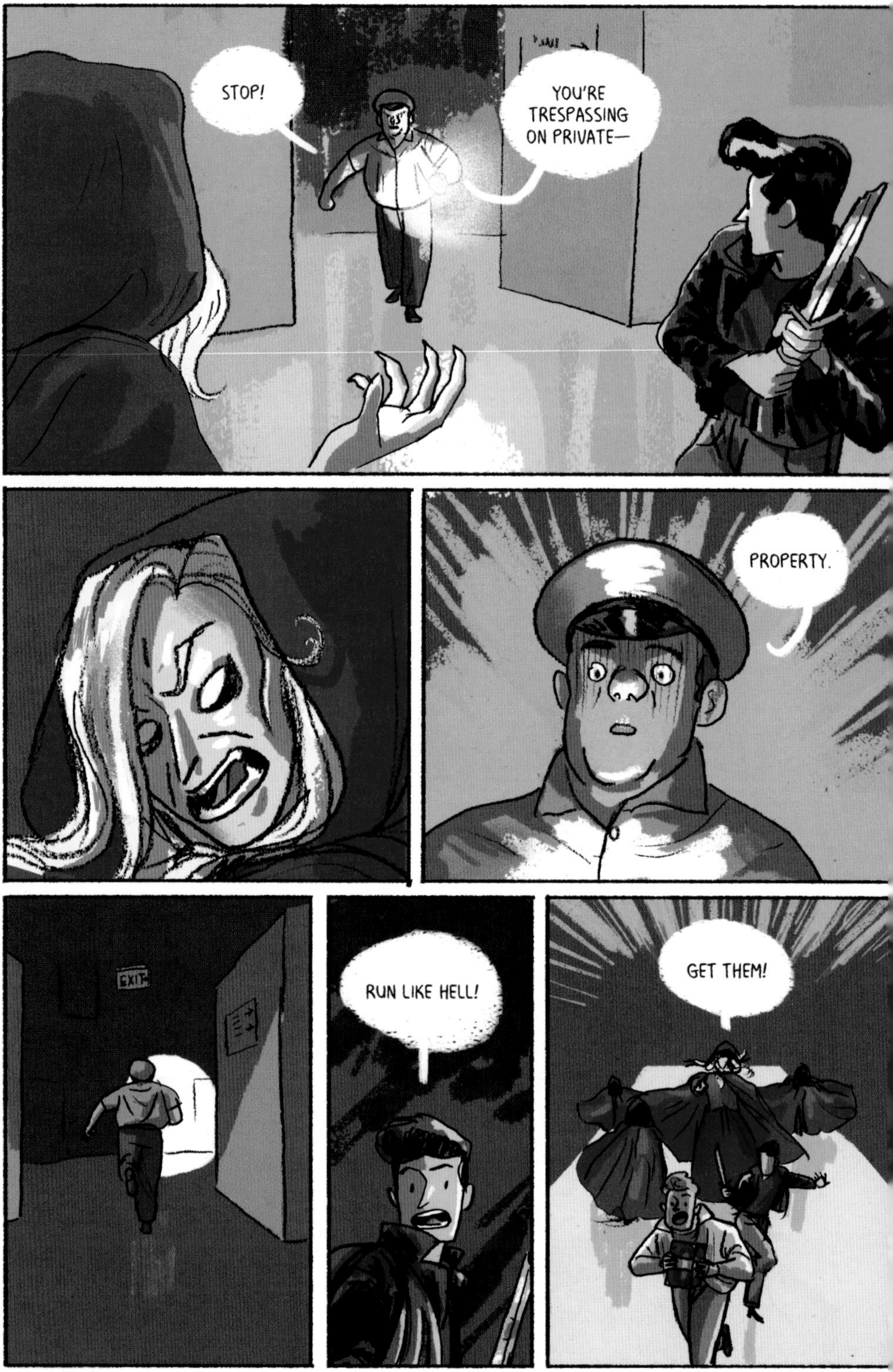
STOP!
YOU'RE TRESPASSING ON PRIVATE—
PROPERTY.
EXIT
RUN LIKE HELL!
GET THEM!

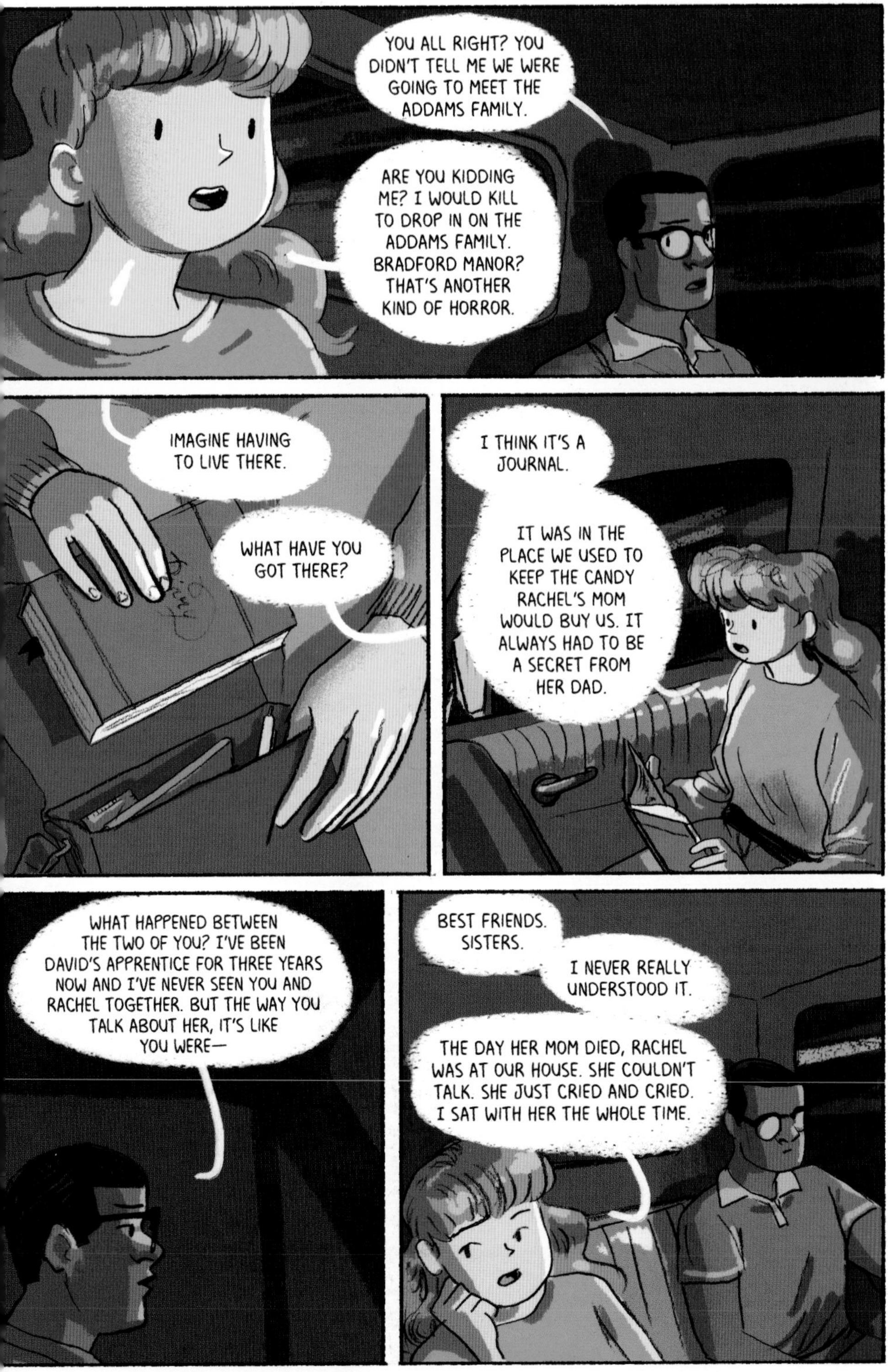
YOU ALL RIGHT? YOU DIDN'T TELL ME WE WERE GOING TO MEET THE ADDAMS FAMILY.
ARE YOU KIDDING ME? I WOULD KILL TO DROP IN ON THE ADDAMS FAMILY. BRADFORD MANOR? THAT'S ANOTHER KIND OF HORROR.
IMAGINE HAVING TO LIVE THERE.
WHAT HAVE YOU GOT THERE?
I THINK IT'S A JOURNAL.
IT WAS IN THE PLACE WE USED TO KEEP THE CANDY RACHEL'S MOM WOULD BUY US. IT ALWAYS HAD TO BE A SECRET FROM HER DAD.
WHAT HAPPENED BETWEEN THE TWO OF YOU? I'VE BEEN DAVID'S APPRENTICE FOR THREE YEARS NOW AND I'VE NEVER SEEN YOU AND RACHEL TOGETHER. BUT THE WAY YOU TALK ABOUT HER, IT'S LIKE YOU WERE—
BEST FRIENDS. SISTERS.
I NEVER REALLY UNDERSTOOD IT.
THE DAY HER MOM DIED, RACHEL WAS AT OUR HOUSE. SHE COULDN'T TALK. SHE JUST CRIED AND CRIED. I SAT WITH HER THE WHOLE TIME.

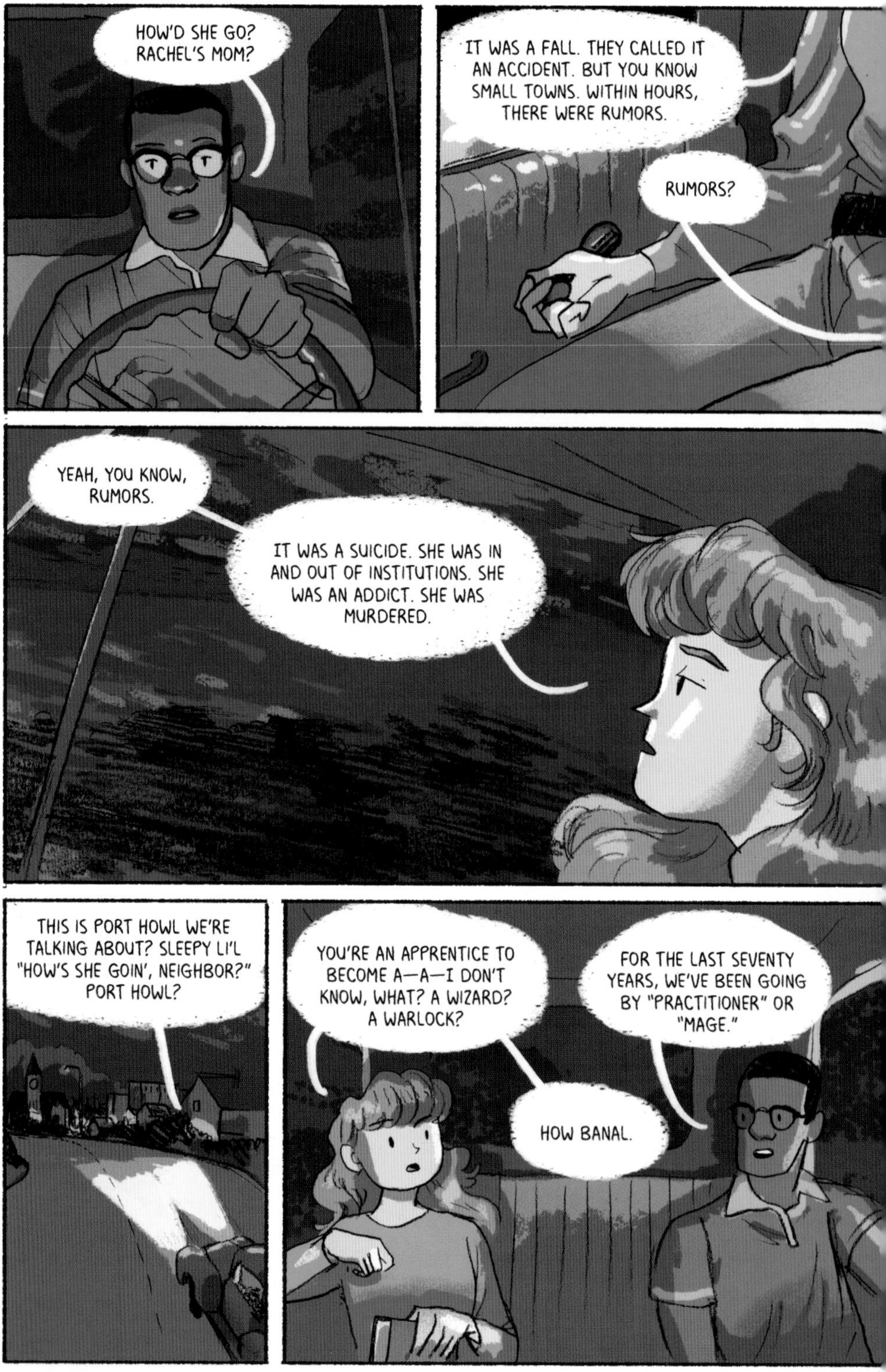
HOW'D SHE GO? RACHEL'S MOM?
IT WAS A FALL. THEY CALLED IT AN ACCIDENT. BUT YOU KNOW SMALL TOWNS. WITHIN HOURS, THERE WERE RUMORS.
RUMORS?
YEAH, YOU KNOW, RUMORS.
IT WAS A SUICIDE. SHE WAS IN AND OUT OF INSTITUTIONS. SHE WAS AN ADDICT. SHE WAS MURDERED.
THIS IS PORT HOWL WE'RE TALKING ABOUT? SLEEPY LI'L "HOW'S SHE GOIN', NEIGHBOR?" PORT HOWL?
YOU'RE AN APPRENTICE TO BECOME A—A—I DON'T KNOW, WHAT? A WIZARD? A WARLOCK?
FOR THE LAST SEVENTY YEARS, WE'VE BEEN GOING BY "PRACTITIONER" OR "MAGE."
HOW BANAL.

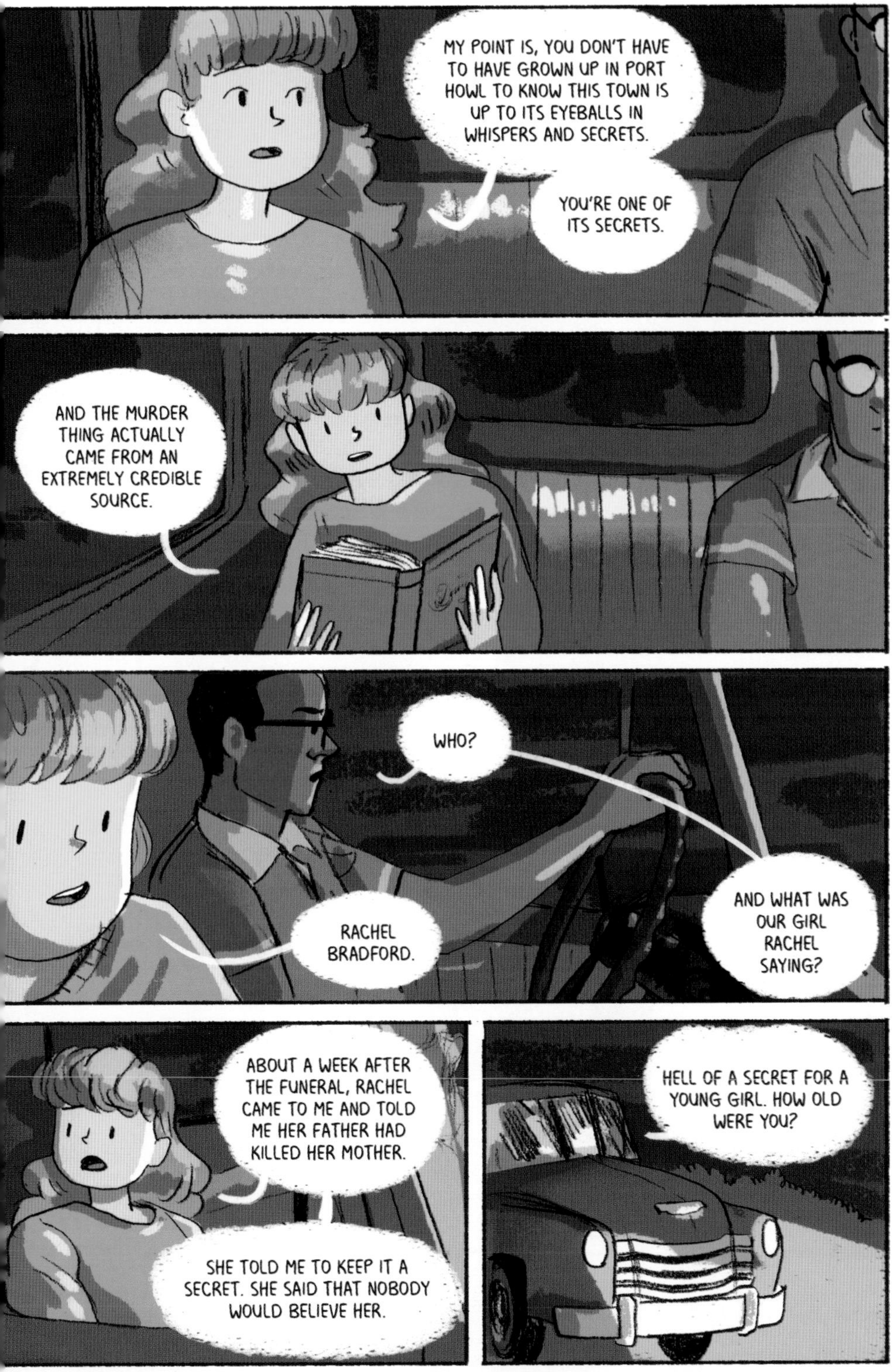

MY POINT IS, YOU DON'T HAVE TO HAVE GROWN UP IN PORT HOWL TO KNOW THIS TOWN IS UP TO ITS EYEBALLS IN WHISPERS AND SECRETS.
YOU'RE ONE OF ITS SECRETS.
AND THE MURDER THING ACTUALLY CAME FROM AN EXTREMELY CREDIBLE SOURCE.
WHO?
RACHEL BRADFORD.
AND WHAT WAS OUR GIRL RACHEL SAYING?
ABOUT A WEEK AFTER THE FUNERAL, RACHEL CAME TO ME AND TOLD ME HER FATHER HAD KILLED HER MOTHER.
SHE TOLD ME TO KEEP IT A SECRET. SHE SAID THAT NOBODY WOULD BELIEVE HER.
HELL OF A SECRET FOR A YOUNG GIRL. HOW OLD WERE YOU?

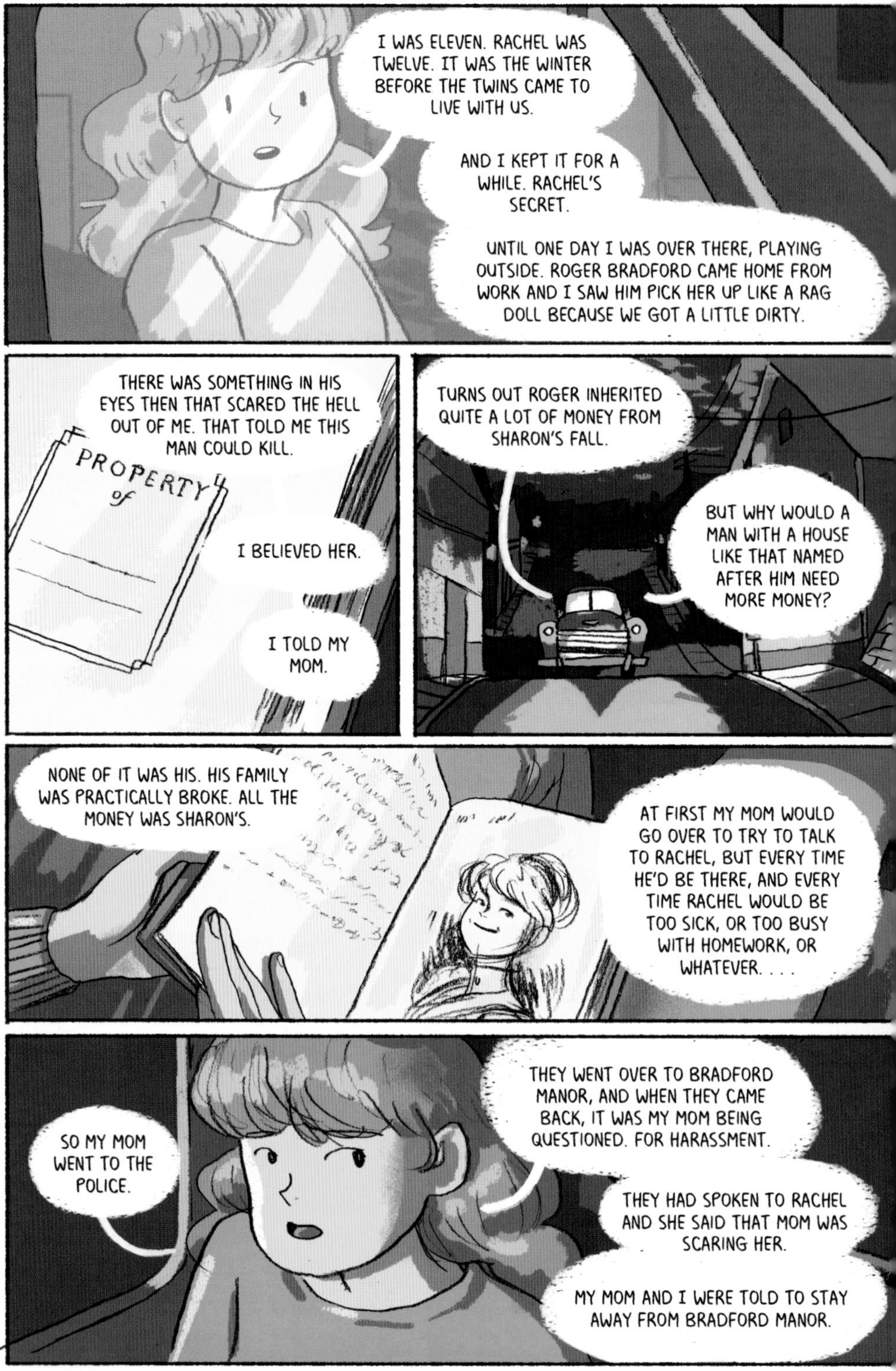
I WAS ELEVEN. RACHEL WAS TWELVE. IT WAS THE WINTER BEFORE THE TWINS CAME TO LIVE WITH US.
AND I KEPT IT FOR A WHILE. RACHEL'S SECRET.
UNTIL ONE DAY I WAS OVER THERE, PLAYING OUTSIDE. ROGER BRADFORD CAME HOME FROM WORK AND I SAW HIM PICK HER UP LIKE A RAG DOLL BECAUSE WE GOT A LITTLE DIRTY.
THERE WAS SOMETHING IN HIS EYES THEN THAT SCARED THE HELL OUT OF ME. THAT TOLD ME THIS MAN COULD KILL.
PROPERTY of
I BELIEVED HER.
I TOLD MY MOM.
TURNS OUT ROGER INHERITED QUITE A LOT OF MONEY FROM SHARON'S FALL.
BUT WHY WOULD A MAN WITH A HOUSE LIKE THAT NAMED AFTER HIM NEED MORE MONEY?
NONE OF IT WAS HIS. HIS FAMILY WAS PRACTICALLY BROKE. ALL THE MONEY WAS SHARON'S.
AT FIRST MY MOM WOULD GO OVER TO TRY TO TALK TO RACHEL, BUT EVERY TIME HE'D BE THERE, AND EVERY TIME RACHEL WOULD BE TOO SICK, OR TOO BUSY WITH HOMEWORK, OR WHATEVER. . . .
SO MY MOM WENT TO THE POLICE.
THEY WENT OVER TO BRADFORD MANOR, AND WHEN THEY CAME BACK, IT WAS MY MOM BEING QUESTIONED. FOR HARASSMENT.
THEY HAD SPOKEN TO RACHEL AND SHE SAID THAT MOM WAS SCARING HER.
MY MOM AND I WERE TOLD TO STAY AWAY FROM BRADFORD MANOR.

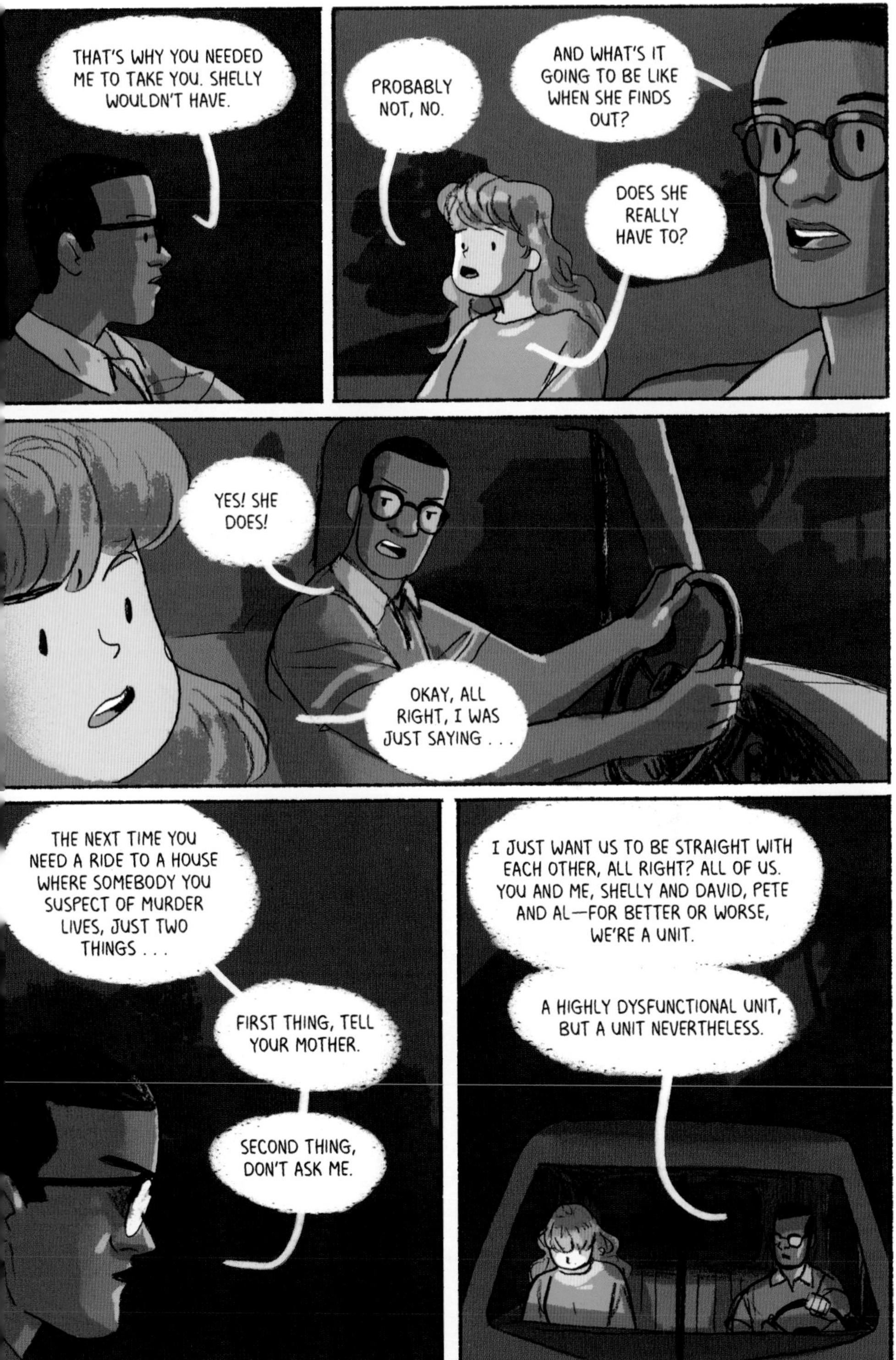
THAT'S WHY YOU NEEDED ME TO TAKE YOU. SHELLY WOULDN'T HAVE.
PROBABLY NOT, NO.
AND WHAT'S IT GOING TO BE LIKE WHEN SHE FINDS OUT?
DOES SHE REALLY HAVE TO?
YES! SHE DOES!
OKAY, ALL RIGHT, I WAS JUST SAYING . . .
THE NEXT TIME YOU NEED A RIDE TO A HOUSE WHERE SOMEBODY YOU SUSPECT OF MURDER LIVES, JUST TWO THINGS . . .
FIRST THING, TELL YOUR MOTHER.
SECOND THING, DON'T ASK ME.
I JUST WANT US TO BE STRAIGHT WITH EACH OTHER, ALL RIGHT? ALL OF US. YOU AND ME, SHELLY AND DAVID, PETE AND AL—FOR BETTER OR WORSE, WE'RE A UNIT.
A HIGHLY DYSFUNCTIONAL UNIT, BUT A UNIT NEVERTHELESS.

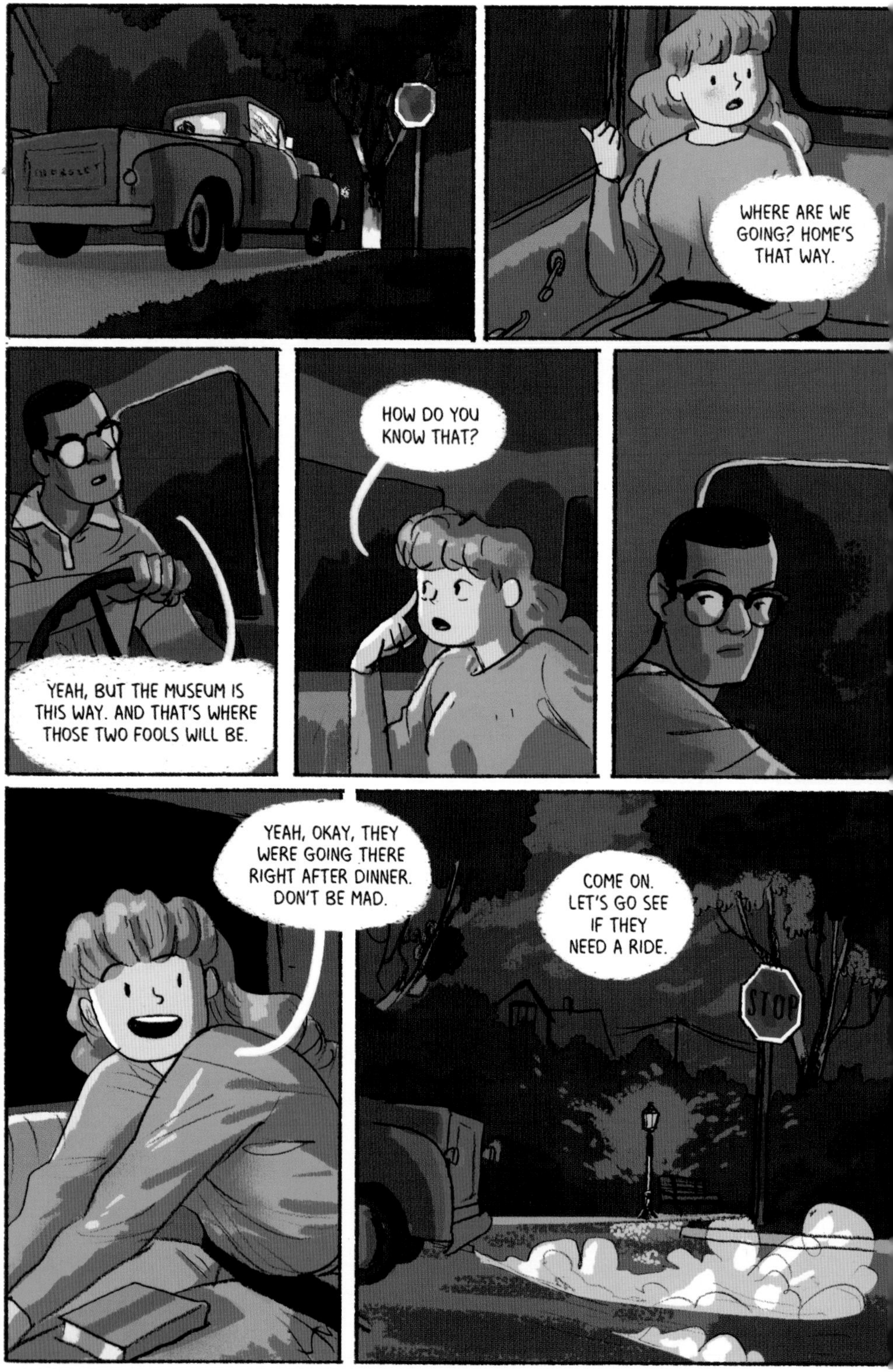
WHERE ARE WE GOING? HOME'S THAT WAY.
YEAH, BUT THE MUSEUM IS THIS WAY. AND THAT'S WHERE THOSE TWO FOOLS WILL BE.
HOW DO YOU KNOW THAT?
YEAH, OKAY, THEY WERE GOING THERE RIGHT AFTER DINNER. DON'T BE MAD.
COME ON. LET'S GO SEE IF THEY NEED A RIDE.
STOP

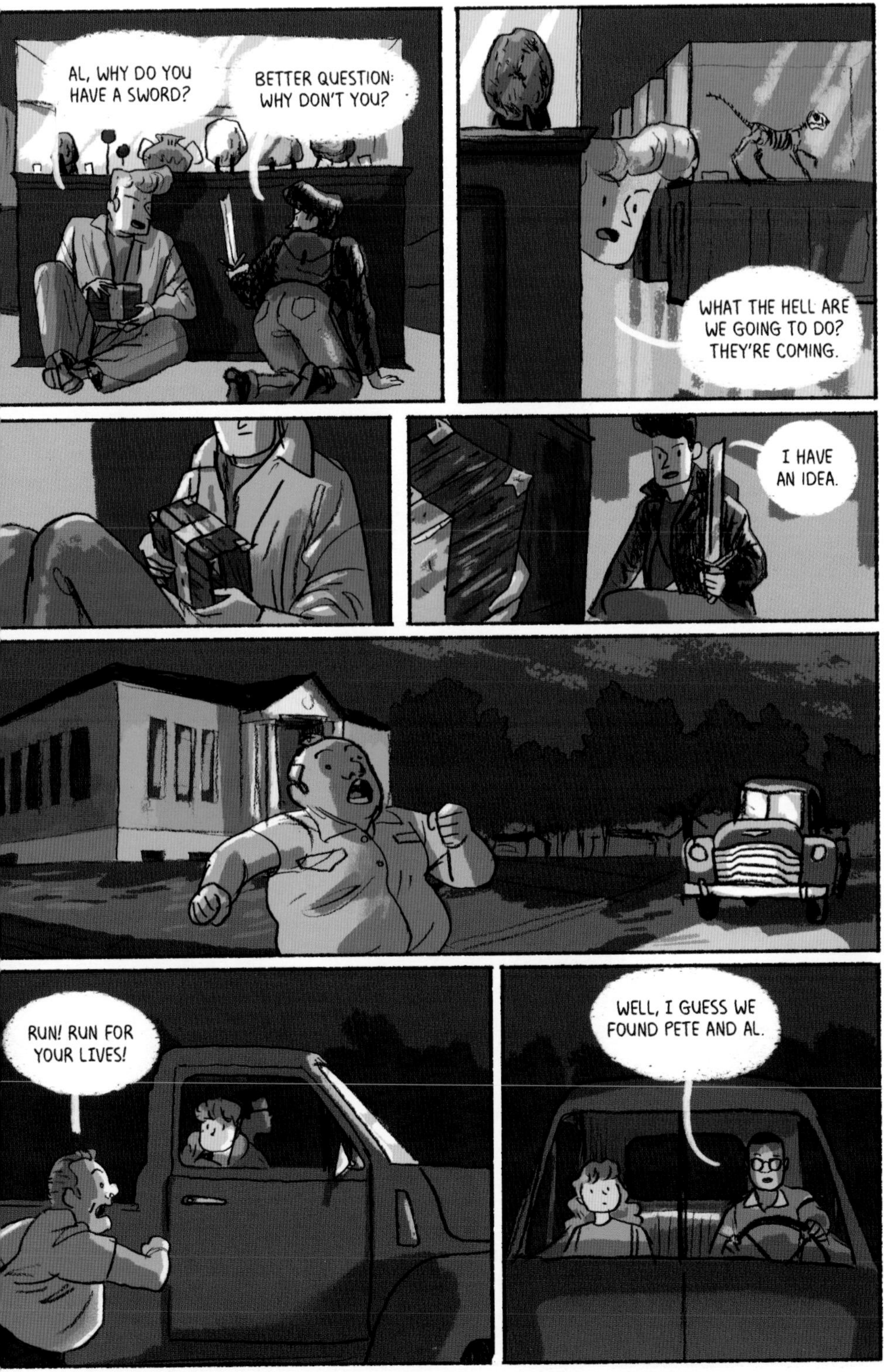
AL, WHY DO YOU HAVE A SWORD?
BETTER QUESTION: WHY DON'T YOU?
WHAT THE HELL ARE WE GOING TO DO? THEY'RE COMING.
I HAVE AN IDEA.
RUN! RUN FOR YOUR LIVES!
WELL, I GUESS WE FOUND PETE AND AL.

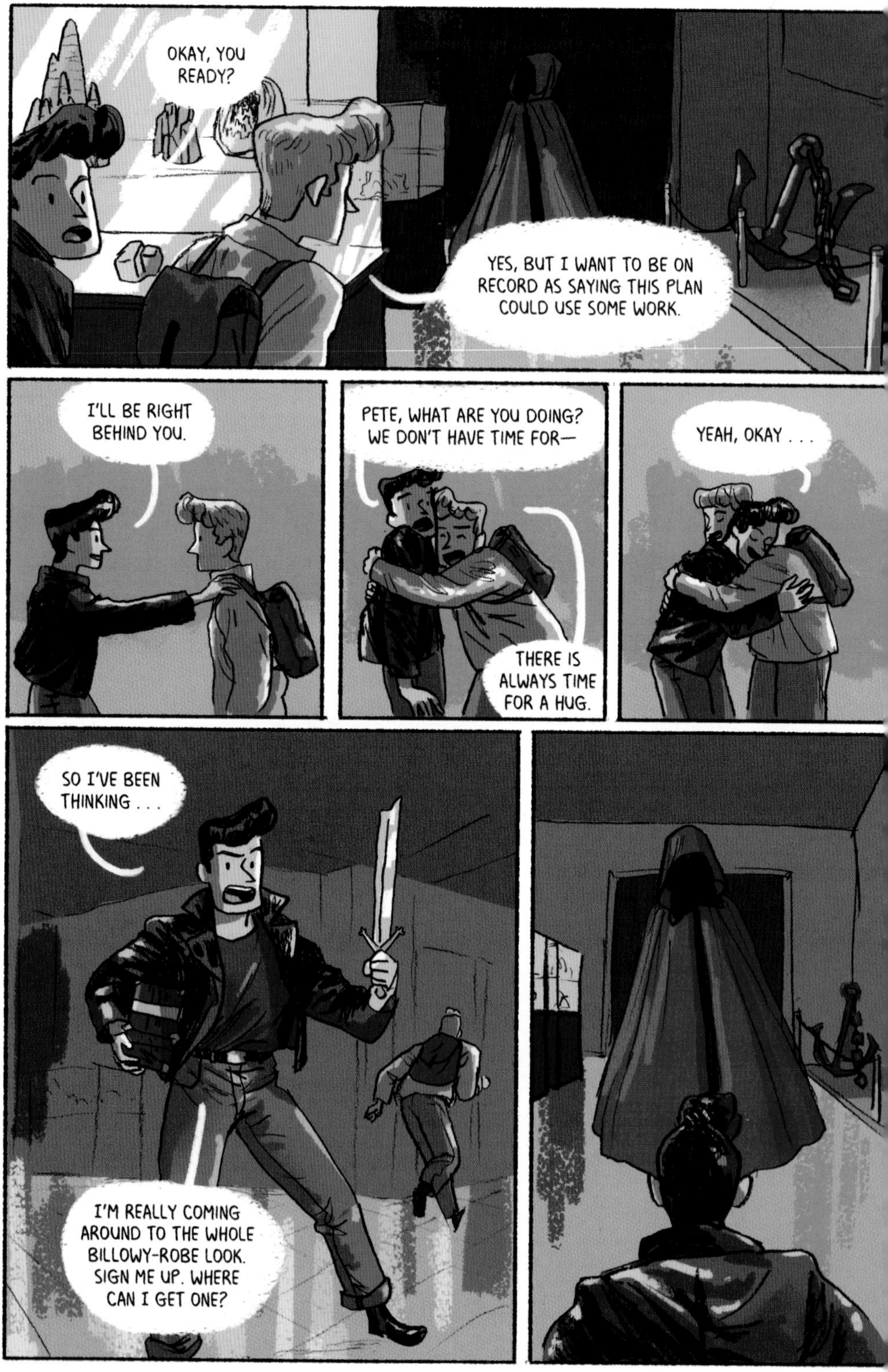
OKAY, YOU READY?
YES, BUT I WANT TO BE ON RECORD AS SAYING THIS PLAN COULD USE SOME WORK.
I'LL BE RIGHT BEHIND YOU.
PETE, WHAT ARE YOU DOING? WE DON'T HAVE TIME FOR—
THERE IS ALWAYS TIME FOR A HUG.
YEAH, OKAY . . .
SO I'VE BEEN THINKING . . .
I'M REALLY COMING AROUND TO THE WHOLE BILLOWY-ROBE LOOK. SIGN ME UP. WHERE CAN I GET ONE?

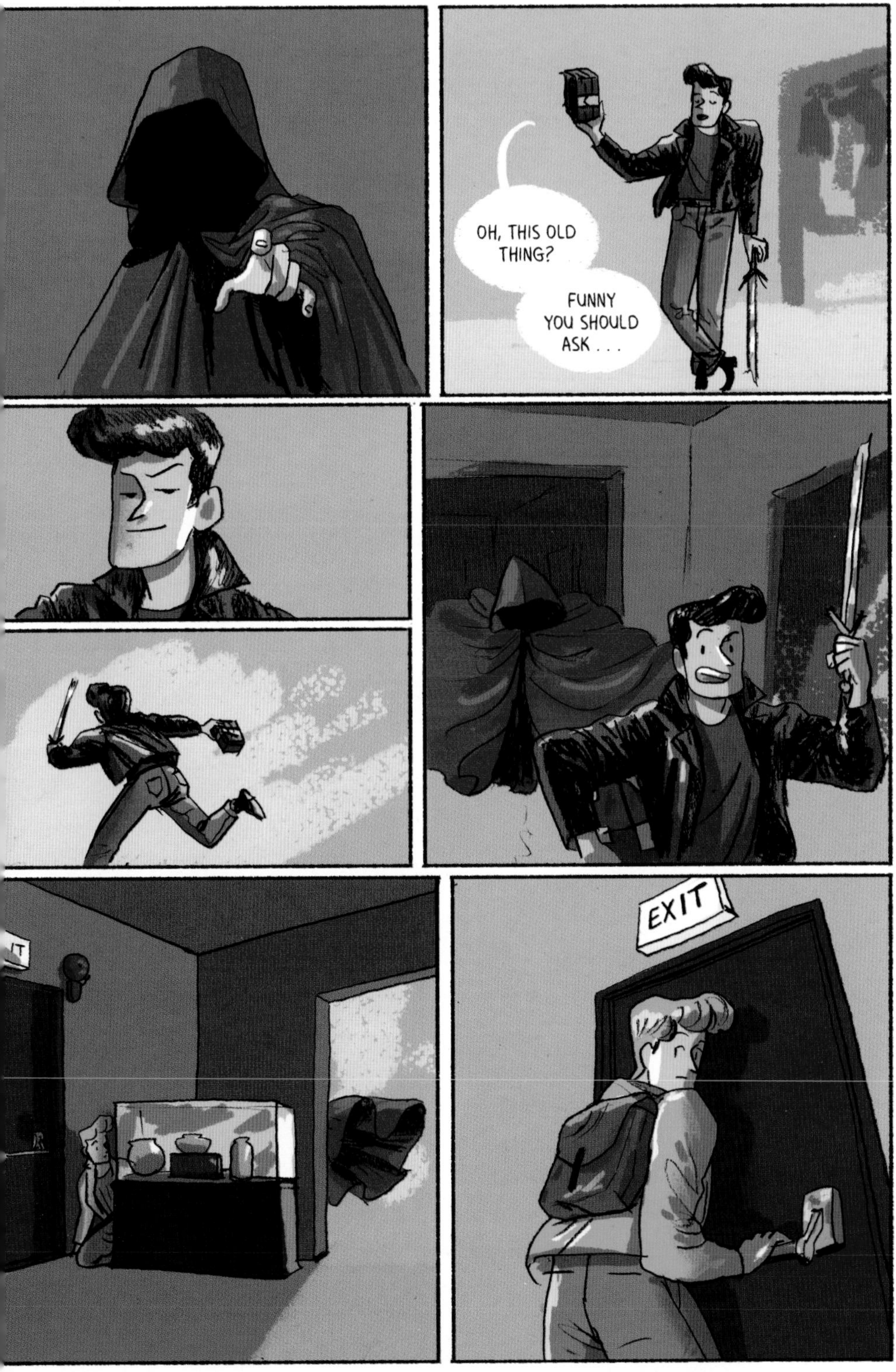
OH, THIS OLD THING?
FUNNY YOU SHOULD ASK . . .
EXIT

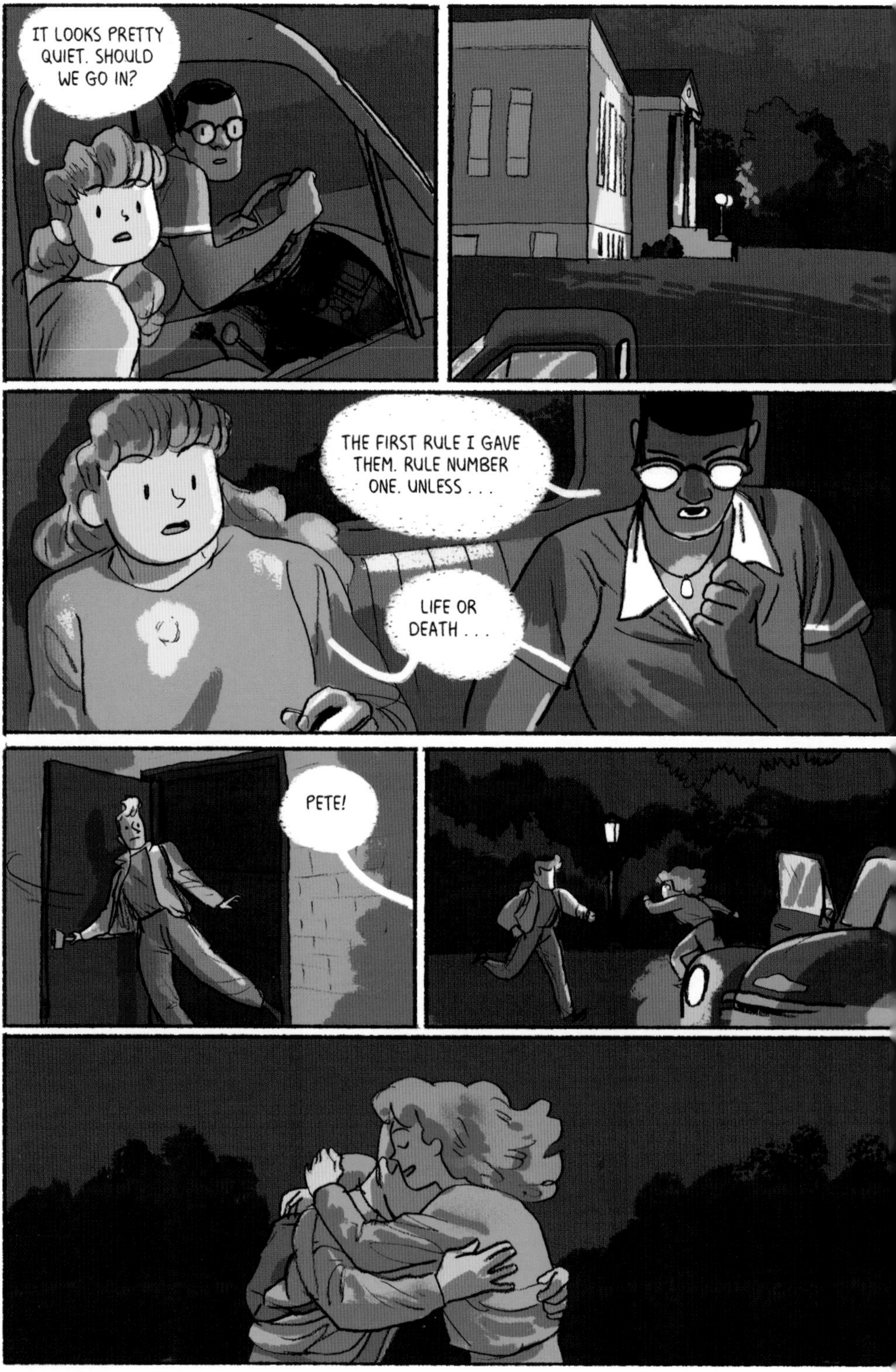
IT LOOKS PRETTY QUIET. SHOULD WE GO IN?
THE FIRST RULE I GAVE THEM. RULE NUMBER ONE. UNLESS . . .
LIFE OR DEATH . . .
PETE!

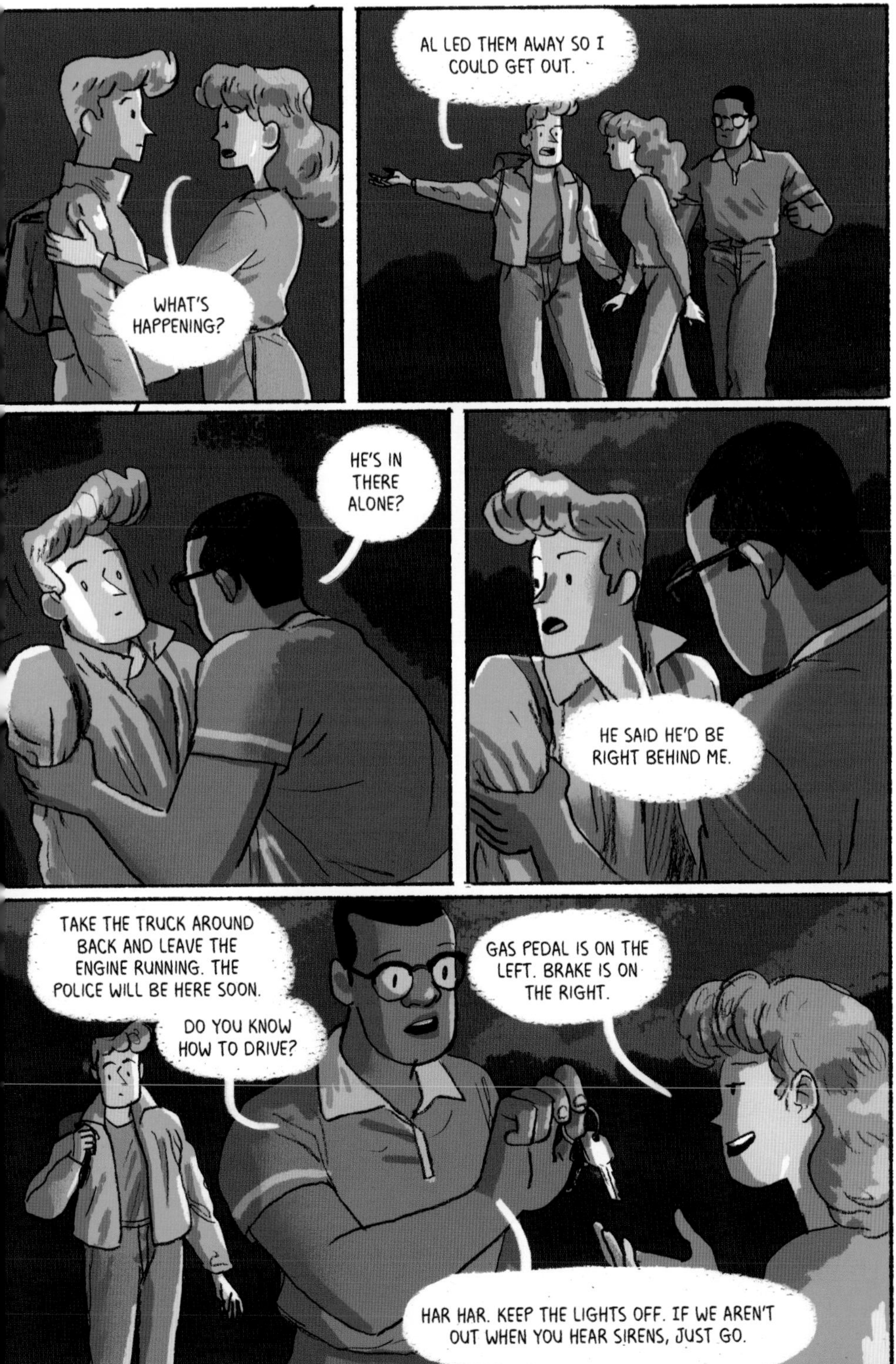
WHAT'S HAPPENING?
AL LED THEM AWAY SO I COULD GET OUT.
HE'S IN THERE ALONE?
HE SAID HE'D BE RIGHT BEHIND ME.
TAKE THE TRUCK AROUND BACK AND LEAVE THE ENGINE RUNNING. THE POLICE WILL BE HERE SOON.
DO YOU KNOW HOW TO DRIVE?
GAS PEDAL IS ON THE LEFT. BRAKE IS ON THE RIGHT.
HAR HAR. KEEP THE LIGHTS OFF. IF WE AREN'T OUT WHEN YOU HEAR SIRENS, JUST GO.

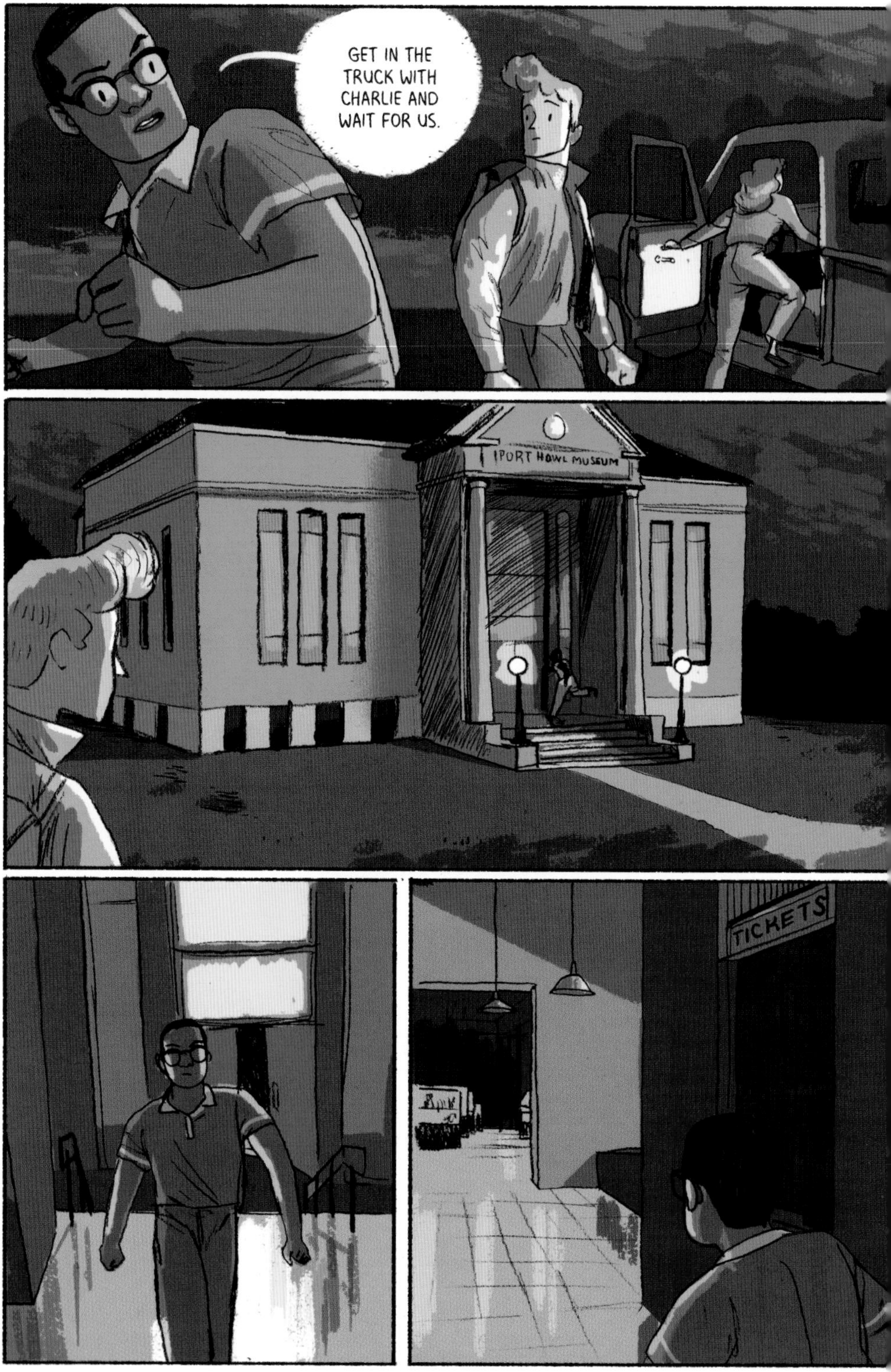
GET IN THE TRUCK WITH CHARLIE AND WAIT FOR US.
PORT HOWL MUSEUM
TICKETS

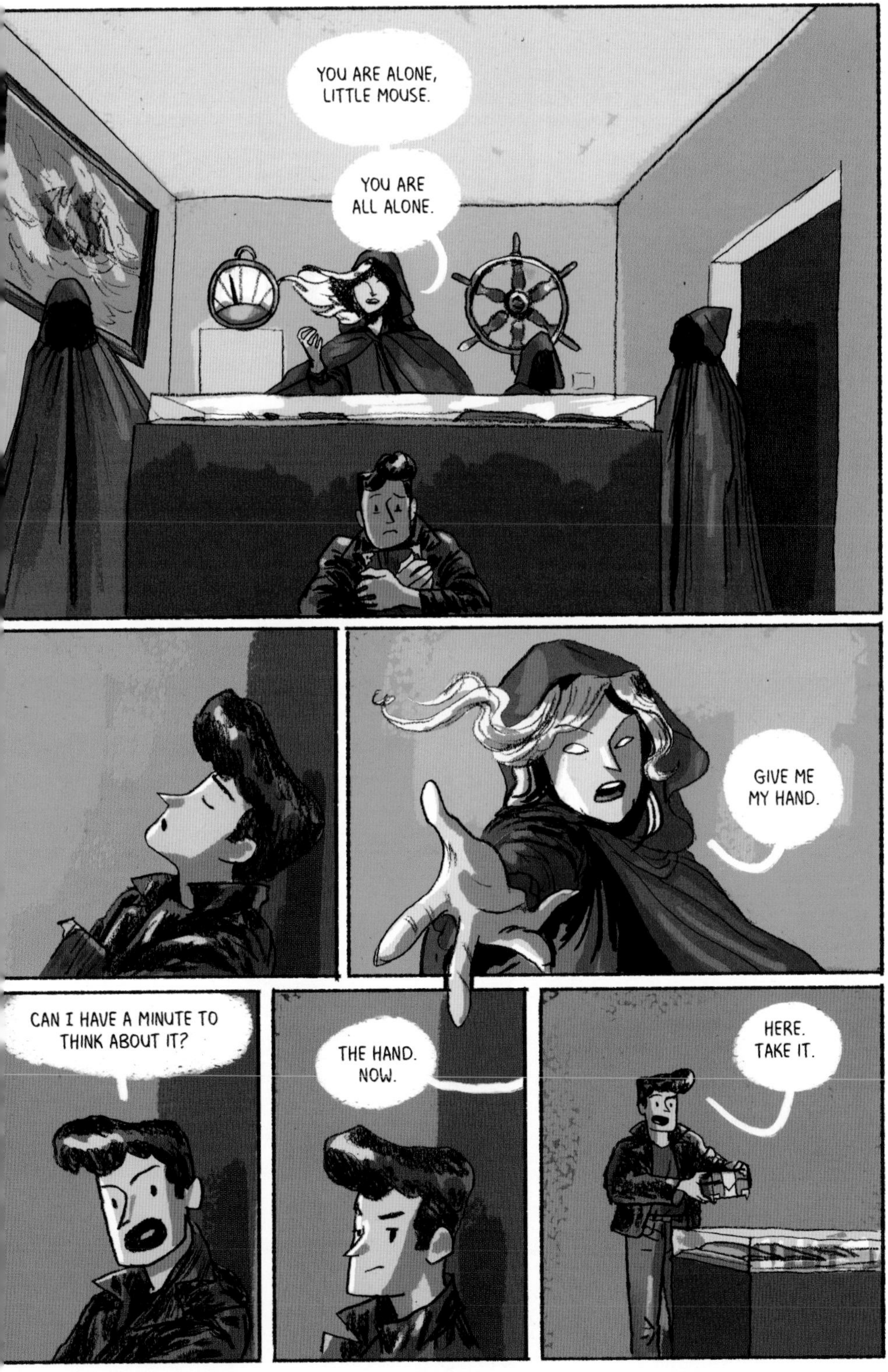
YOU ARE ALONE, LITTLE MOUSE.
YOU ARE ALL ALONE.
GIVE ME MY HAND.
CAN I HAVE A MINUTE TO THINK ABOUT IT?
THE HAND. NOW.
HERE. TAKE IT.

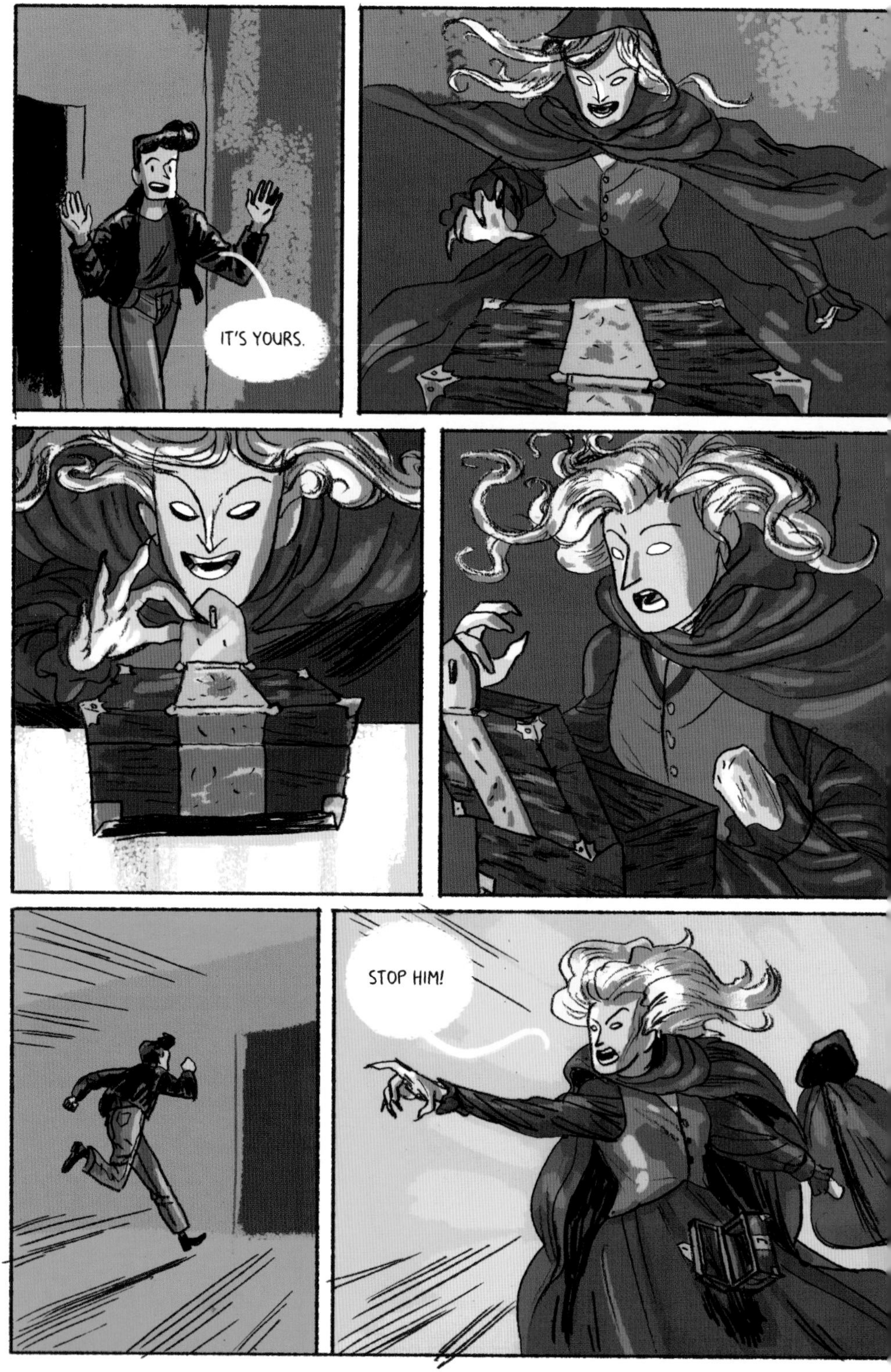
IT'S YOURS.
STOP HIM!

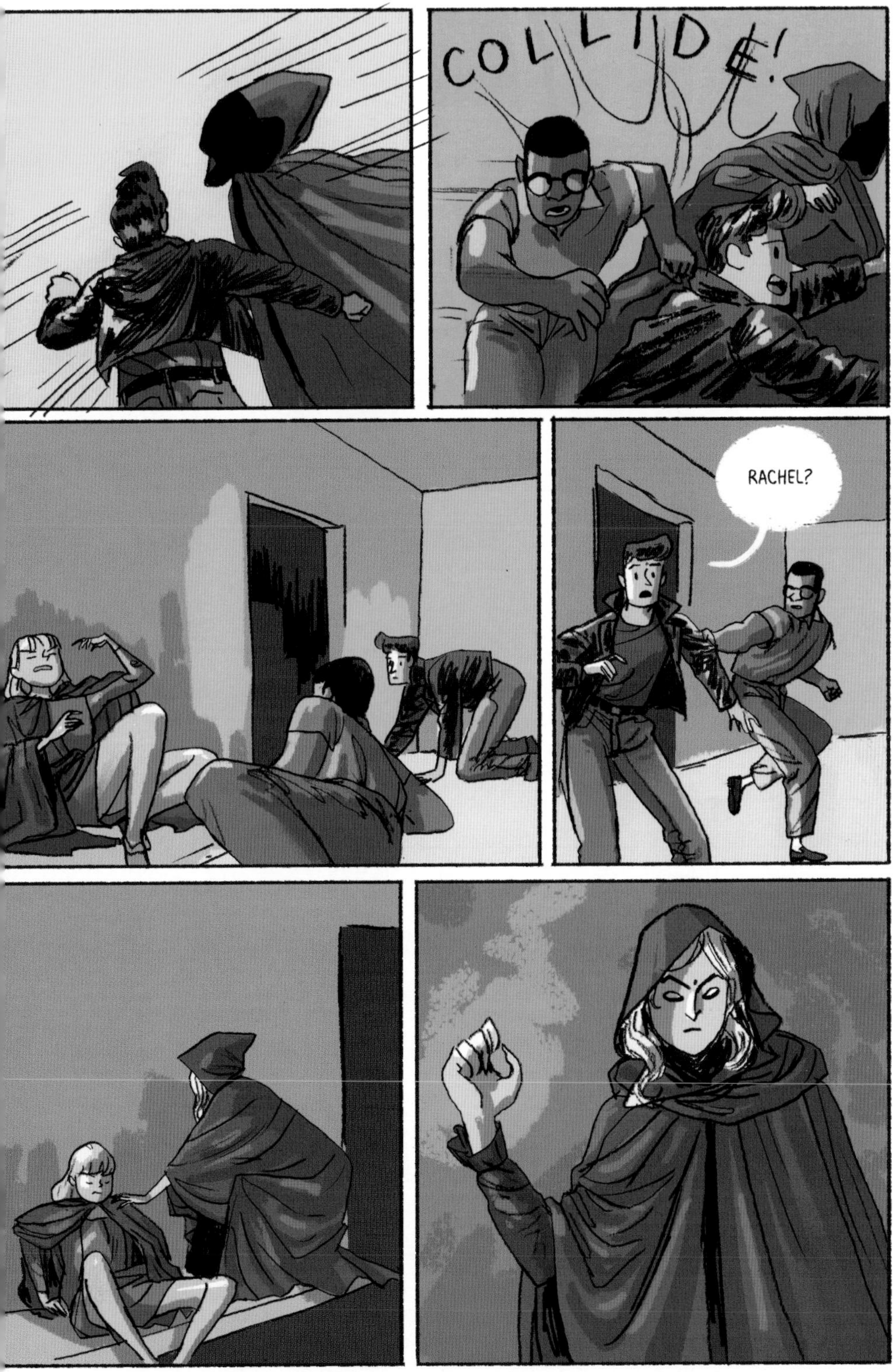
COLLIDE!
RACHEL?

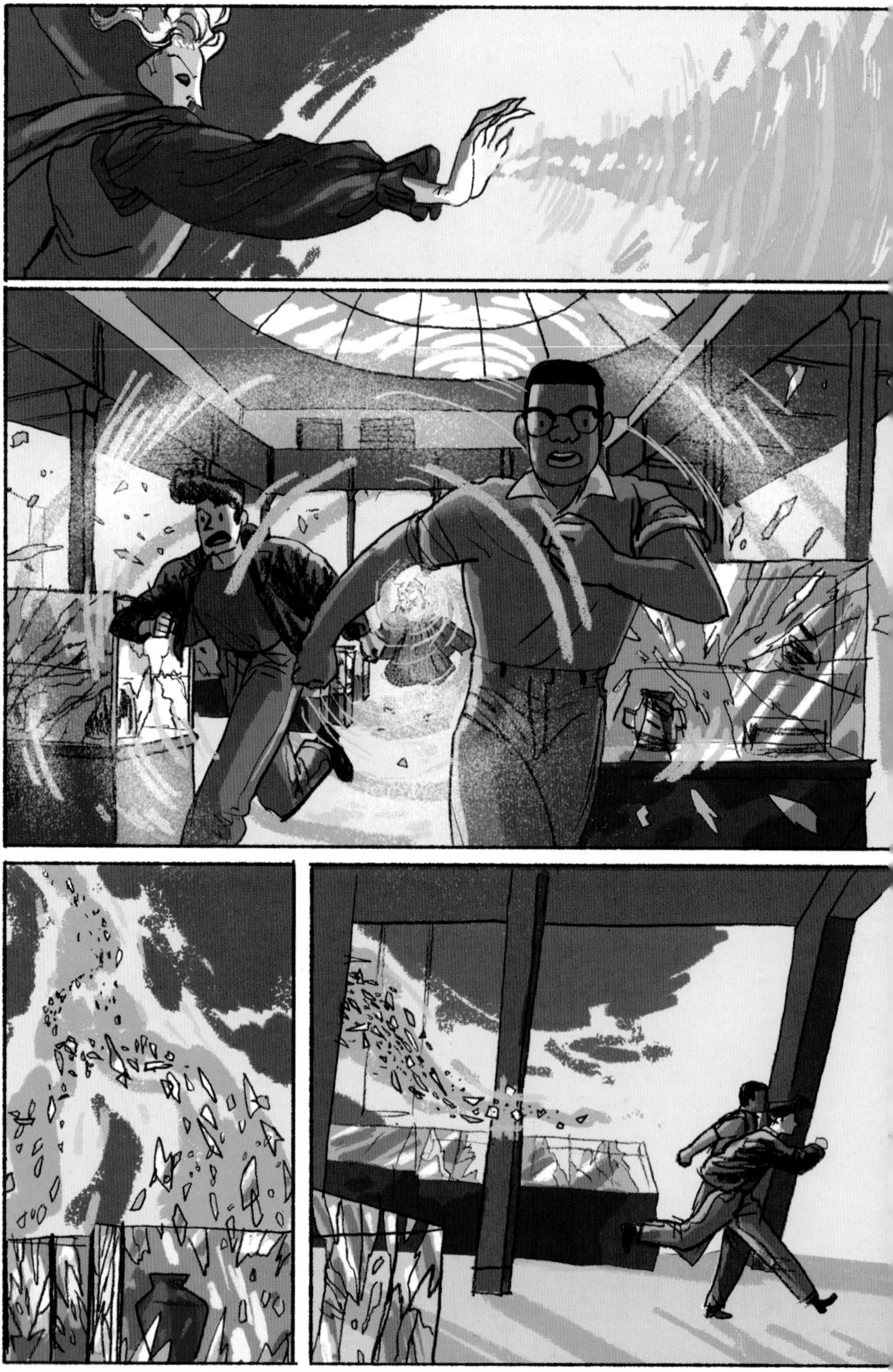

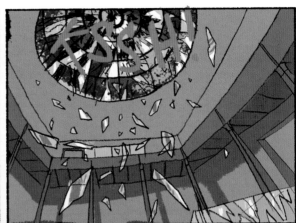

I HAVE TO GO BACK IN!

GET DOWN.

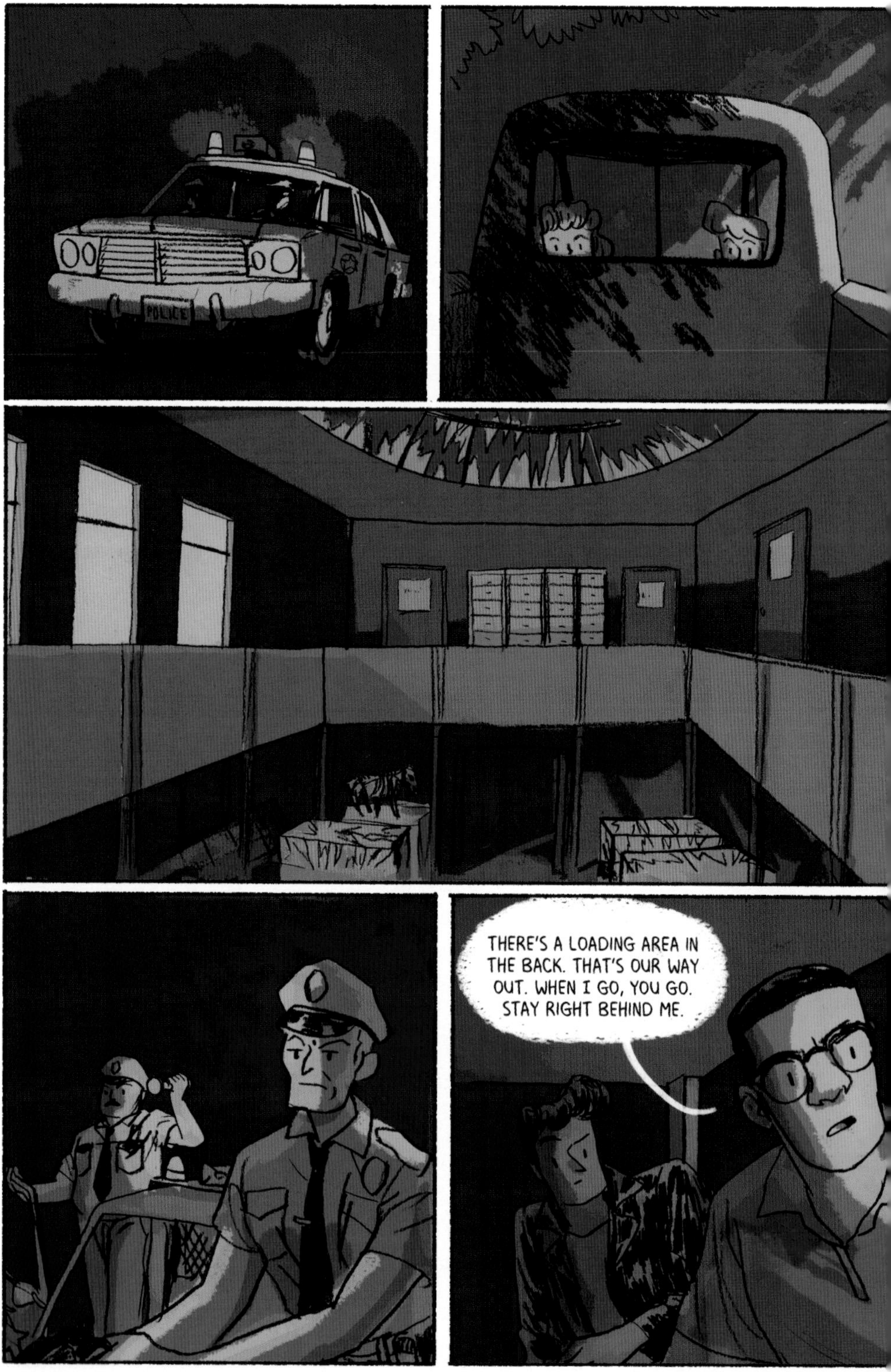
POLICE
THERE'S A LOADING AREA IN THE BACK. THAT'S OUR WAY OUT. WHEN I GO, YOU GO. STAY RIGHT BEHIND ME.

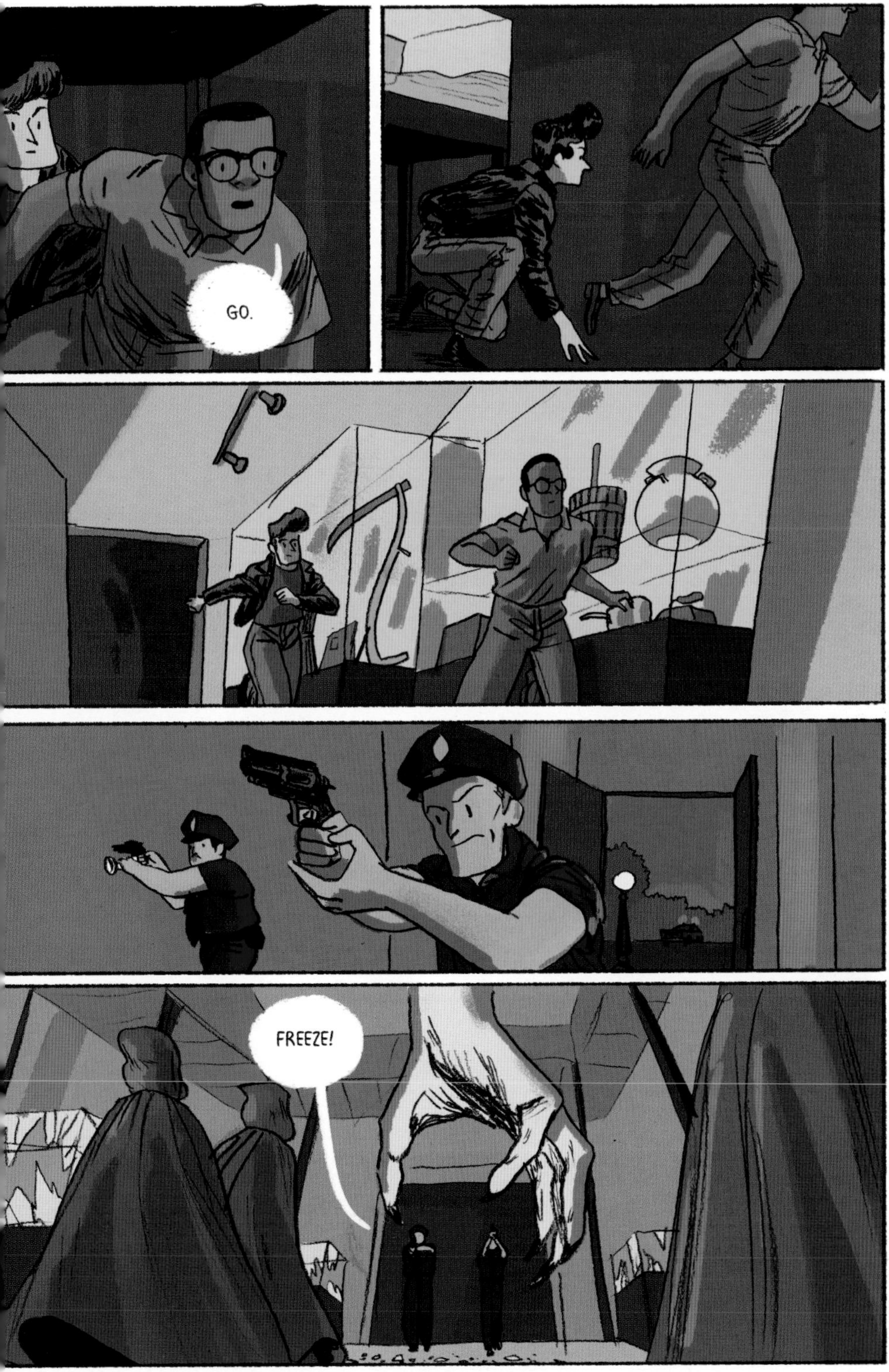
GO.
FREEZE!

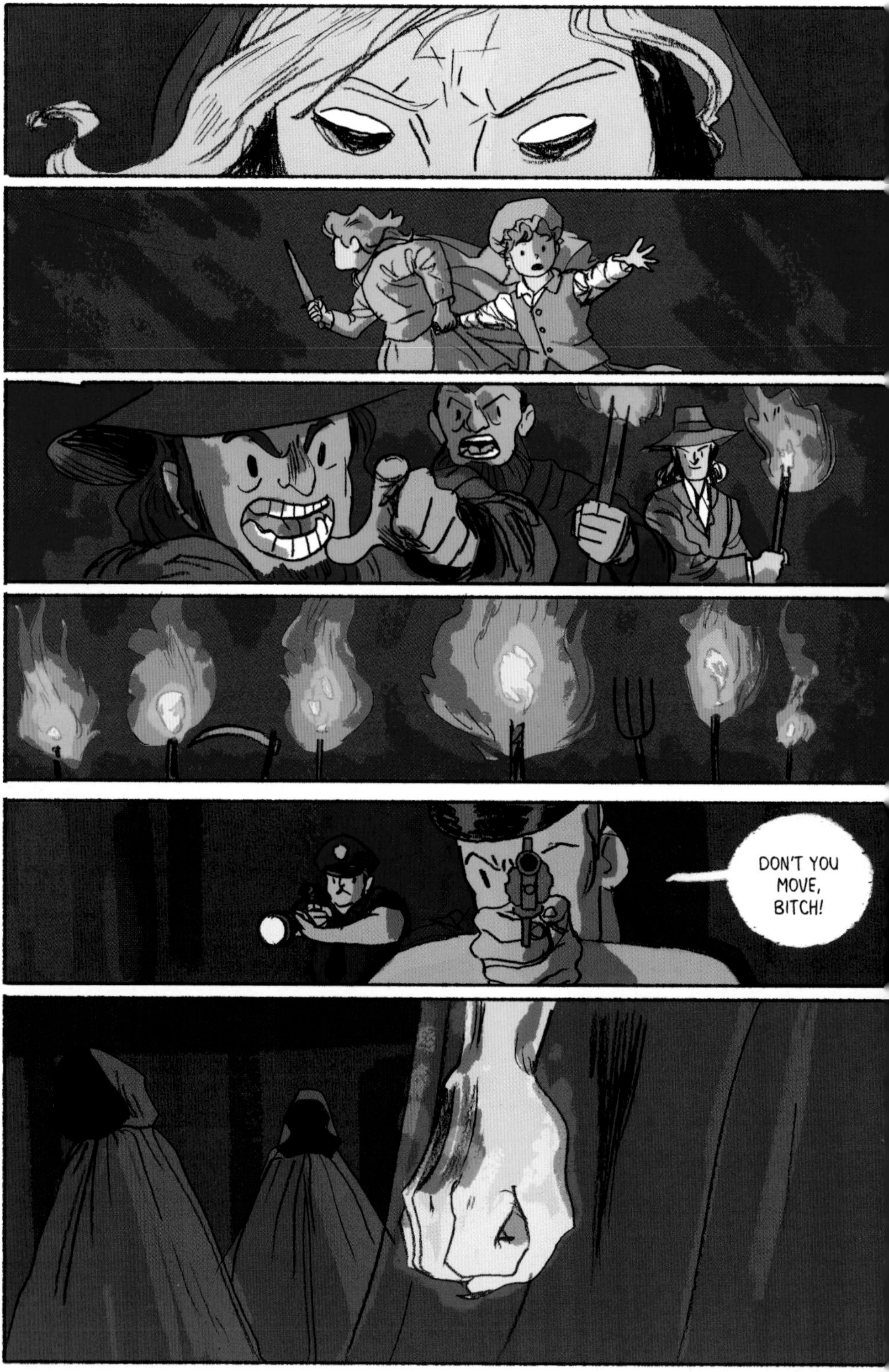
DON'T YOU MOVE, BITCH!

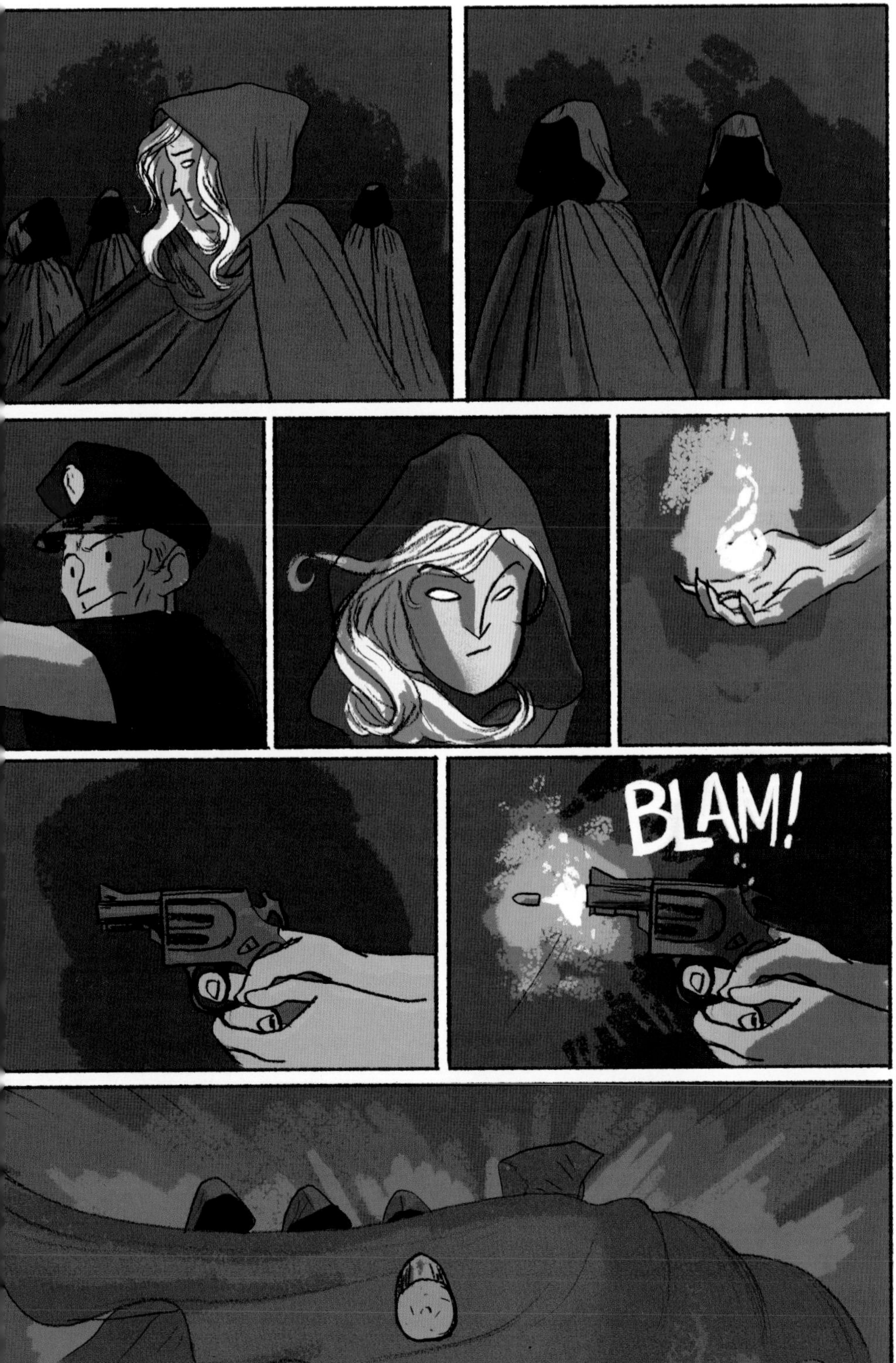
BLAM!

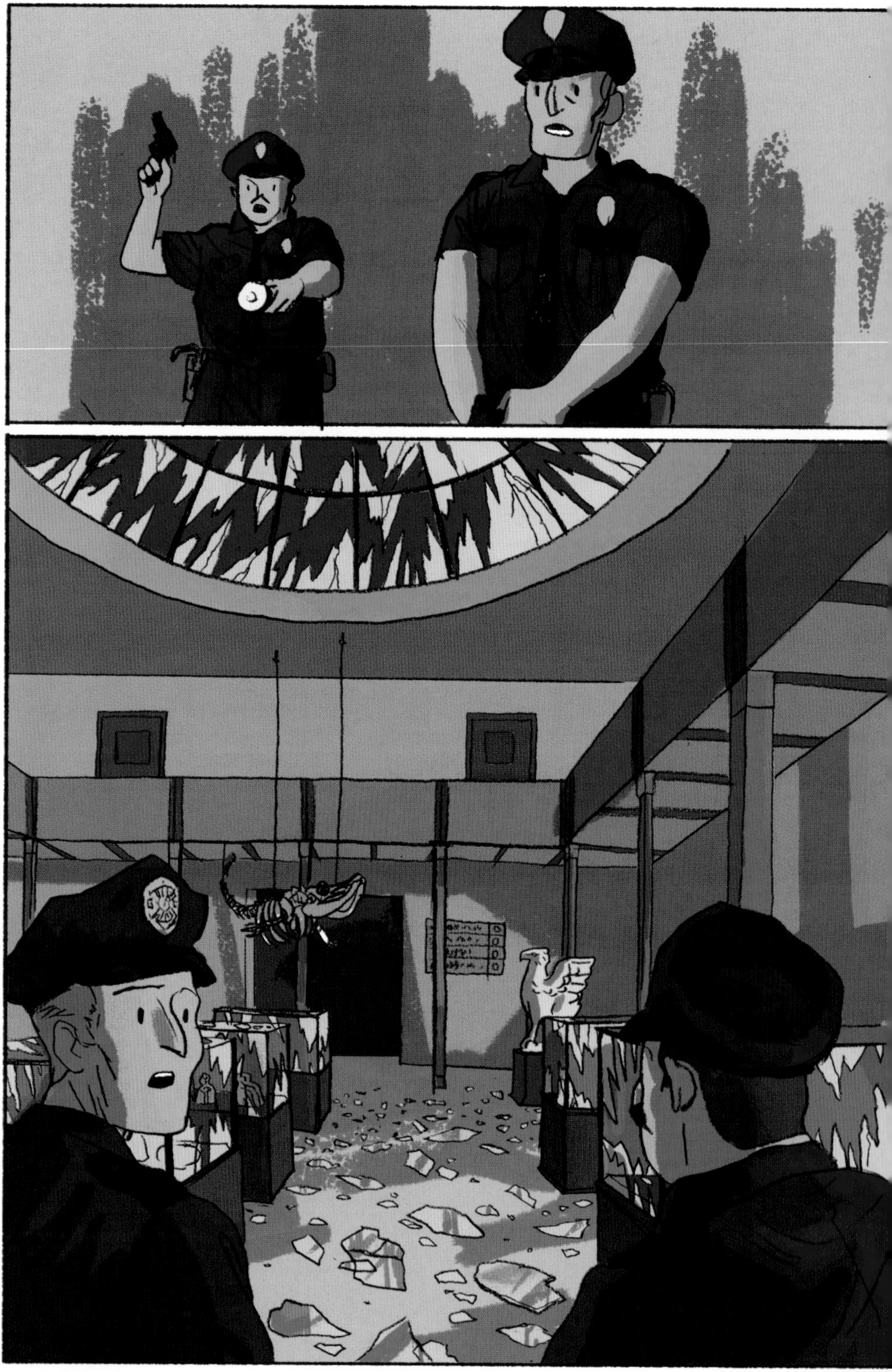

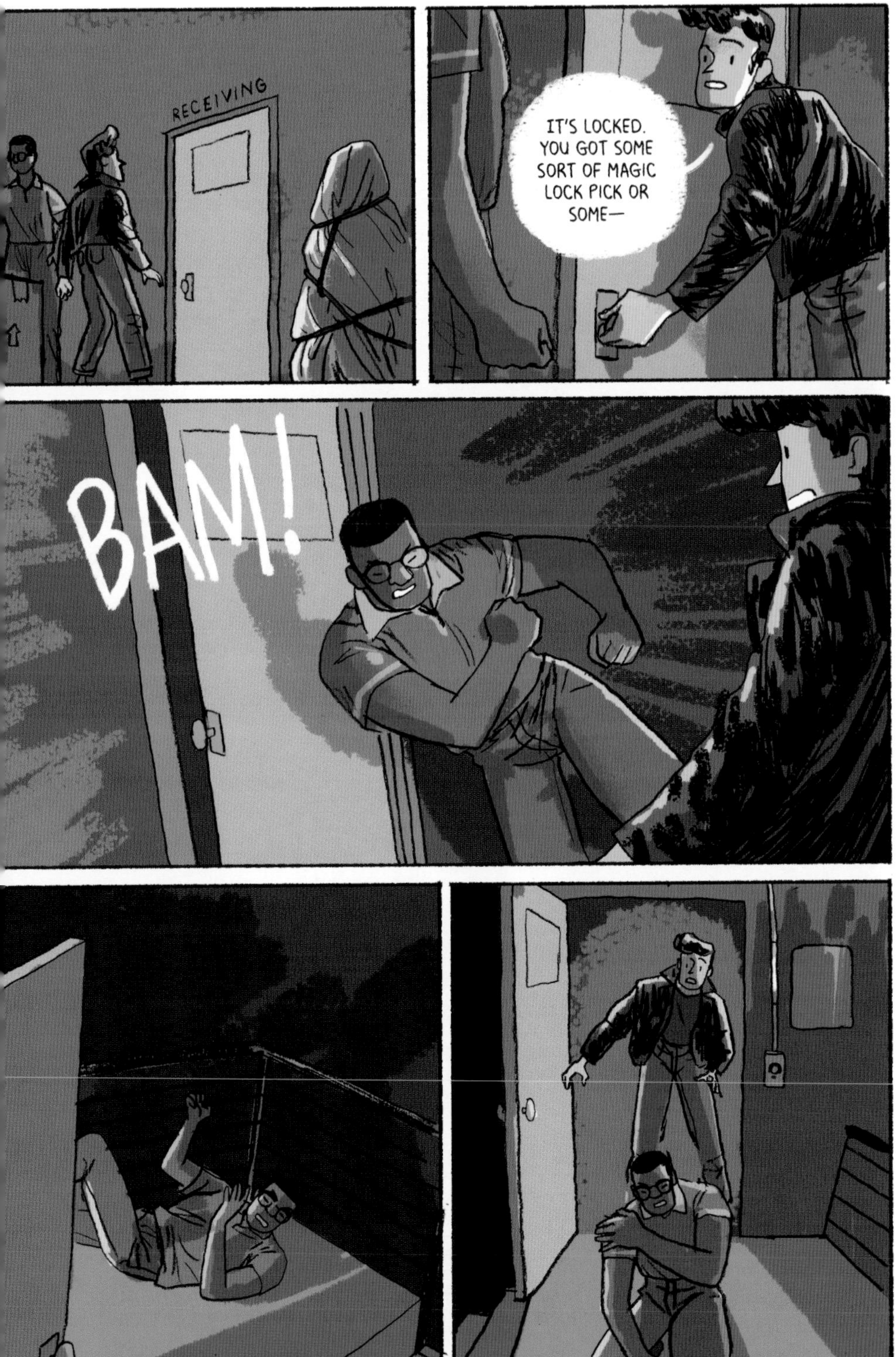
RECEIVING
IT'S LOCKED. YOU GOT SOME SORT OF MAGIC LOCK PICK OR SOME—
BAM!

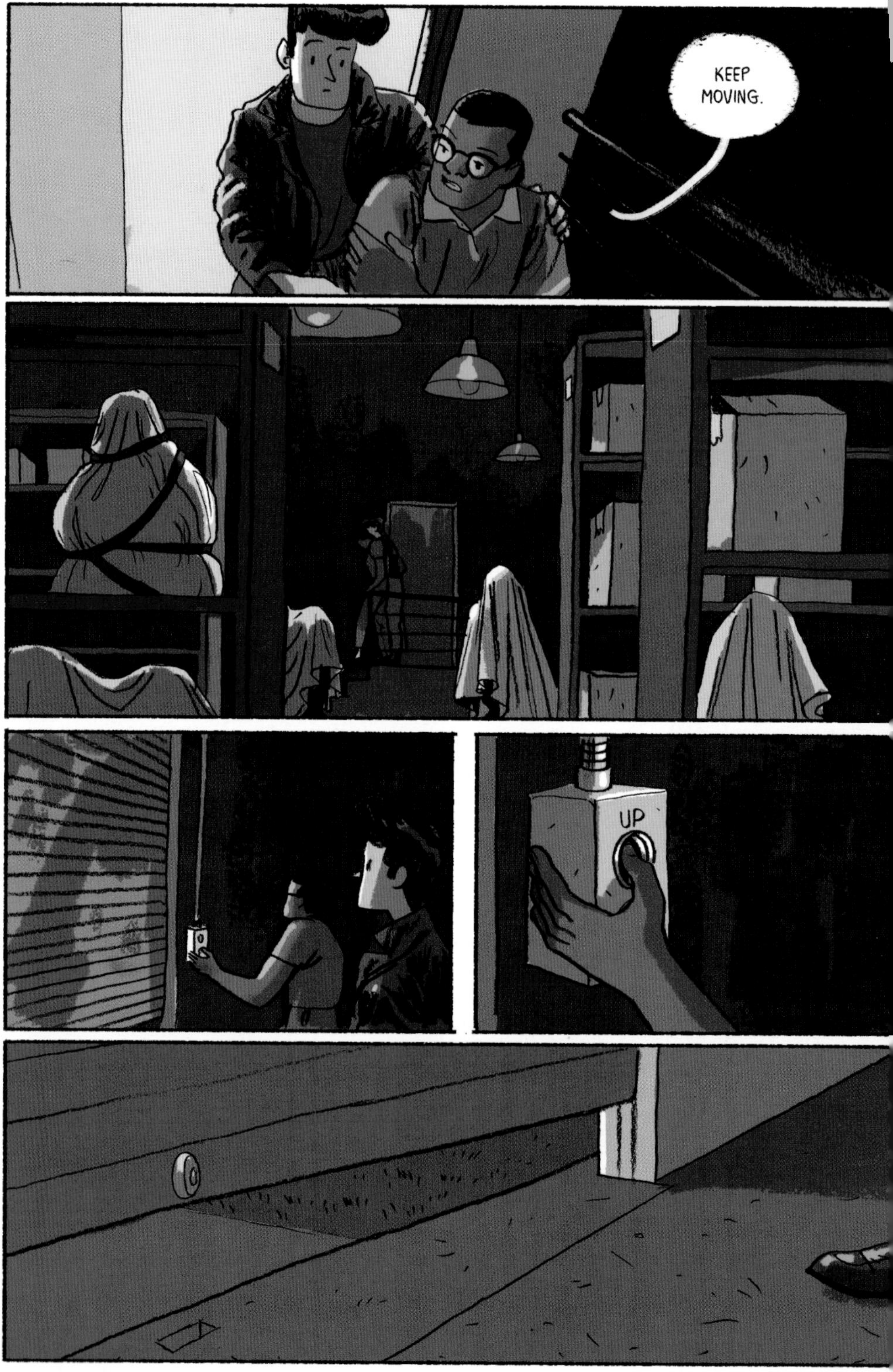
KEEP MOVING.
UP

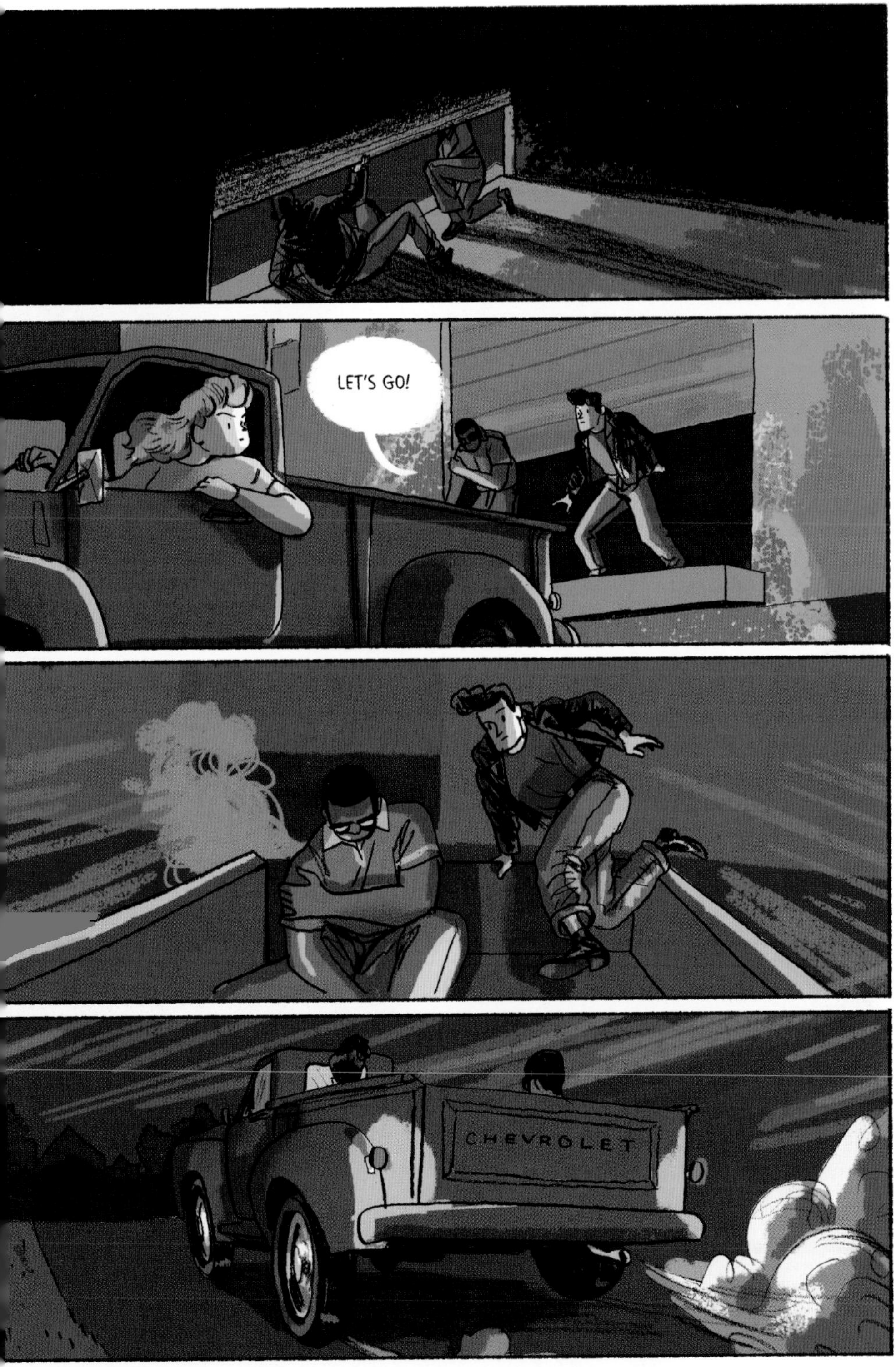
LET'S GO!
CHEVROLET

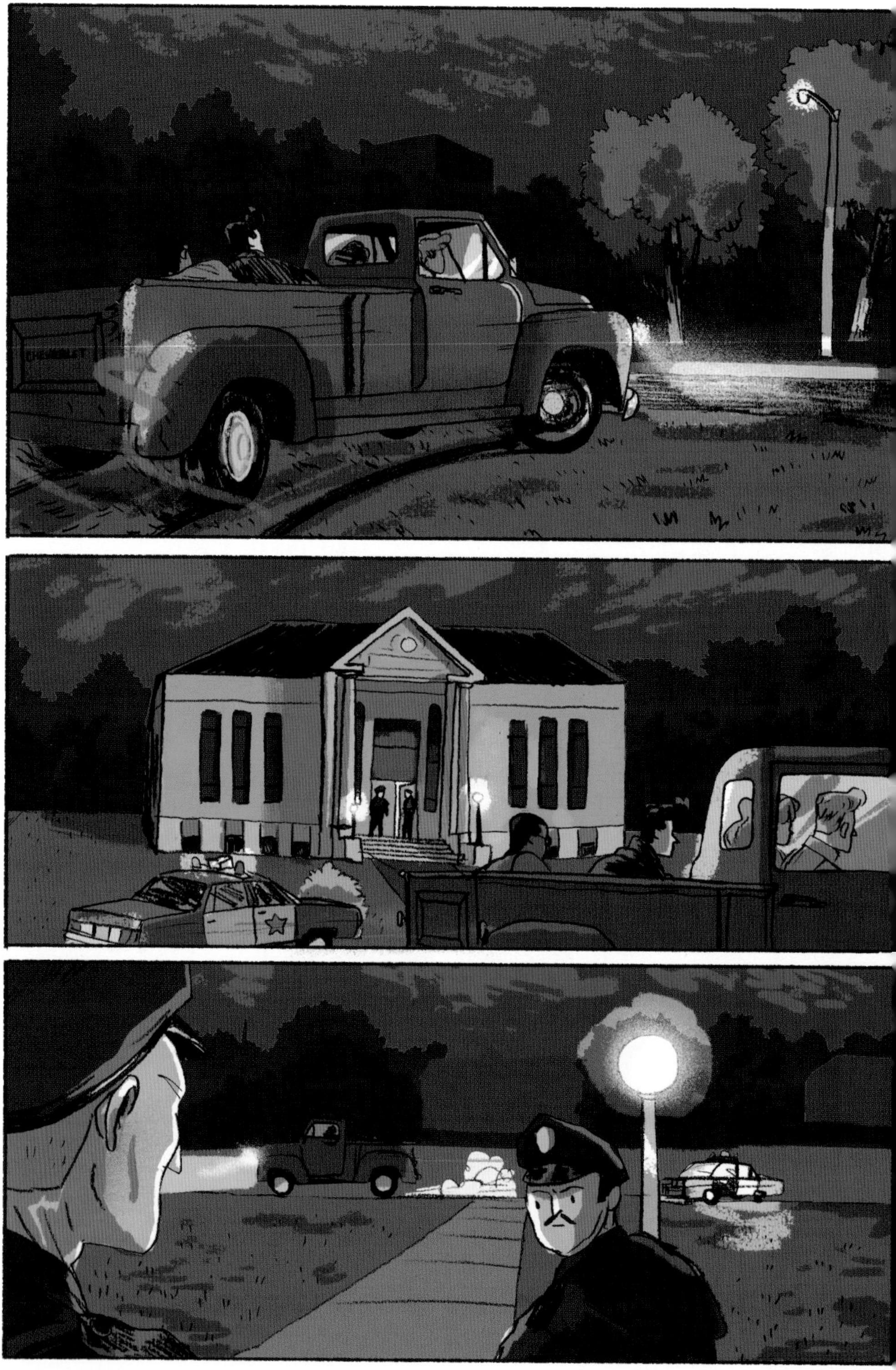
CHEVROLET

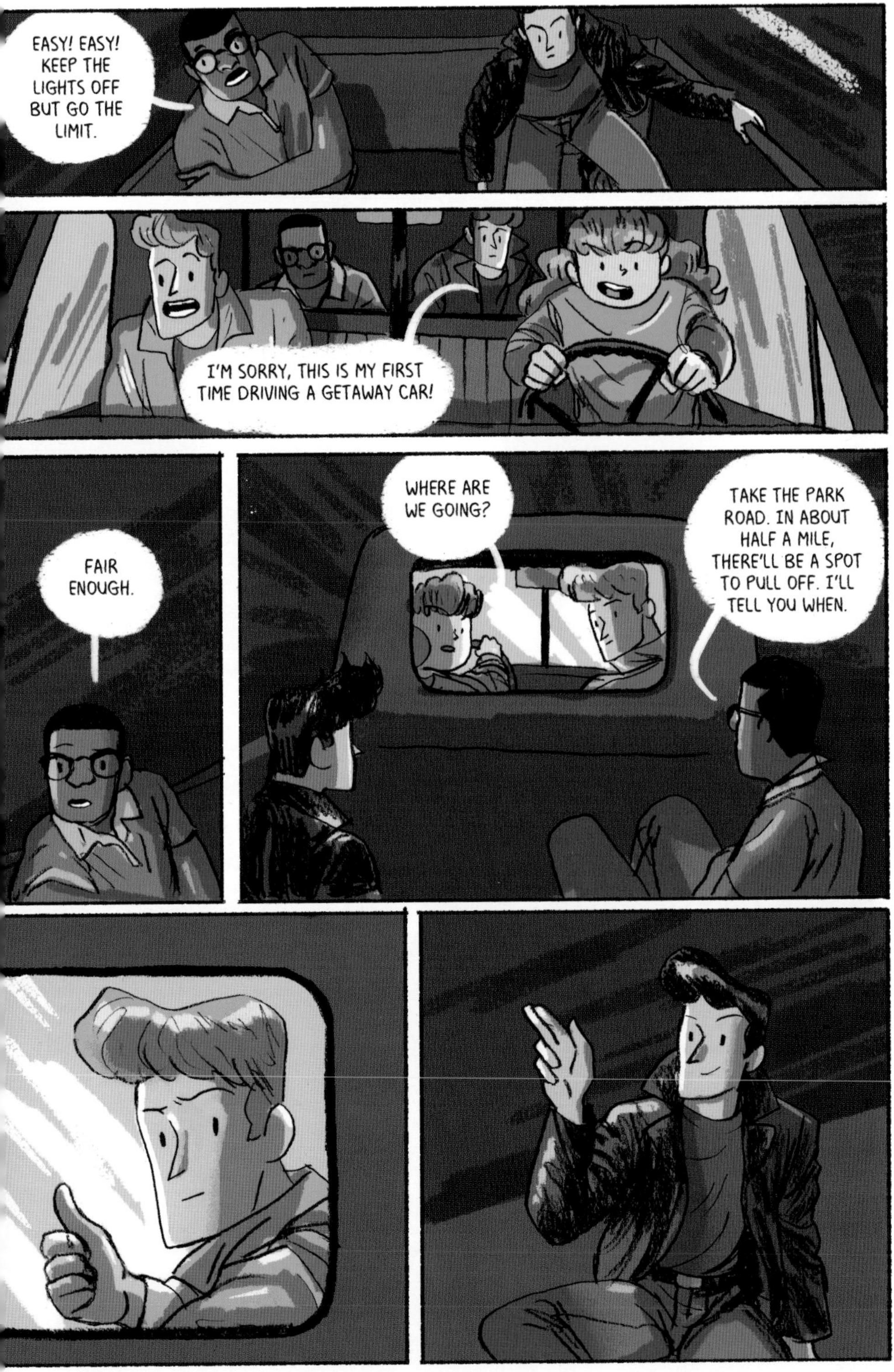
EASY! EASY! KEEP THE LIGHTS OFF BUT GO THE LIMIT.
I'M SORRY, THIS IS MY FIRST TIME DRIVING A GETAWAY CAR!
FAIR ENOUGH.
WHERE ARE WE GOING?
TAKE THE PARK ROAD. IN ABOUT HALF A MILE, THERE'LL BE A SPOT TO PULL OFF. I'LL TELL YOU WHEN.

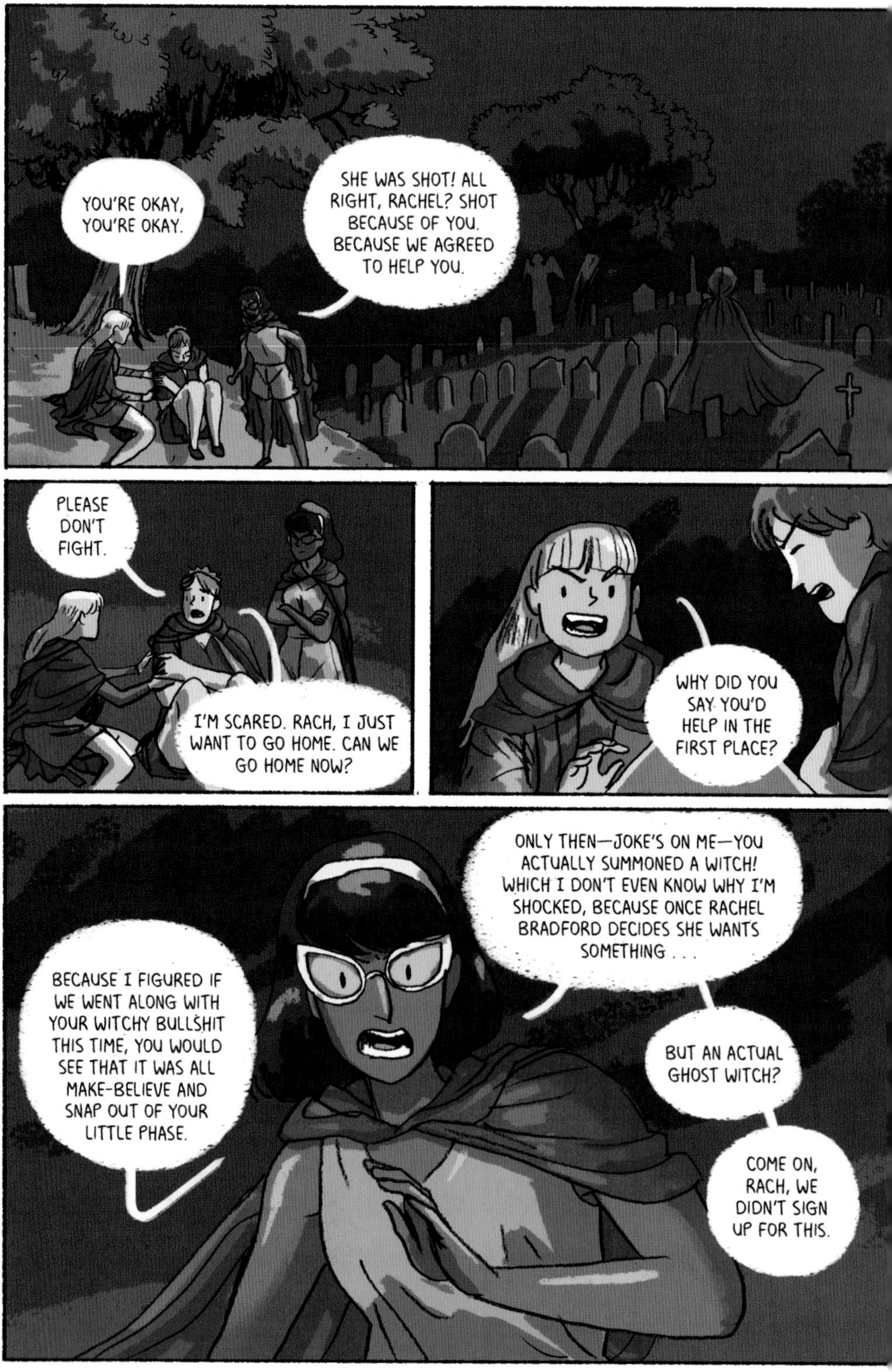
YOU'RE OKAY, YOU'RE OKAY.
SHE WAS SHOT! ALL RIGHT, RACHEL? SHOT BECAUSE OF YOU. BECAUSE WE AGREED TO HELP YOU.
PLEASE DON'T FIGHT.
I'M SCARED. RACH, I JUST WANT TO GO HOME. CAN WE GO HOME NOW?
WHY DID YOU SAY YOU'D HELP IN THE FIRST PLACE?
BECAUSE I FIGURED IF WE WENT ALONG WITH YOUR WITCHY BULLSHIT THIS TIME, YOU WOULD SEE THAT IT WAS ALL MAKE-BELIEVE AND SNAP OUT OF YOUR LITTLE PHASE.
ONLY THEN—JOKE'S ON ME—YOU ACTUALLY SUMMONED A WITCH! WHICH I DON'T EVEN KNOW WHY I'M SHOCKED, BECAUSE ONCE RACHEL BRADFORD DECIDES SHE WANTS SOMETHING . . .
BUT AN ACTUAL GHOST WITCH?
COME ON, RACH, WE DIDN'T SIGN UP FOR THIS.

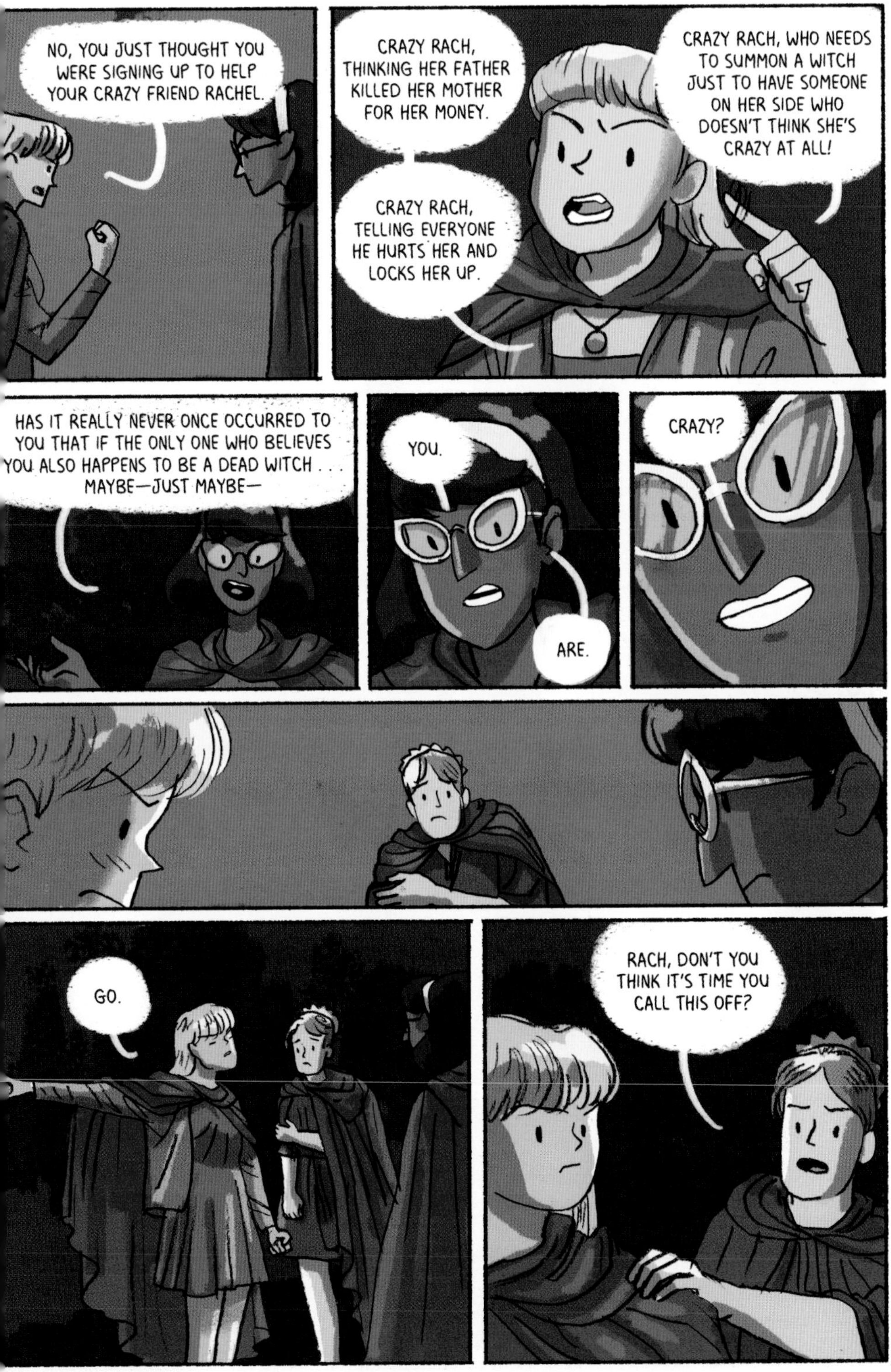
NO, YOU JUST THOUGHT YOU WERE SIGNING UP TO HELP YOUR CRAZY FRIEND RACHEL.
CRAZY RACH, THINKING HER FATHER KILLED HER MOTHER FOR HER MONEY.
CRAZY RACH, TELLING EVERYONE HE HURTS HER AND LOCKS HER UP.
CRAZY RACH, WHO NEEDS TO SUMMON A WITCH JUST TO HAVE SOMEONE ON HER SIDE WHO DOESN'T THINK SHE'S CRAZY AT ALL!
HAS IT REALLY NEVER ONCE OCCURRED TO YOU THAT IF THE ONLY ONE WHO BELIEVES YOU ALSO HAPPENS TO BE A DEAD WITCH . . . MAYBE—JUST MAYBE—
YOU.
ARE.
CRAZY?
GO.
RACH, DON'T YOU THINK IT'S TIME YOU CALL THIS OFF?

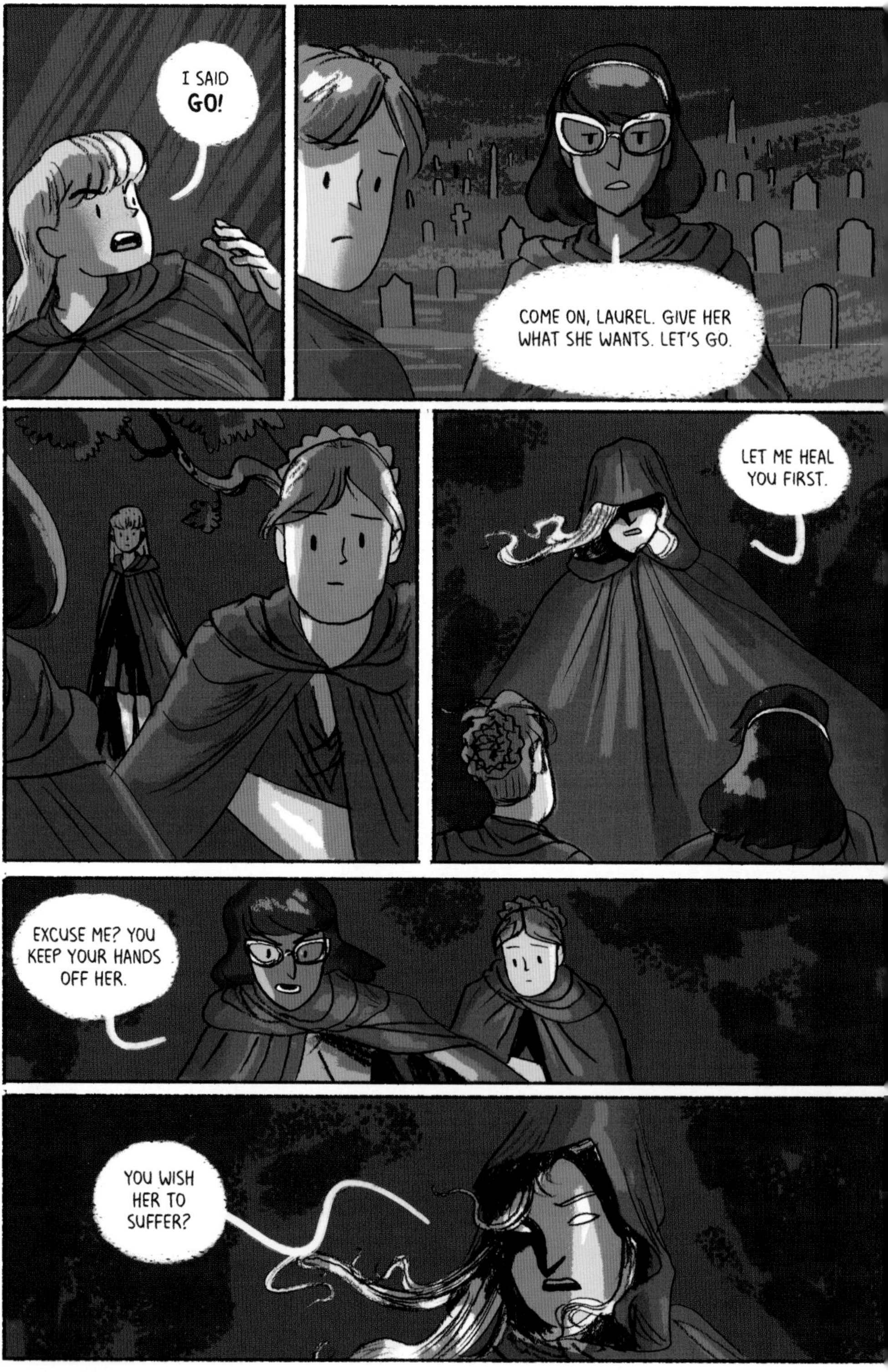
I SAID **GO!**
COME ON, LAUREL. GIVE HER WHAT SHE WANTS. LET'S GO.
LET ME HEAL YOU FIRST.
EXCUSE ME? YOU KEEP YOUR HANDS OFF HER.
YOU WISH HER TO SUFFER?

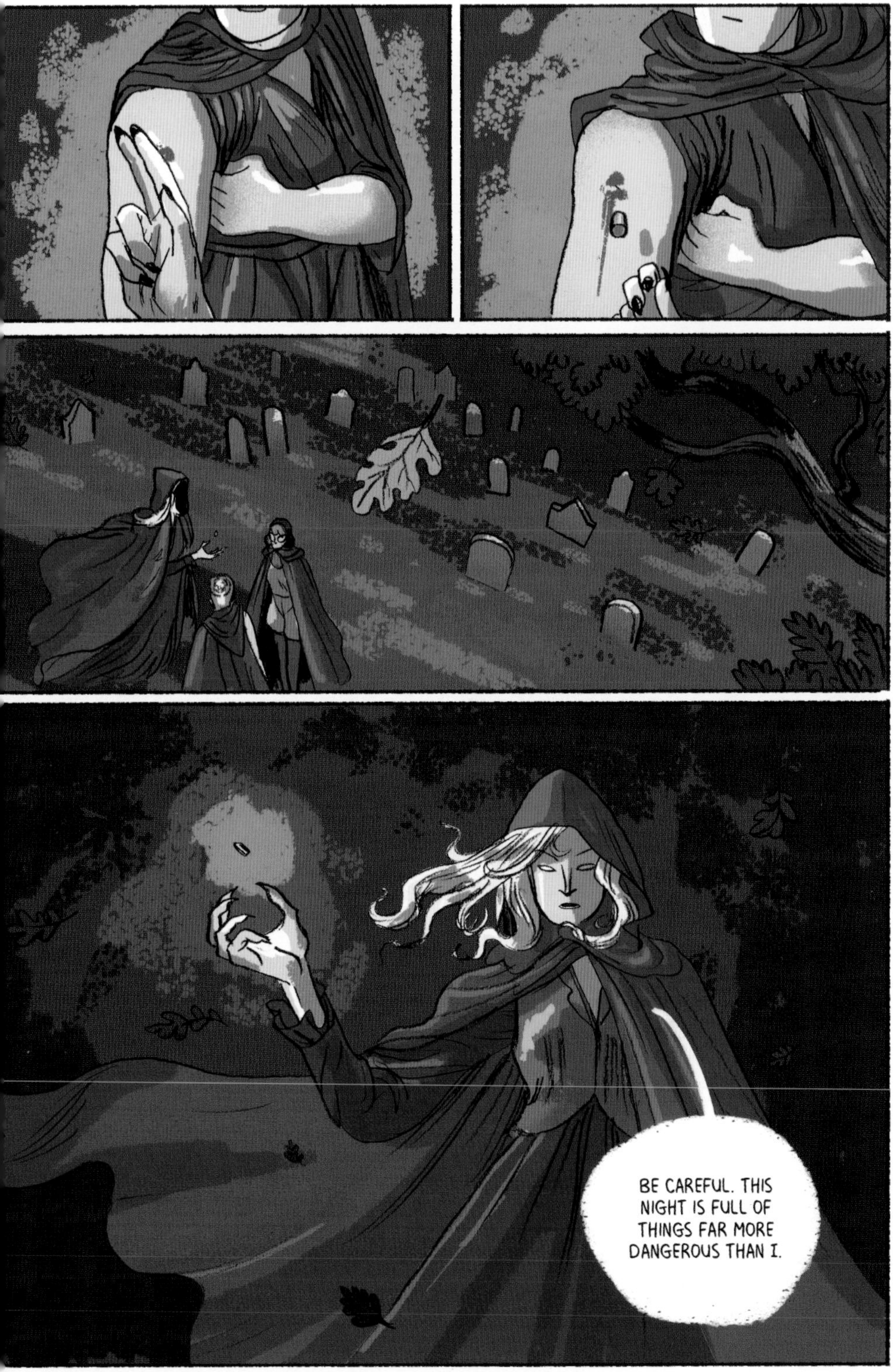
BE CAREFUL. THIS NIGHT IS FULL OF THINGS FAR MORE DANGEROUS THAN I.

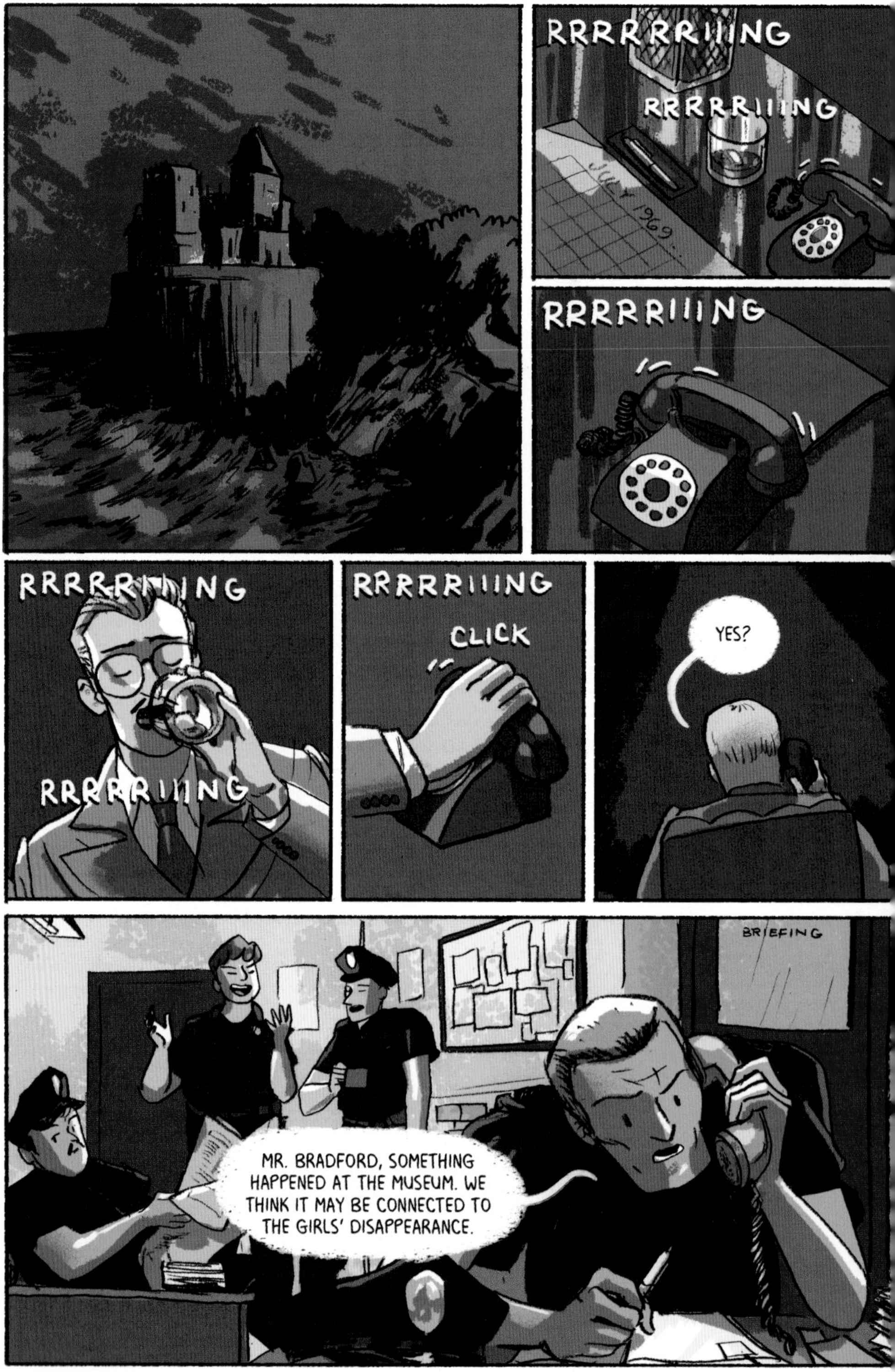
RRRRRRIIING
RRRRRIIING
JULY 1969
RRRRRIIING
RRRRRIIING
RRRRRIIING
RRRRRIIING
CLICK
YES?
BRIEFING
MR. BRADFORD, SOMETHING HAPPENED AT THE MUSEUM. WE THINK IT MAY BE CONNECTED TO THE GIRLS' DISAPPEARANCE.

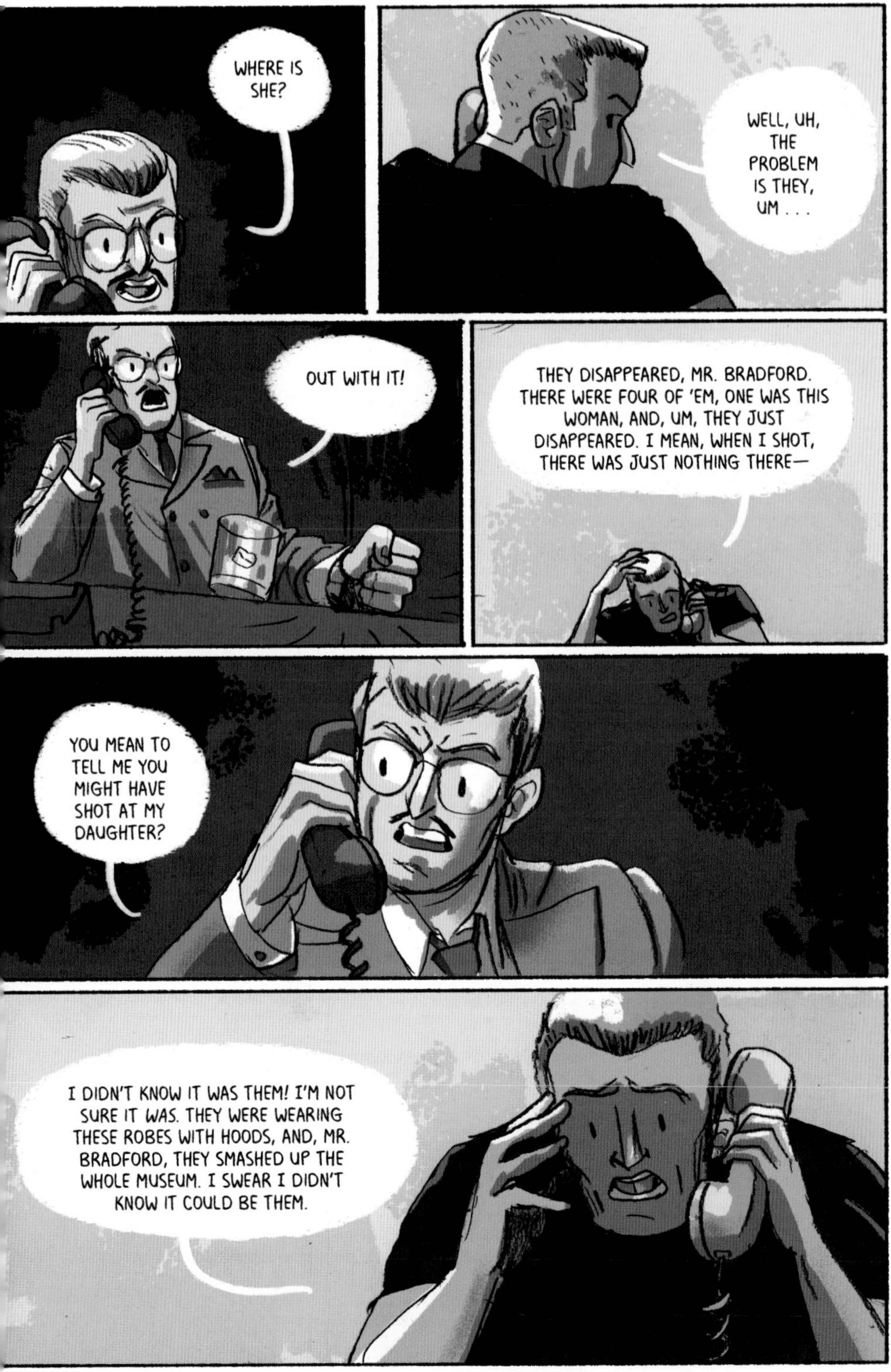
WHERE IS SHE?
WELL, UH, THE PROBLEM IS THEY, UM . . .
OUT WITH IT!
THEY DISAPPEARED, MR. BRADFORD. THERE WERE FOUR OF 'EM, ONE WAS THIS WOMAN, AND, UM, THEY JUST DISAPPEARED. I MEAN, WHEN I SHOT, THERE WAS JUST NOTHING THERE—
YOU MEAN TO TELL ME YOU MIGHT HAVE SHOT AT MY DAUGHTER?
I DIDN'T KNOW IT WAS THEM! I'M NOT SURE IT WAS. THEY WERE WEARING THESE ROBES WITH HOODS, AND, MR. BRADFORD, THEY SMASHED UP THE WHOLE MUSEUM. I SWEAR I DIDN'T KNOW IT COULD BE THEM.

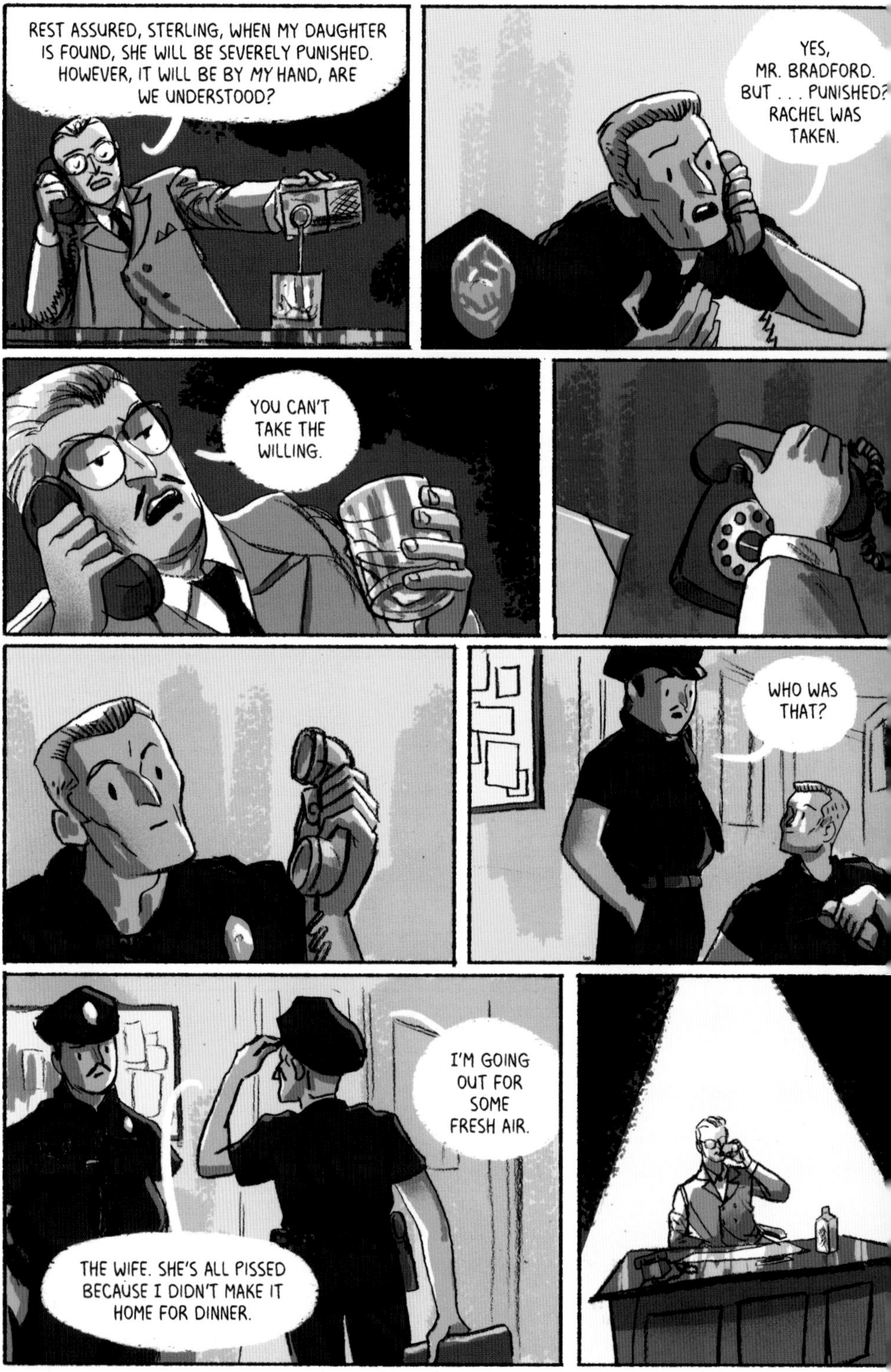
REST ASSURED, STERLING, WHEN MY DAUGHTER IS FOUND, SHE WILL BE SEVERELY PUNISHED. HOWEVER, IT WILL BE BY MY HAND, ARE WE UNDERSTOOD?
YES, MR. BRADFORD. BUT . . . PUNISHED? RACHEL WAS TAKEN.
YOU CAN'T TAKE THE WILLING.
WHO WAS THAT?
THE WIFE. SHE'S ALL PISSED BECAUSE I DIDN'T MAKE IT HOME FOR DINNER.
I'M GOING OUT FOR SOME FRESH AIR.

CHAPTER 5

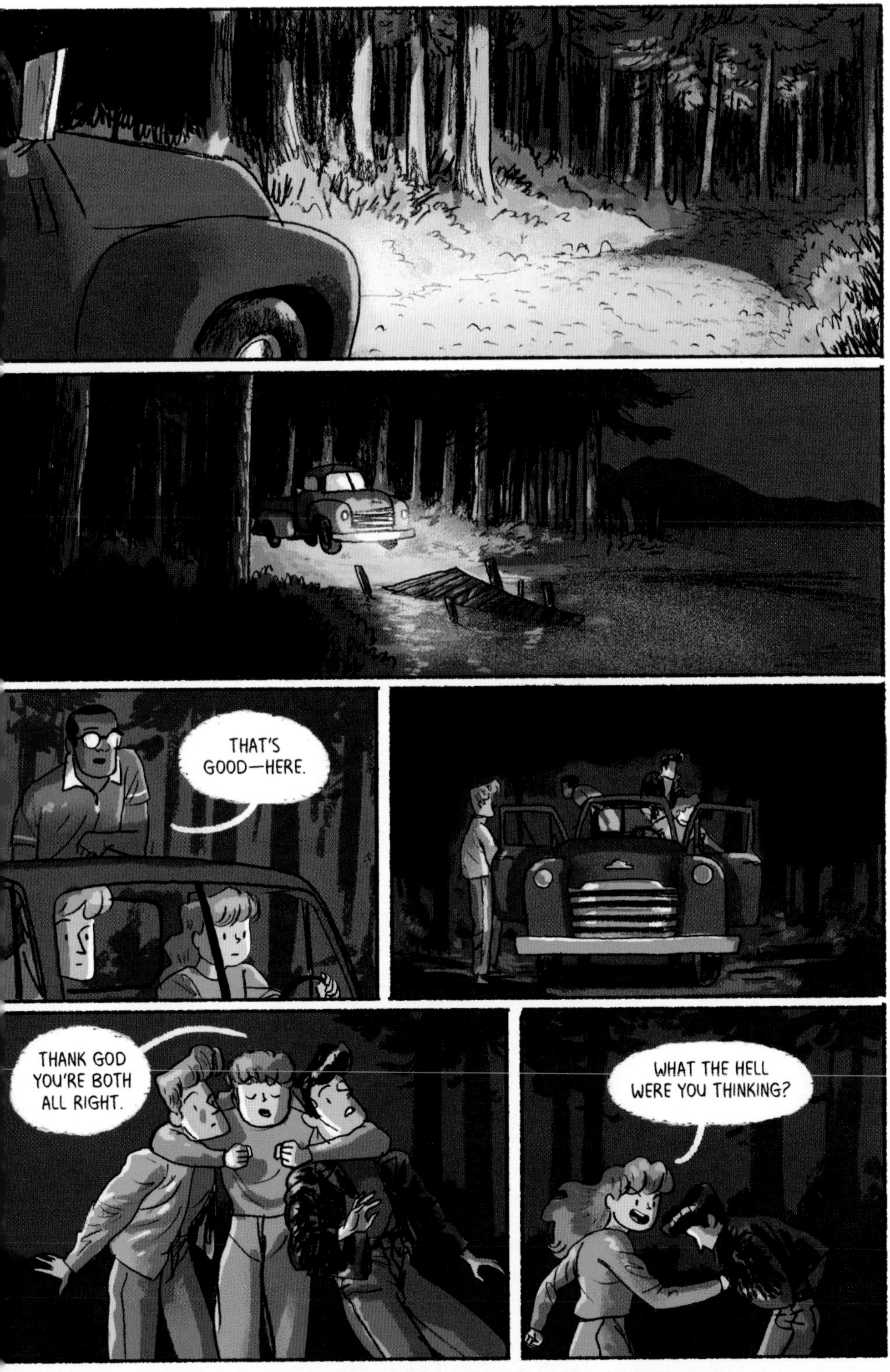
THAT'S GOOD—HERE.
THANK GOD YOU'RE BOTH ALL RIGHT.
WHAT THE HELL WERE YOU THINKING?

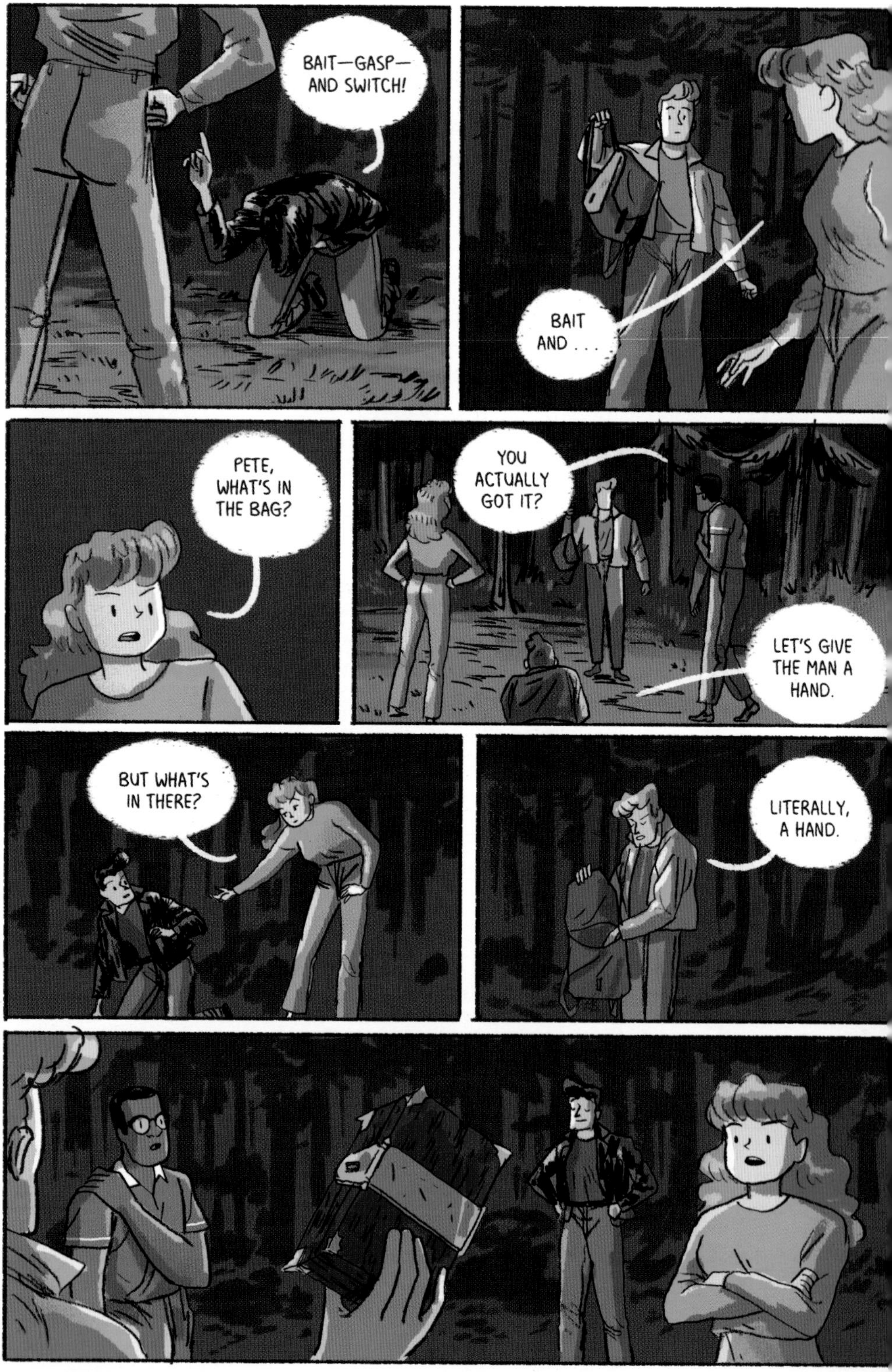
BAIT—GASP—AND SWITCH!
BAIT AND . . .
PETE, WHAT'S IN THE BAG?
YOU ACTUALLY GOT IT?
LET'S GIVE THE MAN A HAND.
BUT WHAT'S IN THERE?
LITERALLY, A HAND.

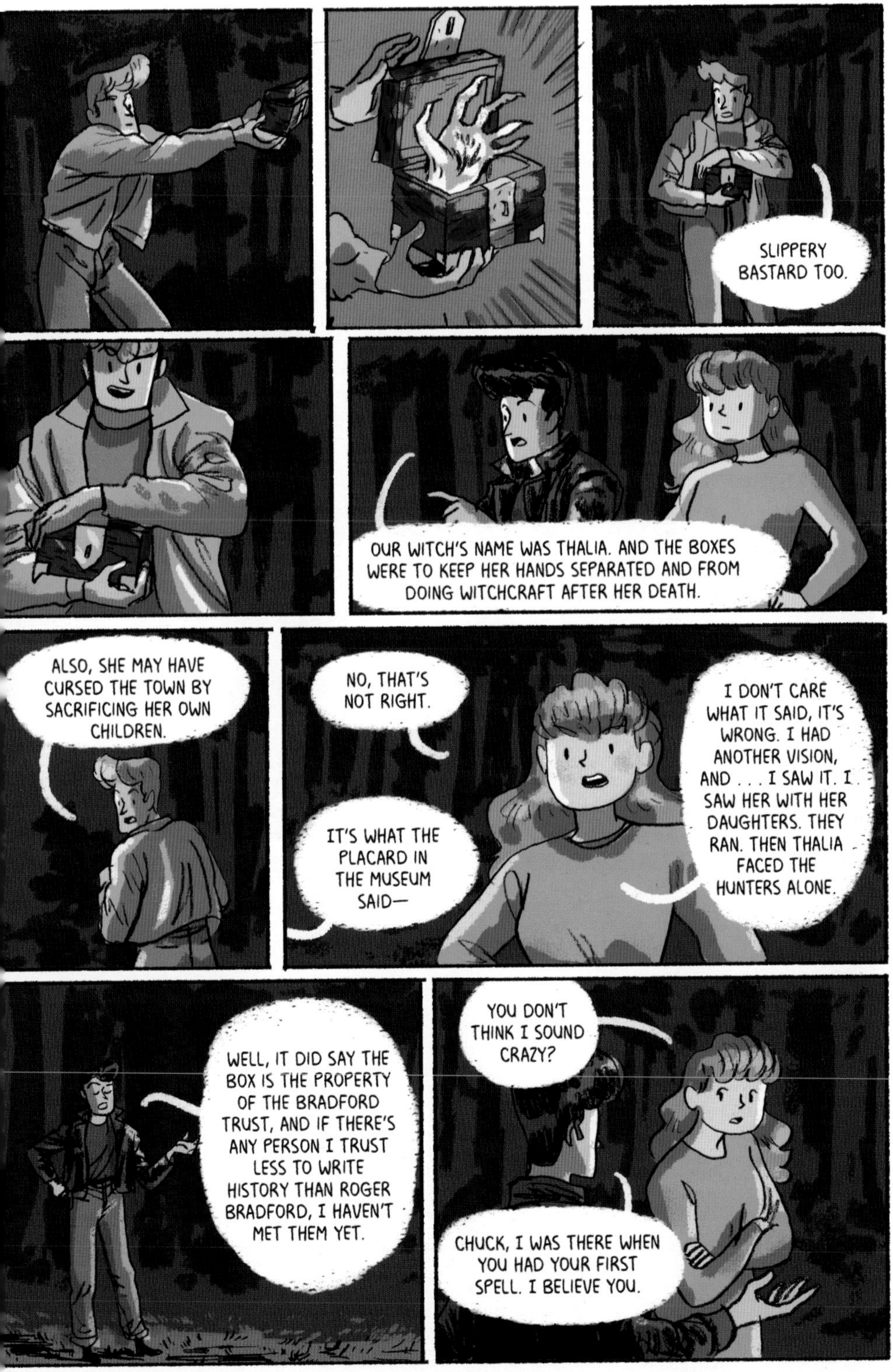
SLIPPERY BASTARD TOO.
OUR WITCH'S NAME WAS THALIA. AND THE BOXES WERE TO KEEP HER HANDS SEPARATED AND FROM DOING WITCHCRAFT AFTER HER DEATH.
ALSO, SHE MAY HAVE CURSED THE TOWN BY SACRIFICING HER OWN CHILDREN.
NO, THAT'S NOT RIGHT.
IT'S WHAT THE PLACARD IN THE MUSEUM SAID—
I DON'T CARE WHAT IT SAID, IT'S WRONG. I HAD ANOTHER VISION, AND . . . I SAW IT. I SAW HER WITH HER DAUGHTERS. THEY RAN. THEN THALIA FACED THE HUNTERS ALONE.
WELL, IT DID SAY THE BOX IS THE PROPERTY OF THE BRADFORD TRUST, AND IF THERE'S ANY PERSON I TRUST LESS TO WRITE HISTORY THAN ROGER BRADFORD, I HAVEN'T MET THEM YET.
YOU DON'T THINK I SOUND CRAZY?
CHUCK, I WAS THERE WHEN YOU HAD YOUR FIRST SPELL. I BELIEVE YOU.

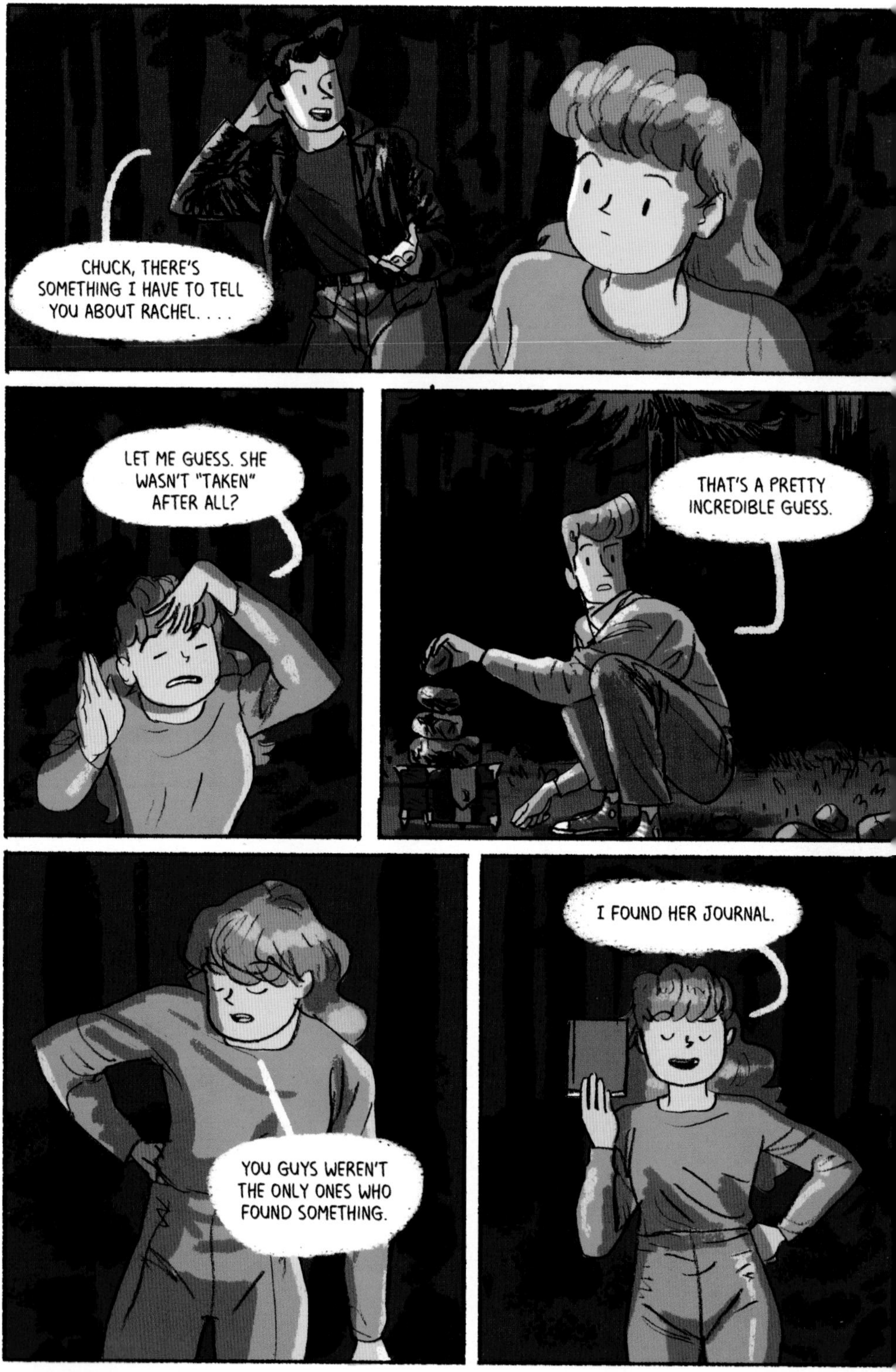
CHUCK, THERE'S SOMETHING I HAVE TO TELL YOU ABOUT RACHEL. . . .
LET ME GUESS. SHE WASN'T "TAKEN" AFTER ALL?
THAT'S A PRETTY INCREDIBLE GUESS.
YOU GUYS WEREN'T THE ONLY ONES WHO FOUND SOMETHING.
I FOUND HER JOURNAL.

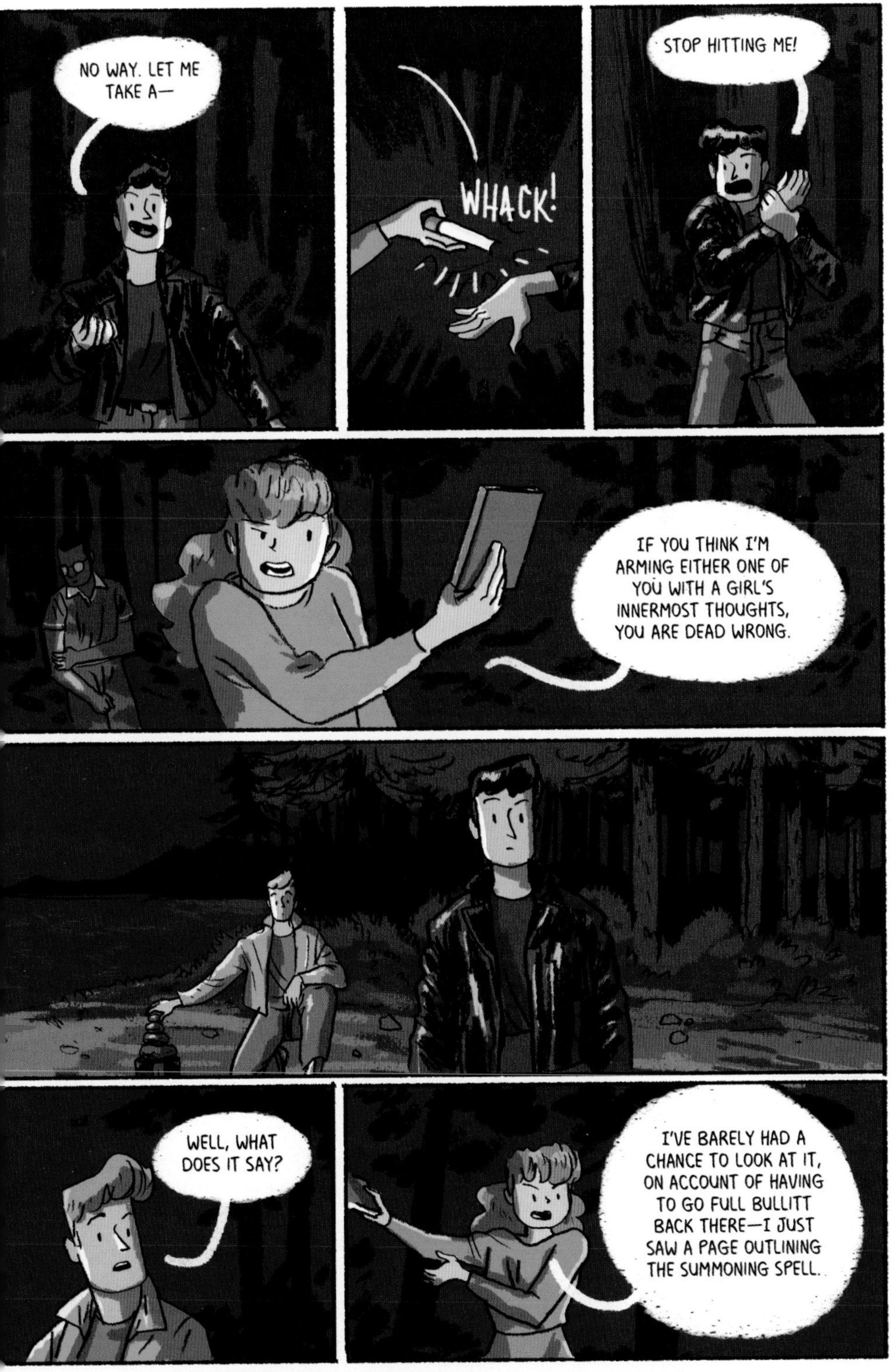
NO WAY. LET ME TAKE A—
WHACK!
STOP HITTING ME!
IF YOU THINK I'M ARMING EITHER ONE OF YOU WITH A GIRL'S INNERMOST THOUGHTS, YOU ARE DEAD WRONG.
WELL, WHAT DOES IT SAY?
I'VE BARELY HAD A CHANCE TO LOOK AT IT, ON ACCOUNT OF HAVING TO GO FULL BULLITT BACK THERE—I JUST SAW A PAGE OUTLINING THE SUMMONING SPELL.

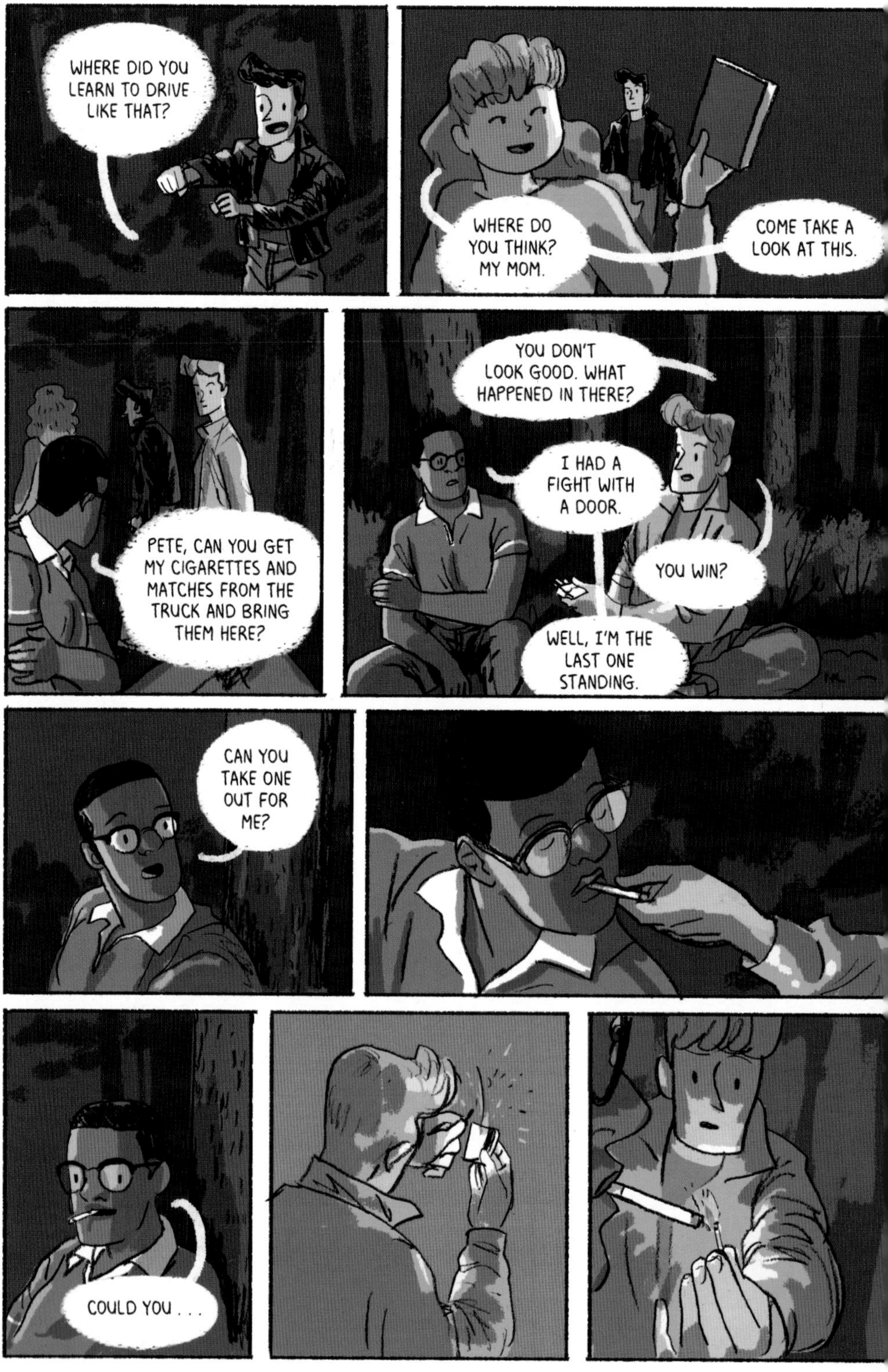
WHERE DID YOU LEARN TO DRIVE LIKE THAT?
WHERE DO YOU THINK? MY MOM.
COME TAKE A LOOK AT THIS.
PETE, CAN YOU GET MY CIGARETTES AND MATCHES FROM THE TRUCK AND BRING THEM HERE?
YOU DON'T LOOK GOOD. WHAT HAPPENED IN THERE?
I HAD A FIGHT WITH A DOOR.
YOU WIN?
WELL, I'M THE LAST ONE STANDING.
CAN YOU TAKE ONE OUT FOR ME?
COULD YOU . . .

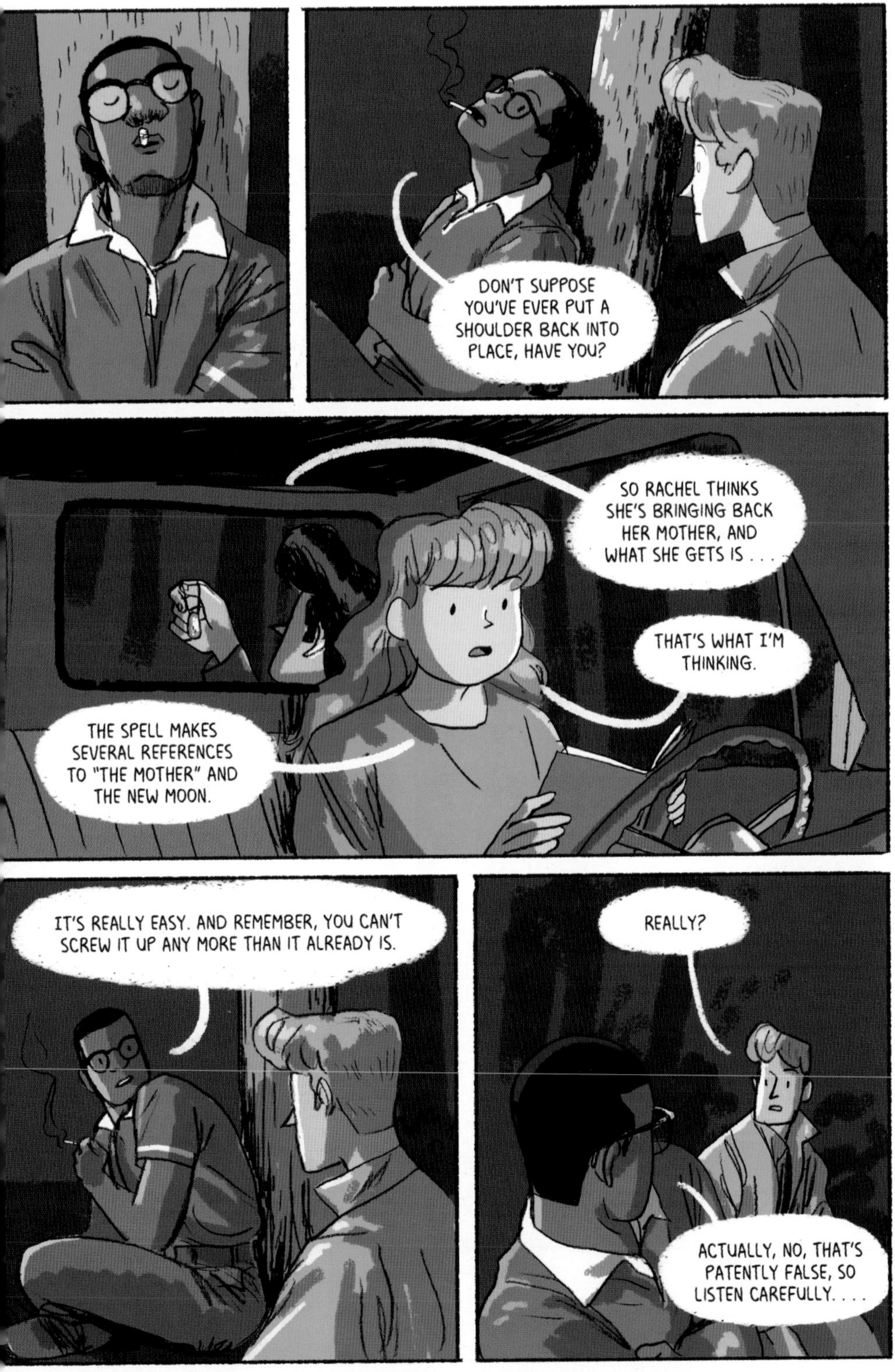
DON'T SUPPOSE YOU'VE EVER PUT A SHOULDER BACK INTO PLACE, HAVE YOU?
SO RACHEL THINKS SHE'S BRINGING BACK HER MOTHER, AND WHAT SHE GETS IS . . .
THAT'S WHAT I'M THINKING.
THE SPELL MAKES SEVERAL REFERENCES TO "THE MOTHER" AND THE NEW MOON.
IT'S REALLY EASY. AND REMEMBER, YOU CAN'T SCREW IT UP ANY MORE THAN IT ALREADY IS.
REALLY?
ACTUALLY, NO, THAT'S PATENTLY FALSE, SO LISTEN CAREFULLY. . . .

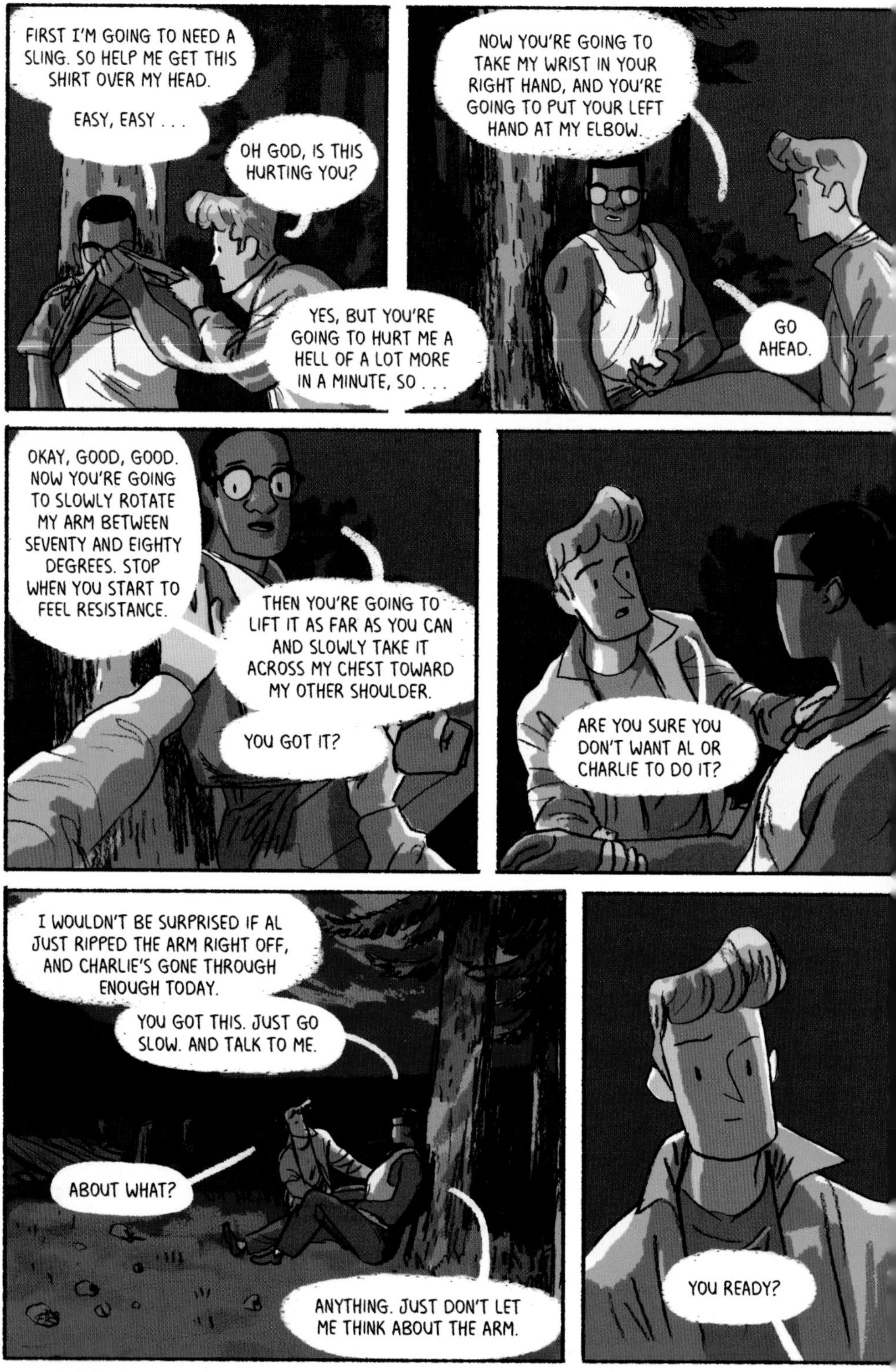
FIRST I'M GOING TO NEED A SLING. SO HELP ME GET THIS SHIRT OVER MY HEAD.
EASY, EASY . . .
OH GOD, IS THIS HURTING YOU?
YES, BUT YOU'RE GOING TO HURT ME A HELL OF A LOT MORE IN A MINUTE, SO . . .
NOW YOU'RE GOING TO TAKE MY WRIST IN YOUR RIGHT HAND, AND YOU'RE GOING TO PUT YOUR LEFT HAND AT MY ELBOW.
GO AHEAD.
OKAY, GOOD, GOOD. NOW YOU'RE GOING TO SLOWLY ROTATE MY ARM BETWEEN SEVENTY AND EIGHTY DEGREES. STOP WHEN YOU START TO FEEL RESISTANCE.
THEN YOU'RE GOING TO LIFT IT AS FAR AS YOU CAN AND SLOWLY TAKE IT ACROSS MY CHEST TOWARD MY OTHER SHOULDER.
YOU GOT IT?
ARE YOU SURE YOU DON'T WANT AL OR CHARLIE TO DO IT?
I WOULDN'T BE SURPRISED IF AL JUST RIPPED THE ARM RIGHT OFF, AND CHARLIE'S GONE THROUGH ENOUGH TODAY.
YOU GOT THIS. JUST GO SLOW. AND TALK TO ME.
ABOUT WHAT?
ANYTHING. JUST DON'T LET ME THINK ABOUT THE ARM.
YOU READY?

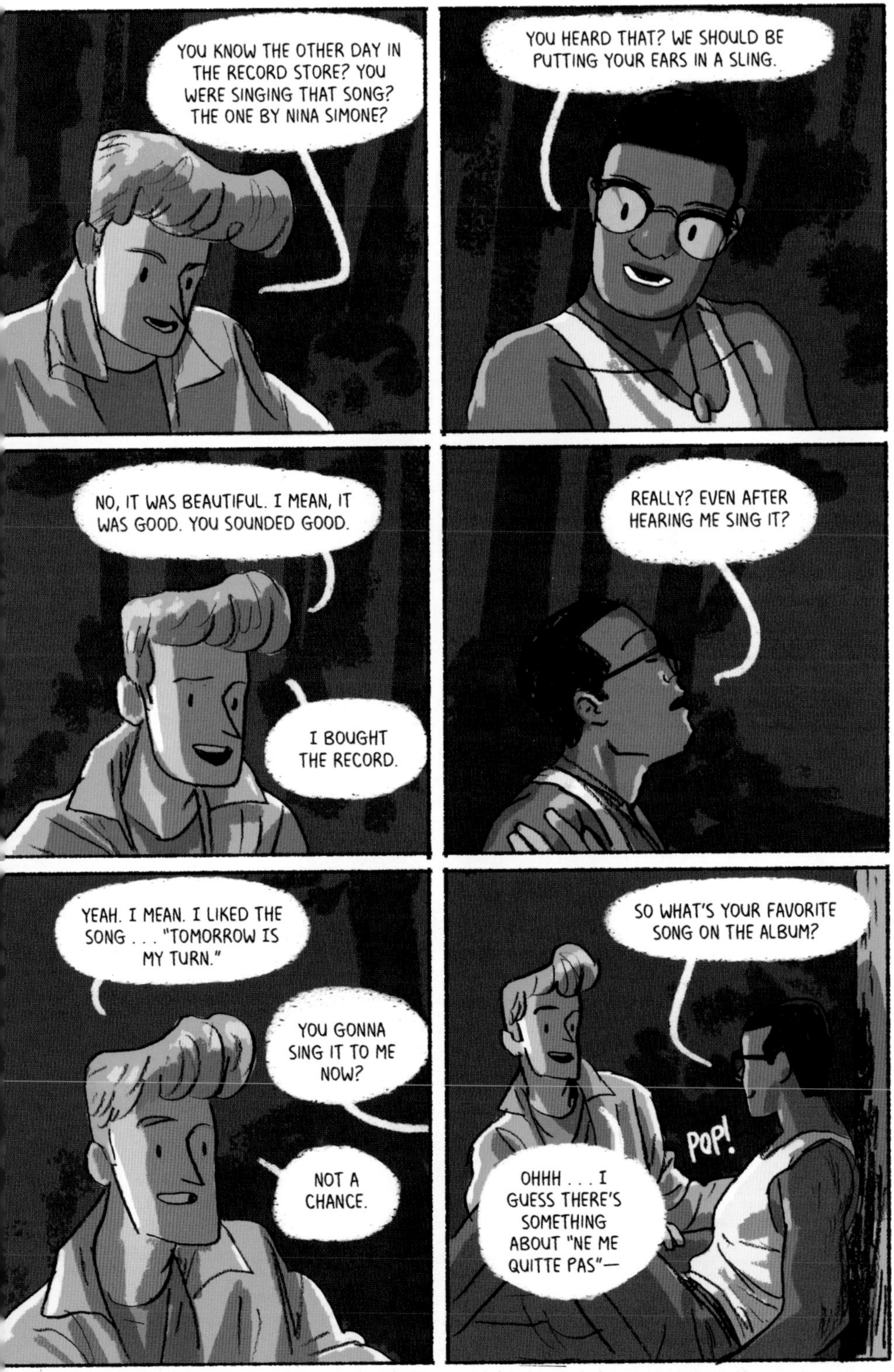
YOU KNOW THE OTHER DAY IN THE RECORD STORE? YOU WERE SINGING THAT SONG? THE ONE BY NINA SIMONE?
YOU HEARD THAT? WE SHOULD BE PUTTING YOUR EARS IN A SLING.
NO, IT WAS BEAUTIFUL. I MEAN, IT WAS GOOD. YOU SOUNDED GOOD.
I BOUGHT THE RECORD.
REALLY? EVEN AFTER HEARING ME SING IT?
YEAH. I MEAN. I LIKED THE SONG . . . "TOMORROW IS MY TURN."
YOU GONNA SING IT TO ME NOW?
NOT A CHANCE.
SO WHAT'S YOUR FAVORITE SONG ON THE ALBUM?
POP!
OHHH . . . I GUESS THERE'S SOMETHING ABOUT "NE ME QUITTE PAS"—

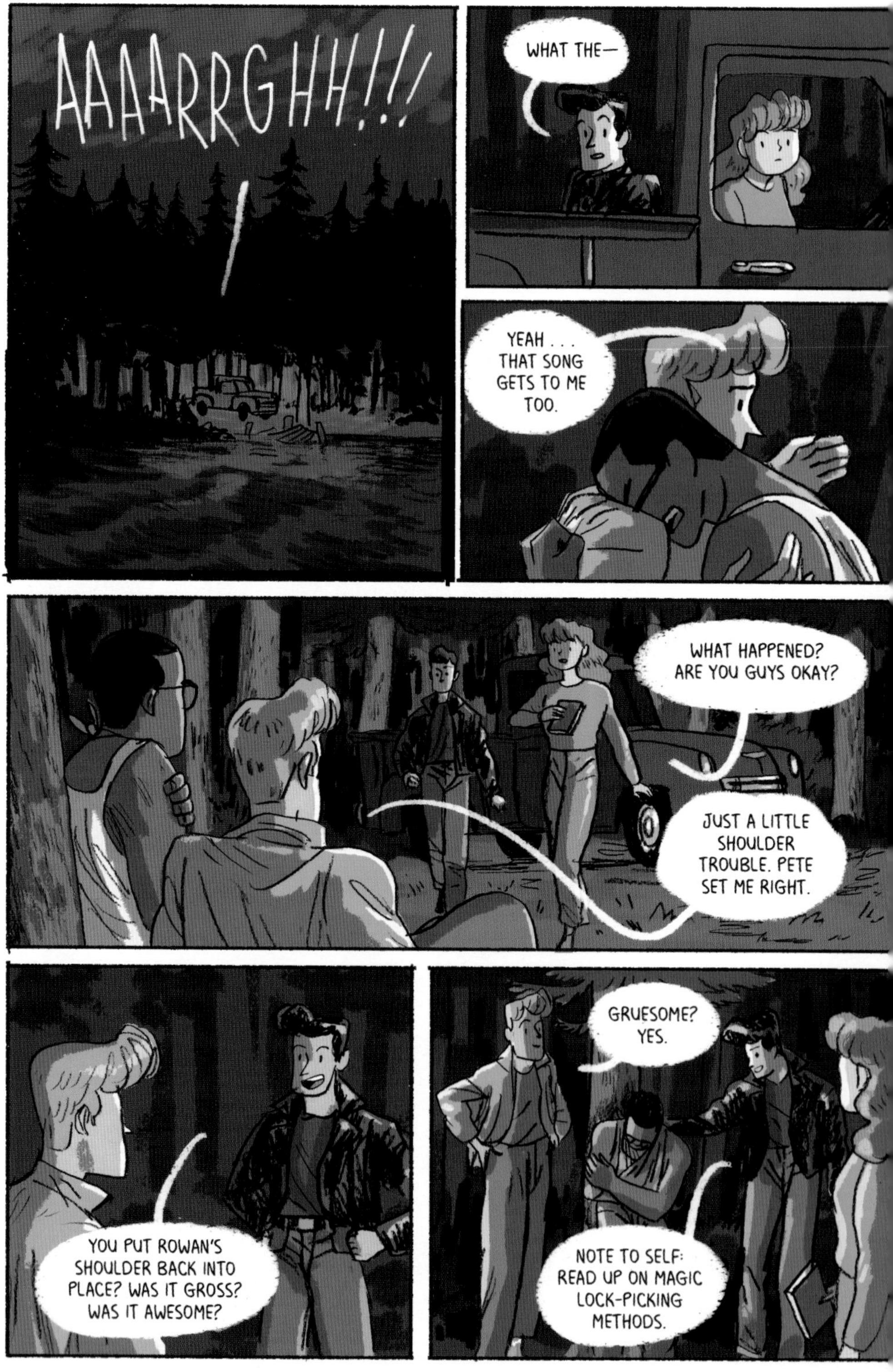
AAAARRGHH!!!
WHAT THE—
YEAH . . . THAT SONG GETS TO ME TOO.
WHAT HAPPENED? ARE YOU GUYS OKAY?
JUST A LITTLE SHOULDER TROUBLE. PETE SET ME RIGHT.
YOU PUT ROWAN'S SHOULDER BACK INTO PLACE? WAS IT GROSS? WAS IT AWESOME?
GRUESOME? YES.
NOTE TO SELF: READ UP ON MAGIC LOCK-PICKING METHODS.

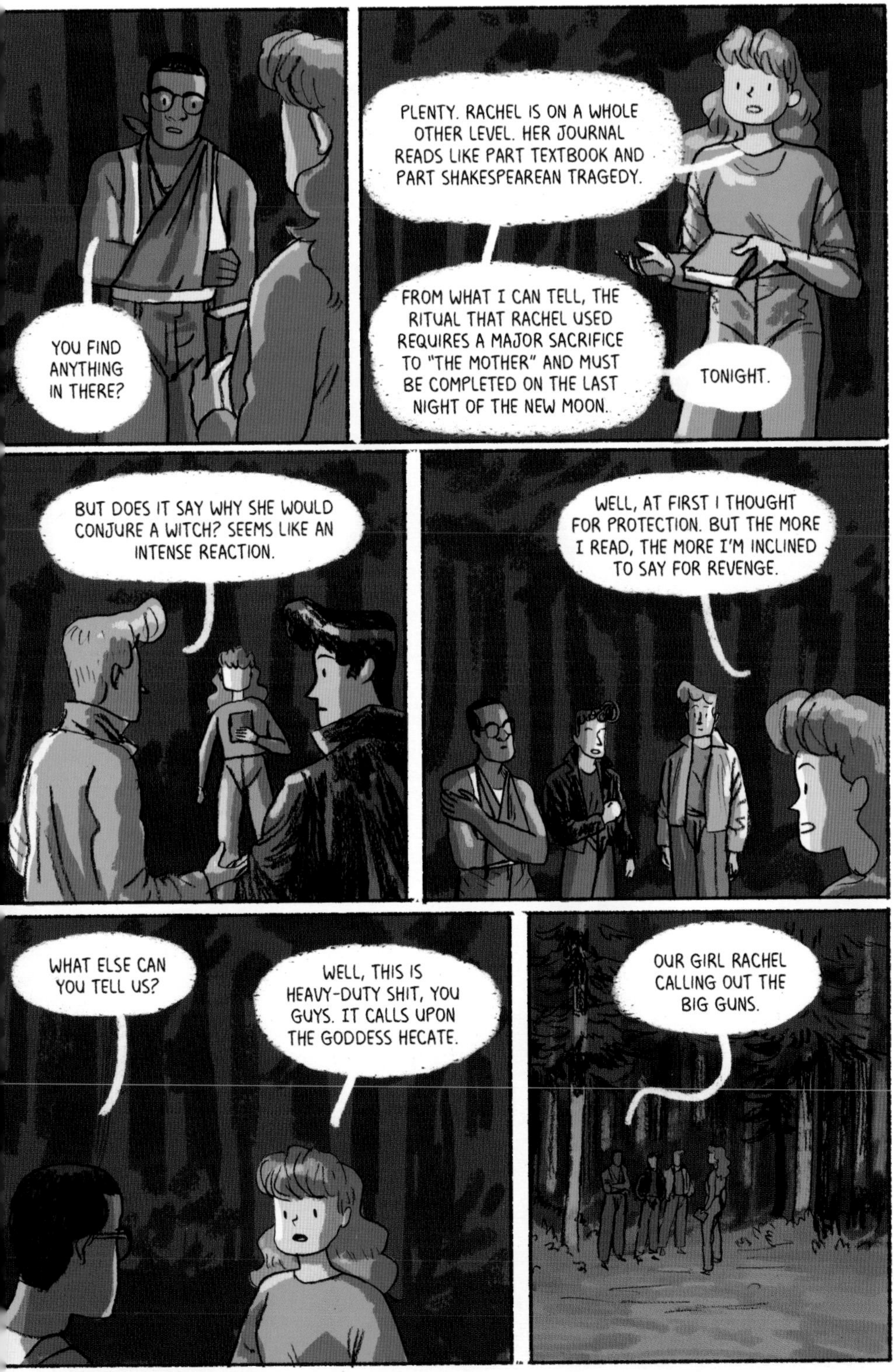
YOU FIND ANYTHING IN THERE?
PLENTY. RACHEL IS ON A WHOLE OTHER LEVEL. HER JOURNAL READS LIKE PART TEXTBOOK AND PART SHAKESPEAREAN TRAGEDY.
FROM WHAT I CAN TELL, THE RITUAL THAT RACHEL USED REQUIRES A MAJOR SACRIFICE TO "THE MOTHER" AND MUST BE COMPLETED ON THE LAST NIGHT OF THE NEW MOON.
TONIGHT.
BUT DOES IT SAY WHY SHE WOULD CONJURE A WITCH? SEEMS LIKE AN INTENSE REACTION.
WELL, AT FIRST I THOUGHT FOR PROTECTION. BUT THE MORE I READ, THE MORE I'M INCLINED TO SAY FOR REVENGE.
WHAT ELSE CAN YOU TELL US?
WELL, THIS IS HEAVY-DUTY SHIT, YOU GUYS. IT CALLS UPON THE GODDESS HECATE.
OUR GIRL RACHEL CALLING OUT THE BIG GUNS.

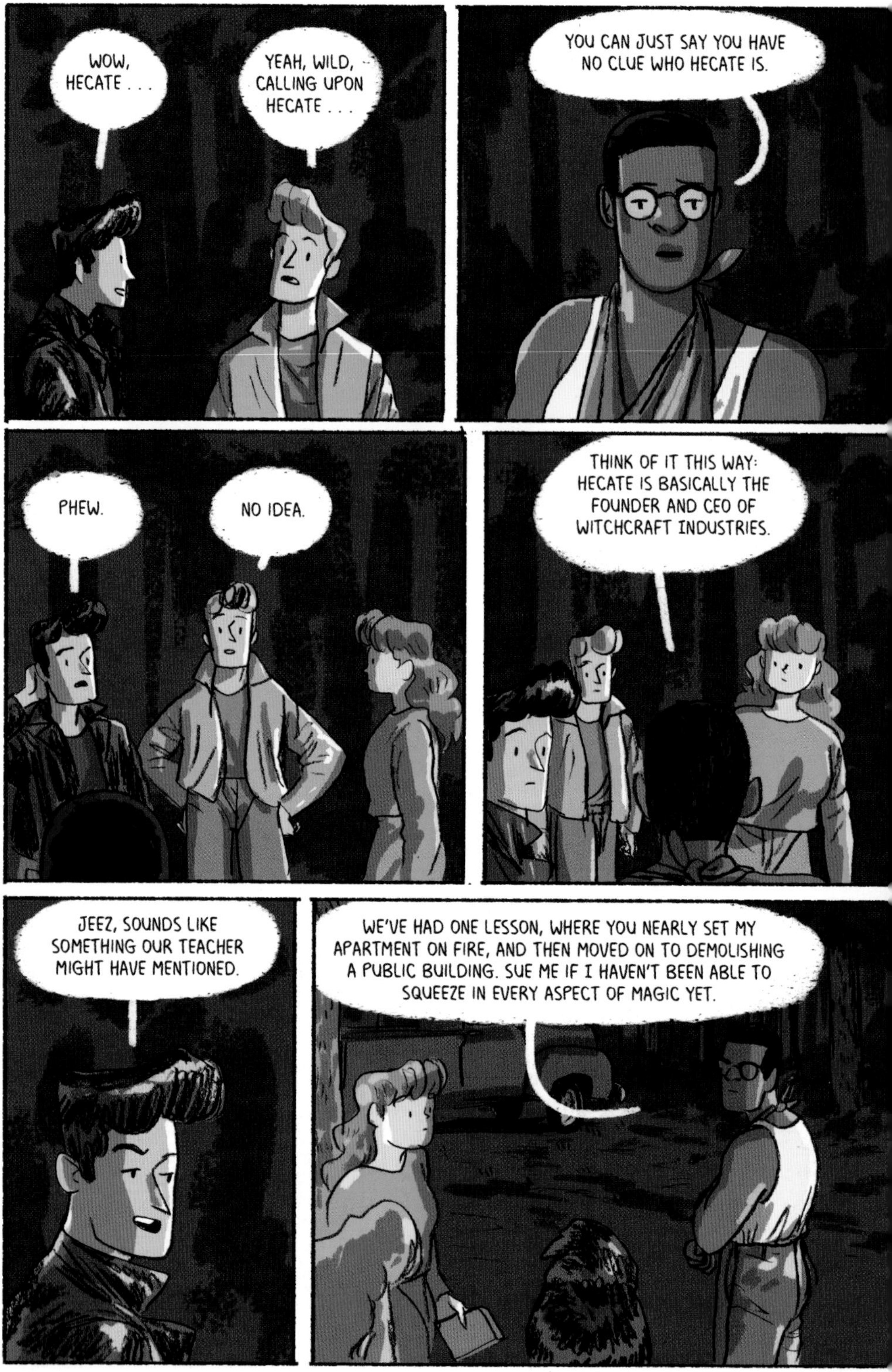
WOW, HECATE . . .
YEAH, WILD, CALLING UPON HECATE . . .
YOU CAN JUST SAY YOU HAVE NO CLUE WHO HECATE IS.
PHEW.
NO IDEA.
THINK OF IT THIS WAY: HECATE IS BASICALLY THE FOUNDER AND CEO OF WITCHCRAFT INDUSTRIES.
JEEZ, SOUNDS LIKE SOMETHING OUR TEACHER MIGHT HAVE MENTIONED.
WE'VE HAD ONE LESSON, WHERE YOU NEARLY SET MY APARTMENT ON FIRE, AND THEN MOVED ON TO DEMOLISHING A PUBLIC BUILDING. SUE ME IF I HAVEN'T BEEN ABLE TO SQUEEZE IN EVERY ASPECT OF MAGIC YET.

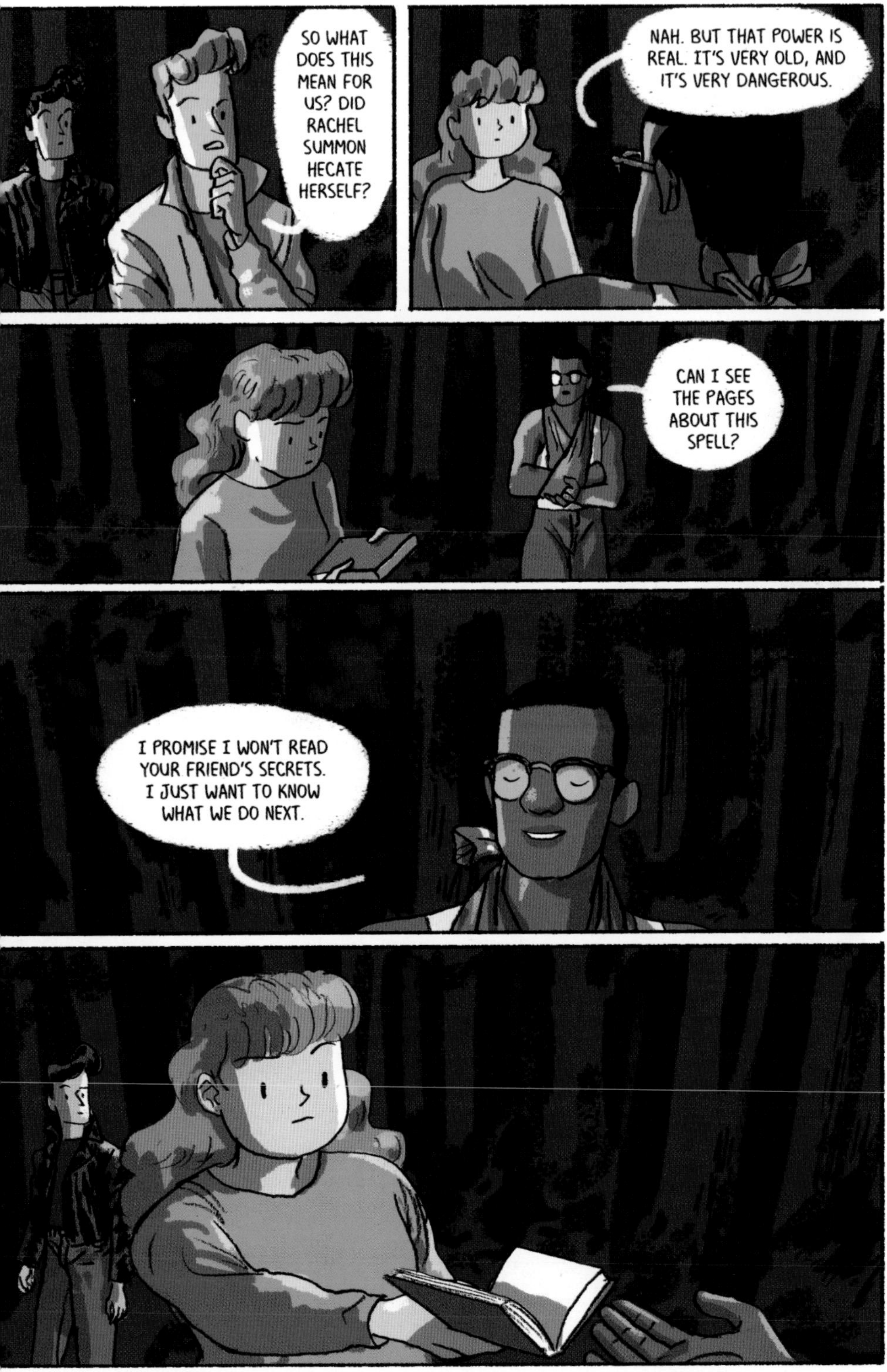
SO WHAT DOES THIS MEAN FOR US? DID RACHEL SUMMON HECATE HERSELF?
NAH. BUT THAT POWER IS REAL. IT'S VERY OLD, AND IT'S VERY DANGEROUS.
CAN I SEE THE PAGES ABOUT THIS SPELL?
I PROMISE I WON'T READ YOUR FRIEND'S SECRETS. I JUST WANT TO KNOW WHAT WE DO NEXT.

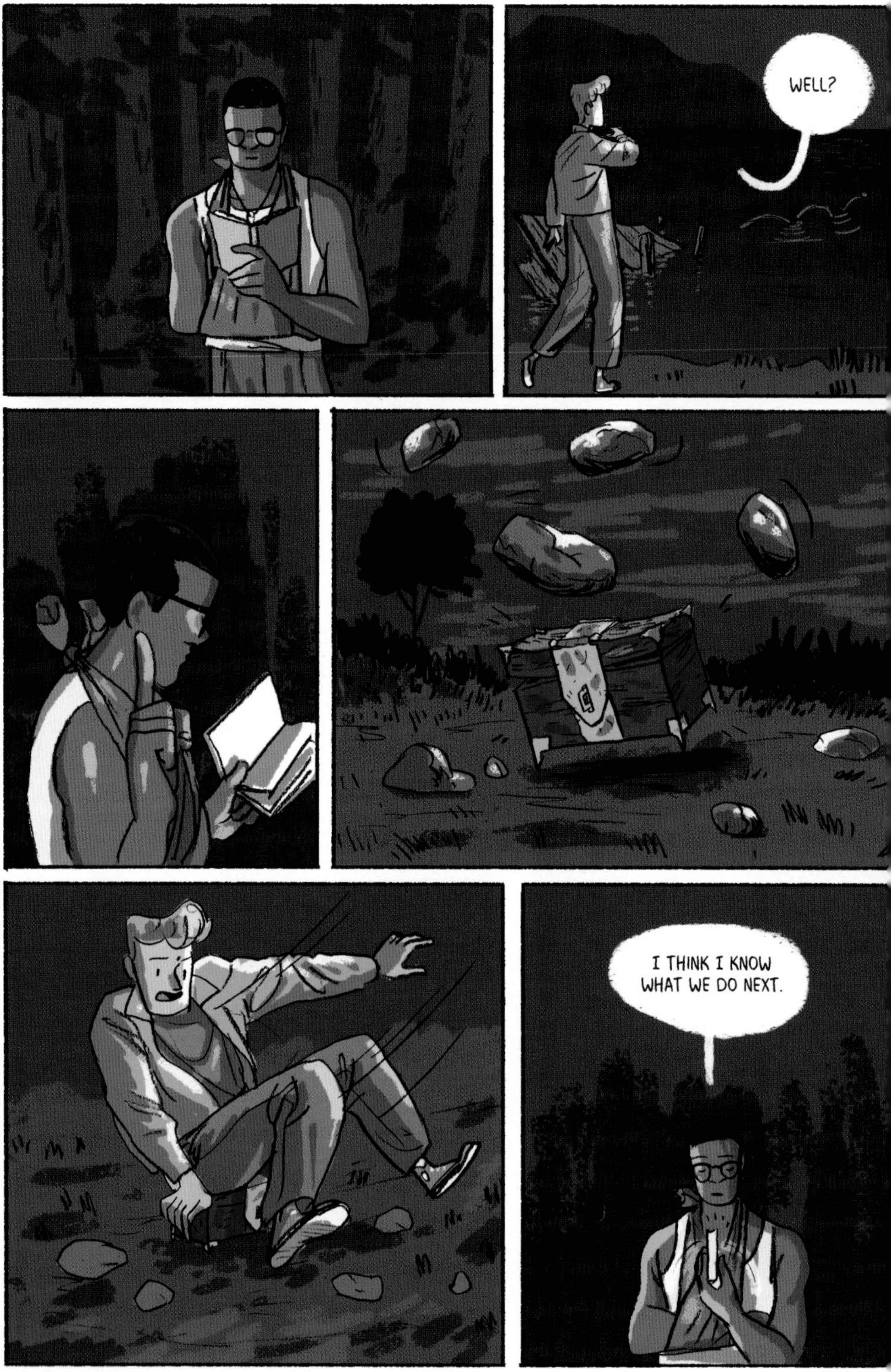
WELL?
I THINK I KNOW WHAT WE DO NEXT.

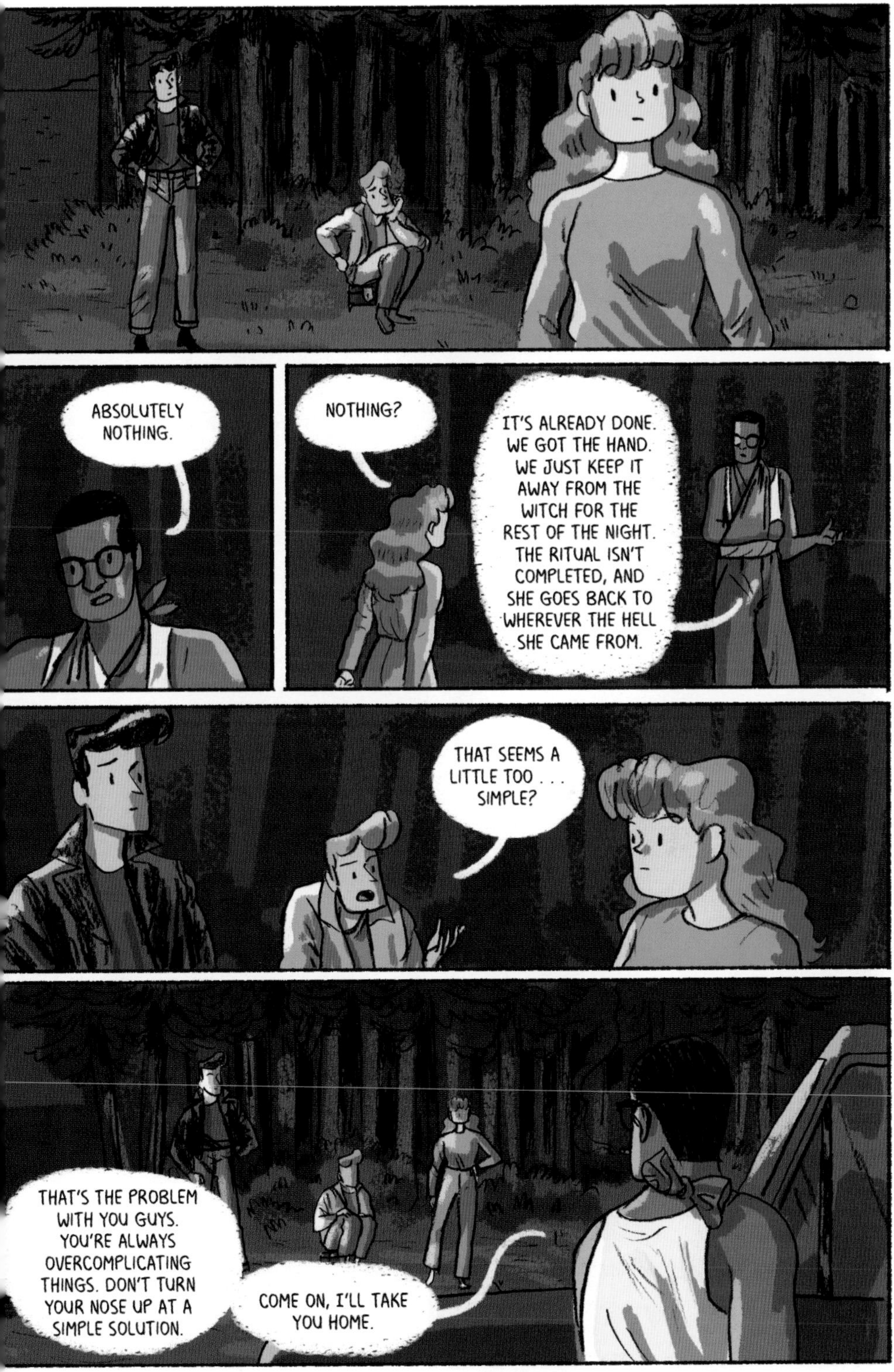
ABSOLUTELY NOTHING.
NOTHING?
IT'S ALREADY DONE. WE GOT THE HAND. WE JUST KEEP IT AWAY FROM THE WITCH FOR THE REST OF THE NIGHT. THE RITUAL ISN'T COMPLETED, AND SHE GOES BACK TO WHEREVER THE HELL SHE CAME FROM.
THAT SEEMS A LITTLE TOO . . . SIMPLE?
THAT'S THE PROBLEM WITH YOU GUYS. YOU'RE ALWAYS OVERCOMPLICATING THINGS. DON'T TURN YOUR NOSE UP AT A SIMPLE SOLUTION.
COME ON, I'LL TAKE YOU HOME.

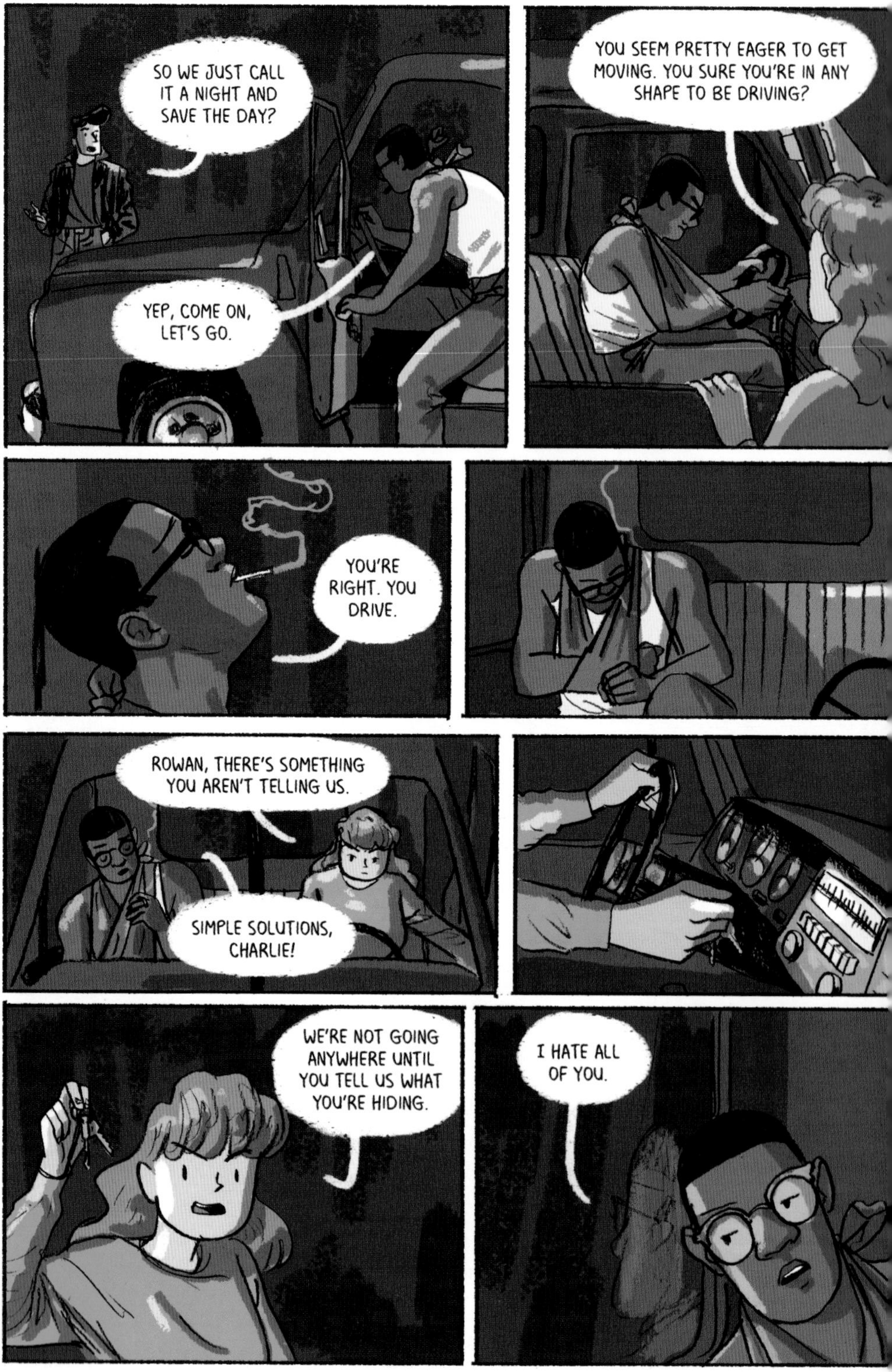
SO WE JUST CALL IT A NIGHT AND SAVE THE DAY?
YEP, COME ON, LET'S GO.
YOU SEEM PRETTY EAGER TO GET MOVING. YOU SURE YOU'RE IN ANY SHAPE TO BE DRIVING?
YOU'RE RIGHT. YOU DRIVE.
ROWAN, THERE'S SOMETHING YOU AREN'T TELLING US.
SIMPLE SOLUTIONS, CHARLIE!
WE'RE NOT GOING ANYWHERE UNTIL YOU TELL US WHAT YOU'RE HIDING.
I HATE ALL OF YOU.

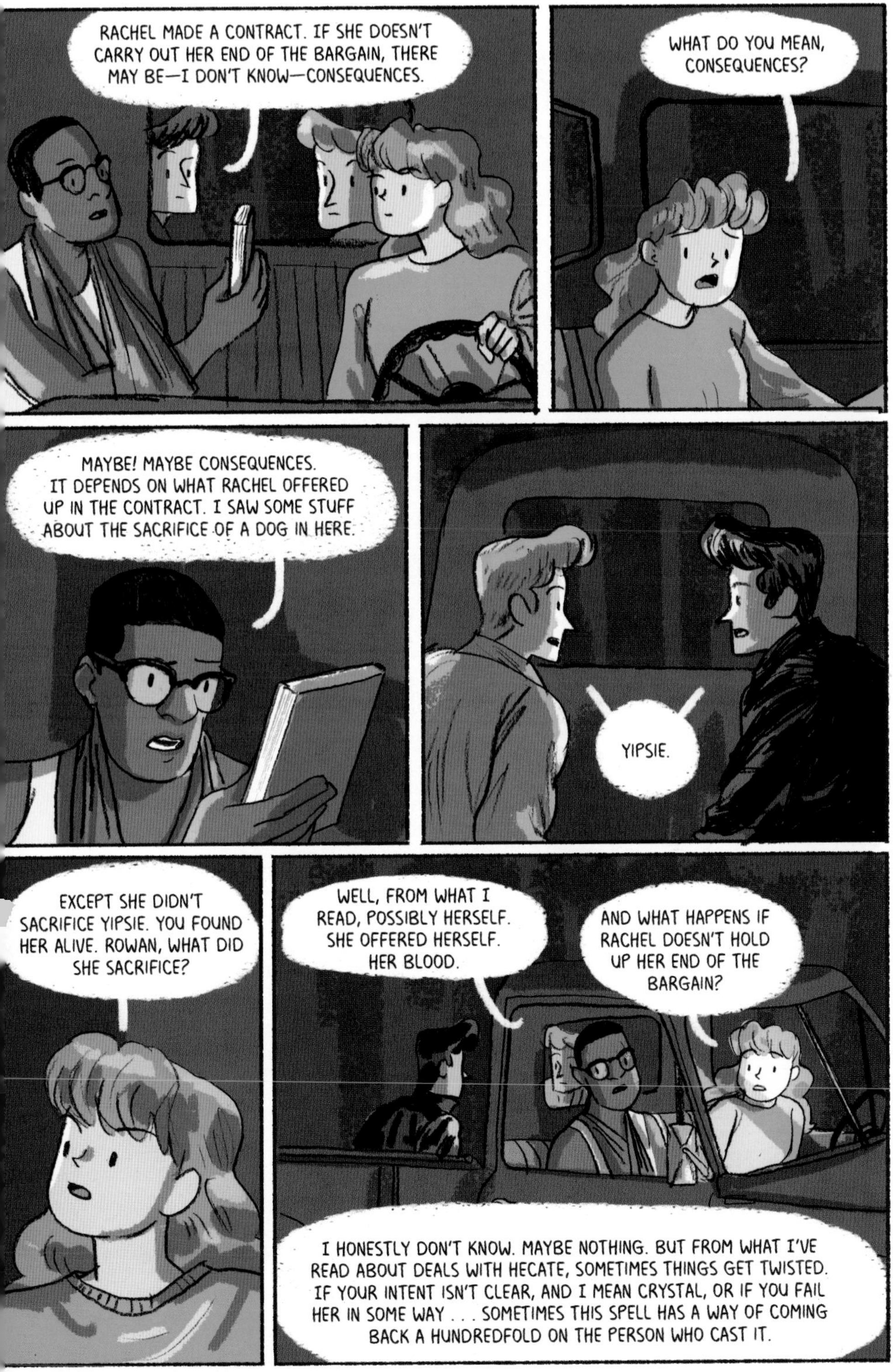
RACHEL MADE A CONTRACT. IF SHE DOESN'T CARRY OUT HER END OF THE BARGAIN, THERE MAY BE—I DON'T KNOW—CONSEQUENCES.
WHAT DO YOU MEAN, CONSEQUENCES?
MAYBE! MAYBE CONSEQUENCES. IT DEPENDS ON WHAT RACHEL OFFERED UP IN THE CONTRACT. I SAW SOME STUFF ABOUT THE SACRIFICE OF A DOG IN HERE.
YIPSIE.
EXCEPT SHE DIDN'T SACRIFICE YIPSIE. YOU FOUND HER ALIVE. ROWAN, WHAT DID SHE SACRIFICE?
WELL, FROM WHAT I READ, POSSIBLY HERSELF. SHE OFFERED HERSELF. HER BLOOD.
AND WHAT HAPPENS IF RACHEL DOESN'T HOLD UP HER END OF THE BARGAIN?
I HONESTLY DON'T KNOW. MAYBE NOTHING. BUT FROM WHAT I'VE READ ABOUT DEALS WITH HECATE, SOMETIMES THINGS GET TWISTED. IF YOUR INTENT ISN'T CLEAR, AND I MEAN CRYSTAL, OR IF YOU FAIL HER IN SOME WAY . . . SOMETIMES THIS SPELL HAS A WAY OF COMING BACK A HUNDREDFOLD ON THE PERSON WHO CAST IT.

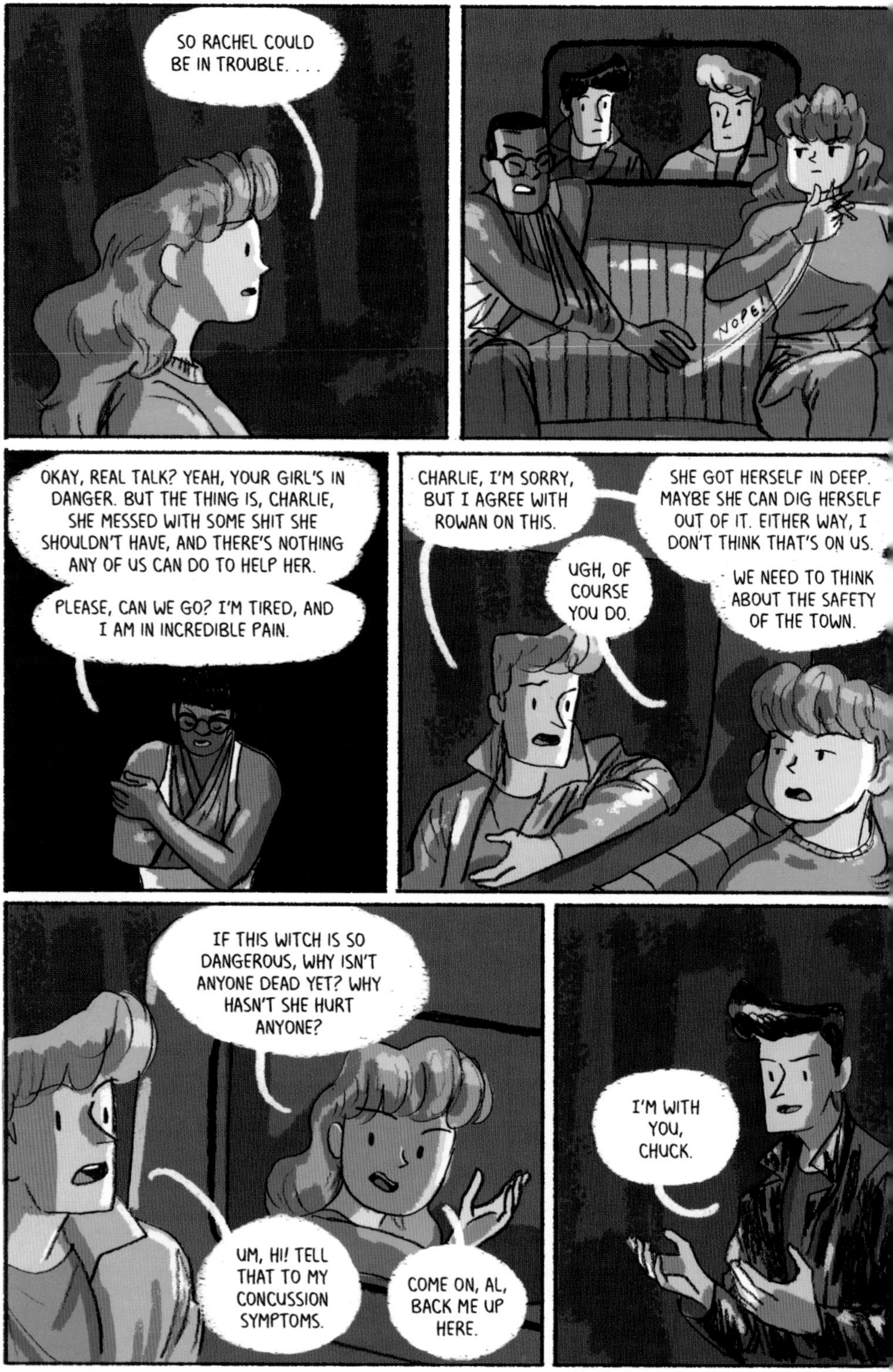
SO RACHEL COULD BE IN TROUBLE. . . .
NOPE!
OKAY, REAL TALK? YEAH, YOUR GIRL'S IN DANGER. BUT THE THING IS, CHARLIE, SHE MESSED WITH SOME SHIT SHE SHOULDN'T HAVE, AND THERE'S NOTHING ANY OF US CAN DO TO HELP HER.
PLEASE, CAN WE GO? I'M TIRED, AND I AM IN INCREDIBLE PAIN.
CHARLIE, I'M SORRY, BUT I AGREE WITH ROWAN ON THIS.
SHE GOT HERSELF IN DEEP. MAYBE SHE CAN DIG HERSELF OUT OF IT. EITHER WAY, I DON'T THINK THAT'S ON US.
UGH, OF COURSE YOU DO.
WE NEED TO THINK ABOUT THE SAFETY OF THE TOWN.
IF THIS WITCH IS SO DANGEROUS, WHY ISN'T ANYONE DEAD YET? WHY HASN'T SHE HURT ANYONE?
UM, HI! TELL THAT TO MY CONCUSSION SYMPTOMS.
COME ON, AL, BACK ME UP HERE.
I'M WITH YOU, CHUCK.

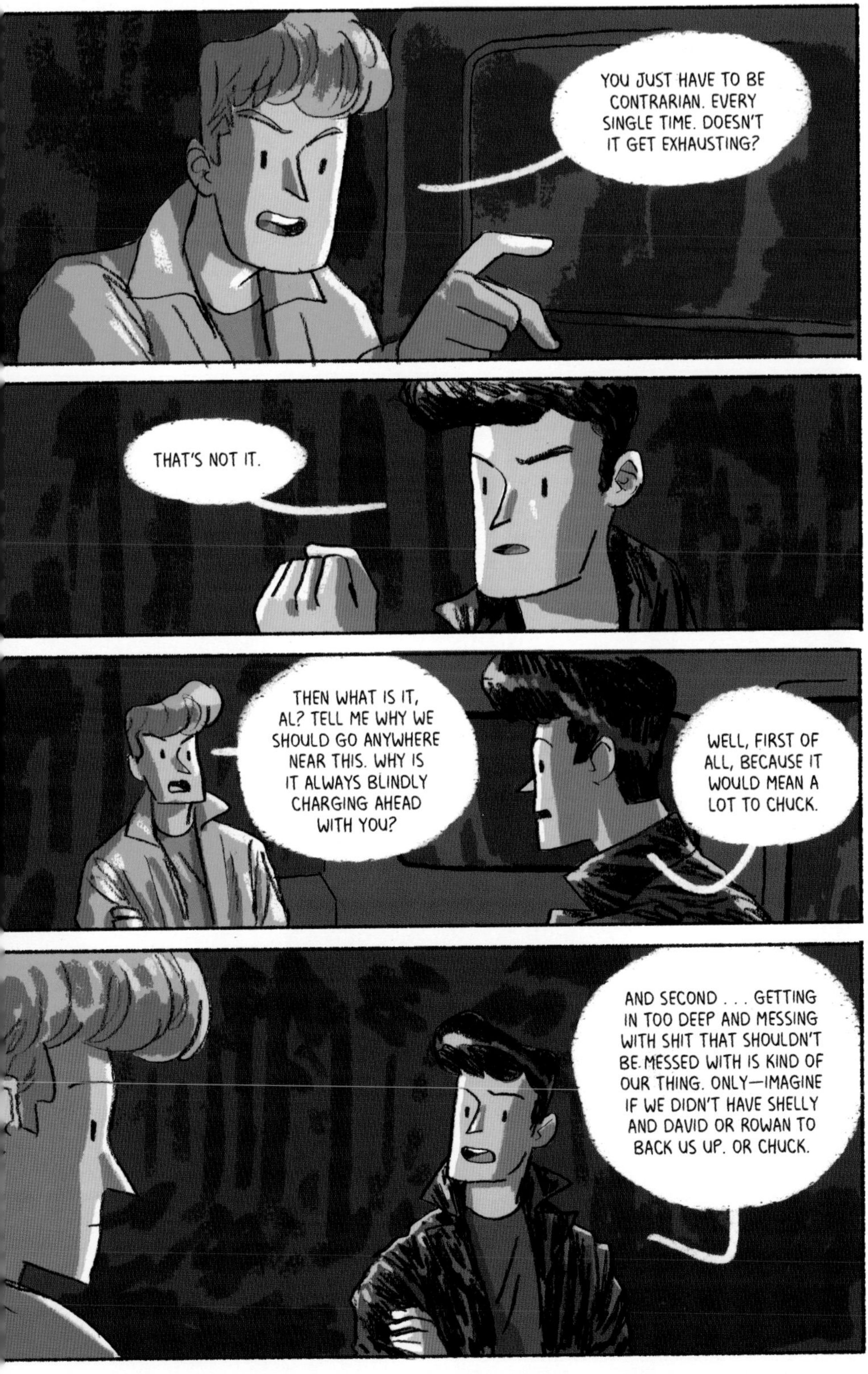
YOU JUST HAVE TO BE CONTRARIAN. EVERY SINGLE TIME. DOESN'T IT GET EXHAUSTING?
THAT'S NOT IT.
THEN WHAT IS IT, AL? TELL ME WHY WE SHOULD GO ANYWHERE NEAR THIS. WHY IS IT ALWAYS BLINDLY CHARGING AHEAD WITH YOU?
WELL, FIRST OF ALL, BECAUSE IT WOULD MEAN A LOT TO CHUCK.
AND SECOND . . . GETTING IN TOO DEEP AND MESSING WITH SHIT THAT SHOULDN'T BE MESSED WITH IS KIND OF OUR THING. ONLY—IMAGINE IF WE DIDN'T HAVE SHELLY AND DAVID OR ROWAN TO BACK US UP. OR CHUCK.

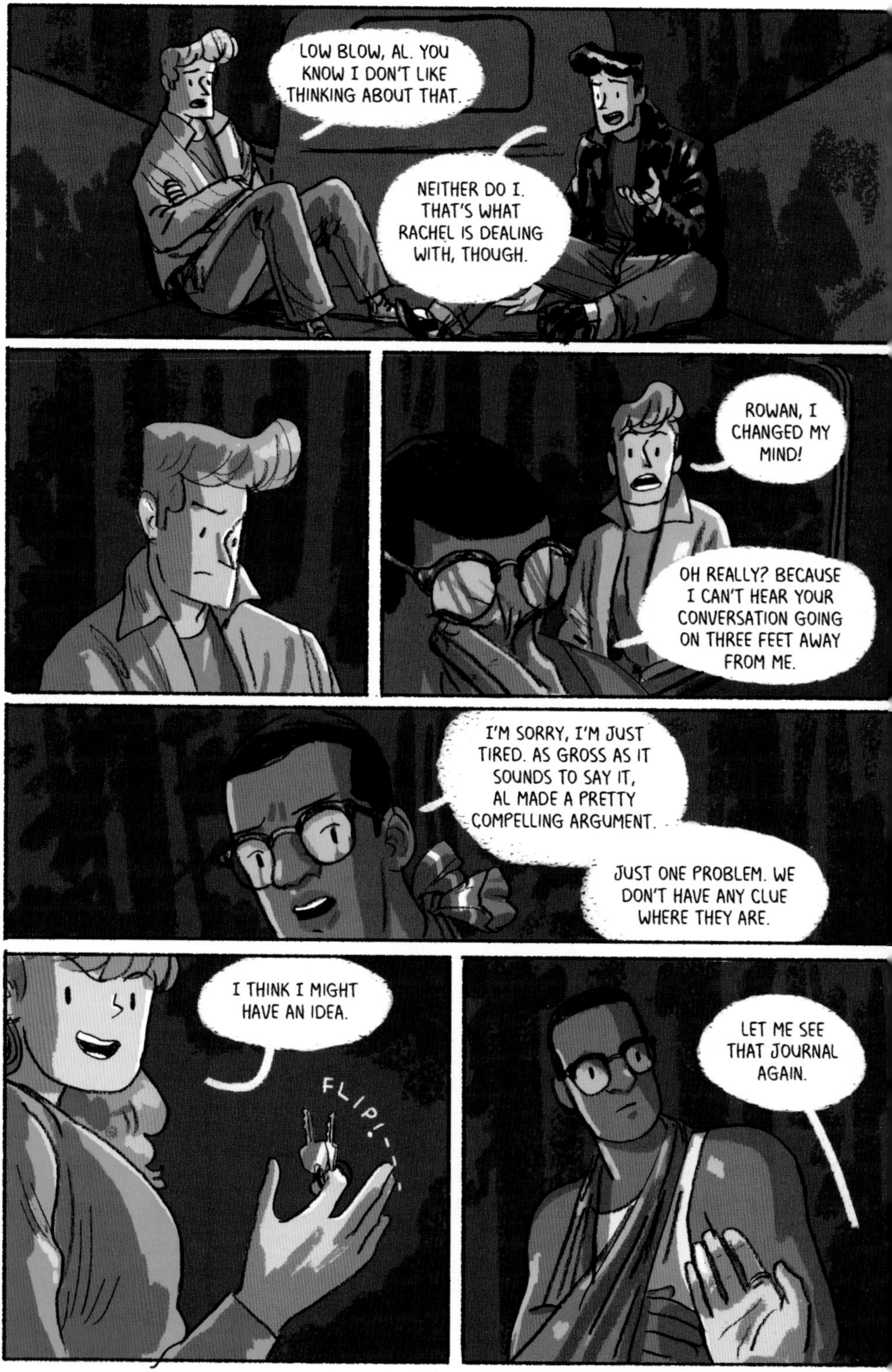
LOW BLOW, AL. YOU KNOW I DON'T LIKE THINKING ABOUT THAT.
NEITHER DO I. THAT'S WHAT RACHEL IS DEALING WITH, THOUGH.
ROWAN, I CHANGED MY MIND!
OH REALLY? BECAUSE I CAN'T HEAR YOUR CONVERSATION GOING ON THREE FEET AWAY FROM ME.
I'M SORRY, I'M JUST TIRED. AS GROSS AS IT SOUNDS TO SAY IT, AL MADE A PRETTY COMPELLING ARGUMENT.
JUST ONE PROBLEM. WE DON'T HAVE ANY CLUE WHERE THEY ARE.
I THINK I MIGHT HAVE AN IDEA.
FLIP!
LET ME SEE THAT JOURNAL AGAIN.

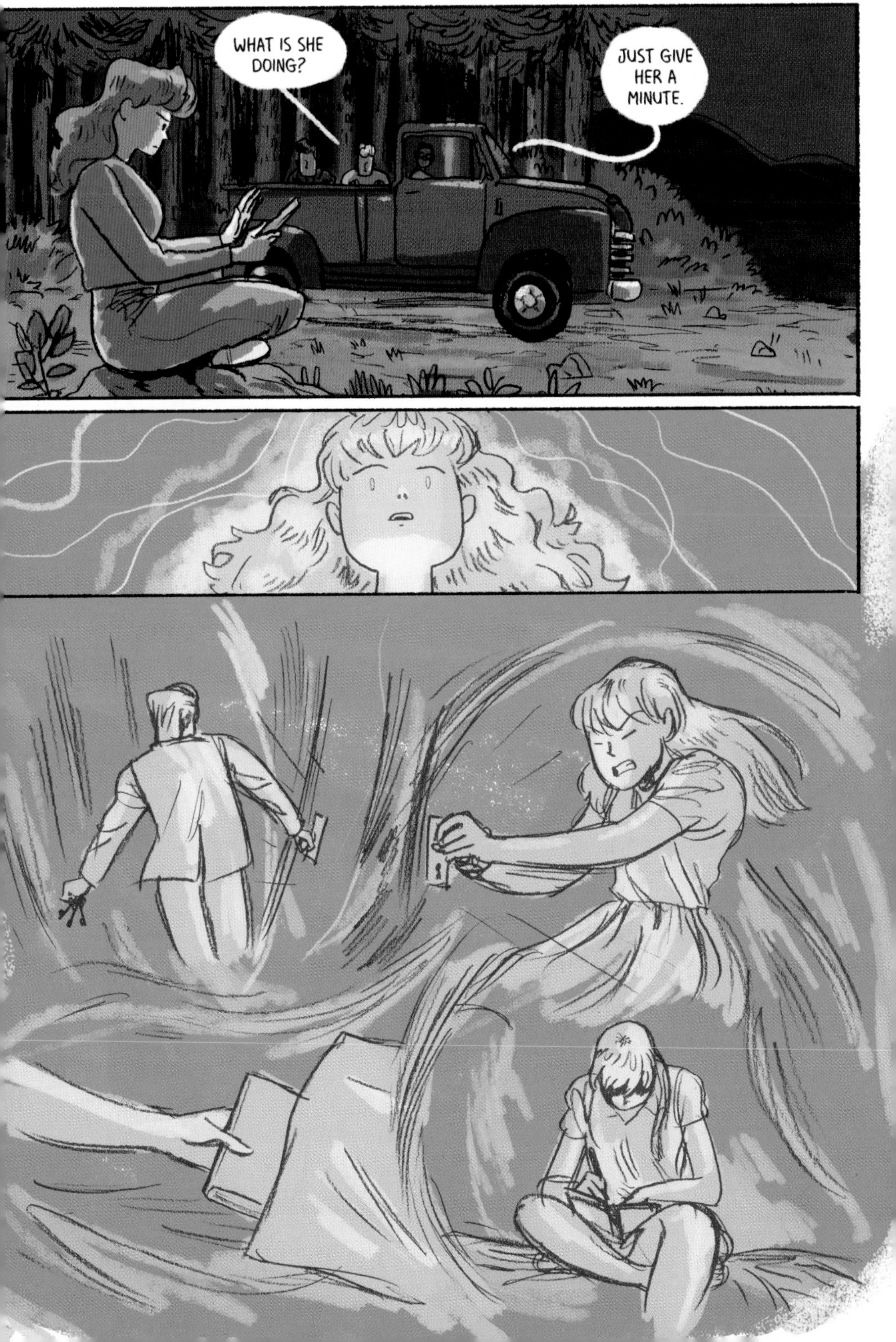
WHAT IS SHE DOING?
JUST GIVE HER A MINUTE.

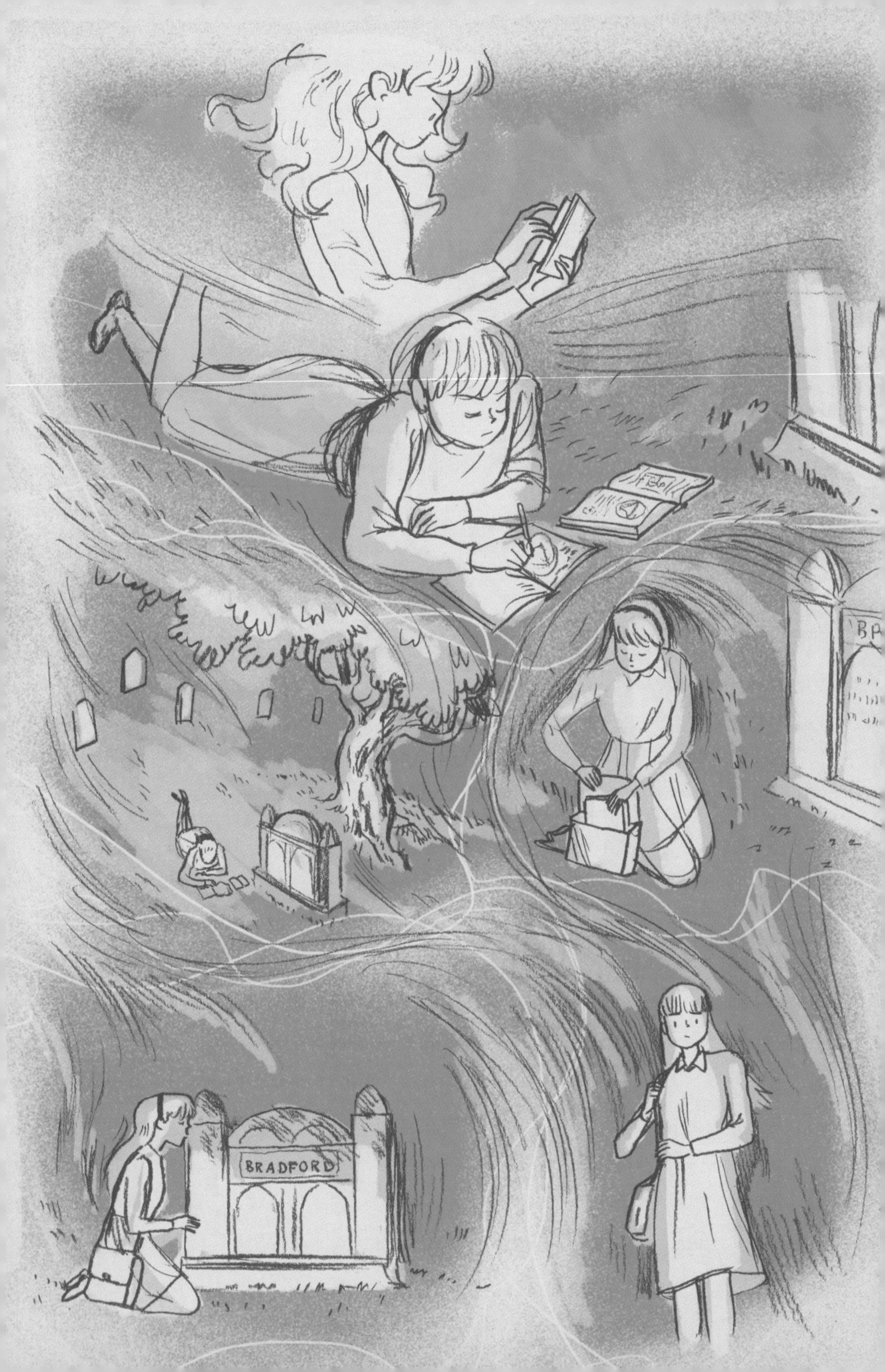
BRADFORD

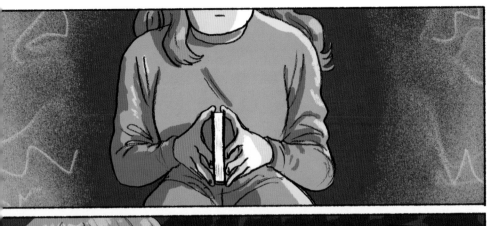

I KNOW
WHERE TO
FIND HER.

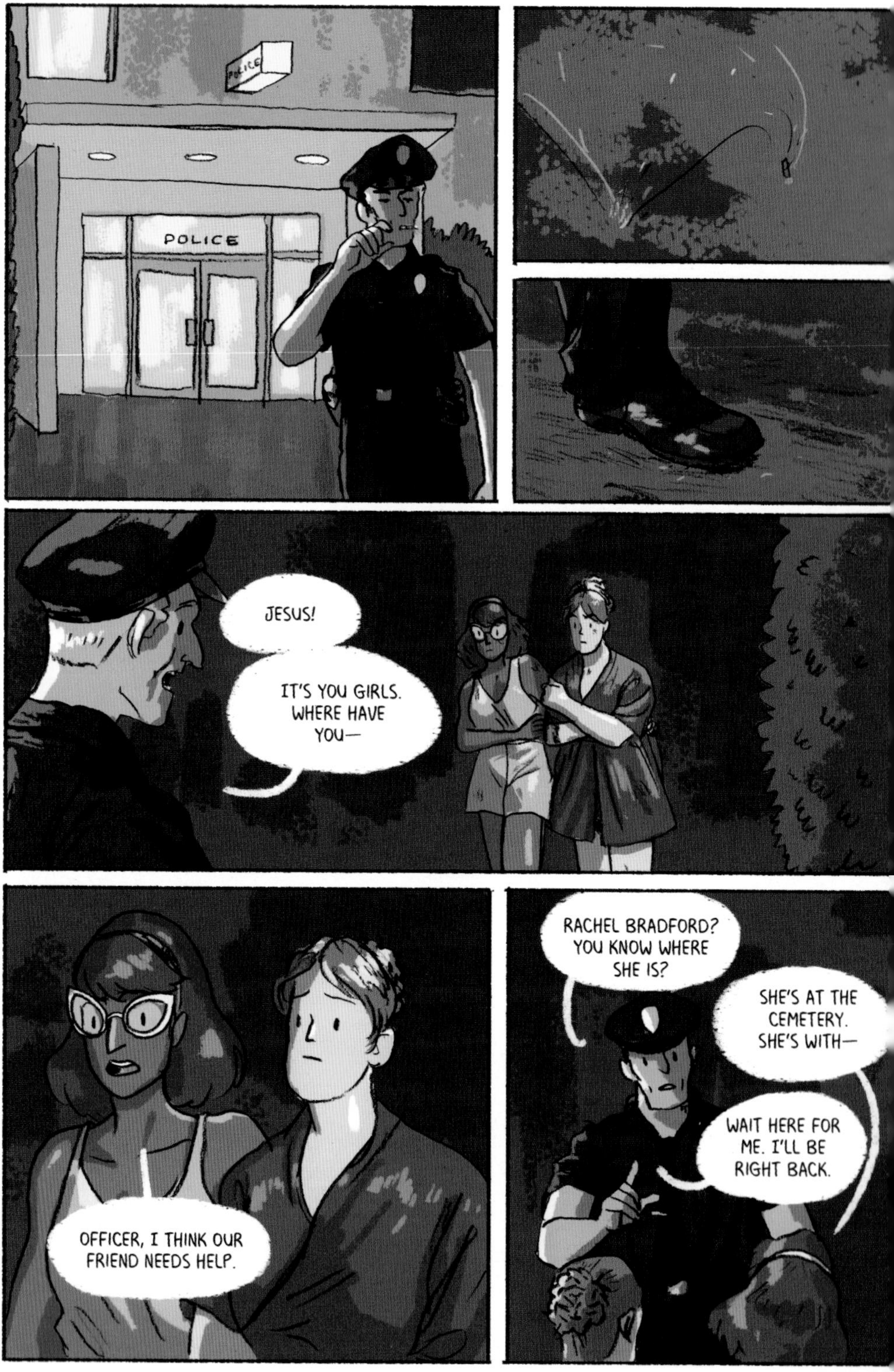
POLICE
POLICE
JESUS!
IT'S YOU GIRLS. WHERE HAVE YOU—
OFFICER, I THINK OUR FRIEND NEEDS HELP.
RACHEL BRADFORD? YOU KNOW WHERE SHE IS?
SHE'S AT THE CEMETERY. SHE'S WITH—
WAIT HERE FOR ME. I'LL BE RIGHT BACK.

WAIT, WHERE ARE YOU GOING?

JUST NEED TO MAKE A QUICK CALL.

THE CEMETERY? I MUST GIVE THE GIRL CREDIT— SHE DOES NOT DO THINGS IN HALF MEASURES.

I'LL BE THERE IN FIFTEEN MINUTES.

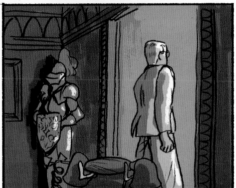

MISS BRADFORD IS IN TROUBLE. SHE NEEDS YOU.

WHERE YOU OFF TO NOW?

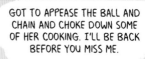

GOT TO APPEASE THE BALL AND CHAIN AND CHOKE DOWN SOME OF HER COOKING. I'LL BE BACK BEFORE YOU MISS ME.

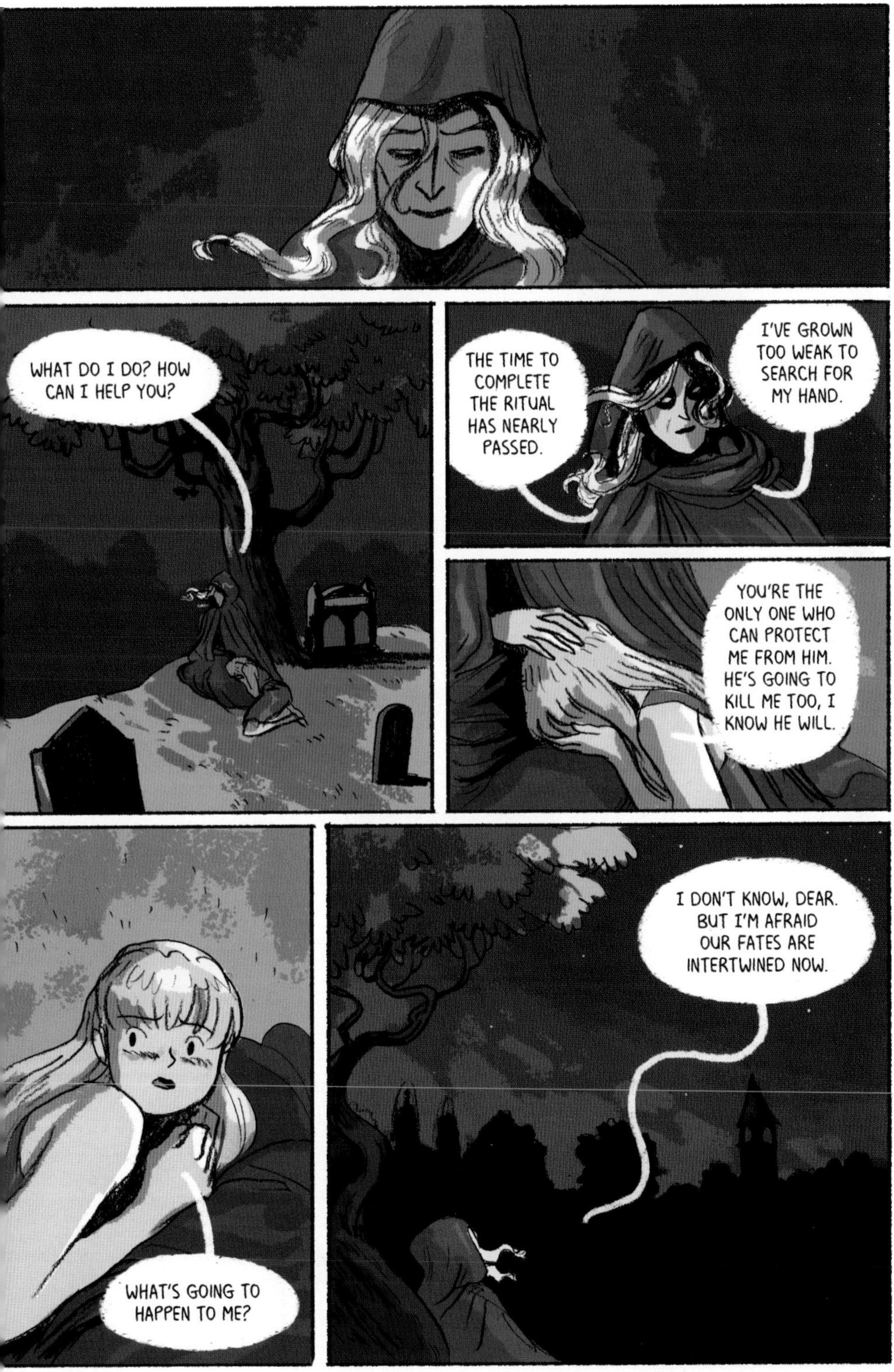
WHAT DO I DO? HOW CAN I HELP YOU?
THE TIME TO COMPLETE THE RITUAL HAS NEARLY PASSED.
I'VE GROWN TOO WEAK TO SEARCH FOR MY HAND.
YOU'RE THE ONLY ONE WHO CAN PROTECT ME FROM HIM. HE'S GOING TO KILL ME TOO, I KNOW HE WILL.
WHAT'S GOING TO HAPPEN TO ME?
I DON'T KNOW, DEAR. BUT I'M AFRAID OUR FATES ARE INTERTWINED NOW.

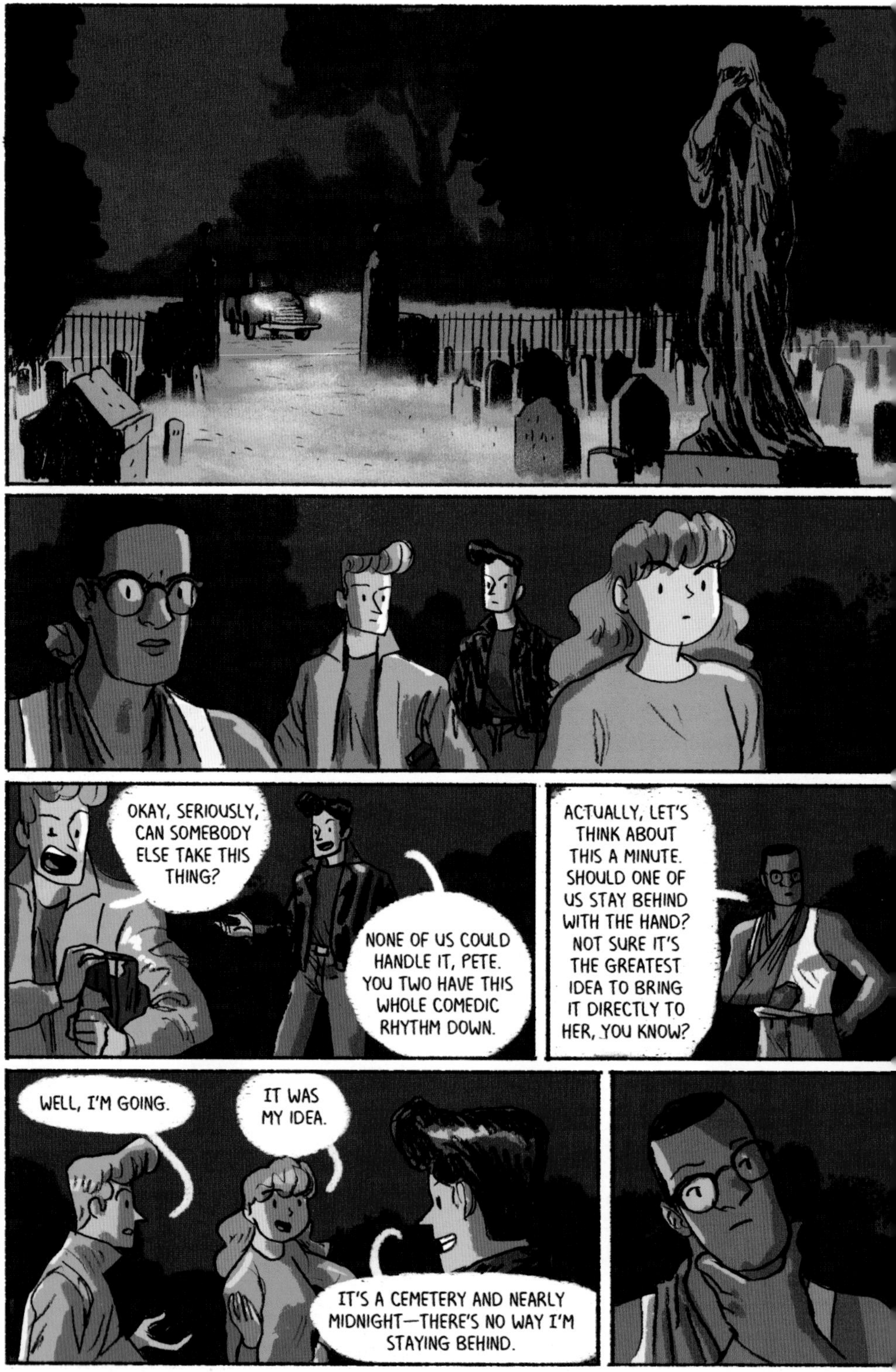
OKAY, SERIOUSLY, CAN SOMEBODY ELSE TAKE THIS THING?
NONE OF US COULD HANDLE IT, PETE. YOU TWO HAVE THIS WHOLE COMEDIC RHYTHM DOWN.
ACTUALLY, LET'S THINK ABOUT THIS A MINUTE. SHOULD ONE OF US STAY BEHIND WITH THE HAND? NOT SURE IT'S THE GREATEST IDEA TO BRING IT DIRECTLY TO HER, YOU KNOW?
WELL, I'M GOING.
IT WAS MY IDEA.
IT'S A CEMETERY AND NEARLY MIDNIGHT—THERE'S NO WAY I'M STAYING BEHIND.

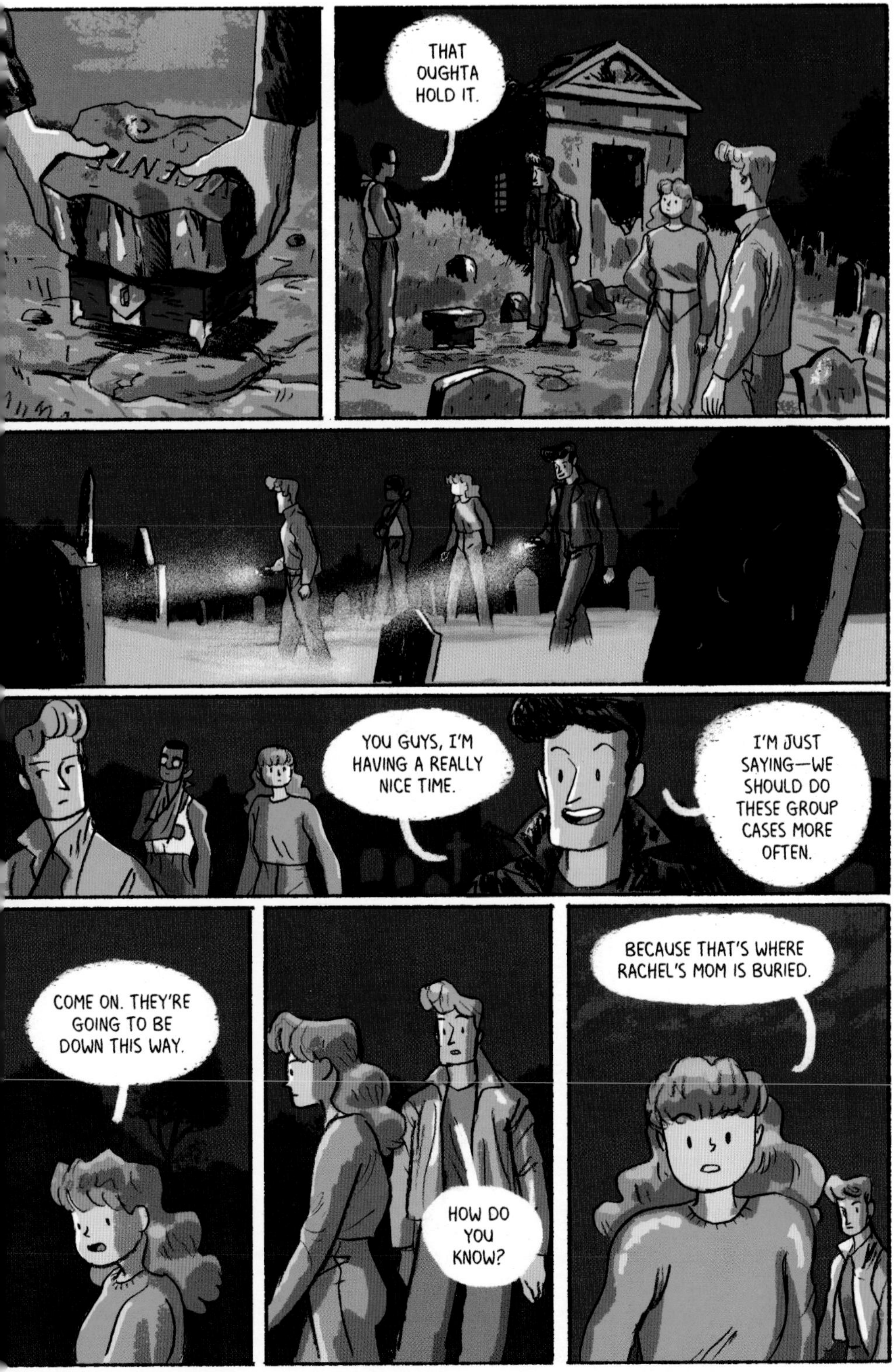
THAT OUGHTA HOLD IT.
YOU GUYS, I'M HAVING A REALLY NICE TIME.
I'M JUST SAYING—WE SHOULD DO THESE GROUP CASES MORE OFTEN.
COME ON. THEY'RE GOING TO BE DOWN THIS WAY.
HOW DO YOU KNOW?
BECAUSE THAT'S WHERE RACHEL'S MOM IS BURIED.

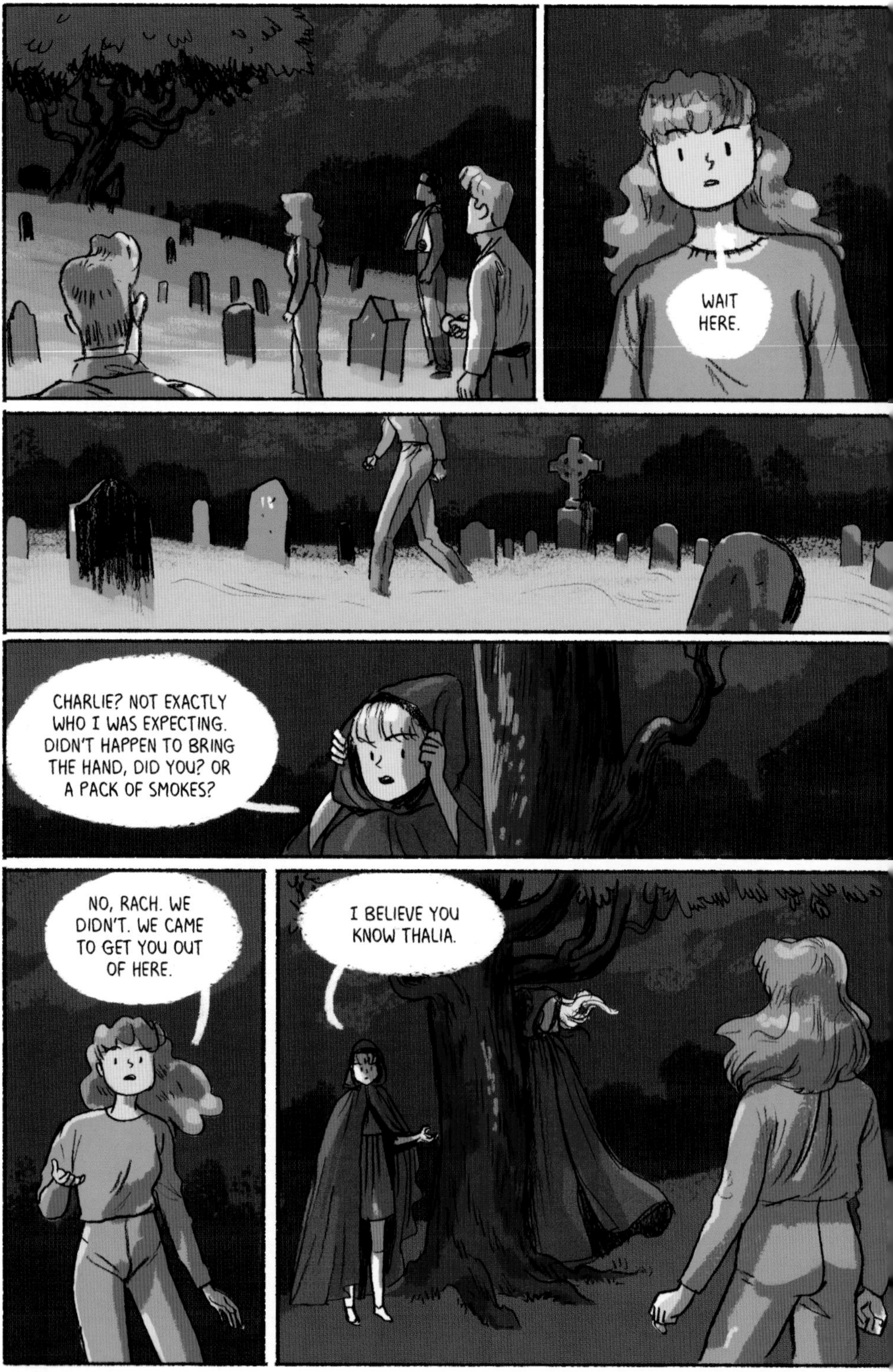
WAIT HERE.
CHARLIE? NOT EXACTLY WHO I WAS EXPECTING. DIDN'T HAPPEN TO BRING THE HAND, DID YOU? OR A PACK OF SMOKES?
NO, RACH. WE DIDN'T. WE CAME TO GET YOU OUT OF HERE.
I BELIEVE YOU KNOW THALIA.

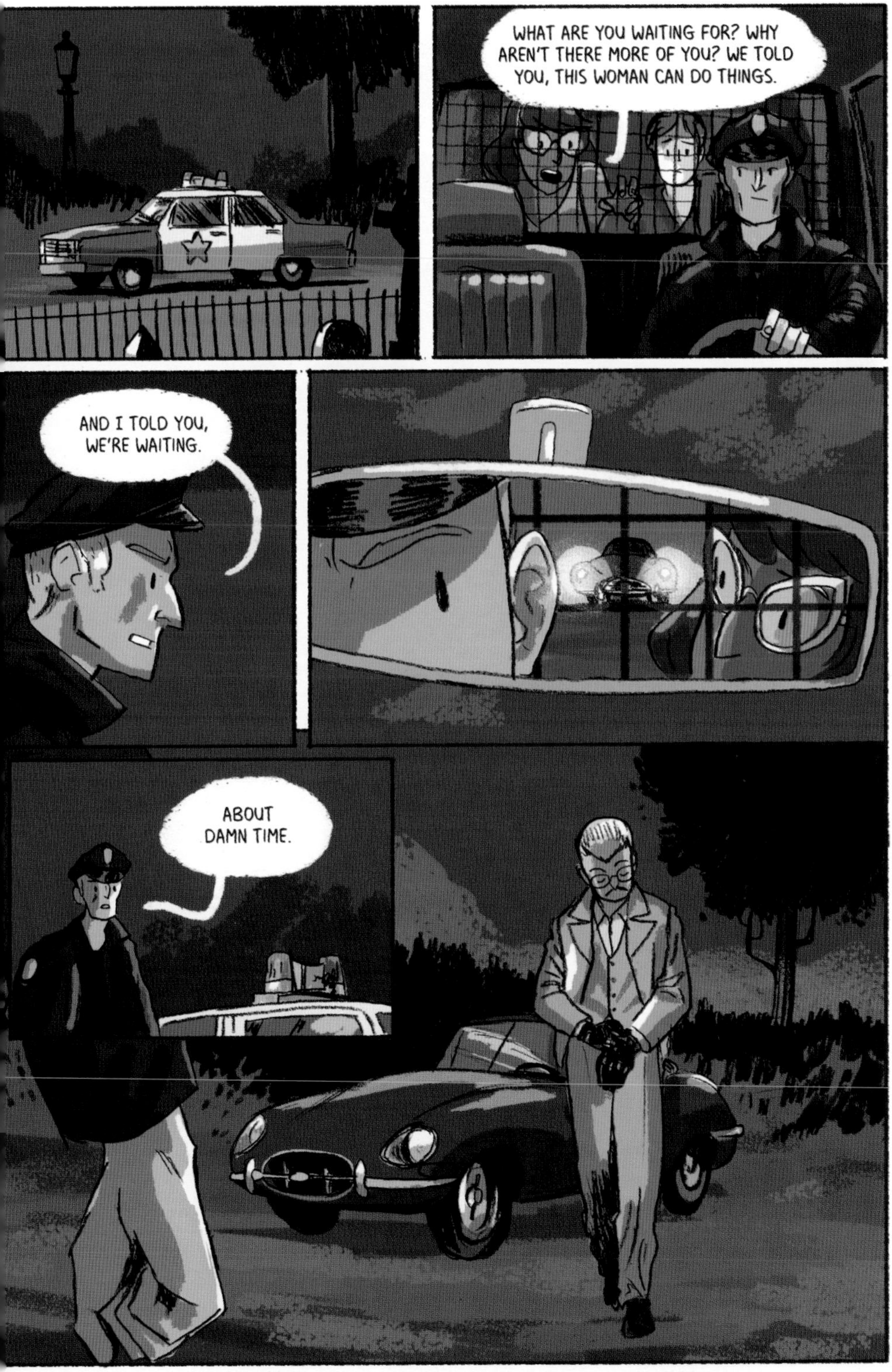
WHAT ARE YOU WAITING FOR? WHY AREN'T THERE MORE OF YOU? WE TOLD YOU, THIS WOMAN CAN DO THINGS.
AND I TOLD YOU, WE'RE WAITING.
ABOUT DAMN TIME.

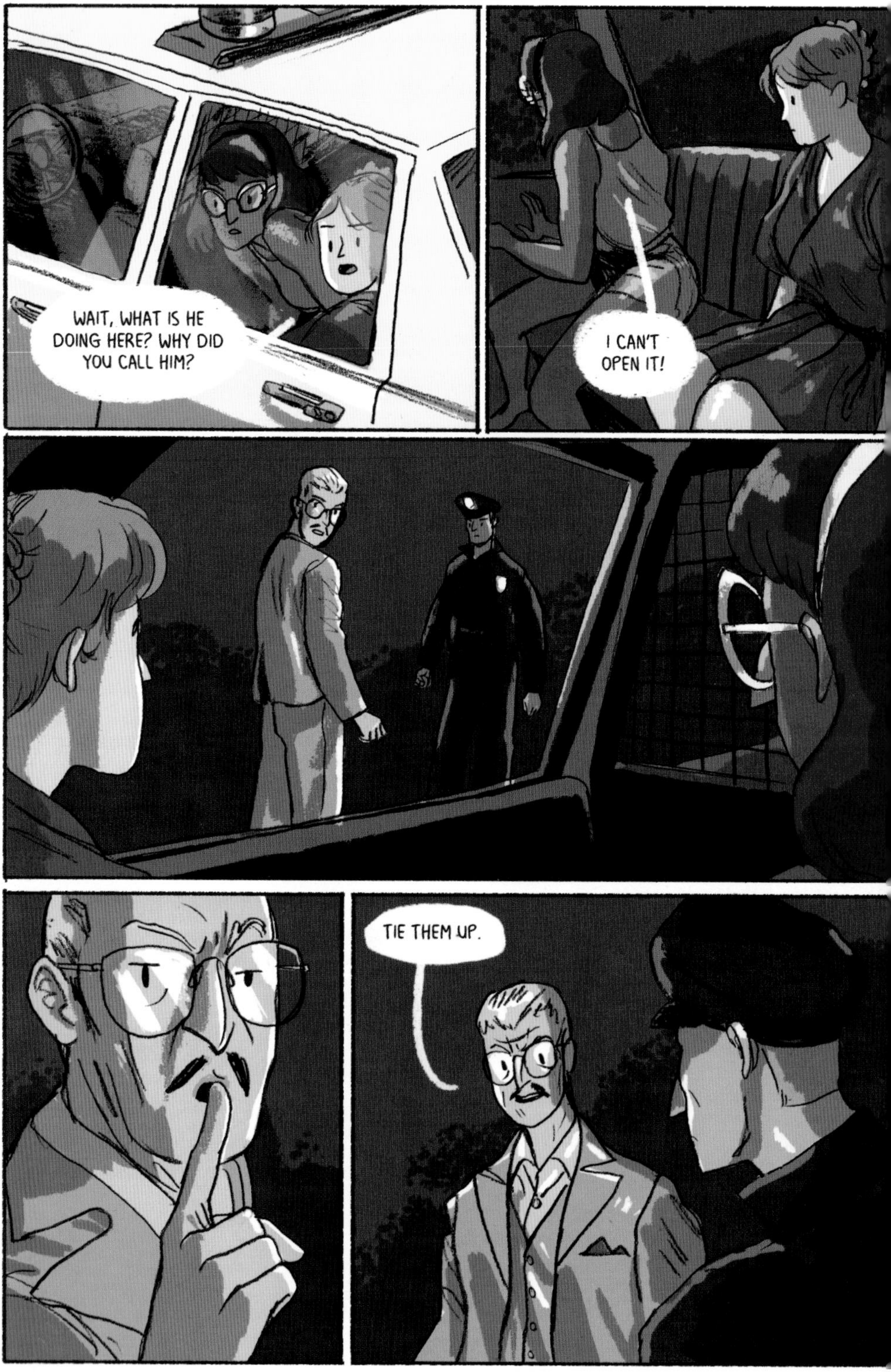
WAIT, WHAT IS HE DOING HERE? WHY DID YOU CALL HIM?
I CAN'T OPEN IT!
TIE THEM UP.

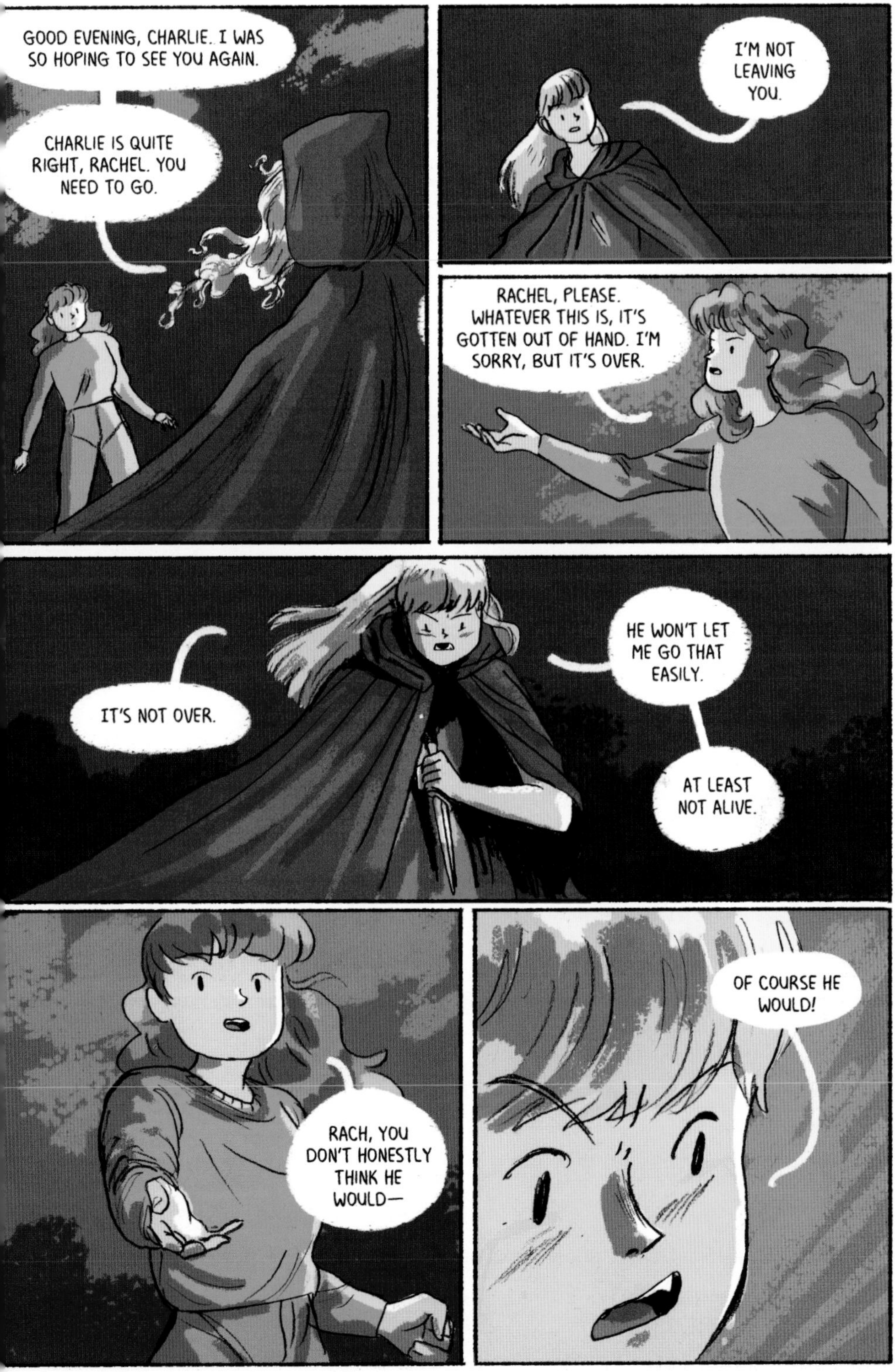
GOOD EVENING, CHARLIE. I WAS SO HOPING TO SEE YOU AGAIN.
CHARLIE IS QUITE RIGHT, RACHEL. YOU NEED TO GO.
I'M NOT LEAVING YOU.
RACHEL, PLEASE. WHATEVER THIS IS, IT'S GOTTEN OUT OF HAND. I'M SORRY, BUT IT'S OVER.
IT'S NOT OVER.
HE WON'T LET ME GO THAT EASILY.
AT LEAST NOT ALIVE.
RACH, YOU DON'T HONESTLY THINK HE WOULD—
OF COURSE HE WOULD!

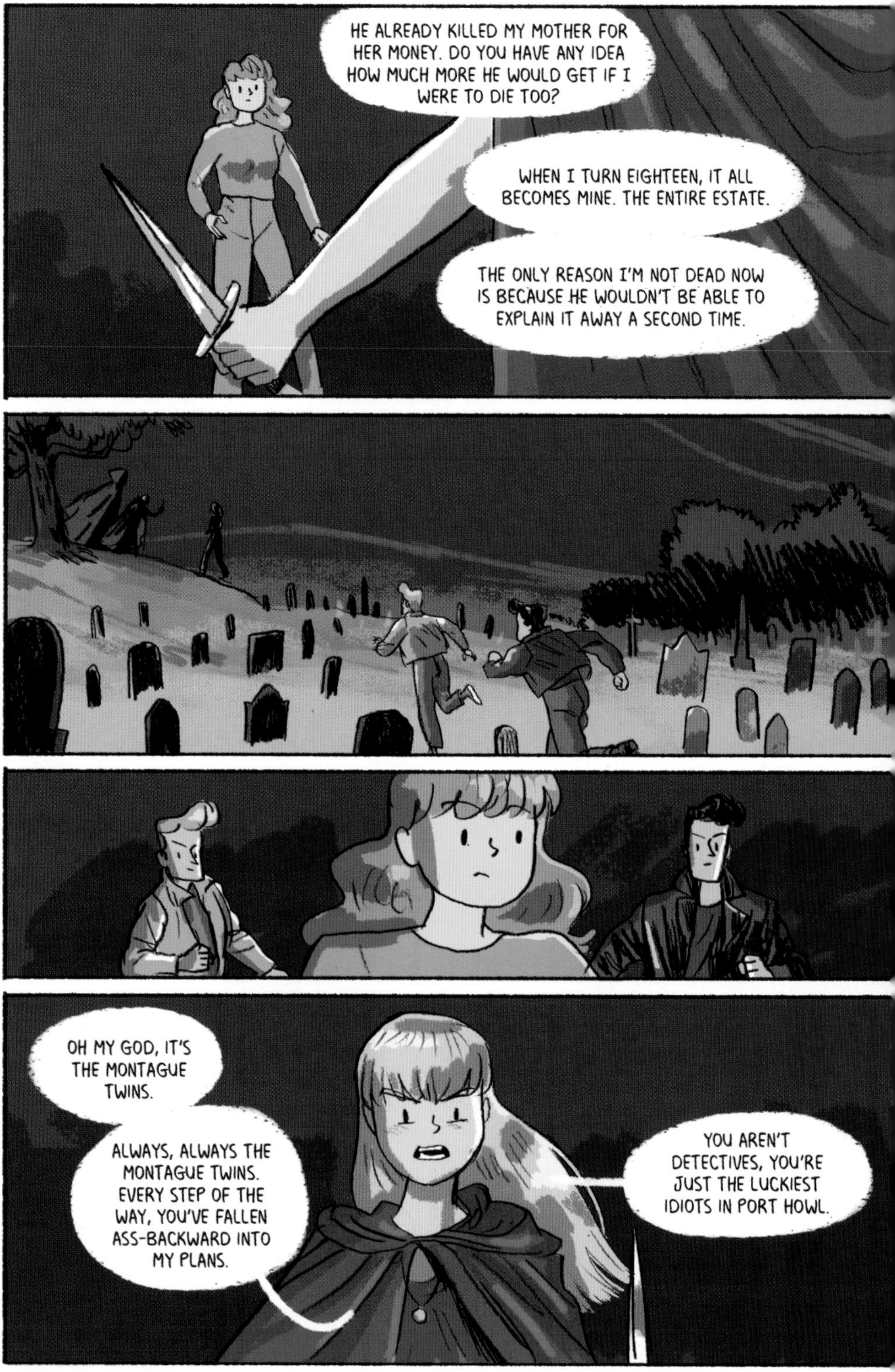
HE ALREADY KILLED MY MOTHER FOR HER MONEY. DO YOU HAVE ANY IDEA HOW MUCH MORE HE WOULD GET IF I WERE TO DIE TOO?
WHEN I TURN EIGHTEEN, IT ALL BECOMES MINE. THE ENTIRE ESTATE.
THE ONLY REASON I'M NOT DEAD NOW IS BECAUSE HE WOULDN'T BE ABLE TO EXPLAIN IT AWAY A SECOND TIME.
OH MY GOD, IT'S THE MONTAGUE TWINS.
ALWAYS, ALWAYS THE MONTAGUE TWINS. EVERY STEP OF THE WAY, YOU'VE FALLEN ASS-BACKWARD INTO MY PLANS.
YOU AREN'T DETECTIVES, YOU'RE JUST THE LUCKIEST IDIOTS IN PORT HOWL.

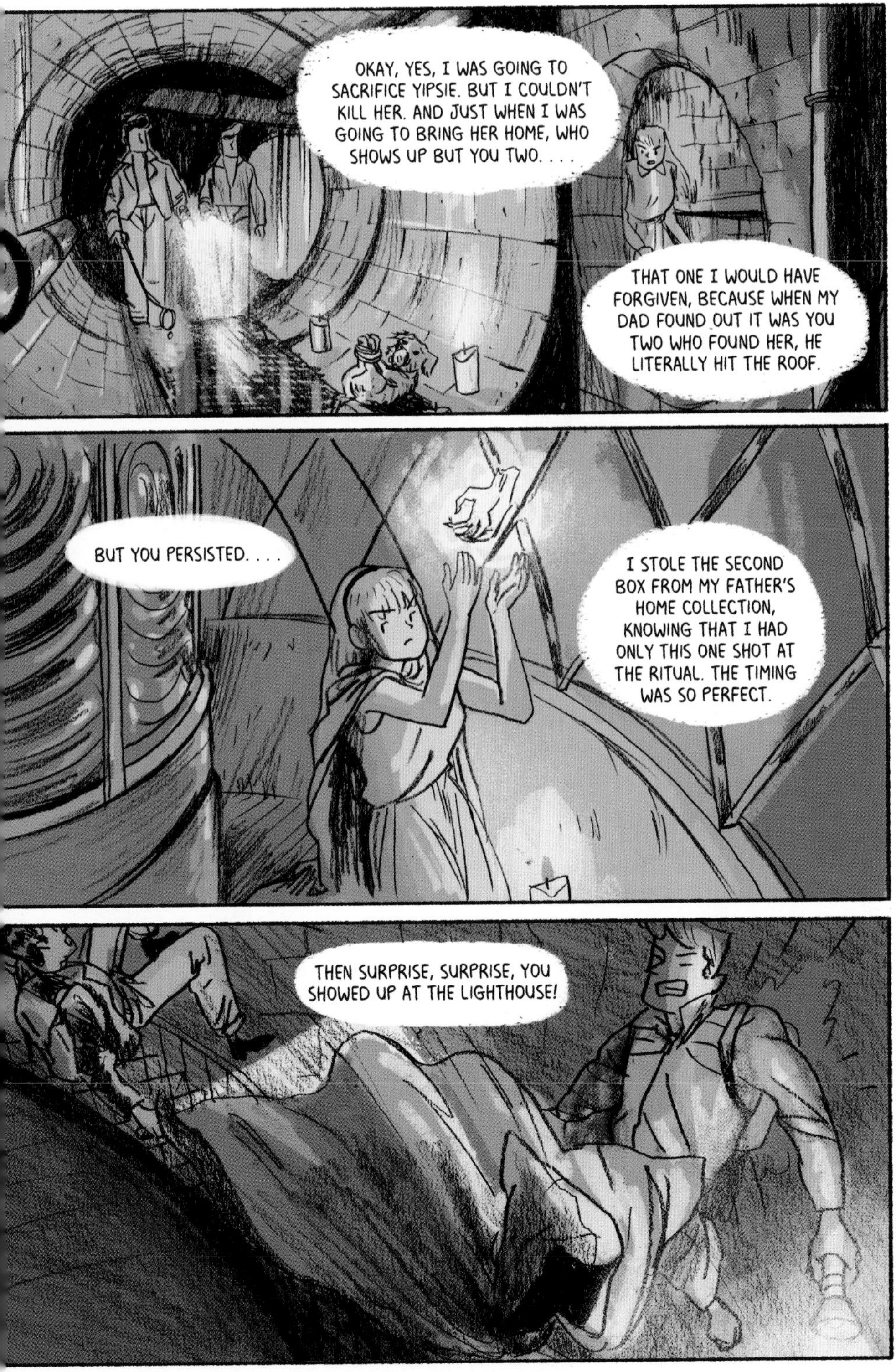
OKAY, YES, I WAS GOING TO SACRIFICE YIPSIE. BUT I COULDN'T KILL HER. AND JUST WHEN I WAS GOING TO BRING HER HOME, WHO SHOWS UP BUT YOU TWO. . . .
THAT ONE I WOULD HAVE FORGIVEN, BECAUSE WHEN MY DAD FOUND OUT IT WAS YOU TWO WHO FOUND HER, HE LITERALLY HIT THE ROOF.
BUT YOU PERSISTED. . . .
I STOLE THE SECOND BOX FROM MY FATHER'S HOME COLLECTION, KNOWING THAT I HAD ONLY THIS ONE SHOT AT THE RITUAL. THE TIMING WAS SO PERFECT.
THEN SURPRISE, SURPRISE, YOU SHOWED UP AT THE LIGHTHOUSE!

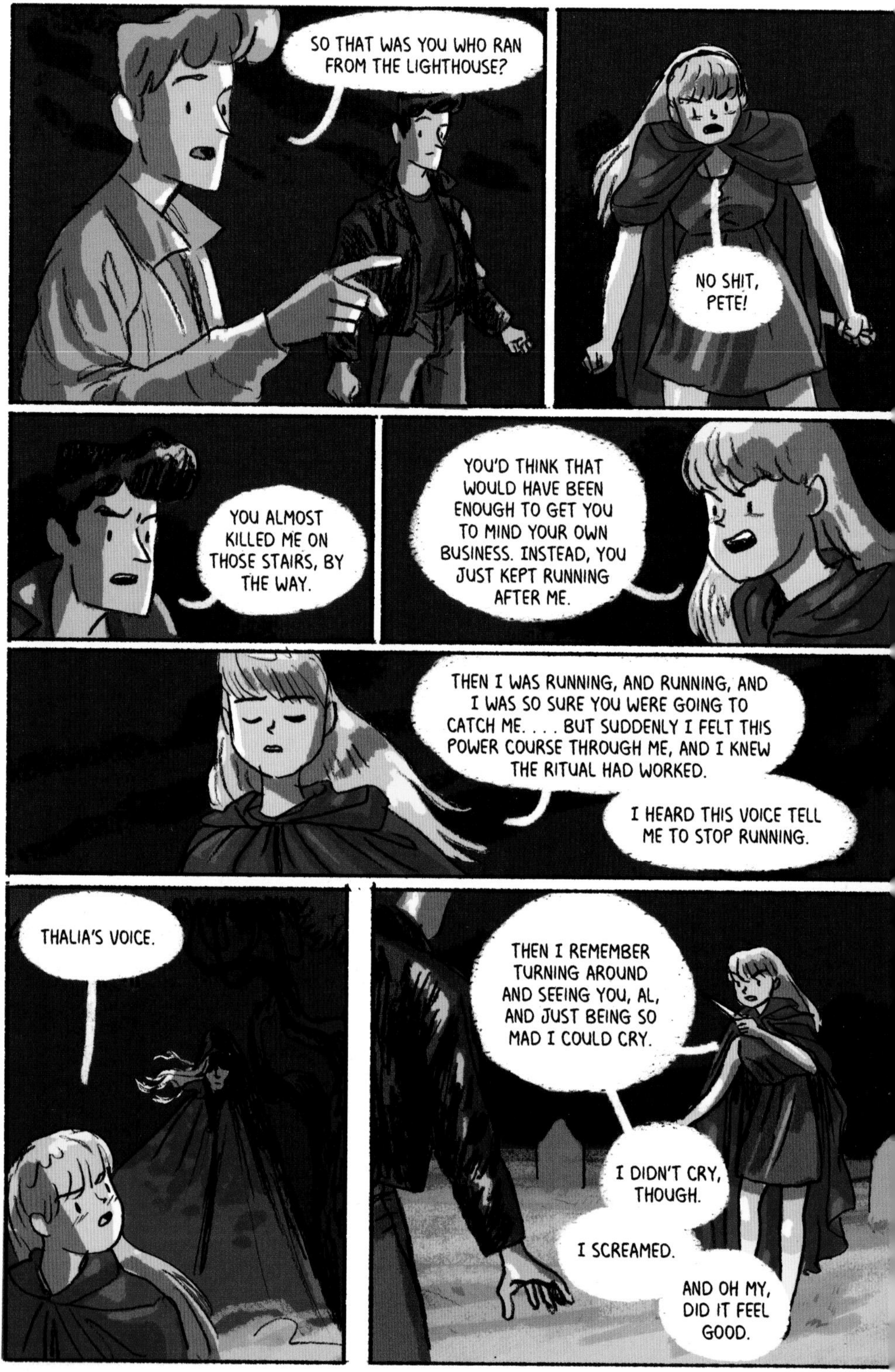
SO THAT WAS YOU WHO RAN FROM THE LIGHTHOUSE?
NO SHIT, PETE!
YOU ALMOST KILLED ME ON THOSE STAIRS, BY THE WAY.
YOU'D THINK THAT WOULD HAVE BEEN ENOUGH TO GET YOU TO MIND YOUR OWN BUSINESS. INSTEAD, YOU JUST KEPT RUNNING AFTER ME.
THEN I WAS RUNNING, AND RUNNING, AND I WAS SO SURE YOU WERE GOING TO CATCH ME. . . . BUT SUDDENLY I FELT THIS POWER COURSE THROUGH ME, AND I KNEW THE RITUAL HAD WORKED.
I HEARD THIS VOICE TELL ME TO STOP RUNNING.
THALIA'S VOICE.
THEN I REMEMBER TURNING AROUND AND SEEING YOU, AL, AND JUST BEING SO MAD I COULD CRY.
I DIDN'T CRY, THOUGH.
I SCREAMED.
AND OH MY, DID IT FEEL GOOD.

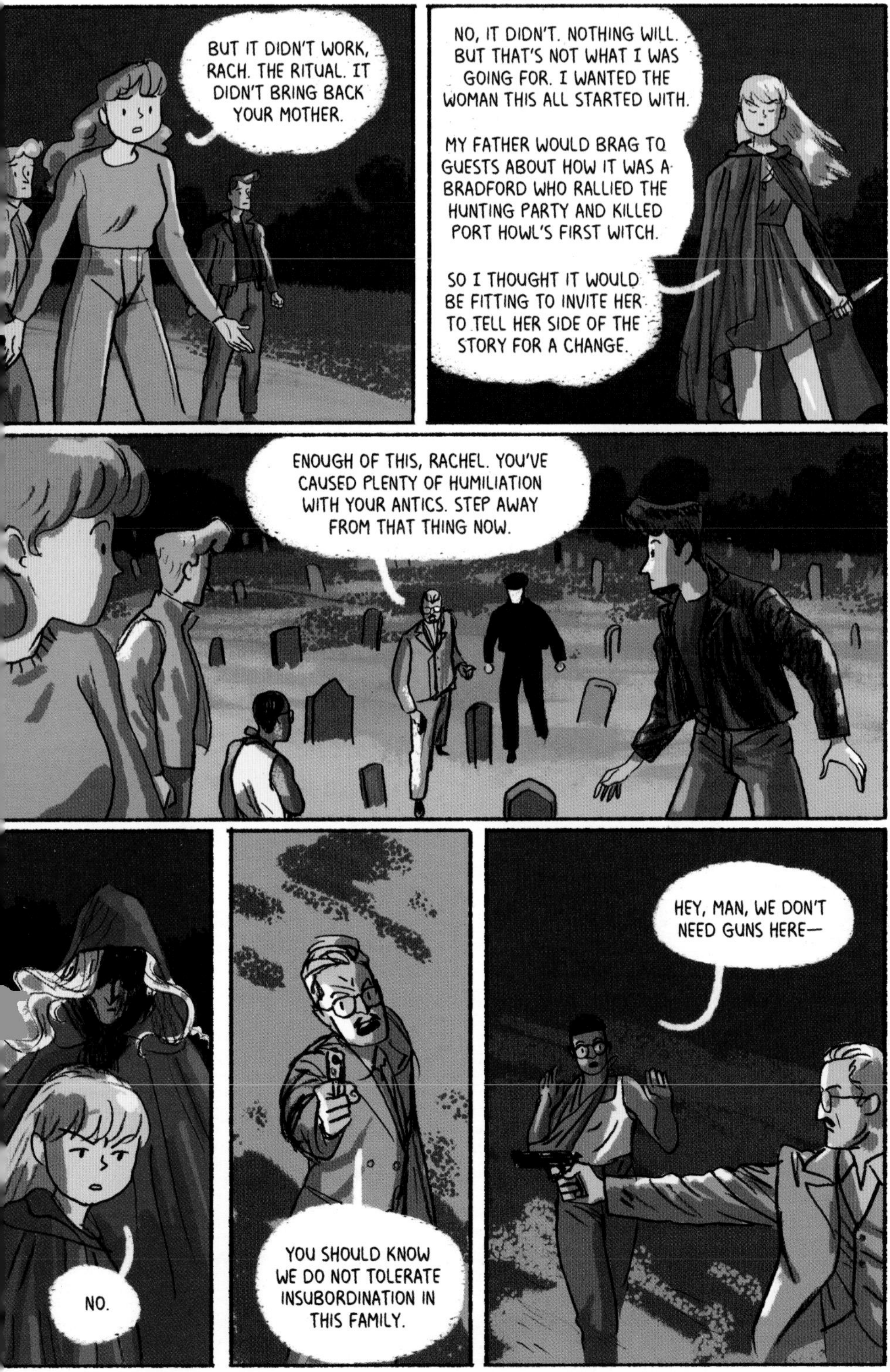
BUT IT DIDN'T WORK, RACH. THE RITUAL. IT DIDN'T BRING BACK YOUR MOTHER.
NO, IT DIDN'T. NOTHING WILL. BUT THAT'S NOT WHAT I WAS GOING FOR. I WANTED THE WOMAN THIS ALL STARTED WITH.
MY FATHER WOULD BRAG TO GUESTS ABOUT HOW IT WAS A BRADFORD WHO RALLIED THE HUNTING PARTY AND KILLED PORT HOWL'S FIRST WITCH.
SO I THOUGHT IT WOULD BE FITTING TO INVITE HER TO TELL HER SIDE OF THE STORY FOR A CHANGE.
ENOUGH OF THIS, RACHEL. YOU'VE CAUSED PLENTY OF HUMILIATION WITH YOUR ANTICS. STEP AWAY FROM THAT THING NOW.
NO.
YOU SHOULD KNOW WE DO NOT TOLERATE INSUBORDINATION IN THIS FAMILY.
HEY, MAN, WE DON'T NEED GUNS HERE—

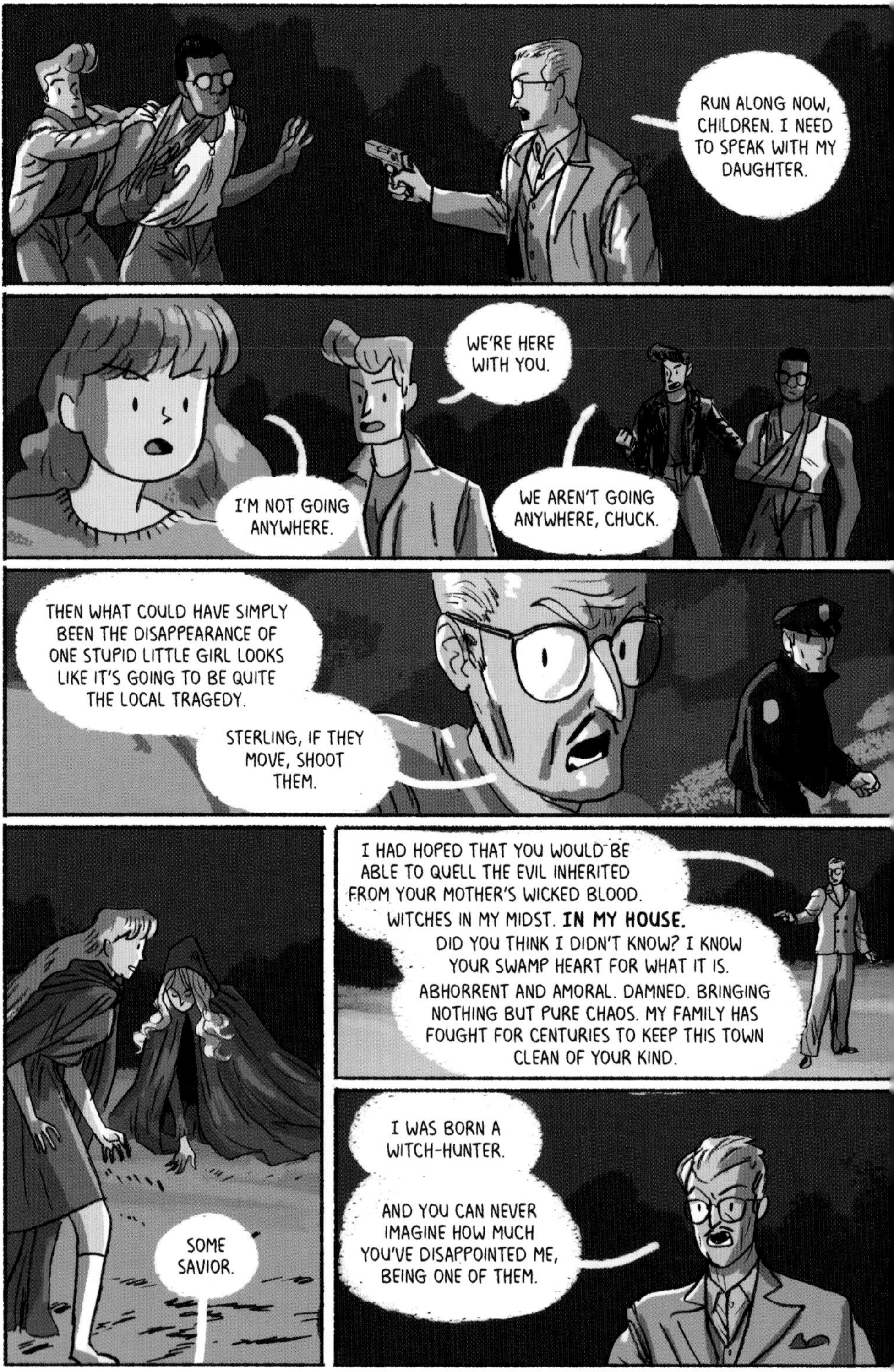
RUN ALONG NOW, CHILDREN. I NEED TO SPEAK WITH MY DAUGHTER.
WE'RE HERE WITH YOU.
I'M NOT GOING ANYWHERE.
WE AREN'T GOING ANYWHERE, CHUCK.
THEN WHAT COULD HAVE SIMPLY BEEN THE DISAPPEARANCE OF ONE STUPID LITTLE GIRL LOOKS LIKE IT'S GOING TO BE QUITE THE LOCAL TRAGEDY.
STERLING, IF THEY MOVE, SHOOT THEM.
SOME SAVIOR.
I HAD HOPED THAT YOU WOULD BE ABLE TO QUELL THE EVIL INHERITED FROM YOUR MOTHER'S WICKED BLOOD.
WITCHES IN MY MIDST. **IN MY HOUSE.**
DID YOU THINK I DIDN'T KNOW? I KNOW YOUR SWAMP HEART FOR WHAT IT IS.
ABHORRENT AND AMORAL. DAMNED. BRINGING NOTHING BUT PURE CHAOS. MY FAMILY HAS FOUGHT FOR CENTURIES TO KEEP THIS TOWN CLEAN OF YOUR KIND.
I WAS BORN A WITCH-HUNTER.
AND YOU CAN NEVER IMAGINE HOW MUCH YOU'VE DISAPPOINTED ME, BEING ONE OF THEM.

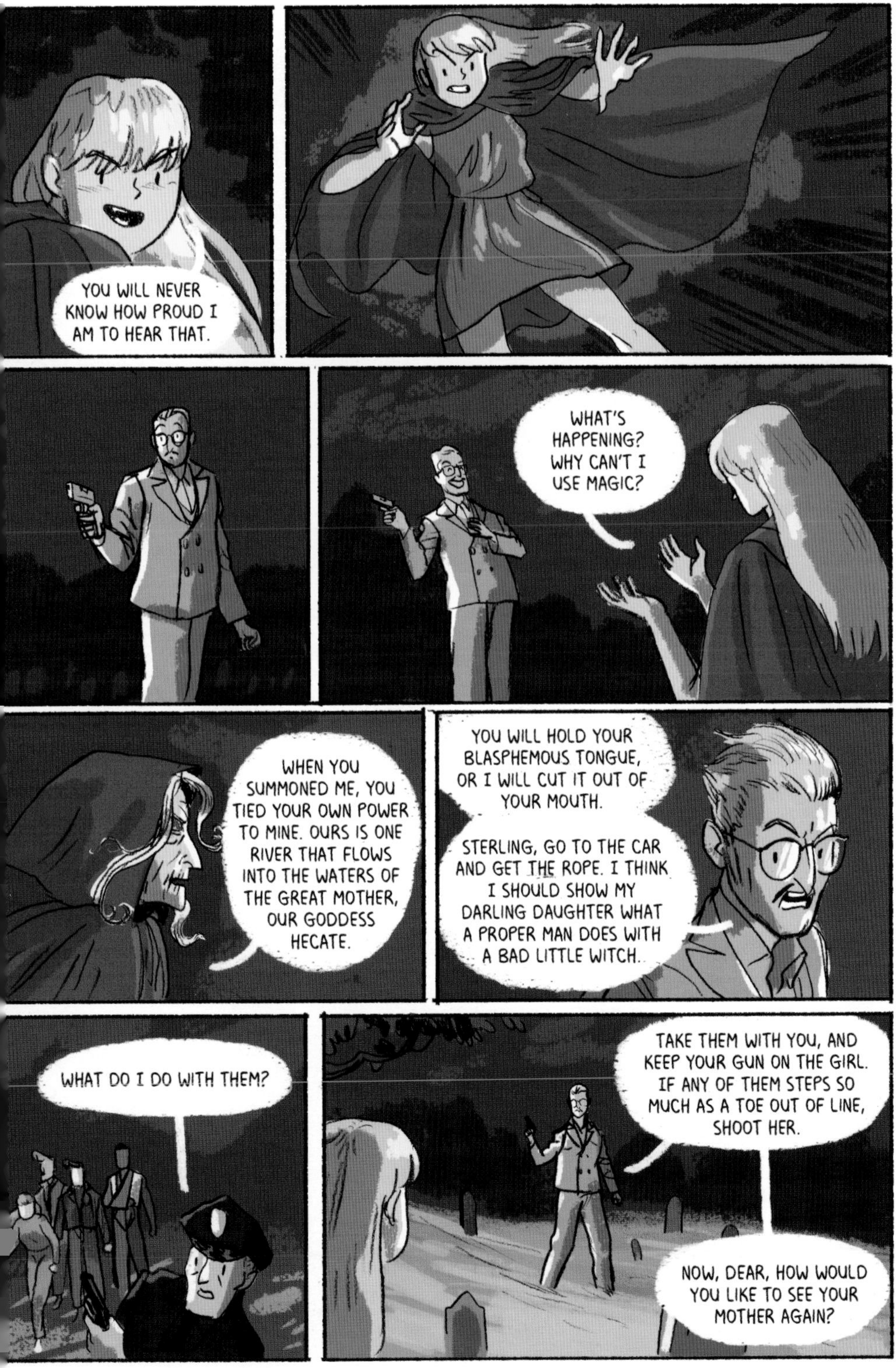

YOU WILL NEVER KNOW HOW PROUD I AM TO HEAR THAT.
WHAT'S HAPPENING? WHY CAN'T I USE MAGIC?
WHEN YOU SUMMONED ME, YOU TIED YOUR OWN POWER TO MINE. OURS IS ONE RIVER THAT FLOWS INTO THE WATERS OF THE GREAT MOTHER, OUR GODDESS HECATE.
YOU WILL HOLD YOUR BLASPHEMOUS TONGUE, OR I WILL CUT IT OUT OF YOUR MOUTH.
STERLING, GO TO THE CAR AND GET THE ROPE. I THINK I SHOULD SHOW MY DARLING DAUGHTER WHAT A PROPER MAN DOES WITH A BAD LITTLE WITCH.
WHAT DO I DO WITH THEM?
TAKE THEM WITH YOU, AND KEEP YOUR GUN ON THE GIRL. IF ANY OF THEM STEPS SO MUCH AS A TOE OUT OF LINE, SHOOT HER.
NOW, DEAR, HOW WOULD YOU LIKE TO SEE YOUR MOTHER AGAIN?

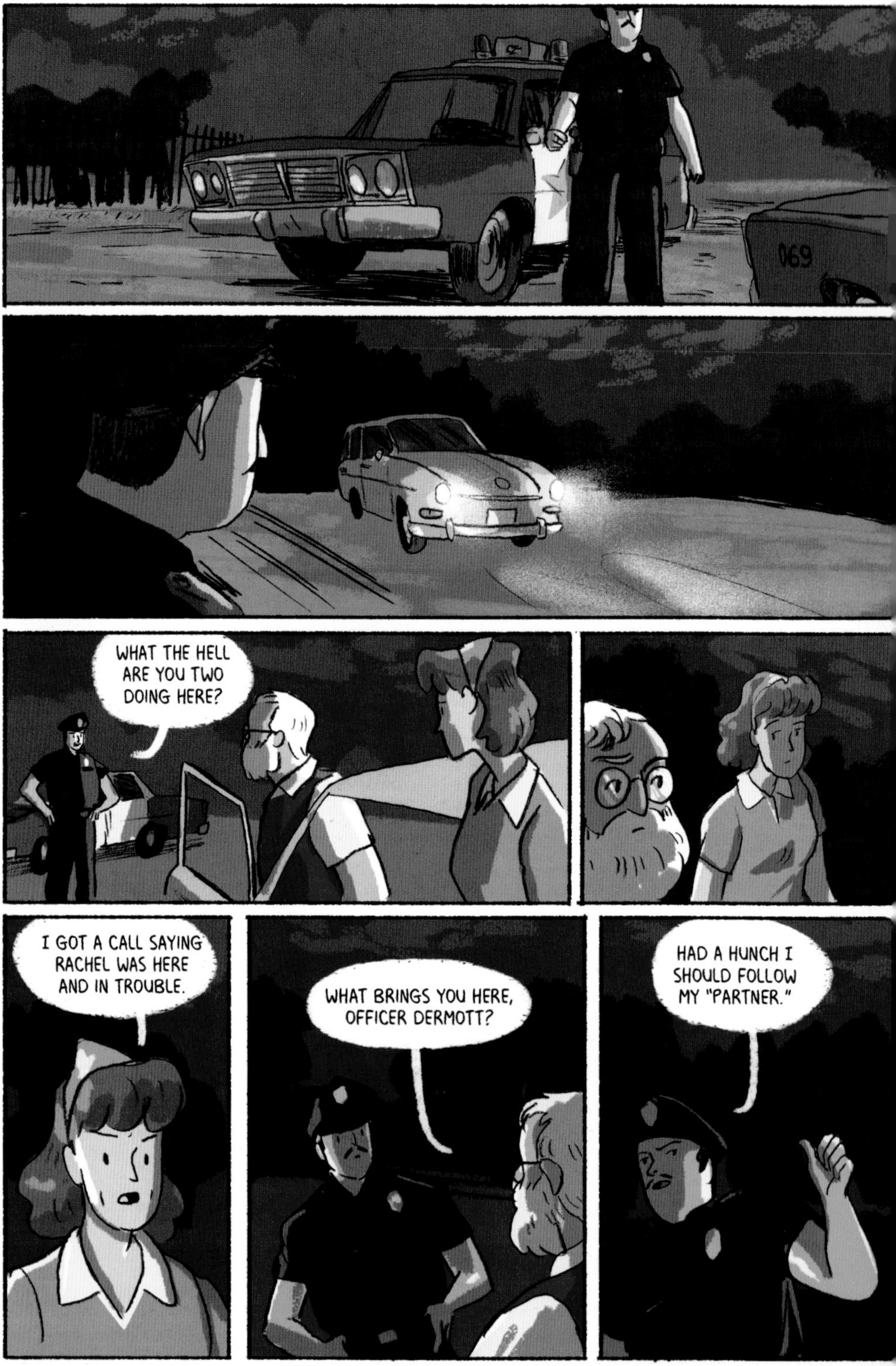
069
WHAT THE HELL ARE YOU TWO DOING HERE?
I GOT A CALL SAYING RACHEL WAS HERE AND IN TROUBLE.
WHAT BRINGS YOU HERE, OFFICER DERMOTT?
HAD A HUNCH I SHOULD FOLLOW MY "PARTNER."

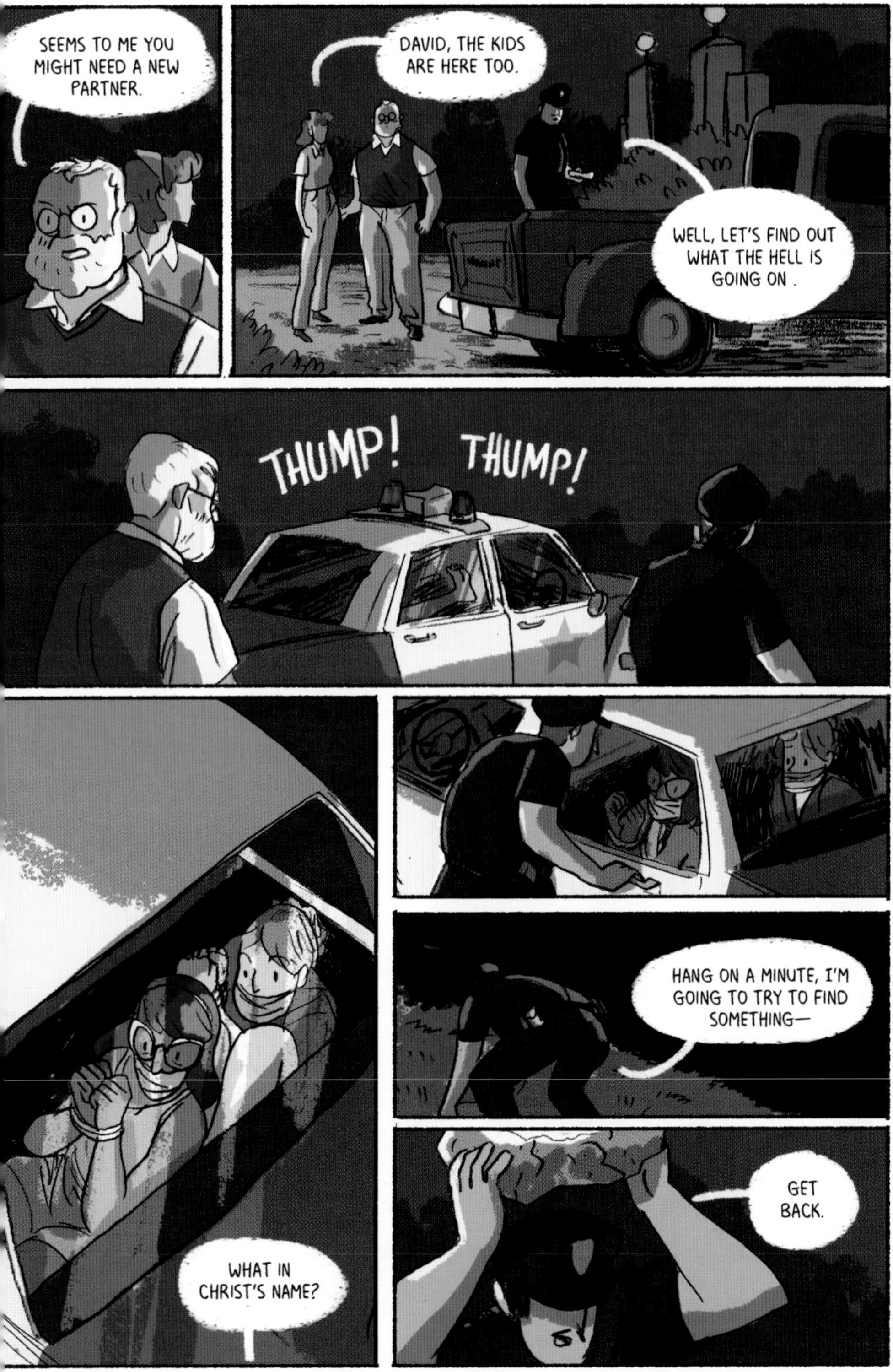
SEEMS TO ME YOU MIGHT NEED A NEW PARTNER.
DAVID, THE KIDS ARE HERE TOO.
WELL, LET'S FIND OUT WHAT THE HELL IS GOING ON .
THUMP! THUMP!
WHAT IN CHRIST'S NAME?
HANG ON A MINUTE, I'M GOING TO TRY TO FIND SOMETHING—
GET BACK.

THIS IS A HELL OF A MESS YOU'RE IN, MAN. YOUR BOY THERE SEEMS KIND OF NUTS.

WHAT CAN I SAY? THE PAY IS RIGHT.

YOU MIND IF I HAVE A SMOKE? SEEMS LIKE AS GOOD A TIME AS ANY.

GO AHEAD. JUST REMEMBER, YOU SCREW WITH ME AND YOUR PRETTY LITTLE FRIEND GETS A BULLET IN THE BACK.

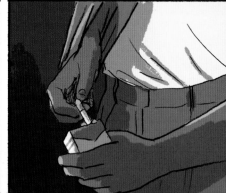

I COULD USE A HAND LIGHTING IT. . . .

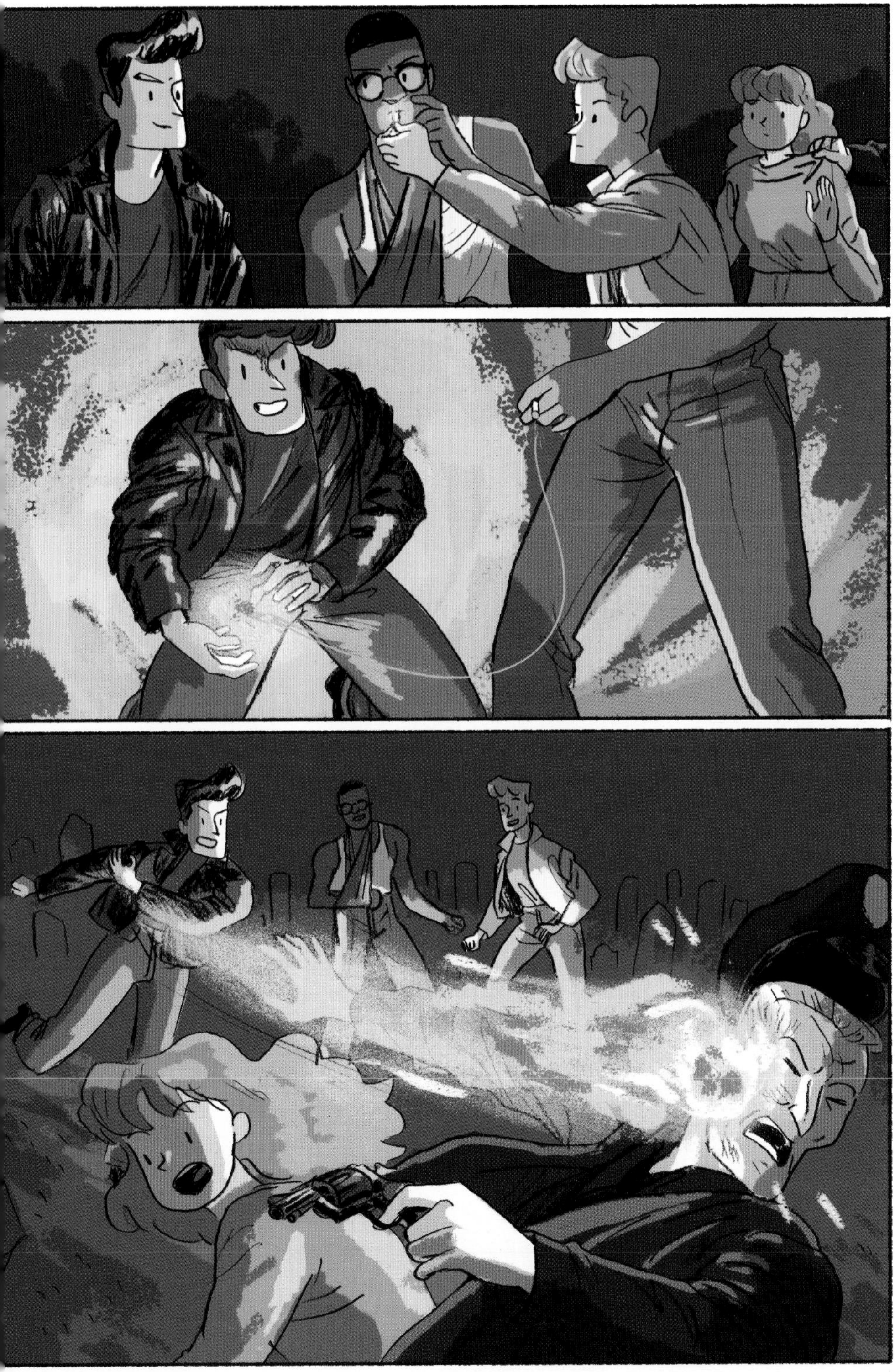

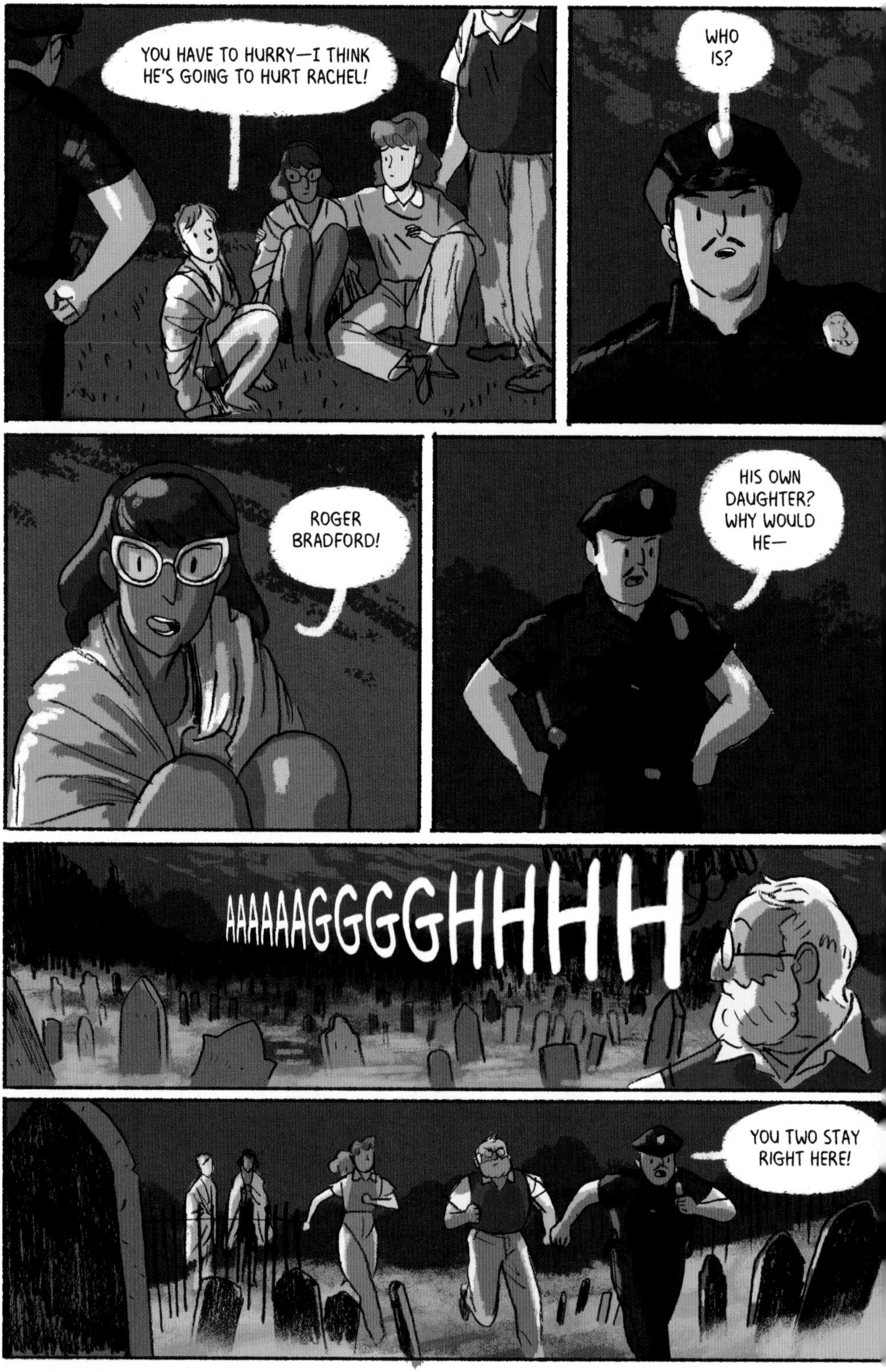
YOU HAVE TO HURRY—I THINK HE'S GOING TO HURT RACHEL!
WHO IS?
ROGER BRADFORD!
HIS OWN DAUGHTER? WHY WOULD HE—
AAAAAAGGGGHHHHH
YOU TWO STAY RIGHT HERE!

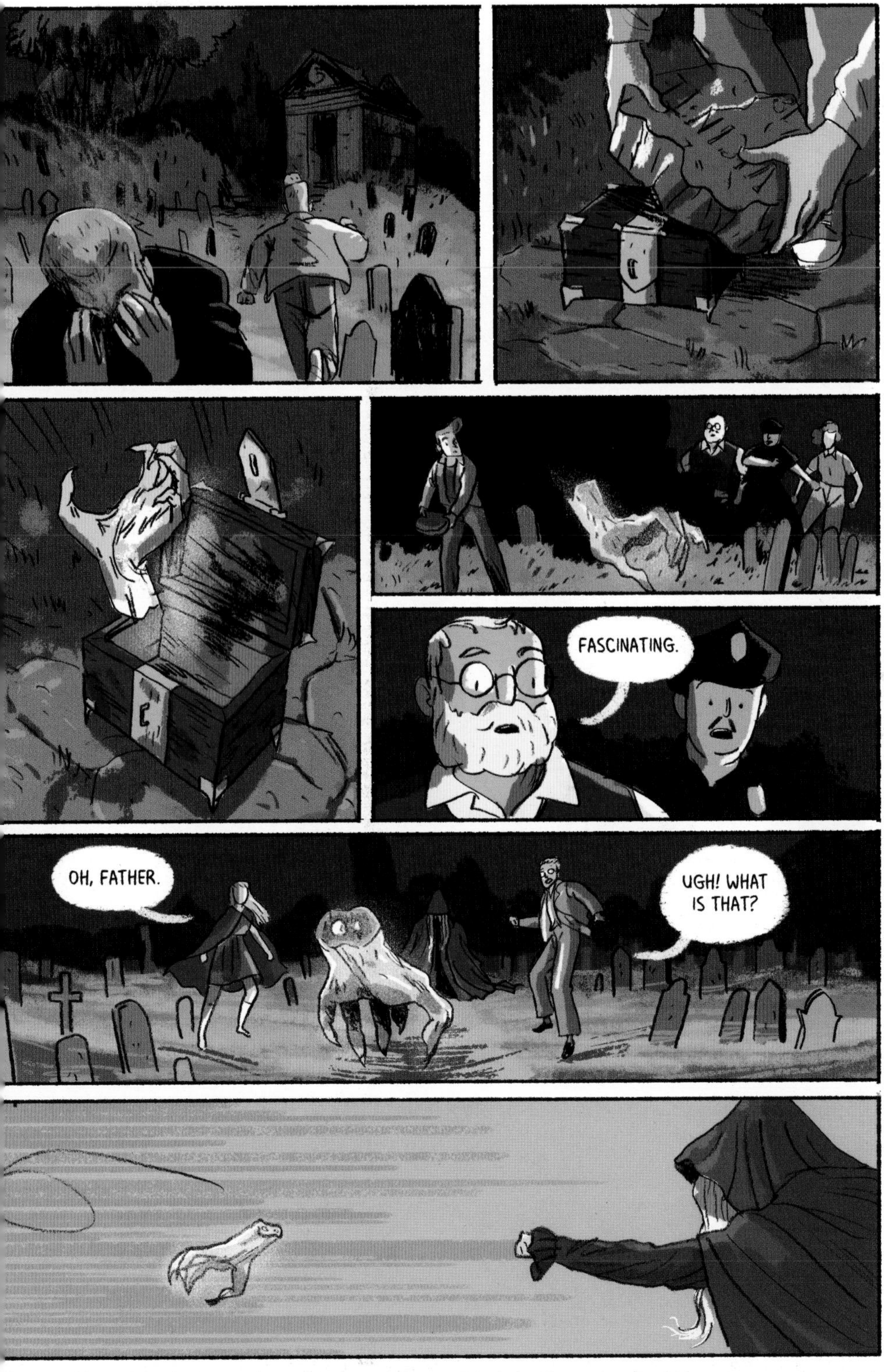
FASCINATING.
OH, FATHER.
UGH! WHAT IS THAT?

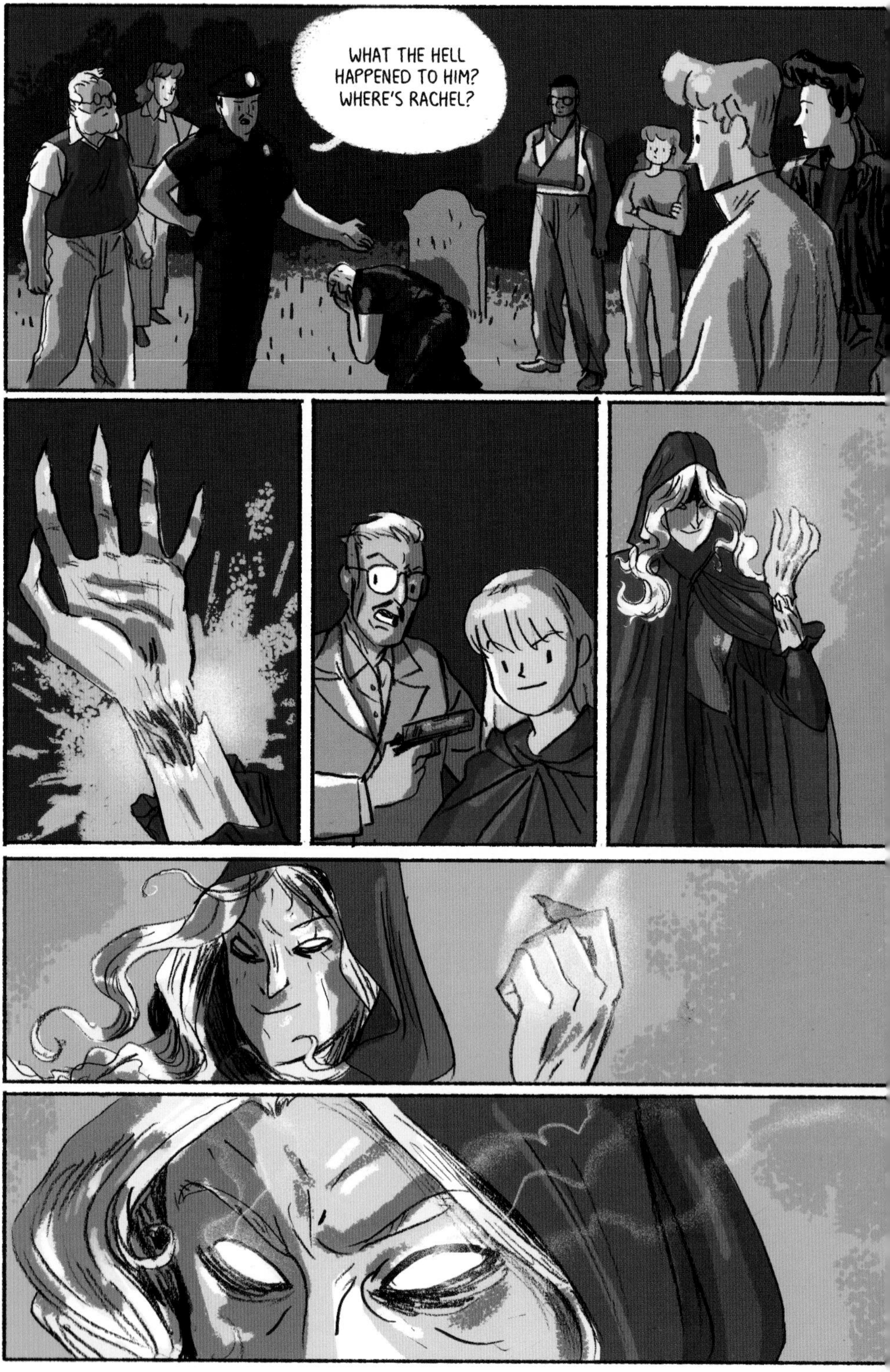
WHAT THE HELL HAPPENED TO HIM? WHERE'S RACHEL?

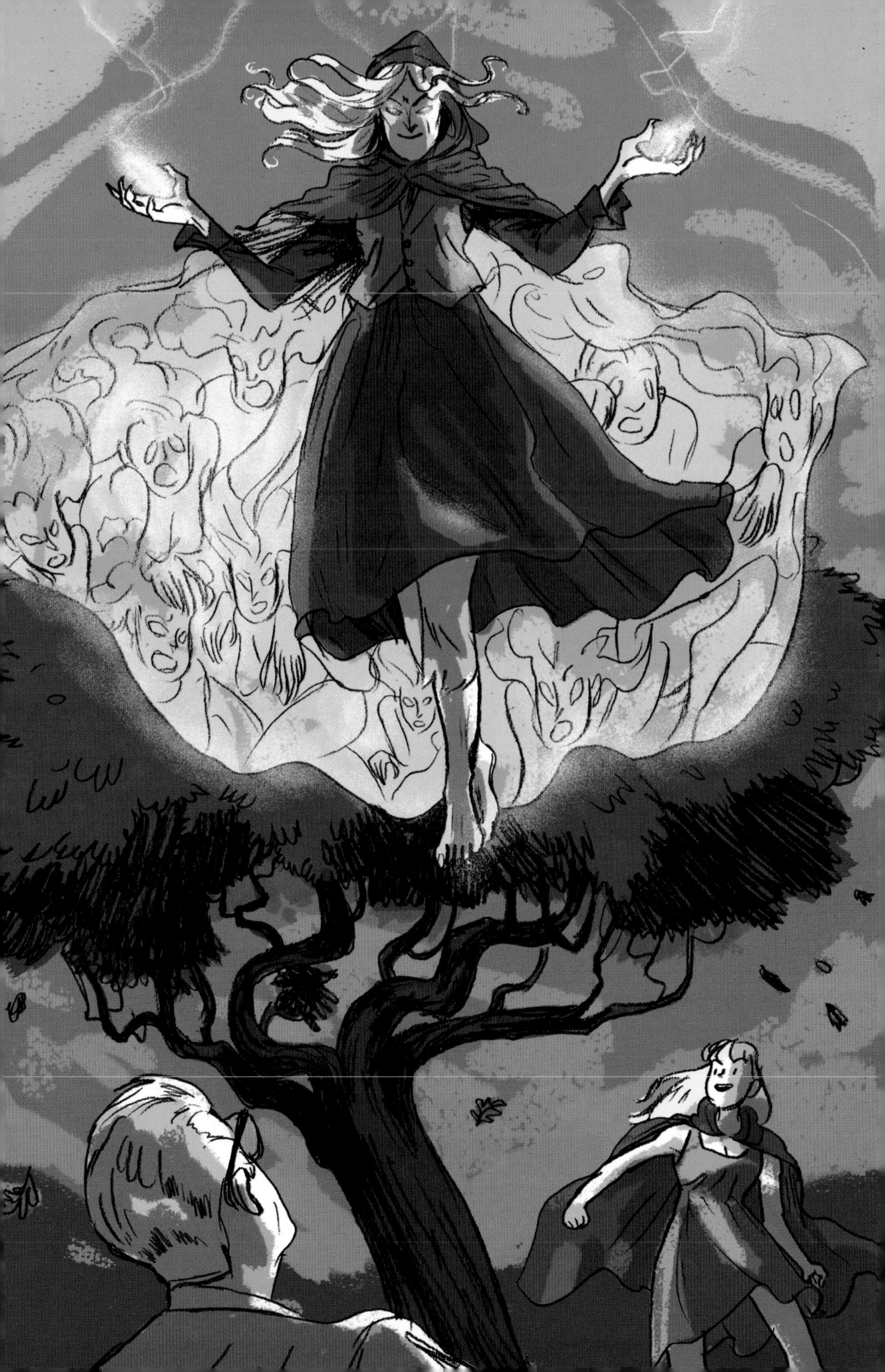

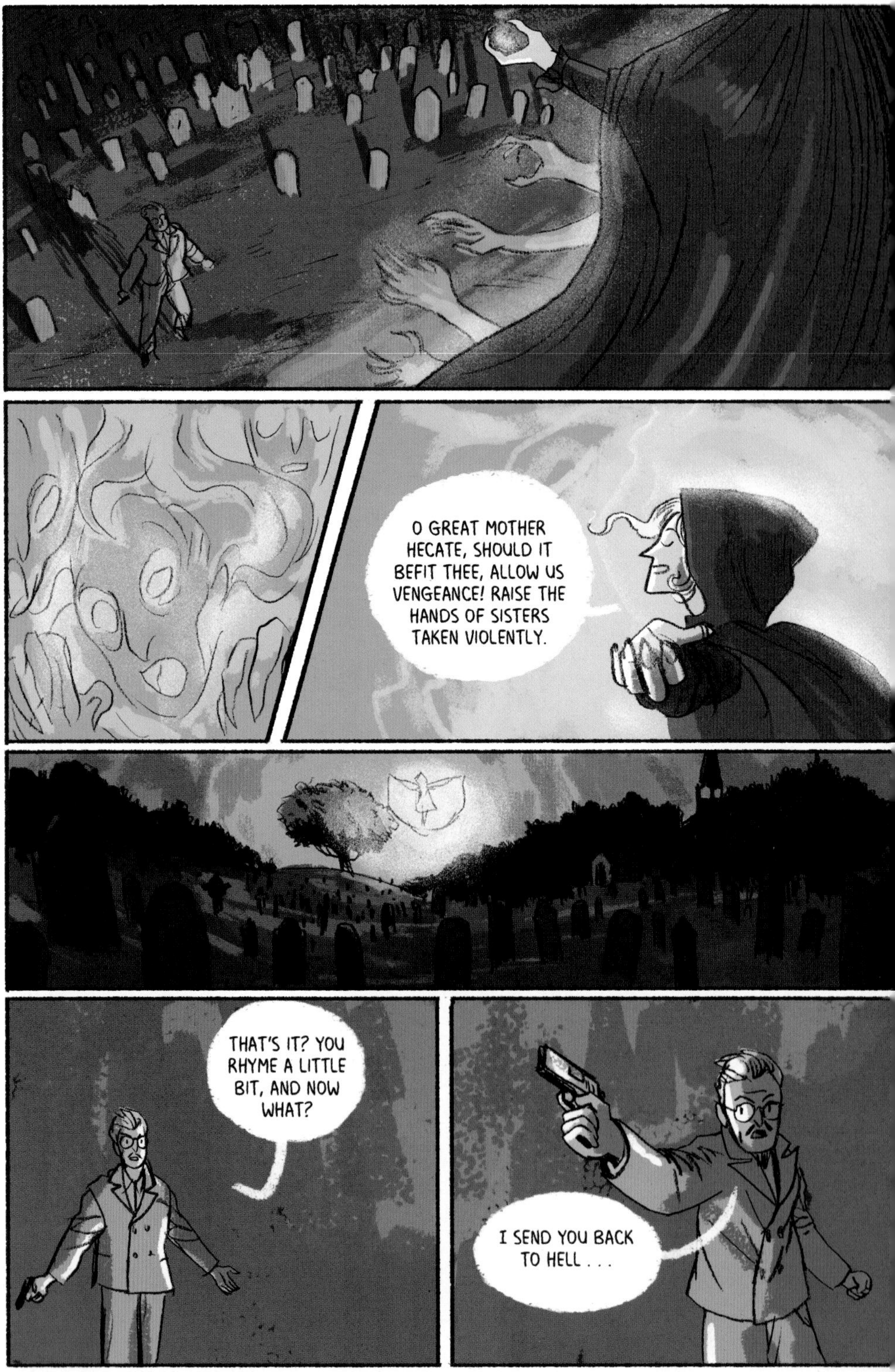
O GREAT MOTHER HECATE, SHOULD IT BEFIT THEE, ALLOW US VENGEANCE! RAISE THE HANDS OF SISTERS TAKEN VIOLENTLY.
THAT'S IT? YOU RHYME A LITTLE BIT, AND NOW WHAT?
I SEND YOU BACK TO HELL . . .

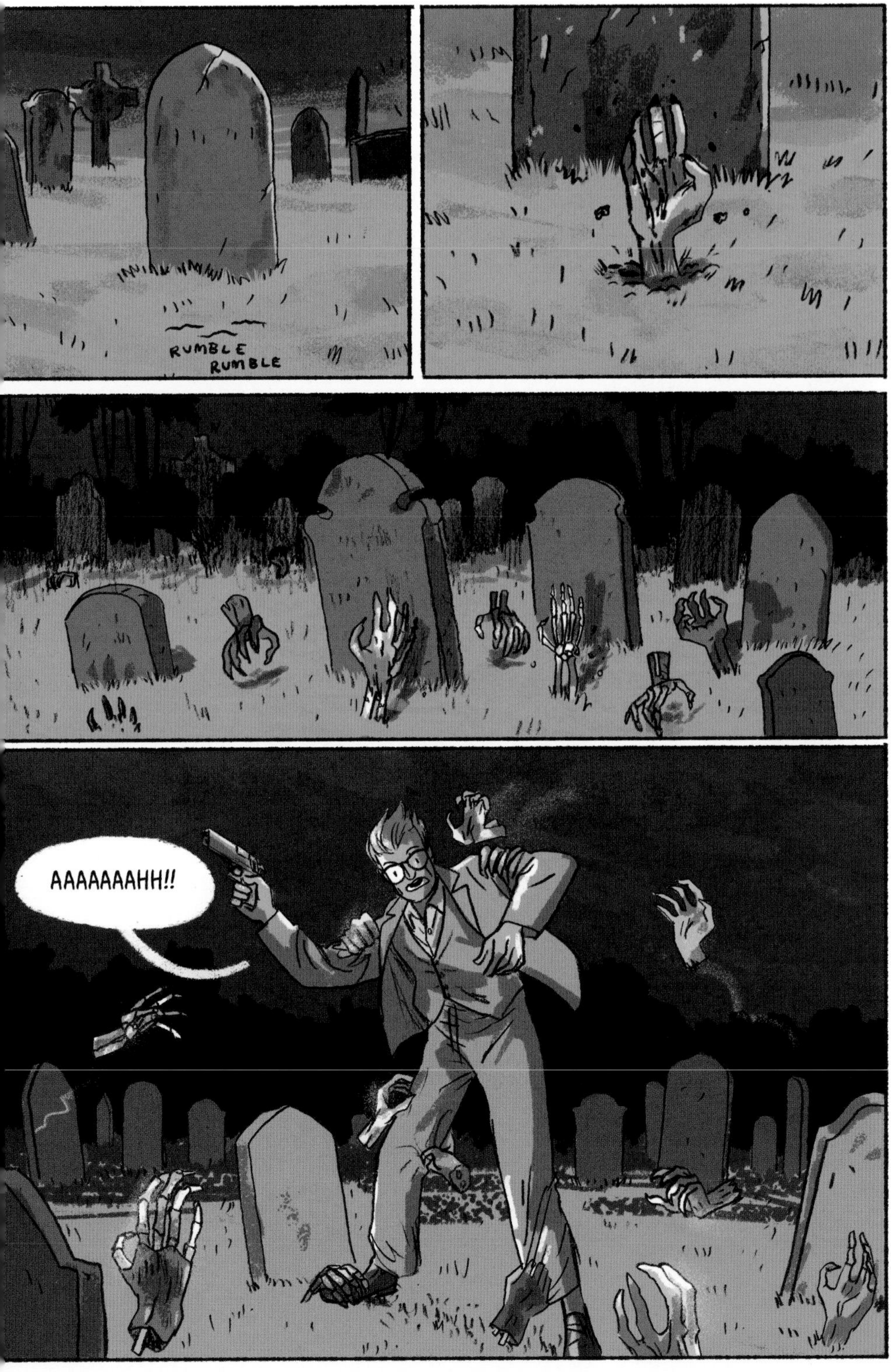
RUMBLE
RUMBLE
AAAAAAAHH!!

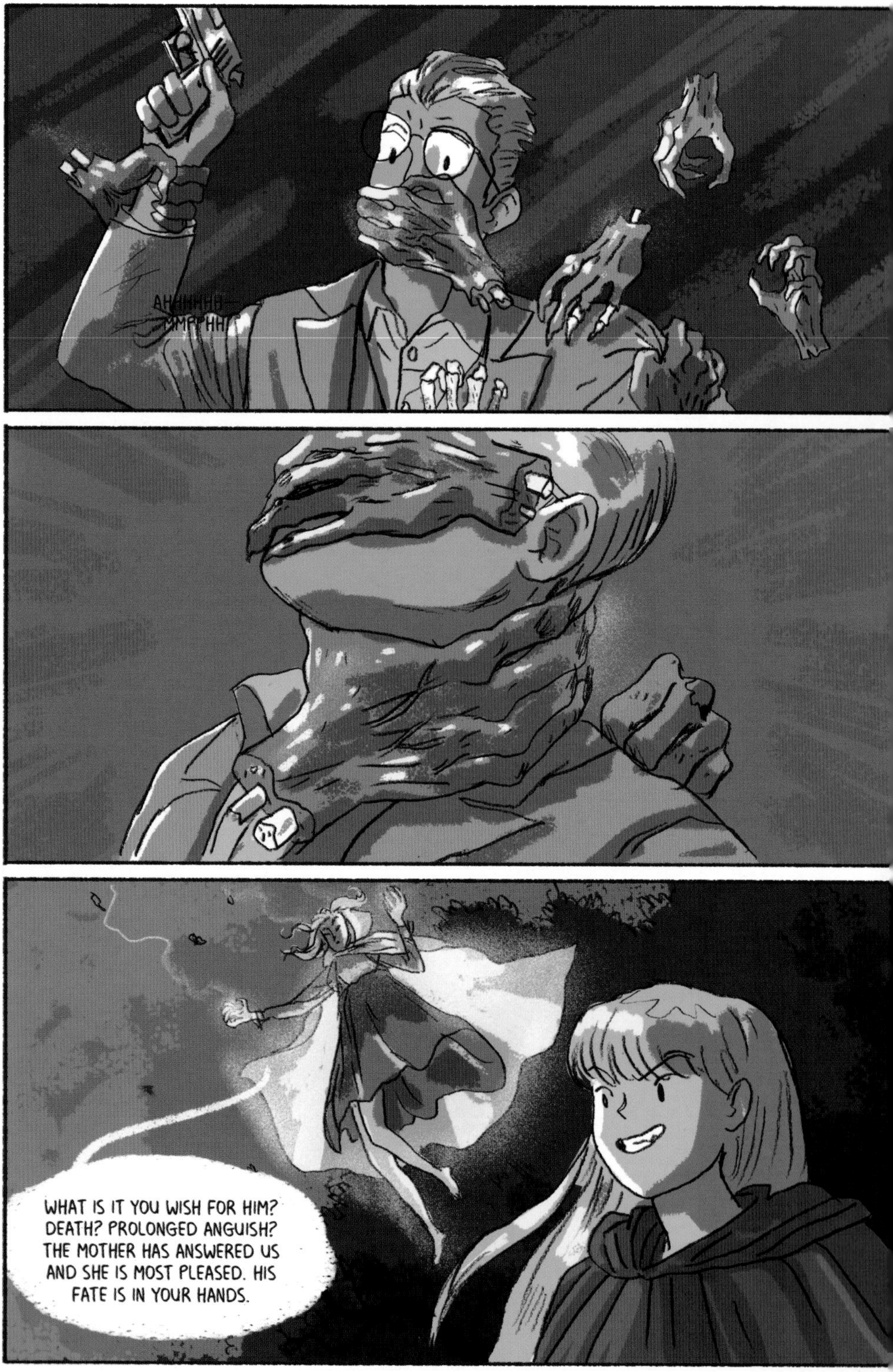
AHHHHHH—
MMPPHH!
WHAT IS IT YOU WISH FOR HIM? DEATH? PROLONGED ANGUISH? THE MOTHER HAS ANSWERED US AND SHE IS MOST PLEASED. HIS FATE IS IN YOUR HANDS.

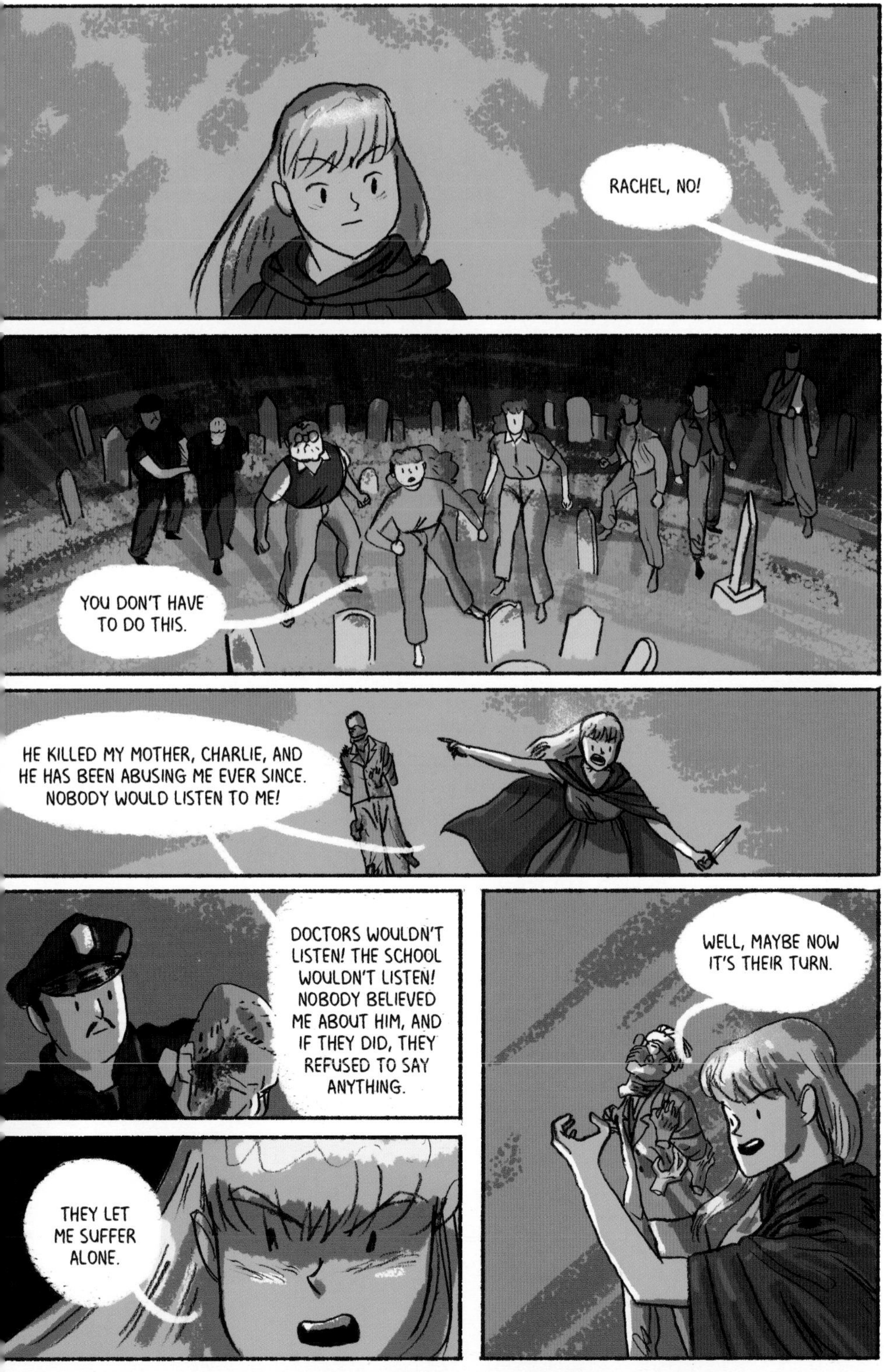
RACHEL, NO!
YOU DON'T HAVE TO DO THIS.
HE KILLED MY MOTHER, CHARLIE, AND HE HAS BEEN ABUSING ME EVER SINCE. NOBODY WOULD LISTEN TO ME!
DOCTORS WOULDN'T LISTEN! THE SCHOOL WOULDN'T LISTEN! NOBODY BELIEVED ME ABOUT HIM, AND IF THEY DID, THEY REFUSED TO SAY ANYTHING.
THEY LET ME SUFFER ALONE.
WELL, MAYBE NOW IT'S THEIR TURN.

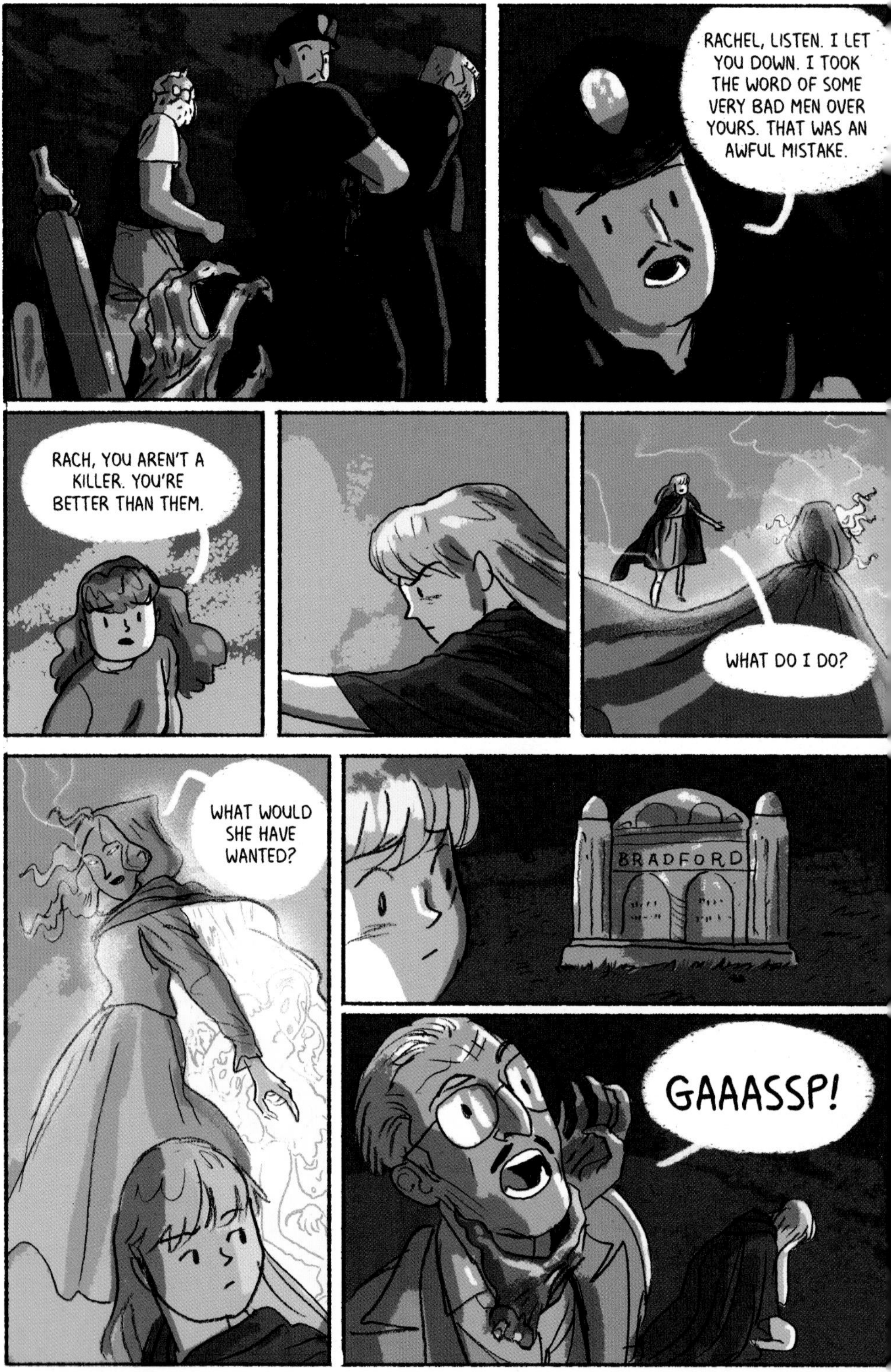
RACHEL, LISTEN. I LET YOU DOWN. I TOOK THE WORD OF SOME VERY BAD MEN OVER YOURS. THAT WAS AN AWFUL MISTAKE.
RACH, YOU AREN'T A KILLER. YOU'RE BETTER THAN THEM.
WHAT DO I DO?
WHAT WOULD SHE HAVE WANTED?
BRADFORD
GAAASSP!

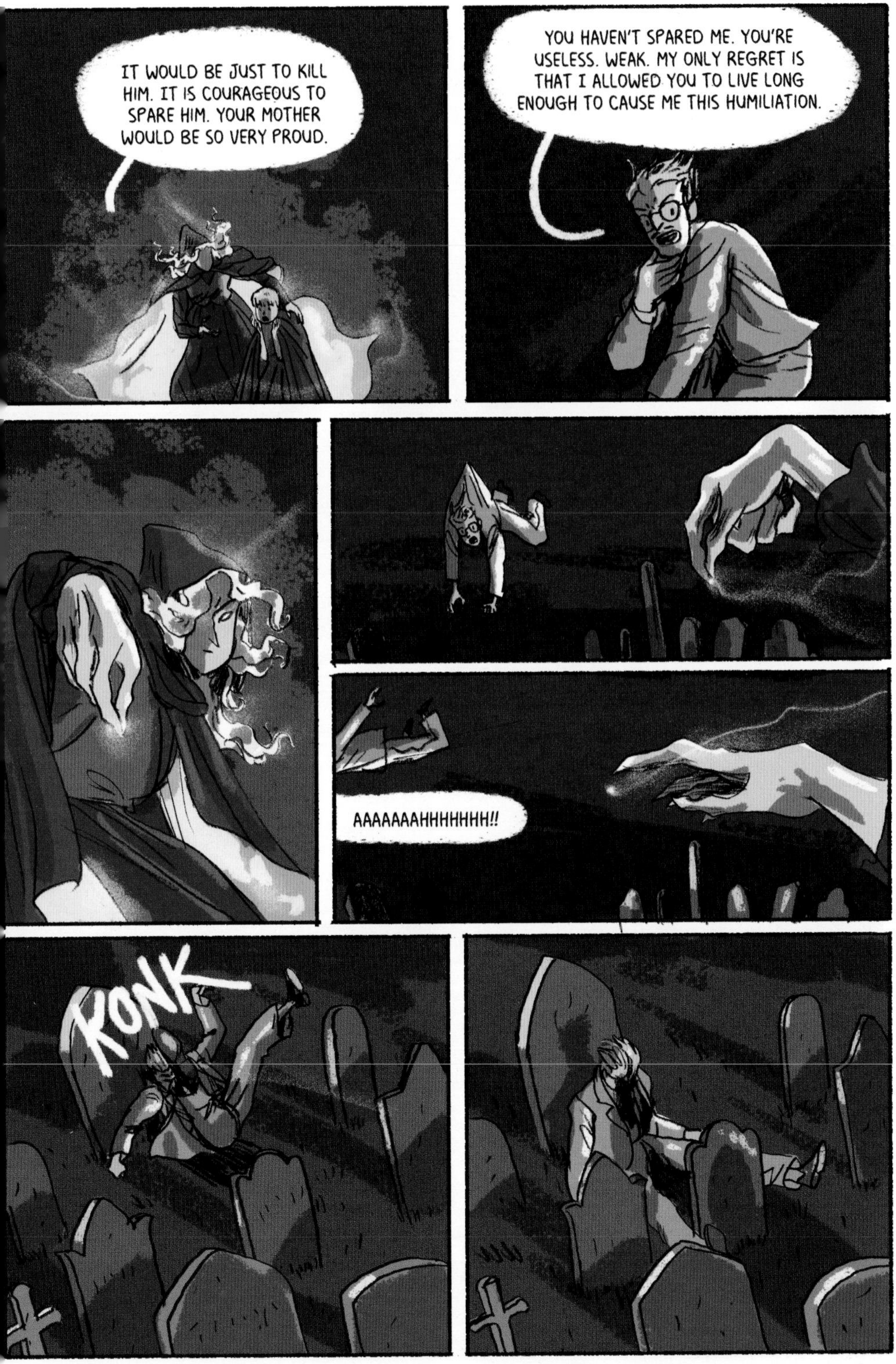
IT WOULD BE JUST TO KILL HIM. IT IS COURAGEOUS TO SPARE HIM. YOUR MOTHER WOULD BE SO VERY PROUD.
YOU HAVEN'T SPARED ME. YOU'RE USELESS. WEAK. MY ONLY REGRET IS THAT I ALLOWED YOU TO LIVE LONG ENOUGH TO CAUSE ME THIS HUMILIATION.
AAAAAAAHHHHHHH!!
KONK

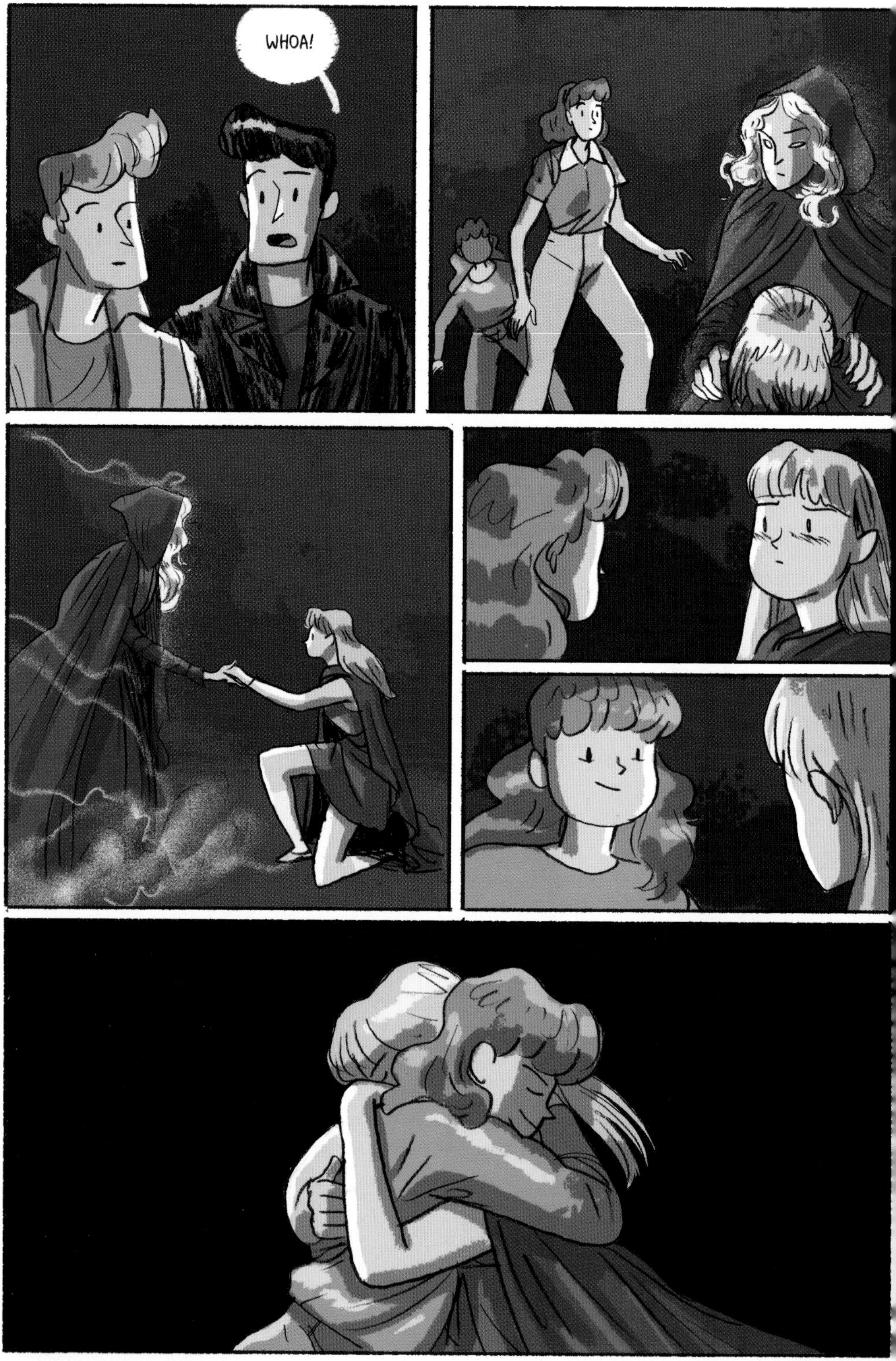
WHOA!

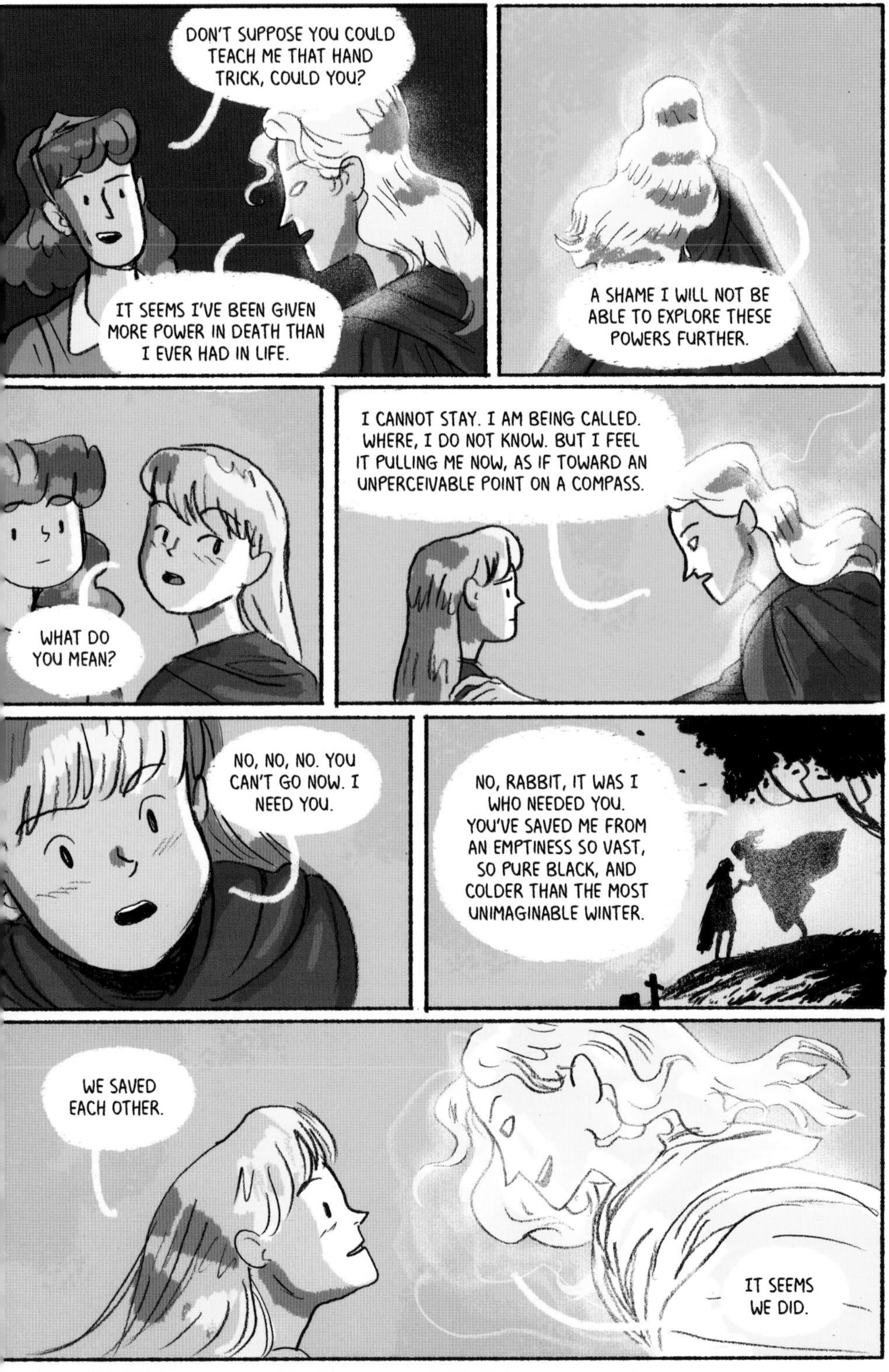
DON'T SUPPOSE YOU COULD TEACH ME THAT HAND TRICK, COULD YOU?
IT SEEMS I'VE BEEN GIVEN MORE POWER IN DEATH THAN I EVER HAD IN LIFE.
A SHAME I WILL NOT BE ABLE TO EXPLORE THESE POWERS FURTHER.
WHAT DO YOU MEAN?
I CANNOT STAY. I AM BEING CALLED. WHERE, I DO NOT KNOW. BUT I FEEL IT PULLING ME NOW, AS IF TOWARD AN UNPERCEIVABLE POINT ON A COMPASS.
NO, NO, NO. YOU CAN'T GO NOW. I NEED YOU.
NO, RABBIT, IT WAS I WHO NEEDED YOU. YOU'VE SAVED ME FROM AN EMPTINESS SO VAST, SO PURE BLACK, AND COLDER THAN THE MOST UNIMAGINABLE WINTER.
WE SAVED EACH OTHER.
IT SEEMS WE DID.

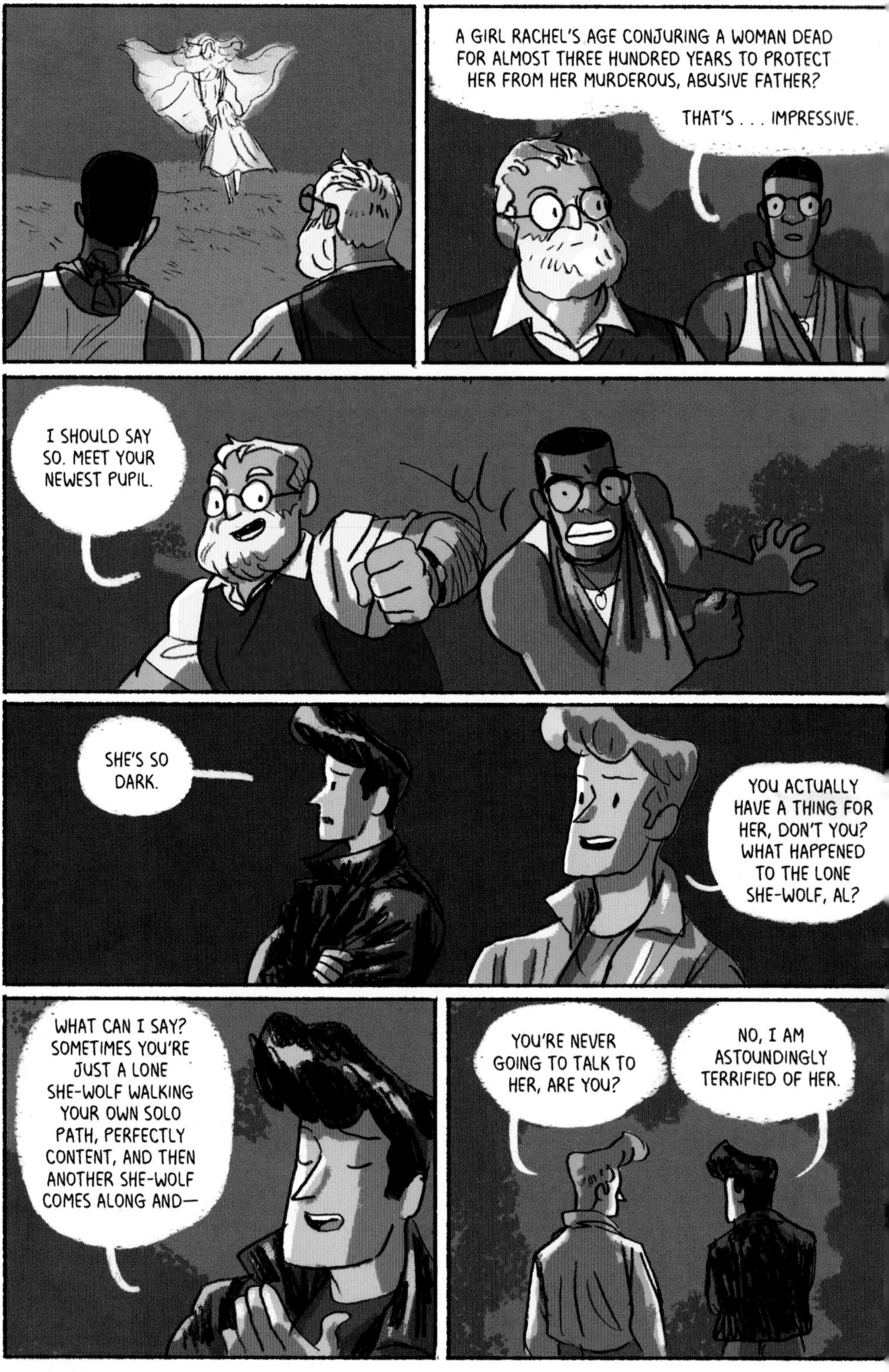
A GIRL RACHEL'S AGE CONJURING A WOMAN DEAD FOR ALMOST THREE HUNDRED YEARS TO PROTECT HER FROM HER MURDEROUS, ABUSIVE FATHER?
THAT'S . . . IMPRESSIVE.
I SHOULD SAY SO. MEET YOUR NEWEST PUPIL.
SHE'S SO DARK.
YOU ACTUALLY HAVE A THING FOR HER, DON'T YOU? WHAT HAPPENED TO THE LONE SHE-WOLF, AL?
WHAT CAN I SAY? SOMETIMES YOU'RE JUST A LONE SHE-WOLF WALKING YOUR OWN SOLO PATH, PERFECTLY CONTENT, AND THEN ANOTHER SHE-WOLF COMES ALONG AND—
YOU'RE NEVER GOING TO TALK TO HER, ARE YOU?
NO, I AM ASTOUNDINGLY TERRIFIED OF HER.

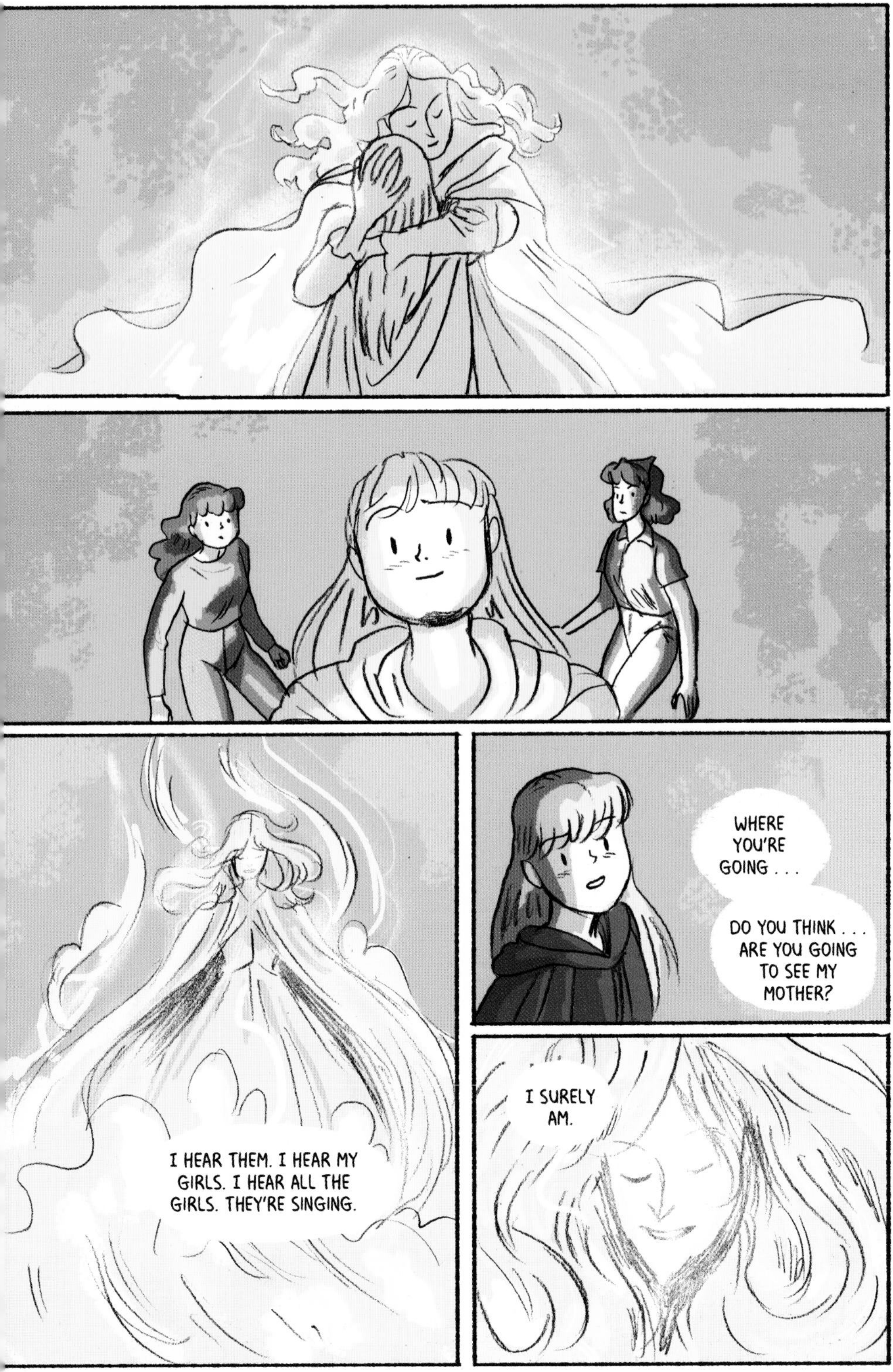
I HEAR THEM. I HEAR MY GIRLS. I HEAR ALL THE GIRLS. THEY'RE SINGING.
WHERE YOU'RE GOING . . .
DO YOU THINK . . . ARE YOU GOING TO SEE MY MOTHER?
I SURELY AM.

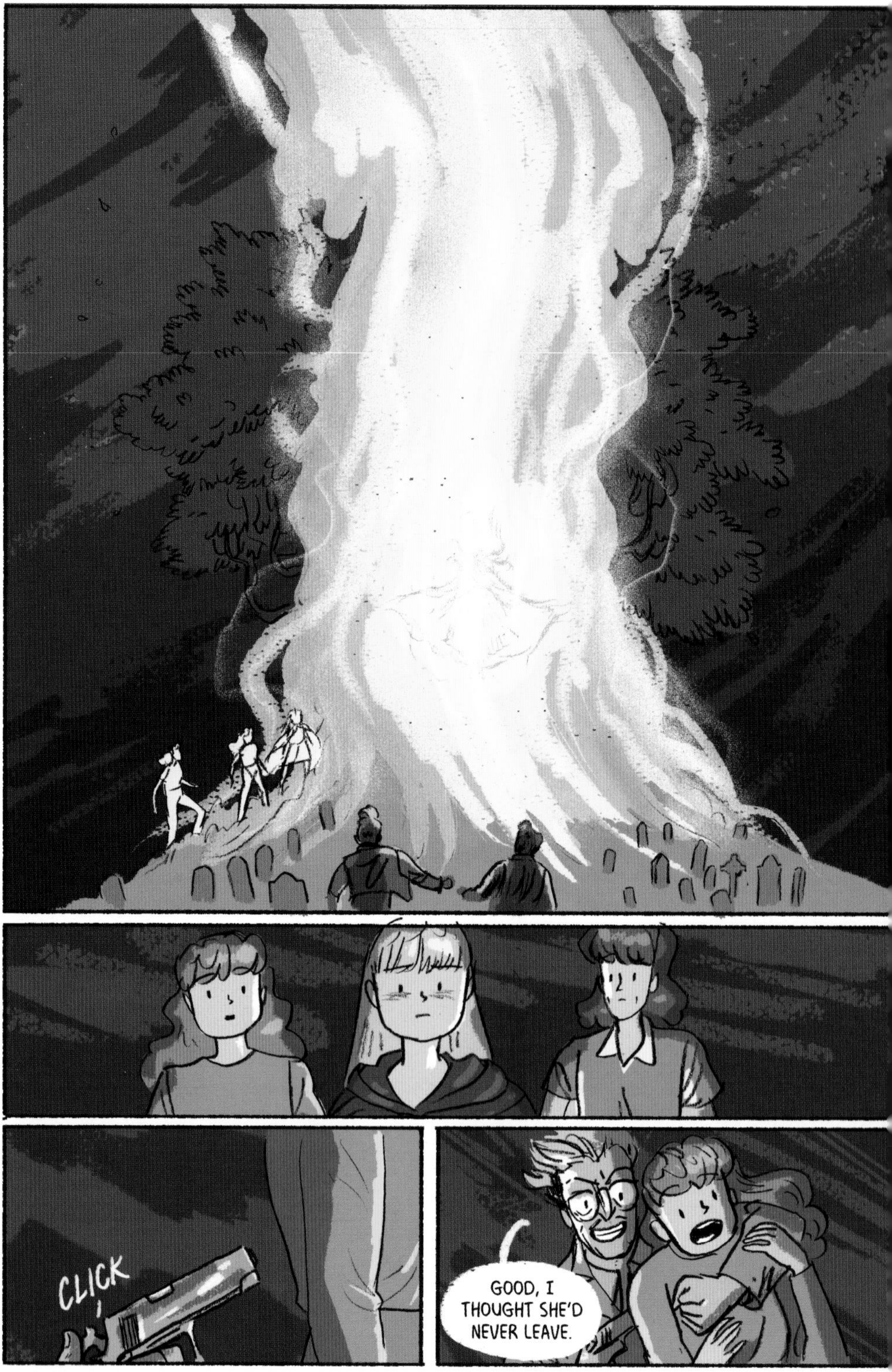
CLICK
GOOD, I THOUGHT SHE'D NEVER LEAVE.

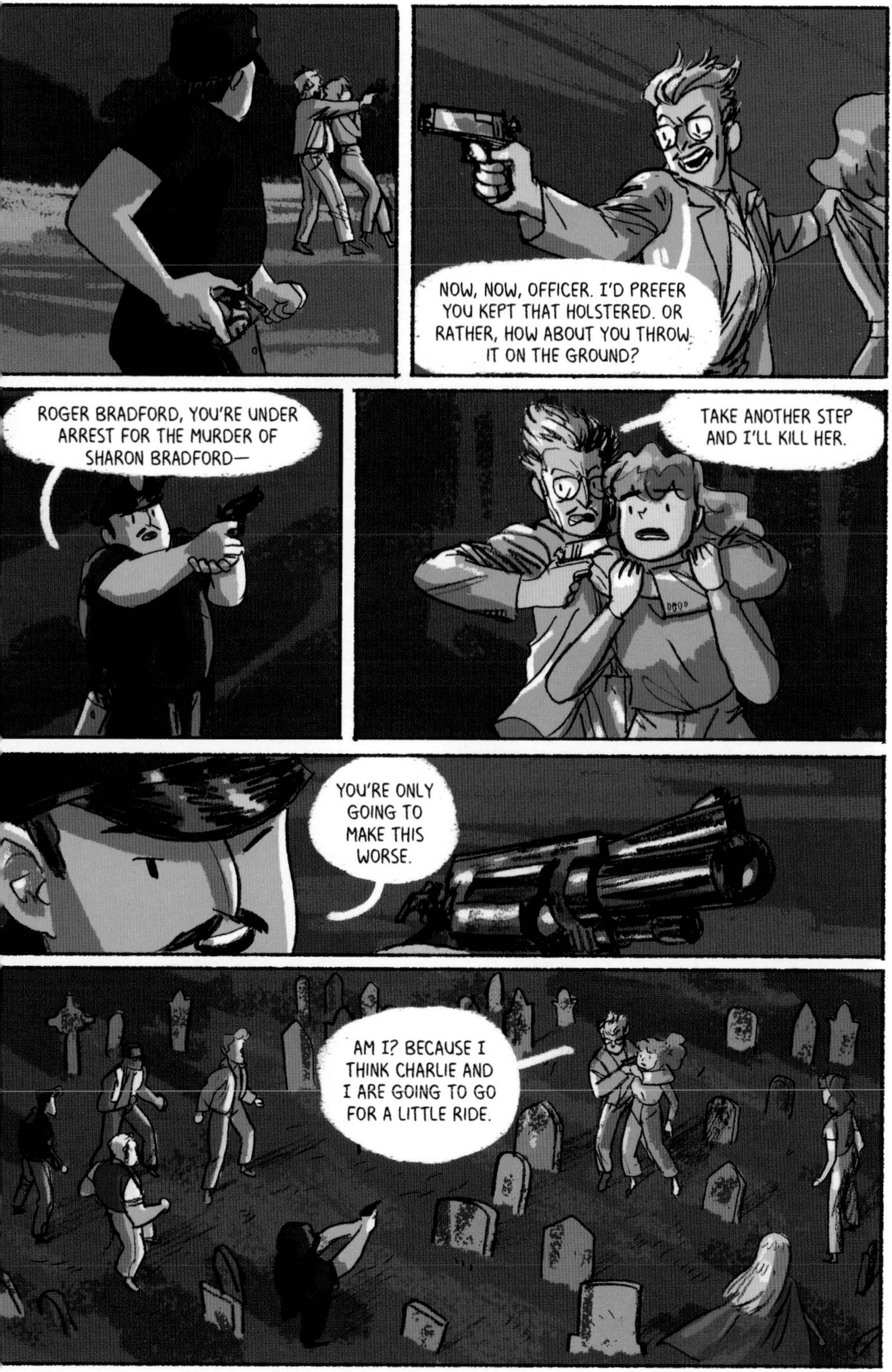
NOW, NOW, OFFICER. I'D PREFER YOU KEPT THAT HOLSTERED. OR RATHER, HOW ABOUT YOU THROW IT ON THE GROUND?
ROGER BRADFORD, YOU'RE UNDER ARREST FOR THE MURDER OF SHARON BRADFORD—
TAKE ANOTHER STEP AND I'LL KILL HER.
YOU'RE ONLY GOING TO MAKE THIS WORSE.
AM I? BECAUSE I THINK CHARLIE AND I ARE GOING TO GO FOR A LITTLE RIDE.

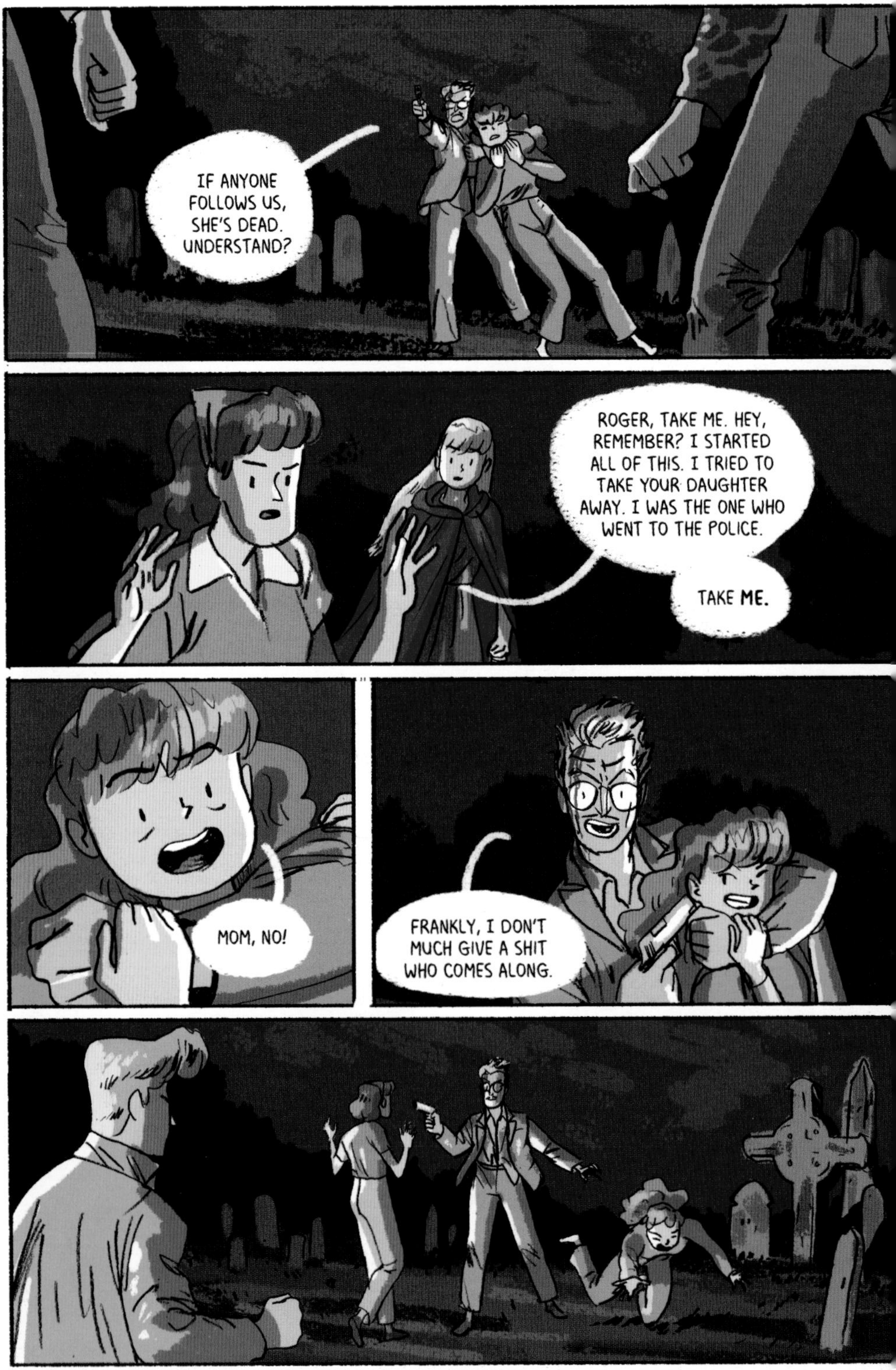
IF ANYONE FOLLOWS US, SHE'S DEAD. UNDERSTAND?
ROGER, TAKE ME. HEY, REMEMBER? I STARTED ALL OF THIS. I TRIED TO TAKE YOUR DAUGHTER AWAY. I WAS THE ONE WHO WENT TO THE POLICE.
TAKE **ME.**
MOM, NO!
FRANKLY, I DON'T MUCH GIVE A SHIT WHO COMES ALONG.

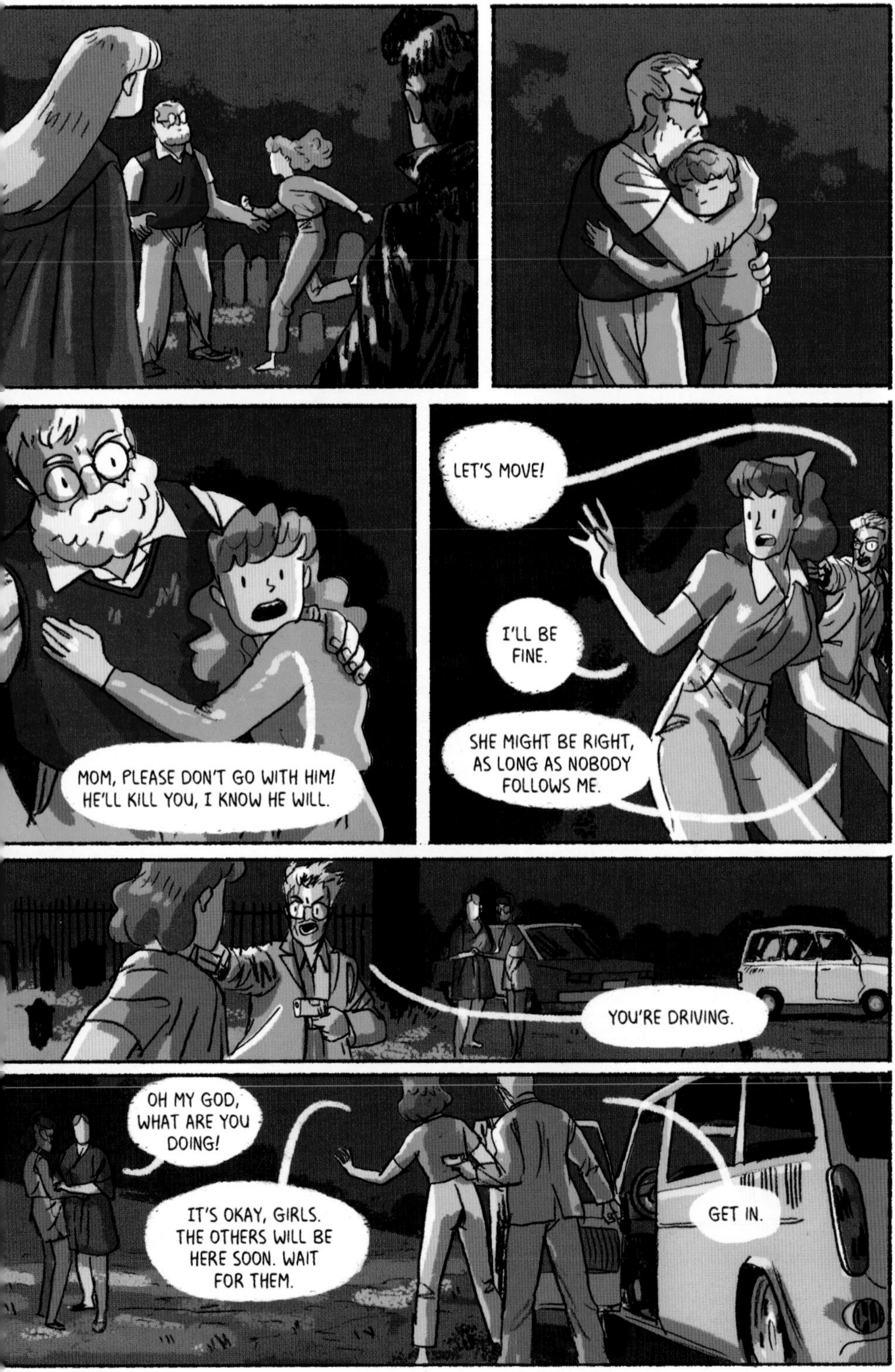
MOM, PLEASE DON'T GO WITH HIM! HE'LL KILL YOU, I KNOW HE WILL.
LET'S MOVE!
I'LL BE FINE.
SHE MIGHT BE RIGHT, AS LONG AS NOBODY FOLLOWS ME.
YOU'RE DRIVING.
OH MY GOD, WHAT ARE YOU DOING!
IT'S OKAY, GIRLS. THE OTHERS WILL BE HERE SOON. WAIT FOR THEM.
GET IN.

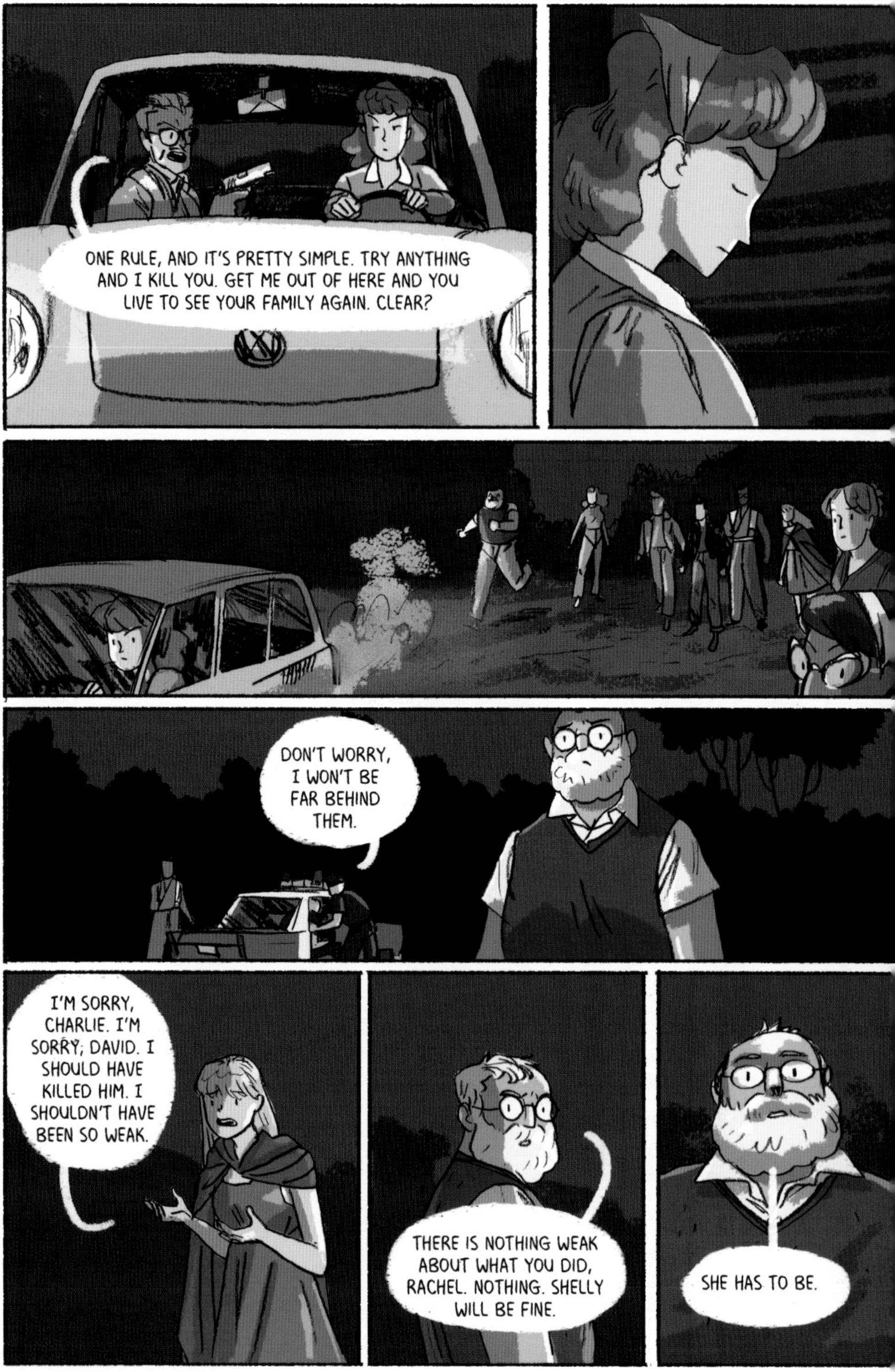
ONE RULE, AND IT'S PRETTY SIMPLE. TRY ANYTHING AND I KILL YOU. GET ME OUT OF HERE AND YOU LIVE TO SEE YOUR FAMILY AGAIN. CLEAR?
DON'T WORRY, I WON'T BE FAR BEHIND THEM.
I'M SORRY, CHARLIE. I'M SORRY, DAVID. I SHOULD HAVE KILLED HIM. I SHOULDN'T HAVE BEEN SO WEAK.
THERE IS NOTHING WEAK ABOUT WHAT YOU DID, RACHEL. NOTHING. SHELLY WILL BE FINE.
SHE HAS TO BE.

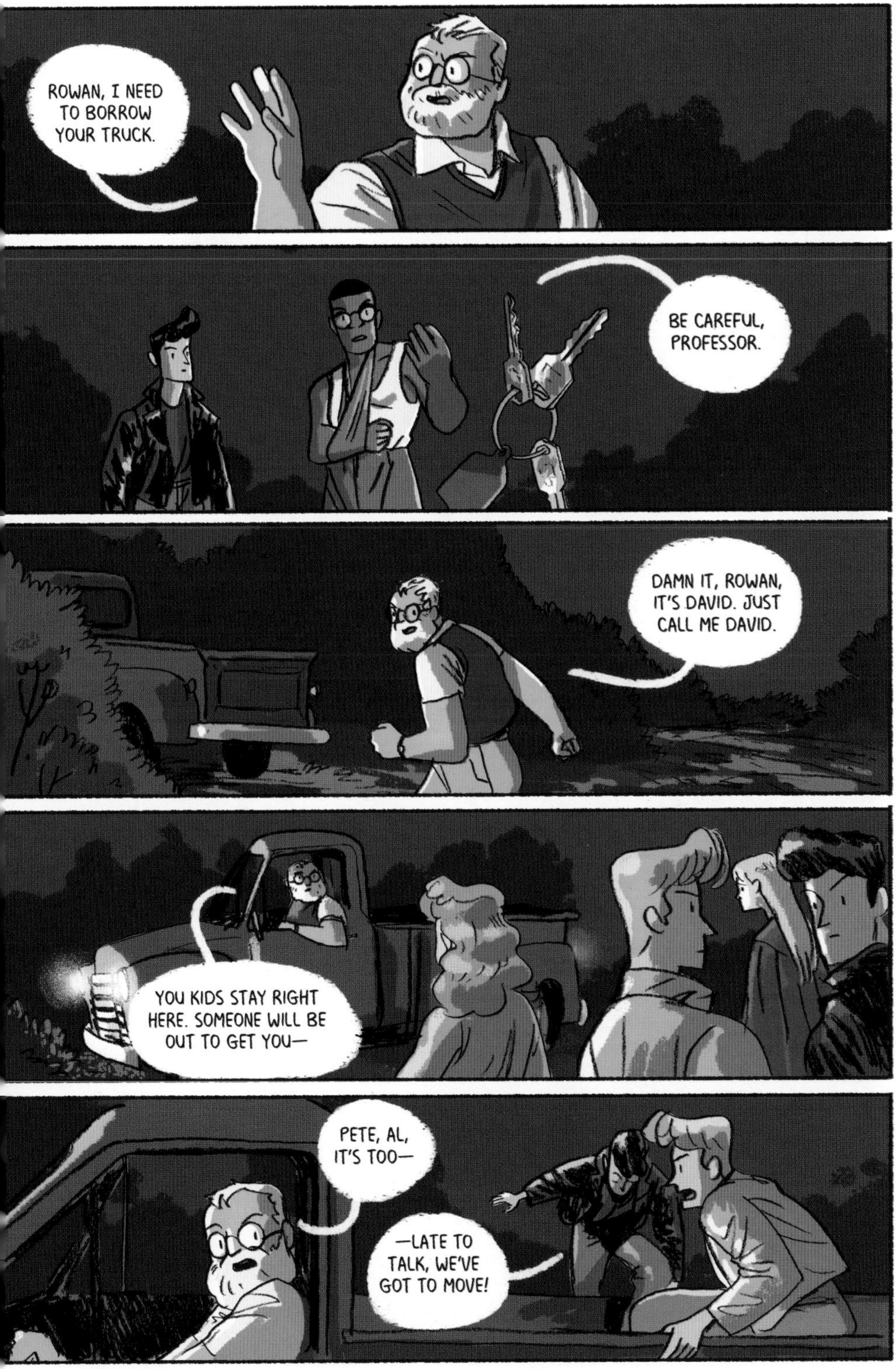
ROWAN, I NEED TO BORROW YOUR TRUCK.
BE CAREFUL, PROFESSOR.
DAMN IT, ROWAN, IT'S DAVID. JUST CALL ME DAVID.
YOU KIDS STAY RIGHT HERE. SOMEONE WILL BE OUT TO GET YOU—
PETE, AL, IT'S TOO—
—LATE TO TALK, WE'VE GOT TO MOVE!

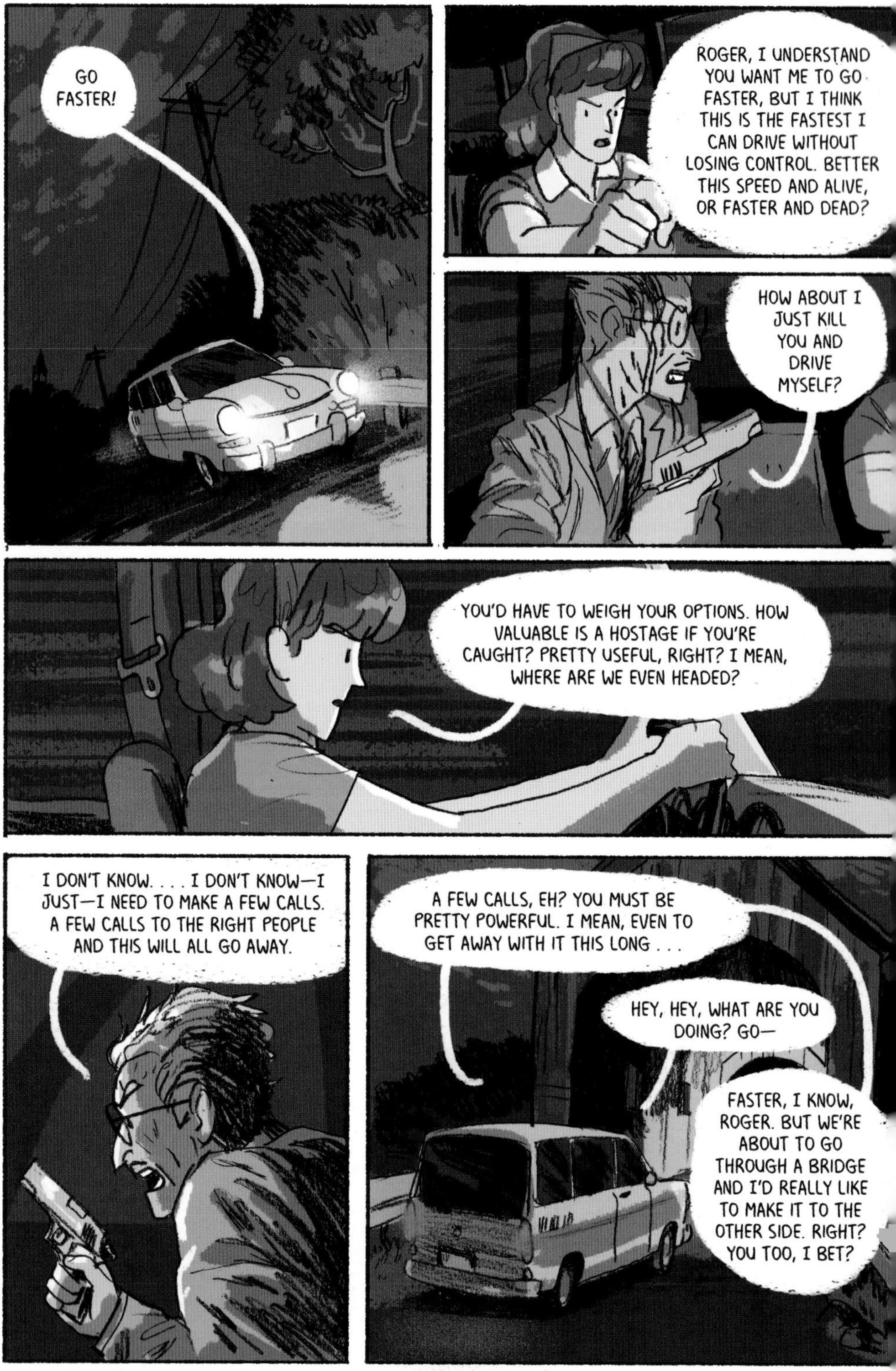
GO FASTER!
ROGER, I UNDERSTAND YOU WANT ME TO GO FASTER, BUT I THINK THIS IS THE FASTEST I CAN DRIVE WITHOUT LOSING CONTROL. BETTER THIS SPEED AND ALIVE, OR FASTER AND DEAD?
HOW ABOUT I JUST KILL YOU AND DRIVE MYSELF?
YOU'D HAVE TO WEIGH YOUR OPTIONS. HOW VALUABLE IS A HOSTAGE IF YOU'RE CAUGHT? PRETTY USEFUL, RIGHT? I MEAN, WHERE ARE WE EVEN HEADED?
I DON'T KNOW. . . . I DON'T KNOW—I JUST—I NEED TO MAKE A FEW CALLS. A FEW CALLS TO THE RIGHT PEOPLE AND THIS WILL ALL GO AWAY.
A FEW CALLS, EH? YOU MUST BE PRETTY POWERFUL. I MEAN, EVEN TO GET AWAY WITH IT THIS LONG . . .
HEY, HEY, WHAT ARE YOU DOING? GO—
FASTER, I KNOW, ROGER. BUT WE'RE ABOUT TO GO THROUGH A BRIDGE AND I'D REALLY LIKE TO MAKE IT TO THE OTHER SIDE. RIGHT? YOU TOO, I BET?

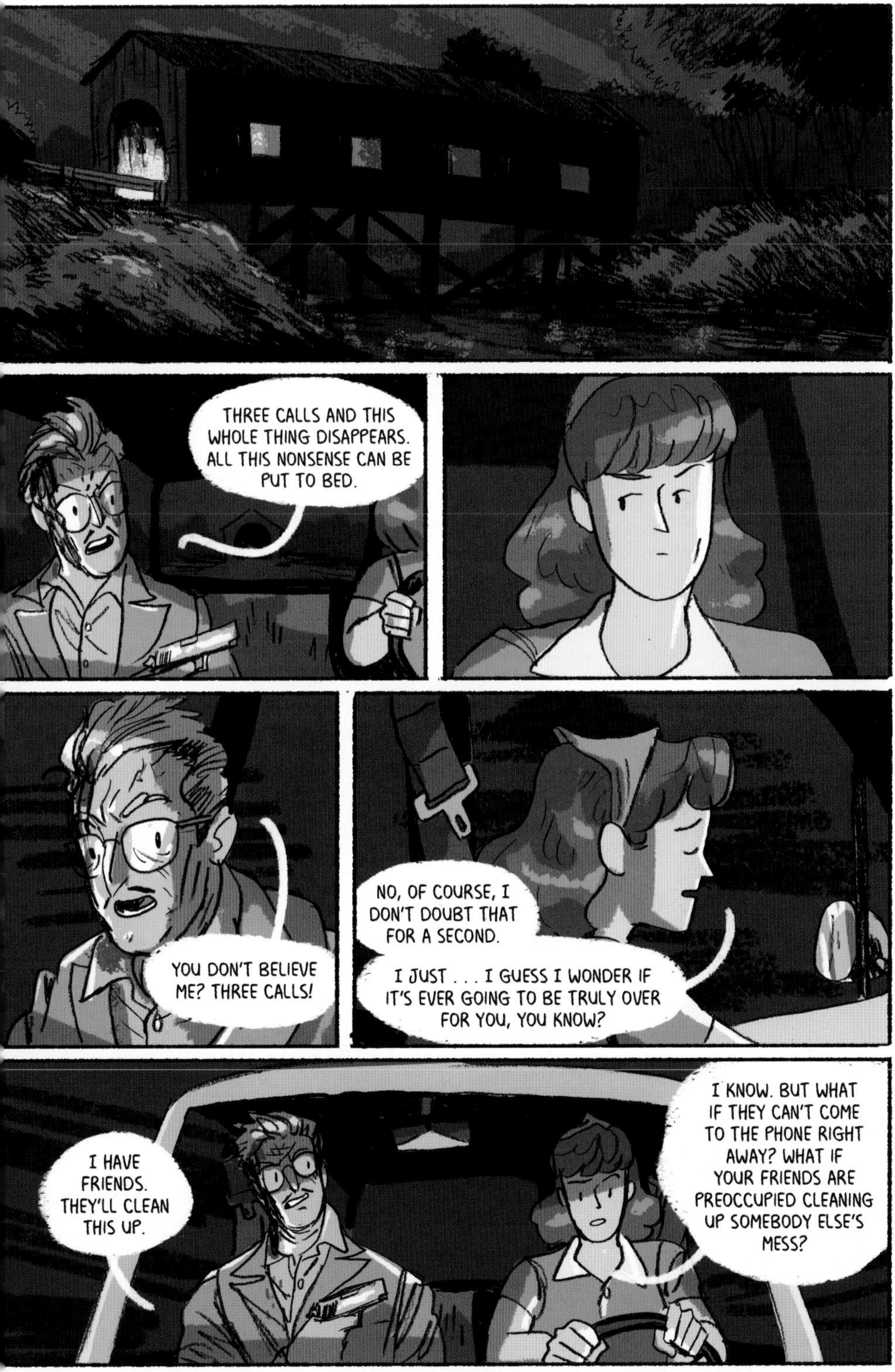
THREE CALLS AND THIS WHOLE THING DISAPPEARS. ALL THIS NONSENSE CAN BE PUT TO BED.
YOU DON'T BELIEVE ME? THREE CALLS!
NO, OF COURSE, I DON'T DOUBT THAT FOR A SECOND.
I JUST . . . I GUESS I WONDER IF IT'S EVER GOING TO BE TRULY OVER FOR YOU, YOU KNOW?
I HAVE FRIENDS. THEY'LL CLEAN THIS UP.
I KNOW. BUT WHAT IF THEY CAN'T COME TO THE PHONE RIGHT AWAY? WHAT IF YOUR FRIENDS ARE PREOCCUPIED CLEANING UP SOMEBODY ELSE'S MESS?

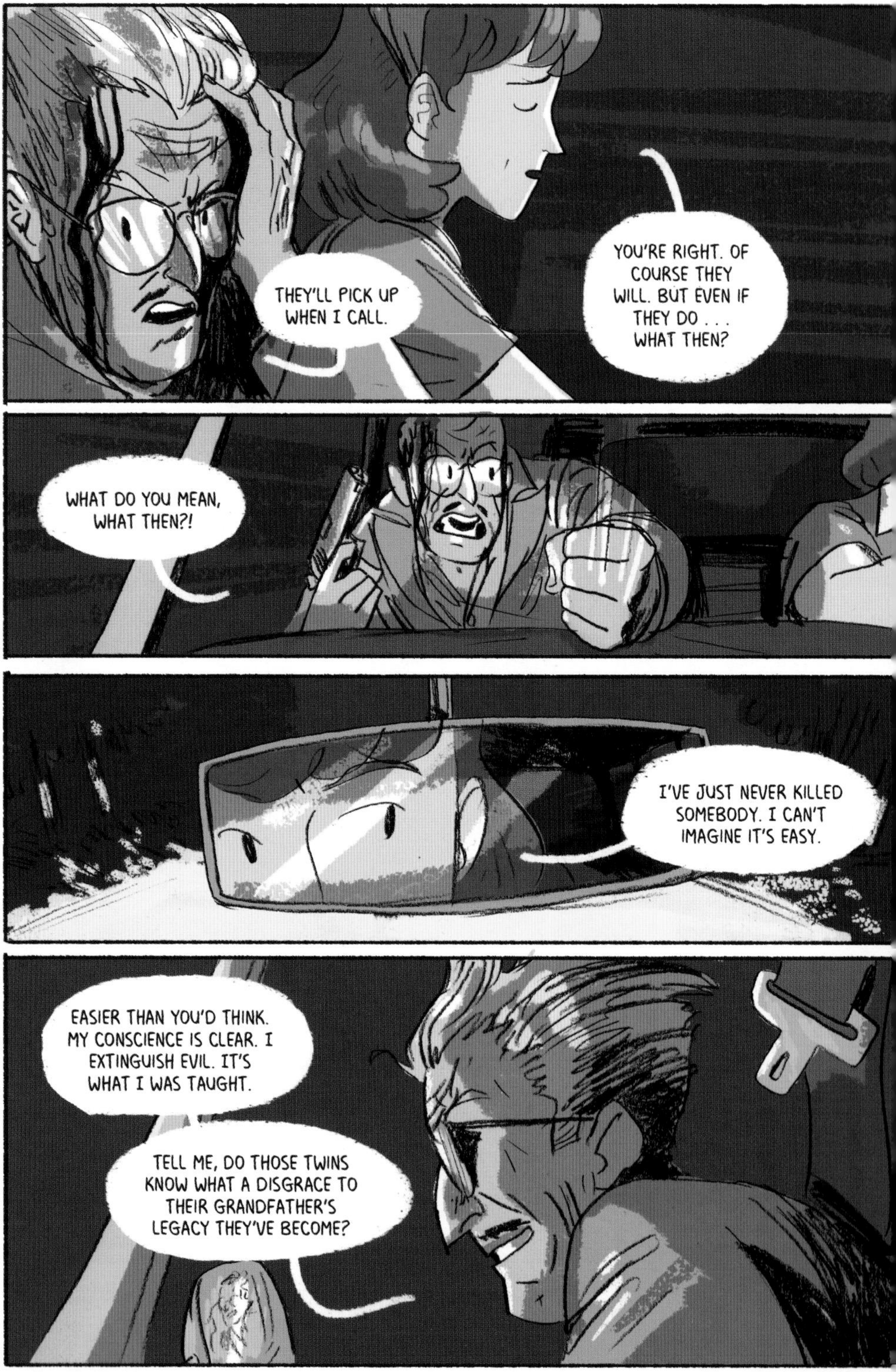
THEY'LL PICK UP WHEN I CALL.
YOU'RE RIGHT. OF COURSE THEY WILL. BUT EVEN IF THEY DO . . . WHAT THEN?
WHAT DO YOU MEAN, WHAT THEN?!
I'VE JUST NEVER KILLED SOMEBODY. I CAN'T IMAGINE IT'S EASY.
EASIER THAN YOU'D THINK. MY CONSCIENCE IS CLEAR. I EXTINGUISH EVIL. IT'S WHAT I WAS TAUGHT.
TELL ME, DO THOSE TWINS KNOW WHAT A DISGRACE TO THEIR GRANDFATHER'S LEGACY THEY'VE BECOME?

NO. WE DON'T CELEBRATE CRUELTY IN OUR HOME. AND FRANCIS WAS ASHAMED OF HIS ROOTS. HE TOOK GREAT PRIDE IN TURNING AGAINST HIS FATHER.

HE WAS JUST ANOTHER MAN SEDUCED BY EVIL.

I KNOW YOU SAID IT WASN'T HARD FOR YOU, BUT . . .

DON'T YOU EVER JUST . . . SEE HER? LIKE, YOU'RE GOING ALONG AND EVERYTHING SEEMS FINE, UNTIL SUDDENLY THERE SHE IS. IN A WINDOW, IN A CROWD, OR MAYBE RIGHT BEHIND YOU? AND IT HITS YOU, WHAT YOU'VE DONE. IT REALLY HITS YOU?

NEVER.

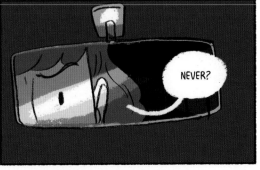

NEVER?

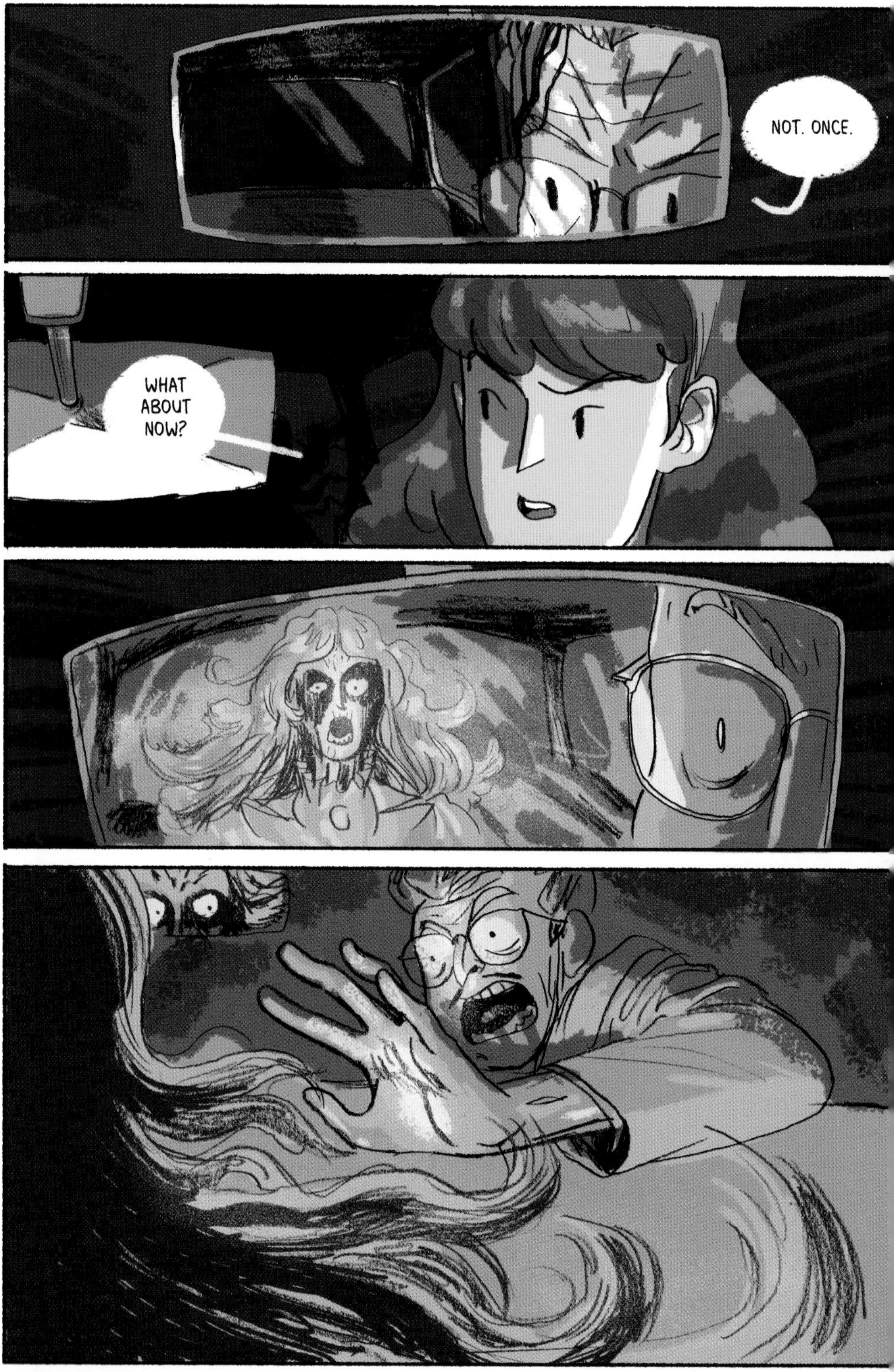
NOT. ONCE.
WHAT ABOUT NOW?

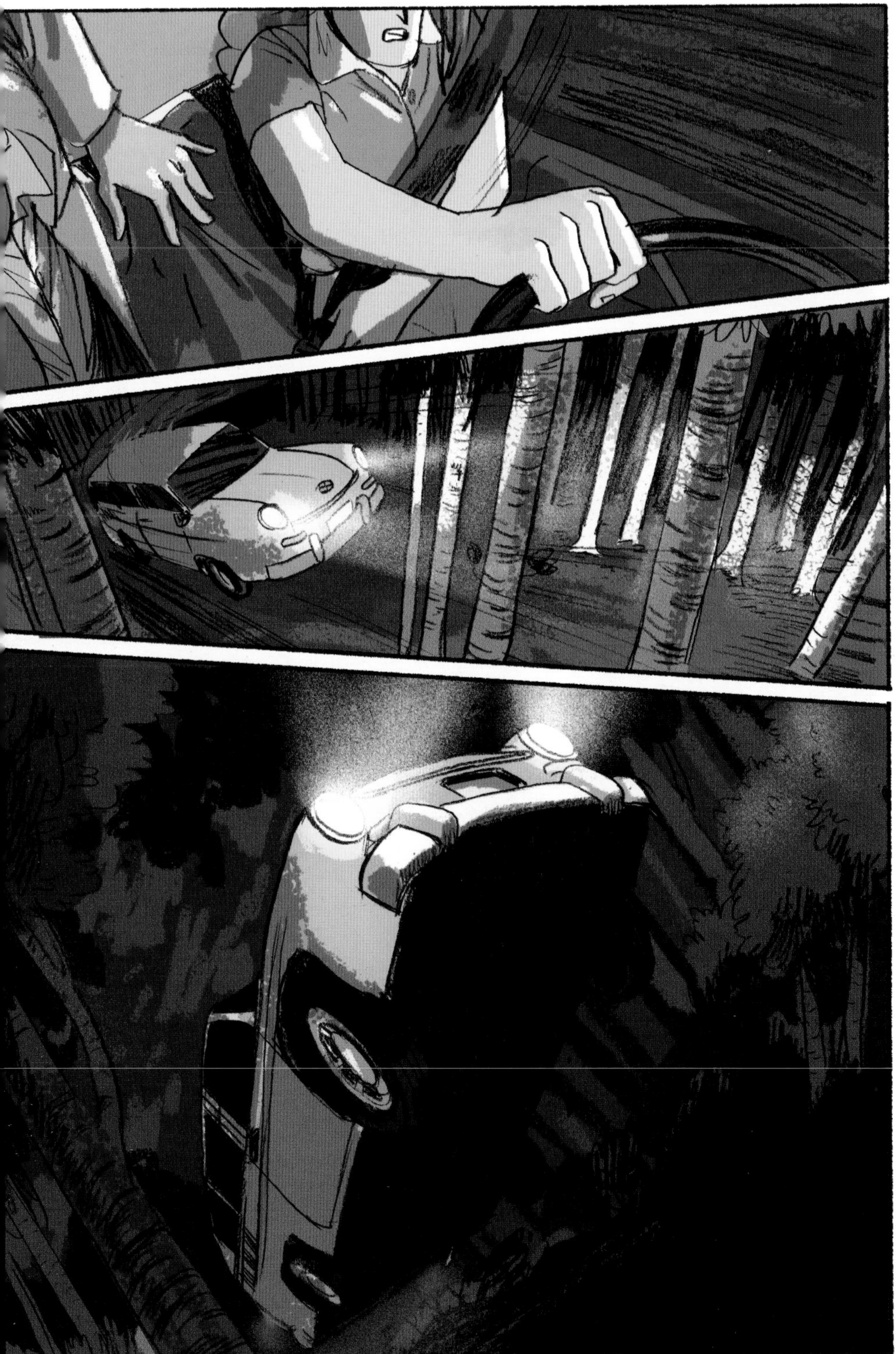

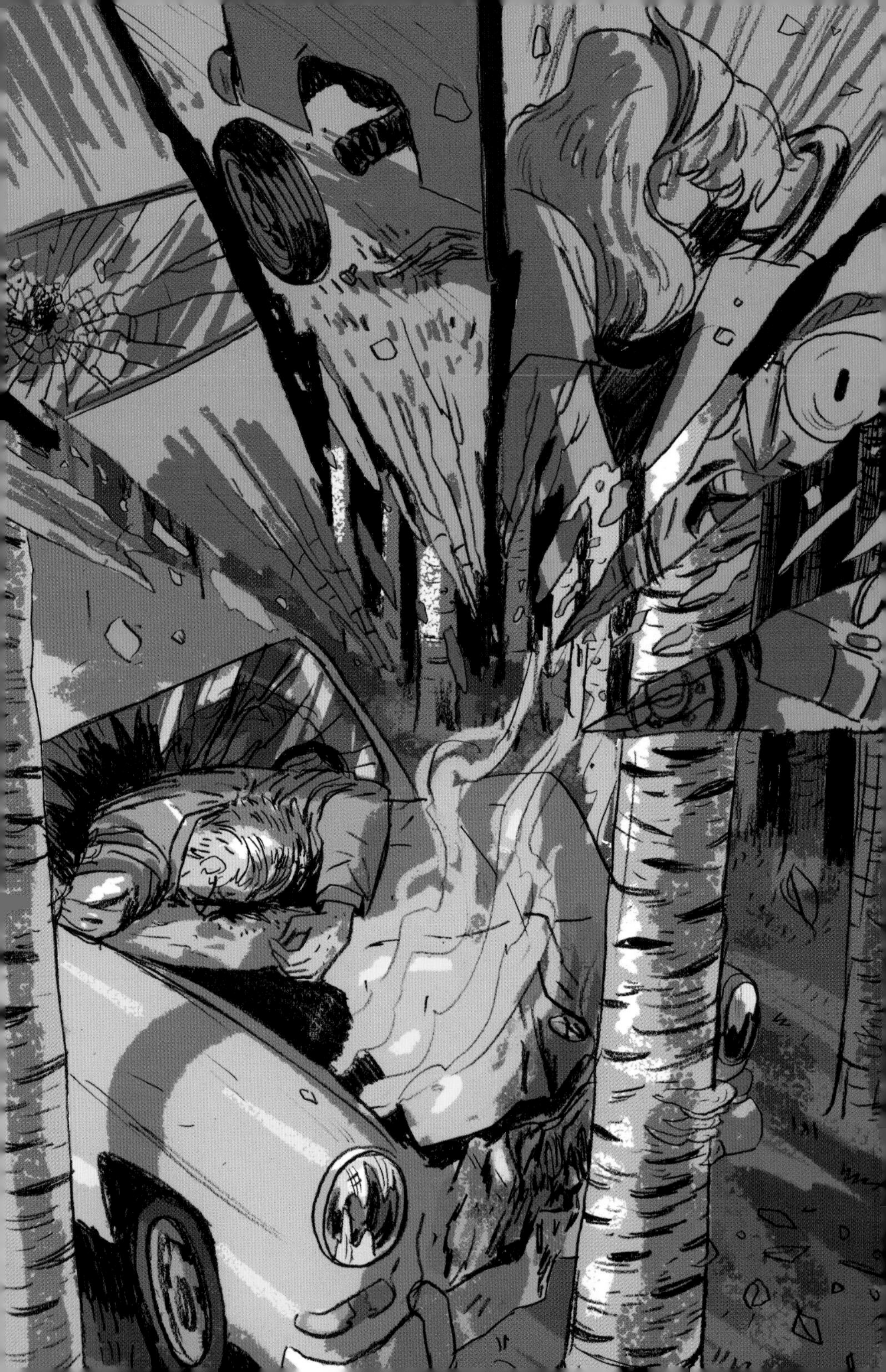

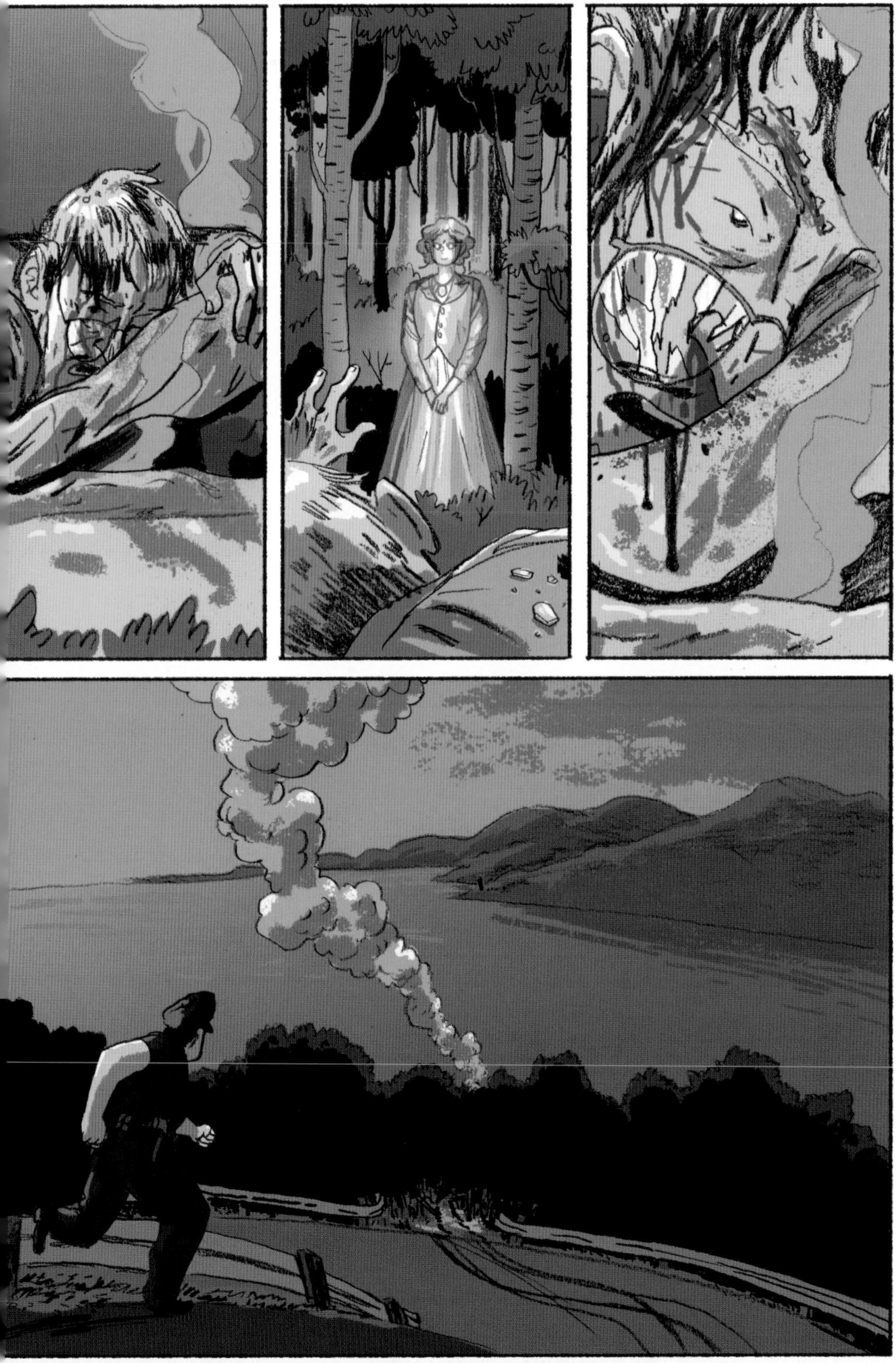

EPILOGUE

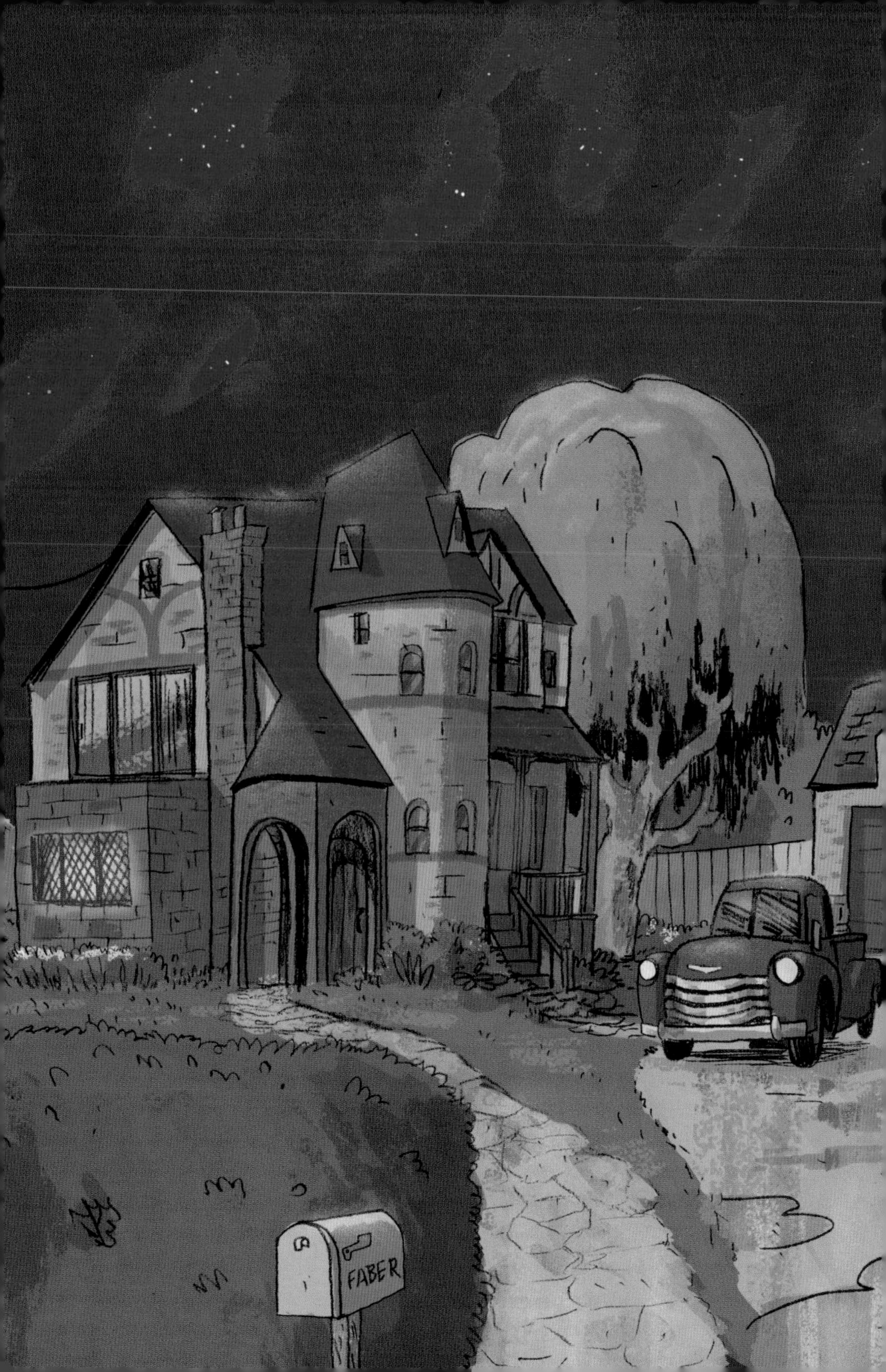
FABER

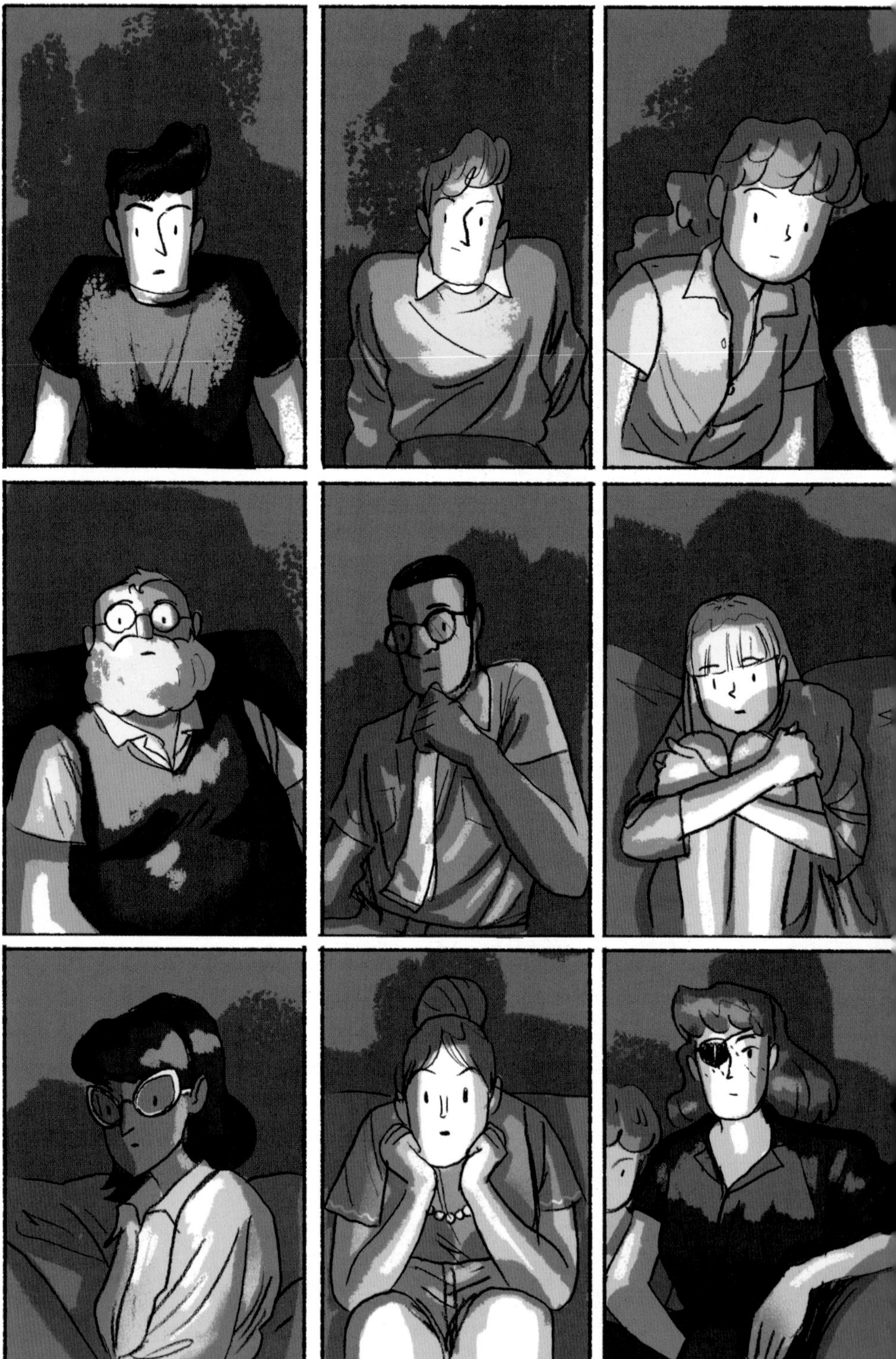

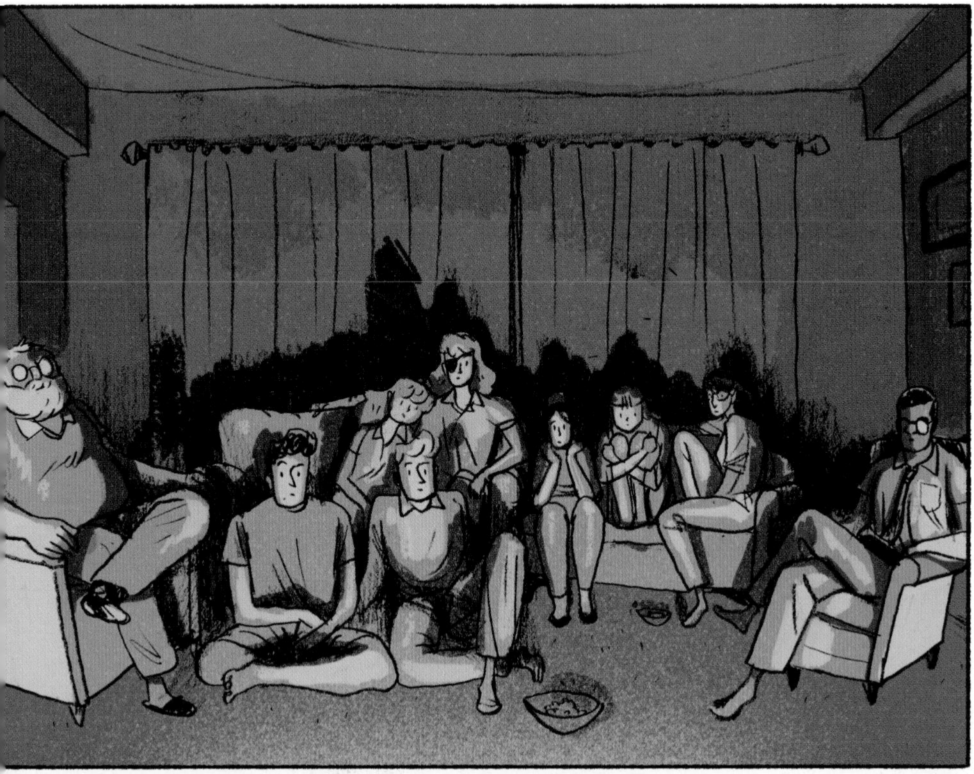

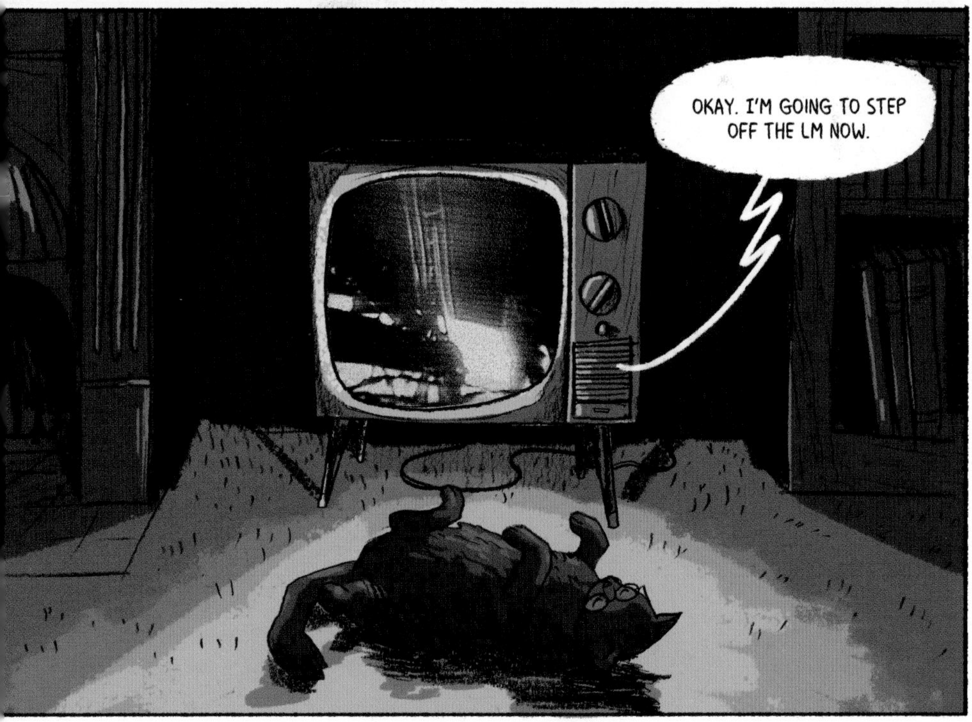
OKAY. I'M GOING TO STEP OFF THE LM NOW.

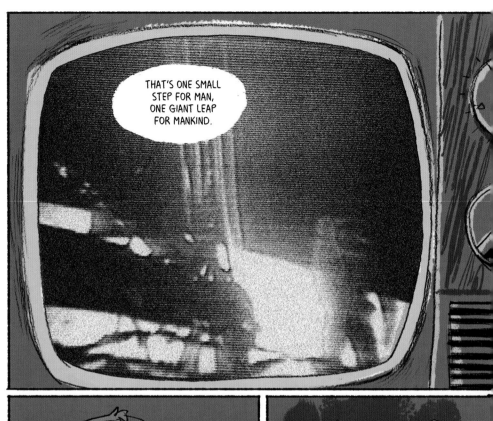

THAT'S ONE SMALL STEP FOR MAN, ONE GIANT LEAP FOR MANKIND.

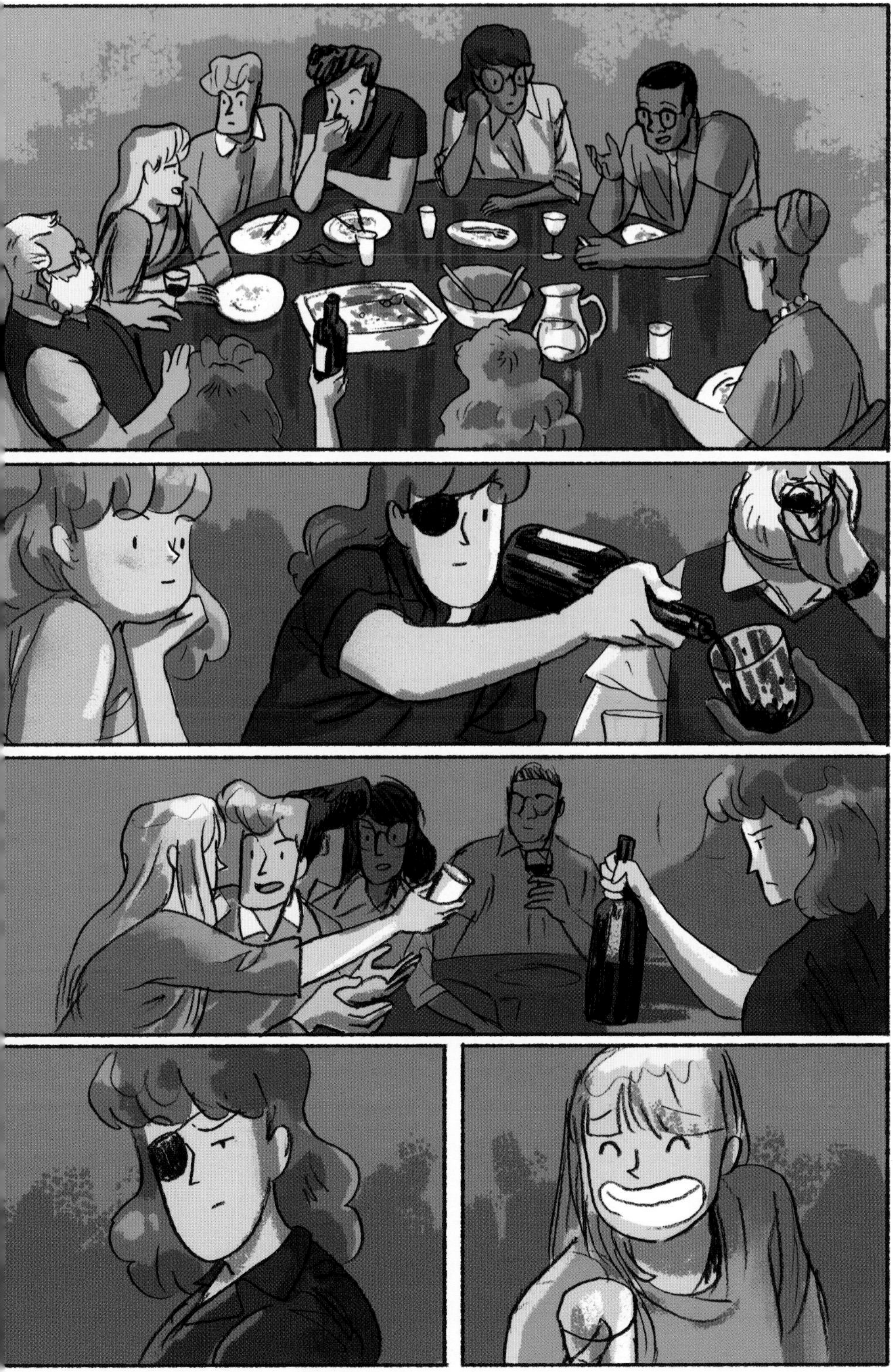

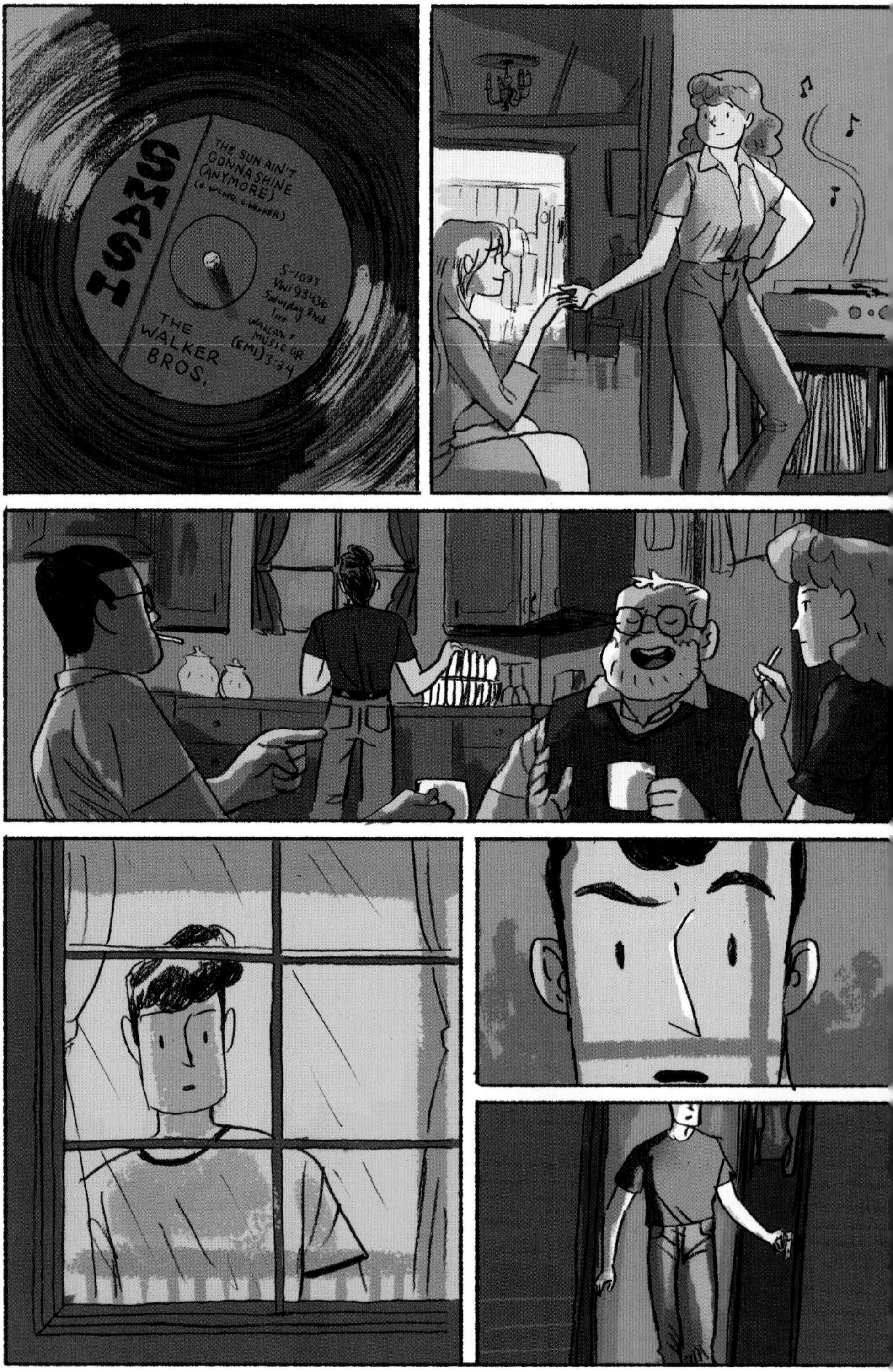
SMASH
THE SUN AIN'T GONNA SHINE (ANYMORE)
S-1037
THE WALKER BROS.
(EMI) 3:34

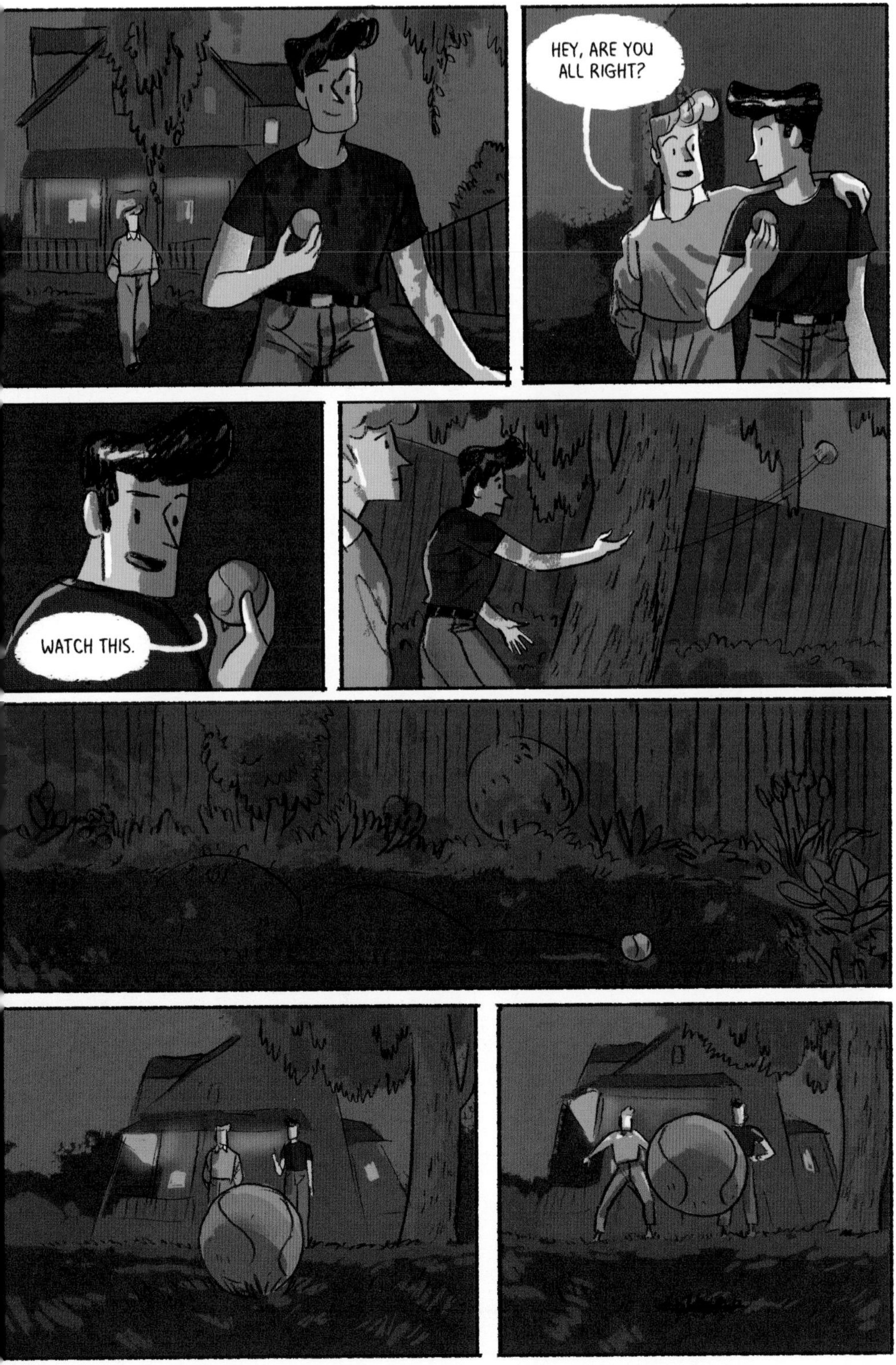
HEY, ARE YOU ALL RIGHT?
WATCH THIS.

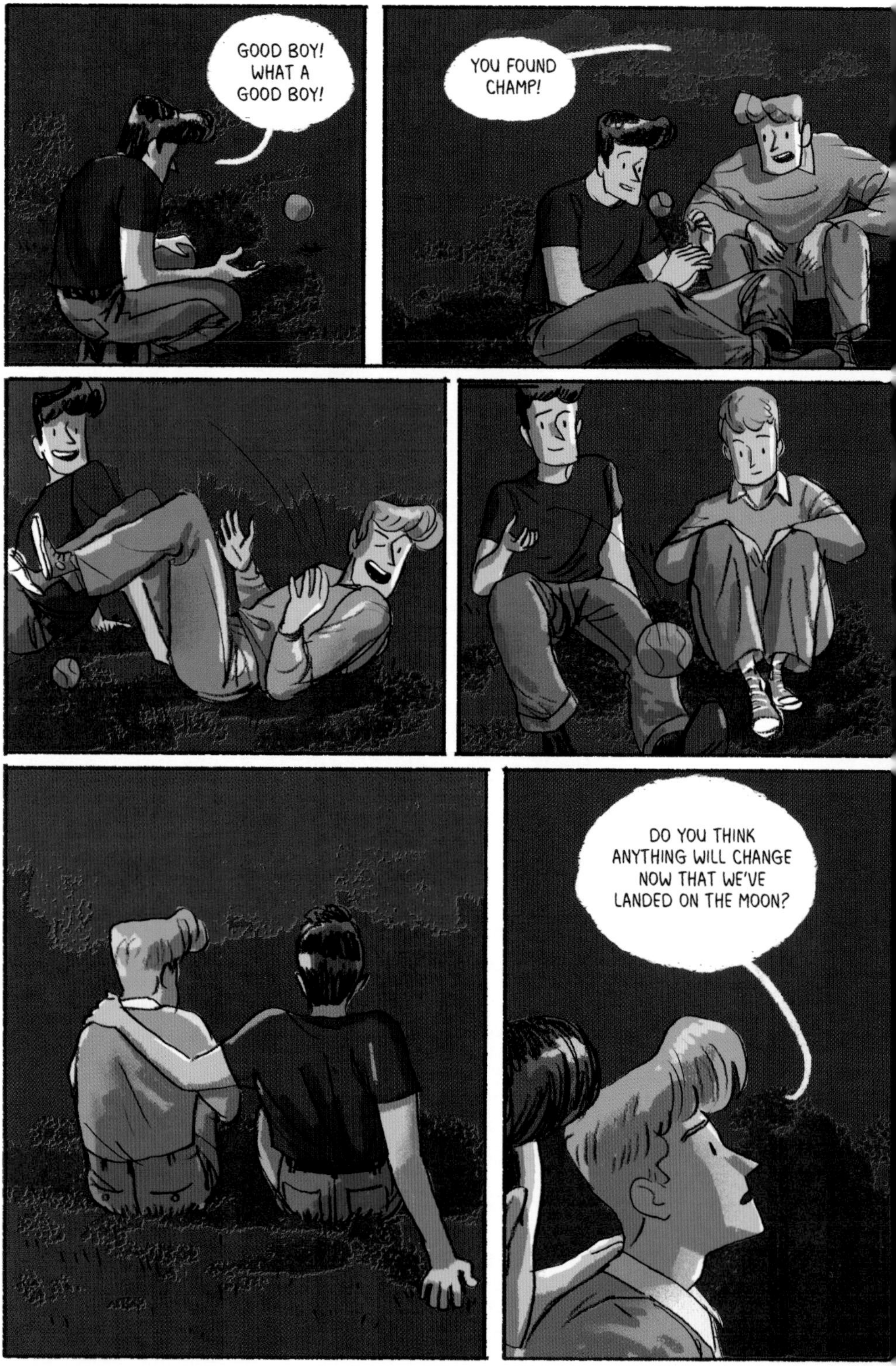
GOOD BOY! WHAT A GOOD BOY!
YOU FOUND CHAMP!
DO YOU THINK ANYTHING WILL CHANGE NOW THAT WE'VE LANDED ON THE MOON?

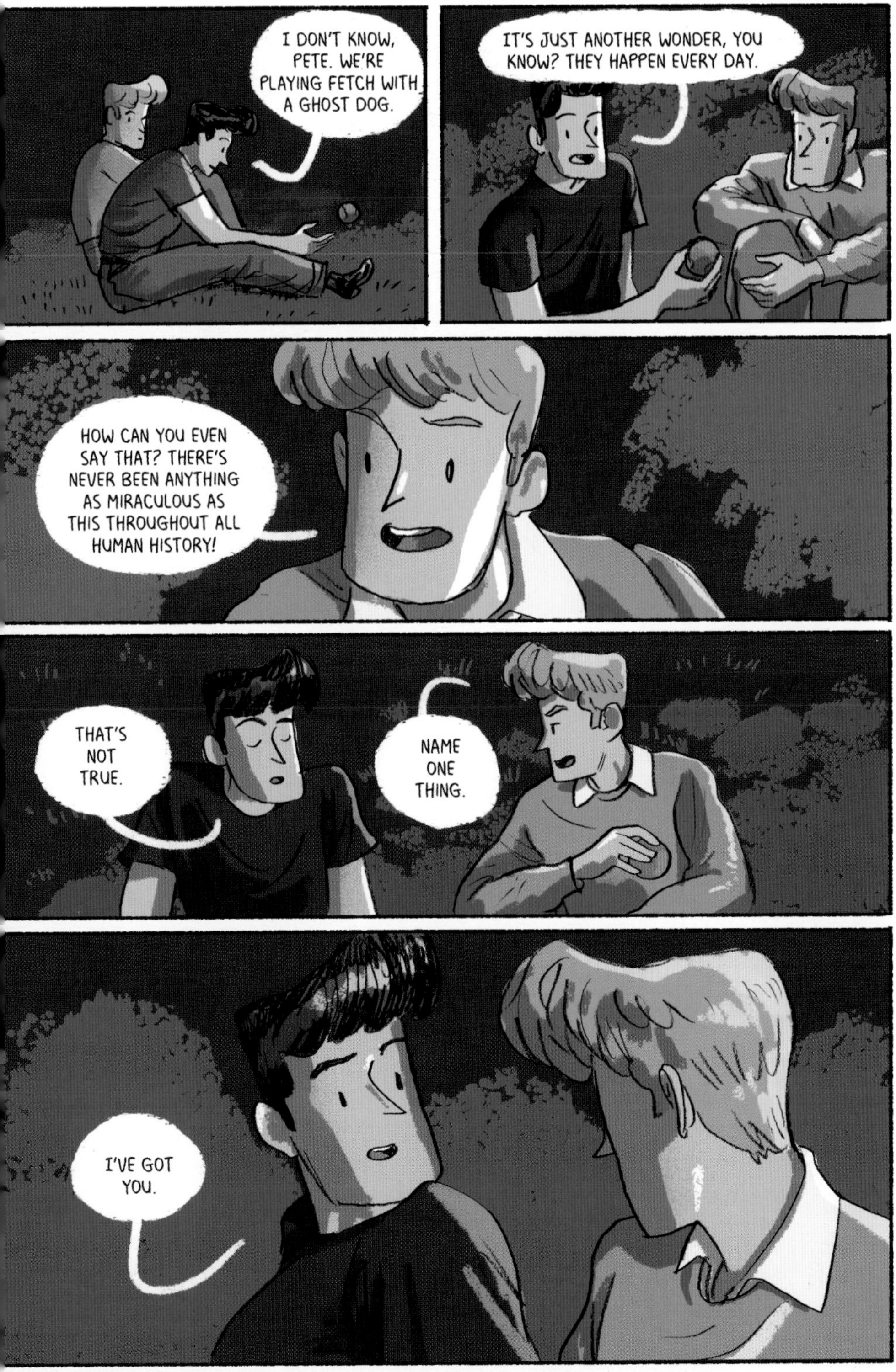
I DON'T KNOW, PETE. WE'RE PLAYING FETCH WITH A GHOST DOG.
IT'S JUST ANOTHER WONDER, YOU KNOW? THEY HAPPEN EVERY DAY.
HOW CAN YOU EVEN SAY THAT? THERE'S NEVER BEEN ANYTHING AS MIRACULOUS AS THIS THROUGHOUT ALL HUMAN HISTORY!
THAT'S NOT TRUE.
NAME ONE THING.
I'VE GOT YOU.

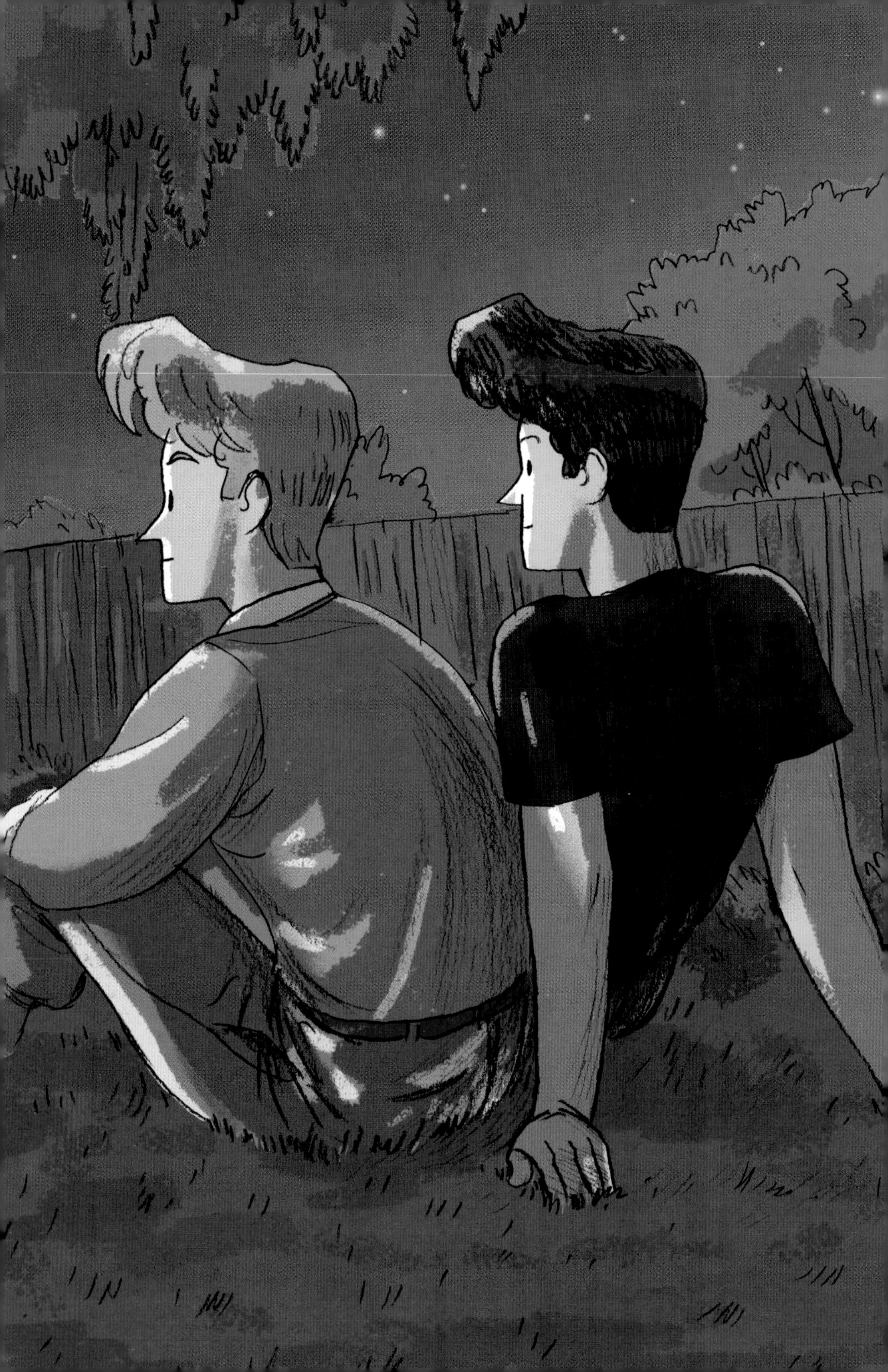

THE MONTAGUE TWINS

WILL BE BACK!

Look for their next adventure,
coming fall 2021!

Visit **montaguetwins.com**
for news, galleries, playlists, and much more!

These are some of the first sketches of Pete and Al, circa 2012. Their quiffs have gotten decidedly smaller over the years.

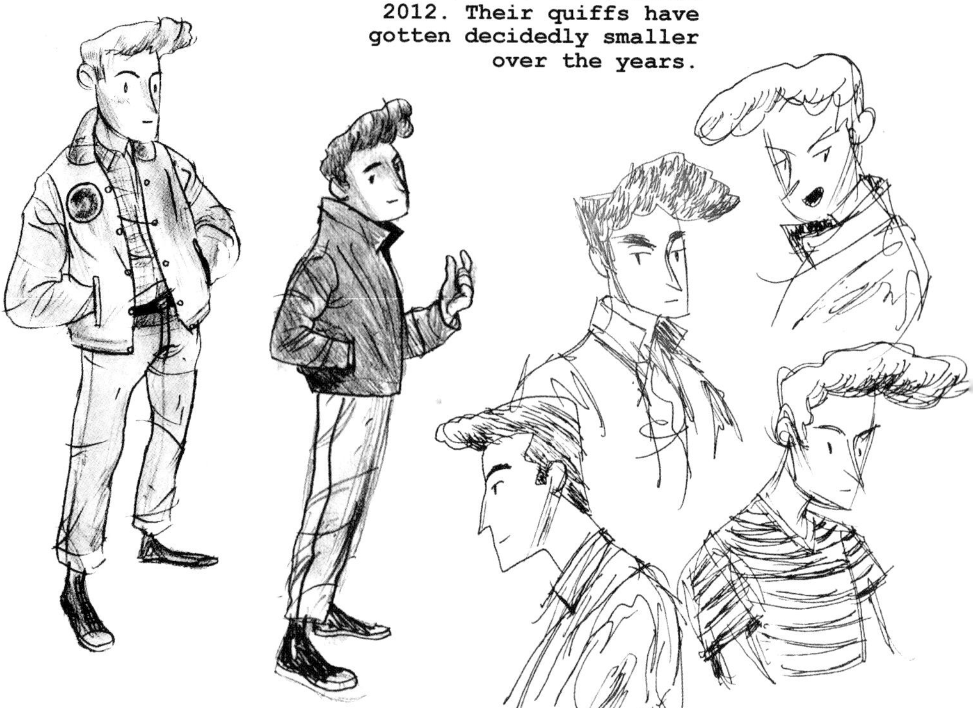

Port Howl is an amalgamation of every small New England town, so of course it's got a Main Street. I forget what town this reference sketch is from...

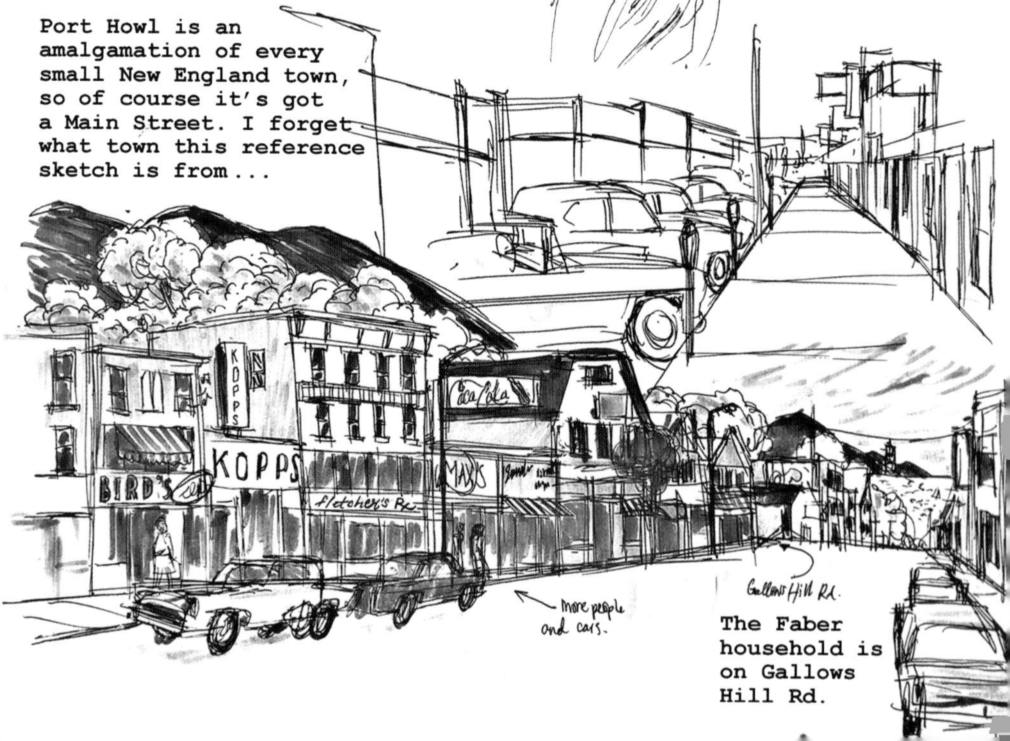
KOPPS
KOPPS
BIRD'S
Coca-Cola
MAX'S
Fletcher's Rx
more people and cars.
Gallows Hill Rd.

The Faber household is on Gallows Hill Rd.

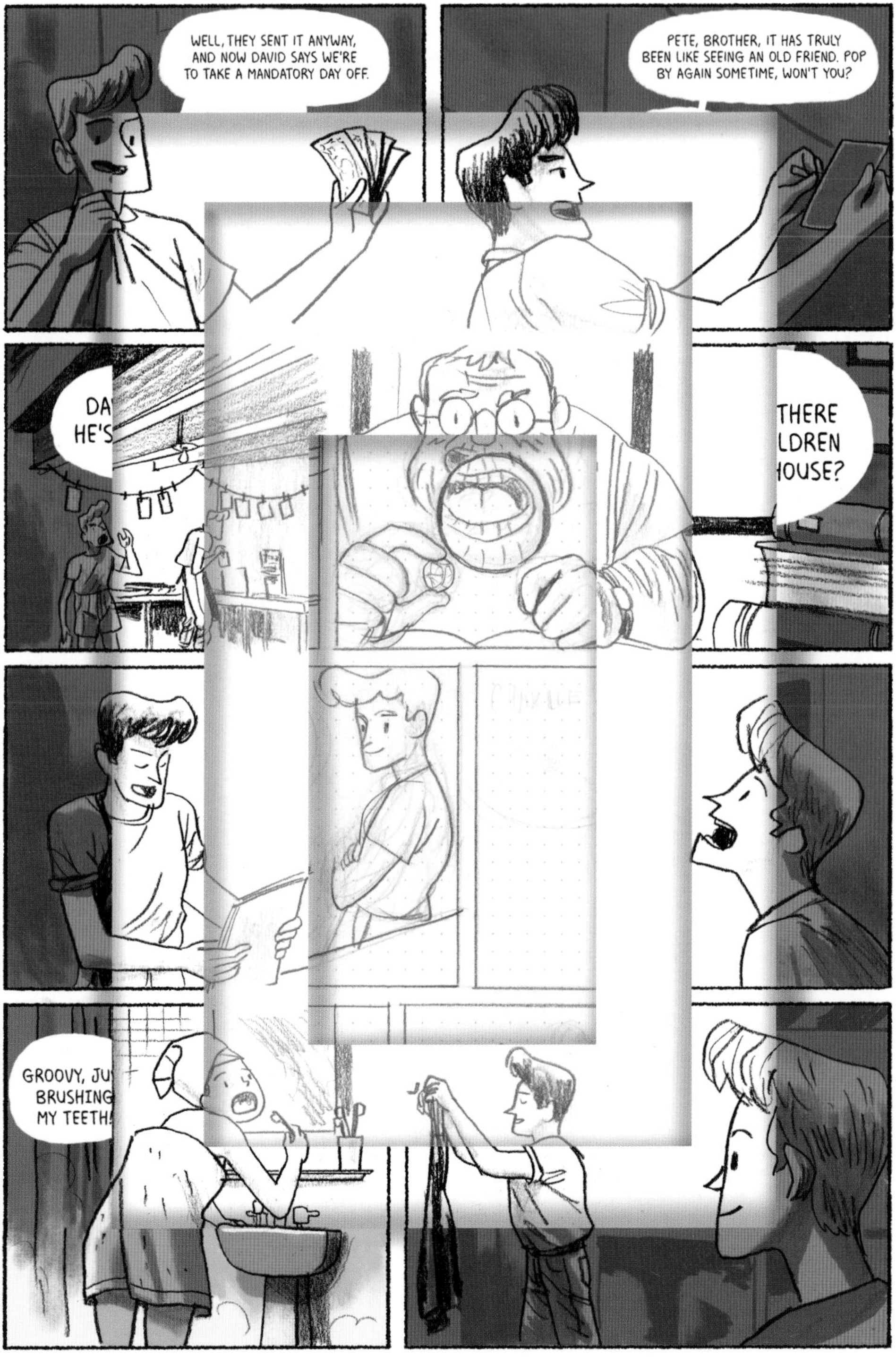

WELL, THEY SENT IT ANYWAY, AND NOW DAVID SAYS WE'RE TO TAKE A MANDATORY DAY OFF.
PETE, BROTHER, IT HAS TRULY BEEN LIKE SEEING AN OLD FRIEND. POP BY AGAIN SOMETIME, WON'T YOU?
DA HE'S
THERE LDREN HOUSE?
GROOVY, JU BRUSHING MY TEETH!

I've always loved reading the original scripts of graphic novels, specifically in the back pages of *Dream Country*, volume three of Neil Gaiman's Sandman collection. This book would never have existed if I hadn't read *Dream Country*. While my writing may pale in comparison to that of a master like Neil, this can give you a sense of what the first step in creating a graphic novel entails. If you're interested in doing it too, I'll get you started:

Page One
Panel One
Go.

Chapter Two
PAGE 53
PANEL 1
Splash.
Exterior shot of resplendent Bradford Manor sitting pristinely apart from the rest of Port Howl. Not so much a house as a modest castle, it looms from atop a solitary hill known simply as Bradford Rock. From its south facing window one can see the entire town and a good bit of the Atlantic spread out before them. A lone gated entrance with a winding drive goes on for a hard mile before arriving at the imposing steps. The grounds are meticulously manicured with monstrous hedges and marble fountains. It is certainly the most beautiful residence in town, possibly the state, but there is something antiseptic about Bradford Manor. One might guess that it was some sort of historic site, that nobody could actually live in a house like this.
The storm that originated on the beach earlier that day has spread throughout the rest of Port Howl. Such a radiant morning devolved into total darkness. The rain is torrential.

PAGE 54
PANEL 1
We are inside Rachel's room. It is lit entirely by candles. There is an incense and cigarette smoke haze that permeates the air. She is lying on an ornate four poster bed. She's got an ashtray beside her. A cigarette is perched between the fingers of her left hand, the stem of a wine glass in her right. Sharing the huge bed, her little spoon, is a record player with the Zombies' *Odessey and Oracle* spinning.

PANEL 2
Realizing her cigarette is down to the filter, Rachel stubs it out.

PANEL 3
She swishes around her nearly empty wineglass. Across from her, in front of a large vanity, are her friends Marnie and Laurel. Marnie is braiding Laurel's hair.

                      RACHEL
            Girls, I'm fading here.
PAGE 55
PANEL 1
Laurel smiles and grabs a bottle off the vanity.

                        LAUREL
              Don't despair, *ma soeur*.
PANEL 2
Marnie gives Laurel's hair a quick tug.

                        MARNIE
              She's got two legs and a heartbeat, she
              can get it herself. Can't you,
              princess?

PANEL 3
Rachel begrudgingly sits up.

                        RACHEL
              You could at least give me plausible
              deniability should my stepmother
              question me about her ever-diminishing
              wine cellar.

                        MARNIE
              Tough love, babe.
PANEL 4
Rachel has gone to the vanity. She dramatically snags the bottle
with jocular severity.

                        RACHEL
              You know how I feel about limits being
              placed on me.
PANEL 5
Rachel takes a cigarette out of the pack with her mouth.

PANEL 6
She looks down at Laurel and smiles. Laurel is shyly looking
away.

                        RACHEL
              You're gorgeous. You both are. Thank
              you so much for coming tonight. I just
              thought it could be like old times, you
              know?

PANEL 7
A smaller panel. Close up of Laurel's hand flicking a lighter
open and the ensuing spark.

Rachel bends down close to Laurel to light her cigarette.

> LAUREL
> Anytime, Rach. It's really good to see
> you. To be honest, we weren't sure if
> you were . . . well, if your . . . uh .
> . .

> MARNIE
> If your porcelain fingers still knew
> how to operate a telephone.

PAGE 56
PANEL 1
Laurel's face has gone all hot. Whenever there is tension in a
room, she internalizes it. She knew Marnie wouldn't be able to
resist bringing up Rachel's absence. It was just so nice to be
doing something together after so long, and now it was going to
be ruined by Marnie's big mouth. So Laurel speaks, hoping to
break the tension.

> LAUREL
> It looks nice? My hair?

> MARNIE
> It looks great, hon. Trust me.

PANEL 2
Rachel has turned back toward the comfort of her record player.
She sways a little along the way.

PANEL 3
Marnie puts the finishing touches on Laurel's hair.

> MARNIE
> Voilà! You can look now.

PANEL 4
Laurel turns towards the mirror and looks at herself. She feels
beautiful. Marnie has her hands on Laurel's shoulders.

PANEL 5
Rachel is reclined on the bed once more.

> RACHEL
> What'd I tell you, Laurel? Gorgeous.

PANEL 6
Marnie leans against the vanity, finally able to relax after two

rigorous braiding sessions. Laurel is delicately touching the intricate braids.

>   LAUREL
>   Thank you. I love it, Marnie.

>   MARNIE
>   Well, now what should we do? I'm going
>   to go ahead and say the drive-in is a
>   bust. Nobody is crazy enough to be out
>   in this storm.

PANEL 7
And cue the elements. Lightning strikes nearby.

PAGE 57
PANEL 1
A blast of wind blows open the French doors to Rachel's balcony. Nearly all of the candles are extinguished.

PANEL 2
Now back inside the room, we are behind Rachel as she throws her full weight into closing the doors, fighting against the wind.

PANEL 3
She is finally able to slam them shut and immediately sets the lock.

PANEL 4
Breathing hard, Rachel stares out at the storm. The room behind her is nearly blacked out now. Her face is brought into silhouette by another shot of lightning landing nearby.

PANEL 5
Rachel picks up a recently snuffed out candle.

PANEL 6
She discreetly runs her hand over it and in that instant the candle burns anew.

PANEL 7
She turns toward her friends with a smile twisting at the corners of her lips. She's holding the candle in her hands, cradling it.

>   RACHEL
>   Who's up for something a little . . .
>   sinister?

ACKNOWLEDGMENTS

This book has been in the making for over six years, and we are so blessed to know so many talented and supportive people who have helped shape this project and have participated in the journey. From the depths of our hearts, we would like to thank the following people:

Maria Vicente

Julia Maguire

Joan Lee

Kyle Mowat

Anne Thériault

Irma Kniivila

Hayden Maynard

Erin McPhee

Matt Coe

Sam Maggs

Jeff Lemire

Amanda Lewis

Annie Koyama

Aaron Leighton

Erika Turner

D.C Nchama

Amanda Row

Paul S. Fowler

Sammy Jamison

Rick Ilnycki

Matt and Laura Rushworth

Marc Whittington and his parents

The ATB team

Ajay Fry

Elvis Prusic

Queen Mob's Teahouse

Evan Munday

Ray, Stephanie